BLACKMANTLE

A BOOK OF THE KELTIAD

BLACKMANTLE
A Triumph

PATRICIA
KENNEALY-
MORRISON

HarperPrism
A Division of HarperCollinsPublishers

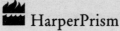

HarperPrism

A Division of HarperCollins*Publishers*
10 East 53rd Street, New York, N.Y. 10022-5299

The songs, poems and rituals contained herein are all © 1997 by
Patricia Morrison for Lizard Queen Productions, Inc. They may
not be set to music or used for any purpose whatsoever without
her express written consent and permission.

ISBN 0-06-105610-3

HarperCollins®, 📖 ®, and HarperPrism®
are trademarks of HarperCollins*Publishers,* Inc.

A hardcover edition of this book was published
in 1997 by HarperPrism.

Jacket art by John Ennis.

Maps by the author.

First mass market printing: September 1998

Printed in the United States of America

Visit HarperPrism on the World Wide Web at
http://www.harperprism.com

❖ 10 9 8 7 6 5 4 3 2 1

To
Jim & Patricia Morrison

For
Silksteel & Fireheart

To the poet & the sorceress. . .
Sailor's son & soldier's daughter
Heir to the serpent clan
& princess of the wolves

ACKNOWLEDGMENTS

To Athyn's friends and Morric's, who are also, ever, ours:
Bruce Abbott, Kathleen Quinlan Abbott and Master Tyler
Abbott, Laurie Sue Brockway, Phyllis Curott, James and
Susan Fox-Davis, Janice Scott Gentile, Lana Griffin, Nancy
C. Hanger and Andrew V. Phillips, Pamela Hannay, Mary
Herczog and Steve Hochman, Susan Harwood Kaczmarczik,
Michael Kaczmarczik and my goddaughter Miss Patricia Susan
Kaczmarczik, Carol Miller, Paul Pigman, Michael Rosenthal,
Ellen Sander, Kathryn Theatana, Armin Wilson, Kristine
Zeronda; to Ripley and Cinnabar and Sheila, and to Steve and
Mary's beautiful Molly and my beautiful Carrokeel Ardattin,
who run now with the hounds of Arawn; to Katherine Kurtz
and Anne McCaffrey and Morgan Llywelyn, for the great gra-
ciousness and generosity they showed, eight books ago now,
to an unknown and fledgling maker; to Christopher Schelling
and Caitlin Deinard Blasdell, for editorial graces past and
present; to Julie Blattberg, for production and patience; to
John Ennis, our first time out, for the indescribably beautiful
cover art; to 'Fiona Macleod,' William Sharp, for the bones of
Athyn's lovesong to Morric at Gwel-y-sidan; to Loreena
McKennitt and Shaun Davey and Enya, for the endless,
wondrous soundtrack; and to all my Kelts everywhere too
numerous to name: glory, praise and honor, and the deep and
loving thanks of the Creatrix, to the true warriors of the
Gweriden—the noblest, best, most loyal and protective of
friends. You will find yourselves herein. Be blessed forever.

And to Athyn's enemies and Morric's, who are—also, ever—
ours: You are here also. Iadsan a dh'àras euceart.

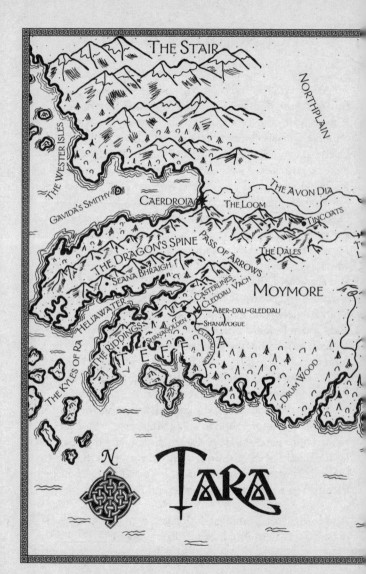

CRINNA: Northlands

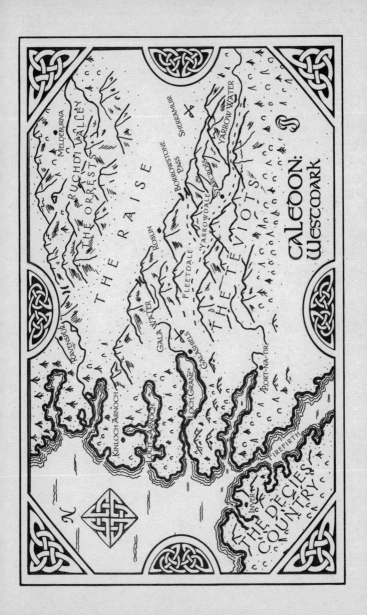

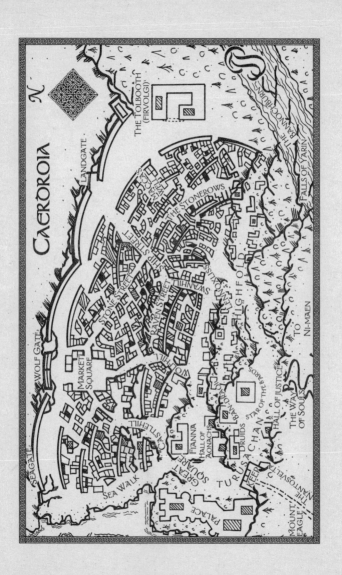

Keltichronicon

In the Earth year 453 by the Common Reckoning, a small fleet of ships left Ireland, carrying emigrants seeking a new home in a distant land. But the ships were not the leather-hulled boats of later legend, and though the great exodus was indeed led by a man called Brendan, he was not the Christian navigator-monk who later chroniclers would claim had discovered a New World across the western ocean.

These ships were starships, their passengers the Danaans, descendants—and heirs to the secrets—of Atlantis, that they themselves called Atland. The new world they sought was a distant double-ringed planet, itself unknown and more than half a legend, and he who led them in that seeking would come to be known as Saint Brendan the Astrogator.

Fleeing persecutions and a world that was no longer home to their ancient magics, the Danaans, who long ages since had come to Earth in flight from a dying star's agonies, now went back to those far stars; and after two years' desperate wandering they found their promised haven. They named their new homeland Keltia, and Brendan, though he refused to call himself its king, ruled there long and well. And Nia his mother, who was of the race of the Sidhefolk, brought to the new realm the grace and magic of her people, so that in time to come the Kelts did call her blessed, and looked to her as saint and protectress of their worlds.

In all the centuries that followed, Keltia grew and prospered, becoming a star-kingdom of seven systems and a power in the galaxy. The kings and queens who were Brendan's heirs, whatever else they did, kept unbroken his great commandment: that until the time was right, Keltia should not for peril of its very existence reveal itself to the Earth that its folk had fled; nor forget, for like peril, those other children of Atland who had followed them into the stars—the Telchines, close kin and mortal foes, who became the Coranians as the Danaans had become the Kelts...

This tale takes place in the centuries between Brendan and Arthur: in Earth Reckoning, around the year 1650.

It is a time when the sovereignty of Keltia stands vacant, when no High King or High Queen rules from the Throne of Scone. In these days the sovereignty does not always descend from monarch to heir as a matter of course but can be contested and won by a successful aspirant, always provided that that one be of the blood royal, however remotely traced.

And, just sometimes, that one might even prove to be the soul best fitted, or most fated, for the task: to ride into legend...

When the aged King Conamail dies, leaving not even a remote heir, the many factions and families claiming a right to the Copper Crown start squabbling bitterly amongst themselves, too bitterly to notice that the Firvolgians, whom Saint Brendan had so decisively cast out of Keltia so long since, have been creeping back like a secret stealthy tide.

By the time it dawns on anyone to think to resist, the Firvolgians—or Fir Bolc as the Kelts turn the name, after an old Earth enemy—are too firmly entrenched to be cut out by swords alone, and they and the Kelts settle down to an uneasy coexistence. A merchant people, the Firvolgians have introduced to Keltia all manner of unwanted innovations, most of which merely stir up discontent and some of which are utterly loathsome, adding nothing of merit, debasing much that has long been deep-rooted in the Keltic soul; they also seize a near monopoly on star travel, so that the Kelts, who a thousand years before had made their great voyagings through the galaxy, now must come and go at the pleasure of others.

Even the nobles, long time the guardians of the Keltic way of life, have grown disheartened, and try to scrape along with their unwanted neighbors—the Incomers, as they are called publicly; Kelts have rather less courteous names for use behind their backs—as best they can.

Over the years fierce battles have often erupted between Keltic lords and powerful Incomers, but nothing ever comes of them, save that the Kelts are left dispirited and drained, less eager than ever to try to oust the insidious invaders. By the time this tale begins, most Kelts have resigned themselves and accepted the situation, without hope, despairing, acquiescent to what they think must ever be.

But not all...

There was a young queen in a far town
Born on field of battle, she came to wear the crown
Her hand in war had earned a warrior's name
And love of justice burned in her like flame.

There was a dark king from the lands west
With poem and song he fought his battles best
He sang to her or ever they did meet
Fate conquered them, but it was no defeat.

They met in winter, joy'd in autumn fair
These fated two did hearts' true union share
Forswearing of all others, free in thrall,
They fell in love, and by love they would fall.

This king rode east alone one day in spring
In golden May he gave his love a ring
He asked if she would be his bride and wife
She answered they would vow past death and life.

Midsummer Day this royal pair did wed
Lay in each other's arms in a bless'd bed
A moonyear's joy they had, all love their own:
Then banished rival made a widowed throne.

This king's true queen in wrath did then arise
Struck down her mate's betrayers and their lies
Avenged him on his slayer with bloody sword
Upon the Low Road sought her lost loved lord.

She found him in that kingdom all folk fear
Saved him alive when none dared venture near
Silksteel and Fireheart: Where all lost faith
By love and valor they won back from Death.

Long years now these two lovers have been gone
Slipped hand in hand away to ride the storm:
Together once, against all evils done,
Together for aye, with all their love has won.

This King and Queen shall never be apart
They gave their souls in giving hand and heart
Two things only kill or heal or save:
Love is first; and then it is the grave.

—from The Ballad of Athyn and Morric,
            by Brahím of Aojun

Taer y gwir an y'n golau.
(The truth is eager for the light.)

—*Lassarina Aoibhell ac Douglas*

ꝼORETꝑLE

By these signs shall a hero be known: an eye to see
the truth, a heart to feel the truth, an arm to defend
the truth. To that I would add: wisdom that strives to
teach the truth, courage that dares to speak the truth,
love by which the truth shall live forever.

—*Séomaighas Douglas Ó Morrighsaun*

She was born among the dead.

Drawn from a dying woman upon a stricken battlefield, she was very nearly never born at all. Her father
had already perished in the terrible fighting, her mother was
on point of following; and she would surely soon have joined
them both had not a weary soldier, wounded himself—a galloglass in the vanquished host, passing footsore by on the bitter
retreat—heard her tiny outraged cries, and turned fatefully
aside.

Scooping her up from the bloody ground where she lay still
half within her mother's body (which not-yet-faded warmth
and unsevered link had surely saved her long enough to be rescued at all—the first, last and only gift, save life itself, the
dying woman could give her living child), he cut the birth-
cord with his own sgian, heard the last faint desperate whispered words and made solemn vow in answer, then swaddled
the scrap of infant in the sword-slashed plaid of a clann that
was none of hers.

Even in his fear and hurt and weariness, the galloglass had
also the rare foresight, or the rarer sentiment, to take as keep-
sakes for the child orphaned at her very birth the brooch and

ring from the dead woman's shoulder and finger, the sword and medallion from her belt and throat, the heavy battle torc from round her neck. He would have taken a swathe of her hair also, but there were reasons why he could not find a tress fit to cut. He left her with a prayer for her speeding and a promise for her child; there was no more that he, or any, could have done.

And even he himself, in after years, could not say precisely why he had done it: why, in peril that very moment of his own life, he had turned aside to save a life that had scarce begun and looked to be almost as swiftly ended, to cumber himself on a desperate retreat-march with a newborn babe that was none of his and not like to survive even her first night. There had been no portents, no omens that he had perceived: no voice in his battle-dinned ear, no shadow against the sun, no wind of a dark and fated wing. But that which he did changed Keltia forever, and more than Keltia at the last.

So he carried the foundling home to his clann and his wife and his children, and she grew and thrived and was happy among them. But the jewels and the sword and the lastwords of a warrior were carefully and scrupulously set aside, given into the keeping of the clann brehon and the bard of the kindred, bound about with fearful oaths of secrecy, until such time as the child should be of an age to value them, and to hear their meager history; for just then that seemed all the heritage she was ever like to have.

Some evil crabbèd souls in years to come did mock the gesture, jeering that the galloglass had but despoiled the unknown dead like any battlefield gleaner, of her child no less than of her jewels. Not only that, they gibed further, but had the infant sickened and died, as seemed for many days the likeliest outcome, he would have simply pouched for himself all the bits of gold and stones and silver. For who knew, they sneered again, that the orphaned lass had even been given full and correct count of her dead mother's pitiful remembrances—it might be that the galloglass, in venality, had kept back more than he gave. Or perhaps, they even dared to suggest, he had lied from the start about the truth of her origins.

So, indeed, some loathly foul-far'd folk did say and think, in after days. But she was never among those who thought so or said so; and being one who did not suffer fools at all, much less gladly, when such mouthings did assail her ear she struck back, and struck hard.

And nor was that the only time she was to do so...

BOOK I

The heart is the hero's weapon.

—*Morric Douglas*

chapter one

It is a truth universally acknowledged, that, as the scaffold sways the future, a romantic character upon the stage of action will sway more parts in the great drama than his—or hers—alone.

—*Davyth na hInclei, called Incleion*

One of her earliest memories was of walking with her father—he was her fosterfather, not her sire, though how he had come to foster her she was yet too young to know, and never for all the years of his life or hers did she call him, or think of him, as aught but 'father'—across spring-green fields near their home on the planet Erinna.

They were bound on an errand of high importance: to choose a horse for her to have for her own, her first; or small-horse rather, her thin legs would have made no dint at all upon the girth of anything greater. She was perhaps six then, or a little either side of it, and she could not remember a day when she could not ride, or was not at home amongst horses: a solemn child with long straight brown-red hair and eyes a deep gray-green under a neat-cut glib; tall for her age, with promise of more height to come, round like a candle but whip-thin. She had lived all her short life as a fostern among six brothers and sisters, not one of whom was the least kin to her by blood. But then that would have been the case for any Keltic child of her age, to be so fostered—though true it was also that few Keltic children were brought to it, as she had been, from the hour of their birth. Few other children had had such need to be; but this too she had not yet been given to know.

They lived in a sprawling stone maenor surrounded by the ancient elm trees that had given the place its name of Caerlaverock, which according to the dialect employed could mean either 'fort among the elm trees' or 'lark castle.' Both were apposite: The towering elms with their rustling foliate crowns were home to shoals of the lovely soarers, and the family, seeing across the fields the singing spirals rise up to greet the dusk and dawn, could time its day by the comings and goings of the birds.

The house itself was big and comfortable, three-storied, with wings going back from the broad front, stepped gables and deep dormers in the tile roof; built in a time when defense was not so needful, mellow with years and ivy clothing alike its walls of warm red stone. The family's lands went on for miles; but the maenor stood proudly in its elm-grove in the midst of vast rolling grasslands, with mountains blue and far to the east and high rough hills much closer by, from which their holdings sloped down like a great grassy saucer to the edge of the sea.

They had lived always in that place, or so it seemed to her. They were farmers, horsebreeders; the Name of Archill had been renowned for centuries on Erinna for excellence in bloodstock. The beasts they raised were various, and to the child all beautiful in their own way—tall elegant creatures that moved as delicately as dancers and had temperaments to match, for lords and ladies to ride and race; tremendous gentle plowbeasts with huge feathered hoofs, bred for hill-farms, massive as hills themselves; patient sturdy garrons and ponies little bigger than the giant wolfhounds raised on the Lanericks' farm that marched with their own lands upwith.

Their nearest neighbor was an Incomer, Nilos Marwin by name. They did not see much of him; he was a quiet, educated man, sparing of his presence, unlike to nearly all his kind in nearly all his ways. The Keltic overlord of the district, Esmer

Lennox, Earl of Connacht, seemed to a child even more remote, as distant as a god, as the lost monarch. Fairer than any, and better than almost all, he was caring and concerned for the many kindreds that looked to him under the old brehon laws. He was scrupulously polite to the Incomers in his ancient domain, who for their part, and for what they deemed good cause, called him Velenax, a word that means in their tongue 'wild boar,' and gave him wide respectful berth. As for the Clann Archill, they did not much more often have to do with him than the Incomers did, or he with them, though her sister Sulior said the Earl and their father were old battle-comrades, and that she, Athyn, had been shown to him as an infant, upon her saining, so that the lord of Connacht might know his liegewoman for the future. She, of course, did not recall, and no other had ever spoken to her of it.

She caught now the scent of horses on the spring air, a warm sweet tang of hide and health, sweat and straw; the wind had veered round to the southeast, over the Elmet plain. Then they came over a last small rise and were among the herds. The patiently cropping knot of horses nearest them were cold-bloods—the fiery throughbreds were kept carefully apart—and among these were the garrons from which they had come to choose.

Solid-boned, hard as iron, lacking the flair or the fineness of the better-bred animals, the garrons were affectionate as hounds, possessed of no chancy temper—in all ways unlike the irritable little ponies from whom she had learned to ride almost before she could walk. As her dignity and saddlecraft alike—on both of which she prided herself—were too advanced by now for those bad-tempered thrawn little creatures, she had insisted on a garron or nothing. She had been so fierce upon it, indeed, that at last her doubtful mother had given in, though not without dire warnings. Even her father, she knew, thought privately that she had overchosen herself, and that there would be tears before supper.

But she was confident. Besides, she could always unchoose later, if it turned out that she was after all over-horsed. True, she would suffer loss of face amongst her forever-teasing sibs— and perhaps worse from her eldest brother, Kier—but she cared little enough for that. Her own judgment was to her what mattered most, and she would thole her own mistakes— so long as she was the one who had made them. So early did she come to that which was destined to sustain her so well for so long through so much.

An indulgent laugh sounded above her, and she looked up. Her father's hand—weathered brown at the end of a muscled arm webbed with fine flat silver scars—still held hers. She had a vague idea that he was a soldier, or had been; someone had perhaps once told her so, or she had overheard it, or then again it might merely be one of the stories she told herself of nights for comfort. But whatever he may have been, Cormac mac Archill dwelled here now, upon the farm of his ancestors that were and his descendants that would be, and seemed content.

He pointed with his free hand. "Athyn? Do you see the horse you would have?"

She looked, and shook her head. Then her scanning eye lighted upon a beast that was watching her from some yards away. Black-maned and black-stockinged to the knees, the little garron had a coat gray as stone, mottled here and there with dark dapplings and a darker spine-stripe. A handsome beast; but she knew already that horses are not to be chosen by appearance, and stepping forward, not looking up for her father to approve or forbid, she held out one small hand, and held her breath.

After a moment's considering—it seemed to be as carefully judgmental a creature as herself, and she rather liked that— the garron came to her, pacing deliberately, not all a-rush like his herdmates. He bent his nose to her hand, mouthing the pieces of apple she offered, then pushed his head hard against her, wanting her to scratch that place between the eyes that on all horses seems ever to want scratching. So small was she, the beast's head near as long as she was, that even so light a shove set her all but off her feet, but she laughed as she was lifted backward, unafraid, and reached up to oblige.

"So, Athwen-fach? Is this your horse then? Are you his rider?" her father asked, watching with some amusement the two half-broke young creatures sensing each other out.

"For now, tasyk," she said clearly, and held out her arms for her father to lift her to the garron's short powerful back for the trudge home. "For now."

They returned to find a household in turmoil. Even her mother, who as a rule was serene as Erinna's moons, sailing imperturbable above even the fiercest rows, was of a fluster, and seized her husband by the arm as soon as he entered the stoneflagged stairhall, speaking to him in a low urgent voice; the child could not make out the words.

Athyn looked up sharply at a hiss from above: her sister Sulior, beckoning urgently from where she knelt by the railings of the gallery that ran all round the front hall. She glanced again after her parents, but they were heading to the back regions of the house, clearly preoccupied, and just as clearly had forgotten her.

"What is it?" she asked breathlessly, as she came to where Sulior was crouching, half-hidden in the lee of the oak balusters. "Why is mamaith—"

Sulior pushed her brown-gold hair over her shoulder and threw a quick fearing look behind.

"The Lord Nilos was here," she said in a dramatic whisper. "He was looking for tasyk. I do not know why."

"You must not call him 'Lord Nilos,' but 'Ser Nilos' or 'Nâr Marwin,'" said Athyn primly. "That is how the Firvolgians name themselves."

Sulior dismissed the correction. "Aye, well enough, clever-clogs, aye, you always know best. But he is coming, mamaith said so. To dine with us this night."

"But why?"

"Why indeed?" came a new voice, and Athyn looked up guiltily. Then she saw who stood there, and shrank back, until she was pressed against the baluster's carving.

Her eldest brother stood at the head of the great sweeping wheelstair, his arms folded crosswise over his chest. Kier mac Archill, eldest son and inheriot of Cormac by his long-dead first wife Kerys, scowled down upon the two younger girls, and even his own half-sister Sulior pulled back now, until Athyn's arm was pressed close to hers. Athyn found that she was shivering, and felt Sulior shaking against her.

Kier saw and smiled. "Where have you been?" he demanded then, glaring at Athyn. "You and my father were gone long enough—"

'*My*' father... Even a six-years' child could not miss the venomous emphasis in that; all the rest made no distinction whatever between their status and Athyn's (as she would make none later; save, forever, between herself and Kier, and what could be fairer than that?). But now Kier took a threatening step forward, and of the two girls Sulior was the nearer to his hand...

"We went to find a garron for me," said Athyn quickly, sacrificing her treasured news to prevent his wrath, as she would toss her only food to a growling dog, a bribe to safety.

Kier, diverted, gave a scornful snort. "You? Little rhisling, little gricemite? I would have thought even that old brokeback brown pony too much horse for you—"

"Well, I have a garron now, and he is *mine*," she countered, surprised at her own willingness to challenge him. "He is in the home barn now, if you do not believe me. Aunya is vetting him." *He spoils everything, why does he have to spoil this too...*

Kier scowled afresh. Aunya nic Cafraidh was Cormac's master of horse; a sunny, shrewd woman, handsome with her emerald eyes and long thick whitesilver hair. She had a great fondness for cats—if none at all for him—and she was the best horsedoctor in the Elmet valley, perhaps in all the province. Even the Earl sent for her at need, and if the bratling said that she was looking over a garron, it was probably so...

"No matter," he taunted. "Even if it is sound *you* will never back it, or not for long, any road."

Sulior intervened in her turn, emboldened by Athyn's defiance. "The Lord Nilos is coming for the nightmeal," she informed him. "Mamaith had word—"

"Then doubtless your mother will understand my absence from her table," he flung back at them, and clattering down the stair out the hall door, slammed it so hard behind him that the sconces shook.

"Why does Kier hate Ser Nilos so?" asked Athyn, more to cover her hurt and fear than out of any real curiosity. "For that he is an Incomer?"

Her sister glanced at her. "Do you know what Incomers are, Athwen?"

The child nodded confidently. "They are not from here. Not Kelts as we are. But Kier?"

Sulior drew Athyn after her down the panelled corridor toward the big sleeping-loft they shared. "Never mind. He may be rude to mamaith—and she is more his mother than ever Mistress Kerys was—but he will not dare risk tasyk's anger by refusing to come to table when a guest is in the gate. But Goddess, look at you! All over grass and dust and horse-sweat—bath first, and then perhaps Debagh will plait our hair for us, if we ask her nicely enough."

Three hours later, scrubbed and shining, their two beribboned thick braids, gold-brown and red-brown, hanging neatly down their backs—their eldest sister Debagh had been successfully prevailed upon— Sulior and Athyn sat side by side at the long board, and bowed their heads, as at the far end of the gleaming waxwood table their father spoke the formal grace that in Keltia ever precedes the meal.

That board was as filled as was usual on nights when the family dined alone: Cormac mac Archill at one end in a massive carved chair upholstered in the clann sett, deep blues and greens with a red line running through; Lyleth his wife on his left, children and household members ranged down the sides. At the other end, Kier in the tanist's place faced his father; and on Cormac's right, in the place of honored guest—

Stealing a look while the grace went on, Athyn saw with some surprise that Nilos Marwin had lifted his hands in a Firvolgian attitude of prayer, and kept them so while Cormac spoke to the gods the thanks of Clann Archill for the meal and the guest who shared it. He was older than her father, perhaps not by more than ten or so years—the Firvolgi enjoy but two-thirds the lifespan of the Kelts—a man of middling stature and build, with dark blond hair as yet untouched by gray, though the neatly trimmed beard was shot with silver. His eyes were a clear light brown, like stones in a mountain pool, and now as the brief prayer finished and the table settled down to the business of supper Athyn saw that those eyes were turned on her.

She blushed and bent her head to her plate—children did not speak at table unless spoken to by an elder, and certainly did not rudely stare at guests however foreign. So she missed the smile that lighted Marwin's features; but neither smile nor look had been lost on Kier.

Athyn was hungry, and across the table from her Aunya nic Cafraidh took care to see that all the younger children were properly served from the lavish board: beef, gammon, salt-roasted porrans, fresh bread, the first spring greens. There were six of Cormac's altogether: Kier, only offspring by his first wife, Kerys; then his brood by Lyleth—Debagh the eldest; a boy, Tigernach; the twins Errick and Galian, a boy and a girl; and Sulior the youngest, more than five years older than Athyn; and Athyn was set apart by a greater difference than age alone.

The meal had been a merry one: Nilos Marwin had praised the food, his hosts, the sleek horses he had seen in the Archill fields as he rode over from his own estate across the valley, the beauty and health and manners of the children, the talents of the harper who played behind the tapestry; and if there were other, darker matters that he wished to discuss he was too polite or too circumspect to mention them over meat.

Down the table's length, Athyn was shyly confiding to Aunya her hopes of a blue leather saddle for her upcoming birthday, when suddenly Lyleth's voice cut across the converse like a whip.

"You shall be silent! Before everyone in the hills hears you! Or else you shall get down from the table!"

Startled and guilty—surely she could not have been talking so loudly, to anger her mother so?— Athyn looked up, and saw at the foot of the table Kier's face flaming with anger and embarrassment, and as she looked he threw his chair over and stood up.

"Then I go! But I will *not* be silent!" He muttered some dark oath too low for the young ones to hear and was gone.

Nilos Marwin never turned so much as an eyelash in Kier's direction, but touched his napkin to his mouth and smiled at his host.

"I hear your youngest lass has a new garron this day?"

Athyn crimsoned as indulgent glances turned her way, and though her mother smiled encouragement at her, and her father bespoke her gently, bidding her answer the Lord Nilos, she could only stare miserably at her plate.

"Athwen," murmured her sister Debagh, "you are being discourteous. Tell the Lord Nilos of your horse."

"Nay, nay," said Nilos smiling. "Let her be. But perhaps she will show me in her own good time."

"Kier said straight to the Lord Nilos's face that all Fir Bolc were liars and thieves and coarser than a pig's back, and that all Keltia thought the very same but did not dare to say."

A chorus of little gasps followed the words. It was three hours past the end of the nightmeal—the elders of the household had all this time been closeted in Lyleth's solar, with the visitor—and the Archill children were huddled like a sheaf of seal pups, in a pool of light on the floor of the vast attic that served them as dorter. It was Debagh who had just now related to her sibs the nature of the heir's offense against the guest, thinking that since surely they would hear, soon or late, best they heard it from her.

Sulior asked the question the others were not quite bold enough to ask. "Did tasyk punish him for it?"

Debagh nodded solemnly. "Thrashed him for it across the horse-trough... Nay, he will *not* take it out on you, I promise! I know he has done so in the past, and my sorrow that I could not always protect you. But tonight you need not fear," she continued. "He has ridden off to his friend Sennen's house, over to Kensaleyre town. He will not be back tonight, and I will go now to speak to tasyk—"

"Nay, do not!" came from Athyn and Sulior in the same breath, and the other three were not far behind. Debagh looked round at them all in turn.

"Do you say—"

"We say nothing," countered Galian, the middle sister, and Errick, a silent blond lad, her twin, nodded solemnly. "It is easiest, and it is usually best."

Later, when the visitor was gone at last and the house was quiet and the children were either already asleep or else disobediently reading in their beds, Athyn sat on the edge of her own bed and stared out at the deep blue night sky.

Save for Kier and Debagh, the younger Archills were not considered old enough just yet for the grandeur of rooms of their own; though each had a particular private alcove with shut-bed and clothes-press and desk, they still slept all together in the long high-ceiled attic with its vault of dark timber beams, and they still took a certain very real comfort in the others' nearness.

Athyn had all to herself a dim corner that none other coveted, well off to one side, tucked beneath the eaves. She thought it perfect: snug and secret and private, her own little space within a dormer where her bed just fit; and by closing the curtains and door-panels of the shut-bed she could make a tiny room for herself out of bed and window and the vast view that the tall window gave on to, of elm-groves and the blue hills beyond.

The heavy curtains of the bed blew in slightly, and she turned to see her mother, a tall handsome woman in her early mid-age, with softly curling brown hair and gold-flecked hazel eyes. Lyleth settled herself upon the pillows with a smile and drew the child into her arms.

"We never had a chance to talk about your garron."

So Athyn woke up again and told her mother all about her day, and then, fighting sleep, twisted in the curve of Lyleth's arm and looked straight up at her.

"Why does Kier hate the Lord Nilos?"

Careful as she was to keep her feeling out of her face, Lyleth's look clouded, just a little. "Well, Lord Nilos is a Fir Bolc, a Firvolgian as they call themselves. They do not rightfully belong in Keltia, and there are many besides Kier who would have them gone."

"How did they come to be here?"

"They fought the great Saint Brendan, of whom you have been taught; fought him for Tara, oh, long ago. He won, you know, and drove them out. Since their name for themselves in their own tongue was 'Firvolgi,' we began to call them Fir Bolc, after our enemies on Erith of old."

"Have they no place of their own they can go back to? No homeworld?"

"Surely. It is called Kaireden, and Katilon Ke Katil is its great city. But they have ever considered that they have a right to our worlds, and down the years we have had to show them over and anew what Saint Brendan once showed them so well: that they do not."

"Do they know we do not want them?" The voice was

drowsy now, and Lyleth shifted the child in her arm, dropping a kiss on hair still damp from the bath.

"Oh aye, hen, but it makes no differ. Not to them... When our good King Conamail died, more than a hundred years ago, he left no heir, and ever since then the kindreds that might claim the Copper Crown have not stopped fighting over which of them should have it. Thus we have no High King or High Queen, and while the Throne of Scone remains empty the Fir Bolc slink into Keltia. And so some of us call them Incomers, though it is not a word I should care to ever hear you using. Now they are well seated here, have gathered estates and brughs; some have even married amongst us."

"But Kier?" Athyn was struggling to keep it in a place she could define.

Lyleth slipped her arm carefully out from behind the child's back and eased her gently down onto the pillows. "Whether they belong here or no, most Firvolgi—like Ser Nilos—are fine natural folk, honorable and good. Many more are not like Ser Nilos; but, whether they be good or evil, Kier and those other Kelts who feel as he does will not have them in our lands. I fear he and they may take rash measures to have this be so. But go now to sleep, alanna. Tomorrow we shall go to see your garron. Find a name for him in your dreams."

But after the child had fallen asleep, Lyleth yet remained, looking down at her. Then with a sigh she stood up and went from bed to bed in the big airy dorter, checking to see that all was well. Last of all, speaking a soft word to dim the lights, she set the tall wolfhound bitch bought of the Lanericks on guard upon the threshold, and went to find her husband.

chapter two

What the Goddess does not wish does not prosper.

—*Rhain mac an Iolair*

The clatter of shod hoofs in the yard beneath her dormer roused Athyn from her nap. She was awake on the instant, dazed by sleep, confused, thinking it was yet morning and she was late to feed and groom her new garron. But no, she had done that, she and her mother and her sister Galian had after long and spirited discussion named him Cloud... But, judging by the shadows and light, by now it must be nearly four, on a showery, blowy spring afternoon.

She ran downstairs. Outside the door in the front courtyard were perhaps a dozen strange horses, with strangers in Connacht hunting dress astride them, each beast crabbing away from each other, and one aiming kicks from his near hind at anything that moved. Then she saw the boar crest on the trappings, the silver crest badges glinting on cloak collars, and the same in gold upon the short riding-cloak of one who sat a tall bay mare.

"It is the Earl Lennox!" said Tigernach, dashing past. "Come to see *us*!"

It was indeed, and Athyn moved aside behind a pillar of the porch, a barn owlet in the rafters for curiosity, peering out at the lord of the province. He was not tall, Esmer Lennox, but strong of build, with gold hair and a full, well-grown beard, and Athyn thought he looked somehow sad. Beside him, mounted upon the powerful black horse that was doing all the kicking, was a lady with long brown hair done in great braided loops; she had a merry face, and she was controlling her fractious mount effortlessly, if not with much success. This must be the Countess Ganor, born one of the great Scotan kindred of Colquhoun...

Athyn's small bright face caught the Countess's eye, and Ganor smiled. "Come, lassling," she called in a clear voice, beckoning, and Athyn began to sidle shyly out from behind her pillar.

But by then Kier had arrived at a run to greet the noble visitors. In passing Athyn he cuffed her sharply, and so swiftly that none but the Countess saw. Athyn, caught off-balance, fell onto the rough stones of the yard, scraping the brawn of her hands and taking the skin off both knees. The Countess flashed a look of fury at Kier, but he had not seen that she had seen, and bowed innocently to her and her husband.

"My lord Earl, my lady Countess," he said, "be welcome of Archill."

Esmer waved a gloved hand. "No ceremony, lad," he said. "We were caught by the rain out hunting, and thought to stop by. Is your father about, or his lady?"

Just then Lyleth came running from the back regions of the house. When she saw who her visitors were, she stopped short, then started forward again when she saw Athyn in the Countess's saddle where Ganor had lifted her—much to Kier's annoyance.

"Countess, has the lass troubled you? Athyn—"

"Not she," said Ganor curtly. "But she *has* been troubled."

While Athyn's scrapes were being washed and salved in the herb-room, the Countess Ganor spoke with point and plainness to Lyleth as to how the child had come by them. Outdoors, the accompanying riders were being served with stirrup-cups, and Esmer Lennox was walking with Cormac in the privacy of the orchard alley. They were speaking earnestly, and of the two it was Esmer doing the greater share; but what they spoke of even the most curious could not tell.

When the visitors had at last ridden away again, Cormac did not go into the house straightway but returned to the pleached alley where he had walked with the Earl, to walk a while alone.

Supper that night was a subdued affair, but after the board was cleared Cormac did not give the customary leave to the children to get down from the table. Surprised by their father's departure from long practice, Athyn and Sulior nudged each other.

"What do you think!" said Sulior. "Tasyk *never* keeps us so—" After the nightmeal, if their studies were done, the children were free to go where they would—the bard Haneria Lauder, in her cottage down the road at Sauchiehall, was a favorite resort. Cormac and Lyleth, for their part, were accustomed to sit on around the table with the other elders of the farm and whatever others might stop by, folk of the four subtigern or tenant families who dwelled at Caerlaverock as habitants in the ancient way, working the farm side by side with the tigerns of Archill. The heads and heirs of all those kindreds were here this night—an unusual occurrence in itself.

"I spoke this day with the Earl Lennox," said Cormac then, "and what he had to tell me was not good. There have been increases in raiding parties of Firvolgian bravos, mosstroopers, all over Keltia—on Gwynedd and Tara they have become most especially brazen—and of late they have begun to make little dabs into Connacht."

"They have never dared come this way before," said Donlin Iveragh, who was Caerlaverock's rechtair, and the subtigerns looked troubled.

"It has been the Earl himself, the fear of his arm, kept them out," answered Lyleth. "But it seems that is changing."

The kienaght captain Gwenda Dalis gave a short laugh. "Brief memories the Incomers must have, to forget Velenax, and what lesson he taught them at Sherramuir! But see, my lord, if mosstroops make inroads into Connacht, to come so far as our valley, it might be best if we were to train up some of our kienaghts into creaghts. To be prepared."

Even Athyn knew what she meant by that. Every lord or liege in Keltia of dúchas standing kept companies of kienaghts in service as household troops; it had been so since oldest times. They were small light companies trained with spear and sword and bow; most troops were horsed, and versed in mounted drill. These days they served more as peacewardens, to deal with such minor offenders as came along, or haywards to round up strayed beasts, or as helpers in time of natural disaster—fire or earthshake or flood. Over the years the need of kienaghts' service had never grown less; but creaghts—armed riders, skilled in catteran warfare and living on the run—were a different story, and Athyn and Sulior exchanged fearing glances.

Cormac mac Archill saw this, and spoke at once to scotch it. "Nay, lasses—all you—there is naught to fear in that quarter, the Earl Lennox shall see to that... But our good captain's word is well taken—do so, then, Gwendal." He stood up. "I wished you children to hear, and to be more 'ware when you are out and about. There is naught to fear at present, and Goddess grant there never shall be. But we must keep sharp all the same. Go now to bed."

As it happened, no raids ever penetrated the Connacht that time. Though the borders were many times tested, the maigen of Esmer Lennox, and the strength of his name, or of his fist, held strong against the mosstroops. But those who lived in the Elmet valley trained themselves to look for raiders; scanning the hills when they went out had become second nature.

Athyn was twelve now. She could ride like a bansha; and in all other ways her life was as that of any maid of her year and station. She had friends among the children of the subtigerns and of other families in Elmet, but her sister Sulior was still her closest confidant, and she had learned all that the local bards and brehons had to teach.

Yet, like every twelve-year-old, she somehow felt a lack, a

nettling, a longing for she did not know what. And, like any twelve-year-old, she had begun spending much time alone, in an attempt to find it.

That day Athyn had a half-holiday from chores, and as soon as the noonmeal horn sounded she had thrown some meatrolls and cheese and fruit and new apple wine into Cloud's saddle-sack and had ridden west, down to a hidden cove that had become her special place. Once there, she had done nothing, or so she would have said if anyone had asked her; the great thing was simply to be away. So she had gone knee-deep in the water—because of the shelving seafloor, and the cliffs trapping the sun, the little rockbound cove was warm as a pool-bath—and then she had worked her way through most of the contents of the saddlesack. After that, she had curled up in her plaid in a grassy hollow, out of the keen wind off the waters, and read, and the strong sun had soon sent her to drowse.

Now she was awake again, and just beginning to think about riding home to supper. As she stared out over the sea just outside the cove, something nearer moved and flashed and caught her eye. Clambering out on a huge flat rock slab, Athyn perched on the overhanging edge so that she could see straight down into the clear green water, and caught her breath.

At first glance they looked like a drift of golden leaves, autumn leaves fallen into the sea, so aimlessly did they seem to be caught up in the current. But each of the 'leaves' was easily the length of her body, with a long stem-tail behind, and they were moving in rhythmic unison, riding the current's stream. It was a shoal of goldencapes, most beautiful of the rays that swim along that coast, their bodies glowing gold against the white sand of the bottom. And in the midst of the soft bright edges slowly stroking, the mantles of the rays baffing and rippling round her, was a girl of about Athyn's own age, swimming with the grace of a silkie, her long brown hair waving like waterweed in the tug of the swells.

They were joined by seawings coming in on the tide, cousins to the goldencapes but silver-gray by contrast. Athyn, watching from above as they went by, was struck with awe and envy in about equal parts. She herself could not swim to save her life, or anyone else's, and this girl who moved underwater with the ease of a sea creature seemed a being of a different race entirely than landbound Kelts.

But perhaps, she thought suddenly, it was the same for this stranger among the seawings as it was for Athyn herself among the horses—a thing so natural that it had ceased to be a wonder. She leaned heedlessly forward, picturing what it must be like to ride the tides as easily as other mortals walk on land— the silver sandfloor, the restless ceiling of heavy clear crystal shot with white foam streaks that was the underside of the heaving waves.

As if she had somehow heard, the swimmer glanced up just then, and saw Athyn through the sunshot water. She knife-dived in a flurry of bubbles, extracting herself from amongst the rays—who seemed unwilling to lose her company, for they waved their cloaks around her with something like distress. But the girl rose to the surface as if fired from a bow, and stood beside Athyn on the rock, the water still streaming off the long brown hair that went down past her waist.

"Morvoren Kindellan," she said, naming herself as was the country custom. "My family live at Seaholt, a maenor twenty lai down the coast; we are sea-ranchers, in liege to the Earl Esmer Lennox."

Athyn named herself and her own dúchas, then remembered her manners. "Are you hungry? To swim all that way— and out of the water you must be cold—"

Morvoren gratefully accepted the offer of a spare plaid to wrap herself in, and even more gratefully a pastai or two and some apple wine. After a shy start they were soon well away, so that Athyn readily found the courage to ask what she had been longing to ask as soon as she had seen Morvoren below the waves. At first the other girl was astonished to the point of speechlessness.

"Not to know how to *swim!*" she said at last. "Well, that is a thing easily remedied—no friend of mine goes as a landswoman to the water."

Her words warmed Athyn as even the apple wine had not, and so eager, in fact, was Athyn to begin that she had all but stripped off to dive, no matter the tiny detail that never in her life had she been in water over her knees. But Morvoren laughed and said nay, there was much to be learned before Athyn could join her below the waves, and any road she must get home before dark; though her parents knew she was well able to look after herself in the running seas, still they would fret, and in any event they liked not for her to be out alone in even the home waters after sunset.

"Though even when the sun has gone, Athyn, it is never dark below—the waterweed in the great beds offshore gives off green light of its own, like sea-candles, to light all the lands beneath. Some of the fish have lights too, along their bodies, and the goldencapes with whom I swam here today look like little sunken moons."

Which only heightened Athyn's wish to go underwave at once... But Morvoren stood up, and shedding with thanks the borrowed plaid she drew herself tall and taut in the westering sun, and then speared the water. Athyn, watching anxiously, for the tide had turned in earnest now and the great combers rolling in were silvery as glass, saw after a long moment a small sleek brown head like a pretty seal's bobbing up beyond the breaker-line, and a white arm lifted to wave.

Athyn waved back, then vaulted up on Cloud and turned for home. But when her mother asked at the nightmeal how her day had gone, she surprised herself by her own reluctance to speak of it; and wondered if Morvoren felt the same, safe and warm at home herself now, down along the coast.

She did tell Sulior, later, before retiring, who had been pleased and interested to hear, though Athyn could not shake off the reluctance she had felt in the hall below. But her sister had understood perfectly.

"This is something completely your own. You have never had something like that before, something unlike to anyone else's. Not even Cloud; for all the rest of us have horses, but none of us has a friend that can swim like a merrow."

And their talk had turned then to farm-talk as usual, of haying, and a new falcon of their brother Tigernach's, and always, ever, horses. But when Athyn fell asleep at last, it was not Clann Archill horses that moved through her dreams but Manaan Sealord's own steeds: endless waves smooth as marble and heavy as silk, riding high against the land, and down among the netted fine red weed that sways to and fro forever in the current and the tide, goldencapes slowly moving, wings rippling, gleaming like a handful of coins thrown into the waters, for luck or for dán.

chapter three

If a woman stir, expect a storm.

—*Selanie Drummond*

hen Athyn turned fourteen, she was advanced to the dignity and responsibility of herdward, spending most of her time out in the fields with the horses, under the watchful gaze of the horsemaster Aunya nic Cafraidh.

Her beloved Cloud had last year been put out to pasture—though he still followed after Athyn like a loyal and loving, if oversize, hound. He had been succeeded by a taller version of himself, a handsome and mischievous dappled throughbred called Tarn, chosen for her by Aunya to suit her great and growing skill as a rider.

Indeed, there was little else that Athyn knew how to do; horses were the only thing she had. She might have liked to become a sorceress, a Ban-draoi; but every time she had broached the possibility to her parents she had been sharply discouraged, and after a while she had learned not to mention it, ceasing to wonder why she should not even speak of it.

She did not yet know it, as she did not yet know so many things about her own birth, but there was indeed good reason that Cormac and Lyleth put the topic so sternly by: In those last terrible moments on the battlefield Athyn's dying mother had laid heavy geis on Cormac; had begged the galloglass to save her child, and if by the Goddess's grace the child survived, that he would by no means allow her to become a sorceress.

She had had neither time nor strength enough to give him her reasons, but even so Cormac had vowed as she wished, and for fourteen years he had solemnly kept his pledge to her, and to her child, unbroken.

He might well have done so even had he not been oath-bound: The life of a sorceress is no easy one, nor by any means always pleasant. Cormac mac Archill had come to love the foundling lass as dear as any of his own—dearer sometimes than all of them—and parents will ever spare their children what they can, no matter that the child in question scorns to be spared so.

So Athyn had been taught therefore only such small hedge-magics as everyone in Keltia knew, useful tricks any village witch could teach, and picked up from books what else she might—skills she had faithfully shared with Morvoren, learning a few water-witcheries in return—but her sister Sulior had more than that, or soon would have. She had gone off to the great Ban-draoi school at Scartanore, on the other side of the mountains from Elmet; Athyn wondered for a while why she might not do likewise, then set it aside and spent even more time with her beloved horses than before.

Then one winter night not long thereafter came for the first time an arwydd, a portent; and the possibility of a very different sort of future indeed...

Athyn came awake as out of deep water; suddenly, completely. A sound? No, the attic was quiet. She sat up, reaching out in a way no book or village witch had ever taught her—no hedge-witchery here, and had Cormac beheld her then, working it all but unconsciously, he would have blanched to the marrow—as if she extended her body and mind together, as one great searching finding hand.

But the whole house slept; in quarters they slept, Aunya and Donlin and Gwenda and the others, the subtigerns in their own snug warm brughs, deep in woods and hollows scattered across the silent winter farm. The beasts slept also, horse and hound and all the rest alike; as far as she could reach Athyn alone was wakeful.

She lay down again, but the feeling grew stronger, as if someone was calling her; out of her bed, out of the house— perhaps even out of herself. She could pretend she dreamed and did not hear, and not go; or she could follow the call—and when had *she* ever misliked to venture out into the deepness and stillness of a winter's night?

So not wishing to disturb Lyleth—who when one of her own was sleepless, beast or human, displayed that eternal maternal instinct that would wake her out of even the most dreamless depths— Athyn drew on trews and boots and tunic as quietly as she could, wrapped herself in her cloak, and then, stealing soundlessly through the dark quiet house, slipped down the back stairs and out through the cookplace.

Once outside, past the kitchen-gardens and the home orchards and into the frost-covered fields—startling a knot of night-feeding deer down from the hills to forage among the stubble—she took a great deep draught of the biting air, and felt her mood lift and take wing.

Earlier a light snow had been falling, but now the sky was swept clean, moonless, clear as black glass and sown as thick with winter stars as spring grass with daisies. Her favorite constellations—Caomai the Armed King, Rhygar the Archer on his great rearing horse, Ariandal's Crown, the Lymphad, the Plough—all blazed overhead, and she stared up at them with sudden longing, seeing the heavens, for the first time, as not so much 'up' as 'out.'

Never in her life had she left the planet of her birth. Save for her father, and the Earl Lennox and his Countess, and Ser Nilos Marwin, she did not even know anyone who had ever been offworld. It was a privilege few could afford, at least in these days of the Firvolgi, who not only had seized a monopoly on interstellar travel within Keltia shortly after their arrival in strength, but charged such high tariffs for it that most Kelts were kept planetbound—one of the things of which her fostern

Kier most bitterly complained. As for travel outside Keltia's borders, well, that was beyond the reach of even dreams; there were even some these days who doubted Kelts had ever done so, claimed no Kelt had ever voyaged the spacelanes—this heresy despite all history to the contrary.

What must it be like, Athyn wondered suddenly, with a thrill that unevened her breathing, *to sail among the stars!* To see the other Keltic worlds, which she knew only from books and farviewers and the stories her father told; to see Tara, the ringed Throneworld with its silver moon and crimson one, and the Crown City of Caerdroia, and the thousands of worlds that lay beyond Keltia, where once Kelts had gone as if by right—even Erith, whence Kelts had come long since... She sighed gustily. Whatever it might be like, it was only an ashling, and of the worst sort. *It is neither good nor healthy to pine for something one can never have...* But she stared at the stars a while longer all the same.

Then, as she lowered her gaze from the heavens, something flashed in her sidesight, and she instinctively whirled eastwards, the direction from which the brief bright blink had come.

That way lay few farms or settled places but only darkness like a breaking wave: the great high ranges of Druimattow, the Long Hills—though that is purest irony, for the tallest of those 'hills' tops ten thousand feet. Queen among them is the mountain called Sheehallion: Long held to be sacred to the Sidhefolk—hence its name— Sheehallion is a dead volcano, a graceful cone that raises shapely snowy shoulders above the rough gray jostle of its neighbors. There is a deep blue lake within its crater, and a precious jewel set atop the perfect peak—or so the story goes, everyone in Elmet knows the tale— which can be seen flashing at noon throughout the district.

To see the jewel flashing at high twelve meant good fortune; but to behold it at night meant either disaster or the onset of greatness. *Or possibly both...* Athyn closed her eyes tightly for an instant, then resolutely opened them and stared at the outline of Sheehallion against the stars. This time there was no mistaking: A lance of light sprang out from the summit and seemed to pierce the long dark miles, dazzling her eyes so that she threw up her hand to shield her sight.

But she lowered her arm almost at once, as if she were commanded, and let the blazing white beam fall full upon her face. How long she stared into it, or it into her, she did not know. But she came to herself in the middle of the frozen field; and as she retraced her steps, very slowly indeed for one who was as cold as she was, Athyn was already resolving not to speak of it to anyone. If disaster was betokened, best none should know of it save herself, so that perhaps then the trouble might fall only on her; and if greatness, well, better still that none should know of it, for no one would believe it, and she would but be mocked for ashlings of grandeur. Indeed, she scarcely credited it herself; and so she would not speak of it, not until much later, and even then only to a few souls. But who can say how it might have fallen out if she had?

Several times a year Athyn went upwith to the mountain grazelands, to take her turn at herding. Even in winter the horses must be toughened on the high hills, and each herd had a particular stretch of upland to which it returned year after year, to the separate valleys and the shielings delved there, those huge caverns hollowed into the mountain sides that serve as shelter in extremes of weather.

All the children on the maenor did herd duty; most of them thought it little better than torture and exile, fleeing thankfully home as soon as their relief had been sighted trudging through the gap. But Athyn loved to be on the mountain, alone with the herds in the high meadow. The horses required very little; Athyn was there chiefly to see that no beast took sick or injured itself or went short of food or water, and the animals seemed glad of her simple presence. Every now and again, three or four together, or one alone, would come ambling over to her for no apparent reason, nuzzle up against her or mumble gently on her sleeve, then when she had made sufficient much of them, go away again, seemingly reassured; their affection comforted her as much as hers did them.

This year she had helped a work party to raise a little shieling for herself, a bield; had delved it deep into the side of a hill, the double door and two round windows sole advertisement of its presence to the world.

Inside, it was as warm and friendly as her old attic nook; she had made it fine with a pieced-fur coverlet on the bed, thick sheepskin rugs on the pale wood floors. There was a quaratz-hearth for cooking and heating, and a tiny pool-room that did duty as a tynollish—the healthful vapor-bath produced of stones and steam that no Keltic home would be without. One wall was solid books; on another hung a beautiful panel of Keltic knotwork that her sister Debagh, already a renowned limner, had carved for her. In a niche stood green bronze lamh-dhia of the Goddess and the God, and one in sea-opal, Morvoren's gift, of Athyn's special protectress Malen Ruadh Rhên. As seemed both prudent and polite, and was traditional in most Erinnach homes, especially in these northern lands, a great pair of shed antlers of the mighty hillstag, ten feet in span, crowned the front door, to honor the God in His aspect as the Cabarfeidh.

It was not all herdwork: Athyn found she had all the time she could wish to practice her handcrafts, or study the pishogues she had been taught by the local witch, or simply lose herself in the volumes of barderies Haneria Lauder had compiled for her. She fed herself on simple good fare: stews and soups, grilled meats wrapped in toasted bannocks; she had even found a new thing to do with the ever-present shakla, drinking it icy cold, made with a mix of fresh milk and the naturally bubbling waters of a nearby spring.

Thus contentedly employed and comfortably housed, she spent endless days listening to the wind slide over the mountain, sometimes hearing voices that were not her own, no voice she knew; it did not alarm her. Often great storms would boil over the mountain barrier and fill the high valley: The sky would howl through a whole season in an afternoon, and gale-borne rain blow horizontal lines like fine steel beads.

But it was all fine: In spring came blustery winds and pink sunsets, and on the damp air the cold fresh scent of life returning to the ground, mist drifting in the bright green hollows and, later, miles and miles of whitest may; in winter the snow-winds puffing around her in the dark, air clean and sharp as wine, snow so dry underfoot that it squeaked when trodden upon, the blackness above the mountains separated from the peaks by a brilliant line of green or purple light, and the Dancers in their bright reel high in the north. But she loved best the autumn with its high blue skies, hard and polished; the cold northwest wind in the horses' tails, waking them up after summer, making them wild to run.

At night in all seasons she had the cool blue omnipresent light of the galaxy, a bowl of stars inverted above her head and the warm sweet scent of grass and horses like a placemarker in the dark. Best of all were the tremendous mountain sunsets, skies richly aflame round to north and south, casting a glow even into the east behind. If autumn was her season, sunset was her time; but in all times and seasons when she was on the mountain, she was so happy she could scarcely speak.

After supper one autumn night Athyn went outside to watch the sun fall westering and the valleys fill with shadow; the hills reared up like islands in the blue evening mist, and the herd was already settled down for the night. A flash of sheeting white light startled her, turned her attention to the sky. *No thunder; what then*— She scanned the deep star-sprinkled blueness like a mariner. Above the hills all was clear. But in one quarter it seemed that something huge had bitten out a chunk of sky, for there was a starless patch in the southwest; a thunderstorm, far off but closing fast.

A whitewing owl baffed by her out of the dark, so close its feathers brushed her cheek. *Only a nightghost*, she told herself, to still her rocketing heart. And then, before she could turn away to go into the bield and ready herself for bed, having promised herself a good long warm soak and a cup of shakla and a new epic-tale after, her heart all but burst from her breast as a giant bronze stallion, his hoofs soundless on the damp grasses, suddenly loomed over her, and on his back a red-cloaked rider lifted a hand and spoke to hail her.

"The greeting of the gods and the folk to you," she said as was custom, heart racing. She felt no menace from the stranger, and indeed he meant none, but she was still near perished with the sheer surprise of it; and a further surprise was that her new wolfhound, Elster, frisked round to greet the newcomer as if he were an old friend. *So much for a bath and my new book and early bed...*

"And to you and your house," he returned correctly. "There is need in my dún, and I ask your help. My horse can carry us both. You will not be long away, and we will see you safe home again after."

Athyn felt a first faint thread of not fear, but wariness, and a certain causeless feeling of awe. She must have betrayed herself, for the stranger smiled just then, and threw back his hood, and she saw the faint silver-blue light that clung about him. Her awe found its focus: This, then, was no mortal man but one of the Sidhefolk; judging by the narrow gold fillet that bound his dark-gold hair, a lord among them.

"You have naught to fear," he said. "I am Allyn son of Midna. I ask your help in Nia's name, and for the sake of Neith ap Llyr."

Neith ap Llyr... Even Athyn knew to whom that name belonged—and no one in Keltia dared refuse anything asked in the name of Nia, who was mother of Saint Brendan and patroness of all Kelts—but she lifted a troubled gaze to the faerie lord. His face bore no sign of the desperate urgency of his plea; indeed, his countenance was a calm and settled one—not hopeful, not expectant, merely watchful. And above the watchfulness, strangely, a look of assessment, of judgment. She hastened to answer before she was judged awry.

"For Nia's sake, to be sure, it is yours. But how comes it that the king of the Sidhe should seek *my* help? Neither I nor any of my kin have ever had dealings with—with those who dwell beneath the hill."

"Truly," said Allyn mhic Midna, smiling. "But if you have not known us, we have known you; and our need this night is for a mortal woman. She whose usual office this has long been is not to home, and though there are others we trust as well, they are not near enough for even a rider of our folk to fetch in time. You are the closest of your kind to our dún, and if you do not come to our assistance we will be in grave strait indeed."

Athyn felt a sudden relief, and well understood the rider's urgency. "A lady of your folk—her time is upon her? I will help gladly, lord, but I have no experience with matters of this sort; well, save only with mares... If that will serve your need?"

Allyn laughed. "You will not be called upon to perform midwife's office; your simple presence is all. And the lady it concerns needs you now."

Athyn was already clasping her cloak at her throat. "But the herd? I cannot leave them unattended—"

Allyn reached a hand to pull her up behind him; as she set her booted foot on his and vaulted up, she was surprised to realize that the Sidhe rode without saddles. Or bridles either, she saw, peering round the lord's shoulder: The tall bronze stallion—magnificent even to her eye—bore only a plumed silver headstall crowning his long cream-gold mane; perhaps he needed no guidance at all.

"Do not be concerned for your beasts," said Allyn, even as the horse reared and turned, and she blushed for the liberty but put both her arms round his waist to hold on behind. "I have spoken to your good hound, and to your two gray friends. With their help, my folk shall ward the other horses well for you while you are gone. A service for a service, as we say, and a gift for a gift. You will not be absent long."

chapter four

None is so blind as he who will not see.

—*Tipherris Inchspell of Greyloch*

She could never afterwards recall how long they had ridden; or even if they *had* ridden, for it seemed to her that at times the bronze horse's hoofs—shod with silver before, and gold behind—had beat on roads of air, not turf at all. Nor could she recollect the way they took; the lands round were veiled in mist, and she suspected that too was faerie work.

Athyn was well aware of the gravity of their errand. Among the Sidhe, a child comes to the birth but seldom, and if, as seemed likely, this imminent babe was the child of some great lady and lord among the Shining Folk—well, no wonder their concern, and the desperation that had forced them to accept instead of a skilled matron whom they knew and trusted, and who was friend to their folk, a maid of fourteen, a stranger who knew only horses and who had never seen born even a human child.

I will do what I must, and I will do my best; there is no more that I can do…

"It is enough," said Allyn aloud.

At last the bronze stallion slowed and then halted. Allyn mhic Midna threw one leg over the beast's neck to dismount and turned at once to help Athyn down. They passed together through a gate in the side of a smooth gray mountain wall, light spilling out from

within, though until they had set foot on the slope no gate had
been there, or at least no gate visible to mortal sight.

Athyn hesitated on the threshold, recalling all the stories
she had ever been told of the Sidhe. Fair but perilous, they had
said; and, Never go within a dún of the Folk, but if you must,
be sure to leave cold iron in the gateway to assure your coming
out again—though she had no iron on her, not even her little
sgian with the knotwork-carved wood hilt; and, Do not for any
sake eat or drink in a faerie rath, should you be luckless enough
to be brought within...

Her companion had turned, smiling faintly as if he knew well
her thoughts. Now that she could see him clearly she wondered
that she had not known him at once for one of the Sidhefolk: an
extraordinary face of great beauty, but that was not the over-
riding impression one took away from it. There was wisdom
there, and sadness, and humor, and a long strange patience that
she did not understand; a face utterly unlike the faces of mortal
men.

"The choice is yours, Athyn nic Bhrendaín. Enter or nay; if
enter, enter by cold iron or by plain trust. Choose thou."

"How if I choose wrong?"

"No free choice is ever wrong. But the choice you make will
determine other choices, and you will not always be the one
who makes them."

She drew in an unsteady breath, then let it out all in one puff.
"My father says there is no victory without venturing," she said,
"I shall trust." And she stepped past him into the dún beneath
the hill. Too proud to glance up, she did not see what was on his
face just then. But it was a many-layered look he bent upon her:
respect, and pride, and, strangely, affection; stranger still, a long
sadness, as if he saw a far and distant day, and a fate with it.

Within, the halls were bright with light and color. All was
silent, and she saw no other of the Folk save her companion
alone, until they came to a chamber outside whose hammered-

silver doors a woman stood. She smiled at the girl and then bent a glance full of meaning and relief on Allyn mhic Midna.

"You come in good time," she said in a voice like a river of bells. Then, to Athyn: "Welcome, maiden, and our thanks. I am called Tarleisio; it is at my bidding you are summoned. Come now within. Naught to fright or fear, no peril on you. This is not a birthing as you might understand it, or have ever seen it. But a child is surely coming, and just as surely you are needed."

Athyn, who had at first taken the woman to be of the Sidhefolk, now was not so certain. The lady was surely fair enough to be: Her name meant 'echo'; her hair was as dark as Allyn's was golden, the eyes a startling amethyst. But she seemed warmer, or nearer, than Allyn's high remoteness, more human and yet less so at the same time. Athyn could not make up her mind about it. Then the silver doors opened, and she forgot fears and questions alike—for each fear and each question were at once replaced by fifty more.

Within the chamber, a woman gowned in gold lay in a wide fourposted bed; and if her travail was so far advanced as the other two had suggested, then labor of bearing for the Shining Ones was nothing like to any labor of which Athyn had ever heard.

First and strangest, there seemed no pain in it, not as she knew was the case among women and every other female creature of the world; no cries were uttered, no convulsive pangs or strivings to bring the coming child to the birth. The woman lay utterly still, in profound silence upon the bed, and though her flame-colored hair grew darker with the sweat of her effort, no other sign of her travail was upon her—she looked as if she slept, or had died.

Yet for all the strangeness, Athyn could see that a mighty struggle was being played out here, and a great mystery. Wherever the woman had journeyed, to fetch her child thence into life, it was a far and perilous place, with pain of its own. But if the destination was a mystery the purpose was ages-old the same, no different for the Shining Folk than for mortals. This errand of birth had taken the Sidhe woman to a place that was no concern of Athyn's, not though it be down into Annwn itself; only the end of the journey mattered. And Athyn suddenly understood her own part in all this. The strength in the world of a mortal woman was needed by the faerie woman in this hour, as a kind of grounding, as the rod will draw the lightning, to bring a child of the Shining Folk into being.

The knowledge discomfited her somewhat, though she could not say why. Yet the strength had been humbly asked, and was hers to freely give. *That*, she could do—all her will, all her purpose, all the strength she had learned in her days on the mountain. It took as much out of her as any physical effort; she could feel herself growing weary with it, her muscles trembling with the long striving. In some strange and wondrous way, she herself was in labor as much as was the woman upon the bed.

And that was truer even than she knew, for without her the faerie child could never have come to the birth. However it had been made in the first place—in the usual manner, presumably, as between male and female of any other kind—it was mortal strength alone could bring it into the world at the last. So Athyn came to learn, as she sat beside the bed, and waited for what, or whom, she did not know.

Nor did the child, when it came, arrive in anything like the usual way: Indeed, when she thought about it afterwards, Athyn could not recall even so obvious a thing as had the woman been big-bellied to begin with; nor did she behold any blood either after or before, nor see the child emerge, if even it did. One moment there had been in the marble chamber only the laboring woman and the darkhaired one and Athyn herself, and the silence and the distance; the next moment there were four persons present, the last a very new one indeed.

"There now," said Tarleisio. She swathed the child in a piece of silver silk and brought it over to Athyn. "See whom you have helped enter into the world of form."

Athyn peered shyly at the infant. She had seen newborns before, if not their actual birthing, and this looked like no newcome child she had ever beheld. His face was pale and perfect; his eyes were open, crystal brown with a clear bloom of light on them, like cairngorms, and she startled back a little, for he looked upon her as if he not only beheld her but knew her.

"And so he does," came the clear soft voice of the woman who lay in the bed. "And will again, as you will know him. His name is Gwyn." Then, seeing on the girl's face the huge trembling question that out of fear and courtesy would never be asked: "I am Seli, wife to Neith."

Athyn bobbed a curtsey, hand to heart, and all her fear came flooding back. This whom she had just helped through her labor was not merely some noblewoman of the Sidhe—daunting enough—but the queen of the Shining Folk herself.

And every tale she had ever been told of mortals who had ministered as midwives to the Sidhe leaped to Athyn's mind. All those tales ended much the same, and none well: Often the hapless woman was kept prisoner beneath the hill; or if the Shining Folk did let her go, they would take away her sight or her speech, so that she could neither tell of them nor find the dún again; and if she escaped from the hill she would find her own world had passed her by a hundred years, a thousand years ago, and fall upon the instant into dust...

"Never happened, not in all time," said Tarleisio, who stood by the bed, and who had been watching the thoughts chasing like clouds across the girl's face and mind. "You have been listening, I think, to the blighted words of folk who know us not. Though I think also that you have never believed those words, not in your mind, still less in your heart." Athyn flushed and lowered her eyes, and the woman smiled. "No shame, maiden, in ignorance. The only shame is in remaining in ignorance."

She was about to say more, but they both turned at a sudden word. Seli the queen was holding her son in her arms; she it was who had spoken.

"Brother will fight brother," said Seli then. "It cannot be altered. Lord of the Dark. Huntmaster. The coming of the Boar—"

What that meant Athyn dared not ask—though Tarleisio seemed to have a fair idea. But Athyn startled afresh at the unexpected touch of a hand upon her arm; and she would have been a thousand times more alarmed had she known how rare it was for one of the Shining Folk to touch a member of a mortal race.

"So then," said Allyn mhic Midna, who had entered silently. "You have heard."

Athyn nodded. "She is your queen," she said humbly, as if she somehow craved pardon for the knowledge. "And the child?"

Allyn's eyes clouded. "This one will be king one day among us," he said, with the slightest emphasis on the 'this.' "Gwyn son of Neith— You have done us, and Keltia, a greater service than you know. But what will you say of it when you return to your folk? Will you have gold of us to keep a silent tongue? Will you have a gift of song, or an enchanted jewel, or a magic sword? We can put a rann on you of forgetfulness, if that will make it easier..."

"You asked my help, lord," said Athyn, anger and hurt overcoming her fear and weariness, not to mention her courtesy, to edge her voice like glass. "You did not buy it—in Keltia, at least among mortals, such help is not for sale but freely given, friend to neighbor, neighbor to friend. I have just now been well instructed that your folk do not commit such things as stupid folk have accused you of, and I will take that word. As for my silence, I can hold my tongue as well as you."

Allyn looked at her a moment, then bowed deeply. "My sorrow, maiden," he said. "I meant no offense. But we do not have many friends among your folk. It is always surprise to us, and joy, to find another, and one so young as well."

Before Athyn could repent of her outburst, he bowed more deeply still, and not to her. Without even glancing round she turned and sank at once into yet another curtsey: Neith ap Llyr, king beneath the hill, had entered the chamber.

Athyn studied him from under lowered lashes as he halted before her. He was a lord dark of hair and deep of eye, who well might be of an age with the hills themselves but looked to have fewer years on him than her own father. He was clad in red, and wore no crown; upon his hand was a ring with a clear gold stone. He smiled at Athyn, though much else there was in the chamber that could have claimed his first attention, and gestured for her to rise.

"And because she does so in full faith, setting aside fear and curiosity alike, asking naught of us in return," he said, "she shall be given much." He spoke to be heard by those crowding behind him, courtiers eager to see the new prince; but to Athyn also. "Our thanks, maiden, and the thanks of ages uncounted. You may never know just what dán, and whose, has turned upon what you have done this night. Ask of us what you will, whenever you will; it shall be granted. My queen and I name you goddessmother and fostermother to our son, and the bond works both ways. Not only our people are in your debt for this, Athyn nic Bhrendaín, but the gods themselves. Do not hesitate, when the time comes, to require that debt be paid."

Then even he was silent, for the queen Seli was sitting up now, fair as the morning, a green shawl covering her shoulders and her hair red as firemist above it. Her birth-ordeal had left no mark upon her; she smiled at her lord and took his hand as he came to look with her upon their child.

"A gift I shall give you," said Seli, looking at Athyn over the baby's head, "a gift from a woman to a woman. One shall come who will be to you both fate and mate together. He will be tall, his hair like the oakbark, his eyes like the sea. A lord with music to his hand, and his own art will name him— Fireheart they shall call him. Your lives will not be as others' lives, nor your love as others' loves. You will be his queen forever, and queen of more than that, if you have the courage; and in the end you shall claim him from the lords of dán in a place where never living woman stood."

Athyn curtsied yet again. "My thanks, lady," she said, in her recklessness of relief even daring to jest. "Though every girl in Keltia has ashlings of such a mate, and such a fate, and sees him in every omen every cailleach reads her in the Samhain flame!"

The queen Seli smiled. "And sometimes even the cailleachs are correct, the ashlings true; how else could they be dreamed at all? But dreaming is not enough: Someone must take dream and forge it into truth, not for herself alone but for all folk; and you, Athyn nic Bhrendaín, shall be one of those who do so."

"And that is a thing I meant to ask of sooner," began Athyn. "I am but the fostered foundling of Cormac mac Archill; yet this night, your highness's self and the Lord Allyn and the King Neith all have named me not nic Archill but nic Bhrendaín. How should this be? My line, though unknown to me, is surely no line of his."

But in that moment a light came, and a dizzying spiral, and Athyn found herself back on her own hillside in the pouring thunder-rain. Amazingly, it seemed mere minutes since she had been ridden off with, for the storm she had seen away in the south had only just now reached her valley. Yet still she heard Allyn's voice in the thunder and the storm.

"What shall be the maiden's fate? Who shall be the maiden's mate?" But to that she had no answer, and he did not give one; or at least not then.

In the morning, when she awoke in her own bed, it seemed a dream: the rider on the great bronze horse, the pale queen and the child, the faerie king and all his folk... *Fostermother to a prince of the Shining Folk! I must have dreamed it, or else I have gone mad with the mountain-ill...*

But she knew it was not so, and as she gobbled half a pas-tai—as all the tales advised she had declined to eat beneath the hill, though now she felt a churl—she remembered that though she had not asked for reward, she had been given one: not only the promises for the future, but the favor of the Sidhe for the Archills' farm. This they had bestowed gladly, for as Tarleisio had said smiling, they had seen how Cormac treated not only his beasts but his folk, and they knew also that he kept and honored the old ways.

Yet when she dashed out to attend to her morning routine, she was brought up short to see that all chores were long done, the horses already out of the shelters and grazing peacefully. Plainly, her charges had been well cared for in her absence—as Allyn had promised.

Athyn shook her head, baffled anew by the Sidhe and their ways, yet also comforted. She had friends now that she had not had before last evening, friends such as few in Keltia could boast, friends beneath the hill; and she turned to her stallion Tarn as he trotted up eagerly. She leaned against his dappled flank, and he snorted and blew her hair around her face and tugged her cloak from her shoulders, as he had recently learned to do.

"What then?" she asked him fondly. "Well it is said, go not to the Sidhe for plain speaking! See you remember that, my Tarn—" *Even so, this is yet another thing I will keep close in my heart…not that anyone would believe me, any road! Indeed, I am not sure that I myself would believe me, did I come to me with such a tale…*

But perhaps she would write her sister Sulior, away at her Ban-draoi college far in the east. After all, she *did* owe a letter.

chapter five

There is more than one yew bow in Gwynedd.

—Alveric Elshender

After Athyn's adventure beneath the hill, life at
Caerlaverock seemed calm and tame, and all the more
to be treasured. She spoke of her experience to no
one, holding herself bound by her word—and even if that were
not so, still she would have kept silence.

The Sidhe too kept faith: Caerlaverock prospered as
never before. No mare died of foaling, no colt perished on
the hill; the farm's stallions were eagerly sought for covering season and all bloodlines thrived. Cormac, going about
his farmwork, sometimes looked at Athyn and wondered;
but if his wonderings ever led him to the truth, or even to a
corner of it, he said no word. As for Athyn herself, her
faithfulness, and her silence, soon found unexpected reward.

On the hill again with the horses, a night of terrible snow and
bitter biting wind. The beasts had all been driven into the
shieling, and having set Elster on guard Athyn went out again
to look for strays.

But after a half-hour's searching she found that all the beasts
were safe, and it only remained to get herself under her own
warm roof. Then as snow slapped her face from an unexpected
direction, a heavy wet hand of ice, she peered through the fly-

ing lines of sleet, and realized with a stab of fear that she was lost.

Surely I came this way, she thought, putting down the rising panic. *See, that is the nurseling hill over there, and the stream-bed…* But when she struggled through the knee-deep blanket of snow and the hip-high drifts, she saw with terror renewed that it was not so. *I wonder does it hurt to freeze to death? I have always heard not, but who knows?* Staggering back the way she had just so laboriously come, Athyn presently found herself at a place she had earlier marked. It was many inches deeper under snow now, but it seemed also the only shelter she was going to find before the cold claimed her: a nest of giant boulders, beneath which was a tiny cave like a badger's or a fox's earth, lined with moss, roofed by the boulders' overhang. *If I can crawl back under there far enough, perhaps it will be enough to keep me warm until morning light…*

But as she burrowed down into the deep dry ferns at the back of the earth, tugging her furred hood down over her face, curling up with her hands tucked into her oxters for greatest warmth, she knew in her heart that it was unlikely to fall out so. *Ah well, perhaps it will be as I have ever heard, easy and pleasant, like drowsing off in front of a fire…* As her terrible shivering began to ease, the cold seemed suddenly very far away and drowsiness started to steal over her. *Either way, sleep or perish, I have no choice in it now…*

Warm. Amazingly warm, much too warm. She had piled too many coverlets on top of her, or perhaps the quaratz-hearth had been set too high, she must get out of bed to lower it, or open a window on a crack before she got a headache. Also there was a strange muttering rumble in her ear, like faraway thunder or the sea… Athyn opened her eyes, and saw above her head not the beamed ceiling hung with drying herbs that roofed her bield, but the veined rough underside of a granite boulder. With some difficulty she extricated one hand from inside her jacket, and rubbed it over her face, and no chill clung to either; then memory came back with a rush. The snow, the dark—but if she had gotten lost in the storm, had spent that howling night in a fox's scrape, why then was she so warm?

As she pondered, she suddenly became aware that the marvellous warmth—and the low vibrating sound—came from a very particular place just behind her. Holding her breath, she slowly shifted until she was lying on her other side, and could see what the source of both might be; and when she saw, she froze yet again.

A giant hill-wolf lay between Athyn and the cold, completely filling the entrance to the scrape, curled protectively against Athyn's back as if she were one of his own cubs. He was awake, watching her steadily out of gold-flecked green eyes; his warmth was what had kept her unfrozen, and his almost purring croon was what had awakened her; it rumbled still, a soft benevolent earthshake. Athyn dared not even blink; but the wolf nudged her with a paw, and then, astonishingly, licked her face with a warm rough tongue.

How magnificent he is—wolves are not rare in these parts, but never have I heard of one as strong and big as this, he must be twice even Elster's size, and for a wolfhound Elster is enormous...

Yet she herself had seen the wolfclanns at play in the high hills, and it was by no means unheard of for one of the shy hunters, more curious than the rest, to come so close and friendly to a human... Athyn lifted a tentative hand to stroke the great head with its black-brindled ruff of mane, and the croon increased, deep in the mighty chest that bore a milky star of silver fur. Then the creature leaped up, and, stretching prodigiously, nudged Athyn with his nose. She was not slow to heed him, but scrambled out of the shelter, stood up and looked around.

Though the snow had stopped, clouds still swagged menacingly above the hills with the promise of more to fling; but the light was clear and the wind had died. Athyn saw with passionate relief that she was but one glen away from her own—in the blizzard and her panic she had miscounted the valley ridges—but now it would be but a quarter-hour's easy walking up the great hollow to reach her bield.

Yet, if the wolf had not been with me through the storm... Athyn turned round, with some confused thought of thanking the creature for having saved her—but again she went rigid, and this time neither with cold nor fear but surprise. The little corrie was empty, and the only tracks had been made by her own booted feet. Prints as clear as if they had been cast in stone, and no pawprints went beside.

"It was your fetch," said Sulior, home at Caerlaverock for a visit, confident in her new magical expertise, and rolling her eyes just a little. "Did you not know?"

Athyn gaped. "I am not a sorceress to know these things, you know, that is why I ask you! But a fetch! For *me*? But how? Our kin have not that honor—"

Sulior's smile was warm but rueful, as if she did not wish to have to remind someone she loved of so obvious a fact. "You are not *of* our kin, Athwen-fach," she said gently. "We forget, because we love you, but you come of a different blood than ours. It would seem, perhaps, a higher blood," she added, and Athyn made an explosively dismissive sound.

"Now *that* I do not think!" But all the same, behind the protest, things were falling into place. "Well, you are the Bandraoi in this family—pray *you* tell me what it means."

"A fetch is a magic beast who attaches himself—or herself—to a particular family. Wolves, bears, bison, ravens, hawks, eagles, stags, serpents, are your common fetchly run, though it can take what form it pleases. The fetch warns its chosen kindred of coming dangers and protects them when those dangers are upon them; it heralds approaching death so all may ready themselves; it advises them, in dreams or even in waking life—it follows no rule or reason but its own.

Sometimes it will be that the family has no history of a fetch, never been blessed by one, but the Goddess Herself, or another of the gods, or even the Sidhe"—here Athyn could not hold back a start—"will ordain a fetch to some member of that kindred. I would say that this wolf of the hills is yours, Athwen, or more correctly, you are his, though I cannot tell you why. But be glad and grateful, for it is a wonder! None of Clann Archill has ever before been so honored."

Not for worlds would she have spoken her inmost thought: *Or so doomed...*

Summer again, a sulterous sullen twilight after a day far too hot and humid for Elmet, the year that Athyn turned sixteen. She had been out with the broodmares and foals in a pasture by the sea—it was Aunya nic Cafraidh's theory that saltgrass helped the mares' milk and the foals' bones alike—and Cormac at her asking had ridden down to the seafield to help her with the beasts. Something had made them fractious and irritable all day long, and Athyn could not cope; and in any case her father's company was always welcome, especially since these days it was so infrequent.

As Caerlaverock bloodstock had grown more and more in demand, so too had demands increased on Caerlaverock's master: Athyn stole a sidewise glance at Cormac where he patiently coaxed a mare and foal to follow the rest of the herd to better grazing. Cormac mac Archill had aged well; the chestnut hair held few silver threads, the soldier's posture was unbowed, the energy undiminished. Yet his fosterdaughter could not look at him without wondering, as she never had in her childhood, what had motivated him that long-ago day on the battlefield, why had he turned aside to save a justborn child that was none of his own. Fialzioch, that fight had been called, a fearful defeat; one of the seemingly endless skirmishes and slashfights fought by Kelts in their ever-vain attempts to dislodge, or at least discommode, the Firvolgi intruders.

But Fialzioch had been followed by Sherramuir, that glorious turnabout in which the Earl Lennox had so decisively thumped Firvolgi aspirations, and won his byname. But now as Athyn watched her father working with the horses he loved, she wondered too did he ever regret those days—or the impulse that had saved her life.

Her musings were broken off by a sudden commotion among the stock. All at once the mares, who had been so reluctant to bestir themselves, bolted snorting up the valley, their halfyear foals tearing alongside. It was some moments before the humans heard it also: a low rumble down from the north, growing swiftly to a roar. *Snowslip?* Athyn knew well that sound from her winters up at the grazeland valleys, in spring thaw only a fool would not have one ear listening for that fatal thunder. *But this is August...* She started to turn to her father, but before she could complete her turn it was upon them.

Afterwards, she swore that the grasslands had rippled toward them, the dark fissure visibly knifing through the fields, swift and deadly, lightning in the earth; it left a slash like a bleeding wound across the land, the rich earth showing red. The ground heaved once beneath her, tremendously, like a horse under saddle going down to roll—yet this was one horse from which she could not dismount.

She could not see her father for the shaking and the dust, could not think for the terror of the roaring. The earthshake's motion knocked her off her feet and flung her from side to side; she willed herself to go limp, and she lay very still until she heard the thing move on. The air was full of blue flashes, and a curious sharp metallic smell as of burned flint.

Dazed and bleeding where stones had cut her hands—and somehow she had lost her boots, she could not think how— Athyn pushed herself up to look for her father; not seeing him, she staggered forward, then ran like the wind in bare feet toward where she had seen him last. But after the roaring, there was only shocked silence; and then there was something else.

The sea was rising in wrath against the land: A wall of glass-green water thirty feet high, child of the earthshake, displaced when the fault line broke beneath the sea, was rolling up the glen from the coast. Athyn had no time even to fear before it was upon her; but as it came, she saw what seemed the veriest terror-born phantasma: her friend Morvoren, riding upon the wave as confidently as ever Athyn had ridden a horse of earth.

No delusion: As the wave broke and hit, Morvoren glided through the raging wash with unhuman grace, catching Athyn into her arms as the waters carried them on. A confused few minutes, both of them tossed like corks, then the wave began to recede, slowly at first, disorganized, then faster and faster, and at the last with a terrible, irresistible speed. As it did so, pulling back out to sea down the steep-walled glen, Athyn could see tumbling in the white and green fury the forms of luckless beasts who had not been swift enough or smart enough to get away—horses, sheep, wild goats—and other forms beside.

Morvoren had with exquisite timing positioned both of them near a ledge in a sea-cliff, so that when the waters receded they were neatly deposited in safety. They huddled there a while, Athyn shivering and silent in her shock; then, when the sea grew a little calmer, Morvoren heedless of the dangers dived back into the waves. She was gone a long time, and when she returned to shore she was not alone: Borne upon a living bier of silver seawings, Cormac mac Archill came with her.

Cormac's was by no means the only life lost in those parts. Several entire villages along the coast had been obliterated—though the Kindellans at Seaholt were, thankfully, spared—and far upwith, where the wave had shot like a sun-gun through the little glens, the damage was terrible.

"Because the valleys are so narrow, the wave did not

spread out," said Debagh bleakly, "but was only funneled harder and higher. It was a miracle of the Goddess that *you* were spared, that Morvoren was so near. Tasyk would have given his life to save you, Athwen; be very sure he is glad you came through."

It was midafternoon of the third day since the earthshake, and Cormac's ceremony of speeding would be held at sunset in the family annat. All the Elmet valley was assembling to pay tribute: Even the Earl and Countess of Connacht were riding over, from their country seat at Graystones. Of near neighbors, Nilos Marwin had been among those who came at once on hearing of Cormac's death, and seeing the through-other state of the Archill household he had unobtrusively moved to assist.

In the immediate aftermath of the upheaval, Lyleth had been frantic in her fear, thinking Athyn and Cormac drowned together. When the girl, face like a glazed stone, leading Tarn with Cormac's body lashed into the saddle and Morvoren walking soberly beside, returned beyond hope from the fields, Lyleth had enfolded her fiercely, in relief and joy too deep for tears. But Athyn gave Tarn's reins to her mother and walked straight on into the silent house, and as she did Kier's terrible shouted accusations rang after her.

She had gone where she always went in hurt and in wounding, up to the old attic dorter, and shut herself into her little bed-corner, curling into a frozen blazing knot of pain and grief, the same refrain running through her mind. Kier had just now blamed her for Cormac's death, and for once he had the right of it: She *should* be lying beside Cormac down in the hall, it *was* her fault—the loss of Cormac, of ten good broodmares and their foals, of the little fishing villages, even; all of which was far beyond the bounds of reason.

Even Morvoren could not help. But when the grieving girl lamented that her friend too had been put in danger for Athyn's wretched sake, Morvoren confided that she had been in nothing of the sort, and for a very particular cause.

"Of the sealfolk? You are of the blood of the *silkies*?" Athyn stared at her friend, caught in spite of herself. "That would explain your featness in the waters, right enough... But how can that be? Mortals do not wed with the Sluagh-rón!"

"The kinship is from Erith," said Morvoren, "not from here. But my family indeed had a sealwife for foremother, before the Kindellans came with Brendan to Tara; and it seems that every now and again her blood crops out in her descendants. And I am one of those ban-rónna... I was in the sea that day by chance, but had I not been of her blood I could not have helped you, nor called on such help to fetch home Lord Cormac's body."

"And I am glad of both," said Athyn in a muffled voice, contrite that she had not yet expressed her thanks to Morvoren as was fitting. But even the wonder of such a confidence could not carry her past the guilt; nor the wonder, even greater, of seeing creatures of the waters bringing Cormac back to land—the seawings who at Morvoren's asking, or perhaps command, had borne him home upon their silver cloaks. "I shall be better amazed, and properly thankful, in a few days, when I am not so— Just now—"

"Just now you have other things to think on," said her friend. "But others there are who need you, Athyn. They deserve of you also, and your father would expect it. It will be easier on you, as well, if you meet it straight on."

Athyn smiled at last. "For a sealwife you are too clever by half."

"Wisdom of the land too," said Morvoren imperturbably, as they went down the stairs arm in arm. "Cows farthest off ever have the longest horns."

Cormac mac Archill's rites of speeding were long remembered in the Elmet valley. Near two hundred folk had crowded into the family annat to honor his going, and thrice as many again stood without, for Cormac had been as

loved as he had been respected, and even in the face of
their own losses no friends of his had stayed away. Esmer
Lennox himself spoke the Last Prayer over the body of his
comrade-in-arms. By Lyleth's order Cormac was buried in
one of the upland grazings, on a southward-facing slope
where shadow never fell, that overlooked the whole vast
vale; and Debagh drawing upon her limner's skills cut into
the turf above the white chalk the figure of a running horse,
hillside-high, that ever after gave the vale its name.

During the ceremonies, Athyn had kept herself apart,
hanging back as far as she could without being accused of
disrespect. But disrespect to Cormac was the last thing she
meant: It was guilt that kept her in the shadows, guilt that
had been with her, a dark outrider, since the instant her
father had vanished under the monstrous wave. Yet she rallied herself now to take loving farewell of Cormac, and
gave to her mother and her sibs all the comfort that she
might.

And was herself comforted, as much as she would, or
could, allow: Morvoren was there with her own parents, and
that was good; and the Earl Lennox had brought his young
heir with him. Not tall, with a heart-shaped face, blue eyes
and silky gold-brown tresses that fell past her waist, Mariota
Lennox was Connacht's Countess in the making. Her fostern,
Sosánaigh Darnaway, a bard in training, at the bidding of Earl
Lennox stepped forward in the annat and took out her harp;
the lament she made there for Cormac mac Archill could,
Aunya nic Cafraidh said later, have wrung tears from the
Sidhe.

It wrung none from Cormac's youngest; not then, not later,
through no fault of its own, or hers. But Mariota and
Sosánaigh and Athyn became fast friends, and that friendship begun in so painful an hour was to last them all their
lives.

And Athyn, who at first had blamed only herself for Cormac's death, now began to blame the Sidhe. *They troubled themselves to send me the fetch*, she thought bitterly many thousands of times in the weeks after, *but neither it nor they could be bothered to warn of the earthshake and the wave... They had known full well it would happen, the Shining Folk know everything that passes in the natural world, and see most clearly of all that which is to come. Despite their promise to care for those of Caerlaverock, they did not warn me of what was to come, as so easily they might have, and tasyk yet might live...*

She persisted in this sullen secret blaming for some months, confiding it to no one; but still there was something deep within her that would not allow her to deny that she knew it all along for what it was: a diversion, dust in her own eyes—as unjust against the Shining Folk as was Kier's cold enmity against herself. Yet it served a purpose; as the weeks went on, the diversion did its work. Slowly, gradually, her heart began to change, until one night Athyn went out through the apple orchards, and stood alone in the fields as she once had done, thinking of that night she had passed beneath the hill, staring blankly, if no longer balefully, at Sheehallion gleaming miles away against the dark.

She lifted up her arms to the distant mountain, as if beseeching forgiveness for her hardness of heart, remembering the night the light had shone upon her from the jewel on its crest. She had no words in this moment, only feelings: But as she reached out in spirit to the holy summit she felt her guilt and anger lift and take wing, never to return; felt she could breathe again, could live again, even. *Not as before, right enough, never that; but again...*

A voice spoke clear behind her, so natural in that moment that she did not even turn round to look. "There are higher crops than heathgrass," it said, and Athyn nodded unthinking agreement, it all made perfect sense. Then she caught her breath, whirling round. *No one there, of course, there would not be...* But as she stared through the twisted darkness of the appletree shadows, she heard, faint and far but very clear, the sound as it might be of a branch of bells, and knew her unvoiced prayer had been heard, and she could weep.

chapter six

The only way to conceal evil is not to do it.

—*Breos mac an Aba*

If Athyn had found herself a somewhat healing in the wake of Cormac's death, her eldest fosterbrother Kier had only grown more wounded. And wounding: He had no comfort for the widowed Lyleth—no surprise there, now that Cormac was gone he did not even trouble himself to be polite—and none for his own halfsibs. For Athyn, of course, there had never been aught save jealousy and hatred and spite, and that did not change now, or if it did it only grew worse.

He performed his duties to the maenor, but with so bad a grace as to make his service more of a help in absence, however more burdensome the chores fell upon everyone else; hard it was even to be in his presence, so black a mood was on him and so little did anyone wish to be around him, not even the gentle Sulior. Athyn he still blamed for not only Cormac's death but even the earthshake that had killed him; but soon he had goleor of others to blame for many things else.

"He has run off," Lyleth repeated, in a voice that gave no clue as to her feelings one way or another on the matter. Looking round the solar at the stunned blank faces, she could not forbear a laugh.

"You look like ducks in a thunderstorm... Well, only consider. My dower rights in Caerlaverock prevent Kier from inheriting unless I cede them to him, and that, for Cormac's sake, I cannot do. Even were I to wed again"—at that the children's eyes went out on sticks, but Lyleth was looking down as she spoke—"even then Kier could not claim the maenor, for Cormac and I were partners in the dúchas as well as in the marriage. Only at his full majority can Kier put forth any claim; and that is not for some few years yet. So he has said he has gone to do what too few Kelts will dare attempt."

None asked what that might be; they knew all too well—the ridding of Keltia of the Incomers, once for all—though precisely how this was to be accomplished Kier had not deigned to inform them.

Athyn found her voice. "So he has truly gone?"

"Aye, hen, gone. And left proper notification to me and to Donlin as rechtair and to the Earl Lennox as overlord, all as the law requires."

"Else his future claim be put in jeopardy," remarked Donlin. The thought in all hearts was the same: If aught befell Kier, of hopefully a fatal nature, Debagh would be heretrix. It was not a new thought for any of them, and an old dear wish for more than a few.

"Well, we can do naught about it even if we would," said Sulior, proud and resplendent in her new robes of Ban-draoi gray where she sat beside Athyn. "He has gone, and there's an end."

But in that she was only partly correct: Kier had gone, but it was nowhere near the end...

When, not long past the prescribed year and a day after a widowing that courting might begin again, it became apparent to their neighbors that Ser Nilos Marwin of Cathures and Mistress Lyleth Kerguethen ac Archill of Caerlaverock were so minded toward each other, few were much surprised, though more were shocked.

For the most part, though, the news deeply pleased the valley folk: Nilos, Incomer though he was, had quietly grown to his place among them, comporting himself as fittingly as any Kelt born. Some even said he had grown more Keltic than the Kelts, as the saying went; as for Lyleth Kerguethen, she had long been dear to all Connacht. Caerlaverock was known to be a difficult maenor to run, and Lyleth had a lively parcel of younglings; small wonder that she should wish to find someone to help her with the work, and if she had found affection also, so much the better. If there was a thread of opinion running through all this that one of their own might have been a fitter choice for mate than an Incomer however warmly liked, it was kept well hid.

Perhaps sensible of this thread, Nilos and Lyleth contented themselves for the moment with courtship only; as they informed both their households, the betrothal—and the wedding—could wait another moonyear. The Firvolgi lord was soon living at Caerlaverock—a steward ran his own estates at Cathures—and had already won to his side those who, after Lyleth herself, mattered most: Donlin, Aunya, Gwenda, the tigerns and subtigerns—and the Archill children, all of whom, save of course the absent Kier, held him in good esteem.

Athyn, who at first had been balky as a little unbroke garron, surprised them all by the depth and suddenness of her capitulation; and Nilos for his part took her up with equal gladness as fosterdaughter, finding in the war-orphan of unknown ancestry the beloved child and gifted student with whom he had never himself been blessed. Teacher that he was, he soon began to tutor her as even the bard Haneria had not: in poetry, his chiefest love, so that if not bard herself Athyn yet grew skilled in wordmaking far above the common run.

From Nilos, too, she became fluent in Volgiaran, the language of his own folk, and the Imperial Hastaic that was used as a common tongue, and Fomorian Lakhaz, and smatterings of more exotic languages still, outfrenne tongues which few in Keltia now cared to learn.

"For you never know, Athnë," Nilos had said one day, when

in a moment of vexation she had flung down her books and called down imprecations on wretched gallaín languages. "It is always better to know more than less, and the more you bring to something the more you will take from it." And she had laughed, and ruefully agreed.

"We are both Incomers, you know," said Athyn to Nilos one evening. "Both of us are foundlings here."

Nilos turned to look at her, startled by both the adult truth of her seeming offhand remark and the casualness with which she had uttered it. But she was gazing straight ahead between Tarn's velvety dark gray ears as they rode home through the fields.

"Very true," he said then, "but I confess I am something 'stonished to hear *you* say so. Though, knowing you, perhaps I should not be, not so much— But since what time have horse-girls turned ollaves, to speak with wisdom so beyond their count of years?"

He was teasing, and Athyn knew it, and smiled back at him. "I am glad you and mamaith are to wed," she said abruptly. "Since Kier left I have been feared for her—feared of what he might do."

Nilos looked at her with sudden alertness. "Where do you think he has gone?"

"I do not know for sure," she breathed, "but I think, I believe—" She broke off as Tarn pecked at a stone, her hands steadying his head through the reins until he had recovered himself; then she turned to look straight at Nilos. "Have you ever heard of those ones who call themselves the Keavers?"

Indeed he had... Composed of the landless, the disaffected, the ones with such a bitter grudge as Kier mac Archill carried, the Keavers took their name from the wild horned cattle of the Caledon hills. The old Scotan word was to do with the herd-bulls tossing their horns in threatening manner, to ward off marauders, and just so did the human Keavers comport themselves, at least with respect to Incomers, and to those Kelts whom they perceived to side with the enemy.

"They hold that Keltia is for Kelts alone," he said at last. "That Firvolgi have neither right nor business here... And, truth to tell, I cannot say I much disagree with them. But, Athnë, we are here now, and we are not all such folk as Kier objects to. Shall we not study simply to rub along together?"

"I know that," she said. "And I would we could. But all Kelts are not like Kier, no more than all Firvolgi are like you. And I am feared for you—and for mamaith—all the same."

Athyn's fears had good footing. In the past year, the frequency of mosstroop raids had increased alarmingly, and in response so too had the activities of the Keavers. Clad in dark-blue cloaks, wide-brimmed leather hats pulled down over their glibs to mask their faces, the Keavers had pursued Firvolgian bravos into the Elmet valley whenever the maigen was crossed, and few indeed crossed back again alive.

In response, the mosstroopers stepped up their attacks, and now they began to single out not only Kelts who stood against them but even those of their own folk who stood too much on the Keltic side—at the least, as the troopers saw it. And of these, Esmer Lennox was a great and prime example of the former, as was Nilos Marwin of the latter.

Hence Athyn's fears; and when the moonyear's wait was up and Nilos came ceremoniously from his own lands to wed Lyleth at Clann Archill's annat, and half Elmet rode to the wedding, her fears did not subside but only grew; and she was not the only one who feared so.

It was shortly afterwards that the rumors began, lying tales of how the new lord at Caerlaverock, Firvolgi Incomer that he was, conspired with the mosstroopers, fed them secret information on the strengths and weaknesses of his neighbors in the valley. As is so often the way with lies, none who heard these tales troubled themselves to think of the logic, or lack thereof, contained therein: Why should Nilos Marwin, an exemplary landowner in Elmet for many years, blameless save for the matter of his race, a friend of the Connacht Earl, now mate to a Kelt, suddenly become a spy for the very mosstroops he denounced? But logic finds barren soil where prejudice has first been cropped there, and indeed the illogic worked both ways...

"How can your own folk denounce you for, as they claim it, selling over to Keltia and working for the Keavers against your own people when the Keavers themselves denounce you for betraying Kelts to your own folk? They cannot have it both ways, the senseless loons, and yet they try, ah gods, they try!"

The speaker was Lyleth, but she spoke for all at the board that night. Nilos, who had refused to take Cormac's old seat at the head of the table but had urged it on his wife, contenting himself with Kier's former place opposite, made no response.

"They even dare think it of Esmer Lennox," said Gwenda Dalis the kienaght captain. "Oh aye, I promise you! I have spoken to some of my folk who have spoken to these Keavers, and they have heard it from their leaders' own lips. Lennox is held to be too much a friend to the Incomers—no offense, Ser Nilos—and therefore must be punished for the error of his ways."

Lyleth turned a hot angry sympathetic gaze on her mate, and Athyn burst forth angrily into a torrent of speech, but Nilos was already shaking his head.

"If once we begin apologizing amongst ourselves for every stupidity either of our races commits, good captain, we shall never have time or breath to say aught else. Let us all take that as read, then... As for you, Athnë, it is a plain waste of good Goddess-given energy, to try to make such folk to understand. They are scut, and they will never hear you no matter how you shout in their ears; see you remember that for the future... Well, clearly the Keavers are more fools than I thought them. My folk have by no means forgotten Velenax at Sherramuir;

for these Keavers to think the Earl Lennox should in any way kiss Firvolgian—"

Lyleth adroitly cut him off before he could utter something too mean in manner for either the dinner table or his own dignity. But as they went up to their chambers after, she slipped her arm through his and spoke for only him to hear, with a desperate unamused laugh.

"So it runs thusly: The Keavers hate you for being Incomer and Lennox for being not enough a Kelt; and the mosstroops hate Lennox for being a Kelt and you not enough a Firvolgi."

"What a world." But though Lyleth was asleep almost at once, Nilos lay long time awake, staring up at where the elms outside threw moonshadows of leafy branches on the ceiling. Not even to her would he confide the presentiment that had, over the past few years, begun to grow to certainty. *For Kelts are not the only race who know dán, or have Sight. For us it is ir'Vanniel, the thing seen far away…*

And he knew he was not the only one, Kelt or Incomer, who saw it: the coming of one who would succeed where all before had failed, and who would drive the Firvolgi out of Keltia forever. There had been no prophecies that he knew of, but history had shown many times on many worlds how such a one was bound to come. *They call us Fir Bolc, Folk of the Bag, for that they hold us fond of nothing but our purses, mock us by what they claim to be our motto—'Everyone lives by selling something; the Fir Bolc live by selling everything.' Perhaps it was true that we first came here for coin's sake, but we stayed for love's… Pray that this one who is coming will see that as well.*

All that week there had been bitter clashes between Keavers and mosstroops, the skirmishes even spilling over the border into Connacht. Gwenda Dalis placed her kienaght troops on creaght footing, though as yet none of the Elmet valley folk had reason to believe the raiders would come anywhere near. The evil rumors that had for some months swirled round Nilos had ceased as abruptly as they had begun, and all who dwelled at Caerlaverock were glad at least of that.

All save one: Athyn for her part was not so sure, and when Aunya nic Cafraidh sent her up into the hills with the herds, she did not take her usual delight in the task but asked to be relieved. Now that this unrest was come so near she would just as soon not be from home; but in the end she went.

Several hours before sunset, which comes very late in those high northern parts in summer, Athyn, on Tarn, was gathering in the herds preparatory to driving them on the morrow over to the next grazeland. The day had begun hot, but clouds had soon come up, and a chill wind; as she looked down the valley, she saw summer fog beginning to form in the hollows and climb slowly up the green sides of the hills.

Though the sight was a fair one of which she never tired, it troubled her now, and for more reason than merely the difficulty it would make with the horses. Hill-mist, however picturesque, was treacherous and dangerous; it could come down out of nowhere, blotting out familiar landmarks until even those who were most seasoned on the hill could lose their way between one tree and the next.

Athyn whistled to Elster, and he obeyed the command in the short sharp whistled notes, going wide to gather in lazy lagging horses, confident and happy as any sheepdog ever whelped. She watched him work for some minutes, then dismounted from Tarn and sent him to await her at the bield, for she could better round up the last few stragglers afoot.

She was just beginning to relax in the chore's completion when without warning the mist was on her, billowing up and down and around, from ground and air alike, and with it came such a feeling of peril as she had never known. Cormac had taught her from a tiny lass that when caught out in the hill-mist it is usually best to stand still; very often the mist will lift as swiftly as it had fallen, and it is safer not to wander. In any case Elster was abroad, and would soon come seeking her.

But the mist swirled and thickened, whitely lapping round

her, close and silent, and Athyn's fear grew with it. *Elster is a gazehound, he cannot see to find me in this, and the drizzle will soon make even my scent cold on the ground...* Yet her fear was not of the mist, nor of the beasts that might go lost in it, nor even for herself, but of something she did not know, for someone she could not see; and it seemed also that she heard the sound of a horn furiously winded, somewhere far away.

Suddenly a darker something came at her swiftly and purposefully through the mist, something of the size and pace of a cantering horse, and she almost sobbed in her relief. *Surely it is Tarn, coming to look for me, and Elster will not be far behind...* Then the towering shape drew clear of the mist, to stand before her, and Athyn saw just what it was—or who—that had come to seek her out.

chapter seven

They are like the Caravat and the Shanavest; bullies and braggarts both, not a pin of difference between them.

—Esmer Lennox

The horn still sounded in Athyn's head, far within— the Crann Tarith, that ancient alarm which had once been a fiery cross and was now instead a ringing horncry to shake the air—when the dark formless shape came looming out of the mist, and took its rightful form before her.

And such form... Others of the drovers, who had gathered lower down the valley, had seen the mist begin to crawl and billow along the hillside above, and guessing Athyn's trouble had hurried upwith on horseback. But now, as they drew near, and saw what she saw, their horses also seeing screamed and climbed the air, rearing in terror, or tried to bolt, or bucked their riders off and did bolt. And so too would the riders have done if only they could—

What stood there on the edge of the mist was a great bonewhite horse, a horse not only white as bone but a horse *of* bones, its flanks insubstantial as mist themselves, its ruby eyes stabbing flame through the murk. It had galloped up out of legend, out of the nursetales told to children on dark winter nights next the fire. But here it was, and it was more real than anything else upon that hill: the Mari Llwyd, the Ghost Mare. It stood before Athyn, a knot of tattered red ribbons hanging from its jaw, where on a mortal steed would be bit and reins.

And Athyn stared, and the Mari Llwyd seemed to stare back at her, though what those eyes of immortal fire saw when they looked on her could not be imagined. Then Athyn slowly reached out her hand, and the faerie horse lowered its skull to the girl's outstretched palm.

As the ghastly white bone muzzle touched her hand, Athyn did not flinch. Then, to the bloodfreezing awe of the onlookers, the Mari Llwyd knelt before her, inclining its mighty shoulder to her so that she might bestride and ride.

If I think about it I shall go mad entirely, I will run screaming down the valley and not stop until I throw myself into the sea... Athyn tightened her hand over where the mane should have been if this had been a horse of earth, and, just as she would have done to mount a natural beast, she sprang all in one fluid motion as the creature straightened, and found herself astride the Mari Llwyd, its withers seven feet above the ground.

She saw the staring drovers grow suddenly dim, as if the mist that had enshrouded the Ghost Mare lay now upon them. How she appeared to them she did not know; but as she looked down to the arched bone neck, to where she forked what had been bare spinebone and open ribs, she shivered in awe to see that those bones were clothed. She sat now astride an enfleshed horse, a giant dark-gray mare with black points, beautiful, the velvety coat the color of a storm-cloud. She rode upon a thing of legend, and did not think for a moment, in that moment, that she was riding into legend herself...

Then the Mari Llwyd began to canter down the valley; the drovers scattered in terror before it, and the few horses who had abided its presence broke and bolted. But Athyn relaxed instinctively into the tremendous stride, to her astonishment actually enjoying the experience. She heard no sound of the creature's hoofbeats upon the turf, only the wind whistling faintly past her ears. They were moving faster than any true horse could gallop; and then the Mari Llwyd began to gallop, and it was as if they had grown wings.

In a very few moments Caerlaverock in its little elmgrove lay before them, so swiftly had the Ghost Mare covered the miles to the lower valley. The Crann Tarith had sounded in Athyn's head all the way, and now she saw why it had blown.

Nilos and Lyleth stood on the steps before the main door, and in the courtyard a half-circle of horsed mosstroopers was ranged before them. The tips of the black-shafted lances pointed directly at the mistress and master of Caerlaverock; above, in the dorter window, highest in the house, Athyn's brother Errick stood frozen, a hunting horn still clutched in his hand.

Athyn laid a hand on the Mari Llwyd's neck, and the phantom horse bent off to the right, biddable as the most docile garron. They stopped on the verge of the elmgrove, and some glamour of concealment must have been upon them, for not even Nilos and Lyleth seemed to note them there.

The leader of the mosstroopers was speaking, threats and bluster against Nilos, his own countryman; blame and scorn for wedding with a Kelt, for not advancing the Firvolgi cause in Keltia, for selling out to Keltic masters, and many other sins beside. Lyleth, for her part, stood silent, though her gaze was fixed not on the leader but on one of the mosstroopers in the back rank.

With a shock of recognition Athyn saw that the trooper Lyleth watched so closely was none other than Kier. Her mind reeled, then cleared: *Kier, among the mosstroops?* It could not be; then the true explanation came to her. Nay, of course, he had joined them under spy-pretext, so that he might ride with them and learn their secrets, then report all back to the Keavers; or so at least she hoped...

She flinched as the trooper leader prodded Nilos with the point of his lance; Nilos did not stir. Then, as if that were the signal it had been awaiting, the Mari Llwyd stepped deliberately forward, and the invisibility seemed to fall from phantom horse and mortal rider both.

Lyleth saw them first, and gladness blazed in her face, a joy not unmixed with awe and fear. Nilos saw and was glad also, though he seemed more mystified than his wife; and Errick in the window high above dropped the horn and his jaw alike.

But now the Mari Llwyd came forward at a slow terrible floating trot, as if it skimmed above the ground; and though to Athyn the beast beneath her seemed by now strangely natural, to those in the courtyard it wore its wonted appearance: an empty cage of bare white bones in shape of a giant ghost-horse, knit together by mist, sighted by eyes like flashing flame. The red ribbons fluttered in the wind of its moving, and it made no sound as it moved.

The mosstroopers, at first frozen in simple disbelief, now fled as one, their screaming horses tearing off in all directions, any direction, so long as it was away from that terrible thing: the nightmare, the Ghost Mare, with a daughter of the house of Archill borne calmly upon its bonewhite back.

Kier too bolted, before Athyn could reach him; but not before she caught a glance from under the hooded cap the mosstroops wore, a glance of burning hatred—fear also, and not of the Mari Llwyd alone—and in that moment she knew who it was had spread those poisonous tales.

But now came to her ears the shouts of pursuit, and the pursuers came into view over the ridge: creaghts, riding hard, swinging out to both sides to intercept the fleeing raiders. Some were clad in the house colors of Caerlaverock, and among them Athyn saw Gwenda Dalis the captain and Aunya nic Cafraidh. Most of the troop bore Lennox livery; as they galloped down the valley she saw the Earl himself come up behind. Checking from the chase, he turned his horse's head to join the group upon the steps—Nilos, Lyleth, Donlin the rechtair, Errick down from the attic.

Real awe came into Esmer's face as he beheld Athyn and that which still bore her upon its back. Then once more the

Mari Llwyd knelt, and Athyn slid off; the moment her boots touched ground, the creature's aspect changed for her yet again. Gone was the storm-colored mare; once more the beast of bones, turf glowing green through the curving basketwork of ribs.

The ghostly head dipped in farewell, again the skeleton muzzle dropped briefly into Athyn's palm; the huge grinning skull laid itself for a moment over her shoulder, and those who were watching trembled. Then the mist seemed to form again, and though none could say that they had seen it go, the Ghost Mare was gone. Not a hoofprint remained; only a small patch of mist that moved swiftly up the valley toward the mountains, and no natural mist had ever moved with such a motion...

Then everyone moved at once. Lyleth and Nilos dashed over to Athyn where she stood a little weak in the knees—and who could blame her—and Esmer Lennox flung himself from his own horse and did likewise.

"You deserve a mighty skippering, do you know that, leaving the drove alone on the hill," said Lyleth, weeping and laughing and hugging Athyn hard and close, "but by the Goddess I would not dare be the one to give it you!"

"Nor I." Nilos hugged her in turn. "Nor I," he repeated, and looked at his wife.

Now Esmer Lennox came up, and he spoke first to Nilos and Lyleth, of that which was perhaps more easily spoken of. "My creaghts have joined your own," he was saying. "We have pursued this particular thrashbag all the way from Graystones." He gestured down the valley to where the creaghts were already returning, a dozen mosstroopers lashed into their saddles with their lances across their backs and their hands bound before. "We shall deal with them as befits," he added with no emphasis; his meaning needed none.

Athyn scanned the prisoners swiftly. Even at this distance she could tell that Kier was not among them, and for all the worlds she did not know if she was glad or sorry. Stealing a glance at her mother, she saw the same twofold emotion shadowing her face; then Lyleth's glance met Athyn's, and the older woman gave the younger a tiny shake of the head.

Then Esmer Lennox turned at last to look long at Athyn, and she was far from easy under the gaze of those keen intelligent eyes.

"Name of Dâna, lass, I confess I do not know where to begin!" he said, laughing. "Save that I think an account of this would go better at my seat of Ardturach, to be told to my Druid and a bard or two..." Turning to Lyleth: "If you would spare her for a day or two, perhaps a week? Nay, you shall come also— Ganor would be glad to see you, and my daughter will bear yours company."

"Go," said Nilos, simply.

So Lyleth shepherded everyone withindoors: Esmer Lennox to partake of Caerlaverock hospitality and to attend to whatever he deemed necessary, Athyn to pack a few bits and bobs of gear, Lyleth herself to speak to Donlin the rechtair and to pack some things for her own use. But she did find a spare moment to slip upstairs to Athyn's dorter room.

The girl was sitting quietly on her unshuttered bed, turning something over and over in her hand; and Lyleth changed her first intent, which was to speak of Kier, for she saw that the thing which Athyn fingered was a piece of the tattered red ribbon that had hung from the Mari Llwyd's terrible jaws.

"It left this in my hand when it—left," she said, gesturing helplessly. "I thought it best to keep it."

Lyleth folded the girl's fingers over the scrap of silk, and wrapped her own hands around Athyn's. "Then keep it," she said gently. "Make a little bag to put it in—this will not be the only talisman you shall come by down the years—and wear it always." She stood up. "If you are ready?" At Athyn's nod: "We will speak later of the other thing—of Kier—but just now let us not keep the lord of Connacht waiting."

*   *   *

"Dialc'h!"

The awed exclamation came from Athyn. The aircar in which they had travelled from Graystones (her first time in such a craft, quite exciting enough) was coming in to land at its destination. Ardturach, the High Towered Place, seat of the Earls of Connacht since the founding of Erinna, was below them on the plain.

Built by Gradlon of Ys—master-builder to Brendan, he who had walled Caerdroia, and delved the Nantosvelta, and raised many another of Keltia's most formidable structures—Ardturach is the Third Great Stronghold of Keltia. Only Caer Dathyl of the Gwyneddan princes and Turusachan itself surpass it in size and strength, and perhaps none else in all Keltia for beauty.

"We have lived here from the first," came a voice over her shoulder, and Athyn looked up to see Esmer Lennox peering out the viewport; what surprised her was that he looked as eager and awestruck as she herself to see the fortress below them. "Oh aye," he said with a smile, correctly interpreting her glance, "it amazes me too, every time I see it—and I give praise and thanks, every time, to him who built it. The Earls of Connacht, of whom I am fifteenth, were the first of the Marcher Lords here on Erinna, and I defend that maigen as best I can."

"Velenax," said Athyn, and Esmer shot her a swift glance.

"Just so." He said no more until they landed; but Athyn felt that keen glance on her from time to time, and wondered to herself what lay behind it.

"After today, can you have any doubt?" Ganor called from the pool-room. "Nay, Lennox, it is as I told you: That lass is dánach, there is a high fate upon her; and if you are as clever as I have always thought you, cariad, you will bind her to us before she gives her loyalty elsewhere. She is of that kind that once she bestows faith or troth, heart or hand, it is given for aye... And I believe she is the one we need, the one we have so long sought. What more proof do you require?"

Esmer was silent. Truth be told, he had long since been of Ganor's very mind concerning the foundling lass his old friend Cormac had brought home as battle-spoil from Fialzioch. Portent and evidence alike told heavily on her side: He had heard in strict confidence from Lyleth of the fetch that had saved the girl from freezing, and of Lyleth's suspicion that something stranger still had happened to Athyn, one time a few years since, up in the grazeland valleys; even the girl's very birth and rescue to begin with. *Born on a battlefield, and borne home by a soldier! If that was not an omen— And now this today...*

"You should have seen it, Ganwen," he said, when his wife returned to the bedchamber, warm from the bath. "The Mari Llwyd! Can you imagine?"

"Oh aye," said Ganor dryly. "I can imagine quite well. But, cariad, hear other counsel than mine alone. I should like to have things well settled at Caerlaverock; at least before Kier mac Archill succeeds to it."

"Whyfor? He cannot turn Lyleth out."

"Nay, that he cannot, but as head of Clann Archill he will be able to turn Athyn out, and I have no doubt but that he will. Before he does so, for her sake, I would she were lawfully lodged somewhere to her liking; and—for our sake—I would that were with us."

"It will not be easy. She loves that farm, would stay there forever given her choice."

"Well, she will not be given it; there is something higher and finer and better in store for her than a horsefarm. But we must choose it for her. As friends of Cormac, firstly; but as rulers of Connacht if that is the only way— I would not leave a hound there to be mistreated by Kier. No matter if he *is* Cormac's son and inheriot," she added. "He has been a bad lot since childhood, and Athyn will be best away from him." She hesitated. "Did Cormac ever say aught to you, of her true ancestry?"

Esmer looked at his wife, surprised by the apparent depth of her interest in one who was, at least on the face of it, a fairly ordinary lass of eighteen or so. But he shook his head vigorously.

"Never. All I know is what we have always known: Cormac found her just born, on the battlefield at Fialzioch, took her up out of pity and brought her home. I was with him at that fight, and my brother Greyloch too; I well recall the grief we had to keep the poor little weevil fed and warm and dry. Yet Cormac never thought to abandon her... There were some trinkets, I believe, which the district brehon and bard have held for her—naught of significance or great worth—but I doubt me there are any clues there, or we should have heard by now." He slid into the huge fourposted bed, waited for Ganor to join him. "Why are you so curious, asthore?"

"Oh, many reasons. No reasons. I doubt *me* it matters much in the end."

But there Ganor told her lord an untruth; for she knew full well it did, and would; and more besides.

Only Esmer's fostern, Greyloch, saw as Ganor saw, and like her he taxed Esmer with it.

"I know that you keep no hounds that cannot hunt, and I can tell, too, when you have a plan—so, braud, tell me. Just what is it that you have in mind for her?"

"Brehon school!" repeated Lyleth. "Do you think?"

"It was the thing upon which my inquestors were most in agreement," said Esmer, "when they questioned her about the Mari Llwyd." The three were in the Countess's solar, and the topic at hand—though she was not there to help plan it—was Athyn's future.

Ganor threw an eye-rolling glance at her lord, then leaned forward and touched her friend's arm, one mother to another.

"M'chara, Lennox understates, to say the least— What

they *said* was that never in all their lives had they seen such a natural bent and disposition for justice. She has the cool mind needed to see all sides, and the warm heart to judge aright for all concerned. That is a rare and powerful combination; great sin to waste it."

Lyleth smiled, but her thoughts were churning. "She has shown gifts in judgment since she was the tiniest lass. It does not surprise me to hear this now."

"It is that which the inquestors consider so extraordinary," said Esmer. "And why they think it essential that she begin her studies as soon as it can be arranged. And to that end I have made some excellent arrangements, which I as lord of Connacht am prepared to implement. If, of course, you and Nilos consent."

"She will have to leave home..."

"She would in any case, Lylo," said Ganor gently. "If you had fostered her she would have been gone long since. You know as well as we do that Kier will never allow her to stay at Caerlaverock—"

Lyleth nodded, but did not look at either of them. "And I shall not be there forever, nor Nilos—aye, then. If she agrees. It is a fine plan. I shall speak to her."

Esmer smiled. "And after her training is done, and she has taken honor as a brehon, she shall come back here to Ardturach, as my brother Greyloch has suggested, and be chaired as Judge of Connacht. It will be good to have a dear friend's child in the seat of the law."

"Cormac would approve," said Ganor, "if he knew."

Lyleth smiled a real smile then. "Oh, he does," she said. "And he does."

For her part, Athyn was much enjoying her time at the Lennox seat. Ardturach was such a place as she had never imagined existed—huge, and complex, and fair, full of purposeful and friendly folk. She and Mariota grew to be fast friends, as both their mothers were strongly minded: riding out together every day, being instructed by brehons and bards, often joined by Sosánaigh Darnaway, who was bound with Mariota for Seren Beirdd, and by Katterin de Cuirteis, a tall glass-blond Ban-draoi from Graystones.

Athyn struck up a warm friendship also with Esmer's fostern, the redoubtable Tipherris Inchspell of Greyloch. Few days passed without her riding over to his keep at Radwinter; everywhere they went they were accompanied by his great white war-hound Liadan, and Athyn, missing Elster, was glad of the beautiful dog's friendly attention. But she spent hours in converse with Greyloch himself, finding him easier to talk to than Esmer or even Nilos, possessed of humor and an ironic judgment; talked likewise with Greyloch's longtime spouse Hutcheon Fraser, a tall brownhaired Fian general who had covered himself with honor in the campaigns against the Firvolgi; and Esmer observing this was well pleased.

Though relieved to have a vocation laid out for her, and more than a little daunted at the interest such high folk showed in her, nevertheless Athyn was a touch cast down at the idea of leaving Caerlaverock. Even the prospect of her first trip offplanet did not lift her spirits much, though all had spoken to her most encouragingly about this change in her fortunes. Greyloch himself had said plainly that it was an unbelievable piece of luck, although he did not use that word, and, if truth be told, believed in luck no more than did his fosterbrother. But, for all her melancholy, on both counts Athyn was inclined to agree.

The night before she was to set out for Dyved, Athyn had been feted at a merry feast, with all Caerlaverock in attendance, tigern and subtigern alike, and from the neighboring farms many who had known her from her infancy. Nilos had made a loving and eloquent speech; Lyleth had watched, torn between tears and pride, too moved to speak.

Now Athyn sat alone in her attic, looking around at the warm familiar surroundings, and, near the door, her travelling trunks—a stack of new clothes within them that would not have disgraced a duke's daughter. She would return here; but never again would it be the same. She was about to step into the world that lay beyond the world that she had known and loved all her life, and though she knew that she did not go unblessed or unprotected, she was more than a little feared.

Still, even anticipation must have rest, and presently she fell asleep, fully clad, on top of the bed. But in the night she woke to a gentle patting upon her arm. Though it could easily have been Lyleth's hand, or any of her sibs', or even Cormac's, despite her drowse Athyn knew better.

It was the velvet touch of a wolf's paw, and Athyn smiled to feel it, at peace now to every corner of her being. *I knew you would not let me leave without bidding me farewell... And I know you will find me to comfort and protect, no matter where in Keltia I might be, or when; on that, at least, I can depend forever...*

chapter eight

Every hand is punished as it deserves; for every living person who gives judgment must have been chosen to it.

—*The Brieve of Ruchdi*

The brehon school of Silverwood lay in the Dysunni valley in the eastlands of the planet Dyved; and still does. Not one of the chief establishments of Keltic juristry, nor yet among the least, Silverwood is a solid school that produces solid brehons, and so had Esmer chosen it. Its masters have ever been men and women of intelligence and honor, if not perhaps of blazing learning or innovative genius or blinding vision, save for the Brieve of Ruchdi who is its greatest jewel. But in the days when Athyn came to it, it was run by a master indeed.

"So you are the Earl Lennox's sponsored pupil." The cool voice from the shadows on the other side of the desk held no hint of how the speaker might feel; merely made a statement of fact, though if the unemphatic words had been 'pet lamb' or 'bought placeholder' they could hardly have sounded more ominous in Athyn's ear. She felt she was known at once for a talentless fraud.

It seemed the voice's owner saw that. "Well. We shall have it out of you soon enough: whether it is justice that lives in your heart, or only the law." The briefest of pauses. "Or merely vengeance."

Athyn found her voice, and her wit. "Surely justice has need of all those?"

"Even vengeance, you think?" The voice held a spark of interest now, as if Athyn's question had both surprised and pleased. "Not to say chastisement does not have its right place in the Goddess's great plan—but to sort one from the other, ah, now that is where brehons are made! Nor is it I that says so, but the Great Codifier, Cennfaelad, who wrote out the law for all Kelts. And the Brieve of Ruchdi, who was the law ensouled in mortal body, who said so again."

Suddenly Athyn felt small and tired, and not up to verbal fencery with this unknown master. The owner of the voice saw this too, and stepped forward into the sconcelight: a woman small of stature, brownhaired and with crystal-blue eyes, who wore learning like a cloak, and looked to have scarce enough years on her to be beyond pupilage herself. Athyn made a suitable reverence, and the woman nodded.

"Welcome to Silverwood, Athyn nic Archill. I am the Archbrieve Bronwyn Muirheyd, and by Arawn Doomsman himself I will make a brehon of you if you die for it." A smile transformed the even-featured face. "Only, of your goodness, do *not* die—my old comrade Esmer would have my guts for greavestraps, and, truly, you know, I should hate that! Now ring the bell by the door, and one will come to show you to your rooms. We have years to know one another, and will not start tonight."

Her studies began at once. At first she had thought to have tutors, as Sulior had told her Ban-draoi students were assigned, but Silverwood was run along different lines, and for the first two terms of Athyn's schooling she would spend most of her days in classes.

She learned more of Cennfaelad, that codifier of the law of whom Bronwyn Muirheyd had spoken. He had been no brehon but a soldier, a Fian on Erith in service of a provincial king. Wounded in the head and hand in battle, he had been cared for in a field hospital, which had by pure chance been set up in an apple orchard just next to a brehon training school.

Now in those days, teachings were oral only; naught had as yet been put on paper, and laws varied from one chieftaincy to another, one king to the next. But as Cennfaelad lay there recovering, bored beyond belief, he found that by some peculiarity of the head wound he had taken he had lost his 'brain of forgetfulness,' as the old texts quaintly put it; so that the lessons he overheard all day long, through the open windows of the brehon school, remained with him and did not fade. As exercise for his injured hand, and diversion for his boredom, he began to write them down; and so unwittingly became not only a brehon himself but the means by which the laws of Keltia were scribed in books.

"And fitting it was that war should be the instrument by which the law came to be preserved; wounds were a means of healing not for Cennfaelad alone, but for us all."

That was Bronwyn Muirheyd on the subject; a lecture to Athyn's sizar class, the first-year students, one startling afternoon. Athyn was to learn that the Archbrieve made a practice of occasionally entering a preceptor's classroom or even an ollave's tutorial, and the instructors welcomed the pre-emption as eagerly as did the students. It was even whispered that if Keltia had a ruler upon the Throne of Scone, an Ard-rían or Ard-rígh as by rights should be there, Bronwyn Muirheyd would be sitting at that monarch's Council table, as Chief Brehon. For the moment, she would have to content herself as Archbrieve; at the least, until a High King or a High Queen came again.

"'The time allotted for advocates to plead is divided by breathings, about fifteen to a minute; whilst the time allowed for each person to plead cause is long or short according to what dignity the pleader might possess; the higher the dignity, the longer the pleading,'" recited Athyn dutifully, and quite correctly.

"And so said—?" prompted her tutor, eyes closed.

"Lanivet, called Tulbrethach, the Hastily Judging."

Redigan Ó Hannay smiled a slow indulgent smile and opened his eyes, very pleased with his pupil. They were seated in one of the small book-lined alcoves of the law library at Silverwood, at one of their tutorials, which to outsiders sometimes seemed less an instructional session than a clash of fell enemies, hurling words before taking their quarrel to the blade.

Ó Hannay was one of the ollaves at Silverwood, a master-teacher. He came of an old brehon family who had served the law since Brendan's day; though he had long been a preceptor here, and had seen many students pass through the refining fires of the law, to none save Bronwyn Muirheyd and Alveric her mate had he allowed himself to exult over the quality of his newest charge, which he and they both deemed pure ore. Certainly never to that charge herself...

"Aye," said Ó Hannay aloud, studying his boots with some complacence—very elegant soutery, sand-colored suede with gold and dark-brown lacings. "See then that you learn something from our man the overimpetuous Lanivet."

Athyn grinned, knowing her instructor was chaffing her. "And that would be—?" she murmured inquiringly, in a very fair imitation of Ó Hannay's own sardonic tone.

Redigan laughed aloud. "Not to mock your tutor, for a start," he said. "Else you might end up as did the High Queen Crestenna."

"And how was that?" asked Athyn, off guard for the moment.

"With a broken crown," said Redigan, suiting action to word by rapping her head sharply as he rose to leave.

Athyn groaned, more at the sally than the teasing tap, but made proper reverence to his retreating back and sat down again, well satisfied with herself. Not often did the stern ollave show affection to his pupils, which made them all the giddier when he did, so hard it was held to please him.

She had been at Silverwood a full sixmonth; she had arrived at Beltain, and it was already a week short of Samhain, the great feast soon upon them. Heading back across the grounds to her dorter, Athyn allowed herself to think of home. This would be her first Samhain away from Elmet, and she suddenly all but doubled up as she walked, seized by a powerful homesickness that clutched at her, clenching her middle in its fist.

Pausing on the steps of the dorter-hall, she looked out at the riverlands below, the tame lovely valley in its autumn dress—bronze and copper trees, gold fields, blue smoke of leaf-fires spiraling up—and inevitably thought of Cormac, all at once missing him very much. He was buried on the chalk, as they said in Elmet; it was how they distinguished between the various hill areas. Was it on the chalk, they would ask, when someone spoke of a place or a farm, high on the chalk, or perhaps low, or was it rather on the hard—meaning on any other sort of ground... Cormac was high on the chalk indeed—a bright dry place for a grave, if a cold one—under a sign that could be seen thirty miles away: the huge running horse Debagh had carved there, white chalk against green turf. Though some said it looked more like a dragon than a horse...

She sighed and went indoors. Debagh was making a great name for herself as a limner now, and who knew when it might be before either she or Athyn came again home? Only the day before, there had been a long letter from Lyleth: Things were well at Caerlaverock; there followed news of the district, such folk as Athyn knew and of whom she would be glad to hear. Then came the burden of the letter: Kier had been sighted once more riding with the mosstroops, so that masque of his, if masque it were, still held. *Much as I detest thinking good of him, it just might be that he does this for Keltia's weal and not his own vengefulness...*

She stopped stock-still on the big goldenoak staircase that

led to her second-story rooms, considering what she had just heard herself thinking, then went on with a quirked mouth and a quickened step. *'It just might be'? Aye—and pigs, indeed, just might fly…*

It was Silverwood's custom to train the students in court practice almost from the beginning of their studies; and to that end mock trials were often held, to which all the school could come as observers. But every now and again, petition was made that a real case should be judged: Perhaps some lord wished to remove a complaint from the purview of the district brehons, or it might be that a defendant felt a fair hearing could not be had from any of the usual courts, and so would seek recourse of the school instead.

This time it was one Countess Loholt who had instituted proceedings, complaining that the sheep of her neighbor, Benna, a wealthy widow, had broken out of a walled pen insufficiently strong to hold them, and had invaded the Countess's estates, where they had dined leisurely and unlawfully on the new woad crops. The Countess therefore had sought damages on the ground that the sheep had been carelessly secured, suing to claim the flock from Mistress Benna, who had promptly countersued, declaring that the woad plantation should have been properly fenced off against just such raids, which were known to occur, and that the Countess was vastly above herself in claiming of the gluttonous sheep.

Clearly, there was right on both sides. The Dysunni brehon immediately begged off the case, not daring to offend either powerful lady by his judgment—whatever he decided, he would be deeply wrong, and deeply doomed—and the problem was then brought to Silverwood. Bronwyn deemed it of sufficient instructional merit to go to trial in the Áras Bretha, the Hall of Judgment, and the whole school turned out to watch.

Athyn had surprised herself by the keen interest the case roused in her, and, with her friends Phaal Torcwyn and

Mihangel Glenrossa and Lira Cromell, had come early to the Hall to secure a seat near the front, the better to see and study the proceedings.

Lira was a bit bemused by her friend's eager anticipation. " 'Tis but a smallcourt squabble, Athwen," she whispered now in her low vibrant voice, as the Áras filled and the combatants took their places. "It is scarcely fíor-comlainn, nor even fíor-coire—"

Athyn hardly heard. Her attention was all for the scene: In the back-court, looking not at all pleased to be there, were the overlords of the Dysunni valley, the Duke and Duchess of Ruthin, flanked by the ranking bard, Druid, Fian and Bandraoi of the district. In the forecourt stood the advocates: Redigan Ó Hannay for the Countess Loholt, and against him Berica Chevyet, a fine arguer with many victories to her credit. As was both custom and law, all parties greeted each other with civility and friendliness; indeed, they could be sued and fined themselves if they did not.

And in the true-court, the center of it all, Bronwyn Muirheyd sat in her green robe of justice in the Cathair-bretha, the judging-seat; hence Silverwood's, and Athyn's, excitement—it had been years since any Archbrieve had taken the high chair at such a hearing, and not a pupil there wished to miss this unexpected chance.

The events were disputed by no one: Benna's sheep had eaten Loholt's woad, and no one was claiming any different. What was being argued here was the degree of culpability on the part of countess and sheepwife alike; which one had been the less vigilant, or the more careless (and in the branch of law that obtained here the two things were by no means identical). As the trial advanced Athyn found herself enthralled. *It moves like a dance, or a duel. Truly, the law is the life of the land, as the old texts say, and the King, if king we had, should be the life of the law...*

At last the advocates retired their arguments, and Bronwyn turned to confer with those who sat in the back-court.

Apparently there was complete agreement, for almost at once she turned round again.

"In law there are five sorts of judgment that may be given," she said in a clear voice, "and they are these: a judgment based on our Draoíchtas faith with its true examples, a firm steadfast judgment between two equally clever pleadings, a straight mild judgment between friends and kinsmen, a discerning stern judgment between cunning false lying people, and a mild soothing judgment between foolish unruly quarrelsome people." She paused, fixing plaintiff and defendant alike with a severe blue glance. "I shall be giving here the last of those five as my judgment on the case at hand, and the high ones of the back-court concur. My judgment is that Mistress Benna's sheep shall be forfeit to the Countess Loholt, to suffice her for the loss of the woad. Thus the beasts themselves shall make reparation for the destruction they caused."

The Countess looked pleased, and Benna crestfallen, but both rose to declare their acceptance. Then Athyn could restrain her judicial instincts no longer; she surged forward to the very gate of the court, and seeing that the fíor-brethas was on her, the truth-of-judging, Bronwyn indicated that the girl should be allowed to speak, herself curious to hear what she would say.

Athyn made brief reverence and spoke eagerly, as if she did not stand with the head of the entire brehon order seated above her, but in any ordinary mock-trial before her fellow students.

"Nay, honors all, the cropping of the sheep for the cropping of the woad! One shall suffice the other—therefore let the wool be given in payment to the Countess when next the sheep are shorn, for the wool will grow again and the woad will also."

She flushed, and looked round her as if suddenly wakened from an ashling, so caught up had she been in rendering decision. *Great Goddess! What have I done?* But she saw the faces of the audience, and heard the murmur of approval, and she flushed again, and hurriedly took her seat.

No matter the unorthodoxy of the delivery, or the youth and inexperience of the judger, it could not be denied that Athyn had given a brilliant and instinctive judgment, plainly the only right one for the case. As Bronwyn noted the feeling of those who heard it—even the Countess Loholt was struck by its perfect correctness, though it considerably diminished her personal advantage—she took note also of her own feeling: how right the judgment was, how right it felt, and gave order that Athyn's verdict should stand and not her own.

For that is fíor-brethas, royal justice, she sent in mindspeech to Redigan. *The kind of justice that only one in whose bone and blood it has long been bred could be expected to give on the instant...*

And only the blood of kings is bred to it, returned Redigan, who had followed her behind-thought. *For only that blood finds judgment so inborn and instinctive as to be unpreventable; as we have seen here, and as you know. The question now is, Does she?*

"I know what you have said, Archbrieve—we all know—but what in the seven hells is it that you do *think*?"

It was evening of that same day upon which Athyn nic Archill had delivered herself of her remarkable judgment. Indeed, all Silverwood was still buzzing with it, and Athyn had by special dispensation been served her supper in her rooms that night, so that she need not face the certain tumult that would have besieged her in hall.

And still Bronwyn had no answer for the question Redigan Ó Hannay had just set her. Her blue eyes clouded as she looked at Alveric, her tall Druid mate, and he spoke in his calm beautiful voice his thought which was also hers.

"Perhaps we may buy ourselves some time. Did Esmer not say that after her time here he plans to send her on to the Fians at Casterlines? You must speak to your cousin Selanie, Bronna, and to her mate Rhain as well. There will need to be steps taken."

Bronwyn did not answer at once. "Another problem for another day, cariad," she said at last. "And you have the right of it as ever; yet in the meantime we must deal with the cast that has been thrown us, here and now. She may well be the one we have awaited. So let me tell you both a thing not even our own Esmer yet knows; and then you may be better able to judge. But first I will have your oaths to Kelu that the secret remains, for now, with us."

When they had duly sworn, startled at the oath she extracted—save for one other, there is none graver in Keltia—she leaned forward and told them, in plain words, what she herself had been told a few months since by a rank-and-file Erinnach brehon who had come, troubled and in secret, to seek his Archbrieve's counsel.

Whatever Bronwyn Muirheyd confided that night to her mate and her most trusted colleague, it was kept among themselves; and if ever they wondered about it they kept that to themselves also.

By now Athyn and most of the class that had entered with her had advanced to the dignity of their sophister term; triumphs and woes unlooked-for befell her, and then one more thing that she had not looked for: She found herself for the first time in love.

It was full winter that year she turned sophister; not yet Brighnasa, no touch of spring upon the land. She was returning to hall for the nightmeal, hungry and tired, hoping the cooks had made something savory and a great deal of it. Halfway there, she passed by one of her favorite places on the grounds of Silverwood, a long alley of pleached elms setting off two grassy swards that in summer were much favored by the pupils to take the sun.

A near sound made her start, and she turned her head. A

young man stood there under the snow-clad trees, a youth with whom a weeping angry girl was trying to have an argument. Athyn knew her: a fellow sophister, one Marsheli by name; she had coarse black hair, was not very witty nor yet very talented, but all the more industrious for it.

The youth was not looking at her, however, but straight past, straight at Athyn. She slowed, looking back at him, touched by a certain prescience, a feeling of fate. And it seemed he was also, for still paying no heed to the tearful Marsheli he stared after Athyn as she went on, long after she had vanished into the lighted doorway of the hall.

That August came her Teltown, that festival by which young men and women are introduced, under the auspices of the Goddess and careful mentors, to the joys and solemnities of lovemaking. As nervous and eager as any of her year, Athyn had gone to the Long Dance with no clear picture in mind of the lad she might favor or fancy above the others, with whom she would learn this new thing; but she had seen him at the same instant he saw her, and they drifted together into the dark fields.

As if by unspoken decision they climbed a wooded hill, and emerging from the trees on the hilltop they found themselves in a tiny grassy clune, no one else nearby, as private as if they had been in a chamber of their own. Only the trees that rustled in the warm wind and the bright stars over their heads were witness, and, shivering a little, they sank down into the deep grass.

"I know you—last Brighnasa," she said. "In the snow—I saw you."

"I hoped you did." He was not much taller than she, perhaps an inch or two, no more, with the darkest hair and eyes she had ever seen, and a tanned skin to go with them, darker than was the rule among Kelts; a Kymro, pure or nearabouts, she guessed.

He began to name himself, but Athyn put her fingers upon his lips. "Later. Later for that."

"Roeg," he said much later, naming himself and kissing her all at the same time.

"Athyn. I am a student at the brehon school."

"And I a bard in training, at Kings Roding down the valley."

There seemed no more that needed to be said just then; and nothing was.

Their romance lasted the rest of the time Athyn was at Silverwood; by the time Roeg was posted to his petty place, and she about to take honor as robed brehon, it was all but ended. After him, though she would have a lover or two, gaysome light-hearted dalliances for the most part, Athyn had the feeling that she was waiting for someone, someone to whom Roeg had been only herald and precursor; and who, when he came, would be the full statement of a theme she had heard, or had been told of, a very long time ago.

I wonder who he is, where he might be—he who was promised me by that one I had better not name, in that place I had better not think on? I wonder if in all Keltia there is one other who thinks as I think, feels as I feel. Who is he, what is his name—and what will they do to him?

chapter nine

Let not the deeds of the guilty touch upon those
whose hands be clean.

—*Cennfaelad*

In fullness of time Athyn's schooling was complete, and
with pride greater than she had ever thought to feel, she
took her formal robing as a brehon. Nilos and Lyleth and
Debagh, prouder even than Athyn herself, and the Earl and
Countess Lennox as well, all came to Silverwood for the
impressive ceremony and the festivities that followed.

Afterward, she and Esmer met in one of the sitting rooms of
the college for a long discussion, over a mether or two, as to
Athyn's future. Esmer was putting a plan together, and he
trusted that Athyn would be foresighted enough to accept it. *If
not, we have still made a prudent investment, and shall find good
use for her gifts in Connacht's service; but if she will only see the
vision as we see it, much the best for us all—for Keltia too, maybe,
even...*

"We have spoken before now of you becoming Judge of
Connacht," began Esmer. But Athyn interrupted him, so eager
was she not to hold him to any promise she imagined he might
regret having made, or not having made.

"Nay, that was but talk, my lord, no need to name me so, I
understand perfectly—"

"Athwen, will you never learn to be still so folk can finish?"
His voice was warm with indulgence. "So quick are you to
decry yourself— As it happens, I have no intention of making

you Judge of Connacht, at least not yet awhile. Bronwyn tells me that you stand at the very top of your class, so that I have no doubts of your ability. But you are very young, and other folk might not be so willing to admit of your judging wisdom. So I have another thought..." He spoke for a while, uninterrupted for once, and Athyn stared at him when he had finished and said the first thing that came to her tongue.

"Surely I am too old!"

"Nonsense," he said cheerfully. "You are but, what, two-and-twenty; too young to serve as chaired brehon, maybe, but the perfect age to train for a Fian. Why should the next ten years, or twenty even, be spent in service to some lawdog who though thrice your age will have not half your skill, clarking and erranding when you might be training as a warrior? A Fian-trained brehon at my side in a few years, at Mariota's side when she comes to be Countess in her own right— Only think! Not only could you hand out judgments, you could apply the strong hand right along with it."

Athyn laughed. "Now that *is* tempting... May I think on it?"

"All you like," said Esmer happily; as Earl of Connacht, and she his liegewoman, he could have ordered her to it, but that was never Esmer's way. "We return to Erinna tomorrow," he went on, "and you shall have whatever time you need. But you are going, Athwen-fach. I have promised Ganor and your mother, and though that may have been rash in the extreme, even I do not dare break my word to either."

For all Esmer's assurances, and her own inclination, Athyn was still undecided; and at last she ate her pride and took her problem to the one to whom she should have taken it first. If anyone knew what way she should go, he would, and could tell her how the instinct for battle she was beginning to feel in her soul of late might best be made to serve the law, or her own inclination.

"So they wish me to be a Fian," she said, ending her recounting. "And I must say the prospect pleases me... perhaps too much. But what I need to know, athro, is how might the warrior's way mix with the law, and punishment with justice, and any of those with magic."

"Ah." Redigan Ó Hannay closed the text he had been studying. *I told Bronwyn long since that this one was going to have a problem with this, and now it is come...* "None of those mixes with any," he said at last, leaning back and steepling his fingers in the teacher's age-old gesture. "And that may be the hardest lesson you will ever have to learn. What is lawful in magic may not be so before the judging-seat; and the same for war. That does not mean these things should not be practiced; only that they must always be practiced according to the rules that the gods have set out for their using. Things are not ever as we might love them to be, or as we think they should be, but that does not give us the right to use magic, or war, or the law, or even punishment, as means to make life fit our wishes, however noble our motives might be."

She was silent for a while, pondering this. "Well; but punishment? That at least seems a thing the law may order."

"Again, not so. What we do when we punish is deliver the criminal, by means of punishment, from the crime. We liberate the evil of the deed from the doer; we do not punish for pure revenge's sake. Vengeance is another matter, and has laws of its own which I shall not speak of here. But mark: Whoever would judge—or avenge—must bear the dán for it; else they have no right to do either. A bad decision from a just judge will do much harm, and work greatly against dán; but so too will a good ruling from an unjust judge."

"Which is worse?"

Her teacher smiled, but not at her; the smile of one seeing a memory, a younger self, an ancient query. "Ah, that is a question many have asked before you, Athyn-fach, and will ask as long as the law lives to be asked of, for it treats of the very difference in nature between justice and law."

"That is no answer, athro!"

"It is not, but it is all the answer I have for you; and the same answer I was given when I asked that same question, myself a new brehon not very much older then than you are now. Each of us must find that difference alone, and, it is to be hoped, in wisdom; as each of us is different, that distinction will be different. But, if justice is in it, the end of those differences will be all the same."

"You speak like a Druid," said Athyn crossly. "I asked you as a judge."

Ó Hannay laughed. "Sometimes we each of us must partake of the nature of other callings, and rules be damned. But good judge or bad, each judge must justify the sentences he or she shall declare; as judge you will be participant in crime and sentencing alike. That too can be punishment, as you shall come to see."

"And if one day I—as brehon, or as warrior—should deem death?"

"Then, brehon or warrior, you must see it done. Brehons are warriors, warriors brehons; sorcerers can be both. But mark: If you have judged correctly, the dán of slaying does not impute to you. And if you have judged awry, you must be willing to accept the altered dán—your own as well as that of the one you have wrongly judged. Therefore judges—and warriors also—are well instructed to consider carefully any death they might effect. Not only can it not be corrected until another lifetime, but it must be the true judgment of the Goddess, and not mere human revenge."

"Not hard," said Athyn rashly. "I can do that."

Redigan Ó Hannay looked up suddenly, and in his eyes was every brehon back to Cennfaelad himself.

"Say that again to me when once you have so judged."

In the end Athyn decided to remain at Silverwood, at least for a time. Taking valor as Fian was a great decision, so great a decision as should not be made in such a time of upheaval. But things had long been ordered other wise, and far away in their secret strongholds, even the Sidhe sighed and wondered, as dán they had long foreseen began at last to move...

Athyn entered the Archbrieve's chambers swiftly and silently, bowing to Bronwyn Muirheyd, who came straight to the point. *It is better for her, so...*

"I have had word from your mother, Athyn. You are to return home at once. Nilos Marwin is dying. I have arranged passage on a ship that leaves in four hours from Port Caradon; you will have just time to pack."

Athyn put out both hands, an unconscious warding-off, a child's instinctive gesture that went straight to Bronwyn's heart. "He is not—"

"Nay, nay. But Lyleth has no hope of him recovering, and he has asked for you." She added in a gentler voice, "You care very much for him, I think?"

Athyn nodded, too proud to let the Archbrieve see the tears that stood just behind her eyes. "When my father—when Cormac died, Nilos took his place, as much as anyone could; he taught me such bardery as I know, and gave me all my great love for it. He encouraged me to come here when even my mother doubted. He is an Incomer, yet I say to you, Archbrieve"—and here her head came up with angry defiance—"he is more a Kelt than many born thus."

"Even so," said Bronwyn. "Go now. I think you will find more awaits you there than Nilos's passing."

"It is not so bad, hurts not at all. He drifts in and out of awareness on his own lifetide. Very often he is awake enough to jest, and demand, and annoy just as he has ever done."

"The healers can do nothing?"

Lyleth shook her head. They were on their way upstairs to Nilos's chamber, Athyn having just that moment arrived home, her cloak scarcely shed.

"We have even had Incomer healers. That insufferable

Rhykeur Pym, from over at Atrohumë, as he has barbarously and brazenly renamed Ardromurchan—you recall him, he has spoken so ill of Nilos these past two years—brought several. But they did no good. It cannot be too much longer now; for his sake I pray so."

Athyn pulled at her mother's sleeve, just as if she had been a child again. "And what of *your* sake? How is it with you?"

Her mother smiled, though tears came flooding to her eyes. "Oh, hen, I shall be well enough—but come."

Athyn was shocked to see how frail Nilos had grown over the past sixmonth since last she had seen him. As sick folk will, he sensed a presence he had been longing for, and opened his eyes to greet her with the old warmth.

"Well, if this is what it takes to get you home on a visit, I must do it more often—"

Athyn laughed, dropping her head to hide her own sudden tears. "My sorrow—I am not much of a traveller."

"I hear you are to take valor as a Fian."

She looked up; he was smiling. "It has not been entirely decided; but do I have your blessing for it, isathro?"

Over against the far wall, Lyleth put a hand over her mouth. *Isathro*... The Keltic word for that teacher who puts a gifted pupil on the path of mastery... *And none deserves it more than he, nay, not even my dearest Cormac, who set her on her path at the first; indeed, who saved her for it...*

Athyn was speaking to Nilos now in Volgiaran, his own native tongue; Lyleth could make out only a few words, loving words, prayerful words. *This is what I summoned her here for; to make that fitting ending with Nilos that she was denied making with Cormac...* She brushed away tears with both hands. *Small comfort, maybe, but small is better than none; or so at least I have always thought.*

But the comfort, if comfort it was, was of brief duration: Three hours later, simply, quietly, one hand in Lyleth's and the other in Athyn's, Nilos Marwin died.

And a bare hour after that, as if he had been awaiting the removal of the one last bar to his homecoming, Kier mac Archill rode into the courtyard of Caerlaverock, to claim his inheritance at last—and to demand that Athyn leave Caerlaverock forever.

"He is of full majority now, he has every right in law to do so. I am no kin here, not formally adopted, nor lawful fostern neither. According to every tenet of landlaw and heirship he may quite properly send me packing. I am a brehon; I know these things."

Athyn seemed less perturbed by Kier's first act as lord of Caerlaverock than any of her sibs. Perhaps she had the advantage of them: She had been expecting no less for years now; for her it was bruising shock, but no surprise. And though Kier had not attempted to oust the others but had banished Athyn only, they were stunned all the more.

"Athyn, is there nothing—" began Debagh.

Athyn shook her head. "Not for me. Only, do what you must, to look after mamaith. That is all you can do; for anyone. Now let us go out and speak thanks to those who have come to speed our lasathair."

The mourners for Nilos Marwin made a goodly number, if not so many as had assembled to grieve Cormac mac Archill some years back. Esmer Lennox had come, and Ganor; most of the neighboring landowner kindreds sent some representative, an elder clannsman if not the chief or the heir.

There were even several Firvolgi friends of Nilos— Teddecin Wenn, a self-proclaimed poet; Darrian Finslock, a holographer; and the pigdog Rhykeur Pym, of whom Lyleth had complained to Athyn—who had arrived together on the morning of the funeral, pompously claiming long and close acquaintance with the deceased, though few at Caerlaverock could recall Nilos ever having spoken of them, or having spoken well of them when he did. Even so, it was an honorable assembly, and Lyleth was glad for Nilos's sake that so many Kelts had come to bid him farewell.

The ceremony was held two days after Nilos's death; not in the annat, as Cormac's rites had been, but in the great hall of Caerlaverock, with burial according to Firvolgi custom. In token of this, the local Druid conducted the rites in uncertain partnership with a Firvolgian prester—few Kelts present had been aware that the Incomers even had priests, nor much cared—and the resultant ceremony was neither good Draoíchtas nor good Jauharah, as the Firvolgi called their own religious practice.

One of the more agreeable Firvolgi funeral traditions is to make offering to the dead—Kelts do likewise, but not quite in the same way—and halfway through the ceremony Lyleth rose to make the first such; Pym, Wenn and Finslock self-importantly jostling to follow her. When all, seemingly, had gifted the dead who were inclined to, Athyn rose in her place and came forward, laying upon the bier a token of her own, and looking defiantly over the hall she spoke in the tones of quotation.

"Though the candles be quenched for him here, yet are the torches lighted for him in another place." She was suddenly silent, her eyes too full of tears to see their faces, her heart too full of feeling to say further, but she saluted Nilos in the manner of his own people and returned to her seat beside her mother, who bent her head to whisper.

"That is lovely; did you make that?"

Athyn nodded. "Yet another thing he gave me. Gifts like that shall never die."

At last the rite was over. Nilos's body, and all the funeral gifts with it, had been reduced to ash according to custom, and placed in the traditional canopic jar, which would be sent back to the Firvolgian homeworld of Kaireden, where Nilos would join his ancestors in the familial shrine.

But here, now, it was the turn of the Kelts, and they were remembering Nilos in Keltic fashion, with food and ale and merry stories, tears and laughter. The Incomers present seemed a little shocked, but did their best to conform, though they stayed only long enough to satisfy custom and decency alike.

Yet one there was who had not shared in either grief or memory, and one there was too who would not let him get away with it... Paying no heed to the stares of the funeral guests but seizing Kier by the elbow—in a grip that she hoped hurt him even more than it pained her—Athyn dragged him into the library and closed the doors behind them.

"Long past time we sorted things between us," she said pleasantly. "I am only sorry it must be across Nilos's coffin."

"Nilos! He could not solve the problems of the rainbow," said Kier with scorn, rubbing his elbow when he thought Athyn could not see. "Nor could Cormac, come to it. But I do not know why I even trouble to speak to you—you have no place here. Indeed, you never did."

Athyn felt a stirring of hot anger, as if some string had been plucked deep inside. But she smiled inwardly as well. All her old nervousness at confronting Kier had gone—so much had Silverwood done for her—and she put down the angry flash that would once have ruled her.

"Ah, that is what I so like to hear: rational argument logically developed... That you would speak so of Nilos does not surprise me; but of your own father? Is that what took you into the ranks of the mosstroops? You know, now I think on it, I do not believe we have ever heard to our complete satisfaction whose name you truly ride there: Keltia's, or Kaireden's."

She was rewarded by the instant flash of fear and fury on his face, and went on.

"Now I like to think you ride with the mosstroops as a secret agent of the Keavers, for Keltia's weal. But I am well reminded, as he whom we sped this day used to tell me, that liking to think is not the same as knowing. Do you think I do not know who spread those lying tales of Nilos, so that mosstroops came into Elmet? Have you forgotten that day you rode with them right to the front door of this house—forgotten what horse *I* rode that day? Brother?" He did not deny any of it, but she was grimly pleased to see him flinch; he had ever been superstitious, and she was only grateful she had a rod as mighty as the Mari Llwyd with which to threaten him. "Well, no matter. We all of us are grown now, and you can no longer hurt us. Nilos, aye, and Cormac too, they are in a place where you cannot touch them."

"But I can still do much to hurt *you*—sister."

Athyn smiled. "Only if I allow it. But listen while I tell you a thing: If you are not utterly correct and compassionate in your dealings with the Lady Lyleth, to the smallest legal particular—well, remember I am brehon now, and I can use all the practice that I can get. I would be most pleased to try charges of false keeping and honor-price violation against any who did not accord Lyleth Kerguethen ac Archill gân Nilos, Nâredd Marwinë of Cathures, all her dower rights in Caerlaverock. Such an offense touches on the heart of brehonry, and the penalties are strict ones."

Kier found his voice again, if not his bluster. "But you will go? You yourself? If I take oath?"

She looked up at him, and he took a step back. "Oh aye. I will go. I have said so. I have little faith in your oath. But I accept it, because I must; and you are warned."

When they returned to the feast, they went side by side and arm in arm, and wore smiles, as if things were well between them; but no one there was fooled, save perhaps the Firvolgi. Only Haneria Lauder, Caerlaverock's bard, who dwelled at Sauchiehall, and the clann brehon, Iolo Forsycht, exchanged glances, and looked at Lyleth, and away again. But Lyleth looked at no one, not even her children, and gave no sign.

* * *

After the last funeral guest had gone, Lyleth, going in search of Athyn, found her in her old stronghold beneath the eaves. The dorter was more of a lumber-room now, its corners crammed with rubble; no one had lived in it since Athyn left for Silverwood, though she still used it on her visits home—as she had last night, curling up in her old bed behind the carved shutters, trying to find the feeling of peace and safety she had known there as a child. But it was gone.

Now she was packing up whatever of her possessions had not yet been removed; little remained in chest or press, even the mementos of Nilos she wished to take away with her were already sorted and stowed. Soon the chamber would look as if none had ever dwelled there; or, if any had, so long ago as to leave no mark of tenure after.

"It is best this way," she said, forestalling her mother's protest. "Indeed, I think it is long past time for the clean break—nay, not a word or I shall weep! You know it yourself, and so did Nilos. Even so, I would not have chosen to leave you now, not with Nilos so newly sped— But thanks to the Lord Esmer I have a place, and so long as I keep away from Caerlaverock, Kier will let you remain."

"I cannot bear to think of him driving you from your home," said Lyleth. "It chafes me that he may do as he pleases, and naught can be done to stop him."

"It is the law," said Athyn smiling, "and I should know."

Lyleth gave a small unwilling laugh. "Did Iolo Forsycht, or Haneria, speak to you?"

"Should they have done?"

"Oh, nay, nay—but I thought they might have had somewhat to say to you. It is of no matter."

Athyn returned to her packing, and the previous topic. "Besides, you very well know how it would be, soon or late, if I stayed on Kier's sufferance, which any road he would never give me... Nay—it is time I went, and it is not you I leave. Nay, do not weep. It is not you."

At the top of the hill pass that leads over Cat Bregion's round green shoulder into the next valley, Athyn reined in Tarn, and the packhorse who followed, and swinging about in her saddle looked back northwestwards into Elmet. She saw below her not her beloved home-valley lying cold and peaceful at the end of a midwinter day but a far vaster picture than that: a realm conquered with scarce a blade having been raised.

It is Keltia no more, but the swordlands of the Firvolgi... Below her was plowgate rather than hardgate; but looking up to the Long Hills in the east and the Twelve Kings in the north, she could see where it changed, from land that had been long under harrow to land that had never felt the plow's steel touch. Elster crouching before Tarn's hoofs looked up at her, and gave a whimper, sensing change, and the strangeness of his mistress's mood.

If only all Keltia could be again that whole and unharrowed! The Incomers gone out forever... That would be a mighty thing. But whose hand could be found to bring us all to such a day?

With a slow, deliberate air of ceremony that seemed to mark some great change—though she could not then have said what it might be—Athyn shook out the folds of a garment that had lain doubled across her saddlebow, a hooded cloak that had seen much wear yet had still much left in it; and there upon the hill Cat Bregion, in the low, blood-gold light of a winter dusk, sun huge and red and ragged in the west, with a strange solemnity she settled upon her own shoulders the black leather battlecloak that had been worn by Cormac mac Archill, that day he had found a newborn infant upon a stricken field.

For a few moments she held the cloak close about her, as if

it embraced her and protected her; as perhaps it did. *I shall wear this until that day comes, and maybe even after...* And rode away out of Elmet, and down into the valley, and the fate, that lay before her.

BOOK II

Side warm against mine in frost-time
Chest my cheek rests upon, shield-broad,
steel-ribbed
Arms around me, oak-strong, sun-warm
Flanks arrow-straight, the downward highroad
Slow honeyed flare of desire spiraling round us
Love, and peace within it:
We are gathered in like grain,
Our harvest each other.

—*Athyn's bridal-song to Morric*

Her breasts are graals achieved
Her skin burns white as snow
Her hair pours down her back
like ruby water

—*from a song by Morric, for Athyn*

chapter ten

The love that I have chosen shall ever me content
And the salt sea shall be frozen or ever I repent.

—*Lassarina Aoibhell ac Douglas*

When she rode away from Caerlaverock at Kier mac Archill's vindictive command, Athyn took the road through Elmet, straight to Graystones to swear liegedom to the Earl of Connacht, as Connacht's Earl had hoped and planned and wished.

And who received it gravely and gladly. Though already he cared for Athyn as for another daughter, and felt keenly for the girl's fresh griefs, it must also be said that Esmer Lennox was secretly, shamefacedly jubilant that things had fallen out so. Now he had no rival for Athyn's loyalties and commitments; there was nothing now to distract from the great plans he had for her.

And so he took her along, and Tarn and Elster came too, when he and Ganor went back to Ardturach, and barely a fortnight later she was on her way to her new home: the Fian school at Casterlines, on Tara, the Throneworld, ancient seat of Keltdom among the stars. But there was another stop to be made first, and, unbeknownst to any of them, the dán that was to meet her there had already taken up its place, and was waiting, smiling, on her coming.

*   *   *

Though many in after years tried to lay some touch of an-da-shalla upon Athyn's first sight of the planet where so much would change forever for so many—surely she must have known, they insisted, upon seeing Tara, what the future would hold for her?—she herself always maintained she had felt not a flutter of Sight, not the tiniest flicker of prescience but only the natural awe of a Kelt seeing the seat and cradle of her people for the first time, the astonishment that anyone would feel at the glory of the sight.

But if Athyn had been awed by her first glimpse of the beautiful ringed Throneworld, she was dumbstruck at her first sight of Caerdroia. Esmer, knowing her excitement, had ordered his ship to come in leisurely over the Strath Mór, that wide green valley also called the Great Glen, thus allowing Athyn a spectacular view of the Crown City of Keltia where it rises from the plain.

Climbing the slopes of the Loom where Brendan built it, flung out along the mountain wall for seven miles, Caerdroia reposes in the lap of Eryri—Mount Eagle of the two peaks—like a jewel in the sun. And on the highest of its terraced ridges stands Turusachan, Place of Gathering, the ancient palace home of Keltia's monarchs. Just now, at the last moment of sunset, the windows flamed as if torches burned behind them, all the panes seeming alight with merriment and life. Then the sun fell below the distant ocean horizon, and the light faded, and Athyn saw with an indescribable stab of sorrow that the windows which had been so bright a moment ago were black and blind, empty eyes of an empty palace. No Kelt had lived there for a hundred years—nor Incomer either—as she very well knew. Yet still, for that one wondrous moment, the palace had been alive for her, and she had looked eagerly to see those who surely must dwell within: the fair lords and noble ladies, the princes and bards and warriors and enchanters, and above them all the one who truly was above them all, who sat—crowned, mighty, humorous, just—upon the Throne of Scone.

But that was an ashling. There was neither High King nor

High Queen now upon that ancient seat, did not look to be any time soon. And still no foresight told her, nor would she have believed it if it had, that one day Turusachan would be much more to her than a sad symbol of long-vanished monarchs; but the Sight of the glory and gaiety and power she had seen behind those briefly glamour'd windows never quite left her, not for the rest of her days.

It was a time of festival, Samhaintide on the planet Tara. Great Samhain, the beginning of the year and the winter together, had been celebrated eleven days before, and the next night was the end of the holy New Year season. Known as Samhain the Less, it is a night of joyful solemnity, when the King of Winter, the Cabarfeidh, the Hornèd Lord, takes up His rule from the Goddess Who has reigned over the summer half of the year. In these days of Summerend, the veil between this world and the next is at its thinnest, and the beloved dead return to be with those they loved in life; and whom they love still, for in the Keltic faith death does not part, but is merely another room in a many-chambered palace of beauty and bliss beyond all words and worlds.

And on the last night of Samhain the tradition Kelts practice is an ancient and a joyous one indeed...

"I would rather not, if it is all the same to you, lord?" Athyn ventured, respectfully but firmly. "I do not think I am in the correct mood for it—"

"It is the custom, as you well know," said Esmer Lennox, even more firmly. "And you shall come. Holy Tree! It will do you good."

And so it did.

They set out from the Connacht palace walking, for that too was custom, and it seemed that half Caerdroia walked with them, down the road that leads through the great Wolf Gate and out onto the wide plain, Moycathra, that stretches for miles below the city walls: the Earl and his Countess hand in hand, Athyn and Mariota behind.

When they reached the little swift stream called Bannochburn that threads the plain until it flows into the mighty Avon Dia, they saw many hundreds of others there before them, high and humble alike, all of them carrying pompions, small pumpkins with carved faces, that bore flickering lights within.

This was the custom of which Esmer had spoken: the soul-sail, an ancient practice that had come from Erith, long since, in the great immrama. All across Keltia this night, such little glowing pompions, charged alight by magic and carved with merry faces or fearsome according to the carver's whim, would be set sailing on black floats down all rivers to the seas, to honor the dead, and to bring to them the words and thoughts and love of the living.

Esmer gestured, and an attendant came up with the pompions he had carried for the comital family to set asail. The Earl took one for Ganor and himself, and then Mariota, and, last, hesitantly, Athyn accepted hers.

She held it in her hands awhile, feeling the weight of it— a pound or two, no more—watching as scores of others launched their small gold vessels onto the flood. All her life she had done this, and had loved it well, every Samhain since first she was able to remember, first with her family and the others at Caerlaverock and their neighbors in the district, then at Silverwood, or Ardturach, wherever the great solemn feast had found her; but never before had she felt such reluctance as she felt now. She stared down unseeing at the pompion in her hands; then, with sudden resolution, she murmured the pishogue to light it, and a glow blinked on as if a candle burned within. Bending low to the dark water that already danced with uncounted fingertongues of light, she set her pompion on one of the small boat-shaped black floats that lay strewn anyhow upon the shore.

Stepping to the water's edge, she gently pushed it out into the current, watching as it joined the great bobbing navy that was already streaming down Bannochburn toward the Avon Dia, and, at last, the sea. The sight filled her with sudden delight, and she laughed aloud with the joy of it: hundreds and hundreds of glowing pumpkins, bobbing on the black water under the sunset sky. *I send you for Cormac and for Nilos*, she thought after her own little vessel as it sailed serenely on, *and for my parents whom I did not know this life round. Tell them...*

She sighed and seemed to give way a little, struck as suddenly with grief renewed as she had been a moment earlier with joy, then she felt an arm round her shoulder, and looked up to meet the understanding gaze of the Countess Ganor.

"They take our messages to those we love; they are the message and the messenger alike."

Athyn's eyes were fixed again on the pumpkin sail, though by now her own vessel was lost in the fleet. "And what happens to the messengers when the messages are delivered?"

"What happens to all things: a natural end when purpose is completed. The magic fades, the little lights go out. Schools of sun-sharks gather to feast on the shells, or they sink to the bottom of the sea, or they reach the sunset itself and come ashore beyond the West... Does it matter?"

And Athyn, watching the fleet of lights sail on undiminished, smiled and shook her head. She was about to say somewhat when she heard Mariota call her name, and excusing herself to the Countess, she crossed over to her friend.

Mariota's voice was eager. "Ah, Athwen! Here is someone I would have you meet—would have meet you."

And Athyn looking up at the tall figure who stood beside her friend felt dán come down upon her like a storm from out the mountains—the dán the Sidhe had foreseen, that had been prepared for her and for many, through many lives, and deaths...

"Athyn, I present Morric Douglas, of Ruchdi on Caledon, a bard made, a friend of mine at Seren Beirdd; you have heard me play his songs. And Morric," she continued, turning to the other, "I make you known to Athyn nic Archill, of

Caerlaverock in Connacht, my very dear friend, and a brehon robed."

Athyn had heard not a word of the introduction past the name. She had stared, then flushed and caught herself, then stared again. But she had good cause to stare so: Plainly put, Morric Douglas was the most beautiful man she had ever set eyes on. Tall, powerfully built, with broad shoulders and the high ribcage of a singer and the lithe grace in gait of a lion just roused from sleep, he had rich pure brown hair down past his shoulders, deep blue eyes, fair skin; though all that was no uncommon look amongst Scotans.

Still, few indeed, in Keltia or elsewhere, could boast the incredible perfection of feature upon which Athyn now stared; but there was a strength in Morric Douglas's face, a tenderness and joyousness and danger and wit, all of which staved off mere prettiness and raised that face instead to the fairness of the Sidhe themselves. *Fairer, even; for the Sidhe are not mortal, and he most surely is...*

And then she saw that his beauty was not the point; it was what had caught her, but not what would hold her; not then, not ever. It was almost irrelevant, even, suggesting as it did a strange and demanding inner life, a plane of existence utterly different to her own—and yet somehow the same, congruent, contiguous, adjacent. *I know him— This is no stranger to me: He is that one I have been seeking, the one I have so long wondered even existed; that one who was promised...*

They reached out to clasp hands in the Keltic manner; and almost in the same motion jumped back, startled alike, as blue-gold sparks showered where their fingers met, the shock passing through them both and into the ground beneath their feet.

"An omen," he said in a deep singer's voice, and smiled down at her.

"A leftover charge from the pompions, more like," said Athyn, in a voice that shook only a little. "Magic will do that—"

He shook his head mock-ruefully, still smiling. "Ah, a pragmatic after all, and here I have been believing my friend Mariota, when she tells me the Erinnach are romantics bred and born."

"Do not let her fool you, lad," confided Esmer with a grin; he and Ganor had been standing nearby, and Morric bowed to them at once. "This is one who has ridden the Mari Llwyd; that is worth a ballad, if I know anything. Get her to tell you of it."

Athyn glanced sidewise at him; though Morric looked intrigued, she herself was not about to rise to the lure Esmer Lennox had so temptingly thrown out. *I shall tell him of that in my own good time, if indeed I ever tell him at all...* "What do you know of horses, sir bard?"

"Not much," he said cheerfully. "They have a leg at each corner, much like a table, and are in the middle less comfortable even than that."

Now it was Athyn who smiled, though she felt as if her insides were a bag of ferrets. "Oh, but there is so much more! For instance, my family breed horses to be used on hill-farms."

"Aye? And?"

"Well, it all depends on the terrain, do you see. If the farm is more up and down"—Athyn illustrated with appropriate gestures—"we sell them horses with forelegs shorter than hindlegs, and if the farm is more side to side, as it were, a less frequent orientation, we breed beasts for them on special commission, with the off legs shorter than the near legs. We send scouts to prospective buyers; if there are many hills it can get most complicated—"

Mariota, who through all this very remarkable account had been keeping no less remarkable a straight face, could keep it no longer, and exploded into laughter. Morric, whose own expression had been growing gradually more incredulous the more Athyn went on, joined her with a will, and with an air of intense relief also.

"I must admit you had me believing you for a moment," he said, still smiling. "You have the bardic gift, you should tell stories. I do not mean that as a slap, truly," he added hastily. "Just that you have the tale-gift."

"My methryn's mate taught me somewhat of the art," said Athyn, allowing a first faint smile to cross her face, though her breathing was still coming a little short. "And I confess I have committed a poem or two in my time. But I have never been trained in it; not as you two, any road."

"Nay," said Mariota, rolling her eyes. "She is a chaired brehon, as I said, and bound for Fianship too, though you would never think it to look on her, would you?"

"Nay," he replied, courteously, "that you would not."

"But really! Side-to-side horses, or uphill-downhill horses, and bow-and-stern, or whatever the hells it was you were rabbiting on about!"

Mariota turned a reproachful look on her friend as they made their way back to the Lennox brugh; Morric Douglas, after a few more exchanges, had bowed and taken seemingly reluctant leave, glancing back more than once. Ganor and Esmer had gone long before, bidding the girls follow when they pleased, but not to tarry, as they had an early morning.

"You knew very well he is that one whose songs you loved so excessively when I played them for you—nay, do not trouble to deny it, you know right well you did—and I tied myself in *knots* beforehand, Athwen, to set you up to him as a brilliant brehon. What must he think of you now!"

"Why," said Athyn lightly, "that I made him laugh."

Whenever they came to Caerdroia the family stayed at Lennoxliss, the splendid town palace of the Earls of Connacht that stands on Highfold, the wide wooded ledge-terrace one level down from Turusachan itself, where the greatest gentry of Keltia, or merely the wealthiest, have their equally splendid dwellings. The morning after the pumpkin sail, at the third hour, the heavy bronze-and-silver gates of Lennoxliss swung open, and a great closed chariot rolled through, drawn by four Vanx grays. Within the carriage were Esmer and Ganor, Mariota and Athyn, Tipherris Greyloch and Hutcheon Fraser, and the Lord and Lady of Ferns, whose family had been friends to the Lennoxes for five hundred years. All of them were riding to the ceremonial opening of the House of Peers, which the Earl and Countess, and almost every other noble in Keltia, had come to attend.

Athyn's eyes were on sticks, as Cormac would have put it, at the magnificence of the surroundings: not only the grand mansions of Highfold but the state buildings above them on the Turusachan plateau—Seren Beirdd, Star of the Bards, directly above Lennoxliss, two hundred feet straight up on the edge of the cliff; the black granite Fianna commandery across from the palace; the dark gray marble brugh of the Ban-draoi and the quiet white cloister of the Druids and the palace itself.

She was as goggled to see many of the folk who lined the way; both surprised and dismayed at how few were Kelts—not more than half, and it troubled her. It was the first time she had ever beheld aliens—save for Incomers—and the gallaín present in Caerdroia were exotic strangers indeed: Fomori and Voritians and Cathanesians, Dakdak and Cassonians and Ganastrians, Fasarini and Numantissans and others too many to count of races she could not identify; all wending slowly in the same direction as they.

Esmer noted her attention. "Aye, lass, *too* many, I am also thinking," he said a touch sourly. "But at least—unlike the Incomers—these ones stay in Caerdroia and do not spread out over the rest of the planet, nor to other of our worlds. At least for now, and so the plague is contained. Yet if there were no hoofs there would be no hoof-rot..."

The others in the carriage startled at his words, though only Ganor called him on it.

"That is not like you, Connacht," she said with a certain roundness, addressing him by his title as she ever did in public.

"Is it not?" he answered, still staring darkly out the chariot's windows at the passing throngs. "What would be like me, then?"

But Ganor, and the others, had no answer.

The ceremony at the Hall of Aonachs had been long and incomprehensible, the reception that followed interminable; and very daunting to one young unknown brehon who was acquent with few of those present. The Connacht party had not returned to Lennoxliss until nearly time for the nightmeal, and Athyn, tired, combative and nerve-jangled, wished only to have some supper in her room, and take a bath, and go to sleep.

But Mariota, intent on showing off her city to her friend, had other ideas; and after the nightmeal she dragged Athyn—in the teeth of the latter's whines and protests—down to the ancient quarter of Caerdroia known as the Stonerows. A pleasant district of low stone dwellings and twisting narrow cobbled streets, the Stonerows had been the first area settled when the City was raised. Now it was inhabited by students and families and artisans, who found the spacious solid buildings much to their liking, and the rentages kind to the purse. The two were bound for a favorite students' meeting-place in a quiet blindstreet: an ancient half-timbered alehouse called Macca's Well, built snugly and safely into the thickness of one of the old city walls.

The cheerful din could be heard in the street. As Athyn saw the minute she set foot within, the place was full of folk; Kelts almost entirely, and young folk for the most part, though there was a fair sprinkling of all ages. Full also of music, the most infectious dancetunes Athyn had ever heard; just to feel the beat of the borraun in the walls or hear the fidil soaring above the merry racketing was enough to set hands to clapping and feet to little tapping half-steps. Her spirits lifted at once, and she looked longingly at the dancers. But Mariota was tugging at her arm, steering expertly through the crowd to a round oak table in an inglenook, in a far and quieter corner of a smaller adjoining room.

"Here, then! Here at *last* is my friend of whom you have heard me speak so much—Athyn nic Archill. And, Athwen, these are friends and fellows, bards all—" She introduced those seated: Cray Jargier, a merry-faced gitternist a dozen years older than the rest, whose wild graying hair and beard made him look like a benevolent bear; a violet-eyed Kymri, Gwencarig, a renowned chaunter, and her singing partner, Tam Blainry, whom Athyn would later hear sing together like the Sidhe in close and soaring harmonies; and lastly another singer, a bronze-lunged woman called Linja Jospin, who when she was in full cry could be heard clear to the Kyles of Ra; a gifted crew, whose disparate styles in music were wonders of their craft.

Bards all indeed, and they welcomed Athyn instantly as Mariota's friend; from the dancing-floor Sosánaigh waved wildly. Then Athyn, looking across the room, saw Morric Douglas standing in the arched doorway, watching her, and it seemed that all fell suddenly still and silent around her, as if a glass bell had been set down, the whole scene caught out of time.

He smiled then, and just as suddenly sound and movement began again. He came straight for their table, greeted loudly by all, and took a seat between Tam and Gwencarig, across the table's width from Athyn.

"Will you sing tonight, Douglas?" asked Cray, tuning his gittern as he spoke.

"Nay, I think not—my musicmates are not here." At the unasked question in Athyn's face: "I have four bandfellows with whom I play, mostly. One is a Kelt; the others are Firvolgi, but they love our music, and play it most well. But perhaps that displeases you, Mistress nic Archill?"

"That they love our music and play it well, or that they are Firvolgi and have no business doing either?" returned Athyn coolly. "My late fosterfather, or rather my methryn's mate, was himself Firvolgi. Art and the love of it, Master Douglas, are scarcely the sole province of Kelts."

Morric bowed where he sat. "I am well rebuked," he said smiling, then rose again. "I shall redeem my disgrace by being useful, fetching more ale; this table looks thirsty, and we cannot allow that—not with a guest in our midst."

Athyn was still looking after him when out of the shadows came a small slight form dressed in Firvolgi fashion—airy floating embroidered panels in mauve and lavender, soft boots of pale pink suede. As the new arrival's face came into the circle of light thrown by the table-sconce, Athyn saw that it belonged to a young woman much of an age with herself, an Incomer, who smiled vaguely and greeted Athyn in the manner of her own race.

"Hal-ya! I am Amzalsunëa—Morric Douglas's wife?"

Athyn, surprised by just how surprised she was at this declaration—and oddly hurt, though that she set aside to examine later—hurriedly named herself to the outfrenne girl, proudly adding her professional affiliation. But Amzalsunëa only nodded, and sitting down in an empty chair across the table took up Morric's ale mether to sip from it, as one who did not need permission.

Athyn looked again at her under cover of the music and her own mether, and despaired. Amzalsunëa Dalgarno—for such was her proper fullname—was the prettiest girl Athyn had ever seen: heart-shaped face, milk-and-water skin under a smear of golden sunsprecks, huge violet eyes, hair a soft red, body whippet-slim...

"And all the depth of a coat of limewash on a Westlands cottage." Mariota's eyes gleamed wickedly as she leaned over, seeing where Athyn's glance was fixed. "Well, rather less, I should say, for I know the Westlanders take great pride in their work. But perhaps she does too."

"What work does she do—is she a bard also?"

The Heir of Connacht snorted cider, and rolled her beautiful eyes. "Sweetling, you may be a brehon trained but you are so green the cows could eat you— Well, how can I put this? In the Firvolgi worlds women are dealt with rather differently than is the way in our midst; and it has long been the very nasty custom there that women may be—bought."

"Bought! You mean, slavery?"

"Not quite; even they would not dare so much. Nay, a more temporary arrangement: the sale of services only."

"Ah." Athyn, untutored in the ways of Firvolgi vice, felt herself blushing, wishing to assure her friend that even such a country mouse as she was had heard of such things. But her ignorance could fairly be excused, for there had been no whoredom in Keltia, ever, until the Firvolgians had brought it in; and even now it was almost entirely an Incomer practice—as was so much else of equal unwholesomeness. A terrible thought occurred to her. "Then Morric—she said they are wed—"

"And I am the Queen of Ruvania! Oh nay, not they! He knows, of course, what she is, and what she does, but it does not seem to trouble him. They are by *no* means wedded, nor does he keep her himself. Nay, with them it was a liaison of youth, you know how it is—only think if you had stayed with, what, Roeg, was that his name? Quite! They met years ago, and have never entirely thrown each other over. I know for fact that she has many, ah, admirers. But whether that was so when first they met, I cannot say."

"By 'admirers' you mean—"

"That is so very much what I mean, my little bundle of grasses—though I *suppose*," she said grudgingly, "most of them are not by strict interpretation customers, just so; perhaps she is more courtesan, as I have heard the Firvolgi call it, than whore. Still," added Mariota hopefully, "that could change."

There were no words for either noisome appellation in the Gaeloch, and the terms Mariota employed were of necessity in the Volgiaran, the tongue used by the Firvolgians amongst themselves; they sounded harsh and uncouth in Athyn's ear.

"I think Morric would gladly be rid of her," said Sosánaigh

who had just now joined them, "if only he knew how—and I must say, he himself is not without ample other companionship; though to the best of my knowledge he has never had to pay for any of it. But they are familiar with each other, at ease in a way that lets them drop pretense and just be their true miserable ratbag selves. There can be a powerful attraction in that."

"Boredom too, surely."

"Oh aye. That is why, however fair she may be, or forgiving of his own indulgences, she will not hold him forever. He is too smart for that. Or at least I have ever thought so."

Athyn feigned massive disinterest. "Ah. Yet another man scuttered by a pretty face. Sad. Perhaps I was mistaken after all; judging by his songs and poems, I had thought better of him."

"Men are often like that."

"And women not?"

"I am thinking, not so much. Though it has been known to happen." Mariota cast Athyn a sly sidewise look. "Has it happened here? Morric is not so hard on the eyes, no more than on the ears—"

But Athyn was still watching Amzalsunëa as she drifted off through the crowd, smiling and speaking to many—men all, Athyn noticed, and noticed too the not altogether pleasant response they seemed to have to her.

"How came she to Keltia?"

"Her parents brought her as a lass," said Sosánaigh, "when they arrived as Incomers; they have had much success in commerce and business."

Mariota nodded vigorously. "You should hear my father on the subject of her father: says he is the Fir Bolc to end all Bagfolk, would let a duergar tup his own mother, if crossics were in it."

"My lord of Connacht must not hold back so," said Athyn laughing, "he must let us know how he *truly* feels..."

Sosánaigh grinned, then set down her mether and jumped

to her feet. "Well, enough of such nasty topics! Where are Cray and Linja? I want to play!"

"And I to dance!" cried Mariota, and fled after.

Athyn alone at the table, watching the dancing and listening with the greatest pleasure to the endless music. She had forgotten her ill humor and Amzalsunëa and her own selfconsciousness so far that she was dancing in her seat, shoulders and hands and legs keeping time to the irresistible rhythms of Erinnach slip-jigs, when suddenly Morric Douglas reappeared out of nowhere to sit down beside her, no word spoken, setting down two full methers of ale. So close had he seated himself that their arms and shoulders were touching, and she could feel his thigh against hers every inch from hip to knee. After a moment she picked up a mether and drank it half off, and, encouraged by his smile and the ale together, blurted out the thought that had been on her mind for an hour past.

"I did not know you were wedded."

"I am not, then."

"Oh aye? Yet that redhaired Incomer woman tells me she is your wife; almost the first words out of her mouth."

He seemed amused by Athyn's bluntness and discomfiture alike. "Oh, she has been known to tell folk so; often on even shorter acquaintance than that."

"And that does not trouble you? That she is untruthful, in public, and the untruth touches upon your honor?"

Morric shrugged. "She may call herself the Ard-rían of Keltia if she feels like it, but that does not set the Copper Crown upon her head. Nor does what she may say have aught to do with my honor, or lack thereof. But nay, lady," he said, with humorously exaggerated exactness, "I have not wedded Melassaun, or anyone else, in any marriage rite of ours or hers or any other race's—no handfasting, no brehon marriage, no precontract or avowal or betrothal; and, though she entitles herself my wife, I tell you again it is no title of hers." He smiled again, a real smile this time, and her heart turned over. "Nor ever will be, though why I am telling you any of this I am very sure I do not know."

Athyn, who was by now scarlet to her hair-roots, felt strangely comforted to hear this, though for all of her she could not think why, nor why she was shivering so inside her skin. *Melassaun*— Presumably a Keltic rendering of the admittedly musical but very foreign 'Amzalsunëa'... She drank off the rest of the mether, and looked at Morric, and swore privately by every god there ever was that never, not once, in this life or indeed in any other, would Athyn nic Archill ever call Amzalsunëa Dalgarno by aught but her full and correct, and irredeemably outfrenne, name.

And Morric looked at Athyn—the stream of dark-red hair that fell almost to her knees, the fair, fair skin, the gray-green eyes with their sword-straight directness under black brows and lashes—and though he had said he did not know why he had told this young Erinnachín what he had just told her, he had a sense that he—and she also—knew very well indeed why he had, and that they both would know even better in time to come.

On Athyn's last night in Caerdroia, the Lennoxes held a grand ball, for the Lady Mariota Lennox and Mistress Athyn nic Archill both. The occasion was quite obviously one for Kelts alone—not a single outfrenne face seen among the guests— and all evening a steady stream of elegant town chariots had been arriving at Lennoxliss, decanting into the torch-lit fore-court gorgeously gowned ladies palisaded with jewels, lords in attire finer still.

Mariota had taken advantage of the great occasion to unveil a brand-new talent. "I am not much gifted for sorcery," she had told Athyn, laughing, as the girls attired themselves in Mariota's solar, "but one can do much with a small gift, you know, Athynnach."

"I will say so," Athyn had murmured admiringly. Indeed, the proof was plain: For reasons known best to her, or perhaps for no reason at all, Mariota had managed a rann or pishogue to have her hair color change magically to suit her mood; so that sometimes she was gold-blond as her father, other times had hair redder than Athyn's or blacker than Sosánaigh's hip-length tangle of coal-colored curls. This night it was shades of brown, from deep rich mahogany at the hairline to ripe wheat at the tips that brushed her knees; her gown was dark gold velvet, her jewels yellow sapphires framed in diamonds.

"Well, I will tell you," she had confided to the fascinated—and, it must be said, envious—Athyn. "It can be tiresome to keep up, but I so enjoy making it hard for people to tell whether I am in good humor changing to ill or the other way round that I cannot seem to leave off." She speculatively eyed Athyn's own hair, as one of the Countess Ganor's women pinned it up in elegant masses and affixed Lyleth's diamond fillet into the deepness of it. "I wonder how would you look with whitegold tresses..."

It was the first time Athyn had ever been to such a glittering affair, much less had one given in her honor, and as she came down the famous wheelstair into the Great Hall—arm in arm with Mariota, who had insisted on a regal double entrance—there was such a shaking within her that she thought she would either faint or upheave. Instead, she had hugged the wall for many minutes, until Greyloch led her out to open the dancing—for a brehon robed, she was all but perished with shyness, though Ganor smiled encouragement and chivvyed her along—while Esmer Lennox partnered his daughter. Then Esmer had claimed Athyn for a reel, and then Lord Declan of Ferns, and Rhodri the Master of Lochaber, and Lord Stellin Ardwyr who was being tipped as a likely future consort for Mariota, and Greyloch's mate Hutcheon and Hutcheon's twin brother Sheele; and after that she had lacked for neither partners nor courage, and found to her astonishment that she was enjoying herself.

So that now, clad in her only best gown—a sweep-trained silk gúna of blue and green Archill sett, worn tonight with the diamond fillet and a new necklace, a chain of dark emeralds with which Esmer had gifted her just before the ball—Athyn, to her own thrilled surprise, was dancing with Morric Douglas.

She had curtsied deeply to his elegant bow when he presented himself before her and requested the honor of the strathspey—sinkingly certain he had asked her only at the Countess's commanding, or beseeching—and had laid her hand on his to begin the first of the dance's figures.

To her wonder, she found that they moved together as if they had always done so, though she had never considered herself more than adequate as a dancer—even their heights were a match, she tall even for a woman of the Kelts, he a head taller—and from the look on Morric's face it seemed he was as surprised and delighted as she. But her hand upon his had trembled, until, not looking at her, he had turned his own to clasp it firm.

Halfway through the strathspey's long elegant complexities, she caught sight over his shoulder of two other dancers across the room. In a copper-gold haze, as if they shone with their own light, they moved through the intricate steps with grace and gaiety: a handsome darkhaired lord, in black and silver and a formal silk plaid of his clann's dress tartan, and a lovely girl with dark red hair piled deep as sunset clouds, skin glowing moonwhite, her face lifted laughing to him over a gown the colors of the changing sea.

What a fine-looking couple they are, she thought admiringly, not without a pang of something like envy. *They look like an elf-lord and his lady, soul-matched to one another; how strongly and how beautifully they go together, how in love they look…*

She glanced eagerly round the ballroom to see them closer to; then with an indescribable thrill and shift of feeling, compounded of equal parts confusion and mortification and something else, something she could put no name to, she realized she was looking at the reflection in the torchlit gold mirror-walls of Morric and herself.

He sensed her sudden hesitation and change of mood, and drew her against him for the last figures of the set, his fingers round hers perhaps more tightly than the dance required; as the strathspey ended, with her curtsey and his bow, he raised her hand to his lips and gently kissed it—which was very much not as the dance required.

It was one of Athyn's favorite tunes, a stately elegant dance which both of them knew well, had heard and had danced to many times before; but this night it was a melody that, suddenly, out of nowhere, with no warning, made her to weep, and him to wonder.

chapter eleven

The truth does not grow untrue by being delayed.

—*Cathárren Tanaithe*

But if dán had indeed begun to move, there on the bank of Bannochburn on the night of Samhain the Less, and had furthered itself in the alehouse called Macca's Well and the ballroom at Lennoxliss, that seemed as far as it was prepared to bestir itself just then.

Athyn, still unsure as to what, precisely, had happened between Morric Douglas and herself, but knowing only that something tremendous had been set into motion, bade farewell to Mariota and Sosánaigh, who remained in the City at Seren Beirdd, and to the Lennoxes; and a few days after the ball she departed Caerdroia for the Fian school at Casterlines, in the southwestern province of Teffia, in high rough hills that edged the Great Plain of Moymore.

Athyn folded back the heavy oak shutters and leaned upon the stone sill, chin in hands, to stare. Below her lay the grounds of Casterlines, as vast and well-tended then as they are today, the old stone halls and tile-roofed outbuildings very red in the flat gray light that threatens snow. Beyond the school's grounds rolls Vantry Forest, a glorious ten-mile expanse of oak and elm and beech and birch; and beyond that again rises the little walled city of Shanagolden on its round grassed hill above the river, perfect and pretty behind its cream-colored battlements, just now unearthly bright as it was spotlighted by a dramatic wash of sun where the dark clouds broke. From this distance it appeared to Athyn as almost a toy city, set upon a carpet in a child's playroom; but that was an illusion, as she very well knew. Keltia's history has not been ever a serene one, and times there have been when even small remote perfections like Shanagolden have had to defend themselves, bloodily and well, if they were to survive. Indeed, not ten miles downriver stand the ruins of its sister city, Shanavogue, which had not and did not...

She had been conducted on arrival to the brugh that housed the new recruits, given a few brief instructions as to meals and what she should do in the morning, and then left to herself. After some wanderings she had found her third-story room, and had begun to unpack the one trunk she had been permitted to bring, when she was caught by the view.

Now a knock upon the door called her from her reverie, and she turned from the window. Upon her quick eager word of invitation, a head, two heads, peered round the door-frame: a fair head at a lower level, another, fairer one about two spans above.

"I am Rhain mac an Iolair," said the owner of the mane of straight gold hair, "and this is my wife, Selanie Drummond. We will be among your teachers, and since few other students have as yet arrived we thought to spare you dining alone on your first night here."

They stepped into the room at Athyn's gesture: a tall man with a sworder's build, his hair pulled back smoothly in a war-braid, an engrain of Morna Rhên, the Battle-goddess in her Eagle form, on his back and shoulders, the knotwork wings extending down his arms; a small pretty woman who barely reached his chest, with green eyes and a beautiful wheat-brown plait, who smiled at Athyn and held out her hands.

"I am cousin to Bronwyn Muirheyd," she said. "But do not let the connection fret you; we are not here to keep an eye on you!"

"Well, truth be told, we are," said Rhain in comical confiding, "but only in the best sense, I assure you. It occurred to Bronwyn that since you might feel something uncomfortable at first, it would go easier if you had acquaintance from the start."

Athyn was grateful of the company, and impressed as well: As she discovered over an excellent supper in the almost empty Great Hall, Rhain despite his youth was one of the premier swordery instructors at Casterlines, while Selanie, a Bandraoi Domina, was a war-witch, practitioner of an arcane and ancient art—the use of sorcery in battle, to confound one's foes and to defeat the sorceries used against one's own side.

"I see you come already Fian-clad," said Rhain with a smile, as they walked back to Athyn's dorter. "That is one piece of gear we need not supply you." At the puzzled look on her face, he nodded toward the black leather cloak she wore. "That is a Fian battle-cloak; you did not know?"

Athyn shook her head. "Nay; I wear it always, because my father wore it—he was wearing it when he found me, on the battlefield where I was born. Must I give it up?" she asked, apprehension edging her voice.

"By no means," said Selanie. "As my lord has said, it is a Fian's garment, and you are here to learn to be a Fian; so, you may wear your father's cloak, and the quartermaster saves the use of a new one. It all works out very nicely."

Indeed, it is beginning to seem as if it might...

In all her before-the-fact hopings and dreadings as to what Fian life might be like, Athyn had never imagined that weariness would hold so prime a place. She had never dreamed she could be so tired, that such tiredness could in fact exist in the world; indeed, it *was* her world, it defined her entire being. Her whole frame ached, her bones and muscles protested, even her hair hurt; sometimes she was so exhausted and so sore, in mind and body both, that she cried herself to sleep. Yet, slowly, steadily, as her training progressed, she found herself becoming harder, tougher, more resilient, and not in body alone.

Much of this was due to her instructors, who if stern were also fair, knowing to the exactness of a feather when their students had had all that they could take; and much again to new friends already made. Sulior visited now and again from her own posting in the eastlands, often bringing with her a young Ban-draoi student called Cathárren Tanaithe. Best of all, Athyn encountered Morvoren Kindellan again, who having finished at the seafleet college now was posted as guardian of the shore to a port town not many miles away, with a new-wed lord, Breos mac an Aba, tall and lithe and brownhaired, and a Fian himself.

All these and more came slowly together in firm friendship round the bruised, battered, unspeakably weary figure of one young Erinnach foundling; and if any of them had as yet an inkling of the purpose for which they were being foregathered, they kept it beneath the Horns. Outside in the greater world, Esmer Lennox watched with growing foreboding as the mosstrooper raids increased and the Keavers moved to match them; as he confided worriedly to Ganor, soon it would be that one could not tell the difference—nor, worse still, even care that the difference could not be told.

At the winter Sunstanding feast, which she spent at Lennoxliss with the Connachts, Athyn met Morric Douglas once again. This time, Amzalsunëa Dalgarno, looking prettier than ever, hung on his arm like a trinket, with ostentatious possessiveness—which, it must be said, Morric did nothing to discourage.

But the festival was in all other ways enjoyable; and after Athyn returned to Teffia, she resolved that she must have been mistaken, that Mariota and Sosánaigh must have been in error, that night at Macca's Well. Surely Morric seemed as chosen of Amzalsunëa as she of him, showing no sign of the disinterest his own bard friends had many times sworn was there, nor yet of the interest Athyn had believed him to have shown in herself, as she, to her own blushes, had in him. Yet there had been those sparks...

That spring following they met again by chance, seemingly, in Shanagolden, at a bardic festival where Morric was chaunting. He was full bard now, with steadily growing repute and fame; so much so that Athyn felt shy and strange in approaching him after his brilliant performance. She had scolded herself for idiocy: *Do you think he will think you but another flutterbye, a bardquain, no better than that Firvolgian mopsy? Surely he is sharper than that, to see the difference! Go and greet him like yourself!*

So she had taken her courage in both hands, and plowed through the admiring crowd that surrounded him, and had been well rewarded for her risk. There had been no mistaking the delight that had leaped to his face, the pleasure he plainly took of seeing her again; indeed, it was at his own oddly diffident suggestion that they shared supper that night at an inn just inside the city walls. Amzalsunëa was not there, and Athyn did not ask. All the same, she had made herself suspiciously fine for the occasion, in a new kirtle of green syndal so thin and close-woven it clung to every curve like moss to a young white birch; her hair was clean and shining and softly done, and at her throat was a torse of freshwater pearls, a birthday gift from Lyleth.

It was a pleasant night, very warm for so early in the season, and they supped out of doors, under a vine-roofed arbor on a walled terrace, with all the Golden Valley stretching away before them. Their talk was eager and full of laughter, the excellent meal all but forgotten in their rush to tell each other things; and Athyn could not but note that he had clad himself with the same care as she, and looked handsomer even than she remembered. But at last their plates were cleared, and they moved leisurely, methers of ale and usqua in hand, to a bench hidden behind a screen of waxflower vines, the five-petalled blooms breathing honey scent upon the evening air.

"We have spoken of almost everything tonight," she said after a while, emboldened by his warmth of interest and the usqua alike, "but not of our kindreds; where we come from."

"Not much to tell," he said, in the deep soft voice she already loved. "At least on my part; it is not a thing I speak of often, and never easily... But, just for you to know, I was born at Meldeburna, in the Ruchdi valley on Caledon; I am the son of a sailor."

"And I a soldier's daughter. We have more in common than one might think."

"More even than that: My parents are both dead, and I have heard from Sosánaigh that yours are also?"

She stirred beside him on the bench, strangely affected to hear that he had taken the trouble to inquire of her from a mutual friend.

"My birthparents, aye. I have never known who they were. But I was raised by Cormac mac Archill and his wife Lyleth; my second fosterfather is dead now too. But my mamaith still lives, in our old home of Caerlaverock, in Connacht on Erinna."

"How did your parents perish?"

She gave a short wondering laugh. "In battle; I know no more than that. My mother died giving birth to me on the field, and Cormac found me and brought me home with him—to his home, I should say."

"Small wonder then you are so warlike." He had meant it to tease, but his smile turned to swift remorse as she raised a troubled face to his.

"The Goddess in Her wisdom has granted me wrath for a virtue; in me it is so. And it is no handy trait for a brehon, I can tell you! Perhaps it is because I was born as I was, upon a stricken field, and all the unspent battle-fury—not of my mother and father only but of all who lay dead upon that field—struck home into me as I came out into the world. Sometimes I feel it so hard, you know," she added in a voice gone small and bleak. "That I could be angry for all creation, and still the well of my anger not be tapped. What use could there be for such a fount or feeling?"

He put an arm around her, gently kissed her hair, then, as gently, kissed her lips, holding her until he felt the edgy crackle leave her, though he half-expected it to go leaping away in blue sparking arcs, as when they first had touched. Both of them were surprised, and not at the kiss alone: Athyn that she had confided in him so freely and fully, Morric at the protectiveness that had leaped in him at her confiding. They were silent a moment, listening to the singers in the tap-room behind them, festival competitors singing now for pure pleasure: the beautiful Kymric anthemic harmonies, unison voices that suddenly split into separate minor-key beauties, ravishing all who heard.

"I do not know," he said then, when the song had ended. "But She Who Made All makes each of us as we are for reasons of Her own; if She means you for warrior, or judge, or both together, then trust to that. There will be a need someday that only such qualities, and only in you, can fill to Her purpose."

"Oh aye," said Athyn after a long silent moment, desperately shamed at her uncharacteristic outburst but feeling his arm round her like a ring of fire, "but sometimes that is what fears me most of all."

She saw him twice more that season, though on both occasions Amzalsunëa accompanied him. But when Lughnasa wheeled round, and then Fionnasa a few weeks after, he came through Teffia once more on bardic circuit, to play some nights in Shanagolden, with his bandfellows of whom he had spoken so often: the Kelt Shane Ó Falvey, a piper, and the Firvolgians Erramun Zedoary, a gifted lutanist, Jaffran Eskendy, a master of the clarsa, and the tamborist Evance Tregar. They were a renowned group now, with a vast following among Kelts and Incomers alike; had even played on outfrenne worlds far from Tara and Kaireden both.

This time Morric was alone: Amzalsunëa was nowhere to be seen, though the others had brought their lennauns with them. All of them alike were dismissive of Athyn when Morric introduced her, which was hurtful, since they knew her not at all, and seemed unwilling even to try.

But Athyn looked on Morric, and listened to him sing, and everything and everyone else went away, vanished like the morning mist with no hurt left behind it. And this time for them it was as it had been the first time they met, when their hands had touched and sparks had leaped in the Samhain night: They looked at each other, their glances crossing with the click of lodestones aligning, and their choice was made, or dán made it for them. When the ceili was over, they left together, no word spoken, for the little inn where they had first shared supper, his arm round her shoulders and hers round his waist beneath his cloak, their heads bent one to the other.

In the night, lying close beside him, she reached out to touch his bare warm chest, laid her hand above his heart to feel it beating, to prove to herself yet again that this was real, that he was there. And at her touch he smiled in the dark and turned to her, and proved yet again how there, how real, they were.

Four days later he left again on his bard-rounds, and neither knew when they might see one another next. But over the next few years, they met, if not so frequently as either could have wished, then with a fierceness of feeling when they did that made up for all the absences. In between there were impassioned missives, sheaves of poems, streams of gifts; if the choice was between having each other in such wise or not having each other at all, both knew there was no choice to be made.

Amzalsunëa continued in the picture, though Athyn resolutely refused to think about her, scrupulously holding to her resolve not even to mention the Firvolgian's name to Morric, much less to question him of her. But whatever may have been the truth of her life with Morric past or present, whatever the reasons for the hold she continued to have on him, somehow Amzalsunëa, the mere fact of her, did not matter; neither could she touch what Morric and Athyn, half unknowingly, wholly unforcedly, were beginning to build for themselves.

In the long months of her lover's absences, therefore, Athyn turned to her studies with renewed fervor, finishing advanced Fian schooling and coming home to Ardturach in triumph, where Esmer, keeping his promise, made her the captain of the Heir of Connacht's guard.

Then, in the spring of that year, word came from Caerlaverock, summoning her there with all speed. Lyleth was dying, and even Kier mac Archill who was lord now in that place could not keep Athyn away.

As soon as Athyn entered the chamber she knew. It did not even take Sulior's single headshake, from where she knelt on the bed's far side...

"Mamaith?" she said softly, leaning over the dying woman upon the pillows. "It is I, Athwen—you see I have come home—"

Slowly Lyleth's eyes came open: dimmed, but with a shine of light upon them that seemed reflected from nothing in that chamber or this life; and the strained muscles of her face relaxed in what would have been a loving smile if she had had the strength.

"Athyn-fach—he let you come. I must tell you—Kier never knew—I promised your father—"

And with that she whispered to Athyn the whole long, all-but-lost tale: the infant's cry that had caused Cormac to turn aside, the dying woman who had just given birth, the sword and jewels he had taken along with the child, to be the only legacy she seemed ever likely to have; the vow, the name, the secrets. The telling took many minutes, and the last of her strength.

"You must go to Iolo and Haneria," she breathed at the end of it, "they will tell you all the truth as they have come to know it." She tugged gently at the girl's sleeve. "Do not be angered with us, alanna—we did the best we could—"

Athyn closed her eyes briefly, but what she shut in behind was more than even she could tell. *The truth, after all these years… nay! She must never know how I feel about this—if I knew myself how I do feel…*

"You did not fail," she whispered into Lyleth's ear, so softly only the dying woman could hear her. "You did most well. You did rightly."

The end came on the third day. Lyleth, who had earlier bidden farewell to all her children gathered round—even Kier, who had the grace at least to feign sorrowful, and perhaps, somewhere even he could scarcely find or name, even felt so— had been murmuring and fretting; then suddenly she grew calm as a glassy sea, looking past them all, beholding something they could not.

"Athyn," she said, reaching out to grasp her fosterdaughter's hand. "A terrible battle, Athwen—the wolf—he has the black bull by the throat—he is wounded, he bleeds—" Her voice sank to a whisper, and a look of joy and pride suffused the wax-pale face. "But—O Loving Goddess—oh my Athyn—he shall *win…*"

And spoke no more.

Athyn had not remained in the chamber beyond the few minutes it took for Debagh, as eldest daughter, to recite the Last Prayer over Lyleth, with all the Archill children—even Kier— hand in hand round the bed.

But she went down to the courtyard in silence, brushing off proffered condolences from those who had gathered below, saddled whatever stood nearest the stable door—Tarn was stabled at Ardturach these days—and flung off over the Archill lands. She rode straight to Sauchiehall, the little hamlet where dwelled the bard Haneria Lauder, and where, she had a feeling, the retired brehon Iolo Forsycht was waiting for her also. *And well I might have somewhat to say to him as regards that precious sibhood of brehonry—something very much to the point, something sharp…*

"Your mother's sword and ring, her torc and brooch and medallion."

Athyn, looking at neither of the two persons present but at the things that lay on the table before her, took a deep breath and asked a single question.

And Haneria the bard answered at once.

"Your father was Conn Strathearn, Lord of Galloway, your mother the Lady Dechtira Aoibhell; they were master and mistress of Kincarden, a great fortress in the Ox Mountains that belonged to your father's family. They both perished on that battlefield at Fialzioch. You came too soon, your birth hastened by the battle, and your mother, wounded, survived only long enough to deliver you right there upon the field; your father had fallen defending you both. Cormac heard you crying, and was moved to turn aside; and so he found you, and drew you forth, and spoke briefly with your mother before she died, to hear the name and birth-geis she would give you. Therefore you are an Aoibhell by birth and naming, as your mother's rank and pedigree are higher and more ancient than your father's."

"The Aoibhells are Princes of Thomond—"

"True," said Iolo, "and you have some kinship even there. But your descent comes in three lines from Brendan himself; and the line that counts is Findhorn, a senior line of Aoibhell to that even of Thomond. You are descended from the union of the Lady Fionaveragh, Brendan's own daughter, with his great friend and captain Donn Aoibhell, a mighty war-lord; you come of the line of their eldest child, the Lady Sithney. You are rígh-domhna thrice over and an undoubted heir to the Copper Crown."

"Why then did not my Aoibhell kindred—or indeed my Strathearn kin of Galloway—claim me after Fialzioch?"

"They did not know that your parents had been slain until many days later," replied Iolo. "Those were troubled times of risings against the Incomers, many records were lost—no great surprise that a child's birth undocumented upon a field of battle should have gone unrecorded."

"And after? When my parents—my fosterparents knew whose child I was?" Athyn hated the high sharp note her voice had taken on, lowered it by main resolve. "They must have investigated—at the very least have had some herald examine these tokens. Did they then not think to return me to my kin?"

"To whom would they have returned you?" asked Haneria. "That branch of the Aoibhells was killed off entirely, save for you alone, in the fighting with the Incomers; the Strathearns were clann-broken in the glen wars on Caledon. Thomond had troubles of their own, and we traced your connection to them only a few years before Cormac's death. It is not a very close link, and they might not have cared to take you in even so." She laid a hand on Athyn's arm, but the younger woman kept her face averted. "Besides, it was already too late; Cormac and Lyleth loved you from the first, and would have fought to keep you against the High King himself."

"And I am of the rígh-domhna?"

"Aye, as we have said. But there are ten thousand folk in Keltia who stand as near the Throne as you," said Iolo. "Still, you have place among them."

Athyn hardly heard him. She was staring at the ring in her hand: It was of heavy red gold, obviously costly—such a jewel as was far beyond the means of the Archill kindred. The huge dark blue sapphire was engraved with a device she had only ever seen in heraldry books, or in the House of Peers, or as a banner carried in some ceremony. She blazoned it in memory's eye with its ancient proper colors: a white wolf's head on a red ground, the arms of the Aoibhells since the first of that line came to Keltia with the mighty Astrogator—who himself was of the Name.

My mother… This ring was hers; and before that belonged to her kindred, which is my kindred… With her death she gave me life, by bearing me before she died, and by giving me into the care of Cormac; and she who was my mother in life, Lyleth, gave me new life upon her own death, by giving me the truth…

"We have known many years now," added Iolo, when Athyn still did not speak. "First, of your finding only; then, later, of your true ancestry. But Cormac charged us upon our vows to our Orders, and made us swear even by the Goddess and the God, that we should breathe no word to you until you came to ask. Even so, we thought this very hard on you, not to mention on us, so when you were at Silverwood, I went to the Archbrieve Bronwyn, and taxed her with my difficulty. Though I did not give specifics, I think the Archbrieve may have guessed the truth. She said no word to you? Ah, well then… Cormac would have told you himself, had he lived; and Lyleth felt bound not to declare of it until she must. And if she had not, we would surely have spoken then."

With a sudden fierce gesture that could have been pride as easily as fury or hatred or defiance, Athyn thrust the heavy gold ring onto the forefinger of her left hand, and, as if she were buckling on armor, or the collar of a slave, she raised both hands to fit the battle torc about her neck. The great wheel-brooch she pinned at her shoulder, slipped over her own head the silver wolf's head of Aoibhell on its chain; lastly she lifted the sword from the table, though she did not strip scabbard from blade. Looking first at Haneria then at Iolo, but saying no word, she slid one arm through the worn leather baldric and settled the sword at her side.

Morric will have a ballad for this, surely, when I have the chance to tell him of it…if I choose to tell him…

"One thing more," said Iolo then; and when he had spoken Athyn nodded and rose and bowed to them both. Swinging up onto her horse she was away, leaving troubled hearts behind her; but none more troubled than her own.

*   *   *

Though at Caerlaverock they were watching anxiously for her return, she did not turn that way but rode up into the hills to the north. If she sought anyone or anything, she was seeking some she had not seen or spoken with for long and long.

But the Sidhe, who had known from the first that this hour would someday come, made her no answer, though she stood in her irons and called until her voice cracked with the calling, all along the upland ridges, late into the night; and folk on distant hillfarms, hearing, looked out with fear and wonder, and pulled their doors and shutters to against the darkness and the cry.

chapter twelve

A man is better than his birth.

—*Morric Douglas*

Esmer, when Athyn went to him straight from Caerlaverock with resolve still fierce within, had the grace not to exult too much, or at least not in his young liege's presence. But alone that night with Ganor, in their chambers, he allowed himself to revel in the revelation.

"Ah, dán works in harness with desire after all! You see, Ganwen, how I was right all along! I am a wonder among flowers, a stag of seven tines, a—"

"You are an idiot," said Ganor; but she smiled. "Listen now, cariad. That fostern of yours and I have not been so idle either." She pressed a carved boar's head on the bedpost; a tiny door popped open, and from the drawer it concealed she drew a small crystal block. Setting it in the bedside holder, they looked together on the words projected at comfortable reading distance on the air.

Esmer devoured the list, hugging himself in his glee, hugging his wife. "Aye, these are Names, right enough, and not just Marcher Lords either!"

"Indeed," said Ganor complacently. "Greyloch and Hutcheon and I put our heads together some time past, enlisting some of our friends far afield from the Marcher maigens, and some of their friends. We knew their dreams for Keltia chimed with our own, and we were careful to choose those who had the resources to make the dream a true one."

Esmer was still gloating. "Some of the greatest names in the realm are here—and I would guess the Aoibhells of Thomond will be even more forthcoming now that one of their own connections is in it." He looked up at his wife. "Clever girl! If this succeeds, Keltia will have the Countess of Connacht to thank for it more than all."

"As I said long since, Lennox," remarked Ganor with pardonable pride, "it was a good plan, and all we needed was the one. And now we have her."

"But these are some of the highest folk in all Keltia—" Athyn was dumbstruck, as she herself went over the list next day, closeted with Esmer and Ganor in their solar. "It cannot be, whatever."

"It can, and it is," declared Esmer. "What is more, with you it *shall* be... Why is that so difficult for you to grasp?"

"Because it is only just a day or so, my lord, since I found out who I was! What I have scarcely yet dreamed of is finding out what I am."

Esmer leaned forward and took her hands in his. "Then let us tell you, alanna, what we pray you might be..."

When he had finished, Athyn said no word straightway. "This, then, is why you had me train as brehon and Fian both," she said at last.

"It is."

"You have had this in mind for a long time, then."

"We have."

"And you knew of my ancestry all that time?"

"Nay," said Ganor, promptly and forcefully. "*That* we did not! But I noted you from a child, as you remember; and after the incident of the Mari Llwyd, we two and Greyloch, and some others, knew we were most likely not dealing with any common lass, and began to think in larger terms. But that you were born an Aoibhell—no. That is as much a surprise to us as it is to you. But you must admit, it makes many things a great deal easier."

Athyn smiled fleetingly; the truth was in Ganor's words, and she herself had never really doubted the Connachts' unknowingness. "Well. I daresay we were all of us surprised."

Esmer settled back in his chair. "Long time now the nobles of Keltia, even more than the common folk, have wished for the return of the monarch; many of us have fought for it. That we have no High King or High Queen is no fault of the Incomers. It is because the rival rígh-domhna cannot cease their differences long enough to agree on one to lead them, and then to support that one with arms and funds and faith enough to drive out the Incomers once for aye, so that a monarch may be elected in peace."

"Would that not be worth it?" asked Ganor, herself leaning forward to take Athyn's hands as Esmer had earlier done. "To free Keltia forever from the Firvolgi, so that a new Ard-rígh or Ard-rían may be chosen? Is that not a thing for which to give up all else?"

"Indeed it would be, if only it could. But why do you think that all these squabbling clanns will find common cause in me to do that?" Athyn's voice carried incredulous scorn, a tone she had never before in her life used to the rulers of Connacht to whom she owed so much. But where did owing end? "To come together for *me?*" she said again. "I am an unemployed brehon, a common or garden Fian—why in all hells would such folk as this trust me to lead them in outworld war, upon—no offense—your saying-so only? For surely if Kelts rise up against the Incomers, it will become soon or late a war between Keltia and Kaireden— I am not the one to manage *that* fight; there are many far fitter than I to be such a captain."

"So folk have said for a hundred years," observed Ganor, face suddenly bleak. "And see what has come of waiting for that one to come along... Nay, lass, it is you or no one. And we—and our friends likewise, and Keltia too—are weary beyond telling of it being no one."

"Even so, we will not force your decision," said Esmer

piously, and was nonplused when Athyn exploded with laughter. "Truly! We do not wish a reluctant hero any more than you might wish to be one. It seems to me, though, Athwen, that you have at least as good a claim to the leader's helm as any, and a better one than most. It is fair to ask, surely?"

Athyn grinned over her shoulder as she rose and bowed and made for the door. "Oh, asking is always fair! It is only the answering that troubles me."

"You did not tell her the whole of our plan," remarked Ganor to her husband, after the doors had closed.

"And if I had," he said after a while, "do you think for one moment that she would be considering it? It would have frightened her half to death, and then where would we be? Nay, the rest we shall leave for another time—a month more, a year, five years. For now, let us be glad we have a leader against the Incomers—or might, if she decides to take down that sword from the wall."

"Aye so," said Ganor. "And count ourselves fortunate, Connacht, for only this morning we did not have even so much as that."

Upon quitting the Lennoxes' chambers, Athyn had gone to her own rooms in one of the lesser towers, brain reeling and soul on fire; and as she readied herself for bed, shedding garments as she paced and thought and paced again, she turned the dazzling prospect over and over in her mind.

To lead a revolt against the Firvolgians, the revolt that, properly backed and planned, could drive the Incomers out of Keltia once for all; not merely to join such a crusade—which she would gladly have done—but to lead it herself! *I did not know they had such faith in me. And I still do not know why... Even though the thing will play out according to their plan, still it is I they seek to be its spearhead...* It was something to be dreamed about; but so far beyond the possible as never to be achieved— or, if it were, surely not by the likes of *her*; nay, it was all ashlings of grandeur, the ravings of one who harbored delusions of glory, traha to boast the favor of the gods...

For all her youth, Athyn had a fine cold judging eye—part of which had come to her out of brehon training and the rest of which was as inborn as the color of her hair—and she knew that though the Lennoxes might set her at the head of the hosts, they would be the ones who drew the reins that moved her, they and their mighty friends. *A fidchell-board, and I but a humble pawn with all the other pawns. . . . Though maybe not so much a pawn as they might think: I will gladly serve as willing tool for the good of Keltia, and even for the blood of Connacht, but not for trimmers and kingmakers, and if that is what those others are thinking, I am thinking they have picked the wrong lass...*

Athyn forced herself to an impartial weighing of her own merits. She was a brehon, and in all modesty an exceedingly good one; a Fian too, if not so good a one as she was a brehon. She was a friend to the Sidhe, or so she hoped, and a friend to the Otherworld. She had learned at last her rightful ancestry; and if her pedigree was not so high as the child Athyn had once dreamed—every lass, foundling or no, with a scrap of imagination dreams of being a lost princess romantically restored to her kingdom—it was quite high enough to enable her to stand before the warring factions and command them with confidence. What counted more was knowing that Esmer and Ganor stood strong behind her, as did Greyloch and Bronwyn and so many others she did not even yet know; and so too might stand Morric Douglas...

Still—she shifted on the window seat where she had curled up to do her thinking—she could bring the clanns together, unite them in common cause; but could she lead them? More than that, would they permit themselves to be led? And, once led, the most crucial question of all: Would they stand?

And that she did not know; would never know, not until the thing was put to the test. *'The only way to know is to go; the only way to see is to be'* ... Goddess, *that bard of old had the right of it; and was not he a Douglas, like my Morric?*

She twisted round to gaze out at the midnight sky aflame with winter stars. *Perhaps I erred, not telling Esmer and Ganor the full of what I was told by Haneria and Iolo: that my birth-mother put the certain geis upon me that she did, though I still do not know why—the bar to magic. There are too many secrets as it is. But geis is a different matter, and if this task I have been offered is geis also, better it is to keep the fates apart, as far as I can, for as long as I can… Or so at least I think.*

"Well then," she said aloud to the dark and the stars and to Keltia. "Aye. I will. Aye. And Goddess help us all. But first I must speak to Morric."

Easier sworn than seen: Athyn had not been in the same province—much less the same bed—with Morric Douglas for nearly four months. Far-famed he was now, a bard of great repute much in demand; he went continually round Keltia—and even outworld—on bard-circuit, and she never knew from where the next letter or gift or poem would be coming.

But just before the winter Sunstanding, Morric sent word to her that he would be playing in the district, and they at once determined to spend that great feast together, and some time alone after as well. So after his bard stint was done they met at Windishaar, a town on the edge of Oriors province where it adjoins Connacht, and took the mountain track into the wild fair country upwith.

"What is this?"

Morric's hand beneath Athyn's leinna had encountered something round her neck he was unaccustomed to find there, and his curiosity had momentarily gotten the ascendancy of his ardor.

It was their first night of holiday, along the famously scenic road that winds into the Deveron Highlands; they had ridden hard through a fierce snowstorm to reach this destination in time for the nights of festival. They were spending the feast days, which began that very night, Midwinter Eve, in a tiny, charming village called White Wellans—built upon the chalk, where its neighbor Vaxan Wellans is not—comfortably ensconced in an ancient inn, a former keep, its walls of native stone fourteen feet thick, its latticed windows, laced with brown dry ruins of the summer's ivy, drifted deep now with snow.

The innkeeper, who knew young lovers when she saw them, had indulgently put them in the most romantic chamber her establishment could boast: a round tower room with carved beams and oak-vaulted ceilings and plastered walls spangled with tiny gold flowers, in which pride of place was held by a huge velvet-curtained bed and an armorial hearth, decked with oak leaves and pine boughs for the season, that was big enough for Morric to stand in without bending his neck. The wintertree, a fine blue ferren hung with candles and gilded firecones and bright-berried holly, stood in the inner corner; each guestchamber had its own. Tomorrow night they would go down to the great hall, where another, much larger tannan stood, and they and the inn's other guests would join with folk from the village for the solstice feast and the revelry that followed.

But tonight they had no wish to stir from their own hearth, on the floor before which they now lay, half-clad and much involved, amidst a pile of pillows and furs in the firelight, with methers of cider and warmed wine, while outside the blizzard raged; hence Morric's discovery.

"That is my new amulet bag," said Athyn a touch defensively, sitting up in Morric's arms and clutching her leinna around her, as the tower shook suddenly with a mighty buffet of wind. "Morvoren Kindellan sent it me for luck-gift. I forgot I still wore it; but then I seldom take it off."

He examined it curiously, lifting it up from where it rested between her breasts: a tiny pouch of black leather on a leather cord, plump with odd-shaped contents and with a carved bone figure of the Goddess as a slide; it was cleverly embossed upon the flap with the device of a rather elegant-looking crowned laighard.

"Whose crest is this? I have never seen its like—"

"I do not know. Morvoren did not know, even; she and Breos found it at a fair in Port-na-tir. Most like it is no one's, or no one's yet... But it pleases me: The laighard knows how to run upon heated sands without being burned, and across water without sinking; it sheds its skin and is renewed, and if a limb or tail is lost it grows a new one. Those are useful tricks."

Morric leaned back, not letting go of the little pouch, so that Athyn must come with it to lie across him; which she, laughing, was nothing loath to do.

"In the bardic usage," he said into her hair, "the laighard is a symbol of everlasting love, and a bridge between the higher and lower worlds; can live in both at once, go seven years without food—though that last sounds suspiciously like something a bard would invent. You seem to have stuffed this one full enough—but let me add to it."

He reached with his free hand into his battered harp-satchel that lay nearby, removed a small screw of cloth. A handful of small rough emeralds glowed limpid green on the furs. "I found them myself, on Caledon, in the Ruchdi valley where I was born; they wash down from the hills in the spring floods. One to feed your laighard; the rest will do for beads, I had them pierced for it. . . And I have yet something else to add, for it seems we think more alike than even I imagined." From a leather wallet he produced another twist of cloth, pressed it into her hand.

"It is earth," she said, opening it with care, a little puzzled. "Gray soil, mountain soil it looks, very rough, and here is a small pebble of blue quaratz—"

"From Kincarden," he said softly, "and from Fialzioch. Earth of your dúchas and a stone from the battlefield where you were born... I was there on a bard-circuit last month, and I minded me of what you had told me. So I rode to both places, and brought some of each away. For you."

When she looked up at him her eyes were glittering with

tears, and then she looked down once more at the tiny crumbs of earth; but still she said no word.

"My sorrow!" Morric was instantly contrite. "I should have known it would trouble you—"

She looked up at him again, and the radiance in her face took his breath away. "*Trouble* me! Nay!"

After they had loved, and Athyn had wept again, and Morric had laughed and teased and kissed her for it, they had availed themselves of the tray of excellent supper discreetly left outside their door. Then, replete and happy, they had taken up the big earthenware keeve of wine and sprawled in the huge bed among the pillows and tumbled silkwool sheets and fur coverlets. Athyn fed Morric grapes and wine and kisses, and they listened to the snow seethe against the windowpanes, the wind howl around the tower walls, talking, laughing, singing solstice carols as the mood struck them.

At middlenight they shyly exchanged carefully chosen solstice gifts—two apiece, a greater and a lesser, which at once became their custom for all such feasts to follow. Hers to him on this Midwinter were a little bronze talisman of the Goddess and the God, three thousand years old and said to come from Erith itself, and a bard-satchel of intricately tooled brown leather, and he gave her a small heart-shaped pendant paved with adamants and a finger-ring set with a sapphire. After making love again—this time in full ritual intent, to call back the light and celebrate the sun's return this feast has ever marked, and not only among Kelts—their converse returned, like the Wheel of the year itself, to Athyn's great discovery, which she had disclosed to Morric earlier that evening: her true ancestry and descent, as she had revealed it to Esmer and Ganor.

"It makes no bones," said Morric calmly, kissing her neck through the fall of hair. "Archill, Aoibhell—it matters not a whit. You are you, and that 'you' I love. What, or who, could change that?"

"There are plans in train already," she said vaguely, and hated herself for not knowing how much she trusted him. She loved him more than her life, that was his now to do with as he would; but she was as yet uncertain how far she might trust him with lives he did not own.

Quick as a cat, he sensed at once her uncertainties. "Then tell me not anything yet." He brightened. "Amzalsunëa will be very cross indeed to hear this. She prefers to think you just one of the usual lightskirts who follow after bards. As if she herself were not, and worse... Oh, she perfectly well knows you are nothing of the sort, but it pleases and cheers her to believe you are less than you are. Perhaps because—well, I do not know why it cheers her. But do not think of it; indeed, do not think of it, or her, ever."

He spoke with that sluttern about me! Has he spoken with her as well about us, about him and me together? Athyn took his face between her hands—he had newly grown a full beard, and looked to her eyes more beautiful than ever—and he turned obediently to look at her. "I have never asked you about her before," she said. "But, Morric—" She took her hands away, stared into the fire. *And I still cannot ask him about her...*

"It is so with young things of all kinds," he said presently, knowing what she needed to hear from him. "Look at me—nay, anghariad, look!" He tugged on the shining hair until she turned unwillingly back to him, eyes steady into his own, gray-green into cobalt-blue. "Listen now: When a chick cracks the shell, it imprints upon the first living thing it sees; its parents, but if they are not about, and a cat or a pig or a person is, then it will imprint on that one instead."

"I was raised on a farm," muttered Athyn. "I know all about it."

"When we are young," continued Morric serenely, though the corners of his mouth twitched, "and fall for the first time in love, we imprint upon that person, and he or she upon us. That does not mean we must remain with them forever—we are free, we change, we grow—but it does mean we remain, in a certain way, forever in love with them. For all firsts are by their very nature forever... You know this yourself, love, from Roeg; you have told me so, even. You have not seen him since your days at Silverwood, but I would bet you crossics to cribbens his name crosses your mind every now and again—once a fortnight, once a moon?"

At her unwilling nod, he smiled. "Well then. And you think nothing of it; though something may mind you of him you are not moved to seek him out. Well, it is the same with Melassaun and me; we met very young, all unformed, and imprinted upon one another like little stupid ducklings. I did not know then that *you* would come along... It does not mean I am in love with her still, but neither does it mean I have ceased to care for her. How could it? I would not be the man you love if it did."

"Oh, you are so very persuasive, as only bards can be," said Athyn crossly. "Yet, you know, it is not the same, Morric, for all that: I have not been with Roeg for long and long, and you are still with—Amzalsunëa."

"It is the same, you know. Also she needs me."

"Nay, *I* need you—but, though I would rather not ever do so, I could live without you; that is the great difference between her and me. She is a lazy sucking blood-bat; if she had not you to drain, she would suck from anyone."

"She has threatened to slay herself if I abandon her completely."

"That is not your dán but hers. And she tells people she is your wife—"

"It is not true. And I have told you so before." His voice remained calm, his tone amused, but she caught a flicker of vexation in the dark blue eyes. It was all the flint she needed to her angry tinder, and she went up like the Crann Tarith, like dry grasslands beneath the lightning.

"You lie here with *me*, and you speak of love to *me*, and yet you are still with *her*!"

"I am not with her this night, am I... Nor have I lain with her since the night you and I were together for the first time in love. From the moment we met, Athynna; those sparks did not lie. I have never felt for anyone what I feel for you. My one irrevocable choice; if that is what you mean by love, then I love only you and have loved no other—gods, even though you are a pest of hell sometimes—some times like now."

He had meant the teasing in loving part, to lessen the fraughtness of the moment, but he had misjudged her mood. Athyn flung herself to the other side of the bed, rigid with rage, her back to him, and though he touched her bare shoulder, then kissed it, still she did not turn; and after a while she was even more annoyed to hear his calm, comfortable sleep-breathing. She kicked the coverlets in fury, then ripped them all off him and rolled herself up in them, leaving Morric asleep naked and unblanketed in the room's growing chill, now that the fire had gone to grieshoch in the grate. It was their first real Midwinter together, and they had been so happy and content and loving, and now—

Let him freeze in his sleep, he richly deserves it—though I must say I am glad to know he does not bed the Firvolgian slampig, whomever else she might bed, for hire or not; and I believe him when he says so. He loves me—again, I believe him when he says so—but yet he will not leave off indulging her... Mighty Dâna! How can men be so stupid about such things and yet so clever about everything else, so desirable and beautiful and perfect and yet so unbelievably tiresome, men in general, aye, and this one in particular? Do they come from some other galaxy than women, are they truly the alien culture they so often, come to think of it, seem? And why a thousand times over could I not have fallen in love with one who came unencumbered by Bagfolk baggage?

She would never know. It was a mystery the gods set women, a test imposed by the Goddess for reasons of Her own. But as Athyn's mood calmed she repented of her theft, and before she herself fell asleep she gently drew up over Morric his share of the blankets, and closed the gap of bed between them, curving close against his back like a paired spoon, her arm arcing round him, to keep him warm beside her in the night.

*   *   *

By morning they had mended the rift, and so well mended was it that where it had been broken it was stronger than before. They stayed in the snow-shut inn for a week and scarcely left their bedchamber, save to take long walks in the frozen silent woods, or to join the other guests for the feasting and merry-making that went on every night of the solsticetide; and no other word of crossness—nor the name of Amzalsunëa Dalgarno—passed their lips.

When the festival days were over, they rode on through the Deveron Highlands; when they parted a fortnight later, back at Windishaar crossroads, they kissed and clung to each other as though they would never meet again, for the first time resentful of the enforced parting, the distance that until now had seemed so useful a component of their lives.

Athyn sat Tarn—the big gray stallion was getting a touch elderly for a war-horse, she would have to find herself a new mount for the coming fighting, and send Tarn to pastured retirement; it would break his heart to hear the war-pipes and know she had gone into battle without him—and watched Morric out of sight with longing eyes. Far down the valley he turned in his saddle—the emerald beads she had strung for him round his neck beneath the leinna, a matching strand circling her own—and raised his arm to her; she held up her own hand, the sapphire he had given her flashing blue in the sun, and then he was gone.

But in the moment of his vanishing down the track Athyn caught a glimpse of black and silver out of her sidesight, and whipping her head round she saw atop a nearby crag one she had not seen for many months: Her fetch, the great hill-wolf, stood poised with lowered head. One huge elegant paw lifted, the magic beast was looking after Morric, and then the maned head swung in Athyn's direction.

Green eyes as cool and clear as the emerald beads held her own; then the wolf gave a chirruping trill, as a cat will use to its kittens, a cheerful sound of affection and approval and encouragement, and before Athyn could answer he was gone. Yet even so she felt strangely comforted. *He came to vet Morric, see if he is suitable… Pray Goddess his protection takes in him as well; I think it must, else he had not shown himself at all. But I wonder what Morric will think when he sees my fetch for the first time!*

Buoyed and perhaps a touch overemboldened by the fetch's unexpected appearance, Athyn took a different route than usual back through the hills to Ardturach: perilous, for this particular pass had been reported of late to be infested with mosstroops. But she was armed and Tarn was swift and it was full daylight, and she judged the time saved to be worth the risk.

Yet it was not mosstroops she encountered in the throat of the rocky defile, nor even Keavers, but, utterly incongruously, the Lady Mariota Lennox riding up cool as a cat in a dairy, seated decorously aside upon a lovely chestnut mare. Though these days they saw one another even seldomer than did Athyn and Morric, they never failed to communicate several times a week, and were the closest of friends. As for Mariota's most notable quirk: Today the magically changing hair was rich dark gold; but what mood that hue might betoken, Athyn dared not guess. And though she had supplied Mariota a brief explanation of the situation into which she had so chancefully intruded—

"How in all the seven hells do you come to be here at all?"

"I was riding to Ardturach myself, to visit my parents," said Mariota complacently, as they turned the horses' heads northwestwards for the pass that led through to the Lennox lands. "And—great minds thinking alike—I thought to take this way to save some time."

"You were coming to see us?"

"Aye; there is a thing I have to tell you all." She looked sidewise at Athyn out of sparkling eyes, her clever pretty face framed by the white fur of her hood. "But not, I think, just yet. And am I mistaken in thinking that you also have something, or some things, to tell us, or at least *me?*"

"Nay," said Athyn presently. "You are not mistaken. But not, I think, just yet."

"You will recall, my lord, my lady, that particular asking you made of me a while since? Well, if the asking is still open, I will make an answer, and the answer is Aye."

Athyn stood before Esmer and Ganor; it was late afternoon of that same day, the westering sun pouring through the windows. After giving Mariota the private time with her parents she had sought, Athyn had gone to the Lennoxes herself, pausing only to change her garb from the riding attire she had worn from Windishaar, where she and Morric had parted that morning.

Only this morning! It seems already years since I have seen him, until I shall see him again… She shook herself and drew herself up, pushed her shoulders so far back they nearly met.

"If you will trust me with so great a task," she continued, face and voice and stance severely formal, "I will gather a suitable company to help me in it—I daresay I shall need all the help I can get—and I will take whatever oath you set me. Does this then suit your honors?"

She struggled valiantly to preserve her stately bearing, but it was no good: Her unfeigned grin broke through, and then Esmer and Ganor were upon her with embracings and kisses and tears and many, many words.

"Oh lassie," said Ganor at last, "it suits *all* our honors, more even than you know—or can know…"

"I shall call them the Gwerin," said Athyn, when the three of them, with Mariota and Greyloch and Hutcheon, were sitting round the fire with methers to toast the new endeavor—and to celebrate Mariota's glad tidings also: that she and the Lord Stellin Ardwyr were newly betrothed, a dainty heart-shaped ruby betokening the pledge.

"Gwerin?" asked Ganor.

"An ancient Kymric word for war-band. Brendan used it for his companions, and now I will use it for those I will ask to be my own. I think it will not displease him, that we should use that name; nor yet the deeds we may do under it."

And as she spoke, Esmer felt within him, running deep and joyous and solemn as a river, that feeling one has when something right and fated makes itself known at last, and knows that it is known.

"Do you know," he said, looking at her, then round the room at the rest of them, "I do not think it would."

chapter thirteen

Better to ride a mule that carries you than a horse that
throws you.

—*Cormac mac Archill*

Ofttimes, when a bulb is planted in a garden, it may lie
dormant season after season, though every condition
of soil and sun and wind and water be right for its
putting forth shoot. Often, too, the gardener, vexed at its
apparent inactivity, may even be tempted to dig it up to see
what on earth, or under it, is going on. But that would be a
mistake. The plant knows best. It alone can tell when is the
right time for pushing upward to the light.

And so it was here, as Athyn often thought of it later. As
always, it had been up to the plant to choose to grow at all; but
once the choice had been made—whether she had made it or
it had been made for her mattered no whit—it unfolded to its
destined purpose as smoothly as any growing thing.

There was no name for what they did, no high-sounding
words to ring like war-pipes to the folk. Even the name Athyn
had chosen for them of Gwerin was but a workaday one.
'Gwerin,' a war-band; but the war they now set out to fight had
not even been declared. Many—and not Incomers alone—
disputed that it was a war at all, and disputed Athyn's right to
fight it even if it were. And yet few fights in all the days of
Keltia's existence would prove more fated...

Indeed, it fell into place as if it had been, well, meant.
Those whom Athyn called came flying to the need; the secret

supporters enlisted by Ganor and Greyloch came through with funds, provisions, material of war, safehides for folk and supplies alike—and she who had been forged as spearpoint to this Lance of Battle gathered it all to her as if she had been born for the task; as perhaps she had been.

Still, for all their own certainty of choosing, and all their love for Athyn, and all their wish for Keltia, sometimes Esmer and Ganor wondered very privately if they had chosen aright; if, indeed, a more biddable and less brilliant pupil might not have suited their purposes better after all...

At first the Gwerin's activities were carried out on a small scale, while bards hand-chosen by Morric and Sosánaigh travelled round Erinna and Tara to sow the thought like wheat among the people: that if they were brave enough, and strong enough, and desirous enough of the achieving, they could drive the Incomers from Keltia forever. Athyn in honest modesty thought it best that none should yet know who was the initiator of this, and Esmer concurred, though his reasons were not the same as her own.

"We are not in this for glory," she said to the Gwerin one day when things had gone even less their way than their worst fears could have held it, "but for high purpose's sake. If we fall in the fight, if we go to the Goddess with none outside the Gwerin ever knowing our names, or to what cause we pledged ourselves, or in whose service we died, it matters nothing, and less than nothing. The word is out, the work is all."

They began in small: Incomers who had been harsh on their Keltic tenantry found their own harshness turned back on them, with an exquisite calibration of justice and vengeance and law. On that Athyn, whose aim in such matters was incalculably better than anyone else's, had been adamant. "It profits us no whit to do as they have done," she had said at the start. "For one thing, it makes us no better than they; worse, for that we know better. But also because some among the Incomers, out of love for our ways and love for some among us, have grown more Keltic than the Kelts. In all our history we have never turned away any who sought us in such manner; and shall not begin now."

But now that the Gwerin had started their campaign in earnest, the Keavers were finding their noses well and truly out of joint, and furiously denounced not only the War-band but any who gave it support, though Athyn had in all hope and honesty expected the Keavers to throw their not inconsiderable weight to her side.

"Fear and jealousy," said Esmer, one day when Athyn despaired of the hugeness of the task and the meanness of the sniping. "The Keavers feel themselves usurped and surpassed by you and the Gwerin—I do not say they have not served a purpose, or at least some purpose, for truth to tell they were very often as much marauders as the mosstroops they claimed to ride against. But now they are as someone who has long time told lies that folk bought as the truth; and you have shown up with the real truth at last to give 'em the lie to their face. You have unmasked their motives, and therefore they attack. My sorrow to tell you, they will not be the only ones who will do so; so do not be surprised, Athwen, when those attacks come, nor wonder at where they have origin. Because you yourself act in honor, do not make the mistake of expecting honorable actions in others."

"I have never held that to be a mistake," she said roundly. "We are all working to the same end, or so at least I had thought—"

"Then more fool you to think it," said Ganor, and Athyn turned to her astonished. "Just as the Incomers soon will be, the Keavers now are fighting for their lives; or rather, they are fighting for their life as they have known it. Because you can do better than they, and they know it; and because you are better than they, and they know that too. And they will never forgive you for either." She smiled, and leaned forward to touch Athyn's hand in real sympathy. "Get yourself a duck's-back against it, cariadol, and soon, lest it burn you up inside. You will need that oil on your feathers, I promise you, for assuredly it will grow worse or ever it grows easy. And easy it will never be."

But Ganor was more correct than she knew when she spoke so, and Esmer less.

The Gwerin very soon numbered in the thousands, as the Gweriden, the inner circle round Athyn—her dear friends and old teachers, earliest recruits to the cause now her chief captains and commanders—brought others in, and those drew in others still. The increase in numbers had rendered a permanent base imperative; so Athyn had besought the secret supporters, and her eloquence in need had untied their purses. A hidden camp was quickly delved, deep in the fastnesses of the Dragon's Spine. Indeed, deep beneath the Dragon's Spine: In the ice-times long ago, water dripping down from the glaciers lying upon the land had hollowed great caverns in the bedrock limestone: halls and brughs beneath the mountains, stone fluted and turned like wood under a carver's hand, rock phantasmas in colors from onyx to blush-white.

This was Seana Bhraigh, the Gwerin's major stronghold. Athyn had sited her camp for proximity to Casterlines and Shanagolden, over east of Heliawater: Even Caerdroia was not so distant as to be unreachable at need; and the beauty of the site fed their souls when there was little else to feed them. But chiefly she had built there because the wild lands roundabouts were unmapped, and had served as refuge for many in troubled times—and would again.

Though in the public eye Morric Douglas had become inextricably associated with the growing rebellion, still he continued to have great success as bard, even among the Incomers. As a spy, he risked himself daily, as dangerously as any sworder. But his secret occupation, though widely guessed at or even strongly suspected, was still largely ignored, and the free comings and goings that this enabled would prove more useful to the Gwerin than ever his blade had done—as it would also prove with another great bard, in later times every bit as perilous. As Athyn said, they had goleor of warriors, and indeed goleor of bards, but there was only one Fireheart.

For so had Morric come to be known, from a lovesong he never sang in public without dedicating to Athyn, the name which Seli, queen of the Sidhe, had given him long ago. The reputation she had also deemed for him was now his own: He was greatly famed, perhaps the best-known and best-loved of his guild since his brilliant predecessor and clannsman Séomaighas Douglas. But quite apart from his calling to the Gwerin cause, Morric continued as bard because he could not imagine a life in which music had no part; and one night in a sea-town in the south of Tara, he learned it all over again.

Tamon Acanis lies on the shores of a vast warmwater bay, with mountains curving round like arms' embrace and a high salt desert on its upwith side. Walled in the Southland style, more for picturesqueness than protection, it had been the first town where Morric Douglas had ever sung to an audience, years since, as a bard in his petty place. And so it was as much for sentiment as on Gwerin business that he accepted an invitation to play there, with his old bandmates. And Athyn, to his genuine surprise, had chosen to accompany him.

"Well, and I have not heard you play to a crowd for long," she answered when challenged. "It is all very fine listening to you sing to me in bed, and I am, I hope, properly appreciative; but it is not the same. I should like to come."

And so she had. But walking at Morric's side into the bard-hall, Athyn felt an unpleasant jolt to see across the room, talking with the lennauns of Jaffran and Shane, none other than Amzalsunëa.

She knew of course that Morric on his bardic travels spent time on occasion with his onetime lennaun; she had even learned of force to live with that fact, and with that extremely peculiar relationship, in a way that was not destructive to either Morric's peace or her own. *But this, nay! He* might *have told me...* Then looking up at him she saw that he was as surprised and unsettled as she, and she felt obscurely better. But that did not last.

Athyn Cahanagh and Amzalsunëa Dalgarno had not met face to face since Morric and Athyn had come to be lovers. Now Athyn, courteous as always, gritted her teeth and her soul alike, greeting the Firvolgian with perfect civility when she longed only to scratch the sunsprecks off that milk-and-water skin with her own fingernails; but Amzalsunëa ignored the outstretched hand and at once began to rabbit on in her clear high childish voice about Morric.

Ah well, what else is to be expected of an Incomer and a light-skirt...

Under the spate of Amzalsunëa's brabblings—and the temptation to fling the truth like firehail into her rival's face—Athyn did not trust herself to speak, so at a tiny pause in the converse she nodded with cool courtesy, turned her back on Amzalsunëa and the others in the hall, and watched only Morric.

He had by this time begun to sing, and as always for her all else fled before the wonder of his gift. *He is more beautiful now than when first we met; he was yet a youth then, and now he is a man. He has grown a strong soul along with that new beard, and I love so much to see them both... But Goddess, the power he raises when he sings, the strength of him; in such moments he stands between the gods and the folk, whether he knows it or nay. The divinity he calls down upon himself, the humanity he takes up into him— and the beauty of the music he makes— Where the spring flows...* And watching Morric, hearing Morric, Athyn smiled, listening to a voice within her that only she could hear, a voice not even Morric's own. She could endure much, all, anything—the bard-followers, the bandmates, the gossip and maligning, defeat and disgracing, capture and betrayal, torture and death, and, aye, even Amzalsunëa Dalgarno—only for this. *Could, and would; shall, and will… Aelodau… O my most beloved…*

Morric, singing and playing with his four bandmates, himself caught up in the tide of music, was only too uncomfortably aware of the scrutiny bent upon him, not Athyn's alone. *Goddess, they are all watching me like a swarm of hooded cave-bats… what do they think I might do?* He did not glance at Athyn—he never did while singing—but he was also never not aware of her, could sense her always, glowing like a jewel or a flame on the edge of his perception. And he well knew her present state of mind, and resolved to amend all after; but then the music washed over him again, and he forgot everything else.

Amzalsunëa, as oblivious of all this as Morric was aware, availed herself all evening long of every chance to be close to him, draping herself over him even in front of Athyn, clinging like a cheap cloak. Morric did not appear to be discouraging her attentions—although to more generous thinking perhaps it was merely that he did not wish to create a scene, to subject Athyn to one of Amzalsunëa's hiss-fits, which by all indications was not far distant.

He was not the only one to think so: To the suspicious gaze, it seemed that the Firvolgian had made use of something more potent than ale or even usqua to alter her mood; Incomers had many drugs for just such purpose. But Athyn sat through it all impassive as a sarsen—at least to the outward eye.

But when Morric at last laughingly declared to the still-clamoring crowd that he had no voice left to him, nor indeed any skin on his harp-fingers, and departed to cheers and praises, he left with Athyn by his side, his arm round her shoulders and hers around his waist, giving Amzalsunëa not even the most cursory of farewell glances. Neither did Athyn look back; but nor did she gloat about it as they went.

*   *   *

In their chamber at an inn on the ocean, Athyn watched Morric beginning to return to lifesize. She had seen it often before: It was something he did after a performance, when he had been reaching his soul out to those who heard him, and now must slowly, carefully retract. But tonight it seemed somehow different... "What is it?" she asked presently. "I know it was not just Amzalsunëa—tell me—"

He did not answer her straightway. "The music had wings tonight. It does not always happen, you know, but when it does— Then, before we left, Jaffran spoke to me, something he said they had been wanting to speak of for some time."

"And that was?" she prompted gently, when he fell silent again.

"They do not wish to continue playing with me. At least, they had been considering telling me, and now they think they are sure of it; or almost sure. And for my part, I am not so sure if I wish to go on playing without them." He gave a short laugh. "Well, nay, I shall, I must, I am a bard, it is who I am as well as what I do... But they are bards too, fine musicians, belike the finest I shall ever have luck enough to play with. Yet though they are musicians they are not the music, and my music will not be over until I can no more draw breath, to live or to sing."

"My sorrow, anghariad," said Athyn. "I did not know. Did they give you any reason?"

"Goleor of reasons, each of them worse than the last, or more stupid than the next. They have not yet decided; they will let me to know when they do." He laughed again, softly, bitterly. "I did not know how much their partnership meant to me, not until tonight when I learned I might lose it... Oh, I shall still do our work, the Gwerin's work, nothing and no one shall stop that. But it is hard, and I do not wish to speak of it. We will talk of it again. But not tonight."

"When you find a parcel of knaves and idiots and drunkards going round together," said Athyn then, "very often you will also find, for some astonishing reason, that one of them is neither a knave nor an idiot, nor even very much a drunkard. No one knows why this should be, but, believe me, it is so. And of you five, I think it is clear to an abundance which that one would be."

"Ah, the truth at last! You always did have a soft spot for Erramun. I can see the reports now: 'Brehon war-lord confesses secret passion; Scotan bard slays bandmate, lover and self'—"

"Well—he does have all that pretty gold hair, right enough—"

When the knock sounded upon the door Athyn hastily pulled her leinna back up over her shoulders and called to the seeker to come in. She was not surprised to see Periel Vailluin— captain of recruits at Casterlines, Athyn's Fian mentor now one of the Gwerin's best commanders—who with a small escort had come with Athyn and Morric to Tamon Acanis.

"My sorrow to intrude," said Periel, brushing back her short dark hair, "but there is word of mosstroops riding into town from the south, and we thought to get us all from here before they arrive."

Athyn was already tugging on her boots. "And from whose mouth do you think they had word that we were here?"

Periel did not look at Morric, but by the sudden lowering of her eyes she might as well have. "Morric's presence in Tamon Acanis was no secret; it had been announced for weeks that he would sing tonight. But it is thought," she said carefully, "that one who was at the ceili alerted the watch."

"You mean Melassaun," said Morric calmly, but he was unable to suppress a twinge—reluctance to agree and certainty that the suspicion was correct. "Have you proof?"

"Only that she left the ceili directly you two did, and was seen to head for the watchtower thereafter, where the night-guard are lodged."

If it caws like a crow, and flies like a crow, and thieves like a crow... Athyn was armed now, and slung on the black cloak of Cormac's that she wore always. "Take two or three of the Gweriden, and lead the rest out by the desert gate. The mosstroops will not suspect we have twigged, and will not think to conceal themselves as they enter the town."

"At once, athiarna." She smiled benevolently on them both and was gone.

"'Athiarna'?" asked Morric, stuffing his music into his satchel and giving her a quizzical glance. "'High One'? Whence comes that?"

She had the grace to look embarrassed. "An old title for a Fian officer. Some of the Gwerin have taken to calling me so, though I have told them not."

"It is as good a word as any."

"Aye, well, spoken like a bard... Given the luck that I have had tonight, seeing folk I would sooner eat my own toes than see, no doubt my stepsib Kier will be leading those troopers in; so let us be out of it before we learn if I am right."

Athyn walking in the birchwoods, up above Seana Bhraigh. It was early spring now, a fortnight after that evening at Tamon Acanis, and her mood was as uncertain as the season. The Gwerin had had a productive winter, yet very little seemed in fact to have been done. *Oh aye, I know we must have a safe and sure foundation before we can launch the lightnings, but still it seems to me we should be farther along by now...*

It was the birds that made her look round: first their loud joyful presence, and then their silence. And Athyn's head came up like a hawk's at the falconer's whistle, for before her in the moss-carpeted clearing was Allyn mhic Midna, and he was not alone.

"The greeting of the gods and the folk to you, Athyn nic Bhrendaín."

"Mathra-dhia," said Allyn's companion.

Athyn stared, hesitant, all the gladness with which she had been about to greet Allyn gone suddenly shy. A youth stood before her, dark of hair, darker of eye; he was an inch or two taller than she, with promise of more height and grace to come.

"Do you not know your goddess-son, Athyn Aoibhell?" asked Allyn softly. "Be known then to Gwyn ap Neith ac Seli, who is Prince of my folk, one day to be king over us."

"Methryn," said Gwyn. His voice was deeper and more beautiful even than Morric's. "I have heard much of you from my mother; and from the Lord Allyn, and even from my father. We make friends too seldom and too slowly with mortal Kelts; but you and I are linked forever now. It is because of you that I am born at all, and born as I am."

Athyn's smile widened and warmed: He might be a prince, and one of the Shining Folk, but also he was a lad of— Her blank astonishment showed on her face, and she made as if to speak, but Gwyn spoke first.

"You are wondering how I can be grown to such stature when in your counting I am not two decades old." His voice held amusement, but it was Allyn now who spoke.

"As we live longer than mortals, so too do we age and grow to a different pace. Do not be alarmed."

"I am not," breathed Athyn, not entirely honestly. "I am only greatly glad to see you. Both you—it has been long."

"Longer than you know," said Allyn smiling. "Or can know... But listen while I tell you that which you must hear, for the good of both our worlds."

What they told her first near froze her heart; what they told her next set it to beating again.

"My sorrow to put this on you," said Allyn at last. "Truly, it shall not come to pass for many of your years, and maybe never at all. But in the Fianna you have a word for it: kethern-a-varna, the fighter in the gap, the one who serves as watcher and warner, then holds the pass against all comers so the rest may safely flee. For us, that is what you are, and will be; you have held the gap for us, a Gap whose true nature few mortals ever glimpse. Held it long enough and well enough for this prince to be born; because of that, he is the one he is, and not another. And because of that, dán itself has shifted."

"Because of me!"

"Because of you; and who you are, and were, and what you did and shall do. You are the lever that moves planets in their orbits, the twig that turns the flood. All Keltia is changed forever for your actions beneath the hill; but the change is not yet at the full, and our debt has not yet been paid."

She drew breath and courage to ask, but in the instant it took her to do so the clearing was empty once more. *Goddess!* she swore feelingly, as many had done before her and would again after, *I hate it when they do that— But can such happenchances—that once, on an autumn night almost two decades gone now, a little horsegirl trusted the word of a Sidhe lord, and went with him beneath the hill—can so seeming small a choice, in truth, move worlds?*

But to her unvoiced question she had no answer. It might have consoled Athyn to know that, many miles away, the man she loved had had the same impulse to question and reflection, and was about to receive a remarkably similar answer.

That need which had sent Athyn to the hills had sent Morric to walk by the rockbound shores of a bay near Tamon Acanis, where his bard-round once again had lately taken him. He had much to think on, so that when a blaze of color caught his eye between sea and sky, he marked it idly but did not note it. *Burning-water, happens all the time in these seas…* Then, a few paces on: *Nay, it is full daylight, the fire on the sea comes never before nightfall… what then is that?*

He looked at her as she approached, as she had appeared to him. Not the wyn-o'-the-wave, the seafire, as he had thought, but a woman, a tall woman in the deep of her age, weathered as a great tree that has seen the blasts only years can bring, wise in the wind's ways, and strong to the roots for it; and then suddenly, confusingly, again not so: A lovely darkhaired girl, with eyes like lilacs in rain and a voice like distant bells, now stood before him.

"I am Tarleisio," came the bell-voice to his entranced

senses. "Do not fear me, Morric Douglas, but hear me. Listen. Hear. And heed. Save yourself from what is coming. Change dán. Now, while still it can be changed, or may be changed. Go back to the one who truly loves you, who loves you more than life or lives. Seize her hand and run off with her, to a castle or a cottage, it matters not what or where. Live with her in love and joy and beauty. Write poems and songs and live forever. Else you will break my heart, and Keltia's heart, and the world's heart; but first of all, worst of all, you will break her heart."

Morric blinked and came back to himself with an effort, looked at her in wonder. "You know my Athynna? But how?" And never wondered that Athyn's name, not Amzalsunëa's, was the one to come instinctive to his tongue.

The woman smiled. "Suffice it for now that she is known to us."

"You are of the Shining Folk," he said, suddenly seeing the truth of her. "What have you to do with our fates? Dán cannot be cheated, surely."

"As well ask what have you to do with ours... And I do not urge you to cheat dán—a vain effort doomed to failure, and to worse dán in store for trying—but to correctly choose the dán that is yours, and the one who is meant to share it. Do so, and more than you can dream shall come of it. Do not, and—"

"And?"

The ban-sidhe, if so she was, was silent. When she spoke again it was in a curiously hesitant voice. "All shall be as it is, as it is meant to be, as it has always been and ever shall be. But you, Fireheart, will not be the only one to pay the price."

The name startled him more than anything else she had said. And in exact replication of Athyn, if only he had known, Morric opened his mouth to speak, to ask, to question; but he was alone on the rocky strand, and the tide was beginning to turn.

*   *   *

And again at Seana Bhraigh, Athyn looked out over the empty valley, and behind her at the empty chamber and the empty bed, and reaching inside her leinna touched a folded piece of paper warm from her body. She did not need to unfold it, she knew by heart the words that had been resting above her heart since he who had made them from his heart had given them to her, but she spoke them now, softly, aloud, for him and her alone to hear.

" 'Silksteel—
My rose of battle
My lily of the sword...' "

chapter fourteen

To disclose the wrong and forgive it is the severest
revenge upon an enemy.

—*Nilos Marwin*

As spring approached, the Gwerin began to quietly
clamor to be allowed to attack some Firvolgian
strongholds, and Athyn was inclined to let them have
their wish. Esmer himself saw no reason to delay, and even the
most cautious of the War-band's benefactors thought it might
well repay them to unsheathe the claws and begin to bat the
Incomers around—just a little.

Their first objective was modest enough: a small
Firvolgian industrial town on the shores of Pentland Bay, in
the east of Erinna. It had long been a blight on the fair landscape, choke-fumed and slag-blackened, and the local folk
had despaired of ever seeing it gone. One night of blackthorn
winter, between dark and dawn, they saw their hope made
real: When they awakened, the town seemed to have been
swept from the face of the land, and when spring came, and
summer after, there was only soft green grass where once foul
walls had stood.

And that sweeping, that clearing and cleaning and cleansing, was the beginning of what would soon be known to Keltic
and Firvolgian history alike as the Outgoing. As fights went in
Keltia, this one was destined to be bloodier than many if
briefer than most; but not for many hundreds of years would
any war be of more import than this which Athyn

Cahanagh—by now she kept her identity as cloaked as she might, calling herself by the name the folk had given her, Athyn of the Battles—now set into motion.

Every day came new supporters; the Gwerin grew and thrived, the Gweriden added new swords to its ranks. Besides Seana Bhraigh, they now had other secret places all across Keltia; and slowly, silently, after so long an ebb, the tide was beginning to run against the Incomers.

"We did very well there at Pentland, d'you not think?"

Esmer Lennox leaned back in his armchair. He was not asking to be answered; he but wanted to hear himself say the words, and to know that Athyn heard.

Since the beginning of what had been—at least to start with—the private war of Clann Lennox against the Incomers, the Chief of that Name had been up to his oxters in all campaigns and counsels, only chafing for the moment when the falcon he had so well managed should be free to fly the flight he had planned for her. But of that flight's final course, or the nature of the high prey at which she would be flown, even the falcon herself was as yet unaware.

Which is, of course, best for everyone concerned... He looked at Athyn where she sat sunk in thought, or what passed for thought, curled up in a deep armchair in the Countess Ganor's solar at Ardturach.

"Not so? Athwen? How is it with you?"

Athyn came out of her study, stretched and laughed. "With *me?*" she said, gently mocking his tone. "I am a pop-eyed rat's-nest of contradictories; every nerve in my body is scraped raw to the sheath, and I think my head exploded an hour past and I never even felt it! How do you *think* it is with me? And howsoever it may be, it is all your fault."

"My sorrow for asking," he said humbly, and she laughed again.

"Nay, that fault I count as greatest virtue! Without you and

Ganor-vaeth none of this had ever been. I only wonder how long we can keep secret your true part in this; I would not see Ardturach invested on my account."

"This old pile has seen worse far than any Incomer could throw at it," said Esmer complacently—and correctly. "But the folk—"

"Aye," she said after a moment. "The folk."

He looked up at a note he thought he had heard in her voice; but she was not looking at him. "We are fighting two wars here," he said then. "Two wars against two enemies: one of whom should never have come here to be our enemy at all, and those are the Firvolgians; and the other of whom were here all along and should never have come to be our enemy, and those are the Keavers."

"Very neat. But I do not see that it gets us any the farther along."

"Then consider: Two such different fights must be differently fought. Small profit to us if we take the same line against the Fir Bolc as against the Keavers, or the other way round."

"I had never thought we should have to be fighting against our own at all," she said bitterly. "But it is on me that we have two greater problems even than these: And the first is the establishment of a standing army for Keltia, such as the realm never has had before, so that the realm shall never have this trouble again; and the second is that long, that ongoing, that seemingly impossible thing—a rightly chosen sovereign once more over Kelts."

Athyn fell silent again, and though Esmer had many thoughts just then he did not allow them to show. *It is not the time, not yet. Soon. But not yet. She has a long road yet to ride before she comes to face that jump, and all of us with her...*

She stirred and sighed. "Well, I can see a way, a possible way, to getting us a standing army. But as for the other: We might just as well wish fish could sing, it would be as likely as our ever having a true ruler again. And *that* is how it is with me, since you did ask; was it not there this conversation started?"

"It was. But all the same, lassling, do not give over just so soon. We may see salmon in the bard-colleges yet."

"Music is better than words," said Morric, in a tone that both baited and brooked no debate, and Athyn sighed, as one who has heard it all before and just now does not want to be hearing it again.

They lay late awake, in their chambers at the Gwerin's newest camp of Nancledra, in the savage range of the Long Hills on Erinna; from the concealed round window they could look out at the moonlight on Sheehallion. They had not been thinking to see one another yet awhile, but battle had given them a brief common tangent, and after the rapture of reunion Morric now was in tearing high spirits, of a mood to tease his lover.

"And why?" he went on, prodding her ungently in the ribs and other more susceptible places when she laughingly refused to answer. "I shall tell you. Because emotion is raised up more quickly."

"Aye, and is over more speedily still," she taunted back. "Words last, songster. Though music is more immediate, I grant; to rouse the unthinking and sway the weak-minded, there is nothing better."

"Ah! Right between the joints of the armor!" He feigned a spearthrust through the heart and pulled her to him, laughing. "Well, I am only a minstrel, trying to entertain drunken halfwits—which sometimes includes me—and I know how I get myself through it. But what do *you* use, to get yourself out in front of the armies and—I will not say lie to them, but, well, lie to them as you do? I know you cannot always believe or even hope that we shall win; a harder question still, what is your comfort when your lie is proved, and the field has not been carried to your liking?"

"Not hard: pride," said Athyn firmly. "It has ever been one of my favorite virtues."

"And your next favorite?"

"Again not hard: anger. You would be surprised how much it can do."

He laughed, it seemed in spite of himself. "But are you never feared of what might be?"

"Nay; what is the use of that? What might be may equally well be what never shall be, and all that good fearing gone for naught, wasting the dán... But, Morric, I tell you without shame, I am often feared to my bones at what *must* be."

"As am I. But how do we live meanwhiles? Is there some trick, do you think, to get round that corner?"

Athyn shook her head. "No tricks, but some comfort: There are places in the waters where there is drowning, and places upon the lands where to set foot is to perish, and places among the stars where dragons wait. Yet if such is not our dán, we will not be directed there. That much is certain. Against that wall we can set our backs; and maybe more even than that."

There was a silence from the other side of the bed, and after a while she glanced over at him curiously. He was lying on his back, staring up at the ceiling, rapt in some deepness; when she trailed a light slow hand downward from his chest he did not even feel her touch.

"When I sing," said Morric slowly, as if he had never before even to himself put so self-evident a thing into words, "I stand for the folk before the gods, and for the gods before the folk. I do not know if it is so for every bard, but that is how it is for me, and I am glad and grateful both to have it so."

"And so are we who hear you," said Athyn, snugging closer. "For it is what you were sent among us to do."

He flashed her his quick shy smile, as he ever did when she praised his work, deeming one word of her praise worth whole screeds from anyone else, but that was not what he sought; just now he was hunting other truth.

"Is that purpose, then—what the Draoícht speak of as sacred intent? I am no priest, but to me it feels so."

"And I no priestess, to answer you with hope of correctness. But, beloved, surely it sounds right to me."

As their love had grown, Athyn and Morric had not studied to flaunt their union; but neither had they troubled too much to hide it. And Amzalsunëa Dalgarno, with animal cunning, was not slow to seize upon it.

Indeed, Morric had himself often spoken openly of Athyn to the pretty courtesan, whom he continued to see at frequent if irregular intervals; though, as he had vowed to Athyn, never again did he lie with his onetime lennaun, and, sensitive though he was beyond the measure of most men, he never did understand Athyn's objections to the ongoing association.

Nor did he perceive the nature of Amzalsunëa's true feeling—nor would he, not until it was too late. But then no man would have seen through her, though almost all women did. She was most convincing: Loudly did she profess to wish Morric's happiness above all else, making great protestation as to how if he, her true dear friend if lennaun no more, had found true joy with Athyn and not herself, well, gods only be thanked that he had found it; and Morric, though vaguely troubled by something in her face or her voice when she said so, took her at her word, speaking her fair because that was the only way he knew.

And so when the evil little stories began to be whispered roundabout, the tiny betrayals began to appear, he did not make the link he should have made, or might have. But Amzalsunëa and her pack of streppochs were not the only ones to turn on Morric for that they felt he had turned first on them...

As his involvement with Athyn and with the Gwerin had grown and deepened, Morric had had less and less to do with his former bandfellows. He knew that his four old friends were dissatisfied and impatient, even angry, with him and at his absences and his new commitments, and seemed angriest of all at the thought of his commitment to Athyn.

It could not go on, and yet none wished to decisively end it. But at length Erramun and Evance and Jaffran and Shane, not daring to tell him so face to face, sent word to Morric Douglas that no longer would they be playing music with him; when he rode in haste again to Tamon Acanis to confront them, they were cool and distant, and set as iron.

"We decided some time since that this was the better way for all," said Erramun, plainly more uncomfortable than the other three, who nodded silent agreement.

"Aye? Well, I do not recall being party to that deciding," snapped Morric.

But they would not be turned, and the more he argued the more sullen and defensive they grew; and at last he sat back, defeated.

"What will you do now?"

Evance started to answer, but Jaffran put a hand on his arm, and said coldly, "We will manage well enough without you. You seem already to be doing very well without us."

Erramun flushed a dull red, and sent Jaffran a hard look; he himself had been the last of the four to forsake Morric, maintaining that they owed their onetime chaunter and former friend a full explanation and a civil answer at the least.

"We have signed on with a company of travelling musicians and actors," he said. "It is run by a Firvolg called Loris Venoët. As Jaff says, we will do well enough. Your way and ours— Well, no two roads run forever alongside. Sooner or later the ground will cause them to diverge."

Morric looked at them, one by one, in silence. None could hold his gaze more than a few seconds, though Erramun lasted longest under that blazing blue regard.

"And you like not the country into which my road is leading me."

But they made him no answer; and as he rode sadly from the súgachan where they had met, he heard behind him through the rain the faint sound of a music he had never heard before, played by those he knew well—or perhaps had never known at all, or who had never known him.

Athyn was well aware of Morric's trouble; but in the fashion of lovers everywhere and evermore, each of them had sternly kept it from the other. But, back once again at Nancledra, Athyn steeled herself to bring it up, and found to her surprise that Morric was not quite so reluctant to speak of it as she had thought.

"Does it not trouble you, then?" she asked, when they had gone over his bandmates' perfidy for what seemed the hundredth time.

He stretched with apparent unconcern. "It troubles me that they feel the need to lie about the reason—and that they have taken up with such road-trash as Loris Venoët and his creatures. But apart from that, nay, it does not; certainly no more than all the lies and slanders trouble *you*."

That last was said with calm blasting irony, and he meant her to hear it. For his part he knew very well how troubled she was by the ceaseless muck, though her fine pretense of carelessness had fooled many even of the Gweriden. Though scarcely all: A few of her closest friends had come privily to speak to him about it, at great pains to ensure that Athyn did not learn that they knew her feeling—still more that they had gone behind her back on it to Morric.

They are brave friends as well as brave fighters; they will have to be both, right enough, if ever Athynna finds out they spoke to me about this and told her not—and so shall I... He watched now from their bed as, well aware of his gaze, she poured water over her hands, then filled a silver bowl with clean water and a small quantity of salt, dipping her fingers and drawing them across her forehead, between her breasts and along the high hollow underarches of her feet.

"What is that? I have never seen you do that before."

She carefully poured the water out before replying. "It is a thing Bronwyn taught me, long ago, at Silverwood; it is how she keeps herself apart from that with which she has to deal as judge. I have come to do it myself lately—since all the evil talk began. It is a purificatory; cleanses away any muck and evil energies thrown at me over the course of the day. Also it turns the badness back upon its source—threefold, I am told, which seems a fair return—and cleanses me for the morrow. You might want to think of doing the same yourself," she added, slipping into bed beside him as his arms opened for her.

"You are not the one in need of cleansing." By the lowered pitch of his voice she knew he was profoundly angry.

"Nay... Well, it does not harm, and it may help. Maybe even them as well as me. Who can say?"

But he was still wrathful. "I would protect you from those worm's-tongues if I could," he said presently. "Though most folk would argue you are the last Kelt there is who needs protecting... But it chafes me that I cannot, that they dare to speak so—"

"I know that... But no more could I protect you from what you felt, when your bandfellows chose to make music without you. They are too stupid to live, anghariad. But we cannot kill them all."

"Can we not?" he muttered.

She shook her head, smiling, and her long hair swept across his bare chest. "My very great sorrow, we cannot! And if we pay heed to any of it, why, Douglas, they have won. Where then is that duck's-back the Countess Ganor is always saying you have, that I should acquire of my own for myself?"

"Oh"—he pulled her down to him—"even oil on one's feathers is not always proof—"

"Aye so? Then let me attend to those plumes myself."

Then, later, when they were lying quiet again: "Mariota said you had a message today? From Erramun, or one of the others?"

"Nay." He paused a long moment. "From Comyn and Havoise." His voice was flat, unemphatic. It took Athyn a moment more to realize that he was speaking of his parents, and then she caught her breath. He felt her sudden tensing, and smiled grimly. "Aye; it surprised me too."

"You have never spoken to me of them; well, only that once, to tell me that they were dead, and that you had no sibs." She was picking her way through the words now as carefully as her war-horse stepped through strewn caltraps. *And this, too, I cannot protect him from...* "I take it that they are not dead, then."

"Only to me, as I to them... Aye, then," he said at last, grasping the blade. "Comyn was a Fian officer, a strategist and scientist, my mother a biddable wife who travelled with him wherever the Fianna sent them. I am their one child—that part was true, I have neither sister nor brother, and I am glad of it, now... My father's god was discipline for its own sake, and my mother's god was pleasing him. And when I was still a very little lad— Well." He took a deep uneven breath, tightening his arm where it curved round Athyn. "So, they are not dead as I have let it to be known; they live on Kernow, in a small port city not far from where we dwelled when I was a child."

He spoke without the least trace of emotion in his voice or on his face; she knew by that very control how deeply it cost him to speak so, and held herself to stillness lest she rob him of what calm he kept.

"When I was old enough to contract on my own," he resumed, in the bard-tone he would have used to tell a story, "I ran away and sought admission to a bardic college; and that was when I began to tell folk that I had no living kin. It was no lie as I saw it; and hear me Goddess, I will never see either of them again—nay, cariadwyn, not if they threw themselves under the hoofs of my horse. That message today came from her; every now and again she sends one, but I do not answer, and she well knows why..."

He fell abruptly silent, his voice taut with the weight of unshed tears; Athyn felt him trembling against her, and her heart bled into his. Yet she dared not ask what she already knew...

So close were they in that moment that he heard even that, for he suddenly turned to her, buried his face between her breasts. "She deserves nothing of me now... Another time. I *will* tell you... Any road"—an everyday voice again—"that was her choice, to sacrifice her child to please her husband, to give him all her power; and his choice was to abuse that power, to misuse it. And my choice—once I had power of my own—was to file quitclaim against them both. Which I did upon achieving my first majority. I have not seen them since."

Athyn hid her surprise, but as a brehon she was shocked, and as one who deeply loved this man she was hurt to the heart for his hurting. The quitclaim was like to a divorce, but between a person and his kindred, and kin being all to Kelts, never was it executed lightly. That Morric had felt the need to declare before the law that he had no family, to make himself by his own choosing an exile of blood because there was no other choice to make... She kissed his shoulder, gently, but he made no sign.

"I never knew my own birthparents," she said presently. "And I wonder now which is worse: never to know how they might have been, or to know them and to have them be as yours were. At Caerlaverock, Kier would beat us, so that my mamaith trained a guardhound for us against him. He hated me because I was only a foundling and yet my parents loved me more than they loved him; but it is not the same."

He shifted on the pillows, and she eased her weight on his encircling arms, but he only held her closer; gathering a coil of her hair into his fingers he kissed it, pressing it to his lips for many moments before he spoke again.

"Near enough... But I am learning—surely, if slowly—that such patterns are meant to be broken and thrown aside; and you are the one who is teaching me. The invincibility of indifference: If one does not care, it cannot hurt. But our own pattern—yours and mine together—that is *not* indifferent, and it is merely invincible."

She glanced up at him. "How is it you always know what to say to comfort me?"

"I am a bard," he said smiling. "I know my audience."

She added in a lower voice, so low he had to bend his head to hear her, "Then how is it I cannot seem to comfort *you?*"

Morric moved his hand round the back of her neck and into the heavy hair, and pressed her head upon his breast. "Ah," he said, "but I say that you have."

"So you will not answer the message?"

"Nay. I will not. Is that too much to ask?"

"It depends less on what is being asked than on whom is being asked," she said after a while, "or on who is doing the asking."

As Morric prepared to ride out the next morning from Nancledra—the Valley of the Sword—he felt a strange prickling touch on the back of his neck, as if someone watched him intently, from hiding. He gave no sign, but finished saddling his horse, then whirled round in the direction from which he had felt the covert gaze. *Nothing, no one—either that, or they are very swift dodgers indeed...*

He rode away from the hidden stronghold, glancing back once. *Athynna was wiser than she knows, to have built this refuge. Seana Bhraigh serves its own purpose, and Ardturach often seems to be serving Lennox's purpose, which does not always seem to be the same purpose as our purpose... But this place is truly ours.*

Halfway down the narrow defile, where the great hills shouldered in on either side and the Clowyn ran white and chuckling in its stony bed beside the road, Morric felt the same neck-prickling he had felt outside Nancledra's hidden gates. Suddenly his splendid black mare Glesni shied violently, almost unseating him, and stood trembling stiff-legged in the road. Though he was no horseman, over the years Morric had learned from his mate; where another might have spurred and whipped the mare to force her on, he slipped from his saddle and came round to hold her by the green leather bridle, close beneath her jaw.

"What is it then, my beauty?" he whispered, in the soft coaxing voice Athyn had taught him horses like to hear, and the mare shivered her fear and distress. "What is your trouble?"

And then he saw what her trouble was, and had no need to ask.

When Athyn herself came riding along the road an hour later, she drew rein sharply to see him sitting on a flat boulder, staring blankly at the hillside above; Glesni grazed beside the stream. In less time than it takes to tell of it, Athyn was afoot with her sword drawn.

"Goddess, Morric, *what*—"

He startled violently to see her; he had not heard the oncoming horse, had not even sensed his lover's presence. But he caught at her cloak, and she put out a protective arm between him and—whatever.

"Above—up there—"

She raked the slopes above them with the thoroughness she had learned in Elmet; nothing to be seen, and she sheathed her blade and sat beside him.

"What did you see, cariadol? Whatever it was, it is not there now."

With her arms round him he felt himself recovering. "It was so—so *real*."

She caught the picture from his mind. "Ah. Now I understand." She tightened her hold on him. "Most people would have said, *un*real."

"Well, they would not be I who said so!" he responded with some heat. "Nay, Athynna, that thing was more real than you and I and the Gwerin and the whole planet put together..." He turned to her. "We are speaking of the same thing, are we not? The hill-wolf? The one the size of my mare? The size of that hill? The one I have the oddest feeling you somehow—know?"

"Well, I will say, he knows me—and he has seen you before." She smiled at his look, and began to tell him all the tale.

chapter fifteen

He that sows thorns, let him not go barefoot.

—*Phaal Torcwyn*

"They are calling me *what?*" Athyn stared at Ganor, who returned her shocked gaze with an unreadable smile.

"Aye, truly, I promise you. You did not know?"

Athyn shook her head. "Nay. I had not heard. But now that I have—"

Ganor laughed. "Lassling, some things there are that even you cannot command!"

After the Countess had closed the door behind her, Athyn glared balefully across the chamber at the cause of all the trouble.

"Blackmantle," she said aloud, experimentally, then laughed; there was nothing else to do. *Well, this will teach me about traha, if anything can! And I have no doubt but that Morric will tell me I should have seen it coming miles away. Folk have ever loved to hang bynames on other folk, and I would guess this was too tempting a one to pass up…* She shook her head, then caught up the guilty garment and slung it on in her customary fashion. *Well—discomfortable as it makes me, it seems somehow right that I should take my name in battle from Cormac's cloak; and certainly I do not intend to leave off wearing it! Perhaps too, it might serve as a handful of dust in the Firvolgians' eye—Athyn nic Archill has disappeared from ken, Athyn Cahanagh they know, and Blackmantle they will know, but that the three are the same, they may not puzzle out straightway, and that might be some protection. All in all, I daresay it could have been a great deal worse. 'Athyn Anfa' was bad enough— Now, if only I can keep my Morric from making a song of it…*

A small castle deep in the mountains of Gwynedd—precisely where, Athyn did not know, as their escorts had prudently taken a roundabout route. The newly bynamed leader of the Gwerin was on her way, with Esmer and Ganor and Greyloch, to meet for the first time the Marcher lords and others who had been funding the revolt, and she was feeling more daunted than she liked.

In that secret keep, past gates and guards, in a tower room lighted by only a sconce or two, and the cool blue glow of the quaratz-hearth, a score of strangers sat round a table. None had bothered to veil themselves with a fith-fath, though several wore intricately draped hoods that concealed most of their faces. And hastening now across the room, a man, tall and spare, his hair the same brown-red as hers, his hands held out to her: Maravaun Aoibhell, present Prince of Thomond—and her nearest living kinsman.

"Athyn—cousin—"

She took his hands as in an ashling, felt his kiss of kinship upon either cheek, heard his pleasant tenor voice speaking of the long estrangement between their Houses and how all that now was changed. She became aware that he had paused, was expecting answer; but she did not know what she might say. *So often have I imagined this moment that now it is here I do not know what to do with it…*

Her diffidence was not rooted solely in private discomposure. In those days, the House of Aoibhell enjoyed nothing near the vast pre-eminence to which it would attain in after times; indeed, Athyn herself would be the root of that pre-eminence to come. But Maravaun, twelfth prince of his line and a great one, was another such as Esmer: vital, forceful, angry, deeply frus-

trated at the inability of the Kelts to come together to throw out
the Firvolgians—and as cunning and devious to achieve his
goals as was his dear and longtime friend of Connacht.

She must have said something suitable, for she saw him
smile warmly and nod. But as she was presented to the others—names with whom she was by reputation well acquent—
she found Blackmantle coming all unbidden to Athyn's aid,
supplying appropriate words for each encounter, proper thanks
for the confidence they had placed in her, the immeasurable
help they had given the Gwerin.

Esmer stood in the shadows and watched; and though he
was not a man to gloat, it could fairly be said that he was, in
this moment, pleased indeed.

"A century now have we been squabbling amongst ourselves,
and the only ones who profit by it are the Incomers. Long past
time, sirs and ladies, that we must ride together to that goal we
all so dearly want."

The cool voice was Tipherris Greyloch's, but the firebrand
sentiments were shared by all—and the warning in his words
well taken.

Maravaun Aoibhell smiled. "Then perhaps the captain of the
Gwerin will tell us how our support has been put to that end."

Athyn collected herself with a start, and for the next six
hours did her best to tell them. Once her shyness had been forgotten—once Blackmantle had made her forget it—she spoke
commandingly; and she was heard and noted, and approved.

Then, near dawn, the night's business completed and a feeling of ease and accomplishment in the room, Maravaun
Aoibhell allowed himself an offhand observation—or what
seemed at the time offhand—and his words struck like arrows
into at least one of his hearers.

"Well enough for all this planning; but for me, I look to
when we have triumphed and the Incomers are gone. I tell
you, m'charai, it would not be the worst fate that might befall

Keltia, did one who has a hand to wield a sword also have a head to wear a crown."

Athyn heard and yet she did not hear. Her immediate thought, which she studied at once to conceal, was that she could not possibly have heard Maravaun correctly; that her traha had wildly overblown itself to think that he could even by the remotest imagining have meant her. She was appalled to realize that she had not misheard, but still she continued to dissemble; in the appearance of ignorance her safety seemed to lie.

Looking covertly at the others, she saw that she had not been mistaken, but they did not seem to twig that she too had taken Maravaun's meaning; the swiftness of her self-control had saved her. So this, then, was why Esmer had brought her here: so that the powers behind the Gwerin might meet—and judge—the one behind whose throne they might all soon be powers. Incredibly, she felt somehow betrayed; even by Esmer and Ganor and Greyloch, whom just then she caught exchanging eyes, a complacent look of tacit agreement.

But she kept her knowledge, and her hurt, to herself; and with dawn now a faint daffodil stain outside the windows, the others beginning to take their separate, secret departures, Maravaun drew her aside into an embrasure.

"I know you have only just recently been told your true ancestry," he began, "and that you were angry the Thomonds did not take you in when your parents were slain—aye, I see you are still. Well, and who can blame you? But, lassie, we did not know you even existed. Oh, we were aware of your imminent arrival: The House's recording brehons had been informed—despite the rift between Thomond and Findhorn, you and Dechtira were still of the Name—and upon your birth you would have been duly entered into the family studbook. As a horsewoman yourself, you cannot doubt *that*!"

He smiled to see her unwilling smile, and went on gently. "When he heard of the slaughter at Fialzioch, and that Conn and Dechtira had been seen on the field, my father, Ruadhan, who was Prince then, naturally assumed that, born or unborn, surely you had died with your mother. And since the Keltic dead of Fialzioch were all burned alike in a great lowe, for fear of despoiling by Incomers or beasts, there was no way of knowing. By then you had been rescued by Cormac in any case... We never received any word to cause us to think other than we did: that you and Dechtira and Conn had perished together upon that field, and that the line of the Findhorn Aoibhells had come to an end."

He put an arm round her, for she was quietly weeping, cold tears slipping down her cheeks. "Now we see that it is not so— and I promise you, as prince and kinsman, things will change, and for the better. You have other cousins, you know, who are eager to meet you, and to have their full share in the work." Maravaun peered down at her anxiously. "Nay, alanna, do not weep—Esmer will slap me silly for making you cry no sooner than we met. Look, we will go out together."

"It marches well, sweethearting, do you not think?"

Esmer and Ganor had retired early following the flight back to Ardturach; the Earl, in high spirits but very weary indeed, had sought his usual remedy, and now was relaxing stressed muscles and nerves alike in the steaming waters of the swirlpool.

"We are sure of this, Lennox, are we?" his wife asked somberly, when he came to bed all pink and puffing from the steam. "True, Athwen is greatly gifted, but still she is very young. And we are requiring her to wrest all Keltia back from the Incomers in a handful of years, when great generals and high kindreds and the strongest princes of the Six Nations could not win back a single planet in more than a century. Not content to stop there, we are planning to punish her for this tremendous deed by forcing the crown onto her head, and we have not even *told* her yet about that part of it... Have we ever, truly, considered what is best for her in all this?"

Esmer looked suddenly deflated, a small boy scolded where he had thought to be praised.

"I thought we had been down that road—why do you doubt again the choices we made?"

"I do not know! But I saw her there last night, with all of you—all of us—and it came to me then that we are using her. She is not a thing, Esmer, not a pawn or a slave... You just now said it: 'the choices *we* made.' Have we ever even asked her what she herself might want to choose?"

"She wants what we all want: freedom for Keltia from the Incomer. She will do what she must to make that happen, Ganwen. She knows that; she chose it long ago." He thumped the piled pillows into a comfortable configuration. "I too wish she could stay with us: to be our brehon, wed Morric and settle down here with him—what ordinary folk are free to do. But she is not ordinary, and no more is he; and even we ourselves are not. If we were, we would never have been called to this venture. And we *have* been called, Ganor. We were not mistaken about that." He was falling asleep as he spoke; it had been a very long day on two different planets, and he was not as young as he used to be. *Maybe I never was*, he thought, and was away.

But Ganor still lay wakeful.

Not many days thereafter, an embassy of Incomers was announced to Esmer, and he agreed at once to see them. *It is always easier when the enemy has a face*... He watched now as they approached him where he sat in his comital chair, Ganor on his right and Mariota in the tanist's place at her father's left.

The local petitioners were no strangers. Lennox named them to himself as they bowed before him and Ganor: Ser Rhykeur Pym, who had over the years annoyed most of Connacht; Ser Leto Novedris, a big bluff blowhard; Dalgu Namani, a slot-faced whitrit; Teddecin Wenn, a spineless trimmer. The rest of the party was known to him by reputation only, and that not good, among them the trader Falxifer Dalgarno, and the Beldam Pharuca T'pettun, in whose Caerdroian establishment Dalgarno's daughter reportedly had a flourishing practice—at least according to Mariota.

Esmer sighed and nodded to his rechtair to let the audience commence. *Ah well—with slugs, who can tell which one is nearest the ground?* He put down his disgust, greeting them cordially, as any Earl of Connacht might greet any who besought him, and Dalgarno stood forth at once as spokesman.

It was suavely done, even Esmer silently admitted as he listened. Under the flag of aggrieved concern, these slinters had come to scout out the depth of his involvement with the doings of the Gwerin. In especial did they want to know of this creature Blackmantle who had suddenly sprung up out of nowhere, bent on stirring up the normal order of things in Keltia, when it need not be stirred up at all, they were all reasonable folk... As the Earl's eyes began to glaze like stones in a winter stream, Rhykeur Pym sailed in on a different tack.

"You, lord, who have been so great a friend to Incomers in Connacht," he said in plump unctuous tones, "in especial to our lamented friend and comrade Nilos Marwin, would be greatly owed the gratitude of Kaireden—"

Esmer allowed himself the faintest frown. "Kaireden's gratitude? Pray what cause, Ser Pym?"

Pym spread his hands and smiled like a spaniel. "If your honor were to put a stop to this harpy's raidings—or at the least use your great influence with other Kelts not to side with her—perhaps even if you were able to find out who she is when she is not wearing that black cloak—"

Esmer sat back, and in the same instant the Countess Ganor leaned forward.

"We understand your concern, Ser Pym," she said winningly, in the smoothest, silkiest voice she could pull from her throat, "and we too deplore marauding—of any sort and origin. Yet we should not wish you to give such assurances out of the air. Upon whose authority do you offer?"

But they turned suddenly coy, perhaps stung by Ganor's pointed reference, which could only mean the Firvolgians' own mosstroops. Dalgu Namani moved to smooth it over, slopping with renewed avowals that should Esmer Lennox halt the rising tide of the Gwerin, truly he would not find Kaireden lacking in appreciation.

Esmer, attending listlessly to this soapy humbug, suddenly sensed the skiving-edge that lay beneath, and, for the first time since the audience began, sat up with something like enjoyment.

"And again I must ask why it is thought amongst you that I might have any greater knowledge of this Blackmantle's activities—or identity—than any other Kelt. She has indeed operated lawlessly within my maigen; but then so have the Keavers, and—no offense, I am sure you deplore their doings as much as I deplore Blackmantle's—so also have the mosstroopers. And I am not privy to their movements any more than I am to hers."

"The Earl of Connacht must have his finger on many pulses," put in one who had not spoken before. Esmer recalled his name and face from one of Athyn's rosters: Lorcan Firdanisk, yet another trimmer. "I myself am only half Kelt, yet even I can attest to that. But we meant no offense in asking."

Ah, and did you not, then? As the others, one by one, put their various cases of self-interest to the lord of Connacht, Esmer slumped down on his spine in the chair of state. *Everything ends,* he reminded himself firmly, *and so too shall this… if perhaps not soon enough to suit me.*

"Mouth-honor only," said Mariota scornfully, when the petitioners had at last bowed and glozed and seeped their way out of the audience chamber. The three Lennoxes had remained, too stupefied to move, and Athyn now emerged from behind the arras where she had been lurking and listening all along. "Respect from the teeth outward; softsauder, and not even artful at that, I have heard so much better—"

"Do you think they believed you, my lord," asked Athyn, with a quick amused glance at her friend, "when you said you had seen never a trace of Blackmantle, and could not imagine who she might be?"

Esmer laughed. "Not for a heartbeat!" he said. "And it alarms me that already they know to seek out Blackmantle as the polestar of the revolt. Goddess be thanked, we took thought for this when we did, so that Athyn nic Archill now is forgotten and Athyn Cahanagh has been kept at a certain distance; nay, do not shrug it off! I know it went hard with you to be seen so."

"What shall we do, then?" asked Mariota. "Spy?"

"Spoken like a true bard! Aye, m'chara, spy by all means. But if I may suggest that the Earl and Countess of Connacht should denounce Blackmantle and the Gwerin, very publicly and very soon, for plunderers and common brigands? Merely some shocked and sad words, deploring this choice to take to the sword a simple disagreement amongst friends... Nay, only listen," said Athyn quickly, seeing their expressions, the words of hot protest already forming on Esmer's lips. "Such denial might serve, at least for the moment, to buy us some time; and I will for my part keep well away from Ardturach, so that you can say in perfect truth you have not set eyes on Blackmantle— should anyone else come asking."

Esmer bridled, as she had known he would, and took many minutes to be persuaded; but as his wife and his heir and his captain all pointed out, the great thing, first, was to win—the rest could be sorted out after. And to that end, or beginning, the War-band was set indeed.

*   *   *

A morning of combat; but nothing yet for the Gwerin had been like to this. This was their first fight in the genuine manner; no simple skirmish or strike-and-run but true planned battle. In the light of a chill gray autumn dawn, atop a windy ridge above the valley in central Erinna known as Arderydd, Athyn sat Rhufain, her new charger, successor to the faithful and now outpastured Tarn.

The giant stallion, foaled at Caerlaverock, had been set aside for Athyn out of the herds by folk still loyal; trained as a war-horse by Aunya nic Cafraidh, he had been recently smuggled to his new mistress under Kier mac Archill's nose. He was a copper chestnut, and bore a startling resemblance to that horse Allyn mhic Midna had ridden that night he carried the young Athyn away beneath the hill—the same dark bronze coat and pale gold mane and tail; a wind-drinker, as such tireless swift racers are called.

Now she patted the arching bronze neck, and Rhufain bobbed his head; her face was as eager as her mount's stance. "Where is our old Gwerin, then, asthore?" she murmured. "Where is our chief Hunter?"

A good question—but she needed no answer. Rhain mac an Iolair was war-lord this day; his shield called Feast-for-Eagles that had flamed black and crimson on many fields had been burnished anew for this one. Her onetime Fian teacher was fitly named, for in the Erinnach 'Iolair' means not only 'eagle' but 'hunter.' And today he who served the Queen of Eagles, the battle-goddess Morna Rhên, was huntmaster of the Gwerin, to stoop upon the quarry.

Some shifting in the mounted ranks round Athyn: commanders leaving to join their companies, gallopers coming up to receive new orders. Breos mac an Aba rode up with Morvoren Kindellan, both of them bright-faced in battle dress. Morvoren's lorica had a green-blue sheen to it, like fishes' mail, and Breos wore the colors of his noble ancient House.

"Blackmantle!" cried Breos cheerfully above the wind. "What do you mean to do here?"

Athyn smiled but never took her eyes from the field. "Why, m'chara, I mean to give the Incomers their Outgoing. A fine thrashing, sirs and ladies; a fine thrashing."

And so fine she thrashed them that day in the valley of Arderydd that before Beltain came there was not a Fir Bolc to be found in all of Connacht, and before it came again not one left on Erinna. But first they must be fought...

It was Athyn's maiden battle. Although she had led routs and raids innumerable, this was a pitched, formal fight; and until that very morning she had intended, greatly eager, to lead the Gwerin into this as well. But too many voices that carried too much weight in her councils had forced a change of plan; and then Esmer had commanded... Her obedience was not uncolored by resentment: *I did not take up the sword to sit in safety on a hill, like some infirm ancient general too feeble to fight! Nor am I the only one here to wear a Fian's black cloak—but, did I ride out ahead of the army, I admit it might not be difficult for even the Firvolgi to figure out just who in fact was Blackmantle—* So that now she sat there on Rhufain among her officers, and watched. *Still, I like it not...*

Below her, the Gwerin forces were splayed out across the valley, provocatively placed to draw the Incomer troopers deep within the glen. In the swales to either side, the war-chariots waited under the command of Stellin Ardwyr on the right and Alveric Elshender on the left, and in the low scrubwoods that clothed the slopes, archers lay hidden, their lasra arblasts tucked deep in the heather, so the Incomers should see no glint of sun on steel.

Unconventional, chancy, foolhardy, lunatic—aye, this just might work... Athyn straightened in the deep war-saddle as the signal was sent from the glen entrance, and reaching beneath her lorica she touched first the heavy silver battle torc that had been her mother's, then the little leather amulet bag that lay between her breasts. Then the lines clashed, and it began.

There is in every battle a moment, an instant, when time stops, when a charging horse seems suspended in air and a shot arrow hangs in flight and a sword descending in the stroke seems forever poised at the top of its shining arc. Athyn saw time begin to move again, and felt herself begin again to breathe, as Rhain, having allowed the Firvolgi advance well down the valley, gave signal; and following a silver rain of arrows and the levin of lasras, the thunder came of Stellin's chariotry rising out of the swales like a landlash, a great destroying storm of war, and across the glen's width Alveric sent back the echo with his own.

The Firvolgi were caught up in the chariot-sweep, their ranks broken in the first charge. They scattered, and that was fatal for their side: The valley floor was broad, but the walls were steep and unscalable; and where those walls could be climbed Rhain had laced them thick with archers. Of the Incomer soldiers who made it as far as the slopes, few set foot on the rising ground, and none at all won past it.

Though small knots of valor held here and there, by early afternoon it was plain for all to see: The Kelts had won their first major victory against the Firvolgians; there in the valley of Arderydd, the Outgoing had begun.

And when the sun had begun to drop behind the ridges, Rhain mac an Iolair, a streak of blood across his brow but his face like the dawn, rode up to Athyn and the other Gweriden, and kissed his hand to Selanie his wife where she stood by.

"Do luathas mar iolair," said Athyn, and Rhain struck bloody fist to mailed shoulder, and bowed from his saddle. "Thy swiftness as an eagle's."

"A feast for eagles," he agreed, lifting his shield so named and clashing his swordblade across it in salute. "Gwerin an uachdar!"

The shout they raised in answer woke the echoes. Even Kaireden heard that shout; in the streets of Katilon Ke Katil the name of Arderydd rang clear.

A sevennight after the battle, Athyn Cahanagh rode alone up onto the broad green breast of the shield-mountain Brondor, and halting Rhufain she dismounted a dozen yards away from the edge of the chalk. Below her the Elmet Vale swept out like patchwork, patterned here and there with gold squares, and those were plowed fields, edged with silver braid, and those were streams.

She looked from the vast vista to the ground before her feet. From this close vantage, the great running horse Debagh nic Archill had cut into the turf to mark Cormac's grave had the aspect many had ascribed to it, a beaked dragon with long elegant limbs and horn-like ears; on one side a crescent moon hung in the green-turf sky, on the other a six-rayed sun. *But never shadow falls upon him...* And Lyleth now lay beside him, as her wish had been.

Athyn stepped onto the horse's eye, and closed her own eyes; already in the Elmet valley it had become the custom to do so and make a wish. *A thousand years from today they will not remember who it was who lies beneath, or who set this figure upon the hill, or the obscure forgotten captain who came here once to pray, but they will still be stepping onto the Eye of the White Horse for luck...* She smiled at the thought, then laughed outright at the idea of how uncomfortable Cormac would have been with it; but she made her own wish just the same.

"My sorrow, tasyk, mamaith, but you were wrong," said Athyn then aloud. "There are some folk can only be reached in the language of blood and steel, and it seems our Kier is one of them—"

For some time she spoke. There was much to tell—the Gwerin, Morric, the great struggle at last begun, Arderydd

just now fought. And finally there was that matter at last to
be set right, of her birth and their concealment. But when
she began haltingly to speak of it, Athyn found to her own
surprise that the anger she had long felt had long gone; for
better or worse, she understood at last why her fosterers—
Nay, my parents, truly!—had done as they did; and admitted,
to them and to herself, that they were right. And a real and
sudden peace came over her, healing as a hand laid upon her
brow...

*Perhaps the countryfolk are more correct than they know, to
stand here and wish. The spirit of the White Horse Vale—or some
spirit—has given me my own wish after all. Whether that wish shall
chime with the wishes others have made—well, we shall just have to
bide the issue…*

She had ridden then to Caerlaverock, or what was left of it—
the first time she had returned there since Lyleth's death and
Kier's accession, and it was no more as it had been. . . Gazing
hard-eyed upon the destruction, picking up an unburned piece
of carven stone from the wreckage to take away with her as
token, Athyn felt the expected stab of sorrow—here had stood
the front steps, there the stables, above her in empty air her
window had opened on the long views, giving her glimpses
within herself of longer views by far. *I wish it had fallen out other
wise…not for my sake alone—*

Over the past year or two Kier mac Archill had kept a very
low sail against the war-clouded sky. It was generally assumed
among his estranged sibs that he lived a friendless life at the
maenor; which, as they saw it, was vastly more than he
deserved. For his ridings with the mosstroops were no longer a
secret, and no more a pretense at spycraft: Like others before
him, and others who would come after, he had turned his
cloak. He had betrayed his kin and friends and people, and had
gone over to the side of the Fir Bolc.

Elmet's riposte to his treachery revealed had been swift

and savage. Three months before Athyn stood where now she was standing, on a night of cloud and wind, Caerlaverock had been destroyed by masked and angry neighbors, levelled to the ground, the maenor's lord barely escaping with his life.

From that night on, Kier mac Archill had given his loyalty, such as it might be, openly to the Incomers against his own folk, and it was no surprise to Athyn that he should turn so—indeed, conveniently ignoring his own guilt, he even blamed her for the discovery of his double-dealing, as he had blamed her long ago for Cormac's death. For herself, she had long since taken from Caerlaverock all that she wished to take, everything and everyone she loved or prized or needed; and what remained could never be taken from her.

Great pity to be so vested in a lie that one would rather eat one's soul up in dishonor, would sooner cling to it in hate, than fairly admit the wrong and sit down to dine at truth's table. But that is a thing that Kier, and the rest of them, will never do.

When she rode out of Elmet, by that same pass over Cat Bregion by which she had left it so long ago—though by the calendar it was by no means so long as events made it—she halted Rhufain now as she had halted Tarn then, and looked back once more.

I do not think I shall look on it again, at least not in this same manner; shall not a third time sit my horse beside the waystone here. At least no more as Athyn nic Archill, youngest of Caerlaverock… That is done with now; it is the sum of all such moments that brings us to the place where dán means us to be. Yet even that is not the whole of it: The final end of choosing is an endless narrowing of choice, until we ride at last the only road left before us. Is it intolerable to be so directed, or is it a comfort? And is it dán, or is it our freedom to choose, that has chosen it?

Beneath her, Rhufain shifted and stamped, and she took his

hint, immediately contrite. "And I a horsegirl from these very grazelands, to keep my mount standing so long! You would think I had never before planted my bottom in a saddle... Aye so, my Rhuvannach. Time we were away."

chapter sixteen

The cat would eat fish, but would not wet its feet.

—*Stellin Ardwyr*

A stormy sea, the rolling billows huge and black and crowned with foam; a ship as black as the waves, with painted sails and decks white as milk, riding the combers, tacking perilously close to land. Upon a beach whose sands were diamonds, red-eared white hounds ran baying at the edge of the waves. But their alarums were in vain: Standing off from that coast the ship sailed by in majesty, close hauled on a nightmare wind, and passing through huge iron gates that stood in the sea it was gone, and the great gates closed behind it; but then an armada loomed ghostly distant over the horizon...

Athyn woke in terror, reaching out for Morric; but the bed was empty. *Yet did he go to sleep beside me...*

It was the third month after Arderydd and Athyn's pilgrimage into Elmet; at which latter Morric still clutched his head every time he thought of it. He had been most reluctant—well, 'reluctant' would not be the word to describe the cold blazing depths of his fear and fury and disinclination, but it was the only word he had—to let her go alone into even her own home lands, so soon after so bloody and decisive a battle. His arguments had been excellent ones: that there could be mosstroops lurking about, or Keavers, or even kedders, those fearful assassins, who might have been hired by her enemies and found their way to Keltia on her trail; that Athyn nic Archill may have been forgotten, but Athyn Cahanagh was known to the Incomers, and well hated; that Blackmantle was known to them also, and now even better hated, for the general who had just presided over the worst military defeat the Firvolgi had been dealt in Keltia since Brendan's day. And she had listened; but in the end she had gone.

Now, heart racing, breath disevened, still half in her dream, Athyn saw Morric standing motionless at the window. Shaken by a feeling of relief stronger than any nightmare, she slipped out of bed and fled to him just as he turned to see what had broken her sleep.

"Cariadwyn," he said, opening his arms, and Athyn went shivering into them. "You were tossing in your sleep like a stirk; what is it? A bad dream? That is nothing."

"Nay," she said, muffled, into his chest. "I fear it is much more." She pulled away a little and looked up at him. In the light that spilled through the two round windows of their bedchamber at Nancledra, the planes of his face were sharp-cut and clean, the moonlight making his brown hair seem pitch black where it fell upon his shoulders and grew fine and straight upon the broad iron-muscled singer's chest. He wore nothing but the string of beads he wore always, that she had made for him of the rough-polished emeralds he had once brought her from Caledon; and even in that moment of aftermath and terror she marvelled yet again at how very beautiful he was, how the beauty of his body reflected the beauty of the spirit it housed. She took a deep uneven breath, and a decision to go with it, and he tightened his arms around her.

"Do you remember," she asked after a moment, "that time when I went with you to Tamon Acanis, when you played with Evance and Erramun and Jaffran and Shane, and we had to flee from mosstroops?"

"I remember well. What of it?"

"I did not tell you, but not very long after that, when I returned to Seana Bhraigh and you went back on bard-rounds, I had a visitor. Two visitors."

Briefly she told him of meeting Allyn mhic Midna and

Gwyn ap Neith in the wood, and with her head against his chest for comfort she never saw the startlement in his eyes. But he held his peace, so as not to interrupt the tale.

"They came to tell me a thing that I have repeated to no other: not Esmer, not my own sibs—" She paused for another steadying breath. "They told me that Seli who is queen of the Shining Folk, Seli who is mate to Neith the king, once had fled the dún and gone to be a mortal's lennaun. And when she returned, she brought with her a half-mortal son—Edeyrn she called him."

"'Edeyrn,'" he said consideringly, though he was astonished at the revelation. "In the bardic usage, that name means 'golden-tongued,' as one who can persuade by power of words alone, be they good or ill."

"Aye, well, according to Gwyn and Allyn, this Edeyrn will persuade by more than words, to more than ill."

Even to Morric she could not yet speak of what else the Sidhe lords had shown her: Keltia ravaged worse than ever it had been under Incomer yoke, the people ground under heel, the royal house all but extinguished, the High King murdered... *And all at the will of this one who stands between two worlds, an heir of the Middle Kingdom and of the Upper World both alike. How much will alter in the time of his sway to come, and whom will the gods send us to turn it back?*

But that was a problem for another age, and others would have to face it. They spoke a while longer; then, as she drew him back to their bed, to sleep a little before it was time to wake again, Morric rallied to jest.

"Goddess! Had I only known, that night of Samhain the Less, what dán I was knotting myself into for the sake of that long red hair—"

Athyn laughed and swooped the coverlets over them both. "Next time be more careful from whose hand you strike sparks."

Though the great fear of many—Kaireden's intervention in strength, in a major interplanetary war that Keltia would almost certainly lose—had never come to pass ("Too costly," opined Esmer, and held his breath in hope), still the Incomers were proving remarkably tenacious. Instead of decamping home, they deepened their presence in Keltia on worlds that the Gwerin did not hold: on Tara, the Throneworld, in especial. Though that would not be so for long; and when Tara was free it would be as if all Keltia were free, and surely then the Incomers would leave...

But if Athyn's dream was a warning, it felt to her as presage, and message, and not merely of woes to fall upon Keltia centuries hence. Never unaware, but at the same time unknowing of what was meant—it was a state that few could have borne patiently, and Athyn was patently not one of them.

Nor was she of that sort who can bear to remain so. So at the full of the Hawkmoon she rode alone—more head-clutchings from Morric—deep into the Long Hills, to find some answers. And there, as if the tryst had been long time arranged, she found awaiting her the one being who could, or would, furnish those answers forth.

Beyond Nancledra's secret valley, away north and east, lie the wild lands of A'Mhaighdean; and in the secretest, wildest part of those lands is the Solway Forest. Not a forest as is commonly thought—trees and brush and the like—but forest in the old sense, a great barren expanse of heath and broken moorland, upon which the hand of man has never yet been lain. Going by the shores of blue and unnamed lochans, moors like purple seas, mountains unfolding before her forever and ever, range after range like rolling granite surf, Athyn rode for three days deep into A'Mhaighdean, and felt herself drawn into it deeper still.

This is a country where man does not rule... It needs naught from us, wants naught to do with us. Yet it will suffer us if we come into it with the proper feeling. Harsh the land may be, yet it is not unkind...

Without warning Rhufain shied, and only the instinctive horsemanship of one bred to the saddle saved Athyn from being thrown. She moved as the stallion moved, and not until the beast was standing four-footed again did she look round for the cause of his alarm. And found it not a score of yards away: Seli, queen of the Sidhe, stood before her, alone on the bare fell's side.

She looked upon Athyn with remembrance and friendship, while for her part Athyn hoped that this time she would remember the queen's beauty as it truly was: the streaming fire-gold hair, the eyes as green as rain. *But the Sidhe never let you remember anything they do not wish you to remember*—and blushed when Seli laughed.

"I would wager much that you have forgotten very little, no matter my folk's hand in your remembering! Now I know that your manners are far too good to ask, so I shall tell you: Aye, it is true. I left Neith to live with Rhûn, a mortal lord, to whom I bore a son, Edeyrn; and that is a tale very much still in the unfolding. Then I went back to Neith, and bore a son to him also; and that is where you come into the tale. You have remembered more than most have ever known, and forgotten more than many remember."

"I have kept the secret," said Athyn proudly, "if that is what your grace does mean. All those years I have told no one. Only when I dreamed of the black ships, only then did I tell my lord... But of that other time, that first time, no creature quick or dead has ever heard."

Seli smiled. "We know how you have kept faith with us, lass. And that telling was no betrayal: For Morric Douglas is caught up in it as surely as all the rest of us... So then"—the cool voice took on a warmer tone—"has that heart of fire I once promised you proved a true and constant blaze?"

Athyn blushed again. "Fire flares and flickers even where it burns the hottest; flame by its nature is never entirely constant—but aye, lady, it burns bright and clear and true. For that, all thanks." She paused a moment, to frame the question.

"But surely that is not why you called me here? For I *was* called?"

"When you did us the great service for which you were brought beneath the hill," said Seli at length, "you were promised whatever gift you asked of us. Many years have passed, and yet you have asked for nothing. Well, that promise shall stand until you do choose to redeem it; but of my own choosing I give you now a gift that has been yours from birth."

"Magic," said Athyn on a long wondering breath, suddenly cold with prescience, a kind of fearing, eager dread. "But my mother—"

"Your mother, knowing she would not live to see you past the moment of your birth, set geis upon Cormac when he found you, that he should not permit you to train for a sorceress."

"I know this *now*," said Athyn, almost crossly, and Seli smiled.

"And my sorrow you could not have known sooner, but do you also now know *why* she did so, the Lady Dechtira?" When Athyn remained silent: "Your mother was a great friend to our folk, a Ban-draoi, a very gifted one. We knew her, and loved her, and we knew of your coming. It is through her that you share kinship with the Sidhe."

"The long kinship, surely, through Brendan's mother Nia; but there are many houses in Keltia who share—"

Seli raised a white jewelled hand. "Closer even than that— and the blood does not always run true. It did in your mother, and it does in you; for that reason we called you to us in our need. When my son was set to come to the world of form, the one whose usual duty it is to preside at births among our folk did herself bid us send for you. And she was besought to do so by one who is mighty among our folk: Melidren he is named, called Melzier, or by some Merlynn, and he is one of those among us who See all turnings of the road ahead, for mortals and for Sidhe alike."

"And what did he see along that road for me?"

"In you he Saw the one to command the Outgoing that has now begun. That task is Blackmantle's, it has been hers or no one's since before the worlds were made; if she cannot accomplish it, it will never be accomplished at all. But I can See also, and it is on me that without magic, Athyn's task must ever go undone."

"But my geis—"

"—should never have been laid upon you. Your mother knew that through her you would be gifted outside the common run, that there would be both need and temptation to call upon forces that ought never to be called upon at all. Not black powers, but certain shades of gray that carry dánach shadings of their own—powers of anger, powers of avenging—and that you in your hunger for justice, or what you saw as justice, would call upon them—because you could. And against that she tried to shield you and protect you; a mother's loving thought, and peace to her on her road, we do not blame her for it. But too much sheltering, and things do not grow. Which is the stronger and the more enduring: the perfect planthouse rose that has been carefully kept from blight and storm, or the oak upon the mountain, twisted and gnarled, but which has withstood both wind and levin?"

Athyn had begun to tremble a little, not far off tears for the strangeness of it all. "Are you saying— What *are* you saying, lady? For by the Goddess I do not think I know."

Seli's voice was gentle now. "Though you knew it not, you have had magic always: wild magic, rogue magic, magic outside the laws of Draoícht; power neither bannachtas nor dróchtas, power which those laws do not, cannot order. Magic of my folk, not of yours. It is not given often or to many, Athyn, and those upon whom it descends must learn to live with it, for without it they cannot live at all. It is a rough magic that you cannot control but which you may command, and you must open yourself to it, so that it may do its work in the world. *Its* work; not yours. You are its servant; it is not your slave. It is lawful to refuse the work—that is a choice of dán, you may make it as you please—or even to abuse the gift, but there is no power under Kelu that can take either from you. Good or ill, bane or bless, it *is* you."

"Then my mother—"

"This and this alone is why Dechtira, herself a sorceress, did not wish you to learn sorcery. You are no Ban-draoi, but you may do such deeds in magic as none other in Keltia has ever done before, or will again after. It is what your mother feared; but also it may be what all Abred has awaited."

"Well, it is far too great and mighty for the likes of me!" said Athyn with some heat. "I may be Blackmantle by the Gwerin's grace; but beneath it all I am still Athyn nic Archill, horsegirl and foundling."

"That is merely what you are, and what you have been. What I ask now is not *what* are you but—*who* are you?"

Seli's words that had been gentle as a fall of spring rain seemed now to come harsh as stone from the deeps of the earth. Athyn went rigid as a statue, eyes wide, unseeing. Slowly she lifted her hands to the moon, elbows bent, palms upward as if to catch the light, and spoke in a drowned voice, as if the words were wrested past some strange lock set upon her speech.

"I am Tywarchwr, the plowing-ox on the turf side, whose tread breaks the hardgate so that the share may pass."

"Who shall come after?"

"After me Trinaethwr, the plowing-ox on the tilth side, whose tread opens furrows for the seed."

"And after him?"

"Comes then Faoltigherna, whose sickle reaps the field."

"Claim the magic, Athyn Cahanagh. It has been yours since worlds began."

And Athyn closed her fingers upon the silver light that filled her palms. As she did so, the night was set on fire, the hill rocked beneath her, a wind tore across the open moor; far off she heard a sound as of bells, and a cry of triumph torn from many throats. Next came a series of brief vivid flashes that

somehow she knew to be true Seeing: a cave, fire-litten darkness, a scent of roses and burning iron; then the shore of a great
water, and there was a sword in her hand, she was fighting
something she could not see, something with eyes, and she was
not winning, and white wings came across her sight; then
darkness again, and Morric standing alone, facing her across a
lake of cold flame, his face pale and stern and beautiful, his
hand outstretched to her, or was it held up to warn her off, she
could not tell... Then blackness; and when she came to herself
she was sprawled upon the damp ground, and she was alone,
and her hands were empty.

Aye, she thought with a certain soberness, as she rose to her
feet again, aching all over, and sought Rhufain where he had
wandered off, *but are they?*

Athyn pressed her face to the glass, a child nosing up against a
sweetshop window; only here the window was the vitriglass
port of a starship, and the sweetshop a vast one indeed—all
the endless starfields beyond. From across the width of the
common room of his swiftest and best-armed vessel, the *Lion of
Connacht,* Esmer smiled indulgently upon her, then continued
his quiet converse with his son-in-law Stellin. While Morric
in the deep-cushioned chair beside her—*The soulless slothel!
How* can *he?*—was actually *asleep...* For a brief instant Athyn
contemplated pinching him, or punching him, so that he
would wake to share her excitement, but he would only be
cross, and spoil the moment, and not even for him would she
risk that.

When Athyn had returned from A'Mhaighdean the
Gweriden had gasped to see her. Something tremendous had
happened to her there, of that there could be no doubt—not
even Morric was ever to hear the full story of what had passed
on the barren fell in the Solway Forest in the wild heart of
A'Mhaighdean—but to Athyn herself it had already begun to
seem an ashling, though she remembered every detail as if it

had been writ with a diamond upon some crystal window deep within her soul. But there had been little leisure for wondering, or pondering, for Esmer Lennox had had other plans...

So that now she clung to the starship viewport. It was her first time outside Keltic space, and she was almost ill with joy. *I am following the same star-roads my ancestors took when they came here with Brendan, I am seeing stars and worlds few Kelts have seen who are now alive...*

But few Kelts ever had seen these particular stars and worlds: Ganaster, the planet of their destination, third world of the white sun Nicanor, showed now below them. In those days it had only just begun to gain the unstained reputation for perfect impartiality that it enjoys even in these latter times, but even so it was often used for discreet councils such as this one that the Earl Lennox had arranged.

For Keltia was by no means the only world to have a history and a problem with the Incomers, and now that the Outgoing had commenced, Esmer could not be blamed for wanting to hasten it along; and to that purpose he sought common cause with those who shared his thought and Keltia's need.

Once they had landed, and Esmer had given leave to his train for a free afternoon before the morrow's duties, Athyn and Morric ran off hand in hand to explore. In the Ganastrian capital city of Eribol everything was fascinating, and not just by virtue of its foreignness: the beautiful public gardens behind the Houses of Justice—which would one day be called the High Justiciary, those who would sit therein swaying worlds they had never seen—the bright fountains, the waterstairs that ran bubbling along the streets, the market square where Athyn purchased gifts for her friends, and more for Morric, as he for her—it was all good and new and full of wonder, and even though they were here in the line of duty, they could not but feel it was a holiday all the same.

The Earl Lennox dispelled that notion speedily enough:

Arriving the next morning at the chambers requisitioned for the parley, Athyn and the other Gweriden looked at one another in disbelief, then looked round them in awe.

The hall was full of gallaín, not just the slender dark Ganastrians but many other races, more than she had ever seen in Caerdroia even in these days of Incomer sway. The tall lupine Welvos, the small feather-furred Chakur-churi, the caprine Valivandans, the humanoid Fasarini, the unspeakably majestic Hail, the Eagle-people— *And every single one of them with a mighty grafaun to grind against the Firvolgians…*

"Who is *that*?" she murmured to Greyloch, who sat on her left.

"That is the queen of Aojun," he whispered back. "The Jamadarin of the Yamazai, as her title is. They are a very great people."

Athyn studied the Aojunese party across the table's polished width. *So these are Yamazai! I have heard so much of them; but never did I think to meet one—much less their very queen…* Not much older than Athyn, Zarôndah daughter of Khareiten had been ruler for five years. She was fine-featured, with long gold-blond hair; beneath a necklace of gold pearls was engrained upon the golden skin the faint blue image of a running deer. Her consort beside her was as sun-bright as herself, with a face of great beauty and sweetness—Brahím, Subhadar of Aojun, like Morric a poet and songmaker.

But while Athyn sat thus musing the meeting had been opened, with a minimum of ceremony and due courtesies all round, and now Zarôndah, as ranking guest, was speaking in reply to Esmer's speech of welcome.

"—have had our own problems with the Incomers. If that word is a true one that my enemy's enemy is my friend, then we are friends already. The name of Velenax has been heard on Aojun before now."

Her words were echoed round the table by the others present, even Sathilano, the tall, staggeringly imposing representative of the Hail. Upon their nations too had come the

Incomer plague: Firvolgians taking advantage of a weak or unguarded moment, to sneak in like mice to a pantry, and make a nest there all under the panterer's nose. To combat this, various strategies had been adopted by various worlds; but in no world had the insidious invasion been more long-lasting than in Keltia—or the resistance more successful.

Athyn took pride on both counts. *They have infested Keltia worse than any other outfrenne realm, and we have no ruler, as they all have, to lead and hearten us; yet we have done better against them in shorter time than all these worlds combined...*

Over the days that followed, Athyn grew familiar with the histories of all those other worlds. They too had been subject to the same indignities as had the Kelts; had names for the Firvolgians more scathing far than 'Incomer,' which seemed now to her impossibly benign. Already she had come to be friends with some of the other delegates—Franca and Jarnithan from the Fasarine world Aquelana, Paonessa of the Yamazai, even the coolly ironic Sathilano—though other some still held their distance, and among those last was the Jamadarin Zarôndah, almost as if she strove against her own inclination. But one afternoon another, older distance unexpectedly closed, and in a fearful way...

"They are neither male nor female, these shape-strongs," said Stellin to Esmer, as they stood staring down at the Sospran's dead bleeding hulk. "And they die very, very hard."

They were standing in the public river-gardens behind the Houses of Justice, where, in broad daylight on a holiday afternoon, crowds of people everywhere, Athyn had just been attacked by a Sospran kedder, only the vigilance of Stellin Ardwyr and Esmer himself preventing its victory. Indeed, so hard had this particular one died that even with Breos and Failenn and Gerr mac an Aba helping, Esmer and Stellin had been sore pressed to bring it down; five armed trained Keltic warriors had only been just enough. It lay now upon the scuffled lawn, still twitching spasmodically—huge, scaled and feathered both, beaked and taloned, utterly alien; so that Athyn, staring at it, could only marvel.

"They are bloodhunters, tracker-assassins," said Esmer then. "They kill to order, and once they are on a blood-trail only their own death can stop them. Many worlds hire them for such work, for their relentless, some would say mindless, tenacity. It was fortunate we were so near—"

"I cannot believe that such a—notable thing as that could have come so close among us, in a garden full of folk, and was not challenged."

Despite the light tone, Athyn was more shaken than she cared to admit. She had stepped only a pace or two from the paved path, to admire a rose topiary, when the kedder struck. She never saw it coming, had not sensed the danger; the first she knew of it was when the blow had slammed into her ribs and sent her to the ground, and then the others had been there... She was not wounded, though her left side felt as if a horse had kicked her, and would be sore for days thereafter: The Sospran's three-edged ritual blade—known as a densaix, and used only in procured assassinations—had turned on the hidden findruinna mailcoat that Esmer had insisted she wear when she was out and about, and before the thing could strike again her friends were on it.

Nay; what alarms me most is that this creature knew me: It was for Athyn it was going, not Blackmantle... And if someone knew enough to send it after me, then what else might not that someone know, or other someones?

"They have a way of shielding themselves," said Breos in answer to what Athyn had said aloud. "They do not change shape, but take on the look of their surroundings, and are all but invisible until it is too late. It is a hard thing to guard against."

And they do not usually fail of their kill... With an effort Athyn turned away from the ghastly huddled thing upon the grass. Morric, still white to the lips with fear, and with anger that he had not been there—he had grown great friends with Brahím of Aojun, and the two had been trading barderies when news came of Athyn's encounter—pulled her to him under his cloak, both arms around her, and led her away.

Esmer set agents on the matter at once, and what they learned was unsettling. When the Earl told Athyn, she was silent a long while, and Ganor looked anxiously upon her. But she shook her head.

"Kier. I might have known. But how did he manage the commissioning—or did he? It is a very costly business hiring kedders, especially to hunt on a neutral offworld; it seems logical that he had help in the financing. But whose? And the great question is, does he—or do they—know me for Blackmantle, or were the assassins sent after Athyn alone?"

Esmer shot Ganor a long cryptical glance, then bent his gaze again on Athyn. "I cannot say, alanna. He is hunted by the Gwerin even now, both here and at home—though I doubt me he will be found."

"He is doing what he feels he must." It was evening of the third day since the attack; Athyn was calmer now, safe with the Lennoxes at the inn to which she and Morric had been newly removed. *Though it was only prudent to do so; if any of those—those creatures are left, they will have known where I lodged, and with whom; and another attack might not have ended so well. If Morric had been hurt...nay!*

"And making a right pig's ear of it too." Across the room, Mariota seethed a while in silence. "I tell you, Athwen, he has become such a mass of grandeur in his own mind that the work he set out to do with the Keavers is long forgotten. But that he should turn to the very ones he hated so long and so bitterly, and make common cause with them to try to— Nay, *that* I cannot understand!"

"No matter, m'chara," said Athyn. "I do."

* * *

Over the next several days three more kedders were tracked down and duly dispatched. The Ganastrians, appalled that such a thing could happen on their well-regulated world, offered apologies and protection, and Esmer accepted both— the latter much against Athyn's will. But she was alone in her protest; and in any case no more kedders showed themselves.

On the eighth day after the attack Esmer spoke at last to the assembly. Athyn, listening with the rest, observing the alien faces turned to him, thought that the problem seemed to be purely one of fear. The others at the table were in concert, no question, with Esmer's aims and goals, and trusted to Velenax's wisdom in war, but still they were reluctant to commit to any kind of union, openly looking to Zarôndah of Aojun for their cue. And though the Jamadarin was bent upon avenging the evils of Firvolgior against Aojun, she was not yet sure as to what action to take; or, if she were, she had not yet chosen to show it.

As Esmer and Zarôndah continued politely to box and bow, dodge and defer one to the other, suddenly it was with Athyn then as it had been once at Silverwood: The fíor-brethas came upon her, the truth-of-judgment, and she rose in her place. Esmer shot her a swift look; she did not even see him.

"I have heard your reasonings, madam," she said to Zarôndah, whose dark eyes were now studying her, "and know your cause. But if you will stand aside in this yet give us speech-support, we in return—should we be victorious—will promise to Aojun an alliance, full, free and fair. So swear I, Athyn Aoibhell"—here the Kelts startled, for never before had Athyn used her lawful birthname publicly; for her to use, in this moment, the name she had been born to was a declaration of no small degree—"brehon, Fian, captain over the Gwerin, captain-general of Keltia." And pushing her sleeve above her elbow she bared her sword-arm as was custom, the wolf and laighard engrains plain against her skin, and held it out to Zarôndah.

It was a challenge, right enough, and Athyn had staked all

upon it: that the Yamazai did not decline any gauntlet flung in honor; a temptation also, for that alliance was a thing Aojun sorely wanted. But more, it was the leap of faith of a heart trusting its own judgment; all Aojun had to do was leap and trust in turn—say approving words and stand out of Athyn's way—and more worlds would be swayed than Keltia and Aojun alone. The moment lengthened unendurably; at the table they kept their silence; Athyn began to wonder if she had read this foreign queen awry, had ruined all Esmer's plan for mere impulse's sake...

Then Zarôndah, after one swift look at Brahím beside her—who raised an eyebrow but said no word—and another, more searching one at Esmer, straightened and smiled; and rising in her place she leaned forward, to grasp Athyn's bared arm across the table, in the clasp of pledging.

"Silsilah Qelitin," she said in her own tongue. "Mirami Yemazain, kirdan khanatim." And the thing was done.

"She said—I am not yet fully fluent in Aojunese, it is a fluid subtle tongue—that Athyn was a chain to the Kelts, Zarôndah the same to the Yamazai, and the pledge between herself and Athyn the clasp that locked the chains together." Morric looked round at the faces of his comrades, together in Esmer's chambers after the day's council. "Well, that is the sense of it. The meaning is clear enough, though I daresay the translation could be more elegant."

"It suffices, amhic," said Ganor with a smile. Addressing her husband: "Oh, Lennox, leave off your muttering, you are like a wee dark cloud at the feast; it will be well, you shall see."

Esmer looked unhappier still. He did not much like surprises not of his own making, and this had been a very big surprise indeed. Not that Athyn had intervened—that he had been expecting, and he was only surprised that she had left it as late as she had. It was rather the nature of the intervention that alarmed him: She was his captain-general, and he trusted her, and loved her as his own daughter; but this had been a chancy moment, and he was not yet sure he quite forgave her.

"An alliance with an outfrenne power," he muttered fretfully, for at least the twentieth time. "And the Yamazai at that—they have never before allied with an outside world."

"No more have we," said Athyn lightly. "Long overdue on both sides, do you not think?"

"It is more a pledge of abeyance than alliance," said Stellin, with a certain disdain for the distinction. "They will stand away from our fight, and keep the others from clogging our sword-arms, yet not get involved themselves. No cost to them."

"Not now, perhaps," said Athyn. "But there yet may come a time when the Yamazai and the Kelts fight side by side. I am thinking of the long term—if I may speak as a former horsegirl before so elegant an assembly, I am out to breed stayers, not sprinters—and it seemed a risk worth the making, and the taking."

And so, long hence, it would be proved.

"Love in the middle of the afternoon," Morric was saying in a mock-disapproving voice; he and Athyn had not ventured out of their bedchamber—indeed, not out of their bed—since that morning's councils ended at noon, a half-day only, a forbearance begged by the Valivandans for religious reasons.

"Disgracefully indulgent," he pursued, "*and* most altogether fine. A religious purpose of our own, too, for look where we worship... But we must get up soon, slugabed. You know how Esmer is if we are not timely to supper."

Athyn did not stir. "Soon enough." Recalled to their earlier pursuit: "Ah, the gallaín say you are a hard man, Morric Douglas, but they have no idea..."

After a while, Morric said in quite a different tone, "I was considering the other day how often the Douglases and the

Aoibhells have come together before now. And how once in especial did they so."

Athyn, languorous after loving, had a look of brightness as she took his meaning. "And belike they will again. But their story is not ours. Well, unless perhaps we *are* they, returned to correctly complete those lives; even our hair is the same color as theirs."

He took the teasing as she had meant it. "Aye, well, if that should be, only pray gods we get it right at last. I cannot speak for you, cariadwyn," he said, and kissed her between her breasts, "but I would very much prefer not to go round the barn with this particular lesson one more time."

"That is as dán shall have it, depends on how well we both shall learn... But if we must come back for yet another go-around, I think next time, Morrighsaun, if it is all the same to you, *I* shall be the famous bard—*and* the man—and let you learn how it feels on this end of our mutual fate."

He laughed, and they lapsed again into drowsy silence, the plashing of the fountain in the garden court the only sound in the room, the scent of summerbyes and late roses wine-heavy in the golden air.

Their cryptical allusions were to a flame-tressed princess of the Thomond Aoibhells two hundred years past, Lassarina, and her darkhaired consort, Séomaighas, another Douglas; the story was one of the great romances of Keltia. They had both been gifted bards, he a poet, she a fabulist; he had died untimely, slain soon after their marriage, and she had lived on many decades without him, refusing to take to herself another lord or lover, holding herself still wed.

Which indeed she was, Athyn reflected. *To choose your mate forever—to know you are not mistaken, and to trust to that sureness past life and time alike...* She herself had never, until meeting the man whose dark head rested now upon her middle, been able to imagine the feeling that Lassarina Aoibhell had had for her own Douglas bard. *Perhaps we are even kin, she and I, or Morric kin to Séomaighas. Not from themselves, right enough,*

*for those two left no heir behind them. They were too much in love
with each other to bring anyone else into it; they would not spare or
share each other with even their own children. It may seem strange
to most but it is a thing I well understand…*

"There is only one Fireheart," she said aloud, in the tone of
a quotation, though she could not recall who had said so, or
when.

But Morric lifted his head from where it had lain, his arms
enclosing her and dán together as he answered her in the High
Gaeloch, the formal tongue of poetry and state and love.

"And he is only thine."

chapter seventeen

Stronger is the thread twined than single.

—*Bronwyn Muirheyd*

The Gwerin were deeply pleased to hear what their captain had to tell them of Ganaster, and had good news of their own to give her on her return. There was a feeling that things were well afoot now: Athyn had secured the help of the Sidhe, at least in such matters as the Shining Folk could or would attend to; and now the Gwerin had outfrenne allies also.

The good news the Gwerin passed on to Athyn was that the Keavers had during her stay in Eribol vanished almost entirely from the picture. Athyn was pleased, but wary: Kier was still out there, for one thing; and who knew how many of his fellow Keavers still felt as he had felt, or would choose to do somewhat about it—as indeed he had done?

Morric too had tidings; his spy network passed on to him what they had heard of late, all of which must be sifted like goldsands in a streambed for the few glittering flakes of pure truth. He did not usually seek word of his former friends; but from time to time, he would receive news of Loris Venoët's company of travelling musicians and guisers—which now boasted Shane, Erramun, Jaffran and Evance in its numbers—and Athyn was not alone in noticing that he never turned the messengers away.

It was a strange and uneven grouping of outworn broken talents, once-beens and never-weres; among the musicians was a tenth-rate chaunter called Juho Alessos, who, finding that these four were indeed the veridical onetime bandmates of Morric Douglas, had begun, extraordinarily, to ape Morric, singing Morric's songs, speaking as Morric spoke, dressing as Morric was accustomed to dress, even coercing Evance to play gittern to his chaunting—all to Morric's vast amusement, and Athyn's profound annoyance.

The Incomers quickly saw the advantage to themselves of sponsoring an impostor to confuse and subvert the Kelts, and for his part Alessos soon began to believe that not only was he as good a bard as Morric Douglas, he *was* Morric Douglas, in his demented fancy even requiring folk to address him as 'Morric' when he sang.

"This Ser Juho," said an exasperated Athyn one day to her mate, when they were snatching an ever rarer private evening in their favorite inn at Shanagolden. "Perhaps I should summon him here, find if he is any more reasonable than you are. I might do better with the counterfeit Morric Douglas than the original."

"You are welcome enough to try," returned that original, peacefully.

"Nay," she said then, with a sigh for that legendary duck's-back of his, apparently as impervious as ever even to her barbs, "if ever I do seek him out it will be to punish him as he well deserves, for his sins of imposture, against you and against art both alike. But, we shall see."

The faintest flicker of discomfortableness crossed Morric's face then, and Athyn turning to look at him was quick enough to catch the expression.

"Oh, *what!*" she cried. "May I not say how much I loathe vermin before I squash them? I could gralloch the lot of them like deer, or cut out their spleens with a toasting-fork, or a tuning-fork, and stuff them in their mouths like apples. Indeed, I may yet. So many slugs, so little time... Their heads on a platter would be a pleasant sight. Many heads. Many platters." She looked at him from eyes gone suddenly gem-hard. "I know what *your* trouble is… You think me too harsh and hard upon our enemies. Let me tell you, cariadwyn, I could handle them all with rougher mittens than ever yet you have seen me use. How is it you do not seem to wish me to do so?"

"Because that side of you affears me," he said at once. "You are a warrior and I am not. It is your trade, and I do not always understand."

Athyn rolled her eyes; but briefly, because she loved him. "What is there to understand, or to fear either? I am a Kelt. Kelts fight. Kelts have always fought. It is what we do. This is not a difficult concept to grasp. The Fir Bolc are here, I want them gone, I will hit them with swords until they are all gone or they are all dead. It is my way. It is what I do. That is not over-hard to grasp either. Besides," she added when he still did not reply, "who is it dares say you are not a warrior? There are ways and ways of fighting, and it is the heart that makes the fighter, not the sword."

"Sword helps, though."

"Oh aye, it helps, right enough. But it is not the only weapon. Perhaps not even the best weapon. But sometimes, so often, it is the only weapon we have. And that of itself makes it the best."

Morric shook himself, and buried his face in Athyn's hair. *There is no winning with her in such a mood…* But as so often when their bodies were close, and many times when they were not, they caught echoes from each other's mind without even trying, and now she found courage to lay aside her shield.

"My greatest fear for you," she whispered then against his bearded jaw. "I never speak of it to you because, I know not, somehow that might make it true, but— You are out there before the people, your name is known; you are so open when you sing, there are such dangerous folk can come far too nigh you…"

He chose his usual weapon against this sort of thing,

though he would not let her see that the thought was no stranger to him.

"You fear someone might put a fork through my throat one night because he did not care for the way I sang his favorite ballad?"

"It is no jesting matter, Morric—"

"I know it is not. All the same, anghariad, I think it by far the least of the worries you should entertain just now." He kissed her bare shoulder. "What is it that Ganor is always saying—'It is well. You shall see.' It is. And you shall."

Before she could get worked up to it again, there came a tiny tapping at the door: the innkeeper, Fleance, his face grave. Courtesy made him lower his eyes, though they were by no means engaged in amorous pursuit. But he would have done the same had they been embracing while fully clothed; in Keltia mere nakedness is nothing. It is intimacy, rather, upon which a Kelt's good manners never allow him to intrude; and so Fleance's did now.

"I would not trouble you, m'charai, but I have just had word from the gate that a band of mosstroops has entered the town. They are asking all over for any Gwerin or sympathizers, and Athyn Cahanagh in especial. Someone must have sighted and recognized you as you rode in."

"Mochyn yn y lliath!" swore Athyn, and even in that crowded moment Morric grinned.

"'The pig in the *milk*!'?" he asked, shaking his head in mock despair. "No woman of mine swears like a mollymop—"

"Aye, well, put your mind to my imprecatives another time. And somewhat else for you to ponder at leisure, tunesmith: How comes it that every time we are together in an inn with romantic intent we are chased off by someone or ever we get to that intent's fulfilling?" She was laughing in spite of herself as they hastily dressed. "It happens *everywhere*, Morric, and I for one am weary of it—Tamon Acanis, Graystones, Caer Dathyl, here... Routed yet again! Mighty Gwener!" She turned to the innkeeper. "Can we slip out without being seen, Fleance?"

"Trivially," he said with pride. "There are secret ways, vennels, that lead down to the river, and some out onto the open plain, far from roads or housen."

"Well," she said as they followed him down to the cellarage, "it is a dead horse that never stumbles. But all the same, I wish we could have gone unnoted."

"There, cariad, you see?" Even in his alarm Morric could not forbear to keep the triumph out of his voice. "You were fretting about someone sticking a knife in me, and all the time there were coursers hot upon your track instead..."

"And what makes you think they are following me?" she threw back at him over her shoulder; but she was laughing again. "I shall not dispute with you just now—*cariad*—but—another thing Ganor is fond of saying—later for you. Aye, later it shall be. Now you are warned."

They came safe away, as ever—in after years Queen Athyn was often heard to remark that it seemed her entire romance with her lord the King was punctuated at the least opportune moments by the vain efforts of the most uncompetent of hunters, who chased and chased and never got anywhere, any more than she and Morric did—and the campaign continued.

There came a day when the Gweriden could not find Athyn at Seana Bhraigh or Nancledra or any other of the camps they had made. At Casterlines and Shanagolden none had seen her; and Ardturach was innocent of her presence. Morric was undisturbed, the Earl Esmer undismayed; but there had been too many attempts on all their lives in recent days for her disappearance now to be entirely easeful to those who loved her—the memory of the kedder attack on Ganaster had not faded in anyone's memory—and the news of her absence was kept as close as the Gweriden could manage, lest it fall in at the wrong ears.

But they need not have fretted.

*   *   *

At the sound of the bell-branch behind her Athyn smiled. *Pray Goddess, all our allies shall be as true as these...*

"You are most careful in your coming, lord; timely, too. Tonight we ride."

Allyn son of Midna stepped from the air and stood before her. They were deep in Druimattow; on every side the Long Hills rose up around them.

"You go to Caledon, to the field at Gala," he agreed. "Aye, we know. We shall be there. And to that end there is somewhat we would give you, and something I must tell you. First, the gift."

Athyn stared down at the thing he put into her hands. It was a piece of soft silver woven as fine as a gossamer scarf, and, though not heavy, heavier far than it looked, and not with mere weight alone.

"It is beautiful! What is it?"

"Armor. Wear it in the fight at Gala Water. Put it on now."

She glanced briefly at him and away again, as if to say Indeed! But he was smiling.

"Nay, truly. Drape it round your shoulders and cross it on your breast."

Athyn raised a skeptic brow, but did as she was bidden. On the instant the silver mail was transformed into a kind of frozen silk: It gleamed like still water under the moon, clung fluidly to her body's curves, covered her front and back, throat to thigh. It moved as she moved, flexible as cloth, and yet was proof against points; so tightly and seamlessly did it shield her that not a gap showed through of her padded battle tunic beneath.

She shook her head in wonder. "It is marvellous," she said simply, spreading her hands, drawing her fingertips over the glittering shell. "But while I think of it, how comes it you know there will even be a fight at Gala Water?"

Allyn turned that aside. "This is a silverskin, the armor my folk use amongst themselves. The corrigauns make it for us; it is proof against most things. This one was forged in Gavannaun's own smithy."

"And therefore has divine provenance as well. I cannot speak the thanks I would, my lord, to you and your kindred, to those who made this armor. But I will take no advantage in battle for myself that my Gwerin have not also."

"A noble sentiment, and one we expected from you," said Allyn, smiling again and shaking his head. "But you may care to reconsider. I know the Gwerin would insist, were I to tell them; as well I might, if you do not give me assurances... Any road, we seldom give silverskins to any but our own."

Athyn looked at him with sudden curiosity. "And why do you do so now? Do the Shining Folk know a thing I do not know?"

"Saving your reverence," he said, and if he had not been of the Sidhe she would have said he teased, "that is very likely. One thing I do know is that very few others of the Gwerin have been sought by Sospran kedders on a deathtrail, whose densaix have a certain name writ in blood upon them, against which a silverskin might be the only armor that could prevail."

"Ah. You have heard about that, have you?" Athyn seemed unconcerned. "Well, any road, they were all destroyed; and I am still here."

Not even to Allyn would she admit how near a thing it had been, though she had a fair idea he knew at least as much about it as she did. True, it had not been her actual blood consecrating those blades to her destruction—though they would have put it there if they could—but she was the one they sought, and only the swords of the Gweriden had kept her blood off the densaix when at last the kedders struck.

More than that, who was it in truth who had bought their murderous service? Kier, working for, or with, the Incomers? Or, though it cut like a tip-whip to think it, Kelts? Kelts who perhaps preferred things as they had been, the status quo ante, and thought the surest way to get them back again was to remove the one who was causing them to change? *It would take at least that much to halt me; I would spend my blood and more to buy those changes for my folk, and think it well spent…*

"What do *you* think I should do?" she asked abruptly, as if she spoke to a brother or a friend and not to a lord of the Sidhe. "You have known me from a child tending horses in an upland pasture; I have now very few others in my life who can say as much. You have seen me at my best times and my worst, and yet you will not judge."

"We seldom do," said Allyn. "All advice and judgment may go awry, yet in this matter I shall take it upon me to say this much, for this is what I was sent to tell you, or to remind you: If ever a task was meant by dán for anyone, this task was meant for Blackmantle; and if she cannot manage it to completion no one can. As to whether *you* can, that is where our judgment must end."

Athyn laughed. "Ah, the eternal ambiguity of the Sidhe!"

"I am thinking of Athyn Ard-rían," said Allyn after a while. "And of King Morric Fireheart at her side."

She flinched as if he had struck her, raised a troubled glance to his.

"Why does that fret you?" he asked gently. "We too long to see the Throne of Scone occupied again, for it is then that Keltia is most truly itself, and we with it… But this you know— Has not Esmer told you of what he has planned?"

"Not in so many words, or those words." She was choosing her own words carefully now. "When first he spoke to me about throwing out the Incomers, he took care to frame it in such wise as would not fright me: namely, only, that I should lead a resistance that he and other Marcher Lords would finance and support, and the expulsion from Keltia of the Firvolgi would be the end to which we strove. And that was good, that was fine, that end I was glad to serve! Not a word was spoken of a crown in store; and if he *had* offered one, hear me Goddess, I would have intemperately fled." She gave a short laugh and a sidewise shrug. "I thought myself the foundling Athyn nic Archill, fortunate beyond dreams to be liegewoman to Esmer and Ganor, friend to Mariota, brehon and Fian to the Name of Lennox—more fortunate still to have Morric Douglas for my mate. Gods hear me, I wished no more, and surely I did not seek it."

"And now?" came the viol-voice.

"And now—I do not know. Esmer still has said naught of the Ard-tiarnas, at least not to me. But from a thousand thousand things he and others have let slip—"

"Does it mislike you so, then? To be High Queen is a worshipful thing."

"Do you know, it does not seem to be altogether me," she allowed grimly, though not without humor. "And certainly it is not why I fight, why I called together the Gwerin, why the Gweriden came to my side—"

"They came because they love you and what you fight for; and because you love them, and they know that also. To accept the Copper Crown, for dán's sake, and Keltia's, and your own—that is much to ask, but what is it when set against all the rest?" Allyn's voice flared suddenly with as near a thing to anger as she had ever heard among the Sidhe. "If Athyn Cahanagh must take the Crown, if that is the only means to save the Keltic way against the outside worlds, then she must take it, and so save it; and if only Blackmantle can bring it about, then that is what Blackmantle must do."

"It seemed all ashlings of grandeur," she said with a shame-faced air. "I felt reluctant to think that it was I whom all the signs had meant; it seemed—"

"Vanity? Vainglory? Delusions of traha?" Allyn smiled again, the anger, if anger it had been, vanished away. "Only the one who was fated for such dán, and humble with it, would feel such scruples. Dán has been shouting out to you all your days, Athyn Aoibhell. Will you not speak back to it at last? Will you not give up the fight-against? It is the noble feeling of a noble soul, and does you great credit in this life and all lives.

But the fight-for will be made immeasurably easier, for you and for others, if you accept your part at last."

Athyn flung out her hands, made one last protest. "But there will be such terrible things that come of it! I have Seen some of them, and I would for no sake cause them to be. Perhaps I have not the courage after all."

"Aye, dreadful things, right enough; but glorious ones too. That is not an argument. Courage is not the absence of fear—only fools are fearless—but the acting in fear's despite. And by that definition, you have never lacked for courage in your life. It will be fearful in any case—that is not yours to rule—but only do what is yours to do, and it will still be less evil than it might have been. That, my folk can promise you," he added, less sternly, "and we do. It is all that we may promise, for we have affairs of our own that need tending."

"Edeyrn," said Athyn. "The Queen Seli—"

Allyn bent his head in assent, but though she waited, he offered no word more.

"What shall I do now?" she asked then. "At the very least, out of our friendship, if it is friendship, tell me that."

"Friendship it is, and it is as friend that I say it: Go now to Caledon, and meet the dán that has been prepared for you and for many. It is waiting."

And with that far from reassuring word he was gone, and Athyn left alone on the edge of the flaming wood. *I have come to the end of choosing,* she thought, and knew that it was true. She looked across the hills to Sheehallion like a mailed fist raised against the sky; nor light nor jewel now flashed from that high peak. *That narrowing of choices—at last it has come down to one; as I knew it must. From here on there are no more choices; they have all been made. It only remains to live them. And is it dán as Allyn says? Did I choose, or was I chosen? And does it matter? Either way, it is on me that we are all about to learn the answers...*

BOOK III

For I am of the children of Forever
I dwell in far valleys and great silences
In strange light and cold air
And on some mornings
I can see a banner in the clouds

—Séomaighas Douglas Ó Morrighsaun

If a wife be denied by her enemies her name
and her love
and her truth
and her honor
She will never forget it
She will never forgive it
and she will want it back.

And she will take it back:
For she will fight
And she shall win
And they shall be destroyed.

—Lassarina Aoibhell ac Douglas

chapter eighteen

Shallow waters make the most noise; shallow souls
cannot harbor deep truths.

—*Morvoren Kindellan*

Though sometimes it seemed that the struggle between
Kelts and Fir Bolc had dragged on since time began, in
truth Athyn Cahanagh's actual campaign had been
underway for little more than seven years, though even Esmer
Lennox was startled and surprised when he remembered that.

But if the span had been so brief, the success had been by
anyone's measure staggering. There were many reasons for
it, Athyn of the Battles herself not least among them. But
even Athyn freely admitted that the chief cause for the
Outgoing succeeding where all other attempts to drive out
the Firvolgi had failed was a very simple one: For the first
time, the Kelts wanted it to happen. For the first time it
mattered more to them that the Incomers be ousted than
who should wear the Copper Crown or have pre-eminence
among the clanns.

And all this had led them to that sword-moment, that
balance-point where neither Gwerin nor Incomers could
afford not to triumph: the Gwerin because they had won
and won, the Incomers because they had lost and lost.
Other battles came after; but that fight beside the Gala
Water was the hinge where history swung: Whether open
or closed, depended solely on which side of the Door one
chanced to be.

*   *   *

The planet Caledon, first world of the Scotan system to be settled, is the largest inhabited planet to circle any of the seven
Keltic stars. Erinna and Gwynedd are much of a size, and Tara
the Throneworld larger than both, but for bigness among them
Caledon takes the palm. A fair world too; not so harshly lovely
as Gwynedd nor so lush as Erinna, but possessed of beauty all its
own, and in places just as harsh and lush and lovely.

Gala province, in the westlin airts of the main continent, is
fringed by the sea on the west and fenced by mountains on the
east. With such isolating topography, no surprise that the sea
plays so vital a part in its life—narrow fingers of ocean reach
many miles into the province's heart, clawing at the land—
and where the young mountains rise up the ground is unstable
all the way to the planet's core. Vast earthshakes are by no
means unknown along that coast, and any sorcerer who can
command the forces which move the lands and uphold the
oceans is welcome to reside.

In those days there were few settlements thereabouts, so
that the provincial capital, the market town of Galashiels,
became Athyn's base for the fight. She moved swiftly; but even
so she was only just in time, seizing Galashiels days before a
strong Incomer contingent was sent to occupy it against her.
Any prudent commander would want to hold it: On the banks
of the broad Gala Water, with an outlet through Loch Grane
to the sea, it was no street-town but a true cashel, the massive
round stonework of Sithney's Keep rising above the red tile
roofs of the housen clustered below.

"It looks more like a keeve than a keep," remarked Morric,
knee to knee beside Athyn on his black mare Glesni. "But if it
holds its contents as it seems able, I shall make a praise-song to
the cooper."

"Oh, it is always about *ale* with you bards—"

They were riding into Galashiels by the main gate; the
Gwerin had taken the town three days before. It was the first

time Morric had ridden to battle with her, and she was not sure how she felt about it: very glad to have him by her, yet feared for the new light in which he should soon be seeing her.

"It will be strange to watch you in battle," he said then, as if he had heard. "It will not trouble you, that I am here? I should hate to have my presence drag on your sword-arm when so much is carried upon it."

"You have never seen me kill," she said in a low voice. "Will that not trouble you?"

He smiled, and reached across to put a hand on her thigh above the high-cut cavalry boot. "Why should it? Aescaileas himself fought at the battle of Marathon— But as I have many times told you, though even I know what happens in a fight, I am no warrior; and as you have many times told me, it is what you do." He tightened his grasp briefly. "But it is not all you do. And any road, nothing you could do can ever trouble me. Have you not yet learned?"

On Lughnasa morning, three days later, Athyn rode out of the gates of Galashiels, between rows of soldiery who flung her name—the name they had been first to give her—against the hills, until valleys ten miles away rang with one word like a great iron bell. *Blackmantle… I seem to have accepted it, and all that goes with it, gods help me…*

Coming to the ground, she swept her gaze over the field placements, noting with approval where Breos mac an Aba— whose own country this was, and so he was war-lord this day—had taken advantage of natural features, that the land itself might fight for them: the hills sweeping down almost to the edge of Loch Grane, Gala Water entering the loch from the northeast, and, broadening, heading out of it southwest to the sea. Those hills now held Gwerin cavalry massed to charge, the slope lending them weight and speed; and standing off the coast beyond the mouth of Gala, waiting only the signal to sail, a fleet of lymphads kept station, black-hulled war-galleys with crimson sails, and Morvoren Kindellan as admiral on the flagship's deck.

Athyn drew rein atop a knoll where the Gwerin standard of a seven-pointed star rolled out on the wind beside her own of the crowned laighard on a black field. Her other banner, equally known in the land—the rearing white stallion, for Cahanagh and Caerlaverock—was borne for her today by her Aoibhell cousin Raffan, Maravaun of Thomond's heir; a tall young man a few years her senior, with the red hair of his kindred and a cheerful nature. Now he gestured out over the ground where the armies were well drawn up, and back to Galashiels behind them, and smiled.

"Cousin, they are all yours."

They were hers, right enough; and she, of course, was theirs... Athyn rose in her irons, and beneath her Rhufain ceased his dancing and stood like a rock in a river. Off to one side the war-hounds of the Gweriden were holding battle council of their own: Athyn's red-brindle wolfhound Ardattin, Stellin and Mariota's golden Mâli, Greyloch's snowy Liadan, Shelia who owned Selanie and Rhain, and Phaal and Cathárren's Sionnabharra, who looked more like a great red bear than a dog.

It was not Athyn's custom in such moments to make noble grand addresses; and any road, it was Morric's job, not hers, to put these things into fine words. But today the land between hills and loch threw back the echoes of a very short speech shouted to the troops; and when she was done, they cheered and settled down to the business of the day.

But not just yet their leader: Athyn was running over the Litany to the Goddess—some of the Lady's more warlike attributes, as seemed suited to the day's need.

"Breastplate of the Gael—Spear of Midna"—unable to escape the thought of Allyn that leaped to her mind, and the guilt likewise, for she had after much thought chosen to leave the silverskin behind, and had ridden to this fight in the same lorica worn by everyone else—"Raven Battlequeen—Caer of the Valiant—Avenger of Blood—"

Breos leaned over, touched her arm, and she started; she had not been aware that she was praying aloud.

"If She is not with us by now, Athyn, She shall never be, though I know She is..."

He spoke truly; but then the battle was joined, and almost it did not matter.

It was sung after, and by more bards than Morric Douglas alone, that at Gala that day no sword slept at its owner's side. In his black chariot Stellin Ardwyr went stroke for stroke against the Firvolgi, as did Rhain Son of the Eagle at the head of his horse. From the lymphads on Loch Grane Morvoren Kindellan raised the ros-catha, Athyn's own war-cry 'Go sian-saoghail!'—'To the world's end!'—as those dark deadly galleys, foaming up the Gala Water from the sea, closed with the clumsy Incomer ships, fighting black swans against ungainly geese.

On the edge of Gala Wood, Tipherris Greyloch commanded the foot, and Liadan in her war-collar ranged ahead, her white coat already streaked with the blood of lesser opponents. On a high slope Selanie Drummond, Bronwyn Muirheyd and Cathárren Tanaithe were linked in a circle, armored in the power of the Goddess as they worked their war-witchery against the enemy sorcerers, flinging back the Firvolgi charms with counterspells like lasra flains.

All the Gwerin upon that Lughnasa field did fight like heroes, and the Gweriden who had ridden with Blackmantle to Gala Mains—Mariota, her hair flame-red for battle; Sosánaigh, harp set aside for her sword; Gerr mac an Aba, brother to Breos, and Failenn his tall mate; Alveric Elshender in his beaked chariot, Mihangel Glenrossa and Robat his sturdy brother, Periel Vailluin and Phaal Torcwyn and Lira Cromell and more beside—well, all they did fight like gods.

Elsewhere too they fought that day of days, not Caledon alone saw their valor: On Dyved, Rhodri of Lochaber led against fierce odds to smash the combined Incomer armies still plaguing that world, and on Gwynedd Micháltaigh Pendreic swept down out of the Arvon hills like the north wind onto the plain—even as, centuries hence, would do also the most illustrious son of the House that he was yet to found, and to a victory as complete.

But between Gala Water and Loch Grane was dán's full theme played out.

"Hujah!" cried one exultant kern, who lived to exult again after. "This is wild work!"

And so it was.

Athyn herself had held back at first from the fight, still constrained a little by Morric's presence; but once the battle was joined she forgot to remember, and as was her wont she led the Gweriden guard into the thickest of the fighting, when and where relief was needed. Morric rode with them, and for all the boasts he had made her that he was no fighter, Athyn was unsurprised to see that he could wield a sword almost as well as he could a song.

It was on one of these forays that she was driven apart, carried on the battle-tide almost to the reed-beds along the loch shore. Cutting her way back to the hill where her own standard still fluttered, she turned to the hail of her byname shouted by kerns who were near, and out of the dust and smoke she saw a familiar face loom, though so distorted was it in that instant that she barely knew him: Kier mac Archill.

And he saw her, and knew her, he had heard the kerns call her by the hated name. *Well, that is it, then. No longer can Athyn Cahanagh stand apart from Blackmantle, or hide behind that cloak...* She felt strangely relieved that the long double masque at last was over. Then all her attention was for her former foster: Kier shouting, Kier running, ignoring all others who stood between them, the huge barbed pike he bore aimed straight at Athyn's chest.

She had time for one gaily rueful thought—*Next time, and I only hope there is one, I shall take my lord Allyn's advice on armor*—and then thought no more but only fought.

In a misty twilight Athyn came to herself again. It seemed many hours later; the battle was long over, the field quiet save for the crying of hawks, or more sinister birds, high above. No one was near, neither quick nor slain.

What woke me? It seemed that someone called; not Morric, not my friends… Memory came back in thick patchy waves: Kier, a blow that connected, a missed parry, a push of pike that had struck hard and bloody. *Well, and a pike is much longer than a sword, I am scarcely to be blamed for that*… After she had been thrown out of her saddle, under cover of battle's smoke she had dragged herself into a ditch that led to a deep fernbrake, and there collapsed; but the same leafy concealment that had saved her from the enemy had also hidden her from rescuers.

She struggled up now on one elbow, peered through the fernstalks. *It looks as if we had the victory, though I cannot tell for sure*… From this low vantage she could make out a little way off, through the evening mist and the blue bonfire haze, some of the Gwerin who were even now frantically seeking her; but she had not the strength to call out, and she was aware of something very much amiss with her left side.

Allyn will be angered that I did not wear the magic armor; but it seemed somehow dishonorable. Blackmantle must bide the battle-hazard like everyone else—but I daresay I would not now be lying here if I had. Well, and I did get in a blow on Kier, though I do not think I killed him. Worst of all is that he knows me now for Blackmantle without a doubt, that secret is blown to streamereens. But then he did not kill me, either…and Morric will be so angry that I might well wish my chiel fostern had killed me. I am so tired, and so cold, and whatever I did to my side, or was done to it, it is noth-

ing good. So, I will sleep, just a little, and then I will crawl out of here…well, unless by then I am dead in this ditch, in which case I shall not…

The thought struck her as comic, and she laughed, and then she burrowed down among the mosses and the ferns, to sleep, just a little.

When they found her she was chill and still, her skin as cold as a frog's. Even her shivering reflex had stopped; her heart fluttered like a trapped wren beneath the healers' hands. They stripped off their own cloaks on the spot, to wrap her in, and the search was called off. But the fear was not so easily put paid to.

The wounds, thankfully, were—some broken ribs and a gash or two the worst of them. More accurately, the thanks were due to Sosánaigh Darnaway's cousin Liaun, a Fian healer who after years of work had perfected, only days before, a wondrous new tool called a skinfuser, a lasra suturer. It sealed tissue and nerve together, so that torn wounded skin and flesh, and even blood vessels, could actually be stitched whole again with light— though doubtless its inventor had never dreamed that it should have been so timely wrought, still less that one of its very first field tests should be on Blackmantle herself.

Athyn would have given greater thanks still if some equally miraculous invention could have spared her from the lacerating scoldings she received from Esmer and Morric; but on the whole she had come away very lightly and very lucky, and well she knew it.

Early evening of the following day. Against all advice of the healers Athyn rode with some of the Gweriden the few miles back to Gala Mains. Sitting Rhufain again—having scorned the chariot they had urged on her—atop the same knoll where she had shouted to the Gwerin the day before, she beheld the ruin of Firvolgi defenses in Gala and Firvolgi hopes in Caledon alike.

Mighty Mother! Only a day and a half gone by since we rode out to make this fight, and see, sense, what change has been here... Her gaze travelled on to the loch, and the new outcrops that broke the shining surface: the huge Firvolgian caravels sunk where the Keltic lymphads had sent them, hulks half-burned, half-drowned, and all within them lost.

"A bonny sight, sirs and ladies—Breosaighed is much to be thanked." *'Fire-arrow'—well has Breos earned the byname the Gwerin gave him for his generalship in this fight...*

But for all her outward calm, Athyn was rocked to her soul by the visible devastation, and by the other, more numinous havoc that overhangs a battlefield on the inner landscape—though none of this would she allow the others to see. Long before the circuit was completed she had begun to tire, though she dared not dismount, praying she could keep her seat and bitterly regretful that she had not chosen the comfortable chariot after all. But she was resolved not to show this either, for they would but crow and send her back to bed.

But at last she could conceal it no longer. Her legs had begun to tremble where the long muscles pressed against Rhufain's flanks, and she swayed in the saddle, muttering to those who were next her some small grudging admission as to how she might not just yet be entirely up to her own mark; might even, perhaps, possibly, do well to rest as the healers had bidden her.

"Oh aye! The Gweriden will believe that when they see it," came a skeptical voice, "and maybe not even then."

Athyn laughed. "Who says so? You, Glenrossa? Well, I daresay you have the right of it; but I shall comfort myself meanwhiles with a sacred text that will tell me how, in other times and other places, my enemies shall suffer greatly, even as I wish, indeed more greatly than myself."

"No sacred text says anything of the sort!" objected Katterin de Curteis, scandalized.

Athyn grinned at her. "Then I shall write it myself. But I *will* be comforted."

*   *   *

They broke the leaguer a day later, and the army began to disperse. Having been conveyed to Roslin Castle, the chief Gwerin stronghold on Caledon, Athyn found herself a prisoner of the healers, with no more say in the matter than the least trooper in her forces. She was not used to being idle and immobile while others did and moved as they pleased, and she did not think she liked it much.

But the healers were as one in their verdict that Athyn should not return to command this side of a sevennight, however fit she might claim to feel. So she had complied punctiliously with their orders, and cheered herself by making everyone's life pure hell.

"And she is so good at it, too," moaned more than one of the Gweriden; but there was none among them who grudged her the game.

Apart from herself, Athyn's only personal casualty of battle had been Cormac's far-famed black leather war-cloak. At first she had borrowed another until it should be mended; but the sempsters came long-faced to tell her it was a lost cause. Cormac's garment was too ancient to be saved, too badly damaged by mud and blood and steel, and Athyn was distressed out of all reasonable measure to hear it.

"I know how you feel," said Morric, though he was not sure he did. "But it had a long honorable service; and it is, after all, only a cloak. A queen cannot be seen in so threadbare a garment, however great her fondness for its former owner; or, if she is fond, all the more reason to put it away in honor."

"Leather *has* no threads! And I am no queen, thank you never so much, and if I have aught to say in it shall never be one—" *No longer to wear Cormac's cloak—still, all things change...* "What then do I put on my back in its place, balladmonger?"

"Something perhaps more suited to the name of Blackmantle— If you choose to answer to a name of legend you must also dress the part; the folk like to see it. And so, I must say, do I."

What he took from the press was a cloak made of black snakeskins stitched together with silver wire; lined with leather softer than silk, and with a weighted hem for riding, it was hooded and collared and trimmed with a deep full ruff of black fur. The cloak was supple as water; when Morric put it upon her shoulders it fell round her like a dark living splendor shot with sparks.

"I did not think it would look like *that*," she said.

"I knew it would," said Morric, watching her in the mirror. "It is sturdier than it looks. Not, say, that you should wear it into battle, or to clean out the stables—but you have not been doing so much of that last, at least not lately."

"Not lately." She grinned. "But as to battle wear it might prove just the thing. If I wear this onto the field, folk may think I am so confident of victory as to be sure my very cloak shall go unsoiled." She looked at him, and did not smile. "Cariadwyn," she said, and the word carried all that was in her heart.

The bed was empty beside her, the hollow cold where he had lain. She rose and wrapped herself in the new cloak—unarguably splendid as it was, still it was not Cormac's, and she was grieved all over again when she thought of it—and went out into the dark of owl-time to look for him.

She found him on the battlements, head lifted, hair stirred by the night breezes. He was looking out across the moonlit expanse of the Teviot Side, up to the great dark folds of the Orrest hills. Over there, she knew, on the other side of those hills, lay the Ruchdi Valley—and Meldeburna, where he had been born. That place where he had lived all his young life, had suffered, had wept, had been forged into the singular soul that she so greatly loved...

It must have been for him like a bow being bent, drawn and drawn and held, the archer's arm trembling with the pull, his fingers bleeding where they kept the arrow on the string, full-drawn to the very barb, until at last the target is sighted and the string is loosed and the arrow flies; or maybe like a ship rising up from a planet, swifter and swifter, until escape velocity breaks the planet's shackles and the ship is free of the stars. But he has been free far longer than he knows...

"Love?"

"Aye."

Who spoke first? Who answered?

And who—or what—was it that did hear?

chapter nineteen

Faults are thick where love is thin.

—*Katterin de Cuirteis*

After the fight by Grane and Gala the Incomer presence on Caledon was broken for good and all. There were small fierceling flareups that continued throughout the provinces, and even Duneidyn, the planet's capital, saw hard fighting in its ancient streets. But by Fionnasa it was mastered, and by Samhain it was done. That harvest tide on Caledon brought a red bitter reaping.

By this time Athyn—and now it was very much Athyn, no longer was she anyone's pawn or prowhead, not even Esmer's, and Esmer himself rejoiced to see it—was becoming pleasantly 'customed to having matters go what way she herself had planned them. As she put it, if things had to be any way at all, why should not that way be her way? And few by now would have dreamed of disputing her; though even Athyn knew that it can be a kind of soul-slaughter ever to have one's own way unchallenged.

As the Gwerin grew in triumph, Esmer Lennox had been by no means idle. As Athyn began to gather the reins into her hands, Esmer—wisely—had let her have her head, and moved his own hands not to the bight but the bit. Few knew precisely what he was about; and when at last he told Athyn of his activities, her reaction was all that he could have hoped for.

"They have named me *what?*"

"You are named by Bronwyn and Redigan as co-arb to the Copper Crown," he repeated. "It is a ranking more than rígh-domhna, less than Tanista. Your line is proven to Brendan's; strange as it may sound, given your onetime obscurity—no offense!—your claim is more valid than most of the others. It is superior even to Thomond's, and therefore Maravaun himself is prepared to avow to you. So that now, with the Prince of Thomond upholding you and the Archbrieve decreeing your pre-eminence amongst the rígh-domhna, not Cennfaelad himself could gainsay you as a lawful heretrix to Keltia."

She had been staring at him aghast, and now she began to laugh. "My gods, Lennox, if anyone ever dares tell me that you have lost Velenax's edge to soft peaceful living I shall throw him through a wall! Listen now: We have never truly discussed this, you and I, so let us do so before we are any older. This is the first time you have ever straightout said to me that I should take the Crown when this is done with."

Esmer looked astonished; or else feigned it very, very well. "You are the one who has worked hardest for it, and longest—did you think we intended another should reap the field you labored, and but leazings left for you? Did we truly never speak of it?"

"Nay," she said, beginning to enjoy herself. "We did not—Oh, I am sure you and Ganor talked enough about it between you; but never did you speak of it with *me*, Connacht—perhaps you simply forgot—and if you had, I should have said—Well, I do not know what I should have said. But unless I in my traha have read things all awry, you have intended from the first that I should become Ard-rían."

"True," said Lennox at once, and shamelessly.

"And for my part I decided, when first I began to twig it was this that you had in your devious mind, that I would be acclaimed High Queen by full voice of the people, or else I would not rule."

Esmer shouted with laughter. "Oh, if that is all!

Athynnach—dear child—do you know how they think of you out there?"

"I know how I am *spoken* of," she said with a certain bitter dignity, "and Morric, and all you with me."

"Amongst the Incomers only! And perhaps too a few exceed-ing stupid Kelts... But that is not what I meant, silly lass; nay, the people, *our* people, already speak of you as the right successor to Brendan and Raighne and Líoch. And that is no empty pufftalk fostered by your man and his way with a tune, but the true feeling of the folk."

Athyn's face changed in such a way that Esmer could not define, and he pressed what he saw as his advantage.

"Have you never spoken—"

"Mari and Sósaun and I have discussed it," conceded Athyn, "and I have talked of it with a few of the others—"

In a flash of clarity he divined the root of her trouble, or at least one of the deeper roots. "But not, I think, with Morric."

She gave him a smile that was sob and laugh, headshake and shrug. "How in all the seven hells am I going to tell him that if we wed he may become King? He will hear that and bolt so swift that the Cwn Annwn could not catch him."

"Is it more that he might be King which so disquiets him," asked Esmer then, "or that you must be Queen?"

Athyn looked troubled. "I do not know," she admitted after a while. "And I am not at all sure I wish to ask."

As human Kelts were not the only Kelts, neither was their fight the only fight; and Morvoren Kindellan, admiral now of all the Gwerin seafleets, had had a great adventure, going where few humans had ever dared to go.

Few others even in Keltia could have gone at all. Her kin-ship with the silkies had proved itself yet again, and at Athyn's bidding she had swum far down to the deep green halls of the sea-folk, where coral castles stand on silver sands, and above them crystal tides like winds do shake the red kelp forests.

With a guard of goldencapes as escort about her, coming before the lords of the merrows and the silkies alike Morvoren had spoken eloquently as a kinswoman, to rally those sea peoples to fight against the Incomer navies. As she herself had said to the Morar-mhara Selattyn, the merrow ruler, who better to fight upon the sea than those who dwelled within it; and the sea-kings had agreed.

Indeed, she had had greater success among the Sluagh-rón and the Moruadha than among some humans. As the need grew sharper, the struggle more desperate, the aid even of Keltia's retired warriors had been sought. Most had been glad indeed to climb back into harness: Captains and commanders, they had heard the Crann Tarith long ago; having missed its call, they rejoiced now to follow it again in Keltia's need. But not all felt so; and Comyn Douglas was one of those who had—flatly, coldly, stonily—refused. The fact that he was also Morric's long-estranged father doubtless had much to do with the refusal.

"He would not help."

Morvoren ran a hand through her tangle of ash-brown hair. She had come to Seana Bhraigh to report to Athyn of the failure of her mission to Comyn Douglas, and was still aggrieved at the rebuff. "As soon as he heard on what errand I was come, and in whose name... He was shut against the whole thing, Athwen, a bolted door had naught on it; heard me out, but would not speak save to deny."

"Well," said Athyn. "It was a gamble at best. Though I had hoped it might have paid out, and other things also be mended thereby—" She cast an uncertain glance over to the corner of the room, where Morric had flung himself, black with temper, into a chair by the hearth, pretending not to hear.

But Morvoren did not note the warning eyeflash, or else she suffered no such constraints as Athyn. "Morric. I saw your father yesterday, spoke with him. I told him of your doings but had no words to give him from you."

"I do not know how that can be," came Morric's voice from the depths of the chair, and he put bite on it like iron in winter. "I have no father. He died long since. I have no words to give one who does not exist."

Morvoren was undaunted. "Well, small wonder then that he would not help us! He is dead, how could he? M'chara, I do not know what quarrel lies between you, but he is, or was, a brilliant strategist, renowned for battle tactics; or so I am told."

"That's as may be. But as a father he was something other. You were wasting your labors with him. Or so I could have told you—if you had asked." He stood up, gave a curt nod and stalked out.

"He has been telling folk for so long that his kin were dead," said Athyn then, "that I think he has come to believe it himself." Not even to Morvoren would she disclose the true reasons Morric had for killing off his parents in his mind; it was not her secret to divulge, not her wrong to right, though she would gladly have avenged it, or healed it, if she could, or if her mate allowed.

"My sorrow, then, to have brought it all back home to him." Morvoren looked as if she were about to weep.

"The fault is mine who sent you." Now Athyn was the one who seemed on point of tears. "It is a thing between Morric and the man who begot him and the woman who bore him. And Morric alone knows if they merit either the hatred or the love."

And speaking of kin-strife… "We do not hear so much these days of Kier," said Morvoren presently. "What is he about, do we know?"

"The same and usual, I am very sure."

"Athwen," said her friend carefully, "you do recall it was Kier struck you down at Gala?"

Athyn laughed. "Aye, I recall very well—my brain of forgetting is not yet that much in command. Well, not just yet…

You would think I had learned my lesson of Kier when I was a child, and he would cuff us all about up in the dorter. And you would also think I would not be surprised that he should try now to kill me in battle, since he could not put an end to me at home…"

"He knows you now for Blackmantle," said Morvoren, "and by this time the Incomers do also. We knew it could not last forever, that leaguer of safety, but you know what the end of it must mean."

Athyn nodded. "Oh aye. And so, I am sure, does Kier."

That winter on Tara was the worst since Kelts first came to Keltia; in the howling nights Athyn sat at her field-desk shivering despite the furs that swathed her. *Beira Queen of Winter is surely fighting for us, for the Firvolgi fear and detest the chill, and we can make inroads while they are sheltering and sweltering withindoors like pigs in a sweathouse…* But suddenly in the deepest heart of the cold Athyn rebelled, and, wild for action—they call such a mood 'clochan-fever' in that part of Tara, where it is by no means unknown—taking counsel of no one she had gone alone into Caerdroia; a fearful risk in anyone's book. She knew very well what would befall her if she were caught; but she had wanted to scout the defenses—and also simply to see the City under snow, and to be free awhile—and she had had her way as she ever did, for in those days she was beyond command.

So she had passed the Landgate—the great Wolf Gate remained shut fast in these uncertain times—and entered the City. She had walked the cobbled streets, where the little stairstepped pavements climbed the hillier throughfares; seen how gallaín were thicker on the ground than snowflakes, and for a moment or two she had despaired.

Drawn by an impulse, she had gone to Macca's Well; but the alehouse was now only a faint echo of its old self. Though the food was still hot and plentiful, the ale copious and good, the music was over. *All those who once did play here took the harp-road for the Gwerin long ago—Cray and Linja who have so sadly perished in our cause, Tam and Gwen and all the rest...* And of those Morric Douglas had chaunted most fiery of all: songs that were a torch to the soul, a Crann Tarith of the mind, lighting fires of Beltain in every heart that heard.

But she went inside all the same, for an afternoon bavour of a pastai or two and a mether or two, rocked by memory. *There I saw Morric standing looking more beautiful than a god, here he sat beside me at this very table, in that corner did Amzalsunëa crawl out from under the skirtins like some painted daradail, over there Cray Jargier and Sosánaigh did play to wake the hills...*

Cast down suddenly, she finished her bavour and quitted the alehouse, and climbing a flight of worn steps just outside came atop a wall. There was a far greater wall now, of course, one of the wonders of Keltia: a full hundred yards thick, so that the Wolf Gate was more a fortified tunnel through stone ramparts than a simple portal. But this that Athyn now stood upon was one of the ancient remnants of the very first wall that had palisaded Caerdroia. Long outgrown as the city expanded, much broken up by streets and small squares and greens, the old wall now was used as promenade or outlook; snug houses, like Macca's, were even built into its scattered outcrops.

Walking on, she stopped to stand at a merlon, gazing northeast over the plain. The Avon Dia, choked with ice, flowed sluggishly nearby, but the huge peaks of the Stair were invisible in the fine blowing snow. Then she turned to look back over Caerdroia, and cried aloud to see it. The city was alive behind her, bright with lights as the blue dusk shut down, each window glowing with warmth. Few were abroad; the snow was small and dry but falling steadily, and there was a light wind from all quarters. A sudden flash startled her: winter lightning, and the muffled snow-thunder rolling down along the Loom. *'Winter lightning, summer war'; but the Thunder Ghost is a good omen...*

"Soon," she said aloud, to whom she did not know, and saw

as she spoke the palace of Turusachan rising like a ghost itself, a few blind miles away.

When she returned to Lennoxliss, it was to find Mariota, unexpected and in transit, who immediately urged Athyn to accompany her away.

"No need to freeze alone in the Wester Isles; freeze in Connacht with us, in comfort, at Ardturach. Where is Morric?"

Athyn looked down. "I do not know," she said after a while. "With the slutling Dalgarno, perhaps. He seems to need to see her now and again."

Mariota began to say something, changed her mind. "Then come home with me. Everyone would be glad to see you; Mâli and Ardattin miss you dreadfully. But listen to me: If you stay on here alone, I shall wager any stake you like against any odds you set that before the week is out you will get into important dangerous stupid avoidable trouble. And you know what they will do to you if they catch you. Bad enough that they know Blackmantle and hate her, and Athyn Cahanagh and detest her; but if they have learned for sure that you are both—if Kier has told them—"

"Then I shall give them no cause to catch either of me."

But Mariota had not been three days departed from Caerdroia before Athyn Cahanagh ran straight into the very trouble that had been predicted; and nor was Blackmantle far behind...

Late afternoon of a cold sunny day; along a small square, Firvolgian civil guards were checking passcards. Never before had Kelts been obliged to endure such indignity, and it was Athyn's own fault that now they were, for it was due solely to Blackmantle's success that the Incomers now took such precautions. So she had only herself to blame, and the irony was not lost on her. Still, the fact remained that she had forgotten all about the passcard rule, and the forged pass proclaiming her to be one Fidelma Venn, of Machrihanish in the Tain, was still, seal and all, back in her chambers at Lennoxliss.

She permitted herself one very curt, very swart oath, then looked around for a way out. She was in a little blindstreet banked with snow. No windows or doors opened upon it but only the mouth of the square; an archway at the far end led perhaps to the next street over, but more likely into a close, and she would be trapped there. Either way, she could not get to it in time, and even if she did her bootprints in the snow would point her path. Then the three Firvolgi civil guards in their gray uniforms were before her, addressing her politely in heavily accented Gaeloch.

"What do you in Caravossa, mistress? Where is your card?"

When she could not produce it, they brought her, and three others who had likewise fallen foul of the rule, to the Tolbooth, the massive, menacing Fir Bolc garrison behind the eastern walls, near the spill-pool of the Falls of Yarin. In all the years of their presence in Keltia, never had the Incomers felt confident enough, or brazen enough, to appropriate some significant brugh, or even Turusachan, for the use of their own leadership, and had made do with rentage. But this they had built, the Tolbooth, and it was like them: solid, stolid, with no feeling for place or art or anything but the use for which it had been made.

Athyn was on her highest alert but not yet much alarmed, and complied instantly and biddably with all the requests made of her: sit here, stand there, explain this or that. *I do not think they know me, at least not just yet—but I would not want to set my life at stake against it. Just what is the Firvolgian way with spies these days?*

She found out soon enough. They put her alone in a bare stone room in which the cold air circulated a little too well; she had only her cloak—a plain shearling such as many Kelts favor in winter, not the already legendary black snakeskin, Morric's gift, which would have betrayed her before she had gotten three paces inside Caerdroia—to keep off the chill. They might not yet know who she was, and perhaps would not discover it, but by the same token they might even now be returning to confront her.

Goddess, I cannot believe that Mari-fach is going to win that wager after all... But it seemed they took her tale for true, for after an hour or two they came and released her, with a cautioning to send her on her way. Then, just as she was leaving the garrison-yard, starting to dare to breathe again, she looked up from the icy footing, and saw Kier mac Archill staring at her from not ten feet away; and Amzalsunëa Dalgarno was clinging to his arm.

chapter twenty

Even the sea can only drown you.

—*Séomaighas Douglas Ó Morrighsaun*

The place to which they brought her, and rather less courteously this time, was far more indicative of the Tolbooth's purpose. On the way there, she noted cells hewn from the living bedrock of the Loom, vitriglass windows with findruinna astragals, síodarainn bars and doors, other refinements suggestive of even darker and more unpleasant uses—all the grim appurtenances of punishment and prison.

Athyn looked round as the grates and gates and doors closed behind her. Though she forbore to rise from the stone floor where they had flung her—*Why bother?*—she did draw herself up to sit more comfortably, tailor-style, her back against the stone-platformed couch that was the chamber's sole furnishing. *Well, at least this cell is warmer than the other one. As for their sudden fit of caution, no surprise that they think Blackmantle more deserving of close keeping than one simple citizen who forgot her passcard...*

"So, nets strung for troutlings seined instead the queen piast. What luck I was nearby to tell the netters."

Athyn watched impassively as the guards unlocked the outer grill for Kier mac Archill to step inside. A second set of findruinna bars formed a small grated cage across the cell's width, in which an interrogator could be private behind the closed door and yet remain safely removed from a prisoner's reach.

"It is always good to feel of use to someone," she agreed.

Kier flushed. "Blackmantle," he said slowly, as if he were seeing an enormity of deed contained in one word. "When I came to know," he said then, "right there in the middle of Gala fight, that the creature sought with such eagerness by so many, and Lennox's minion, and my own father's pestilential charity brat, were all one and the same person, I thought that nothing could surprise me more. How wrong I was. The next time I see you—all three of you—you are stepping out of the Tolbooth's very doors."

"Life is full of bold surprises."

"For us both."

Athyn laughed. "For you, maybe. I find it merely inevitable that the bully who pushed me onto the stones of my own front-yard when I was six should be the same bully who betrays me to the Incomers on the stones of the Tolbooth front-yard three decades later. Dán does seem to be everything."

"Well, a great freight of dán comes due any time now. The folk shall see that if we can make an end of Blackmantle we can do the same to them, and the revolt shall die even as you do."

Athyn had not missed the 'we' he was so careful to employ. "If 'revolt' is what you call it, then you and the Fir Bolc who have bought you are even more lackbrained than I thought; stupider still, if you think that by putting a stop to me you will put a stop to the Outgoing. Vengeance can be a costly business."

"Sometimes one may choose not to count the cost."

"Indeed yes," agreed Athyn. "I myself could easily be spend-thrift in that very market. But you, Kier: You must be very glad to get revenge of me now, after all those years at Caerlaverock when you could not." Leaning back against the granite wall, she stretched her booted legs out in front of her, and smiled at him. "A long time to wait. Cormac and Lyleth and Nilos, not to mention the lady Kerys your mother, will be well pleased to hear of your great doings. I shall be very sure to speak of you to them when I see them."

"Do not mention my mother's name again," he snapped, but for an instant a flash of fear and doubt had crossed his face, and he departed suddenly, and rather more sullenly than he had arrived.

Alone at last… Athyn settled herself on the low couch for a nap or a meditation, however it might fall out; in her present mood it was even odds as to which she might get. But it seemed she was to have neither, for very shortly the outer door swung again, and Amzalsunëa Dalgarno stepped warily inside. Despite all else she had on her mind just then, Athyn was shocked to see how ill her rival looked, and even more shocked to feel well up within her a tiny springlet of—what? Pity? Compassion? Satisfaction? She did not know, and would not try.

But, no question, Amzalsunëa's fragile prettiness had begun to erode: The lovely red hair was orange as straw, and she looked thinner, sharper-featured, more ravaged than when they last had met. Perhaps the ravages were occupational in origin—she had been employed some while now in Pharuca T'pettun's Caerdroian establishment—or it might be that her use of the vile drug hazen, which Morric had reluctantly but honestly confided to Athyn was her longtime practice, was finally taking toll of her.

She is like the pluff-pear in the orchard; fair on the outside, corrupt within. But now the rot is at last showing itself… Still, those who command here have sent her in to me for a reason…

"I told them who you are," said Amzalsunëa then, in a defiant rush; the delicate, slightly prominent chin was lifted, the childish breathless voice the same as ever. "They will kill you for it, they said they would."

Athyn grinned in spite of herself, and put her arms behind her head. "Well, that is one way to clear a path to Morric; but even if I am dead I doubt you will win him back."

"We shall see—well, I shall. And I shall be a Kelt for him at last."

"You are a Fir Bolc and a hazer and a whore," said Athyn in Volgiaran; without heat or hate, as one who but declares that the sun shines in daylight. "No more than that; and it would take very much more than that to make a Kelt of you, or of anyone."

"Nay, when you are dead Morric shall come back to me—"

"You think?" Athyn's tone was genuinely considering. "When he learns that you and Kier were hand in hand in my death—and that business transaction I interrupted? He will gralloch you both alive; or so at least I hope. I would surely do as much for him." She sighed and stretched, and shook her head. "Still, you never know; even the best men are so easily distracted, so quickly they forget..."

The Firvolgian looked at her wonderingly. "But he would *never* forget *you*—" As Athyn's mouth twitched and her eyes sought the ceiling: "Ah. You are being ironical—"

"How in all the seven hells did Morric ever link up with you?" asked Athyn, and now her voice held nothing but honest inquiry. "Oh, he has told me all the tale; but now let you tell me yourself. I should very much like to hear your version before I die."

But Amzalsunëa, warned now against irony, sullenly refused to be drawn. Athyn placidly waited her out; for her, silence was never a strain, and the Firvolgian could by no means say the like. *Ah Goddess! It is not half so much fun as I thought it would be, to bait her; unsporting too, no challenge in it— spearing frogs in a keeve. Oh for one hour of a truly worthy opponent! If I am to die for the rashness of my venture—and I will not say I do not deserve to—then at the very least I should be granted a few last exchanges with an adversary equal to my steel... surely that is not too much to ask?*

"So you are caught at last for Blackmantle, when all these years everyone thought you were only Athyn Cahanagh—"

Athyn smiled, and despite the findruinna bars between them Amzalsunëa stepped backwards a full pace.

"Blackmantle is merely what I do," she said, her smile widening. "Athyn is who I am. If I go to the scaffold five minutes from now it is only Athyn who will perish. Blackmantle they can never destroy, and Morric Fireheart will write songs about her that shall live forever. To my mind, that is no bad bargain. I learned long since that it is always best to command one's own legend; indeed, it was Morric—my Morric—who taught me that, and much else beside. Did you learn nothing from him what time that he was yours?"

But Amzalsunëa only stared silently, and still in silence signalled the guard of her readiness to leave. Behind the bars and bolts and barriers, Athyn stood looking after her visitor, as if she could see through the walls, within the stones; as perhaps she could.

"My guess would be, not," she said aloud, and turned away.

There had been no public announcement made of Blackmantle's stunning and unexpected capture, which surprised Athyn greatly. She had thought the Incomers would be overjoyed to boast of it, shouting exultant vindictive triumph from every toweret in Caerdroia; but Kier enlightened her.

"They are feared the Gweriden, or the City folk, or both, will mount a rescue to fetch you out of here, if they learn that you are held."

"I would never permit them to try."

"You would not command them, maybe. That does not mean it would not happen. The committee of elders will not take the chance; therefore the general populace will not be told, not until the elders are ready to make the example of you that they intend."

It was the evening of Athyn's fifth day of captivity. Though

Amzalsunëa Dalgarno had not returned, Kier mac Archill had been a twice-daily visitor. Athyn could not puzzle it out: Surely the pleasure he had in her downfall, vast though it doubtless was, could not be so vast as that. Or could it? Or was it something else? Perhaps it was not that the Incomers feared a Gwerin rescue, but were rather hoping for it, prepared for it, using her to lure the others in?

Nay, that must never be…

She shrugged, and prayed to sound convincing. "I promise you, before the sun had set on the day I was thrown in here the Gwerin knew where I was. If they were going to make an attempt to free me they had done so long since. Any road, all our Companions are under orders: no ransoms, no rescues, no bargains. There is no privilege for the Gweriden, still less for Blackmantle, that the rest of the Gwerin does not share."

He did not believe her. "Very noble; but you know it is the Firvolgi custom to hang traitors from a long tow off the city walls?"

"I am no traitor to them," she said coldly. "They may hang me if they please and the best of Keltic luck to them, but if they think to charge me with treason best they think again."

"Under Keltic law as well as Firvolgian—"

When Athyn at last stopped laughing, she looked up at him again; discomfiture sat plain and vivid on his face.

"Oh, I do not think so! Who is the brehon-ollave here, braud? Nay," she said, still smiling, "I should like to see them try! If they take this thing to a public trial, or even a secret one, I shall of course stand counsel for my own defense. And I do not mean to boast unseemly, but I will wipe the Tolbooth floor with them and every piece of caselaw they bring against me, theirs or ours. I may end hanged all the same, but in my book it will be well worth it, to discountenance them one more time before I go. I shall enjoy that, very much… Go now, trot off like the good bought dog that you are, and slobber on your masters' hands, and be sure you tell them faithfully what I have said."

On the eighth day she made an attempt at escape, less out of any hope of success than because it seemed expected of her and the chance presented; after that they did restrain her. She had injured her arm in the brief sharp fight, and the bonds were discomfortable in the extreme; and though they racked her endlessly with questions at every hour of the day and night, that was the extent of their tormenting.

I am missing something here... All their efforts for the past few years have been to put me exactly where in fact I now am, or worse—they even sent kedders after me!—and they plainly have no difficulty with the prospect of a public dispatching. So why would they not be over the moons with delight, indulging their revenge in every primitive painful way they can devise? I am very pleased that they do not, of course, but still I wonder...

She turned her mind to even less pleasant paths. *Perhaps time has come for me to begin to accept this as inevitable, as a thing that will be...* In Keltia, save for cases of planned murder and high treason proved on the Cremave, and not always even then, the state has never executed its citizens; while the brehon code, with fines and honor-prices for every conceivable circumstance, has always allowed private persons the private justice of avenging to the death—though that too carries a price of its own. Apart from those conditions, murder in the name of the law has never formed any part of Keltic justice.

But on his most recent visit, Kier had been pleased to recount to Athyn, by comparison, the specifics of a Firvolgian judicial execution, and now she was reviewing them at leisure. There were many sensational touches attendant on such an event, and she was anxious that all the perquisites to which she was lawfully entitled should be observed.

She would be escorted dramatically through the streets to

the walls of the City—a very visible location would have been selected for the scaffold—by train-bands in red robes and tall pointed hoods that covered their faces. The conveyance of choice for an outlaw and a war insurgent—for as such they had charged her—was a black battle-chariot drawn by four black horses, driven by a robed and hooded charioteer. *Well, I think I must insist on that…*

The rest of it was merely grim. Unknown in Keltia, hanging was still on many worlds the traditional end accorded to common felons; criminals of a better class were favored with beheading by axe, and the highest-ranking offenders enjoyed the quick clean mercy of the sword. The good tidings was that it would be swiftly over: The charges against her would be read, the rope would be set around her neck, and then would come the dreadful moment known as 'turning-off,' when she would either step or be pushed—the choice would be hers—from the walls, a thirty-foot drop to her death. Even so, there was a certain comfort in knowing she could never choke, not if the hangsman were skilled at his job; properly positioned, the knot of the noose would snap her neck instantly.

All this troubled Athyn not in the slightest. *It is going to be exceedingly unpleasant, no doubt about it; but dying in battle is as a rule far more untidy and a great deal more painful and prolonged, not to mention unexpected, and I have never had any difficulty facing the likelihood of that…* What did distress her was knowing that she would not be able to make her farewells beforehand. *Oh, I know it can all be done just as well thereafter, but still— At the very least I should like to part fittingly from Morric, for his sake as well as my own, since it is so very much harder to be left than to leave; and it is on me that time is short…*

She shifted where she lay, on the pallet, staring up at the fitted stones of the ceiling; then fell into an uneasy sleep. Awake again, days or hours later she did not know, she was trying to recall to mind the precise wording of a particularly lovely song of Morric's, when the door of the cell opened without warning.

And time, I think, is now...

Emerging into the winter morning sunlight, clad only in a white wool leinna and black leather trews and boots—clean clothing had been sent in to her by unknown providers, and her captors had allowed it—Athyn was pleased to see that the theatrical particulars had been scrupulously observed. Blackmantle was being given a full-dress exit, ushered out of existence in correct lawful style: Two long files of red-robed figures, their faces hidden by tall pointed hoods, were already waiting silently in the Tolbooth yard, flanking the black chariot and horses. Not waiting for the guards, she mounted without effort into the car; her wrists were fastened to the iron rim-rail in front of her. *Not so much to keep me from attempting escape, I think, as to make sure I cannot defend myself against anything anyone might choose to fling...* Then the charioteer took his place at the front of the car, on the seat above the yoketree, and the progress began.

Cold as the morning was, the streets of Caerdroia were thronged with spectators; evidently the elders had announced their plans at last. But those throngs were noticeably sparse of Kelts: Either her own people had stayed away for their own reasons—grief or despair, rage or indifference, sorrow or contempt—or else they had been kept away by Firvolgi civil guards. Athyn could not decide how she felt about their absence. Would it have given her heart and comfort to see her fellow Kelts, for whom she had done all that had brought her to this place and end, or would she have felt instead shame that she had not foreseen or prevented it, guilt that she was leaving them with her work unfinished? And did they blame her, or did they truly sorrow?

Yet these gallaín crowds were notably silent; at the least she had expected jeers and insults, and feared worse. But as the chariot rolled slowly through the thronged streets there was only silence, the car's wheels and the horses' hoofs and the tread of the ghastly escort the sole sounds to be heard; though whether that profound stillness was to honor a noble enemy's last hour or to express ultimate scorn and hatred, Athyn could not tell.

At one point the procession halted, and not by chance, directly in front of a large brugh in one of the broad streets leading down to the Market Square. On the house's balcony stood a number of Athyn's fiercest Firvolgian foes, most of whom had come to the Tolbooth over the fortnight past to visit and to gloat, and to whom she had shown only cold courtesy. The big house in Stone Street was Falxifer Dalgarno's dwelling, and there he stood, with Margiamnë his wife, and Rhykeur Pym, Pharuca T'pettun, Leto Novedris, Darrian Finslock, a few others.

The daughter of the house was nowhere to be seen; then a shutter chinked open, furtively and hastily, at a side window. It closed again as swiftly; but not before the eyes of Athyn Cahanagh and the eyes of Amzalsunëa Dalgarno had met and held, and Athyn smiled.

She lifted her head then and ran a calm gaze along the row of hostile faces upon the balcony, and a strange thing happened. Though the watching Incomers had been a gay and triumphant party only a moment since, merrily pointing out to one another the approaching chariot, their jovial mood utterly at odds with the deathly stillness all round them, not one of them now would meet her eyes; and as Athyn looked upon them they fell silent, turned and hastily scuttled withindoors, heads lowered and averted, that they might not catch her glance.

A lone voice rose up from the crowd to fiercely assail their going; by his accent and appearance, a Fomori soldier, his voice full of scorn.

"For seven years on the field never have you dared to look her in the face; no surprise you cannot do so now!"

And Athyn, who had at the best of times almost as little love for the Fomori as she did for the Firvolgi, found herself strangely warmed by the honest and unexpected defense.

At last the chariot with its hooded swaying escort lines entered the Market Square, which was packed with people standing solid as salmon in a weir, and looking up Athyn could see atop the Wolf Gate the hangsman and a small group of officials awaiting her arrival.

Well, I daresay I am as prepared for this as I can be, though it is hardly the end I expected. And yet in many ways it is... It is perhaps best that it comes so quick and unannounced; but I could have wished to bid farewell to my kin—and they are my kin—in fit fashion. Perhaps some of them are hidden here in the crowd; at least I shall hold to the thought that they may be, to give me strength. But my Morric—he I know is not here, and that gives me strength also; I would not go so easy to my death knowing that he had to watch it...

The chariot drew up in front of the huge gatetowers. Athyn's hands were unfastened from the chariot rim, though left bound in front of her, and she jumped down before they could pull her from the car, glad of the chance to move again. *I will not have them see me shiver; they would think it is fear, when in truth it is but being cloakless in the chill. Though if it were fear, I like to think I would admit it, at least to my own self...nay, it is but the cold.*

Some rigmarole followed at the base of the tower: a legal fuss between the council of elders who had orchestrated all this and the Warder of the Tolbooth, who looked angry and irresolute. At one point some minion pompously asked Athyn for a statement; she replied merely, and loudly, that she had had no trial at all, let alone a fair and proper one, and if that was sample of Firvolgian justice, well, as a brehon she was only glad to be shut of it.

Into the western gatetower then, climbing the twisting

stairs to the top; on the broad battlements above the Wolf Gate, another knot of Firvolg officials stood waiting by a newly constructed scaffold. Athyn looked round, but not even a prester was by to bless her going.

Ah well, if you wish something done right, you do ever best to do it yourself—and that at least I have done. I have been ready for this moment a very long time; I am not sorry, and neither am I afraid...

She was led to the edge of the scaffold, where the hangsman required of her the traditional coin and forgiveness; she gave the one, but, true to form until the end, not the other. The noose was set then round her neck, the heavy knot adjusted—they had left the silver wolf's head of Aoibhell on its leather cord beneath her leinna—and she was asked if she wished a hood or blindfold. She shook her head.

"I had rather see it coming," she said smiling, and they drew away.

She looked out then over the plain and the river and the distant mountains, and Caerdroia, and upon her left the sea— *And so shall Keltia be the last thing in my sight*—and took a deep breath, waiting for the word to turn off into the frightful gulf below her feet; but no word came, and behind her there was only a strange silence. At last she turned round, with greatest care lest she should hang herself by sheer mischance, to see what-the-hells, and saw that something was stranger even than she had imagined.

The watching crowd was not now silent only but frozen, as if a spell had been set on them. *As, perhaps, indeed, one has?* Athyn raked her glance over the motionless scene; time had stopped for all but her. *Or am I dead already?* And then, as calmly and easily as if he strolled through a field of flowers, Allyn mhic Midna walked up to the scaffold to stand beside her; and she divined at once to what purpose he had come. *Well, it does not take a house to fall on this lass...*

"Go away," she said, with a flash of her old manner. "I would just as lief die as escape from here; indeed, by now, liefer. For that too is escape, and, gods know, it is easier."

"You do not mean that."

"Do I not?" Athyn turned her back to him; difficult to do, because of the noose. "Well, hear this: Among the Gwerin we have a rule about what happens to us when we fall into Incomer hands, and rescue is not in it. Many have died for that rule, bravely and gladly, and I would not shame myself before them by presuming that the same rule does not apply to Blackmantle. Indeed, it applies to her all the more."

"But I am not *of* the Gwerin," said Allyn smiling. "Why else do you think I was sent?"

"Then a plague on them who sent you. That is special pleading, lord; I am a brehon, I know these things. And I will not accept a privilege others of our comrades are not offered. I will not go, and you cannot make me do so."

"Nay, 'tis very true, I cannot." He sounded so rueful and reasonable that she turned round again to look at him with deep suspicion; if he was laughing at her he could do it to her face. But he appeared the soul of grave concern.

I cannot believe I am disputing him standing here on the scaffold with a noose round my neck...

"I can scarce believe it, either; or that Athyn Cahanagh would sooner be executed than inconvenienced," countered Allyn; he had heard her thought as easily as he ever did. "As for your scruples, they do you everlasting credit, but the entire Gwerin would sooner themselves perish rather than see you decline a rescue and use them for excuse. I cannot force you. But dán can."

Ah Goddess! He would have to put it so...

"I thought the Shining Folk did not interest themselves in the affairs of mortal Kelts," she said crossly.

"You of all mortal Kelts know better than that: how when we are minded to do so we interest ourselves in whatever we please. Then too there is that matter of a debt. Since you still have asked naught of us, it is a question of our honor not to let you perish with that debt unclaimed."

Athyn laughed, feeling hope unaccountably return. "So,

your honor counts, but mine does not, and to your folk I am only a debt undischarged. Oh, it is well enough! I only ask that I may be certain where we all are; and I remind you, with respect, that since this rescue is done of your will and not mine, it is by no means to be accounted payment. That debt still stands... Well then, if you will divest me of these"—she raised her iron-bound wrists—"let us be gone, so that your ledgers can be balanced. It is doubtless far to the fore of being hanged."

"Doubtless it is," agreed Allyn, "but though I may have power to halt time a while, I have no kinship with cold iron, as you will remember. You will have to shed those bonds yourself."

"And I have no magic; as *you* will remember? I have not the power."

"Not true, and fine you know it. You have always had the power; and the magic also."

Hu mawr! Well, I will try, if only to make him shut up and go away. I will try, and I shall fail, and that shall be the end of it and of me together...

Drawing a deep breath, Athyn raised her hands before her face. There was just enough play in the iron bands for her to turn her wrists back to back in the form of the suncross; she closed her eyes, reaching inside to a place she had never before known was there, calling on a power deep within her that she had not known existed. Her whole frame tensed and stiffened; her hands clenched to fists, the skin across the knuckles shining taut and white with effort, her nails drawing blood from her palms. And after a few moments the iron turned to silver, the silver to ice, the ice to water, and she was free.

She gasped and relaxed, staring at her wrists, flexed her hands front to back, and shed the noose. *Mighty Mother! Good it is to know that I can do such things, untaught as I am. Still—I do not think I much like the knowing, nor yet the doing...*

Athyn felt in that moment strangely sorrowful; as if,

though something of incomparable greatness had been gained, something had been taken away in recompense; as if she had traded away a possession she did not know until then she wished to keep. *It is almost a sort of Teltown: inexperience given up so that in its place may come a great mystery… I wonder if it is like this for sorcerers—the first time of magic feeling so like the first time of love? Neither is a loss—more like accomplishment or achievement, a kind of sharing and joining, an initiation into a larger thing—but it could feel like a loss, I suppose, to those who are untaught or unaware. And gods but it is change…*

"You did that the hard way—but see what you may do when you put yourself to it?"

She startled back to the moment. Allyn, looking pleased and proud, gestured royally, as if he were a king inviting her to some grand festivity.

"Come."

Beyond the quicksilver brightness, the dizzying spinning sensation, cold air slapped at her face. She was standing beside Allyn in the open center of the Market Square behind the Wolf Gate, in the midst of the crowd. Not three paces away stood the great bronze horse of the Sidhe; he nickered gladly to see them, and coming forward rubbed his beautiful head against Athyn's sleeve.

Allyn was astride now, though she had not seen him mount, and reaching a hand he drew Athyn up before him. Wearied by a fortnight's prisonment, dazed with the return from death-readiness and the magic she had wrought, shivering now, she had not even the strength to spring unassisted to the stallion's back, far less ride pillion—and this time Allyn settled her into the curve of his arm, beneath his red cloak.

At an unspoken word from his master, the bronze stallion spun like a war-horse on his hocks, and surged forward straight at the high masoned wall that bordered the square, beyond it the Wolf Gate itself, and the walls of Caerdroia.

Well! It seems I shall not be turned off those walls after all; or not, at least, today. And what will all these do when they come back to themselves, and find that I am gone?

"They cannot see us?" asked Athyn aloud, incredulously, trying to keep her voice steady with the question; though scarce was it a question.

She felt Allyn shake his head, heard the answer within her own. "You ride with *me*"—and that was all he said.

She caught a glimpse of Kier standing immobile and expectant—*Not just yet, brother, nor is this by any means settled between us*—and then they were rushing at the wall, or it at them. The stallion lifted, tucking his forelegs beneath him, neat as any mortal hunter; clearing the towering Wolf Gate as if it had been a five-barred fence, soaring over the empty scaffold and the awakening, angry, baffled, fearful crowd below, he set down again not upon earth but on the air itself.

Then they were galloping the shining track that takes no note of earthbound limits, racing north and east, and in the rushing air all round about them was the sound of small clear silver bells.

chapter twenty-one

What the Púca writes, that also can he read.

—*Rohan Ard-rígh*

W hen word had come to Seana Bhraigh that Athyn had been captured by the Firvolgi, and was being held in the Tolbooth for execution upon Kier mac Archill's betraying word, the Gweriden had leaped straightway into furious terrified action. Those not already in the secret camp were summoned urgently, and came at speed. Indeed, Esmer Lennox arrived from Ardturach so swiftly that his own daughter accused him of time-travel, though this he denied, explaining his expeditious arrival as merely what a good Keltic ship could accomplish when pushed.

"Not that I would *not* time-trip it," he told them defiantly, "if it meant Athynnach could be helped thereby; though I promise you I will slap her silly when we get our hands on her again. But what can we do? And where in all the seven hells is Morric?"

Good questions, and Esmer was by no means the only one asking them. But Morric Douglas had a charge of his own to accomplish, and just then he was well about it. When at last he rode into Seana Bhraigh, weary but somehow peaceful, he bore a strange message indeed to the Gweriden there assembled, and hearing it they wondered greatly. But they did as he bade them, though obedience to such orders went very hard with them all.

                    *   *   *

For the word Morric had brought was this: that by no means should a rescue be attempted, that Athyn would be delivered safe out of the hands of the Firvolgi, that all would be well; but just what assurances he had of this, or who it was who had so promised, he would not say. And the Gweriden of force believed him: Athyn's own lover and beloved, who was for all his commanded, or pretended, calm as terrified as the rest of them, would never take a course that might imperil her; if Morric said she would be restored unharmed then it must be so—but at the same time their helplessness and dread sat heavy as stones. The spies who had sent in the fresh raiment had brought back news of ominous preparations now in train at the Wolf Gate, and though for fear of somehow making it true none would put their fear into words, all of them knew well what that must mean.

So they waited, and fretted, and murmured amongst themselves, some even vowing—Rhain and Sosánaigh and Breos chiefest among them—that if no word, or no Athyn, came to them very presently then even Morric Douglas should not hold them back. But on the seventh edgy day since Morric's return from his mysterious mission, Errick mac Archill came running to the others where they sat in gloomy council, his face vivid with joy and relief.

"She is here, she is safe! And Allyn of the Sidhe has brought her!"

Outside, the faerie stallion stood, unwearied, unmoving, his bronze flanks a little darker where they steamed with the speed of his journey; upon his back the tall Sidhe lord, and Athyn held before him muffled in his cloak, like a lost child now found.

Morric stepped forward, held Allyn's gaze a moment, then bowed, profoundly, to Midna's son. Allyn inclined his own head in acknowledgment, and gently let Athyn slip from the stallion's back into Morric's arms.

She was by now scarce able to keep her feet; but she turned and looked up at Allyn, and she managed a ragged smile.

"Far to the fore," she said, in the tone of someone who has a private understanding with the one addressed, and Allyn smiled back, as one who well understands that private meaning, and bowed to them all from the saddle and was gone. Morric swept Athyn up into his arms and carried her inside.

Out of the chaos withindoors it was Sosánaigh who took charge, summoning healers, medicines, food, drink, quiet; and after those things had been furnished she chivvyed everyone from the room—Esmer Lennox in especial, who seemed reluctant to leave Athyn to the care of even her own mate. But at last the chamber was cleared, and Morric turned to Athyn with all his fear and wrath and worry plain upon his face.

Athyn had been almost totally silent, speaking only a brief word here and there to assure her friends that nay, she had not been harmed, and aye, it was Kier mac Archill who had betrayed her, and aye again, Allyn son of Midna who had come astoundingly among the enemy to save her off the scaffold and fetch her home.

But her silence seemed more the silence of default than of policy. As Morric looked closely on her now they were alone, she seemed small and uncertain, only half-there; in spite of the many calming drenchets Sosánaigh had implacably poured down her throat, she had begun to tremble. And when she looked up at him with haunted eyes, and spoke in a voice that shook like a willow in a windstorm, the thing she asked of him was the last he had thought to hear.

"Tell me a tale."

And he understood, and holding her close—the blistering chastisement he had all prepared for her going unspoken, at least for now—Morric began at once to tell a tale as she had asked him; and bit by bit the terrible trembling began to ease.

"Long and merry ago, there lived a king..."

Next morning, while Athyn slept like a dead thing—the which she had so very nearly been—the Gweriden met and spoke in awed tones of the means by which their captain had been restored to them. What had seemed deepest mystery—Allyn mhic Midna's part in Athyn's deliverance—was soon explained, though only by means of a deeper mystery still: It had been Morric himself had called upon the Sidhefolk for aid; thus, his strange and puzzling absence from Seana Bhraigh, and why, until his errand was accomplished, he had not spoken of it to any of his comrades.

"For though I did not know what else to do, still I was not sure if I did the right thing," he said, though the gladness in his face gave that the lie. "We all know that the Shining Ones have long time been great friends to Athyn—though none of us knows *why* they should be so, and even after yesterday I still have no better idea... To approach them on such a mission, even for her sake—I did not know if they would hear me; or, hearing, if they would oblige. But I knew we could do nothing ourselves; and it surely seemed worth the asking. All they could do was refuse..."

Knowing no other place where he might come upon the Folk he sought, he had gone to that bay near Tamon Acanis where once he had encountered a woman of the Sidhe like the living seafire upon the strand, and there he had called with voice and mind and heart and spirit. And when he could call no more, when he had fallen to his knees in the surf, exhausted, defeated, not knowing if he had been heard and denied or had never even been heard at all, he had been answered.

"I was told to ride home, that what I sought was already accomplished," he said now, concluding the story. "I dared not hope, but neither dared I doubt; the rest you know."

"All save the whereabouts of the sharnclout who caused it: For Kier mac Archill has slipped through our fingers yet *again*," said Micháltaigh Pendreic, Sosánaigh's mate, sounding deeply aggrieved; as well he might, for he had been out all night with those who sought—and all in vain—Athyn's fugitive fostern. But that seemed to be as far as they were prepared to assign blame: Not one of the Gweriden had mentioned Amzalsunëa Dalgarno and her own role in the past fortnight's terror; indeed, they were not certain Morric even knew of the Firvolgian's involvement, and no one wished to be the one to tell him—but she was very much in all their thoughts just then.

In Morric's thoughts as well, if truth were known: He too was thinking of his onetime lennaun, and with glacial repugnance; and though his friends were controlling their countenances as carefully as their minds, he knew very well what those impassive expressions concealed, and why they strove to hide it.

A kind intent, but surely they must know I am already 'ware of Melassaun's hand in it; Athynna herself told me, last night… Well, and why should they not blame me, a little; more than a little, even? I blame myself no less: I was wrong in my dealings with Melassaun, thinking her harmless, keeping friends with her for pity and old love's sake, and now see how she does. She tried to kill Athyn—SHE TRIED TO KILL ATHYN! And Mighty Mother, how very near to it she came… Well, no more…

He ran a hand over his beard, by main force of will concealing the fit of hysterical trembling that shook him head to foot, though whether it was Athyn's deadly peril or Amzalsunëa's equally deadly perfidy that was more the cause of his sudden reaction he could not just then determine.

Looking up, he caught Bronwyn Muirheyd watching him from across the chamber, and was far from comfortable, or comforted, under that steady blue-crystal gaze. But her smile warmed her face.

"Be easy," she said. "It is over. It did not happen; and now it shall not. Dán does not run backward in its course."

For all her reassuring tone, the smile did not reach her eyes; and even Morric could not read therefrom what dán remained to run.

He and Athyn, though, had spoken long, if sometimes haltingly, in the night: Lying safe again in Seana Bhraigh, in Morric's arms, Athyn had been at first much too airily dismissive of her ordeal—by which Morric could read how shaken she was in truth, though he also knew her far too well to hope that this would make her any more cautious in her ways.

Yet even she had fuffed off Amzalsunëa's part in the thing—*to spare my own guilty feelings, or perhaps she but feels it ignoble to gloat told-you-thus, for it is by no means out of charity for Melassaun that she does edit her account!*—and Morric, who had at first been merely silent, had been at last consumed by fury.

"You are every bit as much to blame as she, you know!" he had snapped at his mate. "If you had not gone off to Caerdroia clean against everyone's advising, like the pighead you are—"

And his loss of temper, his shattered control, his fear-born anger, had in turn set free all Athyn's own leashed guilt and fears and feelings, which had been held in check, at least until now, by chains stronger far than those which had held her in the Tolbooth.

"Oh aye, what excellent right thinking is *that*! So: I went to the City when I should not have—a bad mistake, I freely admit it, content yourself to hear me say so—therefore I somehow must *deserve* it that the Fir Bolc should throw me into the Tolbooth? Somehow it is my own fault that my iniquitous fostern and your chafer-brained mopsy should together nearly succeed in getting me hanged? I think not! Unless you are sorrowing now for that I was *not* hanged, and you might have been free to go guiltlessly back to that hazen-riddled little shrike... Well, for all of me you are; so the next time you seek her company, or indeed her professional services, be very sure to tell her I will not make *that* mistake a second time! Only do not think to come to my bed after you do so, Douglas, for I will not make that mistake again either—"

Her fury had flamed up spark for spark the match of his, and they had blazed at each other like balefires until at last Morric had pulled her to him and held her fast; though not before she had glimpsed the terror and relief he had felt and was feeling still. *And that is the true reason he is so angry, his fear for me, and it rejoices me to see it, even though it means a scolding and a quarrel; but for the cause of that fear, and what part Amzalsunëa had in it—oh, aye, I know perfectly well he does not bed with her!—it is all worth it...*

"I will be her death, Morrighsaun, I promise you," she had said then, still unregenerately angry, her mouth muffled against his chest where he so fiercely clasped her, though he also noted that she did not pull away, "that Fir Bolc streppoch of yours, and not even on your asking will I stay my hand."

"She is not mine," he had answered after a while. "And I have not asked you stay it."

But for all the terror she seemed so blithe in face of, the frightful fate she had so very nearly met, Athyn's peril had done nothing to lighten her arm. Not a fortnight after her return to Seana Bhraigh she sent out the Gwerin on five worlds, like hawks from off her wrist, and the quarry at which she flew them—legions of Incomer troops, solid second-line divisions—fell beneath the Gwerin's talons like fatling rockdoves.

Harder to combat were the floods of venom that the Firvolgi, growing desperate, now loosed about their opponents, to so noisome an extent and nature that the previous foul tide of mouthings seemed a clean spring flood by compare. Having all but lost the swordwar, the Incomers thought to triumph instead in a war of words, little recking that their enemy was better armed in that quarter as well; that the Kelts who had all but reinvented words had the advantage of them there also.

"Consider the source, Athyn!" said Mihangel Glenrossa one day, rolling his eyes—some Incomer or other had said or written some new bad thing or other about Athyn herself, or Morric, or the Gwerin, and their captain was in another wrathful mood. "You cannot allow vermin like that to trouble you. You know it is only what they are longing to see."

"And what *I* am only longing to see," said Athyn with great clarity and precision, "is their guts in little steaming heaps on the floor at my feet."

"No good to the carpets," said Mihangel. "You cannot kill them all."

"So I am always being told; but may I not even *try?*"

"Let it go," advised Morvoren calmly from her seat across the table, not even raising her voice from its softness or her sea-blue eyes from her sea-charts. "Send it on. It does not matter. It will not last."

"Oh but that is where you are all so wrong! Not only does that sort of thing last and last, but it has a fell way of growing even stronger and viler with age, a noisome vine that seeds poison wherever it spreads... 'Staves and stones may break my bones, but words can never wound me.' So sing the little children, do they not?" Her face was hard, and her voice shook a little; she was not speaking to be answered. "But when we are older, we come to learn that words can wound worse and hurt longer than any staff or stone there is."

"And when we are wiser, Athyn," said Breos, so gently that tears came to her eyes, "we come to learn that they can only hurt us if we ourselves allow it. We are the ones who give the bullies their victories; they cannot win unless we surrender."

"That is a place very hard to come to," she said presently, the pain of her feeling plain in the care of her pronouncing.

"Aye," he said. "Aye, it is hard."

"But, as long as all you *know* how hard it is—" she stood up, mercurial as ever, her dark mood lifted and flown "—then that is enough for me. Still, I say, if I can, I will slay them all the same. So they shall be paid back for all of it—in their own coin, in my own time. I will never forgive, and I will never forget." She smiled benevolently on them. "It is with them now like a stewpot boiling down; the stock is the stronger as the volume reduces. I am myself an indifferent cook, but even I know how to use the bones that are boiled to make the broth."

"And where is best to break them," muttered Mihangel darkly.

But Athyn feigned she had not heard.

A time came when the Kelts held their worlds clear and clean of Incomers, all save Tara alone, where the Incomers, still not yet willing to admit defeat, had been forced back. And there on Tara, as many had before them and more would after, they had determined to make their stand; to face Blackmantle and the Gwerin with everything they had.

This would be the last stand, and both sides knew it. Bit by bit, foot by foot it sometimes seemed, the Incomers had been driven from places they had held for half a hundred years and more. To their credit, as Athyn herself was neither slow nor grudging to admit, they had fought this fight entirely on their own: Kaireden, with brutal pragmatism, had not lifted a finger to help, though Leto Novedris and Rhykeur Pym and Falxifer Dalgarno, among many others, had run in contraband supplies and arms from the homeworld by secret channels. But the Incomers had more to lose than did their hosts, who now required nothing less of them than total absence; even in Keltia the laws of guestship may be bent only so far, and that limit had long been exceeded.

"And considering they were never invited in the first instance," remarked Phaal Torcwyn, "they can count themselves lucky they had so long a stay."

In any event, the onetime 'guests' had asked for a parley before what bid fair to be their final eviction, and to this Athyn had agreed at once. So she had called in to Seana Bhraigh all those who had had hand and heart and part in the long struggle: her dearest friends of the Gweriden, all those who had come to her when first she called them to her side and had never left it since; Esmer and Ganor, her kinsman Maravaun, all the many others who over the past seven years had brought the Outgoing from ashling into being.

Some crack forces and high commanders had been prudently held aside as a safe-hedge, that all should not be completely lost if matters went awry and Athyn's plan should fail or she should fall, and that was wise; but there was among them no least thought of fall or failure as they set out for the chosen battleground. That warm certainty of dán and doing yoked together to the same chariot rode with them all, and Malen Ruadh Rhên, the War-red War-queen herself, stood behind them in the car.

That last night before the battle all counsels were taken; naught left to do but await the dawn. It had long been Athyn's custom on the eve of a fight to hold a small circle in her clochan for herself and her closest comrades, not to pray for victory but to cleanse her soul and commend them all into the Goddess's keeping; and after that night's brief rite was ended she and Morric spent a quiet hour or two with friends and went early to their bed.

"This is the end of the Incomers," said Athyn presently; the peace and purity the circle had imparted to her had transformed into a kind of wondering exultant certainty, but still she feared to tempt dán. "In all humbleness, it seems impossible for one Erinnach horsegirl to have managed, even with such help and hearts as she was lent. For all the work we have done over the past years, all the dear-bought knowledge that we would prevail, all the dearer ones that we have lost—my soul to the mountain, Douglas, but I am not now sure I ever believed that we would come to it at last."

He drew her gently into his arms. "Then you are the only one to feel so, anghariad, for all the rest of us have taken our faith and cue from you and the certainty you show us. Esmer may have set the thing in motion, and the Marcher Lords and supporters kept it alive, but, horsegirl or no, you have been the soul of this contest, the deep and endless heart of it. And whatever happens when the sun rises over Moymore a few hours hence, that will never change. Take comfort from that; as you give comfort to us."

"Well," she said lightly, though he could see and sense how much his words had moved her, "now I see why princes have ever loved to have bards close beside them when they went into battle! Though whether those other bards were as close beside them as this"—shifting beneath the furs that covered them—"I cannot say."

After a while Morric said, "Poor them if they were not."

So the last great battle between Kelts and Incomers, the fight that was to drive the Firvolgi from Keltia forever, fell out at a place midway between bright Shanagolden and dead Shanavogue. Known as Aber-dau-gleddau, Mouth of the Two Swords, it was a carse, a flattish treeless piece of ground between a riversmeet, where two streams wound across the plain to make one placid water.

And that piece of riverland was to host the bitterest battle Tara had seen in many centuries, or would see for many centuries to come. Not since Raighne's fight against the Fomori, and not again until the still more titanic struggle one would wage centuries hence, not far from this very place, was combat like to Aber-dau-gleddau fought on Keltic ground.

Next day Athyn and her company rode hard and openly to the vast Keltic campment that lay just west of the ground of the parley—the debatable land between the two rivers Cleddau Vaur and Cleddau Vach, the 'two swords' of the placename. There she and a small escort were to meet at midday with the Incomer generals and elders and civic leaders, who had sought speech of Blackmantle before it came once more to the blade.

Among those who had been signatory to the petition, Athyn had particularly noted some of those who had been on the balcony of the brugh in Caerdroia—Dalgarno, Novedris, Finslock, Pym—and others too, who had run arms, who had connived at enormity, who had fostered and festered the campaign of slanders—Baigran Dyoleus, Jirko pen Rhys, Tareba Culloc; and she was deeply not pleased thereby.

And no more, it seemed, were they.

chapter twenty-two

Every horse to his own gait.

—*Aunya nic Cafraidh*

"So that is Blackmantle," said Baigran Dyoleus, watching Athyn approach with her escort over the snow-streaked ground. "I have never seen her before, at least not face to face."

On his left, Leto Novedris shifted in his saddle for the hundredth time since arriving at the parley site. Like most of his kind he was unaccustomed to riding—Nilos Marwin's love of it had been unusual—and he was detesting the necessity of it this day; and, by extension, the one who had made it needful.

"You have told enough lies about her," he said crossly, for the memory of that balcony was strong with him also, "that you should know her by sight."

Lira Cromell, who with Mihangel Glenrossa and Alveric Elshender sat their own horses close by—having discharged their embassy they waited now on Athyn's arrival—said pleasantly in her beautiful low voice, "You had any number of chances to see her ere now, Ser Baigran, if only you had lingered long enough on any of her battlefields."

But they all sat up straighter atop their mounts, even the Incomer contingent under the banner of the Bull, as Athyn's party neared: a dozen riders, Gweriden all, though for once the diplomatic niceties had been ignored, and every single one of them—the Firvolgians also—was armed to the teeth.

Athyn in the center and a little before rode as ever upon Rhufain, her hair in battle-braids, her black snakeskin cloak spilling over the blue leather cantle of the war-saddle, revealing the hilt of Dechtira Aoibhell's sword. *At least I am today in my own proper state, as I was not the last time I faced some of these...* Sweeping her glance over the faces turned to her, Athyn felt a sharp unpleasant jolt, and though her sight seemed momently to have darkened, she inclined her head to speak to Stellin, who rode on her left.

"Is that my brother Kier I see in their midst?" she asked quietly enough. "Or am I having a fit of fancy?"

"No fancy, though fit it well may be, and who would blame you," he answered just as quietly. "No wonder we could not find him; we were looking in all the wrong airts."

"So it seems." With an effort she dragged her glance away from Kier—*Later for you, braud*—and bent it upon the Incomer leaders. Though in the early days there had been Firvolgi generals and commanders who operated private armies under martial rule, it had not been very long into the Outgoing before a committee of elders had been organized to exert supreme authority over the battle forces. And as is ever the case when politics and strategy vie to sit in the same saddle upon the horse of war, strategy had early on been pushed back to ride pillion, by those who were no soldiers.

For which I am much to thank them: Without their endless squabbling amongst themselves, we had not won so many fields at so light a cost. But also these are the ones, these here present, who ran weapons past our blockades, who suborned our own folk, who massacred in battle and randomly slaughtered outside it, who burned crops and villages and polluted the lands and waters, who spread drugs and whoredom, who spewed such muck about us all, who engineered my encounter with the scaffold, who would gladly see me dead—well, as I would see them, of course, so that last is only fair. But, hear me Goddess, I have never wrought with them with such vileness and dishonor as they have wrought with us...

Falxifer Dalgarno had drawn himself up to speak, when another voice spoke first.

"You look well, Athyn, better than when last I saw you," said Kier mac Archill. "But to my mind Blackmantle"—he made it sound more a beshrewing than a byname—"would still look a thousand times better at the end of a rope."

"I can see where you might think it," answered Athyn smiling. "So close you came, and yet here I am, to your distaste... And to yours also, sers and beldams," she said in a voice pitched to carry beyond the farther river, addressing herself to the Incomer leaders. "But you to ours, deeper, greater, longer. Time is past when speech might have had purpose. When you forced our quarrel to the sword you made a pact to bide where the sword should take you."

"Is there no accommodation," asked Dalgarno in his harshly accented Gaeloch, "by which we might avoid this? I know I speak to one who holds no brief for compromise; but many of our folk will perish on this field, and many of your own. To what purpose?"

Athyn looked on him in silence for a long heart-freezing moment; on him, or through him, seeing all the years of Incomer occupation, all the occupiers, all the griefs they had brought to Keltia and to Kelts. Beside her, as her silence lengthened, Esmer made as if to speak, thought better of it.

Then Blackmantle, quietly, in excellent Volgiaran—*Nilos, Nilos*—so that they could not claim incomprehension: "A simple purpose, as we see it... I will tell you again, since the lesson seems so hard for you to grasp. Perhaps it has never been said to you clearly enough. This is not your world. We did not ask you to come here, we have not loved your presence here, we will have you gone from here. I do not know how to put it any plainer than that. Which word is it you do not understand?"

The watching Gweriden saw the impact of those words on blank, stunned Firvolgian faces, could read the thought behind as easily as could their captain: *'We come here in good faith to discuss some way out of this brangle, and see how this intractable blood-drenched harpy deals with us!'* For they did not understand, never did, never would; not in the way that

Athyn would have them understand, and so the one way left was the one now before them.

But if Blackmantle had said all she would, Athyn Cahanagh had not yet said all she wished...

"When I was a horsegirl on a farm on Erinna"—and now she spoke again in Gaeloch, her voice clear and savagely controlled—"I thought things must be as they had ever been, and did not dream ever to have a hand in their changing. But dán fell out other wise, and I learned from great teachers of how things might be altered. Following that dán, those teachings, I thought to make an honest, honorable fight of it, and trusted that you would do the same. And for a time you did; but then you took another road, a bent road, no purpose to it but uncleanness and harm."

Drawing herself up in her saddle, though her seat was deep and her back already braced straight as a spear, Athyn ran her eyes along the line of enemies, and this time they could not look away as on that Stone Street balcony but will or nill must meet her blazing gaze. Athyn—nic Archill, Aoibhell, Cahanagh—had vanished like a taish at cockcrow: Now it was only Blackmantle who spoke.

"For Keltia, I shall defeat you; but for what you have done to me and mine, I will destroy you. I do not forgive, and I do not forget."

Aber-dau-gleddau was not a field of the same sort as Gala, or any of the thousand other battlefields across which Kelts had faced Incomers down the years. Before a single sword was lifted it was already different, for both sides knew it would be the last.

Therefore Aber-dau-gleddau would not be won or lost in a single day, but should go on until only one side was left alive. And because of this, though on past battlefields Athyn had often given over command to one of her sword-arm lieutenants, for this fight she had assumed sole captaincy. *Not for glory! If we win it will not matter who commanded here, for the glory will be to all; but if we lose I would be the one to bear all blame in Keltia's eyes...*

That whole first day was skirmishing only: Keltic cavalry testing the strength of the Incomer lines, Firvolgi foot, in the strange-looking but effective formation known as a turtle, trundling out against the Kelts—few and light casualties on either side. But the next day's dawn saw a vastly different story, as, not waiting for the sun, Athyn gave orders...

Without warning, in the darkness just before the sky began to lighten, the Keltic war-pipes howled their battle pibrochs, and while the Incomers were still scrambling half-naked and wholly panicked out of their tents Athyn sent her heavy chariotry rolling across the Cleddau fords. They went over the Firvolgi lines like boulders in a landslip: armored chariots two and three times the weight of the wickerwork cars that carried the Keltic archers and arbalists, drawn not by the fiery light-boned harness-horses but by destriers, giant plume-pasterned beasts trained to use teeth and hoofs, battalions in themselves.

The Firvolgian frontlines, their turtles useless, went down under the first Keltic chariots like standing wheat in an August hailstorm; the rest stood to the onslaught more creditably and courageously than Athyn quite liked to see. Then the lines met in earnest, and the battle was joined.

Long gone were the days when Blackmantle unwillingly sat out the charge for fear of discovery: Leading her own company of Gweriden horse across the fords, Athyn met with Kier twice that day, but both times they were swept apart before it came to the crossing of swords.

"And perhaps it was as well," she remarked that evening to Morric. "I could slay him; but for my father's sake—for Cormac's sake I would liefer not."

They were alone in their clochan. She had his leinna off, that she might herself heal the cuts he had taken on chest and arms; and now, the task done that she had trusted not even Sulior to perform, she set the skinfuser aside and rubbed a herbal salve over the scars, her fingers gentle where the muscles flinched away.

"The wounds will ache beneath the healing for a few days," she said. "Even a sealer cannot mend that. But did I not tell you before the battle exactly how to parry just such strokes? I did. And did I not tell you to wear a proper lorica? I did. And did you listen? You did not." She jabbed him with a finger for emphasis, taking care not to prod the sore places. "Even I have learned better—you see I wore that silverskin today, and do not plan to go without it any time soon. You *deserve* to be cut to pieces..."

"I am still not so used to the field as you and the others," he said humbly. "For a poet, though, I do not think I have shown myself so very poor a man of the blade—"

"Indeed you have not; Aescaileas would be proud." She helped lace him into a clean war-shirt—the bloodstained one went to the floor to join others belonging to the Gweriden, later to be burnt by Bronwyn or Cathárren lest they should fall into unfriendly sorcerous hands—and leaned into his side, carefully, so as not to lose her healing labors; she was laughing. "Only be sure, cariadwyn, for my sake if not your own, that you get a wee bit *better* in the field? I would not be a widowed queen before I have even been a wedded one. And if you make me so, by the Goddess, Morric Douglas, I shall give you a shirtful of sore bones for it, and whether you are dead or no will be no excuse..."

By the third day of battle the fight was fairly sifted, no clear advantage either way. The poorest warriors had been earliest slain, and the unluckiest, and the least clever; the leaven that now remained was tough and skilled and evenly matched, proof against Firvolgian battle-presters and Keltic war-witches alike.

That night the Gweriden, gathered in Esmer's clochan, had refought the battle several times, and now were warily discussing another strategy: at least until Athyn stirred where she sat, in the shadows away from the quaratz-hearth, and spoke with a curtness few had ever heard her use.

"If we cannot win with such weapons as we have, then we do not deserve to win."

"You yourself have a weapon could turn the fight," said Esmer into the sudden hush, "if only you would use it."

Athyn's face in the sconcelight was white and set with refusal, and she rose and flung on the first cloak she found and stalked to the tent door.

"For the last time, and respectfully— My lord of Connacht. I will not. There is no more to be said."

Behind her the silence pulsed. "Douglas," said Esmer at last, not looking up from the table before him, where he had been drawing battle patterns in spilled wine on the white cloth, "what is your thought in this?"

"I am no Druid, lord," said Morric carefully. "As Athynna has explained it to me, that gift of hers is certainly wild-magic. Just as certainly is it not dróchtas—no black-working in it. Still, it is a power several shades too dark for me to feel at ease beseeching her to use; for her too, else she had employed it long ago on bigger things than a few links of Tolbooth chain. That small use misliked her more than she will speak of, even to me. For myself, I do not think she will ever make a greater."

Sosánaigh looked up, troubled. "But how if one day she stands against something so terrible that she must? She was born with this, you know; the Goddess gave it her, she did not find it lying in the street... She would not use it to save her own life—else the Tolbooth would not still be standing stone on stone—but what if *your* life, say, hung upon it? What might she do in such a pass as that?"

She waited, but Morric remained silent.

Athyn walking alone, bitterly. *Kicking badgers out of my toes, as mamaith used to say... What in all the hells is on me? It is not as if my hands are still clean of sorcery; and the Gwerin know it, aye, and the Firvolgi, and the Sidhe, and the gods… So if I have used it, and am known to have used it, therefore why not use it again, and more nobly? But if it is so natural, as everyone keeps telling me, why then does it feel so very unnatural—like a heavy cloak dragging me down? Hu Mawr, I do not know…*

She was passing the horselines now; seeing Rhufain looking eagerly at her from his picket, she turned her steps his way; and before she thought about it she was backing him Sidhe-style, riding away from the lines. *Well, and how can I go back now? They will only scold for that I rode out alone, in the dark, unarmed, on an untacked horse, telling no one where I went, the Fir Bolc all around—and, of course, they will be quite right… It is cruel to fright them, but, Goddess, they press me so, and I am in no mood to be shouted at— So Rhufain and I will go for a while along the river, and then perhaps I can think in peace… Allavolay!*

After a mile or two of furious galloping, Athyn slid her weight back and sat up straight, and Rhufain slowed through a canter to a long skimming trot. She threw her leg over his neck and slid to the ground, walking beside him hand on mane to cool him down. *I think we both feel better for that! Still, it does not help me overmuch with my problem…*

"Then perhaps you need another way to ask the question."

Athyn grinned and shook her head. "This is not that question, but why am I not surprised? My lord," she added, and Allyn mhic Midna fell in beside her as she walked.

"What do the Sidhe at Aber-dau-gleddau?" she asked after a small companionable silence.

"That again is not the question," he said smiling, "but I shall answer all the same. Well, we are often present at mortal battlefields; not to fight, though times there are when we have done that too, but to ensure that the battle's dán is served, or to serve it ourselves."

"Can war have dán of its own?" she asked, struck by the thought.

"A war can; a battle. Aye indeed."

"M'hm. And how then do you serve it?"

The faint rainbow glimmer that clung round Allyn seemed to ripple and pulse, like the aurora. "Sometimes by watching, only; other times we work another's will. To turn a thrusting blade or the battle's tide, to plant the thought of victory or defeat, to put it in the mind and heart of a tired soldier to save the life of a new-born babe—"

Athyn started so violently that Rhufain beside her climbed the air, bugling his challenge to the foe he thought must be near. Once she had calmed him, she drew a long breath, and turned to face the Sidhe lord.

"I should have known," she said in a voice full of wonder, as if she held all the past like a scryglobe in her hands, could see it all, a mystery long pondered now come clear at last. "And I might have guessed... All those times—all those years— The light, the fetch, those I had suspected. But that it was the Sidhe who saved me at my birth—nay, it was you yourself who saved me! But why? Whose will were you working that night? And to what purpose?"

Allyn's face was brighter now than the moon Argialla; he was smiling. "Always with mortals there must be purpose, high or deep, new or ancient, swift or long—"

"Well? Is there not?"

"Aye, and yet nay also. Listen now: Without Athyn, there would be no Gwyn; without Gwyn, no Edeyrn; without Edeyrn, no Arthur; without Arthur, no Aeron; and without Aeron—" He hesitated, then smiled again. "Not yet for that telling; but if that is not holy purpose, I do not know what is."

"Gwyn and Edeyrn I know; but those others— I know that you, or some of your people, see farther ahead than my own folk, but— You saved me, so that these others you speak of, whoever they are, or will be, *shall* be?" *Ah, Goddess, why did I not just stay in the clochan! And he has* still *not answered my question as to why I was saved, or at whose order—in case he thinks I have not noticed...*

"That is one way of saying it."

Athyn laughed, a brittle sound. "Are there other ways? So the purpose then is yours, not ours at all!"

"Again, aye and nay. It may be that I too was under orders... Or the purpose might be yours and ours together, a greater 'ours.' We are Kelts too, you know; have you never thought of that?"

She blinked, startled. "Why, no; perhaps I should have. And will from now, I promise you... But the magic? The wild-magic? Even Queen Seli said it was mine by right—why then am I so averse to using it?"

"Because it is meant for higher purpose than victory in battle," said Allyn at once. "And this you know, however deep within you the knowledge lies— You allowed it to help you escape from the fate the Incomers deemed for you, but you were not glad of it, and though it was necessary I know that it troubles you still."

"True on both counts. But—"

"You will know," he said, understanding her. "When the time comes for which the gift was meant, you will know it. And I shall be there with you to remind you, in case you do not. But you will know."

Battle-wisdom has it that tired warriors make more mistakes, and those who make the most mistakes, or the worst mistakes, are the first to perish; now, on the fourth day of fighting, the leaven that had been earlier winnowed was being sieved finer still.

Both armies were weary beyond thought, not a soldier on either side without a wound. Athyn herself was as exhausted as any other warrior—like the rest she had taken several sword-cuts—and it showed. She was fighting on foot, as she had done for the past two days. This was now a matter to be contested hand to hand; even the chariots had been held back, for a last throw of desperation should the Keltic lines be forced.

The night before, she had stood humbly penitent under

Esmer's furious tongue-lashing; had steeled herself under Morric's, which came later, and was worse. She shuddered now as certain of his observations came searing back, wholly accurate and deeply unpleasant, little hot molten droplets flung in her face. *Well is it said that bards can peel the skin off you with words! I would not be flayed like that again for any cause in Keltia…*

Turning her attention once more to the fighting, she was surprised anew at how empty the carse between the rivers seemed. *Our ranks have been dangerously thinned, but their strength has been cut to the point of vanishment. It will take but little more to topple them—I think we have it.* She hesitated, constrained by her own honesty. *But I am not sure that they do not have it also…*

The toppling place Athyn prayed to see came in late afternoon, and it fell on the right side: The Kelts, on Athyn's resolute order, overadvanced their right and drove in their own left, and Esmer Lennox himself hurled the last of his horse straight into the enemy center. For a moment, the line balanced, held taut as silver wire; then it burst like a keeve overfilled, and Velenax and the Connacht cavalry were sweeping through to take the Incomers from the rear.

Name of Dâna! Athyn was weeping as she watched. *Goddess, but I thought that line would never break…* But though the battle now was irretrievably swung, the fighting had yet to finish, and she turned round as a knot of Firvolgi foot came running up, swords high. She shouted to rally the Gweriden who were by, and those who heard began to cut their way to her side; but before they could get there a big Firvolgi sworder had engaged her.

She was not ready for him, and though at first she held him off he soon forced her to retreat a little, to where the ground was rough-grassed and uneven. In the midst of a fierce exchange she set a foot down on a tussock, turning her ankle inside her boot just enough to deflect her parry, and from the note of the metal as the two swords met, the numbing shock that shot like the fireflaw from hand to shoulder, Athyn knew she was disarmed.

Athyn Cahanagh and Kier mac Archill had come to the field knowing that one of them would slay the other before the fight was done. While Athyn had sought him at every turn, eager to settle their long quarrel, Kier had just as eagerly kept apart, so that he might meet her with advantage to himself.

Now he saw Athyn backing slowly before the Incomer soldier, her sword knocked from her hand. It was the chance he had been awaiting for days—by his reckoning, all his life. *Even on her best day she is by no means the best of sworders, she can be brought down...*

He poised his own sword upon his shoulder in readiness, and when he saw Athyn lunge to one knee to retrieve her blade, he came at her like a mad thing. First dropping with a flung dirk the man of his own side she had been fighting, Kier swung the huge two-handed claymore in a glittering arc at Athyn's unprotected back as she knelt off-balance, a mighty slashing stroke that had it landed would have instantly cut her in half.

It was never to be known by whose hand Kier mac Archill fell. In the very last instant Athyn sensed the coming blow, or perhaps she saw Kier's shadow on the grass before her; asked afterwards, she could not recall. But there was no uncertainty about her response, and no time for anything else: Still kneeling, she seized her sword left-handed and flung it up in a blind instinctive backward parry, to block the descending blade—barely—at arm's length above her head behind her. The force of the stroke and the weakness of the parry's angle sent her to the ground, her shoulder broken and her blade notched beyond repair. But the claymore did not find its mark—even the Sidhe armor could not have saved her if it had—and on the hilt end Kier was already dead with three Gweriden blades and three war-arrows and a lasra flain standing in him; ten seconds from Athyn bladeless to Kier lifeless upon the field.

She drove the point of her sword into the earth and hauled herself painfully, one-handed, to her feet again, surprised to find it so difficult, until she saw the blood and was more surprised still. *For all the Incomers bent on revenging themselves on Blackmantle before they go, I have been remarkably undamaged. But then, I have been well protected...* She bound her left arm into her baldric, for a makeshift sling until she could get to a healer. *Now I can face my lions without shame—*

Though she told none but Morric after, it had not been a sensing only that had warned Athyn of her peril. As she bent to retrieve her sword, she had seen something flash across her sight; something huge, something like silver and jet, something merciless and matchlessly swift; heard a sharp gruff single bark deeper than the sound of battle. And knew by that brief sight and sound that the Sidhe—and their sendings—had come to serve dán on yet another field.

Aber-dau-gleddau ended definitively but almost as anticlimax, the Firvolgi wavering and then withdrawing like a sudden tide, leaving the Kelts staring after them, swords still in hands and mouths well agape. By the time Athyn had struggled to her feet again the fight was over. It was as if a call had gone out that Kelts could not hear and Fir Bolc could not ignore, some hai atton that instead of rallying on had rallied away.

Not that there were many Firvolgi left to call from the fray: The Gwerin had swept over the land between the rivers like a steel flood. Athyn stood on a small knoll, her broken arm held fast beneath the baldric strap, her sword with its notched blade to bear her up; stared and stared, and still she could not believe.

"Swordplain, they are calling it." Esmer had come up behind her as she stood there, pain forgotten, transfixed by the sight. "A name that shall cling, if bards have aught to say in it, and we know they most generally do—"

Athyn smiled, but in truth she had scarcely heard him.

Aber-dau-gleddau, of which the bards will sing forever; Mouth of the Two Swords, where the Incomers were driven from the land. It will not change; cog we never so well or ill, it shall remain as it is. It is done, and it is well done…

She looked where Esmer pointed. Some of the Gweriden had staked out the captured Incomer standard on the ground nearby—the black bull on a red field, symbol of Firvolgior, slashed and cut now by many Keltic blades—fixing it with four spears driven deep into the churned and bloody earth. And a memory leaped to mind that Athyn had not thought of for many a year: her mother, Lyleth, dying, and words that she had whispered, words about a great struggle that would come to pass, between a wolf and a bull…

The bull on the banner—see how the tatters let show through the red fabric behind the black. It looks as if swords, or claws, have torn long wounds in the bull's flanks, ripped out its woven throat… Is that what mamaith foresaw—the wolf bringing down the bull at last? My wolf—or me? Or is Keltia itself the Wolf that has fought and won? What was it, then, that Lyleth had true Sight of?

"Even at the last he could not face you in fair fight, but only dared strike from behind," said Tigernach after; he had been one of the swordsmen whose blades had cut down Kier. "I am glad we do not know which of us slew him. I am his brother, it might well have been I—"

"Or Failenn, or Rhain, or any of the archers— We shall never know for sure. Comfort yourself, braud."

Athyn smiled as she spoke, but ran a hand over her face. She was in her clochan with some of the Gweriden; it was early evening, and coming on to rain. Her shattered shoulder had been mended—under the force of Kier's stroke the bones had splintered like glass, and it had taken Sulior and two assistants over an hour with a bonewelder to put them back together—and her other wounds tended. She had walked the lines, to praise and cheer the Gwerin, to give words to the wounded and blessing to the dead, and now she waited only on Morric's arrival to ease her mind completely.

"Perhaps it is best we do not know," she added after a while. "I am only glad so many swords were so anigh me." But she knew how close it had played out to a very different end. *And so we see again how dishonor is paid back by dán, though perhaps not often so swiftly as this…*

Shortly thereafter Morric came in alone, his handsome face all the more so for the weariness that lay upon it. Despite the demands of battle, and battle's aftermath, he had retained his mood—*Not hard, since we did carry the day*—and had expected Athyn to uphold her own. But something had apparently overtaken her: She sat now cross-legged and barefoot, huddled under the famous cloak, and she did not look at him; she had dismissed the others some time since, and was alone in the dimness. He sat close beside her, though he made no move to touch.

"What then?" he asked, his voice pitched to soothe, and in spite of herself she shivered. "Cariadwyn, we have won—*you* have won… It is finished. That should mean all to you."

"Much. It means much. But also it means that if Esmer has his way," she said haltingly, "and knowing him I do not doubt for a heartbeat but that he shall get it, I must be High Queen over Keltia. I did not make this fight for that purpose; hear me Goddess, that was never my wish or my will. I have never wanted it, never worked or hoped or planned or prayed for it; and yet it seems it must be mine. And if it is mine, and if I am yours—"

Ah, so that is what is on her… Morric felt relief sharp as a sgian, and, just as fierce, tender loving pity for her difficulty.

"Anghariad, this is no new thing; he has had this in mind long time now. We have spoken of it, even… How does it sit upon you?"

She laughed unsteadily. "Like a sack of gravel across my shoulders, dead weight, the balance ever shifting as the pebbles move within! I must do it, you know that—and I will do it. But what fears me more than all the rest—how will it sit upon *us*? Upon *you*?"

Morric smiled, and took her hands in his. "I cannot tell; how can we know, until we begin to feel the weight and make shift to bear it? But a burden shared is a burden halved... To ease that burden, then, before it comes down too hard upon us: Wed me. Handfast me at the stones. I will love you and you alone, and I will stay with you forever."

She did not look up at him; neither did she withdraw her hands from his.

"And if you must be King for it? Consider carefully: It may well be a worse sentence than that one to which the Incomers almost brought me. Certainly it will be a longer... I would not doom you to it; I love you too much for that."

"I am but a Scotan bard," he remarked presently. "I have no lands, no kindred, no title, no fame or dower save that which my harp has won me. I am no king, could not dream of asking a queen to wed—yet I cannot be a king until we are wed and you are Queen. It seems a stall-mate." When still she made no sign, unheeding even of the smile in his voice, he solved it for them both; kept hold of her unresistant hands and knelt before her. "This is a dán we face and fare together: King and Queen alike. But if I am not yet king, nor are you yet a queen, and so I ask now, bard to brehon, before my beloved turns queen entirely..."

And he asked again, and Athyn looked into the face lifted to hers; and tightening her fingers round his she drew their joined hands to her, and gave him answer.

She stared down at the ring he slipped upon her left mid-finger: a band of ancient findruinna—softly gleaming, untarnishing, the warrior's metal—engraved between its reeded edges with old-style round-letter, in fashion of a poesy.

"'Love Is Enough,'" she read aloud, and smiled for the tears that came stinging to her eyes. It was the refrain from a favorite verse of hers that the bard Séomaighas Douglas had written for his own Aoibhell lady, Lassarina; engraved inside it in delicate scrollscript, 'Silksteel and Fireheart.' *How well he knows me...*

"You must have been very sure then of your suit, my lord bard, to have come so well prepared."

"I have been carrying that ring around with me since before you went to Caerdroia," he confided. "I was waiting on the right and perfect moment. Then when you were held in the Tolbooth, and we did not know what might be done to save you, and we had word that—" Morric paused, took a deep careful breath as his smile faded. "I saw then that such a right and perfect moment might never come; worse still, that it might not come because you were no longer here to answer my asking, and if only I had asked sooner..."

"Hush." Athyn put her fingers across his lips, and he kissed them. "I am here. No one can deny it, or us. If we must fight for it, if we must rule for it, if we must die for it, no matter what else betide"—she held up her hand with the ring upon it, closed it over his—"we shall love for it. And this from now I wear forever."

Yet though she spoke from love and a high heart, no Sight to cast a chill, even Athyn of the Battles might have been daunted in that moment to know in what place, and on what errand, she would come to wear that ring in days that were yet to be.

chapter twenty-three

I pity from my heart those who have never been in
love, or in hate.

—*Athyn Cahanagh*

smer Lennox had commandeered the old inn at
Shanagolden to serve as field lodgings for the
Gweriden commanders, and on the night of the
victory at Aber-dau-gleddau Fleance the innkeeper himself
proudly bowed Morric and Athyn upstairs to the best chambers in the house. He had known them for years, first as ordinary young lovers, later as Fireheart and Blackmantle; he
had kept their secrets either way. But Morric drawing him
aside spoke privily, and Fleance beamed and nodded and left
them; and turning aside they walked on down the hall, and
went up a turret stair to a smaller tower room that they knew
well.

"Who says men have no romance in their souls?"

Spreading her fingers wide, Athyn turned her hand so that
the findruinna ring caught the sconcelight. "The first night
ever we were together, it was here, in this same inn—this same
bed—and so many nights thereafter. And you remembered."

"Oh, I remember well enough," said Morric peaceably,
drawing bars and bolts across the door, though two Gweriden
guards stood below at the foot of the little steep stair and the

inn was stiff with warriors. "I was there too, as *you* may remember."

"And what woman would forget." She hesitated a moment, then: "Now that our union is a thing assured, shall we tell the others?"

Morric laid his sword to hand at the bedside, and shook his head. "I think not yet a while. If we do all Keltia will only clamor for a royal wedding, and you not even crowned."

"And that is *not* a thing assured! It must still be put to the vote."

"But you will accept, if they ask?"

She was silent a while. "Aye," she said then, quietly, "I will. Aye. And yet, oh Goddess, I feel such darkness shall come of it."

"Never," he said at once. "Not through you the Dark. From before you knew it, you have served the Light."

Athyn closed her eyes, spoke as one who sees a great truth and loves it not, though she knows it to be truth all the same.

"You cannot stand in the Light without casting a Shadow; that is fact unalterable. The trouble comes when you refuse to admit that you possess a Shadow; for then *it* has possessed *you*. This deep truth is a thing that the great run of folk cannot understand, and so they make the fatal error of confusing the Shadow with the Darkness. Yet even the Dark was not evil at the first."

"And will not be evil at the last; aye, so we all have heard, many times. Some have said to scorn me that I am too much in love with darkness, that it is plain in all my chaunts how I have chosen the side of the Dark."

"And what do you say?"

"What do I say?" He smiled, but not at her. "What so many have said before me, and will say again after: No Light without an equal Unlight; in the end we *must* choose the one or the other, all of us shall come to that final choice. But the brighter and whiter that Light in which you have just now said we all stand, the deeper and sharper and blacker the Shadow it will cast. It is the Light, not the Dark, which creates that Shadow; and the Shadow is ourselves as much as is that Light. And when we cannot see where that Shadow might be, it is bound to be behind us, its fingers reaching to close around our throat."

"Morric—"

He was looking past the walls of the chamber, as if at something far distant that only he could see. "Nay, love... There is a great and final difference between the Shadow and the Dark—I am in thrall not to the Dark but to the Shadowplace, that fine and burning edge where Dark meets Light, fire on the one side and night on the other: the exact place where the two are balanced, neither one having mastery, no safety or surprise. Out where all the interesting things happen."

"They call you Prince of Shadow, from your songs, do you know that..." She looked at him, wanting only to protect him, to keep him safe forever in her arms against all dán and danger, knowing how futile a wish that was; knew too that she must not let him see this, or her fears for him. As to those fears, he would laugh, and for the futility he would scoff, and any road neither of them had ever been a safe sort of person. "But only stay with me, and I will make you King in the Light."

Morric shook his head, eyes closed now. "Not I. Not that for me. That dán is to another." His voice, so clear and deep in song, now was the veiled voice of prophecy; she shivered to hear it, as with sudden cold, though their chamber was warm. "But, Athynna, I *will* stay."

The next night on the plain at Aber-dau-gleddau Athyn Cahanagh was acclaimed as High Queen by the armies of Keltia assembled. Those who had fought the Incomers cared no whit for niceties of law or billet-box; to them, the thing was simple. Athyn had defeated the Firvolgians in Keltia; she deserved the Copper Crown, and, this night, they intended to make sure she would come to wear it.

No Keltic monarch had been made by acclamation for nearly three hundred years, not since Darsúlaith Ard-rían had been cried up to the crown over the Fian general Eldrydd who challenged her. But the Gwerin had read history too, and they knew how it should go...

Athyn came to Aber-dau-gleddau at sunset, by torchlight and afoot. The Gweriden made an aisle for her, a double line for her to pass between, with the rest of the host behind them to either side. She looked at the long corridor open before her, and though she paused she did not hesitate. *It is Inadacht-na-laithe, the Path to the Kingship, but it seems that I have been walking that path all my life. What are first causes, any road?* As she stepped between the first pair of facing warriors, all swords flashed out as one and crossed, ringing, to form a silver arch above her, and Athyn began to tremble. But she kept it within, and, head high, walked proudly beneath the roof of swords, knowing and loving each face she passed, her own face set as steel and wet with tears. The last pair of crossed blades was held aloft by Esmer and Morric.

She recalled little of what came next: not the Copper Crown but an oakleaf garland set upon her head, Coron-catha, the war-crown of victory and rulership; for scepter, instead of the Silver Branch, a slim gray-feathered arrow; not the Throne of Scone to sit upon but a high seat of spears and sarsens, to which the Gweriden raised her with their own hands; no coronation robe but the dark and fabled cloak from which she had her name.

It was a night for feeling, not discourse; but Esmer Lennox spoke, and Maravaun Aoibhell, and lastly Athyn herself. What she said then to her Gwerin was no great address of flaming words and wingèd, such as a captain will make to a battle host, but a speech of love and thanks, as one indebted will offer to helping friends; and as friends they received it as gladly as they had given. *I am in their debt indeed, for only by their labors, and the blood of many, am I come to this moment. Now comes the time for me to repay, and glad I am that I may do so.*

Morric, watching half as observing bard, half as proud anxious mate, thought it made a picture of the most indescribable drama, and the bard half of him began to frame it in words, so that later he might set it down in song: the young queen raised high upon the throne of stones, the torches like yellow diamonds strewn over the plain, the oakleaf crown green-bronze against bronze-red hair, the two rivers silver in the moonlight and the torchlight and the glow of the Criosanna high above.

Then across the exultant horde his eyes met Athyn's, with the same click and spark as the first time, as the last time, and he smiled from the fullness of his heart; and, after a moment, she did also.

On the first of May, Athyn entered a liberated Caerdroia at the head of the Gwerin armies. She rode in upon Rhufain proudly stepping, through the Wolf Gate off which she had so nearly been hanged, Morric beside her and the Gweriden behind her and the banners of the star and laighard borne before, with a baleful glance to her left for the Tolbooth glowering under the eastern walls. *I will have* that *place down around its own ears before I am many days older! I would not doom even an Incomer to a stay behind those stones; perhaps the Fianna may have a use for the site...* She went up through the thronged streets to Turusachan; and all the Kelts who had not watched her go to the scaffold were there now with all their kin, to see her enter in at the gates that had not opened for a Keltic monarch in more than a hundred years.

The palace itself had been hastily restored. No longer did blank windows stare blindly out, no more did cracked lintels crown rusted doors or frost-heaved paving-stones play host to weeds. Life had come back to Turusachan, that long-ago ashling of Athyn's now made real. But more than a palace needed setting in order before ruling could commence...

Three days later, in the Hall of Aonachs, before the House of Peers and the Senate and Assembly all convened,

Maravaun Aoibhell, Prince of Thomond, cried his cousin Athyn's name and rank and deeds before the gathering, as he had done at Aber-dau-gleddau before the Gwerin host. 'By right of blood and conquest': That was the double ground of Athyn's claim to the Ard-tiarnas; and Esmer, acknowledging that a kinsman's nomination had precedence over a liegelord's, and a prince's over an earl's, contented himself with briefly seconding the naming—though none in that chamber was ignorant of who it was had architected this moment.

Then Athyn rose to speak. Wearing the plain Fian uniform that had seen her through the campaigns—its wound-rents healed even as her own—she stood silent a moment, recalling the first time she had seen this hall, as a very young and unemployed brehon in the train of the Earl of Connacht: the great chamber with its ancient vaulted oakbeam ceiling and its elaborately carven stalls lining both sides in triple tiers, above each of which hung the banner of the incumbent noble.

Almost dreading what she would see, knowing she must look, she let her gaze travel down the right-hand side, to a dark empty stall. Dusty, stiff with age but its colors distinct, the wolf's-head banner of Aoibhell still hung above the two high seats; below it, impaled upon a faded pennon, the cadency mark of Findhorn and the arms of Galloway still declared of a union long ago. Athyn smiled gently, and heedless of those who watched she curtsied to the empty box, a daughter's reverence to Conn Strathearn, Lord of Galloway, and his lady Dechtira Aoibhell, heir of the Findhorn line of the House of the Wolf.

Every eye in the room was on her, and she was well aware of the nature of the gazes. Many faces she knew, many more were known to her by report only; but in this moment all were alike in the looks they bent on her—expectant, impartial, waiting to hear what she would say. *And that is as it should be—I want no favors here, in especial from those I dare to call friend...*

"I am not the flower among warriors," she said into the silence, "nor the jewel of judgers, nor a queen of sorcerers.

Until only a few years since, I did not even know my own kin and bloodline. But I am a Kelt, raised as many another in the humblest of estates and the deepest of those ways to which our folk have held. For too long we could not come together to throw out those who had crept in uninvited. With the help of the gods, and the Sidhe, and the Gwerin, and all right Kelts, all that now is changed."

She relaxed a little into the moment, sensing approval and support, and taking heart from both.

"The enginers and artificers will tell you that there is one pillar upon which even the greatest hall must hang. No special virtue belongs to the pillar itself: It does what it does, it serves the task for which it was made. None may ever see it, even, save the builders who set it there. It is meant for work, and not for show. Yet it supports the edifice without, and lacking its support the noblest keep must crash into rubble. I am not here to make a battle speech; that need is now behind us, and for that I give thanks to all gods. No special virtue obtains to me in this; if it had not been I, then it would have been another. But I was there at the moment such a pillar could be raised, and the edifice of Keltia renewed. If other support is now more suited to the task, I will gladly stand aside. I shall not stay for the vote, it would not be fitting. But if you choose me for Ard-rían, my oath to Kelu, I will serve you until I die. And also after."

She ceased, and casting one final glance round the chamber she bowed in silence and left alone. But she left behind her a very different silence than she had found there. And the pronouncement, when it came, though she had thought herself prepared to receive it, fell on her like a sudden swordstroke; and that pronouncement, it need scarce be said, was Aye.

So it was that a moon-month after her battlefield coronation at Aber-dau-gleddau, a fortnight after her acclamation in the Hall of Aonachs, the Kelts themselves voted Athyn Cahanagh to be their High Queen, by right of descent and conquest alike; by clann-right and sword-right, as the law-books had it.

As she had not stayed for the verdict in the Hall, neither did she tarry in the House of Law, where the results were being tallied from brehon jurisdictions all over Keltia. She had made her say to the peers a fortnight since, she had cast her vote today like any other Kelt, though she alone knew that her billet had been a blank one—to have voted any other way seemed the height of traha, and bad luck besides.

Now, in her new favorite place on the battlements atop the Keep, Athyn leaned, arms folded, upon the parapets. The sparkling day gave a view for fifty miles and more; across the glen, the blue monsters of the Stair looked within arm's reach. *Oh, this is a fair land! It makes no differ what fate is being decided across it—I shall keep that word I gave: that I will do my best for it, until I die, and after...*

Athyn straightened at the sound of the opening door, but did not turn round; and it seemed to those who emerged from the turret stair—Ganor and Esmer and Morric only, though all the Gweriden had begged to come—that somehow she already knew what they had come to tell her, for her carriage held a hint of new apartness, even the set of the back of her shoulders had a distance that never Blackmantle had worn. But that might have been in their eyes rather than in her; and then she turned.

"Ard-rían," said Esmer Lennox; Morric and Ganor had insisted that he should have the honor, or the burden, of saying it to her first.

They saw it thump home into her like a spear: a ragged indrawn breath, a flinching of her whole frame, as if she had been struck to the heart—as perhaps she had been. Then she was herself again; but a different self from the one that had been only an instant since. It had been Athyn nic Archill they had come to see; but she was gone forever, her they would never see again. Athyn Ard-rían stood before them in the sun.

Then Morric came forward, and looking in her eyes that for

him were unchanged he raised her hands to his lips and kissed them. And Ganor held out her arms, simply, and Athyn went into them without a sound, like a child that has had enough of being brave. And last the Queen of Kelts turned to the Earl of Connacht, and they looked long upon each other.

Then Esmer, perfectly, straightfaced: "Told you."

It broke the fraughtness and the tension as nothing else could have; and after they had laughed and cried they went down to where the Gweriden impatiently awaited them in the chamber Athyn had chosen for the Queen's council to meet in, if she should be that chosen Queen. It was a beautiful double-cube room, long unused, with leaded glass ceiling and plain stone walls. Tempting dán, she had ordered a table made to fit it, of dark polished waxwood—in shape of a wain-wheel, so that there was no head, and all who sat down there would sit in equal honor.

"The table is good, the table is fine—but the room needs more," said Mariota to her friend, while the Gweriden's jubilation went on all around them. "Wall-paintings—tapestries, perhaps."

"In good time," said Athyn, and promptly forgot. But others had heard Mariota's words, and, much later, would recall them...

That evening in Mi-cuarta, the great banqueting chamber, boundless revelry. Athyn, seated in the presiding place at the high table, more than a little daunted by such public pre-eminence—though she would have gutted herself with her own fork sooner than show it—bore with all the merriment as long as she could, then quietly signalled that the revels should go on for as long as those present had a will to it, and left the hall alone.

Ganor gave her a half-hour, then went up. The chamber was dim in the spring twilight, no sconces glowed; Athyn sitting in the window seat spoke without turning.

"I chose this chamber for this very seat and view; it minds me of the attic room that I had as a lass at Caerlaverock —"

"A farther view and a wider prospect than you had before you then— It has been a long day, cariadol," said Ganor, sitting down behind her and drawing her charge into her arms, most motherly. "For you and for the rest of us, and for the High Queen most of all... But we have all our wish now, and all our will, and that is a thing we never were sure of until today. So I ask you now, for your sake, and for Lyleth also, since I am here for you in her place: Is there happiness for you in this? If not, it is by no means a yoke I would have you take upon you; you have done more than enough without. There is room still to step aside."

Athyn turned to Ganor all a-rush, and the Countess saw what she had not seen until then: the woundingly young, the tremulous and shining face of joy.

"Nay, too late for that! And it would not be the word—not for this!—but it is all the word I have. Aye, methryn, I am happy. Until the vote was in I did not know, truly, how I wished it to fall out; I am full glad it is as it is."

"But?"

"But I wonder if I am up to it after all. I was meant to be an Erinnach horsefarmer, at least I was until you and my lord Esmer got your meddling paws on my life..."

"Nay," said Ganor laughing, though her face grew grave again. "You were meant to be High Queen; else you would never have come to it in a thousand lifetimes. The dán is yours, lassling; ours was but to serve it. And yours too is to serve it... When one does a great thing one often finds that one grows to the size of it. There is no road back now to that farm on Erinna; the young oak cannot be stuffed again into the acorn."

Athyn's smile flashed to light the room. "What is it a countess I know is ever heard to say: 'It will be well. You shall see.'"

"And as a young friend of that countess is ever heard to

answer," countered Ganor, with a smile to match, "'I daresay
we shall.'"

In after days Athyn Cahanagh was often heard to describe
those first weeks of her queenship as like being brought to
battle on a dozen fronts at once. First and chiefest of those
fronts was the matter of the Incomers: no small task, to
begin the shifting of many hundred thousands of sullen
embittered folk suddenly declared unlawful and outcast in
the only homeland many of them had ever known; and, just
as chief, the 'customing of the Kelts to the rule of the Ard-
tiarnas, to the fact that once more they had a monarch, a
fact to which they had to adjust every bit as much as that
monarch herself; and a thousand and one other tasks
beside.

In the midst of all the changes, Morric and Athyn were
striving somehow to settle into their new life together, and
their new home. Though as yet naught had been said aloud,
it seemed common if tacit knowledge that as Athyn was
now High Queen, so Morric Douglas was King in all but
name, and that name would not be much delayed in the
bestowing.

So those who had prepared Athyn's rooms in Turusachan
had taken care to make them Morric's as well, and the result
was a wonder. The couple had marvelled at the unaccustomed
lavishness of their new surroundings—a huge bedstead carved
with their intertwined monogram and impaled arms, swagged
and curtained with Douglas tartan; in the pool-room, a water-
wall of opals, a slab of granite paved thick with iridescent
stones, flashing blue and red and green sparks through the
coursing water.

They had explored a while, and then they had loved; now
they stood at the windows, watching the sun go down in
cloudfire and speaking of the future that was even now upon
them. Westaways on the edge of sight, on the volcanic isle

known as Gavida's Smithy, far out in the bay, a great plume of flameshot smoke was rising from the peak.

"See, Gavannaun too will wake this night... We might join once more with Erith," Athyn was saying, "though so vast an undertaking must wait new exploratories—we have no idea of how things stand with them." She nudged her mate where he stood behind her, one bare shoulder shrugging backward. "Perhaps you yourself might manage the realliance, as the particular province of King Morric."

Morric shook his head and tightened his arms around her, returning the nudge with a pinch on her breast. "The last two words I had ever thought to hear addressed to Morric Douglas of Meldeburna... Never shall I get used to that. I am after all but a songsmith."

"And I only a horsegirl; what knowledge I have of matters of state was learned from watching Esmer run Connacht, or my father Caerlaverock."

"And know this, love, those are no bad models—though it is on me," he added grinning, "that you have been modestly trotting out 'only a horsegirl' just a touch often of late... Well, if it helps, think of Keltia as a large—a very large—horsefarm. You, as chief horsemaster, have stock for riding, for racing, for battle, for farmwork; you need to find stabling, feed, tack, new grazing ranges; you must keep or lease the fields and the hay-barns, hire trainers to gentle the horses and teach them their particular uses, and to work with them after they are trained, to keep them active and happy; you will need to concern yourself with breeding matters, so that the best lines thrive and the new foals are strong and healthy; you must give employment to farriers and fence-setters and horsedoctors and saddlers and feed merchants... And once all that is in place and running, you must maintain it. Who better than 'only a horsegirl' to do it?"

Athyn laughed. "Very neat, very clever; I see you have learned a wee bit more about horses than you knew when we met, and you seemed to prefer furniture over even the kindest beast... But know this from that same modest horsegirl: Horses are tricky creatures to keep; they are endlessly taking sick, have any number of little quirks, can do odd things for no reason—or at least no reason you can see. Sometimes under saddle one will take it into its head to bolt, or to roll, or to scratch against a tree, and care nothing that it has a rider on its back. They will throw you, or rear and fall with you still in the saddle, or even turn round and bite you on the knee."

"What do you do when they try that?" asked Morric, diverted; and startled too, he had never imagined this as among horsemanship's many worrisome perils.

"Give 'em your boot across the snout. And pray to Rhiannon Rhên that you keep your seat—and your knee-cap."

"Well. Glesni and I may need to talk. But as to the rest of it—"

She turned in his arms, looked up into his face. "Glesni is a kind and well-trained creature; she knows what you want of her when you ask it, and because she loves you she is glad to do it. That is another thing with horses: Once you and they have sorted out who is to run the ride, everyone has a fine time of it."

"Even the horse?"

"Especially the horse." Athyn rested her head against his chest. "Yet Keltia is not one horse but countless many, and they may not always wish to obey leg or hand or bit. A chariot is harder to manage than a ridden beast, and a quadriga harder to manage than a chariot."

Morric said thoughtfully, "I have heard even Aunya nic Cafraidh say that every now and again a light—a *very* light—bit of stick behind the girth is not unthinkable, just to get the horse's attention."

"I have never needed that with any horse I rode," she said with pride. "At least so far."

"This is a horse of a very different feather." He lifted her in his arms and carried her back to bed. "Might need more leg than hand, and more stick than leg."

"I have ridden worse; and I have never yet been thrown."

"Never yet."

And dán, listening, made careful note.

Athyn had brought with her to Caerdroia all her friends and kindred and supporters—the great rise in the fortunes of the Lennoxes, Pendreics, Douglases, Drummonds and many other families dates from this time—and now that things were well in hand she and Morric began to order themselves and Keltia alike.

In her first official act as High Queen, Athyn declared Keltia free of Incomers; in her second, she raised Esmer and Ganor to be the first Prince and Princess of Connacht. All the Gweriden were ennobled of various degree; indeed, all those who had followed her received due reward—titles, dúchases, what they would—not excepting the humblest member of the Gwerin, nor forgetting the kindreds of the lowliest slain.

For his lady's queenmaking Morric Douglas wrote a new royal anthem. So beautiful was it that the first time Athyn heard it played for her, a private performance, she wept; and two thousand years later they are playing it, and weeping at it, still. For the rest, she balked at any further pomp, saying that the crowning the Gwerin had given her on the field at Aber-dau-gleddau was coronation sufficient for any ruler, and any road Keltia was in no state just now for elaborate and costly ceremonial.

Yet even Blackmantle could not escape certain demands of ritual and law; and so one cool spring morning just before dawn the Gweriden solemnly escorted her by torchlight up the Way of Souls to the ancient stone circle of Ni-maen, and there before a small knot of friends and witnesses, in the presence of Archbrieve and Archdruid and Ban-draoi

Mathr'achtaran, Esmer Lennox placed the Copper Crown upon Athyn's head, and Ganor put the Silver Branch into her hand; and leaping to the top of the Lia Fail, the Stone of Destiny, Athyn Cahanagh set her bare foot in the hollow at the stone's gray heart, where Brendan and Raighne, Conaire and Cadivor, Lorn and Líoch and all the others, Ard-rían or Ard-rígh alike, long gone or yet to come, had, or would, set likewise their own.

But what came after the fighting had taken as heavy a toll of Keltia's new monarch as the fight itself. So she had shaken Morric awake one midnight and fled with him from Turusachan, telling only Esmer of their destination; and coming to the lake region of Armoy in the south they had been welcomed in secret hospitality by Maravaun Aoibhell, at his beautiful country castle of Witchingdene. It was an old redstone keep, not great in size but many-turreted and peak-roofed, and Athyn fell in love with it on sight; in its chambers and gardens, for four days she and Morric, sometimes conversing eagerly but more often speaking in the silence that lovers have shared throughout time, took refuge with and in each other, and she felt her ravelled edges beginning to knit up again, a firm brave weave.

Across the valley from Witchingdene, on the far bank of the little river of Alligin Water, rises the range known as the Licat Annir. It is an old range, the hills for all their height as round as breasts; near the top of one, there is an open clearing in the clothing woods, grassed and sunny, in shape of a heart, and from this the mountain has its name.

Up Heart Fell, then, Morric and Athyn set out one green-and-golden morning; and when they had climbed to that high meadow, in the cool lovely light of May, white blossoms drifting on the spring winds, he asked her again, in formal asking, to wed.

"Though this time it is the High Queen herself I ask... Glad I am that I spoke for my Athyn while yet I dared."

"And your Athyn is glad to have so been spoken for, and to speak for her Morric in her turn; but since our lives are changed so vastly since that asking and answering, I do not hold you to it."

"Foolishness," he said, and turning over the hand he held he kissed her palm, and the findruinna ring he had set there after Aber-dau-gleddau, and the great glowing heart-shaped ruby he had just now set beside it.

"Nay, Morric, but listen— Though we love immoderately, shall we be able to live—much less reign—side by side, day and night with each other and not drive ourselves mad? We are neither of us easy folk, though it is true we have never even quarrelled—well, not over aught that mattered," she added hastily, for he was laughing. "And it will not be for us as it is for others: not mate and mate alone, which, Goddess knows, is hard enough, but King and Queen also—"

"No fear," he said comfortably, and lay back again in the sun-warm grass. "Even if you had become Judge of Connacht, and even if I had kept to my bard-rounds, and even if the Incomers had not been forced back to Kaireden—"

"Then—?" she prompted, pushing him with her foot when he fell silent.

"—we still should not have had a life like others' lives, or a love like others' loves. We knew that, cariad o'nghariad, I think before we had ever met."

And because—sharply remembering the words of Seli the queen on a night many years gone by, the very same words he had just now spoken—she could not have disputed him even if she would, Athyn glanced instead at the leather satchel she had given him that Midwinter at White Wellans, and to her great surprise said something very different.

"It seems long since you have made music—"

"Not true! It is only long since you have heard me make it."

He pulled the little telyn from the leather bag and, not moving from his easeful place in the warm grass, balanced it between knees and chest. "But listen now."

They returned next day to the world and their work and worries; and though they understood each other perfectly their next quarrel came soon enough. No surprise to either, it was Amzalsunëa Dalgarno, even in her absence, who was the cause: Some injudicious remark had set Athyn off, and had sent Morric straight to that place of unassailable calm he always sought in such moments, putting on the armor of amused unconcern that to Athyn was more maddening than any wrath. But the angrier she grew the quieter he became. *Arguing with him is like punching pillows! It wears you out, and the pillow is unchanged...*

"You are as a man who waits and waits for fine weather," she snapped at last, "and then when it comes, waits some more in case it might grow finer still!"

"I cannot answer that," he said, spreading his hands in a gesture that might have been arrogance or apology as easily as admission. "What would you have me say? You know I have no skill at quarreling; I never learned the art from those who know it best."

"M'hm? And who would that be? The pigbitch Firvolgian cutsark, who did her best to have me executed because she thought she could get you back if I were dead? Who if she knows what is best for her is on her way to Kaireden even as we speak? Before I can get my hands around her throat?"

"I have seen her once only since your time in the Tolbooth—to tell her you and I would wed—and she wept to hear it."

"Piast-tears!" *Goddess! Why are even the best men sometimes so stupid...* "Hear me, Douglas: Those tears of hers—I tell you, if ever you think to wipe them away they will cost you your life."

She spoke in metaphor; and though their quarrel was soon over and mended, as was ever the way with those two, it was not forgotten—and that too was their way. But metaphors, unlike dreams, have a way of coming real. And sometimes dreams also.

chapter twenty-four

Two roses went across the moon, a red one and a white.

—*Morric Douglas*

orric was an eager bridegroom, and Athyn a joyful bride.

The day before Scotan Midsummer, they took ship to Caledon where Morric had been born—the Gweriden having gone on before—and next morning rode into the mountains of Westmark. They were near to the field of Gala.

Athyn swung herself about in her saddle and looked with approving eyes at the savage landscape. This was Fleetdale: a steep-sided granite gash with rough bastions on all sides, running back to a high hub of peaks and knife-edge ridges where no road leads save that of the hill-goat and the wild deer.

No hearthsmoke taints the winds that blow across these scaurs, no window looks out upon these high fells… We are riding to be wedded! And he who is my lord and my love shall be my King also… For a nameless foundling orphan lass, I have not done so badly—she said, with all the arrogance that has been, indeed, attributed to her…

She laughed aloud at that; and where he rode upon her left, between her and the sickening unfenced drop to the valley floor two thousand feet below, Morric smiled to see her gladness. The track they now were riding is a very old one, running straight on and up to the Borrowstone Pass, though they would be turning aside long before that into the Yarrow Valley, headed for the ancient nemeton of Starcross where they would be wed. On the other side of that pass, where Westmark falls away into the high plains of the Raise, was Roslin Castle facing the Orrest Hills, where they would stay for the brief bridetime that was all they could steal just now from their new duties. And at the back of the Orrests was Morric's own birthplace at Meldeburna, in a valley named Ruchdi for the great Caledonian moon.

As the horses went round a great curve in the track that opened on a hundred-mile view, Morric looked out over the dark walls of Westmark, and raised his eyes away northeast; sighed, then smiled.

"You are watching me like a cavebat again, I can feel it... Well. When I was a lad I ran away to these hills once, to escape my father after a beating. The flight was not what you could call well planned: I had some vague idea of taking refuge at a cousin's hill-farm—never considering that they would have packed me straight off home as soon as I knocked at their door—but I lost my way, and even when it grew dark, and I grew cold and hungry, I was still so angry that I would sooner have died on the mountain than gone home again. So I lay down and cried myself asleep in the moonlight where I found myself—and that was Starcross."

He smiled again as she reached her hand to him in sudden aching empathy; caught her fingers and kissed her palm.

"Nay, cariadwyn, it was long ago— Any road," he resumed, "I woke up in the night, or at least I thought I was awake. I was huddled like a puppy at the base of the largest of the stones, and I *was* warm, wonderfully warm, not hungry even, and there was a woman in the sky looking down on me with love. It was the moon, but the face was my mother's."

"It was the face of your Mother, right enough," she said gently.

He threw her a quick smile. "I was twelve years old, and a lad; what did I know of the Goddess? But I slept safe and warm all that night; I felt protected, as if by my true mother, as never my own mother had made me to feel. So I have never failed to make my duty to the Lady upon Her holy days; and that is why

I wished to wed here and not at Ni-maen. I have never forgotten."

Athyn drew over to her the hand she still held, and kissed it. "She has never forgotten, either, beloved—and, She has promised us, She never shall..."

Before high twelve they had turned off the track and ridden down into a new glen, where lay their destination: Wyvis Yarrow, where the Gweriden waited—a beautiful old redstone maenor in the valley of the Yarrow Water, below Belnagar upon whose crest rise the stones of Starcross like a gray and ancient grove.

The lands roundabout belonged to the Macosquin lairds of Yarrow, foster-kin to Ganor Colquhoun ac Lennox. When the Lennoxes had heard from Athyn of the betrothal and Morric's desire to be wed at Starcross, Ganor had at once sought hospitality of her old friends; and not only had they gladly consented but were boggled with the honor of it all: that the Ard-rían and the King should be married from their house.

That house and its lovely wild setting minded Athyn sharply of Caerlaverock, though this was more shut in than the Archill lands had been; and when she beheld it for the first time she had had an undeniable pang or two. *It is so like to my home! Yet it still stands and lives, and Caerlaverock does not... But if I cannot be wed from my own old home, then a dwelling that might be its cousin will suit well enough. If my own parents cannot give me to be wed, and Morric's will not, to give him, then Esmer and Ganor who have been more than parents to all of us will more than suffice us both...*

Midsummer Day itself was spent alternately in fierce bustle and calm contemplation. Athyn was closeted with the women all day long, attending to bride's business, while the men rode out with Morric on a manly errand of their own. But at last all was done that needed doing, and at sunset came the sound of a horn to summon them, high and sweet and clear and ringing; the note carried for miles in the soft air.

So in the gathering evening mist Athyn Cahanagh and Morric Douglas left the empty house, and walked together up the hill Belnagar to the stones; as they reached the circle, as if on cue the mist blew back and the clouds parted. A blue velvet vault, still stained with the last of the sunset, arched above; the crescent Ruchdi, horns sharp as sgians, rode high in the south, and his light through the veils of remnant crimson cloud silvered the mountains that ring the Yarrowmere like a crown.

Inside the nemeton all the Gweriden were ranged round, a circle of souls within the circle of stones within the circle of the mountains, below the sickle circle of the moon. They were wrapped in cloaks as gray as the stones, and stood unmoving as the stones; each of them held high a lighted torch.

Other guests were foregathered there as well, kin and friends to the clanns of Archill and Lennox and Aoibhell. Morric's Douglas relations were notable only in their utter absence; but he had been as iron on the matter, that they should not come, should not even be told of the joyful event that was toward, and he had been obeyed—as he would have been on his wedding day even had he not been King. Nor were his bandmates present; or so many others present in spirit only, but present even so—Kelts all, friends all, a soul-family come to witness this joining in ceremony of two souls they greatly loved.

And then, hand in hand, robed in black and naked beneath the robes, silver torcs about their necks and the emerald beads from that long-ago Midwinter, barefoot and with crowns of oak and willow upon their hair, Athyn and Morric passed between the gateposts guarded by Rhain and Selanie with drawn swords, who saluted their entrance and sealed the circle behind them; and entering the sacred precincts they came to stand before the priestess and the priest who served this holy place.

The priestess was tiny and ancient, the priest tall and white-bearded, no less ancient than she; he it had been who had winded the horn. But both of them were strong beyond age and ages, rooted in the power of the Goddess and the God; and as the couple halted before her—Athyn handing the peony-sheaf she carried to her brideswoman Mariota, whose hair was pure gold for the occasion, and Morric his own garland of ivy and laurel to Stellin his groomsman—the priestess waited a few moments, looking from one to the other, then spoke in a clear carrying voice.

"What do we see in this circle?"

Morric and Athyn answered at once, in strong steady unison. "A man and a woman who have come to wed."

"What is the cause of thy journey and thy story?" asked the priest.

"To be married to this man"—("woman")—"of my choosing and my love."

"What clann and ancestry have they?"

The priestess answered. "Their ancestry unimpeachable, of the Kelts Keltic; as to their clanns let themselves pronounce."

"I am of the House of the Wolf," said Athyn, softly, proudly; for the first time it felt right to declare her Aoibhell descent, and she sensed presences hearing and approving as a lost daughter of the Name claimed her place at last in the ancient line. "Uí Fidhgheinte, the People of the Deer."

Morric's voice, deep, no less proud than hers, for though he was lawfully sundered of his parents he had never disseevered himself from the honored clann to which he had been born: "I am of the House of the Serpent; Uí Muirgheasain, the Sea-chosen."

"They are worth and fit to wed," pronounced the priestess, and now a faint smile warmed the sternness of her face. "Let them be set handfast one to the other according to our way and law."

*   *   *

So the bridals began that would be sung of for a thousand years thereafter. Morric and Athyn were marked with mystic sigils in burnt ash from the thirteen sacred trees, the wedding-rune drawn upon their foreheads; they were smudged with herb averin and asperged with sacred water from the Goddess's own spring; they passed their right hands through the flame of needfire that Mariota and Stellin kindled upon the altar. Air and water, earth and fire: The elements were present; and the gods also—a silverblue light seemed to rise up from the ground, or out of the stones, the circle crowded thick with mighty presences.

Morric took the sgian from the altar—his own, a gift from his bardic tutor upon his achievement of ollaveship—and made unhesitatingly the two tiny cuts upon his left wrist, in shape of the rune Avren, Firstrune, the Sign of Beginnings; and though Avren is a rune of beginnings also it is a sigil of completion, third and last of the Three Cuts which mark the three great ceremonial moments of a Kelt's life, when what is done is done forever, and for all gods to see.

Thus Morric; and as he did so said for Athyn alone, "The blood of my heart bind me to thee. So are two made one." The few droplets of blood were caught by the priest in the silver quaich, and Morric looked at Athyn and smiled.

She took the blade from him, did and said the same; and the priest set the quaich gently upon the altar, and blessed the contents. A sigh so faint it was scarcely to be heard, like a shivering wind, ran round the Gweriden where they stood; it was as if the stones themselves had sighed.

The priestess lifted her staff of ash and struck the ground once, and the silence deepened to absolute stillness, a hush that stretched between the worlds; and even the most earthbound of those within that circle knew that they were by no means the only witnesses attendant to this rite; this joining was seen and sealed in far places. Then the priestess spoke for all those worlds to hear.

"Who claims this man?"

Athyn laid her right hand over Morric's heart, where the robe was pulled aside to bare his chest.

"I claim this man to wed him from his kindred," she said, her eyes seeing nothing but him, her voice pitched to ring against the stones. "I Athyn wed thee Morric with hand and heart, with blade and cup, with ring and vow. I swear by That by which my people swear, to take thee for my wedded mate, to bear to thee true faith and all love, in this life and all lives. If I break faith with thee, let the sky fall upon me, let the earth gape beneath me, let the fire rise around me, let the waters roll above me. Naught can part us save lack of love alone; not man nor woman, Dark nor Light, death nor life, hear me gods."

And, looking only at Athyn, Morric vowed the same to her, splendidly, his deep voice soft yet strong, the ancient words in the High Gaeloch rolling out among the stones and down into the earth, his sword-hand brown against the blue-whiteness of her breast. Then the priest struck once with his oaken staff, and as Stellin lowered Morric's sword where he had held it high Morric slipped the silver marriage ring from off the point.

"I Morric take thee Athyn for my wife and mate and lady," he said, and placed the ring on Athyn's finger. "I wed thee with this ring, with my love and my oath upon it, in the presence of these who attest and witness, to Kelu and to thee. Hear me Highest. Hear me gods and Kelts. Hear me thou."

The Gweriden watched with joy as Athyn, receiving the gold ring from the point of her own sword that Mariota had borne, set it upon her lord's hand. Her ring-words came softly, full of love, spoken for him alone; and looking up at him she thought again how very beautiful she found him, within as well as without, and never knew that she herself looked just as fair.

Esmer and Ganor, and Ashlinn and Maravaun, standing in

the stead of the absent pairs of parents who should have performed this joyful task, came forward to tie the wedding spancel, a braided red silk cord, round the wrists of the couple where their hands were joined. Then the priest brought the quaich again, consecrated wine now mingled with their own blood, and Athyn and Morric pledged each other joyfully.

"Thugamar fein an samhra lin'!"

'Tis we have brought the Summer in!'... They drank alternately until the quaich was emptied; Athyn poured out the last drops of wine upon the earth, and the knotted spancel was slid off and set aside. Marriage documents, great curling parchment sheets, were placed upon the altar and signed by principals and supporters, their signatures duly witnessed by Bronwyn as Archbrieve of Keltia, and while this went on Gweriden bards harped a wedding anthem to those assembled.

One last thing remained: As the wedded pair turned from the altar, Sosánaigh and Micháltaigh stood forth smiling, holding between them at knee-level a great black-bladed sword. Laughing and clinging to one another, pelted with flung flowers, Athyn and Morric stepped over it together to end the rite, and in a joyous disorder the others followed them out from the holy place.

They had not far to go: The merry procession came to a revelground in a sheltered grassy hollow ringed by trees, where folk from Wyvis Yarrow had labored all day to set out boards and benches. Those boards were now laid thick with such food and drink as well befit the marriage-feast of a royal couple who had not been born to the throne, and who had very strong feelings indeed about such things as pomp, and pretension, and overmuch fuss.

But at last the rejoicing wound down to happy exhaustion. Morric and Athyn, standing in the nemeton gateway, thanked the guests, who kissed the bridal couple and departed, leaving them to speak to the gods alone and then to retire to the dower house, deep in the nearby woods, that had been romantically prepared for them—or perhaps, as those new-wedded often did, to stay all night within the circle precincts, there to have union in holiness and love for the first time as wedded mates.

But those who happened to glance back at Belnagar from the valley below, or looked up at Starcross from the windows of the great hall of Wyvis Yarrow, where the revels continued unabated till dawn, might have seen lights dancing amid the standing stones, and the glow of moonfires as the Sidhe came to the sacred circle to bless the marriage of their friends.

When Morric and Athyn returned to Turusachan from their bridemoon at Roslin, purest honey for all that it had been a sevennight only, they slept for the first time in the new tower rooms that Athyn had chosen for them to share.

"I know we had only just been settled in the other chambers—not that those were not fine or grand enough," she had explained carefully, "but I wished to make all new for us, as Keltia is new, as this is new"; and Morric, who cared little enough where he slept so long as the pillows were ample and Athyn's head was on the ones beside his own, had indulgently agreed.

He was pulling off his sithsilk leinna when a sudden yelp made him whirl. Fighting the shirt that entangled him, he emerged looking wildly round for the cause of her alarm.

"Gods—Athynna—what is it?"

His bride who but a moment since had slipped between the sheets now stood beside the bed, clutching her filmy nightrail about her, regarding the coverlets with wariness and suspicion.

"In the bed—something sharp—"

He drew his sgian and with the other hand flung back the bedclothes; and both of them stared, and Morric laughed, and Athyn wept.

From their bridebed the perfume of roses was rising: a carpet of roses, white ones and red ones, strewn between the silken sheets, among the wild-swansdown pillows, beneath the velvet coverlets. And the Gweriden, who had joined in joyful conspiracy so to welcome them home, had as one, in their complete dazzled unity of romantic purpose, forgotten all about the thorns.

Athyn lying half asleep. She raised a hand to the place between her breasts where she was 'customed to find her amulet bag, to touch the bag for luck and prayerfulness as she often did; but for once the battered little leather pouch was not there, and her fingers brushed something new, for an instant unexpected.

And she smiled then, well remembering the moment it had changed, the morning after the handfasting. She had proudly bestowed upon her mate the tinnól, the morning-gift she had chosen for him; then Morric in his turn had brought out somewhat on a gold chain, and had clasped it round her neck. Athyn, who as he did so had been looking only at him, when challenged had not even been able to tell him the color of the gem, or indeed that it was a gem at all. When she did glance down she had gasped to see the biggest emerald she had ever heard of, set in a gold frame: a cushion-cut stone the size of a kestrel's egg, dark glowing green in color; deep within it, a flaw caught the light and danced like a tiny flame.

"I found it in that same place on Caledon whence came those little beadstones," he had said. "I saw it through the water of the stream, and took it up, and had it cut and set and polished. No other stone of such size has ever been found there; the Goddess must have meant it for us."

She had smiled up at him then through her tears. "As well She might: Green is the Goddess's color, the livery of love."

Not even to their closest friends had they chosen to show a gift more intimate still: two small gold lockets made at Athyn's order, unremarkable on the outside, but within... On the left-hand side, beautifully exact, was the semblance of a man's lover's parts carved in sapphire, and that was Morric's month-stone; on the other side, in matching fineness, a woman's in emerald, and that stone was Athyn's; when the locket closed the two gems had union even as did the two they represented.

Now Morric looked over at her as she lay beside him in the firelight, the emerald glowing between her breasts like a great green star, the engrains she bore on breast and arm and hip and shoulder vivid against the whiteness of her skin. *That day is wasted, when one has not been moved to laugh, and weep, and love… For the rest of our lives, I vow we shall not fail, each day, to do all three…*

"What?" she asked, coming back to the moment, her own smile widening and warming to his, snugging closer.

"I have lain tonight with a crowned queen in her own palace," he said straightfaced. "My wife is a jealous woman of most fiery temper, her anger will be terrible when she hears."

"Oh aye, very like," she agreed as gravely. "But no more than my husband's, when I boast to him of how I have slept with a king, and in his own bed too, now that the thorns are well out of it…"

In the night, words, and neither of them ever knew after from whose mouth which words had utterance, which of them did speak what syllables—the ancient and beautiful Erinnach wedding-words, spoken aloud when none were there to hear them but they themselves and the stones of Starcross and the Powers to whom they had offered their love and days and worship:

"Cuirim fad beannacht na greine thu—" *I give thee the blessing of the sun…*

"Cuirim fad beannacht na gealai thu—" *I give thee the blessing of the moon…*

"—na mhara—" *—of the sea…*

"—na reanna—" *—of the stars…*

"—na Dé—" *—of the God…*

"—na mBan-dé" *—of the Goddess…*

*　　*　　*

Next morning Morric entered with Athyn into the Hall of Heroes, in great-aonach, and there he was crowned in the presence of nobles and commons alike as King of Keltia. Attired as she had not been even for her own queenmaking, the Copper Crown gleaming redly against her hair and Morric's bridegift blazing green at her throat, Athyn said the words of investing, and received Morric's oath, and set the cathbarr of Nia the Golden upon his bent dark head.

It was an all but legendary treasure of Keltia, the tinnscra Nia had had of her own people, the Shining Folk themselves, when she wedded her mortal lord. The cathbarr had made its own immram to Keltia; and ever since it had come and gone across the centuries. A band of heavy silver knotwork set with clear crystals, in the frontlet piece a cushion-cut stone larger than the rest, the coronet had such virtue, or such magic, that it fit every head deemed fit to bear it.

And now it was again a gift from the Folk of the Hills, the People of the Star, given to Morric and Athyn on the night of their wedding from the very hands of Neith and Seli. Yet never was Nia's crown given to mortals out of the guardianship of the Sidhe but to some great purpose...

Now Athyn held it high a moment, then set it gently upon Morric's head, and kissed him, and he rose to stand beside her for the first time, Morric Rígh. So fair he looked that day, splendid in a richness of black and red and gold, his beard freshly trimmed, his dark brown hair flowing upon his shoulders and the ancient silver coronet about his brows: the very image of a Keltic king.

Yet Athyn Ard-rían had more in mind this day even than her mate's crowning, and now she lifted her hands to command silence.

"As a marriage boon, we, Athyn Ard-rían and King Morric Fireheart"—so she herself was first of all who were to call him so down the centuries—"do grant a choice to certain of the Incomers so lately made to be Outgoers. Justly made, make no mistake: All Fir Bolc present in Keltia have been rightly and lawfully cast out. They may depart in peace, with their goods and their gear and their gold, and we wish them safe home. But in the past few weeks I have received desperate petition from some who have great wish and will to stay: Perhaps they have taken mates from among us, or had children by Kelts, wed or bred. And to these I say now: If you stay, and swear to us, and obey our laws, and take our ways upon you—for that I will make you Kelts."

Athyn ignored the sudden hiss, like a giant nest of serpents unpleasantly disturbed, as her hearers caught back their breaths in shocked surprise, and she continued serenely, her voice raised only a little.

"So that those who do so will be known no more as Incomers, but Comelings—a word we have for a stray animal that attaches itself to a person or place, a wanderer that, once lost and finding at last a refuge or a friend, will choose to stay, and is received." She placed her right hand over her heart, to honor the promise. "So say I, Athyn Queen of Kelts, hear me gods."

She had known this decision would cause bitter feeling among the folk, had discussed it with Esmer and the full Gweriden and her new High Council at great length beforetimes. But she knew also that the Comelings, whatever numbers they might make, would be in the end vastly the exception, no more than a few thousands at most. The paramount majority of Firvolgi unreservedly now wished to leave, and from one end of Keltia to the other they were going about it as quickly as they could.

And who could be surprised? thought Ganor, listening to Athyn. *But this is a gift: an act of mercy tempering justice, and only the true ruler can bestow it...* She glanced aside at Esmer, and met his eye, and knew he shared her thought, and was content.

But the Firvolgi were not the only ones who sought to depart: Indeed, Kelts who had had insalubrious or unlawful or otherwise suspect dealings with Incomers and now feared reprisal had already petitioned the Throne of Scone for permission to leave. Even though Athyn had many times made it plain that she had declared a full amnesty, would tolerate persecution of neither Comeling Fir Bolc nor collaborator Kelts, in the end she allowed them to go as they did wish.

But her clemency was to find its reward elsewhere. Comparatively few Firvolgi, as it turned out, were to take up her offer; but those who did were the best of their kind, and they became in the end, as the Kelts say, "more Keltic than the Kelts." Their new fellow countrymen—once the Comelings had settled down and been accepted, largely because they and Athyn alike were determined on it—opined that it seemed plain enough that these Comelings had been Kelts in former lives, who, for typically inscrutable reasons of dán, had been reborn away from Keltia, and who now were returned home; it seemed as good an explanation as any.

"In a few generations it will matter not a whit," said Athyn to Esmer and Ganor. "They will wed us, and we them, and soon only the bards will have a dusty record that once—a hundred, five hundred, five thousand years ago—a Comeling entered into a Keltic family for love of Kelts and Keltia. And that is as it should be."

And—*the true reason I did so*—*Nilos would be pleased to see it done; I think, I hope, proud of me also, that I have done so*... But this she did not say.

The Comelings were not the only ones to settle in well after unlooked-for starts: Morric and Athyn ruled happily and without incident for a full moonyear of great joy and bliss. The Outgoing was far advanced, the Firvolgi grimly performing under the law what they had been forced to accept under the sword, their numbers in Keltia dwindling as the ships left laden for Kaireden and returned to Keltia for another ferrying run.

Even if they would have been, which was not the way they did things, the Queen and King were far from idle that first blazing year. The very air of Turusachan was alight with bright plans and fervorous talk: how the new reign might change things for Kelts; how indeed things were changed already, as they had not been for a hundred years and more. Keltia once again had a young monarch and consort upon the Throne of Scone, a High Council to advise them; the Incomers were vanishing like snow in spring. Alliances had already been made with outworlds, most notably with the Yamazai on Aojun; plans were well in train to re-establish trade in many galactic sectors, trade that Keltia desperately needed to put itself back on the independent footing it had once enjoyed. Grand high matters of state all of these, and rightly worth prime attention; but there were small private matters that needed attending to also, matters just as important to the folk upon whom they bore...

Esmer and Ganor, as first Ruling Prince and Princess of Connacht, went home to Ardturach to attend to the province's affairs; then, leaving Greyloch and Hutcheon as regents, they returned to Caerdroia to take up residence at Lennoxliss, though by exasperated count of their rechtair they passed more nights in the royal palace than in their own; which was not to be wondered at, since Athyn had named her guardian and mentor as Taoiseach for her reign.

Of the other Gweriden, though Athyn would as lief have had them all at her side forever, many returned to their own worlds soon after the wedding, there to do the work that called them. But of the inmost circle, most remained with Athyn and Morric in Caerdroia, or else, if they left, returned so swiftly and so frequently that, as the cailleachs say, they were never gone long enough for folk to notice they were gone at all.

Athyn had given the Firvolgi two years to settle their affairs and be out of Keltia, and that was generosity above even the honor of the victor. But that grace was not to be abused, nor her tolerance presumed upon, for after that time they would be turned out by the Fianna, not packing-time allowed—and it was Blackmantle who had made this very clear. By the time of the first yearday of Athyn's accession, most of the Fir Bolc had already left for Kaireden, some to behold their own ancestral world for the first time. Many of those who had most maligned Athyn and Morric and the Gwerin down the years were gone also; though some few yet remained, and upon those the Gweriden kept a close eye.

But if old enemies were vanquished and vanished, new friends—though by another reckoning these were older far than even the ancientest of foes—were being seen in the streets of Caerdroia for the first time since Brendan's day, and their return was to Kelts a wonder and a joy.

For, always in small numbers, under cloak of night or their own magic, the Sidhe began to come as they had promised. Though their friendship with those they knew was real and natural, the faerie visitors had little commerce with ordinary Kelts, save for chance encounters in the woods of the Loom or beside the Falls of Yarin or down upon the sands and saltgrass at the mouths of the Avon Dia; and those fortunate enough so to meet them found them only courteous and fair-spoken.

But the Shining Folk knew well their effect on most mortals, and few of the citizens of Caerdroia came so close to them as that. Yet even those who only glimpsed a glimmer as of starlight on the hill-shoulder behind the palace, or heard ringing from the sea-cliffs at sunset a song no mortal bard could match, or had a word of greeting and salute offered by a red-cloaked rider on the high moors or in the empty windswept streets at dawn or middlenight, felt blessed and honored to know that such guests were near, and hurried home to tell their dear ones of the moment, that they might share the magic's gift.

On the first yearday of their handfasting Morric and Athyn returned to Witchingdene, in Armoy, where more than a year before—June on Caledon is July on Tara—they had climbed to the Heart and pledged to wed; again as before, Maravaun Aoibhell was there with his Princess, to welcome them with kinship's kiss.

"Oft is it said 'I would not call the King my cousin,'" he observed slyly, "but this time I think I can call him so indeed, and with a fair degree of certainty too—"

They laughed, and entered in, exchanging greetings and small news as they did so; just the right amount of ceremony, and no more. But at table that evening Maravaun glanced at Ashlinn his wife, and she nodded smiling.

"If the Ard-rían and the King would do us the honor of acceptance," he said then, "we would have the honor of bestowal: that you should take this castle as your own, for tinnscra, for crowning-gift, for yearday gift. You two have no place that is yours alone, and since it was here you pledged to wed and planned your rite, it seems fitting to us both that you should have it, as gift for kinship and love from Thomond to Findhorn."

Athyn protested long and fluently, and Morric no less, but in the end it seemed less churlish to accept than more gracious to refuse, and their thanks were then as fluent and as many as the protests had been.

"Besides," confided Ashlinn later, as she and Athyn luxuriated in the tynollish while their men swam in the rock-walled pool, "my lord has ever keenly regretted that you were lost so long to your kindred; and I think this is by way of honor-price for the clann's failing." At Athyn's startled splutter of protest renewed: "Oh aye, I know! But it is how he feels, and you know how men can be. We are here so seldom, any road: When you and that handsome minstrel boy of yours hid yourselves here last year, that was the first time we had been in residence since Raffan was a lad, and even then we came only to host your guesting. It pleases me very much," she added, "that it was here you two did swear troth. The castle will be glad of you. It should be a place of love; it was for love that it first was built."

*   *   *

"Do you know the story of this place?"

Morric shook his head, lazily but firmly, and snuggled him under the coverlets. "I do not; but all my bardic instincts warn me I am about to hear..."

"Hush. Well. A lady Tarnaris, of the Clann Lochiel, built it for her beloved, Arran, a lord of the Clannrannoch who dwelled nearby. For reason of ancient enmity their families forbade the match, but they were resolved that they should not lose each other, not though death itself should bar the way. And so she would come here in secret, and set a light in a certain window, which seeing he would ride over to join her, and stay with her until the end of the night."

"And did their kindreds not notice this ever-so-subtle signal, and ride over sword in hand to put a stop to it?"

"Hush. Any road, nay, cynical one, not so; for their meetings went on until he was slain in battle—not with her kin—and then she came to live here until she herself died. But all those years she dwelled here alone, every now and again the light was seen to burn in the tower window as before, from dusk to dawn. And to this day, every now and again, that light can still be seen shining from that same very window where once she had set it to call her love to her."

Morric was silent a while. Then, shifting on the pillows beside her: "What window was it, where that light was set?"

Athyn laughed. "Now that is just exactly what I told the Princess Ashlinn would be the first question out of your mouth; always with you it is curiosity over romance."

"Not always. But you never know when a song might come wanting to be made, and it is as well to know." He paused so long that she turned to see if he had fallen asleep. But in that same moment he spoke. "What would you do if I should come to die?"

Athyn caught her breath at the question. He was not looking at her, the blue eyes were hooded; but she knew very well why he did not meet her gaze, and why, too, he had asked. And though she was also 'ware that every millim she was silent was a millennium to him who waited to hear what she might say, even so it took her a moment or two before she could answer.

She leaned over him, placing her hand upon his heart as she had done when they were wed. He looked up straight into her eyes; his own were haunted, and she put all her strength and all her love into look and face and voice, to drive that haunting back forever.

"She did most well; I would do more. I would ride to Annwn to fetch you back from Arawn himself. We have bound ourselves in more than memory: I have knit my soul with yours. The weave cannot be unpicked. The gods themselves may not undo it. Do you hear?"

And dán, listening still, heard well, and noted yet again.

It had been raining all that day, soft fine rain from clouds like billowing gray and white silk, hurrying by so low it seemed to Athyn she could reach her arm out of the tower window and touch their hem. But she had run out into the rain to gather late lilacs, with only a thin cloak to cover her nakedness, and Morric had watched her as she moved in the garden below: her arms unearthly white in the rainlight, her feet bare in the wet emerald grass, the gray cloak now and again swirling open showing ivory or russet beneath.

She lay now very still upon the bed, between her breasts Morric's latest gift—a fiery opal the size of her palm, cut in shape of a heart; graven upon its back, in his own hand, was his private message of love to his wife.

Kneeling above her, Morric shook out one of the lilac branches from the sheaves that filled the chamber, so that the purple flowerets fell upon her bare body like a shower of tiny amethysts, and the rainwater also, that clung to branch and leaves and blossoms like little round diamonds. He bent then to kiss the flowerets away, blowing gently to clear them from her breasts and groin and swelling curves, kissing, his mouth lightly brushing where the blooms caught or drifted, drinking the raindrops where they stood upon her skin.

"Silksteel," he said, his voice deep and quiet in her ear.

"Not Roselily?" she murmured presently, pointedly, and he shook his head, laughing.

"She named herself so, though she is neither. I call you Silksteel, and you are both. Though in truth," he added with bardic judiciousness, "you are every bit as red and white as she; more, for she is sunsprecked, and your skin is clear as milk."

Athyn sat up with a snort of laughter, scattering the lilacs, and gave a shrewd tug to the corner of his beard.

"Ah, Goddess, the tongue of a bard! Yours had rather more useful employment a moment since—"

"Well," he said, a little embarrassed. Then, teasing: "Perhaps I am still daunted, thinking to bed with a High Queen."

"Well"—teasing in her turn—"it is then your Queen's command that you put aside such daunting; for she will lie with no man of lesser rank than King of Keltia."

"Then I must obey my Queen, so that she does not lie alone; for we are wed for life and lives, so we did swear before the Goddess and the God."

"Some even of our own people think that promise excessive and strange."

"How?" He was suddenly cross, but not with her. "Swans and wolves and other beasts will mate for life—both their lives—and if their partner is slain they will take no other after. And are not humans held of at least as great nobility as beasts in Kelu's plan?"

"One would like to think. Still, liking to think is by no means the same as knowing."

He laughed and kissed her hair, restored to loving humor as swiftly as he had been thrown out of it a moment since.

"Nay, I will tell you what it truly is, and it is a fearful terrible secret: Most wedded folk prefer the state of being married to the person they have in fact wed. Aye, it is true, I promise you, stop laughing and listen now... Oh, they love their mates, but to them the being wedded is the important thing, and many another congenial woman or man would suffice as well. If a mate dies, they will mourn correctly, and then happily find another and wed again. And that is well for them; we do not hold it against them. But we are made differently: For us it is the soul and heart that make the marriage; our faithfulness and choice are fixed upon the mate, not the state. This is what they cannot understand; but they know it deep within, and they are chagrined they cannot do likewise."

She stirred against him. "It is very true. If I had not met you I should not have wed at all. I would not have settled for less than you, for less than what we have between us—next best is not good enough. And if ill befall you, which Goddess forfend, I will never wed again, because I would still be wed to you. That too we have promised."

"It is why I never wedded Amzalsunëa"—he felt her sudden stillness, and kissed her hair—"nor was much troubled that she styled herself my wife; it did not matter. She was of my choosing—once, long ago, do not vex yourself!—but she was not my choice. Then I met you—and I learned that it mattered very much, after all, which woman went round Keltia saying she was wife to Morric Douglas... Now your House's own symbol is a wolf, and that well befits your faithfulness; but we together are swans, you and I, and so I give you this."

He reached over to the bedside chest and took up a small leather box; opening it, he lifted out something that shot silver sparks in the firelight, and clasped it around her neck, settling it into the hollow of her throat, above the great opal. She touched the cold splendor of it: a heavy collar of linked silver swans, their wings upraised, their necks elegantly curved, their feathers deeply carved with finest vaning.

"O rare black swan..."

It was to be the last gift he gave her in that life; the next time he was to see her wearing it, it would be in a blacker place than any swan's dark wing.

*　　*　　*

In the exploding smother-enfolding fire-shot dizzying darkness, Morric heard a silver voice chanting, beneath, before, behind, above; a rann of love and passion and union beyond the body's own. *With us it has never been merely bodies alone, fierce and fiery and wondrous though that be—but always, ever, more. Indeed, all...*

"Thou the axe, I the helve; thou the plow, I the share; thou the sword, I the sheath; thou the force, I the flame; thou the source, I the same..."

He knelt upright upon the bed, pulling her hips up to him, so that they touched only where their bodies were joined, and their minds, and their hearts; she arched her back like a drawn bow, to take her weight and his motion on her shoulders and her heels and her outstretched arms. She it was who chanted, and yet not she alone, and the words spun about him and her together both web and wonder.

"Thou and I," he said in the night, in the High Gaeloch, in the voice he kept for her alone. "We are not much unlike."

"Nay," she said as softly, in that same stately tongue, tears glittering upon her cheek, silver swans glittering around her throat, "we are not much—unlike."

chapter twenty-five

Argue as you please, you are nowhere. The Queen disposes.

—Sosánaigh Darnaway

"She asks *what?*"

Though Athyn hoped that surely she had misheard, that Morric could never have just now said what she thought he had said—*We have only just been wed a full moonyear, how can he even* think *to do this?*—when she turned round to look at him, she knew that she had not, that he could, and, indeed, he had...

"Melassaun begs me come to Kaireden, to help her." Morric's voice was even, unstressed; and with a terrible certainty Athyn knew that no matter what she herself said, he was going. "She is in desperate straits, Athynna; read for yourself, here, see, she is to be pitied. She says she knows that now you and I are wedded she has no right to ask, but she needs my help and mine alone, and if I go to her this one last time she will never trouble our path again. Says that for sake of our onetime love I must help her change her life now or she will die, unless perhaps she should slay herself first."

Now that *would save us all a sword-edge...* "I thought she had found herself a wealthy baron for 'patron'?"

Morric had the grace, and the supreme wisdom, to look uncomfortable. "Melassaun lands ever on her feet, she has that talent; but this time— It is the hazen, you know."

Lands ever on her back, more like... "Aye," she said, her rising anger putting an edge on her voice that she hated to hear, and knew he hated. "I do know. You are so 'customed to this it no longer even seems strange to you; you have been hearing this from her endlessly, and in honor and chivalry you have endlessly answered; but has ever your 'help' helped her? She whines like a hedgepig, sucks life like a blood-bat from you and everyone. But when does she learn to tend her needs herself? Compassion is the gift of a noble soul, King Morric; but she has fed on yours for years, like a kite on the slain of battle. Fed and fed; and still she does not grow. And by every god that was or is or will be, are you not *yet* tired of dealing with her? And still you refuse to understand why it so angers me..."

He was silent a long while. "I understand well enough," he said at last. "I have told you before the common cause of the hold we had for each other; though she herself seldom speaks of it, being a woman of few words."

"Since she knows so few to begin with!" snapped Athyn, then seeing his surprised recoil instantly repented. "My sorrow! But, Great Goddess, men can be so— I do not say it did not happen even as she claims; but I do say that Amzalsunëa Dalgarno would spin any plausible tale she can, to keep her hold on you alive past the time it would have died of old age, like any other first love. Very like she was the first pretty lass who ever paid you any serious court, and you were taken by her, and who would not have been, for she is very pretty indeed, far prettier than I; but that is where it should have ended—indeed, it did end there, for it grew not one inch more. Such things are never built to last. You grew; she did not. Let it go."

In spite of his woes, Morric grinned. Athyn held ever to a certain grim punctiliousness in referring to her Firvolgian nemesis by her proper name. For her it was always 'Amzalsunëa,' and never once 'Melassaun'; it was as if she wished to emphasize the unbridgeable distance between Incomer and Kelt born. *Though doubtless there is more to it than*

*that, since with her there always is; still, she is not far off the mark
in any of this…*

"It takes nothing from you that is yours," he said then. "If
she has prettiness, you have beauty—and more beside. I never
thought I should ever have so much with anyone as I have
now with you—but from the day we met, and this I take oath
on, I knew that never would I have it with another. I love you;
man to woman, mate to mate, king to queen. I have taken
oath upon all."

"And oaths are the flower of honor, not the root. Which
means—"

He had that look on his face now that she had come to recognize to her detriment: a flat, shuttered expression that told
her no matter what she said or did or felt, he intended to do
just exactly what he was intending to do. *Name of Dâna! It is
that pillow thing again—and he says I am stubborn as a gauran…*

"I have made promises to her also. Would you have me
break them?"

"Nay… But you are King of Keltia," she said; defeated now,
and both of them knew it. "Morric Rígh has a certain value to
many besides the Ard-rían, far and above that of Morric
Douglas the handsome gifted bard; not to mention that bard's
value to his most put-upon, long-suffering and sainted wife… I
do not understand why you must go—well, I do, but I do not,
if you take my meaning—but if go you must, then you shall
take some of the Gweriden with you."

It was a lover's capitulation, but also a queen's command,
and Morric though he felt keen relief to hear the one put the
other by.

"I will go; but alone and unannounced. Nay"—he put his
fingers across her lips to halt the protest already forming
there—"it will be better so; safer too. I shall go and come again
home unremarked by any."

"Well," she said against his fingers, and kissed them, "I
yield; however I do so against the stream of my resolution
quite, so make sure you note that well, because, Morrighsaun,

I am going to make you pay more dearly for this than you have ever dreamed."

He was laughing now. "I never for one instant thought that you would not."

"And see to it also that I do not have to come to Firvolgior to fetch you home. That would be more than I think I could quite encompass, or yet endure."

And Morric, not knowing that he lied to her for the first time and the last, faithfully and lovingly promised her that she should not have need.

The object of all the disagreement between the Ard-rían of Keltia and her King had left that realm almost before the Outgoing had begun. Amzalsunëa Dalgarno had naggled her parents endlessly to depart at once, so that she need not be forced to witness the nuptials of Morric and that harpy who called herself a queen. Even the hazen could not dull her rage: at Athyn for marrying Morric, for having red hair, for turning the Firvolgi out of their fat comfortable niche in Keltia; at Morric for his treachery in wedding her.

But in the press of uprooting his affairs Falxifer had found himself unable to leave for some time, and Margiamnë his wife would not travel without him, so Amzalsunëa had fled to Kaireden alone.

There on the homeworld of Firvolgior she had promptly sought out the Beldam Pharuca T'pettun, who had already relocated her zareer to a certain district in the capital city of Katilon Ke Katil, and who was well pleased to take Amzalsunëa once more into her employ. Indeed, she herself was filled with cold sullen anger against Athyn Cahanagh: Once the Gwerin had taken Caerdroia, one of the first things Blackmantle had done was to order the abolishment of the vile trade in flesh and hazen which the Firvolgi found so lucrative amongst themselves—though, thankfully, few Kelts had ever been tempted to succumb to either—and the

Beldam's trade in those commodities had suffered considerably.

But if the Beldam filled want of both, Amzalsunëa had need of both; indeed, as so often fell out with hazers, the need of the one forced the practicing of the other. And as she fell deeper and darker into hazen and hatred both, the Beldam and she talked long together, and found they shared more than whoredom and addiction alone. And together they, and others with them, contrived a plan of darkness unparalleled, by which they hoped—if so fair a word can be used of so foul a venture—to avenge their wrongs on those they held to have caused them. And, for a while, it would even seem that they succeeded...

In spite of her apparent grace in defeat, Athyn had resolved not to see Morric off when he left for Kaireden; though even she did not dare to defy his wishes and send Gweriden with him. *Truly, I am tempted; but he will surely twig, and then I will be for it; let it be as he will have it...*

So on the morning of his departure, after a night of couplings that were combat every bit as much as passion, she had stonily feigned sleep when he had bent over her and kissed her farewell, he knowing full well she was awake, and she knowing he knew. Then at the last moment, overcome with remorse and ill with foreboding, she had changed her mind and dashed out to Mardale, bursting onto the spaceport field just as he was bidding farewell to his escort.

They looked long at each other, eyes striving, contesting even as swords, faces mutinous and vivid with love and conflict and contrition alike. *We have known such flashing bliss this year past— Goddess, do not let us part so ever again...* The thought shone between them like a road to the heart of the sun.

Athyn fetched a deep breath. "Thou and I," she said then, as he had said to her once before, and tears stood in her eyes. "We are not much unlike."

"Nay," said Morric low and close upon her words, only a

breath away from tears himself. "We are not much—unlike."

They kissed then, as they would have were they alone together, and for all the note they took of the others round they might as well have been. Then, holding Athyn's glance, Morric raised her hand to his lips and kissed her fingers, where the findruinna ring and the silver one were side by side.

"Cariadwyn," he said; no more, and she watched him walk away to the waiting ship. He did not look back, and she did not expect it.

"He is lucky to have you," said Morvoren severely, who having been coaxed to court for a while had attended Athyn from Turusachan; though, as ever, she was not best pleased to be so long on land.

Athyn breathed a short laugh, half moan and wholly mirthless; she was looking after Morric with desperate eyes as he vanished into the ship. *I would know him from all other men by his walk alone, he ambles like a throughbred, or a tiger...*

"Indeed he is! But I am luckier to have him... Still, there is no such thing as luck, or else we create our own."

"Is that true, do you think?"

"I know it is. Oh, sometimes we are given a great and splendid gift, all perfect and shining, and we think it comes out of nowhere and nothing, and so we call it luck. But when we look more closely, we see what the true reasons are." She was silent a moment, watching Morric's ship rise up from the field and streak out past the Criosanna; she held her breath until it winked like a star into the overheaven, then sighed. "Still, I did not wish to part from him in anger."

"Sometimes it is the better so; makes reunion all the gladder."

And so, oftentimes, it does. But this time was not to be among them.

Well, if the whole of their homeworld is like this, small wonder the Fir Bolc prefer Keltia—did I dwell on such a drear planet I too would choose to leave...

Morric looked out the viewport of the ferry shuttle that had met the Vyonessan starliner just outside the atmosphere of Kaireden, which now was bringing him down to the world below. The main of the planetscape he beheld was barren and sere: scrubby hills clothed with low trees and gray-green brush, the scars of recent wildfires on the slopes. The city toward which he was descending looked faded and shabby; its very air seemed brown. *Most grandly built, once, but poorly kept; the older buildings are tumbledown, and the newer lack all grace and style…*

He had travelled to Firvolgior not as King of Keltia but as a private citizen, everything about him calculated to attract the least possible attention. So the Keltic ship in which he had departed Tara had taken him to a wayscross, a free-zone space-hub where ships of all stellar nations landed and embarked passengers, and—reluctantly—had left him there alone.

He had boarded a Vyonessan liner bound for Kaireden, and no one had taken more than casual note of him: merely another tall, well-dressed traveller, his garb of quiet good quality but otherwise undistinguished, his documents declaring him to be one Séomaighas mac Mór, knight, an Erinnach landowner with business interests in Firvolgior. Not even the Keltic embassage in Katilon Ke Katil had been informed of the King's presence on the Firvolgi homeworld, lest his safety be set at risk.

So far he had gone unremarked. One unexpected boon of the Outgoing was that he had not had to disguise himself as a man of some other race: There were still collaborators leaving for Kaireden on every outbound flight, Kelts who preferred to throw in with the Incomers rather than risk reprisal from their own. The peril was that any chance-met Kelt might know him, and he was glad of the lookaway that Cathárren and Selanie had put on him. *Not that I much love having magic on me; but they did assure me it is merely what the name suggests—a kind of compulsion on casual beholders, that though they may look, they shall not see…*

But the lookaway worked only with strangers or the casually acquent; those who knew him well—and Amzalsunëa was not the only one in the Firvolgian capital with whom he had history—would see him for who he was. *It is a risk, but too late now to alter; and for all that, I think not so great a risk as Athynna fears... Any road, I shall not be tarrying; I shall find Melassaun, and help her as I can, and be home again with my Athyn by the week's end.*

The thought that he might not, that it might be long and long before he once again beheld his lady, or she him, never for an instant crossed his mind.

He found the place almost at once. It was in a backstreet quarter of Katilon Ke Katil that, judging from the marble columns that fronted the houses and the gardens the houses stood in and the fountains that graced every square, must once have been very grand indeed. But on closer inspection Morric saw that the marble was chipped, the columns listing; the gardens were weed-filled and unkempt, and it had been years since water leaped where now the fountains held only rusty stains.

He went in at the address he had been given—'*At the sign of the Bow-trellis, Number Seventeen, Street of the Limeflowers*'; *a fair name for a foul throughfare*—and entered an atrium that like all else there had seen better days. But the proprietress, the Beldam Pharuca herself, greeted him with no surprise, and had word sent up to Amzalsunëa that he was come.

When she came downstairs to him at last, taking the curving steps one at a time, two seconds to a step, he caught back his dismay; though it was doubtful she would have noticed. *It is worse than I thought, or feared... Even Athynna must pity her, if she saw her now...*

But the truth was plain as it was unpleasant: His once-pretty love-of-youth was a full-blown whore, shredded by hazen into a ravaged wayward flink. And as she led him to a bench in an alcove, that they might talk in privacy, Morric looking round noted that his onetime lennaun was not the only one known to him, and was all the more dismayed.

They were arranged languidly on benches and broad couches scattered throughout the open rooms of the zareer's ground floor. He knew almost all of them by name: Rozenath, Jalior, Lyrin, Junoth, Najén—who one ghastly night had thrust her hand beneath his trewsflap, right in front of Athyn, who had coolly ignored it—Nellis Vantesso, Davengra, Veziëba, Tanja Malis. Lennauns of his old bandfellows, bard-followers and hangers-on, even a few old one-night-jinks of his, bedded in moments of boresomeness or foolishness or drink taken; perhaps a dozen or so in all. *They have turned to whoredom to support themselves— No matter that they slandered and lied against Athyn and the rest of us; however vile they proved themselves, no evil merits such a fate as this...* He saw others he knew—the Coranians Prochuldalith and Haëvristes, now prinking male harlots, the eunuchs Bilbelhal and Jaltorry, failed bards turned jealous scoffers—with most of whom he had hoisted a mether or two in youth, and was revolted afresh.

Was this the best they could do for themselves? Was this all that they had within themselves to call upon, that they should come to this in the end? They did not have to choose so, surely... Well, Athynna is right again, as usual, though I certainly do not love the prospect of admitting as much to her...

As for Amzalsunëa, the ravagement of her prettiness had taken toll on her spirit, or such of it as she had ever had. Deeply in hazen's thrall, she was by turns limp and drooping as a broken-stemmed flower and bubbling as a stream in spate, possessed of little more substance than the windpuffs children use to tell the time on summer days.

Though he was shocked to see the change in her, Morric bespoke her gently, and in her lucid moments she told him things to make him weep. Her much-boasted-of noble patron, a young baron, was merely her best customer, an enthusiastic fellow hazer. She owed the Beldam Pharuca for her passage from Keltia; Morric settled the debt on the spot. She had not been sent by her father any funds for her keep; Morric gave her what she required many times over. She needed more hazen, and stronger, purer than what she had been using; seeing her growing agitation, much against his better judgment Morric paid a slaved gytresh, a shoggling thing called Taggerlin Tumbolgy that served as a zareer drudge, to go out and purchase a quantity of the noxious draught, if only to calm her— and only enough for that.

And ever she wabbled on about him, and herself, and how it had been for the two of them together in the old days; and though it was but vagaries and sad conceits, hazen-spun moonwash as fanciful as any fable, because he had loved her once he listened to her with patience and with pity, for as long as she had need.

That night Morric found himself lodgings at an elegant inn in a far pleasanter quarter of the town—he would not stay in the Beldam's house had it been the last lodging on the planet, nor had he for a micromillim considered remaining with Amzalsunëa—and after a bath and a surprisingly good supper, he went out to a small music-hall not too far distant.

He had a purpose beyond entertainment in so going—it had been the Beldam who had suggested it to him—but all the same he felt an unpleasant shock to see them: Erramun Zedoary, Jaffran Eskendy, Evance Tregar, Shane Ó Falvey. As he walked in unnoted—the place was little more than a catchhouse, not much larger than the súgachans they had had their start in—they were playing a song he knew well, for it was of his own composing, and they had played it often together in their days on bard-circuit.

He sat at a table in the rear and listened for the space of an ale or two, then when others had their turn he rose and went back to where the performers took their ease. *Strange it is to be behind-stage again; it has been a very long time. Perhaps when I am home again I will do somewhat to alter that—though the Queen may have more than somewhat to say about it…*

Erramun saw him first. "King Morric of Keltia—a long way to come for a royal performance. We are not what we were; but then, who is? Still, we had a chaunter once—"

Shane and Evance, who were by, looked at him and then looked away, attending to their instruments, and Morric wondered why he felt sudden cold danger in their lack of emotion or surprise.

"I am not here as a king," he said, "or even as a bard, but as myself only. Melassaun asked me to come to her in her need—"

"Aye, well, she would—"

"How do you all here, are you well?" asked Morric after a long silent uncomfortable moment. *It seems uncivil not to ask about their ladies, but they doubtless know I saw them at the Beldam's—hence their unsurprise—and perhaps they do not wish to be reminded…*

"As you see. We are still with Loris Venoët's company," said Shane. "What else? You may recall after you left us—"

"Left you! Nay, it was you packed *me* off! In Tamon Acanis—"

"—we struggled to make what music we could without you."

Morric began an impassioned reply, but Shane stalked off unhearing. Erramun looked after him and shrugged.

"You know it as well as we do: The music we made without you was neither very much nor very good; and as you just now heard, most of what we play these days is yours in any case. Your songs are much favored here; that should please you."

Morric had no words, and after a vain attempt to find some he murmured farewell and unashamedly fled. Walking back to his inn through the silent streets, he was haunted by his band-fellows' fate. *'Please' me! Nay, great grief to see them so, in such state, their music lost—but though in youth there was never a moment when I had no time to wallow in their mires, I was always well aware, I think, of what they were. But what we had together as bards—not even this can lessen that memory. Still, I am so very sorry all the same…*

Yet that night, when he had stripped for sleep, he mixed salt and water in a pottery bowl—salt he had carried from Keltia in a little cloth sack, and, in a silver-capped cut-crystal bottle, sacred water that had been blessed at his wedding—and dipping his fingers into the bowl Morric brushed the water across his forehead, over his heart and upon the arches of his bare feet, and poured the rest out over his hands, as Athyn once had taught him.

As she says, might help, cannot harm; and any evil sent my way is sent back whence it came. But at the least I feel cleaner so… He drew up the coverlets, reaching out for Athyn as by instinct, rueful when he remembered, and touched the gold locket that hung on its chain round his neck, the locket Athyn had ordered made to mark their wedding. *My side is cold without her—gods, but I shall be glad when I am gone from here, and once again home…*

He went back to the zareer the next morning. Amzalsunëa was dull and sullen, far from the mercurial creature who had greeted him the day before, the false sparkle of the hazen replaced by the morbid torpor that ever follows.

And full of shriekings and lamentings and crossness beside: "I should not have asked you to come here, now you must surely hate me—"

"Nay, not so, would I have come all this way if I did?" His voice was gentle. "But I hate that you feel you must do what you do… You shall have help, Melassaun, I promise—look, I will find you healers—"

But she flouted and spurned, and batted him away.

"You are with that swordslut—if you do not hate me *she* most surely does—"

He kept his tone soothing, did not accuse. "Well, you tried to *kill* her, Mela; no one would be best pleased at that…"

She frowned and squirmed and ran her hands up and down her thin arms. "Aye, well, but she escaped, you know—they were wild when they found out, no one could puzzle out how she did it... And they knew already, before I told them, knew that she was Blackmantle—no fault of mine, I told them nothing they did not know—and then she took you away—" She brabbled on a while, and Morric listened in sorrowful silence.

"She is my wife and my Queen," said Morric at last, gently still. "She has nothing of me that was not hers alone from all time. Naught of what is hers in me was ever yours, Mela, and naught of what is yours in me can ever be hers. Be at peace with that."

She looked at him out of mad amethyst eyes, and dán itself paused waiting on her choice. If he had said one word differently; if a word was not said that should have been, or a word spoken that would better have gone unsaid; if he had smiled, or not smiled; if a cloud had crossed the sun or a star danced—who can say how it might have gone? But it went as it went, as it must, as it had always gone and had ever been meant to go...

"Here." She thrust the little stone vial at him, suddenly, her decision taken. "You look weary; the voyage here must have tired you more than you thought. Or perhaps seeing the others last night troubled you, who could blame you if it had— It is like to dubh-cosac, as is used on Keltia; nothing harmful. Take it. It will not hurt you, I would never hurt you. You will feel better, easier. Drink some wine, to go with it, wine is good. Then go back to the inn and rest. It will not harm. Take it now."

And he, because he was indeed a little weary, because she seemed to need him to trust her, because he trusted that she would never harm him, took it.

Morric felt nothing but the weariness Amzalsunëa claimed she had seen, not until he was back in his chamber at the inn, where she had bidden him go; he had even drunk a little wine, as she had suggested. A few hours later it came down upon him sudden and hard, sending him reeling, and he fell fully clad upon the bed, his marriage ring pressing sharp against his hand. *Something more than dubh-cosac, I think; and I think too there is very little time—the later the symptoms, the more surely fatal the dose. Strange how not surprised I am, how it seems I have always known this is how it would be...*

He was dying, and he knew it; and there were things to be done, he knew that also. But words kept getting in the way, words of someone, someone who knew Athyn, he could not remember who. Yet the words came clear: "Go home. Go home to the one who truly loves you, who loves you more than life or lives. Save yourself. Seize her hand and run off with her; to a castle or a cottage, it matters not what or where. Live with her in love and joy and beauty. Write poems and songs and live forever. Else you will break my heart, and Keltia's heart, and the world's heart; but first of all, worst of all, you will break her heart."

Would that I had heeded your words; I would heed them now, if only I could. I cannot save myself—nor yet her, but though her heart be broken she will not be, my Athynna does not break—and at the least, at the last, I can go home...the Low Road, the Low Road for me...

But the words he heard were different than the words he remembered, and it troubled him that he could not remember how they differed, or even who had spoken them. There was music—his voice, his songs, though he knew it was not he who sang them. *Cariadwyn...* He could see her clearly now: her hair, her eyes, the slow sidewise smile, as he had first seen her; bright and dangerous as a blade, as he had last seen her; the way she looked glowing up at him as she walked beside him, as she lay beside him. *I will go home, then, and maybe even now I might be saved...*

And because he wished himself there, because he loved her, because it was the place he had forever chosen to be, he lay down beside her, eyes fixed upon her face, his hand reaching out to touch her across the darkness, her face ever brighter and brighter as the mists drew in.

Athyn—my Silksteel—my lily of the sword—

And went home to the heart that was his forever.

In Caerdroia, in the owl-time of night, Athyn started awake with a cry out of a deep sleep. Morric stood beside the bed, and he looked more beautiful even than ever he had looked to her. She sighed in relief to see him, holding out her bare arms to him, smiling, never thinking for an instant other than that he had arrived home unexpected and had come straight to their bed. But in that same instant she knew the truth, and reached out instead in desperate denial, as across a widening gulf, a dark rushing river that ran between.

He smiled at her, bent to kiss her; she felt his mouth warm and hard on hers, his hand upon her hair, his beard and breath soft against her cheek, heard his voice in her ear; and he was gone.

She did not move for a long moment; felt nothing but a great endless Nay, a distant welling ache upon body and spirit, as though she had taken a great wound and did not even feel or know it, except that someone had told her, somehow, long ago, far away; knowing already that this was a wound would never be healed, might well be mortal itself, wishing it could be, that she would not have to endure what she knew was even now upon her. *I cannot feel it just yet, too early to feel the pain of it, too deep a hurt for tears; yet that will change... O love— Morric—my Fireheart...* She made no sound but shivered once, like a sail that a strong wind shifting had suddenly left empty, and drawing herself into herself she toppled over onto Morric's side of the great bed and curled herself round the pillows as around his body, and a blackness took her far away.

When they came to tell her at dawn, the news having come from Katilon Ke Katil, they found her sitting huddled in the window seat, wrapped in one of his old tunics, her hair loose around her.

Mariota said, in a voice that told all in one word, "Athyn—"

"I know," she said, in a voice that told more; she did not turn, and when she did, and they saw her face, they crumpled as if they had been struck. "I know. He came to me before he left, he took the Low Road— I followed him out as far as I could, I would have ridden with him all the way but they forced me round, to turn for home."

The others looked swiftly from one to another, and almost she laughed to see it. *Nay, that would upset them beyond all measure, best not; there will be time for laughing later, any road…*

"Speak," she said then, with the greatest weariness she had ever known.

It was a command, and Esmer chose his words with paramount care. "Amzalsunëa Dalgarno, who was with him just before he died, has claimed that after he left her and returned to the inn where he was lodged, he took a sudden heartstroke, and though help was summoned he could not be revived."

"Aye? And?"

Closing his eyes briefly, Esmer sighed out a long breath, waited longer still before he spoke.

"It was murder. She gave him hazen," he said at last, and lowered his eyes so as not to see the look that crossed Athyn's face. "Morric thought it was dubh-cosac, or else she lied and told him it was; either way the dose of it, its purity and strength, killed him." He paused for another steadying breath. "It was common knowledge at the zareer that Amzalsunëa planned to give it him: a plan she cobbled up with some of our old enemies who were glad to conspire at his murder; to strike at him for their own reasons, but chiefly to strike at you by striking him down. We have the story from several sources— including the healers who were summoned to try to revive him— and our spies, and our own ambassador to whom she herself brazenly reported his death. There is no doubt. She has fled now into hiding, in terror of what you might do."

Athyn had mastered herself again. "Not so stupid as she has, in fact, seemed... Well, it shall avail her nothing. But for now: If I am widowed Queen, I am Queen still; I will have his body brought back to Keltia, to be barrowed at Ni-maen as is fitting for a king."

"Dalgarno had him buried in secret, before she fled the city."

Athyn shut her eyes then, but the picture behind them could not be shut out: Morric lying dead upon a bed not their own, the dark hair disarrayed; she had seen those who died of hazen—the paleness, the blood from nose and mouth. *Dead without me, on a foreign world, under strange stars—but thank the merciful Goddess, thank all gods forever, no pain in it for him... It shall be very much otherwise for them...* She opened her eyes, and the sky darkening before a storm was less terrible to behold.

"I will find him."

"How, lassling?" Ganor, so gentle a voice. "He has gone—"

"I will find him."

"Athwen—we would not leave you alone—"

"I know that." She turned back to the window. "But leave me. I am not alone. And he has not gone."

Because they loved her, and him, they would not have left; because she was Queen, and he had been King, they obeyed.

The costume of control broke later, when none was there to comfort or to see. When she thought she could weep no more, her gaze moving round the chamber would fall upon the bed where he had lain beside her, or a tunic he had tossed over a chair, or some scribblings that waited to be made into a song or a poem and now would wait forever, or her marriage ring upon her hand, and she would weep anew, crumpled upon the bed, the floor, huddled in a chair or the window seat, all the ground of her being cut out from under her, until she was done with weeping; and then she would weep again.

It was sometime during that long terrible day and night and

day again that she called upon the magic that was in her; called in earnest, as she had vowed she would never do, as she had not done to save her life or win her war. She called upon it now for love, in love, to do a thing that none in Keltia had ever done before, and it was done. Not even on Erith had it been seen, not in Eruinn, not in the magic realm of Atland, not even in Núminôr that was father and mother of all magics; but Athyn did it now, and never regretted the doing.

None of the Gweriden ever knew how she spent those hours, and Athyn never told them; but two mornings after Morric's death she entered the Council chamber and took her accustomed seat against the northern wall.

They had not expected her, and though they had stood up at her entrance, as swiftly as if a sword had been drawn, they were appalled at the look of her. She was gaunter than she had been three days since—the trays of food sent up had gone untouched—but perfectly composed, clad in the stark white of formal royal mourning; her only jewels were her marriage and betrothal rings, and the seal ring she wore as Queen, and the opal heart Morric had given her on a black velvet cord round her neck.

She looks like a white birch in an icestorm, thought Esmer, *prisoned in a sheath of glittering frozen water, branches ready to break at the least breeze. I would not shatter that fragile—balance; I do not call it peace, for I know it is no such thing…*

"Ard-rían—" began someone.

Athyn shook her head slowly. "Do not. Do not… I have already determined of my actions, have come here only to inform you of what shall be."

"And that is—?" asked Esmer.

"You have left me very little sword-room," she said curtly, looking up at them at last, and they flinched at what they saw in her face. "At first I thought to go to war against Firvolgior, but this you will persuade me from doing, saying Keltia is not strong enough to win such a fight, that it would only hand over to the Firvolgi on an ashet what they could not win upon the field. And you would be correct. Any road, even I know it is hardly Firvolgior's fault. He was there in secret, and not as King, and his death was not by policy. Therefore, no war."

A wave of relief, hardly hidden, ran round the room; and Athyn almost smiled to see it. *Aye, well, that shall not last long...*

"No war between our two respective nations, that is," she added with perfect timing, grimly amused to see them tense anew. "As for me, I have declared private war against many, not merely his murderer alone. And, hear me Malen Rhên, I'll make them all dance Jac Lattin before I've done. But Amzalsunëa Dalgarno I will slay with my own hands. I told him once that I would have her blood; it seems I am so made, that I must keep my vows."

For one blood-blinded moment Athyn thought she could not have heard correctly. Then:

"*Precontract!*" she said when she could speak again. "Are they making some obscene vile jest, or are they but mad?"

"Firvolgian law," said Bronwyn Muirheyd, severe face belying her own disgust, "allows Falxifer and Margiamnë to claim precontract of marriage between Morric Douglas and their daughter, and on this they base their suit, offering as evidence the time Morric and Melassaun spent together in youth—and the fact that though she went round Keltia calling herself his wife, he never put her word to the Horns. Further, they claim that any marriage Morric may have made after is therefore invalid; unless, of course, for proper consideration, Melassaun might just be persuaded to dissolve the alleged union unilaterally after the fact—in much the same fashion, I doubt not, that she just now unilaterally declared it after the fact, knowing Morric cannot gainsay her to her face. I need not remind my star pupil that such claim has no merit under our own law: I have already ruled against them in two courts, and would not have troubled you; but they seek to take the appeal to you, as Queen."

"They are claiming that Morric validly contracted marriage with Amzalsunëa, because they slept together on occasion long ago," said Athyn, slowly, carefully, as one who repeats a message in gibberish, or in some foreign tongue that she does not speak, but must get it right even so. "I wish to be very clear on this... Yet no syllable of such a claim was ever heard whilst Morric lived."

Bronwyn shook her head. "There was never a claim, any more than there was ever a contract. But out of it all they seem to think Melassaun is owed."

Athyn's fists crashed down upon the table, so hard that one of her rings splintered the wood and drew blood from her hand; she did not feel it, and leaped up in the same instant to pace the room.

"*SHE MURDERED HIM!* She is owed, right enough! And I vow to all gods there ever were, in all worlds there are or ever shall be, that I will see to it she is paid in full... As for their time together constituting marriage, or even precontract: Much as I love him, if marriage were provable on such terms for every random lass Morric Douglas sluttishly bedded in his extremely misspent youth, he would have had by now wives in quantities to rival the Coranian Emperor."

"It is undoubtedly not Amzalsunëa's idea; she is not clever enough to have thought of this herself. But, I tell you, Athwen, never have I seen the like."

Athyn gave a short laugh. "And you say you have fought the Fir Bolc all these years! But leave it to Amzalsunëa to show us a new benchmark: Perhaps her professional skills do not bring in enough to keep her in hazen, and this is but her little way of making sure she does not go short." She looked up, caught by the quality of Bronwyn's silence. "There is more, then."

"I fear so; and if no worse it is at least of the same rank of badness."

"Then let you tell me, and be done."
And Bronwyn did.

At the end of the telling, Athyn was unsure whether to laugh
or weep, but she was sure beyond all doubt that she wished to
kill. For Bronwyn, as swiftly and simply as possible—*True it is
that she must know, but, Goddess, how much more must she bear,
or can she*—had informed her that the Douglases, Morric's parents, had for their part elected to countersue the Dalgarnos
and the Crown alike. Their son's estate as bard-ollave had
been substantial, and of course he had been King Consort as
well; they seemed to have forgotten that not only had he won
quitclaim against them but had told anyone who had asked
him that they were dead.

"So, they crawl out from under the graveslab Morric set
over them," said Athyn, "now that he himself is dead in truth
and cannot bar them... Do you know what they—nay, well, I
shall not betray his secrets now, save to say that for what they
did to him they *should* have died. And if I have aught to say
about it—come to think of it, I do!—they will yet... Hu mawr!
He told no lie when he told folk they were dead; they may
have bred and breathed, but never were they ensouled."

Perversely, Athyn suddenly found herself looking forward
to the coming confrontations; deep within her something
seemed to chuckle darkly. *It is fíor-comlainn and combat both,
and more beside— How little folk know of true grief, and how less
of real revenge! How much of both I am going to so gladly teach
them! Aye, they shall learn whole new kingdoms of mourning and
vengeance before I am done... And yet it seems somehow fitting:
What is it the cailleachs say—'Be 'ware of what you ask, for surely
you shall get it.' Well, they have asked, and I have asked, and now
all of us together are about to get what it is that we have asked for.
And if that is not justice I do not know what is.*

More than that she would not say or show, or at least not to
those around her. But when she lay awake deep into owl-time,

in the bed she had shared with Morric, weeping and anguished, all the pain hid all the days long from all Keltia overcoming her at last, she turned to the only one who could comfort her in the blank white depths of grief, spoke yet again to that one to whom she had never once ceased to speak since the day they first had met; and though the other side of their marriage-bed was empty he was with her all the same.

Beloved—this is not ended, I promise you! So I shall rule as judge, and judge as Queen; and then I shall act as woman, as lover and wife and widow, as Athyn Aoibhell ac Douglas gân Morric would be expected to act, as Blackmantle mate of Fireheart could be foreseen to act. They will not understand why I do this, they are going to be more afraid than they have ever been; but it is all part of what must be. And so the dán begins that my own mother tried with her last strength to spare me; and what do you think we may all of us learn from that?

But Morric, if answer he had for her, kept his words for her alone to hear, and she was well content that he should do so.

BOOK IV

BOOK IV

What I began with others
I will end with you.
What lives, loves.
What chooses, changes.
What doubts, dies.

—*Morric Douglas to Athyn Cahanagh*

Three things to keep in mind of death and bards:
It is death to mock a bard, death to love a bard,
  death to be a bard.
A journey have I endured, and to the gate
  I now am come.
The hall I will enter and my song I shall chaunt;
my truth I will pronounce to silence lying tongues.
I will destroy them!
Upon them I shall break as water strikes the shore.
Let the fools be therefore silent
and their falsehoods fade away,
and death to them who thought to mock a bard:
for vengeance of a bard who loves a bard
  is come upon them.

—*Athyn's Song Against Liars*

BOOK IV

chapter twenty-six

Light and shadow we bestride
Rage in darkness by my side.

—*Morric Douglas*

For all Athyn's valiant scouting of the trial to come, by anyone's measure the cruelty of it was beyond belief: the kindreds of Douglas and Dalgarno, at bitter odds in all else, uniting to make Athyn, newly widowed, rule as to whether her wedded lord had not been in fact wed to another, to adjudge on the rights to his estate of the parents who had spurned him and the woman who had slain him.

It would have tried and tested the soul of a hero or a god. Even Esmer thought it was beyond her strength, and with all the Gweriden's voices added to his had begged her to decline; she had that right under law, could designate a regent to declare on the matter in her stead. But Athyn, stonefaced, had refused.

"They have sought the High Queen's judgment. They shall have it."

On a morning not long thereafter, a small company of Gweriden knights escorted four persons into the chamber where Athyn was wont to sit in hearing-court. She was already in her high seat, robed in the green of a master-judge, and she did not look at the King's empty chair upon her right. The escort, led by Rhain, saluted and withdrew to leave the plaintiffs standing alone before the low dais.

Two of them Athyn had seen before: Falxifer and Margiamnë Dalgarno, of whom Amzalsunëa was sole spawn, bowed to her, and avoided her gaze. *It is the balcony in Stone Street over again; only they now are the ones in the chariot, and still they will not meet my eyes...* She turned her head then to the other two. Comyn and Havoise Douglas, Morric's parents, held themselves rigidly correct. Havoise had hair not far off the color of Athyn's own, and seeing Morric in his father's countenance—the strong bones, the deep-set blue eyes— Athyn flinched, and touched her fingers to the emerald at her throat. *When my Morric is the same age as that, he too will look so...*

"Dâr Athnë," began Falxifer, after Bronwyn Muirheyd had opened proceedings, though properly he should not have addressed Athyn before she herself had spoken, and Margiamnë curtsied again in Firvolgian style.

For one white instant Athyn thought she would slaughter them where they stood, rip out their hearts with her bare hands, lift a finger and call down skyfire to blast them out of existence. *I could do it, and I can do it... But I will not do it—at least not just yet. But Malen Rhên give me strength! She killed him! They know it well, know how I must feel, and still they dare come before me—me!—to claim what they believe is their lawful due... SHE KILLED HIM! They pretend away the blood on their daughter's hands: What manner of souls are they, if even they are souls at all? And she! If she did not harm him, if she feels so strongly the innocence of her deeds and the correctness of her case, why does she not dare come back to face me?*

For Amzalsunëa had not presented herself in court but remained in hiding on Kaireden; for which absence Athyn was grateful, since had she found herself within arm's-reach she knew she could not have kept her hands from the Firvolgian sluttern's throat. *Any road, I already know the answer to my question; know also what my judgment shall be. I have committed the worst sin a brehon can commit: I have judged this case before ever I put on my robe and took my seat. Worse still, I do not care…*

She cut her glance over to where the Douglases stood, and though they at least had sensibility, if so it could be called, to bear themselves more fitly, to look upon them was for Athyn more difficult still; remembering what pain of Morric's she was witness to, holding him while he wept to tell her what they had done to him… *These have even less excuse than the other two—and all of them grubbing for crossics in his grave…* She bit the inside of her lip until the blood came, for she did not trust herself in judgment; and yet she must judge.

These were Morric's parents, by law of handfast marriage her own parents this moonyear past. Yet what they had done to him seemed to preclude forgiveness. *Though perhaps true royalty would mandate more merciful treatment; but I am only Athyn, and his wife, and I was not born a queen…*

Easy to judge; or so she in her traha once had thought. She had even so boasted. But now the words of Redigan Ó Hannay, spoken one quiet afternoon in a library at the school where she had learned the law, came back to her full force: 'Say so again to me when once you have so judged.' *Ah athro, I cannot say, as you well knew; but I must judge, and I will, and that too you knew…*

Of the four standing before the high seat, only Comyn Douglas met her eyes, and he wished at once that he had not. *That glance could strip back your skull, peel flesh from bones without a quiver. No human regard—those are the eyes of the Sidhe or the merrows or the dark-elves. Not even that, for those are feeling beings: They spoke truly who said Blackmantle is past feeling, my son's wife*—never seeing that the all-encompassing look Athyn bent upon the father of her mate was not the soulless stare of one who could not feel but the stark and endless gaze of one who feels too deeply.

Athyn, withdrawing her glance at last from Comyn's, nodded for the arguments to begin, and settled herself to listen. *I have condemned myself to hear this through to the end; let be…* Knowing from her days upon the war-trail that it is ever best to face the more fearsome foe first, she had elected to begin with the precontract case; and as she listened, much to her own surprise she found her calling superseding her feeling; the law, and not her very human enmity, winning paramount in her mind and heart, instinctively—almost, even, against her own will. *'The law's hand uppermost'; they did not teach me falsely, nor did I falsely learn…*

Even so, as the case unfolded, she could not help but marvel at the natures it limned out. Wondered too—though by no means was she surprised—at how, despite all claims to the contrary, love for Morric, or grief at his death, appeared so remarkably absent in these very cold equations. *They care nothing for him, his life, his death—nor ever did, not one of them—but only for what they can now get from him…* But she listened all the same.

What she heard was a matter of record: depositions from the principals there present, and from those, like Pharuca T'pettun and Lorcan Firdanisk, who had plainly followed Amzalsunëa's lead and stayed prudently away. What she felt would never be known, for she spoke of it to none thereafter. *I would not have them see how it hurts me; no outside eye should behold that… But in the end it all comes down to this: Do I take the word of liars and bawdmongers and profiteers, who have never spoken a single unbent word in all the time I have known them, or do I take the word of the man I love, who has said he loves me, who fought for me and beside me these seven long years and more, who wedded me with ring and vow and whom with my own hands I crowned King? She killed him! Once, long ago, I have no doubt that there was love between them, for his sake at least I hope there was; but then, as he himself did say, there was only pity and habit, and now only grasping and greed. Whatever was between them died long since; and when she would have seen me hanged, and he knew it, then and only then did he come to see it needed proper burial. She killed him!… He declared his heart to me, I was not wrong to believe him… But, Goddess, what some folk will not do for crossics—* He married me of his own will before the gods, but Amzalsunëa had to kill him before he would 'marry' her…

And then the fíor-brethas came upon her, not as formerly, with a stunning clear rush; but quietly, firmly, with a certainty that never in her most tempted moments could she mistake for wishful thinking. Athyn laughed aloud in spite of herself, a bright sound of health cutting across the unclean feeling in the room, and the court looked scandalized. All at once she had heard enough. *More than enough, and none can gainsay me—good it is to be Queen!* Drawing herself up in the Cathair-bretha, leaning forward as if she were setting a course at a stone wall atop her favorite hunter, Athyn began to deliver judgment on the rotten case set before her: 'a discerning stern judgment upon cunning false lying people'—as she had learned at school.

"Whatever Morric Douglas may or may not have said to Amzalsunëa Dalgarno," she said in a plain everyday voice that was one of the greatest achievements of her life, "or whatever she thinks or wishes or deludes herself that he said, or whatever she may have told others that he said, never while he was alive did he tell folk they were wedded, by precontract or brehon marriage or any other sort of marriage. No one has here produced a shred of evidence: no ceremony, no documents, no witnesses, no declarations, no contracts, no untainted testimony. She may swear from now to Nevermas that she considered herself Morric Douglas's wife; and whether she truly believed so, or whether all this is merely fabrication after the fact, it signifies naught. There is no proof that *he* considered her his wife—and in this matter his is the only word that counts."

She met their eyes, and they knew now how she looked in battle. "And that word Morric Douglas gave to me and no other, before the gods and witnesses alike. His ring on my hand, and mine on his; our blood in the holy quaich; our vows heard, our signs-manual witnessed and attested." She leaned back, steepled her fingers and set them to her chin, and smiled. "And the only woman Morric Douglas ever wedded may now, in Keltic law and in Keltic justice, bring certain claims against his killers."

Out of the corner of her eye she saw Bronwyn's sudden glinting glance, and laughed inwardly. *Ah, I know that look! 'Where the hells is Athyn going with this?' Well, she shall see with the rest of them…*

"You have dishonored yourselves and your people," said Athyn to the Dalgarnos, on point of shedding her green robe then and there, scarce able to bear the touch another instant of the color of justice in improbity's presence. "And you have insulted me and mine." She drew herself up still and tall in her chair. "'Lex est ata regis'—the law is the armor of the king. Hear then the judgment of Athyn Ard-rían: The alleged pre-contract is dismissed with the contempt it merits, and the claim on the late King's estate also; murder makes null all claims. As for the countersuit brought by Comyn and Havoise Douglas: I remind you both of the quittance Morric Douglas won against you when he was eighteen years of age. In law you have no standing as his kin, and in attempting to claim against him you have incurred honor-price violations of your own. For that, your estates and possessions are lawfully seized, to be used in helping Kelts made homeless by the Outgoing; and also for that when at my command the Gwerin sought help and advice of Comyn Douglas, my emissary was denied, and that is a crime against the Fianna—that a soldier refuse his sword to another in war."

"You are not a soldier!" said Comyn, speaking for the first time.

"I have been a soldier, and I am a soldier's daughter. I am your son's wife, who may rightfully claim against you my mateparents, for his honor as well as my own. I am the Ard-rían whose armor is the law, whose justice you in your traha did call down upon you. But above all else I am a judge paramount, who cannot—not in law, not for this, however much I long to—give order for your deaths." The four who faced her gasped as one. "Though perhaps in justice, or even in conscience... But I shall not put myself in the law's reverence for such as you."

Nay, they do not see it even now...that death might be what price my honor, and his, might require. Which proves how little they do know me; and how littler still they knew him, or what sort of mate my mate would choose...

"Thou two," she said in the High Gaeloch, indicating the Dalgarnos, "being not Kelts but Incomers unlawfully present in Keltia, I deal with according to the ancient rule. It is a matter of offense from the sea, as a wrong committed upon a true Kelt by one who had washed ashore in Keltic lands of Erith. When I declared the Outgoing I adjudged that the Fir Bolc had washed ashore unlawfully in Keltia from the very first, with intent to conquer. You could not win of me then before the law who paid you so beneath the sword, and you cannot now. You had my warning—that once you left Keltia, you might not return—and you chose to flout it, and now you must bide the issue."

Athyn paused, watching Falxifer struggling to control his anger. The law she had cited superseded all rulings, and was the one by which she and Bronwyn and Redigan had justified the Outgoing—not that it needed justifying, but as the saying went, 'Better the word with the sword.' But now she turned to the Douglases.

"Thou, being lawfully mine, as Ard-rían I can for your offenses lawfully banish, and this I do." Her face and voice were expressionless now. "I banish you all four to a cloaked and barren planetoid well off even the most far-flung star-routes. No one will find you. You shall cry no rescue. You will not escape. I banish you to your own company, and the company of each other, and the truth of your crimes. I leave you four in number, but with food and shelter and clothing sufficient only for two. How you divide it amongst you is your own concern. Also I leave you, lastly, the means with which to slay yourselves, or one another. That too is your concern."

Into a charged and profound silence she lifted the Silver Branch, the Scepter of Llyr, from where it had lain across her knees, and balanced it across her upturned palms.

"So say I, Athyn Ard-rían, Queen of Kelts, called Blackmantle, Dâr Athnë n'Kueltoi in the Firvolgian tongue, wife to King Morric Fireheart, Dâredd Moriadoc who is avenged—in part—herewith."

Falxifer found his voice. "Athnë Atrais, you mean! My people named you rightly! You cannot do this thing!"

"Ah, but I can. And I do. And it is done. This is not Firvolgior but Keltia, not Kaireden but Tara, not Katilon Ke Katil but Caerdroia." Athyn's voice held no emotion, the voice of a judge in the service of the law. "I have deemed here as Ard-rían, and brehon-ollave, and Fian; but also I am Athyn gân Morric, and now I claim in his name enech-clann and corp-díra, such an éraic as has never been seen before. Against you and yours I claim it, and against any other who had hand or heart or part in his death; and by all gods I shall have it. I name myself clannstalker, Am Bladier, Dioghaltair-cheart. Hear me, Arawn Rhên, Lord of Annwn."

She spoke these sword-words into a profound stillness, her hands upraised in the attitude of oathtaking. For those who stood by, their surprise was as vast as their silence: Those titles Athyn had just now claimed were ancient ones indeed, and never assumed lightly—as many could attest, had they yet lived to do so. Dioghaltair-cheart the Just Avenger, Am Bladier the Avenger of Blood, clannstalker...they were oaths and quests as much as titles; and once declared only death or achievement could release the avower, for it was to the accomplishment of lawful final vengeance that he, or she, had declared.

And Athyn had sworn by Arawn himself—Arawn, the Doomsman of the High Dânu, Arawn Deathlord, Arawn Lord of Annwn, Firstborn of the Absolute. If Justice bears a divine face, it is Arawn's is the countenance; in his realm of Annwn the souls of the newly dead face their own deeds, good and evil alike, with no self-deceiving mortality to excuse and explain. In Arawn's calm stern presence no false motives or wishful tunes are heard, but truth alone is lord. Though he is called Doomsman, Arawn never judges, but merely watches one judge oneself, as he has received the sacred charge from the Highest; and no judgment in his presence is ever less than perfect and correct.

And I as brehon swear by him who is the Brehon of the Gods; if I am faithless or forsworn let Arawn be the judge…

"But my daughter? My little Amzë?" Margiamnë, caring about none of this save as to how it might work upon her child, shook off her husband's restraining hand and came as close to Athyn's seat as the guards allowed, fears and tears alike upon her face. "Majesty? You would not—"

Athyn's own face did not change. "You I would pity if I could," she said, "for I think that of all you four your hands may be the cleanest. But if you did less evil, still you did no good. As for your daughter, she shall receive the same justice, and the same mercy, as she herself has shown. That is fair, surely. But know this: I will perish upon my own sword by my own hand sooner than allow my lord's slayers—whoever they are, and however many—to live."

She looked then at the Douglases—Comyn white and silent, shaking with rage; Havoise helplessly weeping, though whether she wept for her own plight or for her slain son or for what she had done or had not done would never now be known—and seeing only Morric before her Athyn's heart was full. *Judgment stands…*

She raised a hand, all at once sickened at the continued sight of them; Rhain mac an Iolair stepped instantly forward. "Take them hence, my lion. You know my will."

"You have heard the Ard-rían," said Rhain, and the banished four bowed to the widowed throne: with anger, with terror, with hatred, with bewilderment or resignation. Athyn did not acknowledge them, but watched them walk away; when the chamber was empty once more she rose from the chair.

'Athnë Atrais'— And 'Atrais' in the Incomer tongue signifies 'reprisal'... Well, very like I deserve it; and surely Nilos will not be best pleased with me, but there it is, and this is not the end...

She sank down again into the high seat, turning her head for the first time to the seat beside her own that had been Morric's—now draped with a sash in the dress sett of Douglas bordered with the white of formal royal mourning—and reached out a hand to touch the chair's carved arm; only then did she notice that she was trembling from head to foot. *How could they look upon his great empty chair and still do as they just now did? I should have killed them right here...*

But her fingertips could only just brush the darkly shining wood, and as her hand strained across the space that separated the two thrones she saw the gleam of her marriage ring. There was another ring beside it now, glowing dark gold: Morric's own ring, that had arrived home from Kaireden only that morning, brought straight to Athyn by the Keltic ambassador to Firvolgior himself.

He had had it of an unnamed messenger, who came to his door in Katilon Ke Katil three nights after Morric's death. Recognizing the token, and not wishing to trust it to another, he had taken ship at once to Tara, his shaking hand dropping the ring into Athyn's steady one, though her fingers closed so tightly upon it that blood ran down her wrist where her nails pierced her palm; the ambassador bitterly lamenting that he could not have brought the King home to her as well. But though strenuous efforts had been made by the embassage staff—and every Keltic spy in Firvolgior—to learn where Morric had been bestowed, none could find his hidden grave, nor yet could track down Amzalsunëa Dalgarno, who alone knew where she had barrowed him.

For her part, Athyn was grateful beyond hope for the ring's return, but she refused to speculate as to who that mysterious messenger might have been, and kept her thoughts as far as possible off Morric's lonely grave. Though try as she might, that last was beyond even her powers: The vision haunted her, it hung before her eyes open or shut, waking or sleeping, it burned itself into her brain and carved itself upon her soul; it would not die until she did.

My thanks to all gods that the ring has come back to me... But I cannot think of it now: If it were not she who returned it, then that is well; if it were, still I do not repent of my intended course. She killed him! *Naught is changed there, for any of us; at least not yet. But it shall be...*

"So, then," she said aloud to Morric, knowing that he heard, and her voice echoed in the empty chamber. "O my beloved—"

And though she was not in the least degree sorry, nor ever would be, still she found she could not say that she was glad.

After the judging Athyn seemed to return a little to her own old self; or at least so those closest to her did hope. Though fitting rites had been held for Keltia's slain King, and Athyn comported herself with faultless correctness, clad ever in unrelieved mourning, in private she continued to speak of Morric as if he were still alive, and this troubled more Kelts than a few. But no distraction however great could draw her from the track of her pain; and even had she ever forgotten for an instant, the which she never did, still there was ever something there to remind her...

As she went by an oriel one afternoon, she overheard Mariota and Sosánaigh, and struck by the few words she caught she stopped to tax them with the rest of it.

"Naught to fret yourself about," said Mariota firmly, not wishing to add to her friend's pain; but under the steady pressure of Athyn's gaze she sighed and gave in. "Merely some stupid words spoken on Kaireden, someone giving it as opinion that Morric and Amzalsunëa had been so much alike they were male and female of the same person."

"That's as may be," said Athyn, with a smile of purest irony for the folly of it all, though the words had stabbed her to the heart. "But mating with yourself is a sterile exercise at best. He and I did rather better than that. And as a former horsegirl, well I know that a throughbred stallion does not belong in the same pasture as a she-ass. I was not wrong there."

Mariota looked after her as she went. "That was a stupid cruel word," she said aloud. "You did well not to tell her it was Erramun Zedoary who spoke it."

Sosánaigh nodded. "As if *he* would know... Well, perhaps it was so, for a while, long ago, in their youth, before they changed; before Morric grew in the Light and Amzalsunëa not only did not grow but turned to paths of Darkness. Male and female of the same person, maybe once; what of it? Morric and Athyn are male and female of the same soul—as he himself did sing. Their pairing meshes strengths, where the other simply mirrored weaknesses. And though mating with one's own self makes for a sterile union, as Athwen just now said, more than that, it breeds mules of the spirit."

"And as a former horsegirl—"

"Just so."

"I wish to kill something."

The Gweriden looked round at one another, and though Athyn was shivering withinwards she laughed unforcedly.

"Oh, not *you!* But I wish to hit things until they die, and I wish those things to be my enemies and Morric's, for only then will this—" She could not go on, drew a deep uneven breath. But if they did not all of them agree with her they surely all understood, and their love reached out to comfort her and carry her, bearing her upon it like a great warm wave.

"You might do better to forgive," said her sister Sulior, so gently. "I do not say forget, and would not ask it of you, none of us could—"

"Then that is well, for I forget nothing and no one."

"And forgive?"

Athyn smiled. "Nothing and no one. And I will hang a piece of them on every tree in the wood."

It was a summer evening on Tara, a month since Morric's death. The Gweriden had come to the council chamber at Athyn's summoning, and sat now round the great wheel-table. And there before them all had Athyn Ard-rían just now given the governance of Keltia into the hands of Esmer and Ganor Lennox, naming them stewards of the realm—she had stripped her signet from her finger and put it on Esmer's hand—with the true Companions to help them in their new and, it was to be hoped, very temporary task.

All of them, not just the newly named stewards, were still reeling from the shock. This was nothing that any of them, not even those who had known Athyn longest and best, could have ever expected. She knew well what their objections would be, and spiked their guns methodically aforetime, bringing to bear on her Council all the considerable charm and charism she possessed, and they were as powerless against her as they had ever been.

"What of the world?" asked Greyloch quietly, when all the argument seemed done, and naught had changed one inchling.

"The world!" Angry tears stung, hot and unexpected; Athyn dashed them away with fury and impatience. "The world takes everyone three coils away and leaves them there— that is not what I will have for him!"

"Then what of the law?" asked Stellin.

Athyn hesitated. "I have used the law to my own purposes," she said presently, "as indeed I was warned against at Silverwood, and whether that is sin or no I cannot say. But though I would gladly do as much again, still I feel that scales must be cleared that swing heavy now, and this shall require stepping down a while from the Throne."

She smiled at their protest renewed, her countenance suddenly bleak as a winter moon seen through midnight flying clouds.

"Not for long! And I swear upon my love for him and you alike that I will return. See, I leave stewards, not regents, to hold the Throne whilst Morric and I are gone."

'*Morric and I*': Even Esmer exchanged a troubled glance with the others at that. Athyn saw, but chose not to call them on it. *Best they grow used to hearing that, for while he is from me I will not cease to say it; and when he is once more with me I shall not need to cease to say it...*

"And we?" asked Miach Pendreic. "What must we do?"

Athyn turned in the door. "Wait for Samhain. If I have not returned by then—choose yourselves another ruler, and follow her, or him, as you can, or will."

It was to take less time than that; yet by another reckoning it would be Samhain seven times round before she returned, and still they chose no other while she was gone from them.

So began the Long Hunt, Athyn Cahanagh's terrible vengeance on those who had wrought so terribly against her. Between Lugh's Feast and Summerend they died; they who had done the harm as she saw it now paid the price as she told it. The Gweriden had the gravest doubts, and did not stint to remind her; but in the end, those who loved her did not let her hunt alone.

The list was not so extensive as it might have been; Athyn had exercised restraint in that at least. But those whom she held contributory to Morric's death, or guilty of the worst lies against her and hers, or responsible for war crimes that even the strictest tribunal would not have faulted her for avenging—massacres, arms dealing, drug trafficking, whorage, smuggling—all were quarry for her Hunt. In Keltia, public law has ever allowed for private justice, and as brehon Athyn knew it; as for the dán, she had long since determined she would bide the issue. *I will not be turned; I shall answer for it when I stand before Arawn, and we shall then see who is adjudged, and how, and of what...*

She rode out on Rhufain early the next morning, before Caerdroia woke, heading east along the mountain tracks round Loom-end, then south over the Plains of Ellertrin, following the way some of the fleeing offenders had been seen to take, toward the river Drumna.

'Beyond the Leap, beyond the law': That was how it was set down in the oldest statutes of Tara. If a fugitive could take, and make, the fearful leap across the Drumna, he would be safe forever from the law's toll for that offense. But he must make the leap at the one place, a chasm through which the river raged white and tumbling, a hundred feet below; and of those who tried not all leaped to their chosen end, and that was justice too.

Beyond the law, maybe. By all means let them think it, for in that comfort they will soon grow fatal careless. But though they be beyond the law, they are not beyond my law; and most assuredly they are not beyond justice. There is no Leap in the universe is wide enough for that...

Her first quarry was swiftly run to ground. She caught up with Ser Leto Novedris in a market square in Tamon Acanis, where he lingered with others of his countrymen spinning out their full allotted time in Keltia. He knew her at once when he saw her; and though he tried to slip away under cover of night, in a packtrain bound for eastern ports, she was waiting for him beyond the town. The packdrivers did not interfere.

For a Fian it was no work at all: She bound him to a horse, and they rode several days over high mountains, crossing a salt desert where none dwelled. By now he was more subdued, though still mutinous enough to attempt escape, and at last, exasperated, she pulled off his boots and scored the soles of his feet, two quick slashing chops each, so that he could not walk.

She led his horse while he crawled beside her own, under the brutal white sun on the glaring salt pan—*Why this country is called Farranfore, the Cold Land, must surely be purest irony*—

pleasantly discoursing to him as to just why this fate had come upon him: for the lies he had told, the betrayals he had made, not only of Morric and herself but of other Kelts, even of his own people.

In the end he ceased to crawl; even death was preferable to listening to Athyn one minute longer. She was nothing loath that he should choose so, and setting up a small pavilion to shield the horses and herself from the sun she sat calmly watching Ser Leto dry like a piece of meat, his tongue growing thick and blackened in his mouth. *Cruel, aye; but so too what he did to us...*

"You perish by sun and wind," she said aloud, "greine 's ghaoithe... No cairn for you; for your crimes against Morric I will set you no stone."

He died shivering in the blazing sun, his skin still shining where she had kept it well oiled; she had a purpose in so doing. She waited until he was quite dead before she flayed him, though it cost her a struggle to tarry.

Next morning, a leatherman at a tanyard just outside Tamon Acanis looked up incuriously at a sudden hail, and a rider on a splendid bronze horse threw a large bloody bundle unerringly at his feet.

"I have need of a riding rug made from this particular hide," said Athyn. "I shall be in the town until week's end; craft it well, but swiftly, for I wish to ride from here with it beneath my saddle. A matter of honor."

The man, who had been unwrapping the bundle, thinking to see—at least judging by the abundant dark pilosity—the usual unscraped cowhide or perhaps summer pelts of fox or bear, suddenly leaped back in terror.

"Mistress—this skin is—it is *human!*"

"Do not trouble yourself." She wheeled Rhufain rearing, turning him back along the road to town. "He was Arlan-zar, the Beast that Walks like a Man, and he well merited what he has received. And do not think, either, to bury it with the respect he does not deserve, and fob me off with some cow's hide. Trust in it, leathermaster, I'd know his pelt in any tanyard—and if you cross me I will have your own."

When she left Tamon Acanis at week's end, the rug, beautifully tanned and finished and tooled with certain runes, lay between saddle and saddlecloth upon Rhufain's back. Looking down as she rode away, Athyn smiled, admiring the handiwork—hers and the nervous leatherworker's alike—that had gone into its making, and thinking of him who once had worn it.

The only way he would ever lie between the same thighs as Morric; great pity he is not alive to enjoy it…

But Leto Novedris was merely the first; one by one, all across Keltia, Athyn's enemies began to fall. By now it was well known on Keltia how the King had died; the folk mourned with their Queen, and as good Kelts they approved her errand. And though hers was the hand by which most were brought down, often the task of avenging was done by the Gweriden, who wished to spare their friend and Queen what they might.

Either way, of the many Incomers and bent Kelts who had offended, not one there got out alive; and of those who had hoped that removal to Kaireden might save them, none also—though that was yet to be.

So Rhykeur Pym, Firvolgian profiteer, was boned like a pike by Rhain and Selanie: every bone in his body broken and extracted through small slits in his skin, until he was a mass of guts in a sack of flesh, gasping and flopping on the ground beside the pile of his own bloody bones, until he died.

Another such, Dalgu Namani, was hunted down by Mariota and Stellin, who fed him through a winepress and danced on his face when it broke on through to the other side of the rollers. Stellin nailed his flattened skull to the walls of Ardturach to serve as warning, as a farmer might hang upon the garden gate or boarden a ragged weasel carcass or a stoat's, and, without a note even, sent the crushed body home to Kaireden to serve the same.

Tareba Culloc, a slanderer and war criminal, was brought to an end peculiarly apt: Her nose and ears were sealed shut, then her mouth was piped full of bees, and her jaws bound behind the angry insects with a gag of hot soft lead. The bees having nowhere else to go began to crawl down her throat, even into her lungs and stomach, and into the passages of her ears and nose, stinging furiously as they went, until bees and offender died alike.

"Stings for the stings of her base lying tongue," said Mariota, reporting the event to her father afterwards. "Still, I am sorry for the death of the bees."

"Then again," said Stellin, "they *were* Incomer bees..."

All that burning autumn Athyn rode in search of those who had wronged her worst and most, and wrought upon them all, fittingly, as they had wrought against her—she even sent the spinebones of the turncloak Jirko pen Rhys to the Fian silversmith Ádriagh Errwen, to make Rhufain a breastplate ornament that would complement the riding rug. ("Not much there to work with, Ádri; he was a thing of very little backbone.") Ádriagh carved the bones with Keltic interlace and set them with rubies and pearls, for Morric's blood and Athyn's tears, and Rhufain bore it amongst his war-tack—a great success.

But while Athyn kept herself so occupied the Gweriden too were not idle, and wherever their quarry strove to hide, it strove in vain: Teddecin Wenn, Buticularia, Hunfrith—profiteers all, dispatched by various Gweriden; Baigran Dyoleus, who for war crimes was hunted down by Greyloch, and Liadan ran him to earth and tore out his throat; the eunuch Bargeld Almont, a failed and bitter bard who wrote lying books and had maliciously promised one on Morric, cut to pieces and fed to the geese; one Marberek, stamped flat between two grind-stones by Miach Pendreic; the whore Jin Tenarë, buried up to her neck in firesand by Sosánaigh Darnaway, and that neck sawed at with a sedge saw by any passersby who cared to: all of them dead, and well dead.

"They knew what would be the honor-price of their lies," said one of the Gweriden, when taxed by a nervous observer. "But they had not a shred of honor amongst them; not for them to complain of our accounting."

But for all Athyn's swiftness and starkness upon her quest, many of those who had offended worst had already departed Keltia; and her friends feared that she would not limit the Long Hunt to the confines of her own realm: that in pursuit of justice she would go far strange ways to bring it home.

And they were by no means wrong to fear so.

Summer was almost gone. As the news of Athyn's bloody Hunt had spread among her terrified quarry, some hearing of her approach had most unwisely tried to flee, and some coming face to face with her had even more unwisely tried to fight; either road a vain one, as Athyn could have told them—and, before she killed them, she almost always did.

One of those last, the half-Kelt Lorcan Firdanisk, surprised her considerably—and by no means unwelcomely—by daring to draw sword against her. Though he claimed old friendship with Morric, and had profited handsomely off the claim, he had been guilty of some of the vilest of the slanders. But it was for his betrayal of her mate that Athyn tracked him now; and early on the morning of the feast of Fionn, she came up with him at last, at Ranza on the Donn.

She did not speak; he knew why she was come. *He called Morric 'friend,' yet took his dignity, made him look a drunkard oaf; and because they had indeed been friends in bard-school there were many who took his fleering lies for truth…*

"Not wise the thought," he gabbled, backing like a cornered whitrit, "to strike a Comeling."

"Not wise the deed, to cross a queen," countered Athyn smiling, and drew her blade from its backscabbard; the metal chimed faintly, as if to arm her words. "And nor are you any Comeling; do not think to hide from me behind *that* mask. You had a Keltic parent, you are lawfully a Kelt—fight like one, then." She raised her sword to the salute, and her smile fled. "Bas no beatha, cupshot filth—Death or Life."

Life or death, it was no fight worth the name: Ten passes later, Athyn stepped up to his prostrate form. Setting her boot upon his chest, she pulled her sword out with little effort, wiped the blade clean upon his own tunic, sheathed it. Once more she looked down at the splayed-limbed body, and the lines of her own hardened again.

This—thing *dared to claim Morric's friendship, and yet did not stint to fail him and make him look a fool. Even had he done him no ill he did him no good; thus are false-friends served, and rightly too, for a true-friend would spend his last strength in the service of the friend he claimed to love*…

She spurned the bleeding carcase one last time with her booted foot. "Cross no swords with love or vengeance. Remember that for next time round."

But, though love is forever, vengeance must some time have an end; and as the red leaves began to fall, and An Lasca, the Whip-wind, sent them southward across the long dark miles under the autumn stars, with those leaves fell the last of Athyn's enemies in Keltia, and in Keltia the Long Hunt wound to an end; already it had passed into legend. Having kept her word to Morric and to herself, Athyn now kept her word to the Gweriden, and before Samhain was in she rode home to Caerdroia, where her friends had returned before her.

The folk rejoiced to have her back; though they approved

wholeheart of the task that had kept her from them the past
months, they had begun to grow restive at the doubly empty
throne. She knew their thought: 'Bad enough to have lost our
King, must we lose our Ard-rían also?'

For her own deeds, the road of blood that marked her
hunting season, it was hard for her to speak of even now—
ever and aye the vision of Morric dead without her, lying
down to die upon a bed not their own on a world they did not
rule, came to slam her yet again into white silent petrifaction.
So though she gave account of her own dispatchings, and
heard approvingly the Gweriden's tallies, little more was said
either side; but once, to Bronwyn Muirheyd, she spoke her
heart.

"I have heard it said that each time you kill, you lose a little of yourself."

"And do you feel you have so lost?" asked Bronwyn quietly.

Athyn turned to her onetime teacher a face that shone like
the morning. "Nay, I feel that I have *found*! Found a part of me
that had been somehow reived away. If the cause is a true one,
I think, perhaps, it can be so. Never in attack. A balance of
blood, in blood, to right a wrong."

"So it was not revenge?"

Athyn shook her head. "Nay, it was revenge, right enough;
I do not let myself off that lancepoint. But it was also justice. I
could do no other, and I will bide the dán. You and Redigan
taught me that. And also grief is a great teacher."

Not to even her dearest soul-kin had Athyn yet spoken of the
next journey she must make, still less of the far greater one she
knew must follow; a briefer pilgrimage took precedence of
both. Samhain was at hand, the first since Morric's going, and
she knew she must escape Caerdroia. *I cannot stay here for it, I
do not think I could bear it; not so much the curiosity—though that
would be bad enough—but the sympathy, and the love. I would be
alone for this, with none to see my pain but Morric only: What I*

*need is sanctuary, a place for me to hide; I can set a light for him
anywhere in Keltia, and I will...*

So she went southeast again, alone, to Witchingdene in its
wooded valley beside the Alligin Water. Though some might
have thought it the last place on any Keltic world that she
would wish to be, Athyn straight from her Long Hunt fled
there swift and surely, hunter now hunted; fled like a wounded
vixen to the one unstopped earth she knew.

chapter twenty-seven

There was never enough where nothing was left.

—*Lassarina Aoibhell ac Douglas*

Just before sunset on Samhain night Athyn set a lighted candle in the western tower window of the castle of Witchingdene, stood back and watched the flame dance its loving message into the dark, feeling as she did so a sudden deep kinship with the castle's long-dead mistress, Tarnaris of Lochiel. *Only another woman who has lost her lord too soon can understand—though where there is love even a thousand years would be too soon... Both of us, in loss, sought refuge here, both of us have mourned, will mourn; but I have made a promise, to my lord and to myself...*

The day had been warmer than was wont for November Eve, windy, full of thunderstorms; then in the afternoon a line of squalls had marched through like cloud-armies, heralds of a cold front, and though the temperature had plunged the wind and rain did not abate.

Athyn had spent the day in the chambers she had shared with Morric. She had prayed, and wept, and laughed, and remembered, wrapping herself in an old tunic and leinna of his, to feel the nearer, curled up in the window seat, looking from time to time back into the chamber, as she had so often done before. All those other times she had seen Morric there, seated at the paper-strewn table in his great purple-upholstered chair, or stretched out on his stomach in front of the fire, writing, or singing to himself, or to her, or laughingly prisoning her in the window-niche until she yielded to whatever his wish might be—love, or supper, or a walk. Yet now, as she read poems he had made for her scribed in a book she herself had given him, when she looked up from habit, smiling, to share with him the beauties of his words or a thought of her own, the room was barren of him, and she caught a shivering breath, each time, on the edge of tears. *Goddess! When will I learn he is not here, will not be here—shall I be looking to see him forever? Well—I cannot see him with my eyes, perhaps; and yet I think he is here even so… I must learn to open my eyes a little wider, sharpen my Sight to see beyond the seen.*

The light was going; Athyn closed the book, hugging it for an instant to her breast, then set it tenderly aside and lighted a few sconces. Suddenly unable to bear herself withindoors another instant, flinging on an old cloak of Morric's that still hung behind the door where he had left it, pulling the hood close around her head—her face buried for an instant in the rough gray hodden, where the scent of him still clung to it—Athyn ran down the stone stair, out into the empty autumn gardens and the rain.

On Samhain night the veil between the worlds is vanishingly thinnest. Portents flare, banshas weep, the Sidhe ride out from their hollow hills, the beloved dead return to be with those they themselves did love in earthly life; a solemn night, a night of joy and sadness both. Samhain is the giant beating midnight heart of faith; it holds promises between the worlds, its mighty door stands wide and open to any either side who love enough to pass.

Athyn walking in the rain-filled gardens, where not long since she had gathered lilacs in which Morric himself did clothe her. *I told no one my true reason for coming here, though anyone with half a brain and any heart at all will have twigged. But it is so that Morric will know where to find me, and so that we may be alone together. And I know he could find me no matter where I went; still… But if Tarnaris of Lochiel and Arran of Clannrannoch do care to join us, they will be no unwelcome company upon this Samhaintide; or any tide…*

At her command none had accompanied her from Caerdroia. Taking another leaf from Tarnaris's book, before her arrival she had dismissed on liberty even the few folk who were caretakers in her and Morric's absences, so that no one might know the Ard-rían had come there, and Athyn was alone in the little castle with her grief and her love. But on this greatest of all Keltic feasts there are things must be done of which even queens cannot scant the doing—and as sunset came on she turned her steps down through the darkening gardens, to the banks of the Alligin Water.

After the rain, the evening was thick with mist and cloud; the moons were hidden, and the Criosanna were only a lightening smudge far down the waste places of the sky. Then the clouds parted before the rising wind, and the sunset flooded through the gates of the rain. For a long time Athyn stared blindly at the black stream rushing by, her thoughts as tumbling-wild as the waters; then leaning forward she slowly drew a small pompion out from beneath her cloak. With a gesture she kindled it aglow, then bent to set it on the stream, and straightening up again she looked after it as it went its way to the sea, gazed and gazed, until the tiny flickering brightness was lost downriver in the night.

If pain is the price of memory, then by all gods I will gladly pay it; it is anguish untellable, but also it is the reason I care to live at all—to have been with him, to be with him still. It cannot be other; might as well wish he and I had never been born, never had met and mated, bedded and wedded, never shared dán each with the other…and that is a thing neither of us would ever wish to be.

She drew a deep and cleansing breath, clear to the core of her, and smiled, as she felt the old year lift and take wing into the past, a hawk called home to the wrist of that Falconer who had sent it forth. Peace came down upon her then, or else peace's calm cousins that are weariness and gentle resignation; either way it seemed a thing achieved, and surely she had fought for it long and hard and brave enough to have fairly won it now.

But the light had gone, and the mist and rain came on again. As she retraced her steps to the castle behind her, wandering weeping through the gardens in the dark, she saw dimly through the mist another cloaked and hooded figure moving silently some yards away. And though she knew herself to be alone at Witchingdene it never crossed her mind to be afraid; never once the thought that this might be no loving spirit-presence but a corporeal and hostile one, some enemy that had learned of Blackmantle's whereabouts, and had come to do her harm on Samhain night.

She was not alone now. Yet there was no danger for her from this silent escort; that, her soul had known straightway. A figure that never came too near yet kept companionable pace with her, moving as she moved, the cloak of hodden gray swinging with that long, unhurried stride, a stride remembered; a tall figure, man or woman she could not tell, the face was hidden within the deepness of the hood. Who walked with her in the rain?

She reached out a hand, a name, her soul. *Morric—*

She was not alone; but then she was suddenly doubtful. *The Lady Tarnaris, come to condole with me, or perhaps her lord Arran?* Or was it some other—one she had not seen since first her Long Hunt began?

But who walked with her, in the gardens, in the rain?

And then the white moon Argialla ran out from the flying clouds, turning all the wet leaves to silver, and she saw him, his long dark hair upon his shoulders where the wind had thrown back the hood of his cloak, his face clear where the flooding light touched it. His eyes were blue fire in the night and the mist, blue as burning copper, blazing into her own, as they had done in life, in love; he was smiling.

*   *   *

Back in the tower, shaken and solaced alike, Athyn stripped and went into the pool-room for a ritual bath; then, naked save for her rings, the silver swan necklace and a pendant that had been Morric's which now she often wore, she returned to their bedchamber to set out the Samhain candles.

She had brought with her from Caerdroia the familiar altar gear that had come from Caerlaverock before that; sgian, quaich, censer; and for Samhain, an ancient bronze candleholder in shape of a stag's head, a candle cup on the topmost point of each antler, each of which held a tall black taper. Behind the altar stood an iron candletree in the form of the circled suncross, topped by a white taper, and that was for death; then two red candles on the east and west arms of the cross, and those were for mourning, and for love and loss; and a green altarcandle, and that was for love alone. Set round the floor were twelve candles more, black, white, green, purple, red, gold all together.

One of the loveliest parts of the Samhain ritual is the Calling-on, the invoking and the inviting in and the thinking with joy on the beloved dead, recalling bright loving moments; and the loving dead do come. In the blasting welter of memory that came on her as she chanted, Athyn recalled suddenly how, only a fortnight or so after Morric's death, hearing by ill chance one of her favorite songs of his composing, she had wept and laughed alike to recall him telling her once how when he was a youth he could not make the music he had heard within him, not until the bards taught him how to set it free. He had been so envious, he had admitted laughingly, of his friends Jaffran and Evance, who had only to look at an instrument, seemingly, to know how to play it; and so grateful to his bardic teachers, to have been given at last the skills to make music of his own.

Song and memory alike had moved her to wild weeping, and no one could console her. But she smiled to recall it now, and took up a pen... And though Athyn Cahanagh was never the poet her lord was, and was ever the first to say so, the love of poetry that Nilos Marwin had labored to instill in her found flower in the ground of her grieving, so that the coronach which Athyn Ard-rían made for Morric the King, the 'Cumha Dubhglais,' the lament for Fireheart—written by her that very night of Samhain, copied with her own hand into the brown leather-bound book filled with the love poetry he had made for her—still stands today in Keltia with the 'Marúnad Séomaighas' that Lassarina Douglas made for her own murdered lord, a benchmark of sorrow and of art.

The candles burned down serene and still, all save three: The two red crosscandles balanced streaming gold flames the length of her forearm, and the flame of the white taper topping the iron tree danced and writhed and twisted like a living thing. Outside the wind had died; there was not a breath of air moving in the chamber to cause the candles to behave so. *How wild it is*, she thought; then, as wildly as the flame itself, *Morric*—and the flame leaped again.

What is it, cariadwyn? What do you wish me to know? That you are here? As soon as she thought it she felt it; love around her like a cloak, so warm and fierce and strong she all but crumpled beneath it, laughing and weeping in one. *Never would I not know whose touch is that, whose the arms about me... Never could I mistake him, he is engraved upon the very tips of my fingers, seated deep, I see him not with my eyes but with my skin, to the center of my being...*

And she knelt in the center of the candles, she danced in the ring of fire and of light, she spoke to him who was there with her. *It is you, and that I know forever... But what would you tell me? That you love me? Beloved, I know that... That things were left unfinished? I know that too. It cannot be left so. You cannot be left so... And you shall not be. I swear it by the Goddess and the God and the Alterator, by all gods, even by Kelu's Oneness—to do what I must, and will...*

And dán—listening still, hearing always—made the third

and greatest, and gravest, of its notings; and then at last decreed.

Back at Caerdroia the day after, Athyn opened a battered old brass-studded leather trunk that she had not unstrapped in many years. It had been hers at Caerlaverock, contained treasures of those dear times; but it was not for sake of mere memory that Athyn went delving in it now.

She found it almost at once: a Firvolgian passcard and identity crystal made out in the name of Athnë Marwinë. Upon his marriage to Lyleth, Nilos Marwin had registered Athyn, alone of all the Archill children, as his legal ward according to the law of his people, and out of respect and sentiment she had kept safe the proofs of that wardship all the years since.

I remember how strangely I felt when he showed me this, and told me what he had done; though even then I knew it was done with love, and to protect me, because I had no other lawful status that he knew of; and for his sake I never used it when I might have, against the Incomers…who knows, it could even have kept me out of the Tolbooth! But now I must use it, to board a Firvolgian liner—oh, not here, to be sure, they would never permit me even to embark— and to pass where I will on Kaireden. And a lawful ward of a citizen of Firvolgior is a citizen herself; as such, Nâreddin Athnë Marwinë may make certain claims that Athyn Queen of Kelts, much less Blackmantle, might not—and that is a thing I may find very useful to my purpose. Strange: Nilos always knew that some-one would rise up in Keltia to bring the Outgoing; we even spoke of it from time to time. Is it irony, or merely dán, that I should have been that one he knew would come? Well, the thing is met, no mat-ter now; he will not be entirely glad of heart that I shall be using his gift to do what I must do—but I think he will understand, will be pleased that I shall come to his world at last. Even on such an errand as mine. Even as he knew I would.

*   *   *

"Are you mad *entirely*? To throw your life away merely to spite that cutsark flink, those lying fuddocks? Has your own Hunt taught you nothing? You think the Incomers here detested you—do you know how you are hated on Kaireden itself? Even your status as Nilos's ward will not save you; they will tear you to pieces in the street if they find out who you are—"

Athyn let Esmer berate her as long as he liked; then, when he ran down at last, and before he could gear up again for another round, she said only, calmly, as once she had said similarly to his daughter, "I will take the greater care then that they do not."

But truly it should have come as no surprise to the man she thought of—even more than Cormac or Nilos—as her father; so well did Esmer know her little ways. Since the moment she knew of her beloved lord's murder, there had not been a moment when Athyn Cahanagh had not intended what she had just told Esmer Lennox she intended: to go to Kaireden and to take there the last of her vengeance, fulfilling her oath—and slaying Amzalsunëa Dalgarno with her own hands.

Indeed, at first she had planned merely to go and tell no one, and if she fell, she would fall alone; and then she would be with Morric again, which was all she wanted. But through that long Samhain night, the light shining out from Witchingdene's tower window across the empty dark miles, the one for whom it shone so close beside her, around her, together with her, she had sensed as clearly as if he had spoken it, as so often she had done in life—*And gods know* that *was often enough!*—that same beloved lord's extreme distinct disapproval of her plan; and so she had made a new plan, and if King Morric Fireheart discountenanced this one as well she had long since stopped her ears to him—as, again, so often she had done in life.

Well, one way or the other, I shall be with him again; I have sworn it, and if I may not go to him, then— But even she could not yet frame the rest of that intent in words. Yet as much as she could, she confided in Esmer only, binding him with most fearful oaths, as her Taoiseach and steward, now her Regent, not to divulge her intention—not even to Ganor or Mariota—until after she was safely offplanet.

And though he railed against her going as much as he might, knowing even as he did so that it was no use, Esmer kept his word, and told no one—not his Countess, not his daughter. But the instant her ship left the ground of the spaceport all oaths were off.

Not for naught did I study what way to hide my trail or mark it; has Blackmantle forgot in a mere few months of Queen Athyn's reign those lessons learned over all those years with the Gwerin? I do not think so!

So, by way of hiding trail, Athyn went first, in secret, to Mistissyn on the Yamazai homeworld of Aojun the More, where Zarôndah the Jamadarin and Brahím her consort welcomed her warmly. Indeed, Zarôndah informed her how she herself had slain the Firvolg Darrian Finslock, who had come slinking to Mistissyn, seeking to tell and sell lies about Morric and Athyn—"His error, Athani; the Yamazai suffer such creatures no more gladly than do the Kelts"—and Athyn had been grateful.

She remained there for only a night, guesting with Brahím and Zarôndah in Khed Anjaval, their beautiful palace in the lovely towered city all of wood, enjoying their company and Brahím's music, so different from Morric's who had been his friend. Then, against their protests, she had departed Aojun for the Numantissan spaceport of Vari Zion, in guise of a crewman aboard an Aojunese cargo vessel.

This was a compromise all round, and it pleased no one. Faced with Athyn's legendary pigheadedness, of which she had only ever heard, the Jamadarin had finally given in, thinking that it was best to have Athyn go, since go she clearly would, in the safety of an Aojunese ship over which Zarôndah would at least have some command; though she was already learning that with Athyn 'command' was a word others very seldom got to use.

"Is it because you are queen?" Zarôndah had asked, defeated, as so many had been before her, and would be after; not a thing that often befell with her, queen that she was herself. "That you must ever have the mastery?"

"Why, no," Athyn had said, surprised, "it is because I am a horsegirl. Because I am the one with the reins."

But that horsegirl, however much she would have preferred the complete anonymity that some nomad freighter would have given her, was content enough to sail on the Yamazai vessel, where only the captain and her first officer knew the new assign's identity; and after the waystop at Vari Zion Athyn went on to Kaireden, aboard the luxurious Firvolgian liner *Star Elephant*.

This was the part of the trip that had given her most pause beforehand: the moment when she must stand forth, face bare—she was clad now as a traditional Firvolgi widow, all in black, face hidden by a heavy veil—and declare herself, backed only by her passcard and her crystal and her nerve, under the name and rank of Nâreddin Athnë Marwinë; praying all the while that the port officers, or the liner crew, or even a fellow passenger, would not somehow recognize the name, or her face, and slaughter her on sight as Blackmantle, who was by no means out of Firvolgian thought even so far from her own ground. The danger was fearful, and she was prepared every instant for discovery.

Yet, though Nilos had never boasted, Athyn knew that the name of Marwin was an ancient and a noble one, and she had relied on that, that any member of that kin might travel unquestioned and unchallenged in Firvolgior. The quiet deference Athyn now received was not only the special courtesy her widow's weeds commanded but the genuine respect due the Marwin name, and it was doubly shaming: to her sensibilities as a Kelt—her honor and her honesty, that would not let her sail under false colors however useful or becoming they might be—and to the loving regard she bore to Nilos. *He would never say so, nor even think as much, but it feels to me that I am using him, that I*

*am cynically trading on his love and kindness for my own selfish and
terrible purpose…*

Many times on that voyage she all but spoke up, irrationally
tempted to surrender and confess and make an end of it, but
that would have given away more games than hers alone; so
she thrust off her constraint and her disquiet, for on that name
of Marwin not only did her own safety hang but the greater
goal as well. *He would only tell me that though it does me great
credit to scruple so, it is sleeveless and bootless and crabbèd, and he
would bid me do exactly as I do. I know very well he knows why I
do this, and for whom, and he would cheer me on…* But she did
not love the way it made her feel.

Her brief voyage was smooth and uneventful, and under
any other circumstances—say, had she not been bound to a
hostile city on a foreign world that would like nothing better
than to see her head on a spike above its gate, where her mate
had been murdered by the whore he had trusted, where her
lord and her King lay dead and alone in an unknown,
unmarked grave—it would have been a most pleasant one. In
a deeply soft, enfolding, velvet-cushioned blastchair, Athyn
stared through her black veil out the *Star Elephant*'s padded
viewport, at hyperspace streaming by; then smiled, and
touched the great emerald that hung between her breasts,
beneath her leinna. *Still, now I think on what else it brings me
to—my last avenging—I find it something pleasant all the same…*

Upon arriving in Katilon Ke Katil she had gone at once to the
same inn where Morric had found lodgings, and by bribery and
sheer strength of will, and perhaps a force greater even than
both, had obtained for herself the same rooms in which her
mate had slept and died. It was not as easy a matter as she
would have thought; she sensed that for some mysterious
unspoken reason the innkeeper was strangely reluctant to rent
the chambers, even though he did so at last, and for a price by
no means reasonable.

I do not think he has twigged me for myself... though I did well to change from my weeds before I came here. Most likely it is that he thinks me some morbid gravesniffing curiosity-seeker, thinking to stay for the sake of a thrill in the rooms where Morric of Keltia met his end— Well, it makes no differ what is in his mind, so long as he has let me the chambers—and I would have paid a good deal more than I did to make sure of it...

Now, alone in the cool spring morning, she looked round the spacious bedchamber, her eyes wide and haunted and flint-dry, face shut as iron, all her senses open and straining, to the bone, to the nerve, to the pain. *Oh, but he was here, right enough, this is the place... He died here. He died here. From here did he go out... He is not here, it is too long since his going; and yet he is here all the same, and I will do what I must to find him... Mighty Dâna, help me!* The reality of where she was, what she was come there to do, suddenly overcame her: She reeled, dizzied, and caught herself up just as she started to collapse upon the bed; she was not yet ready for that, to lie where he had lain and dreamed of her, where he had lain and died...

So, slowly, she sank to her knees beside the great oak frame, and put out a hand to touch the huge footpost carved in shape of an alaunt. *In the bardic usage alaunts signify faithfulness of heart; they are steadfast in the hunt, and kill their quarry cleanly at the end, not for sport. Worse creatures far to take for model 'havior...*

Her control shattered without warning, and the post took all her weight as she clung to it in weeping desperation, bearing her up as a lost spar from a foundered ship will lift a stormwrecked sailor through the surge and wave. *Goddess—I do not know if I can endure it, upon my soul I do not—this may well be the thing to overmaster me at last. But I needed to see this place, I could not not have come here. It was from here that he went out, and so it is from here that I begin to follow. But not yet. There are things I must know before I ride out to draw this foreign covert: word of my quarry, my ground, all the stops and earths and*

*checks and fences; and any road I wish to be home from the hunt
before tomorrow's sun has set—I shall not stay here any longer than
I need, will not leave him here one night more than I must. But
tonight—tonight I lie here with my love. This night I will sleep again
with him.*

For a district of such notorious character it proved surprisingly difficult to locate, even with the excellent plain
directions she had been given. But once she had found it,
upon the stroke of next day's noon, there was no more mistaking.

As Morric had done before her, Athyn hesitated, looking
doubtfully up at the crumbling façade of the once-elegant
building in the Street of the Limeflowers—*No limeblossom
has been here, not for a good long time*—the leprous white
patches where the stone had flaked away, the ornate tracery
vainly trying to mask the rot, the ragged bow-trellis that
gave the place its address. *Aye, it seems about right; and no
more than I expected…* Within, a small dusty lobby opened
upon a round atrium screened by elaborate fretwork, in
which amber panes and copper mirrors were set; trade
seemed at a lull. *Perhaps there has been a lack of traffic since it
was learned that Keltia's King was given his death here. The
usual run of patrons might risk the pox for a paid tumble, but few
will care to risk poisoning—and Morric was not even here for the
usual purpose…*

She entered unchallenged; there was little curiosity in the
few glances flicked her way, and those mostly aimed at her
attire, which though she had done her best was not entirely
local, and uneasily, or perhaps unwisely, too like herself: tunic
and trews and boots, her mother's shortsword, though the
snakeskin cloak had been left at home. Perhaps they thought
her a prosperous foreigner seeking a morning's diversion, an
early patron; if they even thought on it at all.

But she found it hard to think of aught else: There they

were at last, or those that were left of them, there before her in the little atrium, those she had hunted so long and so far, sitting sprawled in unflattering postures such as one would not believe could tempt even the most deprived, or depraved, among potential customers. Garishly painted, women and men both, attired in cheap and none too clean clothing, hair frailed out into the tangled masses held for fashion on Kaireden, they sat dull and bovine under the influence of hazen, or perhaps other more noxious substances still.

Athyn found herself as revolted as Morric had been. *What man or woman of decent parts or clean appetites would suffer the unalluring touch of such as these, who of any brain or worth could sink so—either to resort or be resorted to? Is it merely the drug after all? If so, I shall be doing them all a kindness…*

She had fee'd informants lavishly the day before, a steady discreet stream of bought spies coming to her chambers from noon to sunset and going away again heavier of purse; and all the vile story had come pouring out at last. *Like lancing an infected wound, so that it might free itself of all the festering poison, and the pain ease a little, and then to cleanly heal…*

So, sitting in a chair, veiled again, her back to the light, she had heard at last the full and terrible truth of it: how Morric had come here even as he had told her he would, purely to help Amzalsunëa, purely for old times' sake and out of the pity that was the gift of a gallant heart; how he had been betrayed; how his own old bandfellows, and the playmonger Loris Venoët and his company, and all the inhabitants of the Beldam Pharuca's house, and the Beldam herself, had every single one of them known, or at least strongly suspected, what Amzalsunëa intended. Indeed, some of them had even suggested how she might lure him out of Keltia, had helped her with hints as to what she might say to best ensure his coming and his trust, though those same some would deny they meant his death. But the ones who did mean it—they had killed him to requite Blackmantle, to take revenge on Fireheart. And not a finger had been lifted to stop it, not one word of warning, not one syllable to save him...

All this had Athyn heard; and Blackmantle also. She had listened to each informant with a face of stone; she had paid the last of them as she had paid the first, with the same calm demeanor, the same quiet thanks; and then she had barred the door, and what she had done and felt in the hours that followed none but she herself, and Morric, would ever know.

Now, in the zareer, she looked around her, and closed her eyes briefly, as in great pain or great resolve; both were there, and in that moment even she could not say which was the greater. *Here it begins: Here then is where I take that step upon the path my mother died to turn my feet away from, that same path the Queen of the Sidhe did reveal... But right or wrong it is my path, which I will take for him where I would not take it for myself; and later, well, later we shall see. Aye, we shall see.*

Athyn opened her eyes and raised her hand, and all around her the doors and windows of the house quietly shuttered, folded, bolted, locked themselves behind her. Even then those who sat there did not look up; and it would not have saved them if they had. Her last coherent thought flickered like a dark flame across her awareness: *How easy it is to draw upon the Shadow; how fatal to do so for less cause...*

Of the moments that followed, Athyn afterwards remembered very little; and perhaps that was best. To judge by the evidence, her enemies had apparently attempted self-defense, which only enraged her all the more; though by numbers alone—at the least twenty to one, far above the odds to which honor demanded even a Fian stand—none could say the fight had not been a fair one. When she came to herself again she was standing unhurt in the thunderous silence, sword in hand and dead bodies thick as fallen leaves about her boots: whores, eunuchs, the young baron who was Amzalsunëa's chief customer and fellow hazer, even the shambling gytresh who had at Amzalsunëa's own bidding bought the hazen with which she had killed Morric. *Coin that he did give her out of pity purchased death for him instead—soon now, very soon, we shall see what it buys her; and I for one shall not be counting crossics…*

Apart a little from the rest lay the Beldam Pharuca, beheaded and cut in half side to side with the lightning back-stroke of the first blow, and then split in half again top to bottom before the head or first-cut halves had even hit the blood-drenched floor. Athyn did recall slaying her: *Give false testimony in my court, will you…*

She went forward then, passing the amber mirrors, to the inner zareer, where cowered the surviving slutters who had most cause to most fear her hand. Looking round at the slack faces, even as Morric had done, she knew them all by name. Her eye picked out four from the rest; of those present they were the ones had offended most grossly, and she addressed herself to them.

"You four were pleased enough to vaunt knowledge of my lord, and to revile me at every turn. But here: such garb as, I remember me, you did much love to wear; a last little gift in Morric's name and mine. Wear it now."

Athyn flung each of them—Jalior, Najén, Vantesso, Junoth—a shawl of heavy gold silk, deeply fringed, richly embroidered; the wraps seemed to have been pulled from the air itself.

As they caught them instinctively, acquisitively—though it seemed to the others watching that they had no choice—their faces changed from smirks to purest terror as the shawls, with a sudden life of their own, wrapped round and clung and held; and though they tried desperately to rip the garments from their shrinking raddled flesh, the more they clawed the closer and tighter the shawls did cling. The silk seemed alight, glowing, blazing, giving off heat; the screams were terrible, and when at last there was silence again in the zareer, only four small piles of frothy ash remained. Junoth and Vantesso, Jalior and Najén, all were gone, and the shawls, not a stitch of their embroidery snagged or singed, not a fringe torn or tangled, were silk once more, lying upon the floor where they had fallen beside the little heaps of ash.

The other harlots stared from shawls to ash and back again, as uncomprehendingly as cows, and Athyn looked upon them, her face the face of the judge she was. *Light skirts, light heads— and yet even these must be taught that truth is truth...*

Athyn waved a hand, in anger and impatience, and shawls and ash were gone alike. She looked on the remaining strumpets for a long time as they crouched dumbly, numbly waiting. *Ah, Goddess...*

"I shall not kill you," she said aloud, and saw the fear on their faces ease a little into a kind of dull hope. "I will even leave you your minds and reasoning faculties—such as they are—unimpaired. In punishment, for you do deserve to be punished, I shall put upon you the outer form of what your souls reflect. But in mercy I shall give you also this: If there comes a time when the truth wins out in your hard hearts and meager brains, if you admit and repent of the wrongs you have done, this shape you are now to receive—the shape your actions have proved is the only one you merit—shall fall from you, and you shall regain your mortal molds. If not, you shall stay as you—are."

And on that word Athyn lifted her hand and stretched it out before her, and then in the chamber of the zareer were no more five cringing harlots but four of the prettiest little pigs one could ever hope to see. They veered and climbed and tumbled over one another—Tanja, Veziëba, Rozenath, Davengra—ran round and round on their short little legs, shivering and scurrying, squealing loudly every time they caught sight of their reflections in the amber mirrorglass. At last, still squeaking, they darted out the back door of the zareer, which Athyn had by now thoughtfully unbarred, and trotted frantically off down the alley in a long string, dogs barking, street-lads shying stones.

One human form remained huddled on the floor, resigned and dully unexpectant of mercy, staring up at Athyn out of blank eyes under a fringe of matted hair: Lyrin. Athyn turned to her, and the truth-of-judging, the fíor-brethas that had ever marked her dealings, that had never deserted her from the moment it first had come to her, in a crowded court-hall at a brehon school, long ago, came once more upon her.

"I do not know if you have ever maligned my lord or myself," she said quietly, "if ever you have done us the hurt and harm your sisters have. At the least, if you did, I have never heard so. Therefore I will give you this grace: If that be the truth—that you have thought or spoken no lies or hatefulness of us—then you shall keep your mortal shape. But if ever you have shared in the others' malice, then seven days hence you shall share in their fate; and five little pigs there shall be to trundle through the backstreets of Katilon Ke Katil—if indeed you last so long in such poor and hungry quarters, pork on the run. You shall share as well in the mercy I gave them: If you repent your evil and your lies—if you have committed any— the magic will spare you. Seven days you have to search your memory and your heart, before the fate you have earned shall come upon you; it is all one to me. Now go."

Standing in the door of the silent house, Athyn watched her flee while still she had human legs under her. The pigs were by now vanishing into the countryside beyond the gates at the end of the street, though it seemed that already one was being borne squealing off to meet a savory fate; Rozenath, it looked like, and Athyn smiled.

Fortunate they, that so many Firvolgi deem swineflesh unclean, and will not eat it. Then again, it is only fitting that such muck-souled creatures be clothed in an outward guise to match their inner selves. Truly, they are much to thank me, for I have given them a mercy they never showed to Morric or to me: If they admit their sin, and repent of it, they shall be restored to human form; and that is justice. If not— Well, if they end up smoking on Firvolgi tables, I cannot say I shall too much sorrow for it—save of course that I shall not be here to share the meal. I am fond myself of sausage of a morning… And that is justice too.

chapter twenty-eight

If the heart be right, small matter where the rest may lie.

> —*Athyn Cahanagh, when told of Morric Douglas's secret burial in an unmarked, unknown grave*

Amzalsunëa Dalgarno, paying well for the information from the very funds Morric Douglas had supplied her, soon had what she did purchase: the timely and altogether certain word of her doom's arrival, and further news of what had befallen at the zareer, even though the Firvolgi authorities and the Keltic embassage were working hand in desperate glove to muffle all of it as secret and as quiet as they could.

For once both governments were utterly of the same mind: Blackmantle loose like an avenging firedrake on Kaireden? What would Firvolgian citizens do if *that* news got out? What would Keltia do, if something befell their queen at Firvolgian hands whilst she was killing Firvolgians? A Firvolg had already slain Keltia's king...

The possibilities of interstellar incident were volcanic, the climate volatile; and the politicians all hastily agreed, as only politicians can, that by far the safest course would be to let Athyn take the revenge even the Firvolgi conceded she had the lawful right to take, and for the Kelts to get her the hells off Kaireden as speedily thereafter as they might. After all, they temporized, she was slaying only those who had wronged her, and by their best report only her consort's actual murderer was yet left alive, so in effect she had saved Kaireden the cost of many trials and much administering; not to mention another war, which none of them would mention, and a war that would be fought on Firvolgi home earth; then too, she might even weary of avenging, it could happen so...

Thus, piously, or impiously, did Kelts and Firvolgi pray together for a successful conclusion to Athyn's quest; but that she might leave off her avenging, no, there they prayed in vain.

But Amzalsunëa Dalgarno, whom no prayer to any deity would avail and well she knew it, had fled Katilon Ke Katil and the bow-trellised house in the Street of the Limeflowers long before, knowing as the politicians did not, as only the truly guilty can know, that Athyn Cahanagh would surely come, would never abandon the hunt, not if all the seven hells together barred her way, and she would be bringing Blackmantle with her.

And against that double coming Amzalsunëa had prudently concealed herself in a secret place deep in the tangled empty valleys far beyond the town. Yet in the end she was not hard to find.

An old roadhouse in a narrow steep-sided canyon where sage and scrub pine grew; behind it, a whitewashed cottage, a brokeback brown horse in a paddock, a yellow mongrel asleep on a sunny terrace, a grove of orange-trees in fragrant bloom round about the walls.

Athyn stepped out of the air—*One thing about using Sidhe magic is that you get to travel as do the Sidhe themselves, a great convenience*—and looked calmly upon the refuge where Amzalsunëa Dalgarno had thought herself safe hid.

Very charming; who would have thought her such a country lass at heart? Yet scarcely, I think, defensible. But then she is no soldier; nay, nor sorcerer neither... She swept a level hand before her, and the air round the cottage began to shimmer like heat-haze on a summer day; the dog on the terrace whined and bolted, though the old horse continued to doze, oblivious. No one would disturb them now; to all outside eyes the cottage was no longer there. Even those accustomed to the sight of it would not notice its absence.

Walking across the rough grass to the front terrace, Athyn came to a door—round and fretted, made of ruddenwood, it was ajar, opening on a solar—and she went inside, hand on swordhilt, raking every corner of the untidy room with a wary glance. *Empty; where then—* A stone-built archway opened on the left; going down three steps she went along a paved passage to the kitchen.

Amzalsunëa Dalgarno sat at a round wooden table in the center of the room; she had a blue bowl before her, but she seemed uninterested in its contents. Her hair, banged and crimped as was the fashion in Katilon Ke Katil, was now garish orange, no longer the soft pretty red that had caught Morric's eye so long ago; the pale skin, still smeared with sunsprecks, showed the blue ravages of hazen. Her eyes were lowered, and Athyn could not see the look in them, the truths they might conceal, the depths they lacked.

She seemed aware and yet unaware of Athyn's presence. *Perhaps she thinks I am but a hazen-dream; rightly did they name that noxious substance, calling it for the glazed look that comes in the eyes of the newly dead...* But that was far too close a touch upon the bleeding wound, and her thought swerved sharply away before she could feel the full screaming pain of it, could see before her own eyes the picture it so inevitably conjured. Neither woman spoke.

Presently Athyn took a seat across the table's width, and watched her for a while in silence, seeing the last remnants of prettiness that had somehow survived not only harlotry and hazen but murder and guilt alike.

"I have wondered long what I should say to you in such a time," she said, after a silence that felt strange for that it did *not* feel strange. "It seems that there is no court strait enough, or punishment sufficing."

"Morric had many ladies," said Amzalsunëa, and the

patronizing note in her childlike voice was plain to be heard, though she would look neither at Athyn's face nor at the rings on Athyn's hand, "but Athyn Cahanagh was very special to him."

"On a world of the star Suka Vellanor," said Athyn after another silence, in the bardic voice she had learned from Morric, "there lives a bird called the pamma; lovely, graceful, swift-flying, with feathers the color of the setting sun. Only one 'crab,' if I may speak so, has this bird, and that is that it lives solely on the blood of others. A long time ago, it survived by grooming the wingfeathers of the tarnachan—a bird renowned for its beautiful song—and eating the seeds or parasites it found there: a benign relationship from which both birds benefited. Then, perhaps accidentally, one pamma learned that if it pecked with its sharp hooked beak as it groomed, it could draw the tarnachan's blood; and blood was both food and drink to it, better far than grubs or seeds. So this one pamma began to groom and peck together, drawing just enough blood to live, not enough to harm its source. And all the other pammas, seeing this easy new way of feeding, very quickly learned to follow suit."

Athyn's eyes on Amzalsunëa were clear and cold and steady, and though the Firvolgian trembled at what she heard in the other's voice, and felt the weight of the glance, still would she not look up.

Well, she has learned the irony lesson, right enough, which alone is greatly more than I expected—but let us just make sure...

"Except that sometimes, every now and again," continued Athyn in the same pleasantly narrative voice, "a pamma will peck too deep and drink too much of a tarnachan's blood—out of haste or greed or fear, out of the wish not to be forced to feed itself—or else perhaps the wound will not stanch and close, and the blood continues to drain away even after the pamma has fed to fullness. Either way, the host perishes; and if the tarnachan dies the pamma dies with it, since it cannot fend itself. You would think that even the stupidest pamma ever hatched would know this, by low cunning instinct if naught else; but the result is the same so or no, and now there are fewer tarnachans in that world, and less song—for a dead tarnachan's mate will die as well, since those creatures pair for life. And pammas still compete to feed off the tarnachans remaining, for they still have not learned to feed themselves... This habit so far is limited to this one bird, this pamma, but who knows what other animal might not follow suit? Or may have already done so..."

"I did not mean to harm him," she said then in a dull unemphatic whisper. "I thought the drug was dubh-cosac, as I told him..."

"Do not lie to me," said Athyn, with the first flash of anger she had allowed herself since arriving on Kaireden, and it cracked like sudden thunder in the quiet kitchen. "Do not—not in this moment. Or by all gods I will bring down this house around your ears—your bleeding dead unhearing ears—and then bring down the planet around the house."

That made Amzalsunëa raise her eyes at last. "You are not queen here."

"No. But I am still Blackmantle, and even in the brief time I have been here I have seen why Kaireden did not make shift to help the Incomers when I fought them in Keltia; and because I now know that, I could be queen here within the year if I so chose... But I do not choose," she said then. "For that is not why I have come."

"You have come to kill me," said Amzalsunëa in a dreaming dozy voice. "As you did the others, in Ruca's house—Blackmantle killed them all, others told me—"

"Not all of them. But aye, I did kill; and aye again, I have come here to kill you. It seems much to be preferred to killing myself."

"I have *said* I am sorry," she flared, with a kind of peevishness, "and you should not feel so cast down over Morric; but you have always hated me—"

"That is not so," said Athyn, when she thought she could

trust her voice again. *Not to be 'cast down' over Morric's death? Is she mad entirely, or merely too stupid to live? Which last I can remedy very quickly...* "When first I learned of you I wondered what someone like Morric could see in someone like you, and looked to know. Then, the more I learned, aye, the more I did come to hate—not you yourself, but what you did; and when I knew that you had slain him— Well. There can be a kind of purity in hatred, a simple perfection that other, more blended emotions know nothing of. Kelts, by and large, are not great believers in forgiveness; we do not turn the other cheek, we rip off both of yours. It is one of the many benefits that came of paying no heed to Rome's cowherd Pátraic. Or, if we do forgive, it is a kind of forgiveness that needs another name, for there is no absolution in it; rather, it marks down the transgression and reparation alike, upon a balance-sheet unlike all others, and allows both parties to go on. But the sin is surety for future actions, and neither side forgets. Honor-price is well and good, but sometimes, do you know, it is simply not enough." She. paused, looking into the empty, pretty face turned to her. "Do you have the least tiniest idea what I have just now said? Any greater idea than this wall has, that bowl, this chair?"

Amzalsunëa's sunsprecks stood out like begriming smudges, mottling her paleness like some dreadful skinplague, an ugly contrast to the orange hair.

"I am not stupid, Athyn!" she said in her high, petulant little-girl voice. "Though you and Morric ever liked to think so— If you kill me Morric will be angered with you. He did love me first, you know..."

Athyn laughed aloud in real amusement. "And as the Goddess is my witness, I have never denied it! But it is the last love that counts..." The smile died away, and the light that came then in her eyes made Amzalsunëa startle. "Besides, I would venture to say he is perhaps not best pleased with you just now: *You killed him.* You gave him hazen, with intent to slay, or to punish, or in an attempt to drag him in to share your noxious practice. Both your law and mine hold you guilty of his death. Or, in your hazer's fog, have you forgotten that too?"

To control and conceal the fit of trembling that suddenly wracked her, Athyn leaned back in her chair, put her booted feet up on an empty bench.

"I told Morric once, back when you and my late unlamented brother Kier almost had me hanged from the walls of Caerdroia, that I would be your death one day, that even his asking would not stay my hand from your blood. And do you know what he said to me? He said he had not asked that I should stay it."

"That is not true!"

"Two things I am too proud ever to do: I never sing, because I cannot, and I never lie, because I will not... Nay, he said it, and aye, he meant it; for he knows me, all of me, he knows my moods and my mind, and he knew very well what I would do... They are all dead, you know; and the ones I did not kill, my true-friends killed them for me. You are the last, and now I shall kill you."

"And what will you do then?" challenged Amzalsunëa.

And as once long ago in a cell at Caerdroia, in a building now levelled to the ground by her own command, Athyn smiled, and Amzalsunëa shrank back a little.

"I?" she asked. "Why, I shall bring him back. What else?"

"You came all this way for that?" The Firvolgian's voice held honest bewilderment. "To bring back his body? You do not even know where he is—"

Athyn shook her head slowly. "Ever do you listen, never do you hear... Once again: I am come to bring *him* back. Him. Not his body only. Him."

The other stared, and her voice when she managed to speak was a shaking whisper, and for the first time Athyn saw fear in her face.

"That is not possible..."

"It is not usual," agreed Athyn. "But it can be done. I will

do it. I would do more than that, even, to right things where
you have wrenched them awry. As for my not knowing where
you have bestowed him—I will find him. Nothing and no one
can keep me from him. Not you, not anyone. Have you not yet
learned? Then let us sit here together—and, I think, without
your hazen—until you do."

A long while later; the white sun-pools had crawled down
from the walls and onto the worn unswept floortiles. The need
for the drug had won out: Thwarted of it by Athyn,
Amzalsunëa was rocking back and forward now, hugging herself, rubbing her thin arms as if she were cold, talking in a high
rapid singsong voice about Morric.

"I wish to get him back; or, if he will not, at the least I shall
make *him* a hazer as well, to punish him for that he chose that
redhaired swordslut over me; and then he will not scorn and
pity me but love me, and I will not feel the guilt so much, and
we will be together again as we were before. But if neither of
those things can be— This is how it will be, he will come
back to me..." Her words turned and redoubled, small and
indistinct, every sentence repeated over and over again; she
rose and began to pace and bat her hands at nothing, at herself.

With a sudden sick horror Athyn realized that
Amzalsunëa, in her guilt and hazen delirium, was back in the
moment months since, the moment just before she gave
Morric the drug. *These are the thoughts she had then, the reasons
she killed him. If thoughts and reasons they may indeed be
called...*

And as she listened Athyn began to shiver uncontrollably.
*Ah, Goddess, I cannot! I cannot hear this—it is as Esmer warned
me, at last I have found the thing that is beyond my strength. This
is harder than it was to force myself back from death, when I stood
on the scaffold above the Wolf Gate and it would have been easier
to die than to come back among the living... To hear how she killed*

him? Why she killed him? Nay, if I listen to her very much longer I shall run as mad as she...

"Melassaun"—the first, last and only time in either of their lives that Athyn broke her own oath and used that name to her enemy, and she used it with command—"Hear me. Come back to the now, to where we are. I will give you time. I will count it out for you, even, count you back. In your very own tongue, too, so that you see I do not miscount. Han, thu, sar, ruva, zal, sechri, tabari, nechero, derecho, vix..."

But the other murmured on in a passionless droning voice about Morric, and the hazen, and how he would be hers again, pacing frantically back and forth as far as the space allowed; and Athyn, her face impassive now, her shivering done with, taking a long deep breath rose to her feet, slowly, and as slowly drew her sword.

Amzalsunëa turned to her and smiled, and just for an instant, though her will was no less set, no whit more shaken for the seeing, Athyn glimpsed the last radiance flash out of the young spirit that once had been, saw what had caught Morric so long ago, and after love was gone had held him still in pity's chains; saw what Amzalsunëa could have been had she had the grace and strength and will to become it, if her inner beauty had matched that which was without; saw too what had set Morric free of her in the end, set him free to love elsewhere.

She chose to squander that spirit, elected to turn beauty into bane; choosing death for herself, she gave him death also. Souls do not live on promise; and though he danced with the Shadow the death-reel was a tune he did not call, and she was no fit partner...

With a defiant gesture Amzalsunëa threw back her matted hair, and halting her pacing she looked straight up at Athyn, who topped her by half a foot. Not once had she glanced at the sword: Perhaps she did not see it, or something kept her from seeing it. Under the smeared facepaint the violet eyes were mirrors of madness and at the same time clear and sane as the evening sky, though there was something like a drop of burning ink about Morric at the back of them, and something about Athyn that writhed like a nest of vipers. And also, astonishingly, a plea for freedom and release.

"Aye, then! I killed him!" she flung at Athyn. "Are you content to hear me say so? I killed him, and the others helped me, and I am glad of it, for if I cannot have him you shall not have him either!"

Athyn stood a moment more in silence, looking upon Amzalsunëa but seeing something very different; standing motionless, finding without surprise that her body and soul were both strangely at peace, seeing all that had been before and all that would come after, and she knew that all of it was meant.

No revenge is great enough, no torture sufficient, to requite her as she deserves for what she has wrought against my lord. Not though I tortured her for ten thousand thousand lifetimes and ripped her soul from her body to send it on a tour of all the seven hells... There is not time or pain or punishment enough in all Abred to avenge myself upon her as I wish to: Sudden death is a sudden lesson; sometimes it is the only way such souls as hers can learn. Make an end, then; the clean quick way best for all— So I shall send her where perhaps she may find the wisdom she does not yet even know she seeks. Sometimes the defect may only be mended at the place where it was made; the cracked keeve must be thrown back into the kiln, the bubbled glass mass again to hot gather on the blower's pipe, the bent blade melt back to metal in the forge...

Then at last she stirred. "Ah," said Blackmantle quietly, clearly, softly; the voice of a judge with the look of an avenger. "But I shall."

And flashed her blade through Amzalsunëa's thin white neck.

*   *   *

With that death came the fulfilling of Athyn's oath as clannstalker, Am Bladier, Dioghaltair-cheart, the Just Avenger. She looked upon the body before her, and the head that had rolled a little way away, and her face did not change. Nor did it change as Amzalsunëa's yellow mongrel, emaciated, rib-scarred where his mistress had whipped him, crawled in on his belly to lick up her fountained blood, crouching between the stare-eyed head and the lopped crumpled trunk, loyal as only a dog can be even to one who had abused him, trembling as he gazed up at Athyn to see if she would hurt him, but not moving even so.

I would not strike the smallest blow upon you, poor cur, do not fear me. Though it would be mercy to put you out of your misery, as I did your mistress just now—but I cannot. She did the same to greater far than you, treated them the same who were wiser than you, who could flee… I am so tired—and half sick of vengeance. But vengeance is done with. Now I can go to find him. Now at last I may take him home.

Athyn knelt and rubbed her fingers together, making the small soft encouraging sound that is universal in this galaxy, seemingly, to coax the dog to her, thinking to heal his hurts before she went. Though his tail swung uncertainly, his eyes showed an agony of fear and indecision, and in the end he would not come.

So she set out bowls of meat and meal and water, which plainly he very much desired, but he would not eat while Athyn was there. *I trust there is enough for a day or two, or that someone may come by before the creature starves. Perhaps the folk at the roadhouse will take him in. Goddess forbid he should be so hungry that he is forced to feed off Amzalsunëa, though now I think of it history is full of stories where evildoers were devoured by their own hounds, and what a lesson for them, too—*

Casting one last look at what lay dead upon the floor, Athyn quitted the empty house, the place of her avenging; the door stood wide behind her.

*   *   *

An even wilder, narrower canyon, a savage gash through hugely folded and striate stone, a mile away from the cottage in the orange-groves. Athyn halted before a massive swelling rockface colored like a frozen sunset, a buttress thrust straight up from the planet's core. *This is the place, and no mistaking...*

Over the past weeks there had been moments when Athyn had felt, as never she had felt before, or ever thought to feel, that she had come to the end of herself. She had thought herself destroyed when she knew of Morric's death, had thought her strength gone from her with the Hunt's end in Keltia, or, just now, consumed finally with the slaying of Amzalsunëa. And yet each time she had known that it was not so; had rallied, and gone on. Not by any virtue or choice of hers: Something, or someone, else had pulled her along further, or higher, or deeper.

Now, as she stood in the shadowed canyon, the blood of Amzalsunëa Dalgarno not yet dry upon her sword, and stared up at the wall of stone in which she knew her mate lay entombed, she knew too that there was something within her that had never yet been touched or tapped by any of it, something that patiently waited to be drawn upon, needing only to be asked. And she feared that unknown something; feared it more than anything she had ever faced, for it was greater than all those things, and greater than herself, and yet within herself. But it was hers; she would ask it, and use it, all the same.

She lifted her head, then raised a hand and thought her will. Without a sound, the entire hillside obediently peeled itself back like the skin of a fruit. And a small mocking voice came from far within, and others joined. *And that, just so, is why your mother put geis on you not to become a sorceress. Easy it is for you to do such things. Too easy. For you. Drawing upon the Shadow. Well now. Magic of the Sidhe. Wild magic. No surprise. So afraid...*

Athyn shook herself, angrily, impatiently, and the voices ceased. "For that is not why I am here!" she cried to whomever might be listening. "I have come only for what is mine, to bring him home. If there is aught of the Shadow in that, there is none of the Dark! And if you will not help, then at the least I bid you do not hinder."

But no voice made answer, and presently she turned again to face the hill. *O love...* She straightened, held out both hands before her, palms forward, fingers wide. In the hours after Morric's death, when she had kept her chamber alone—though in truth she had been nowhere near her chamber but riding beside him every step of the way—she had set a staying-spell upon his mortal form, wherever it might lie; the mightiest magic she had ever worked, or had yet worked; and perhaps that too was geis broken, but she no longer cared. So he would be as she had known him, fair as in life, as if asleep, untouched by death; but even if he were not she would be neither feared nor repulsed to look upon him once again.

And if geis is in it, who is to say that this is not how it was meant to be all along? That he must die, and I must avenge him, and, in the end— But though she had boasted of it to Amzalsunëa she had not admitted that last even to herself; not yet, not entirely. *And yet it is not only Morric I avenge here—and is that dán, and if it is, just who was it decided that Athyn Cahanagh should be dán's mirror? Did I, in my traha, decide it? Or was it truly meant? I am a judge by profession; to what other court am I called? The Long Hunt has brought me to this place, but it took Lughnasa to Samhain to get me here—I could have come sooner, first of all, straightway upon his death, nothing simpler; but the journey is as important as the journey's ending. We are together again, and more even than that before I've done...tomorrow's dán to tomorrow.*

She shook herself again, as a horse will shiver itself to throw off a cleggan, or a rider, and strength flowed into her like water, from the air, from the ground, from every direction at once, sinking through her skin, turning her bones to findruinna and her blood to flame; there was a deep drumming sound that seemed to roll in on a spiral from nowhere, her own heartbeat. She could move the planet itself with a flick of her finger, could juggle the moons like hurley-balls; but instead she held her arms out straight before her, then with her right hand made a slow, infinitely graceful gesture of beckoning, of summoning, the first two fingers close together, the others arching loosely to the palm.

For a count of three long breaths nothing happened; and then, slowly, silently, a stone coffin emerged from the solid rock of the mountain, where by sorcery it had been made one with the natural stone. It did not so much appear as emanate, sifting out of the cliff wall like mist or groundwater. One moment there was only the hard folded stone, impenetrable clear down to the mountain's roots, the next moment the very rock seemed to have melted away, and the coffin was there, floating down toward her now as lightly as a thistlepuff. It settled to earth before her, near enough for her to touch; a long gray kist, plain solid stone and sealed with lead, no mark of any kind upon it.

So much, then, for Firvolgian sorcery... But it needed no name graven upon the mute marble to let her know who it was who lay within.

While Athyn was getting herself to the far shore of her vengeance, her friends had been meting out the last of their own. When she had left Keltia outbound for Aojun, some of those who were closest to her acted at once upon the word Esmer Lennox gave them, and pursued her to Firvolgior themselves.

So swiftly did they follow that it could scarce be called pursuit, for they arrived on Kaireden three nights in advance of her—whose arrival was of necessity more circuitous—and once there they had set straightway to their work.

And as Athyn was dealing with those who had dwelled at the sign of the Bow-trellis in the Street of the Limeflowers, moving on to the cottage among the orange-trees and the stark canyon beyond, and the Keltic embassage in Katilon Ke Katil was trying desperately to keep a rein on it all, Mihangel and Sosánaigh, Breos and Mariota, Rhain and Cathárren had already completed a few little small random tidying tasks of their own.

They did not have the resources or indeed the resourcefulness that just now so well did serve their Queen, but they did have the inestimable advantage of Esmer Lennox's bottomless purse, and employing that to the fullest they soon knew as much as did Athyn herself, and on certain matters even more. Armed with what they had learned, outraged and revolted and cold with purpose, they divided into hunting pairs, as they had often done in the earliest Gweriden days; and knowing that Athyn and Blackmantle now were a paired brace of hounds themselves, set to run down Amzalsunëa as relentlessly as the Cwn Annwn, that éraic against Morric's murderer was well in hand, the best hands for it in all the worlds, they took it upon themselves to remove the last of the quarry from the trail.

So Mihangel and Sosánaigh tracked Jaffran Eskendy, Evance Tregar, Shane Ó Falvey and Erramun Zedoary from the spring warmth of Katilon Ke Katil to a distant snow-covered city far in the planet's north; and, after some brief consultation as to what might be a fitting fate for bards who had connived at the death of one of their own, had tied them up in a bell tower, so that they might die by music who had failed to live by it.

"I have heard it said that bells can break false weather," said Mihangel, peering through the open arches at the snow thickening outside. "Let us see if they can break false friendship as well."

When the presters came to raise the bells for the dawn peal, the four in the tower above did not last long enough to hear the half of it. They died from the ringing, died mad and shrieking, blood pouring from ears and eyes and noses. The falling snow shut in the sounds they made and the sound that killed them—only the rhythmic pain, the tearing claws of vibration, while the bells rang on, rejoicing for the return of the light.

*　　　*　　　*

As is so often the loathsome case upon the demisings of the great or renowned, a certain morbid interest had been sparked in Kaireden by the news of Morric Douglas's death, and the playmonger Loris Venoët had seen in it the chance to revive a dreadful historical of his own creating, a play that had once angered Athyn to fury, and at which Morric had only been amused—now with a new, hastily written ending alleging to depict King Morric's last hours on Kaireden. And singing Morric's own songs, in the intervals, was none other than Juho Alessos; grosser now than ever, still aping Morric, whom he still fancied he resembled.

"Not in his dearest dreams, save that they are both male humanoids," muttered Mariota venomously, "and even that is debatable. Goddess help me! He as Morric! Only if those who watch him, the stupid witlings, do so with their fingers in their ears and a sack over their heads."

"And their heads up their—" The rest of Breos's swart rejoinder was lost in the sound of the play resuming.

But even that was to prove no respite: The actor presuming to portray Morric—a preening Coranian, Kelviram—had less art and presence in his whole being than Morric Douglas had had in one fingertip; as for the actresses playing Athyn and Amzalsunëa, the best that could be said was that it was good work in a bad case. Good work too that Athyn herself was not there to see them, for if she had been, Katilon Ke Katil would have been a smoking crater in glowing ground by the time the sun came up.

But her friends had attended the play for other purpose... Behind-stage, after, Kelviram, the playmaster Venoët and the strutting Alessos were dumbstruck alike to hear Breos and Mariota invite them to a very private dinner. In their boundless vanity they were not slow to accept; but unlike to a play, this was life: There was no black-robed, gold-masked chorus standing in the wings to bid them warning...

"Well," said Mariota, upon leaving the ghastly table two hours later, at the inn where the obliging tavernkeeper, a

Keltic spy, had been pleased and honored to close the premises to all others and allow his common-room to serve as shambles, and to clean away the blood and bits thereafter, "any night the universe can be rid of a few more offenders against art is a good night's work in my book. Any halfway well-writ tragedy would have told them all as much. But then they would have had to be halfway artists to have seen it..."

Like their Queen's, the Gweriden's work now was all but finished. It was Rhain mac an Iolair did slay the last of the last, who had been also one of the first and worst...

Ser Yalarin Nao had been summoned in panic by Amzalsunëa on Morric's death, and he had done well for her. It had been Nao who had secretly brought to the Keltic ambassador Morric's marriage ring to be returned to Athyn, where Amzalsunëa had been all for throwing it into the sea—having persuaded her that Athyn might be too distraught at the token's return, or too thankful, to pursue vengeance; proving only how little he knew of Kelts, and how less of their queen. He had helped Amzalsunëa remove Morric's body from the inn to the country cottage; and then, seeing that she had plunged into hazen and was of no use whatsoever—whether out of guilt or no he could not say—Nao had wrought one wrong more, last and greatest. He had hired sorcerers to bury Morric in the rock, fusing him into the solid stone where no ordinary seeker could find him. But he had not reckoned on the seeker who came; nor on those who came seeking her...

When Rhain rejoined the others, reporting the completion of his errand, the six vowed among them that knowledge of Nao's complicity must be kept at all costs from Athyn, for a long time to come, perhaps forever. It might be that last feather laid upon an already intolerable burden, and even if not it could only cause her pain; she had suffered enough, and more than enough. All now had paid the price of their faithlessness and traha and slander and hate; let be. Athyn herself would make an end; and once she did, it would be the Gweriden's last task in Firvolgior to bring her and Morric away and safe home.

In the lurid flooding light of the Kaireden sunset Athyn looked at the kist before her, and then at the marriage ring that had left her hand only once since Morric set it there. It was of his own designing—he was as deeply gifted in that art as in musicmaking—and the beautiful pattern of two hands supporting a crowned heart already was gaining great popularity among the folk, who loved it for the sheer high romance of its creating as well as its richness of meaning, calling it calon-dal, or claddon, or clondagh—all meaning 'heart-hold', though Morric had been wroth that others should presume to name a thing of his own making, and one that he had, moreover, made for his lady. Indeed, when the immrama-tuathal began again, as soon they would, the ring would even find its way to Erith, destined to be known there under a name not so unlike.

Her ring was worked in heavy silver, the Goddess's metal, Morric's in gold for the God; she wore both now on the same slim finger, hers keeping his, much larger, safely inmost in place, nearest her heart—the one time she had removed her own ring, to put his there. *I will wear them ever so, until I come to*— But again she shied from that, as from a great jump that she knew she was not yet collected for, not yet set to leap. *Yet it is the part for which all the rest has prepared the way. I know very well what I must do; and so, I think, does he…*

When the Gweriden arrived, they found her sprawled weeping across Morric's coffin. With infinite gentleness, and a certain inexorability, Breos raised her up and held her; she stood leaning against him, weeping still, seemingly drained, while the others scanned round for dangers, and Cathárren brought the ship down from its hidden orbit, to land below the hill.

They drew Athyn gently aside then—she had not been surprised in the least to see them—but impatiently she broke free of her comforters.

"*I* will do this! Mine it is to do..."

She lifted her tearstreaked face, and her hand, as she had done before, and again the kist rose in the air and bore itself into the ship. Before they could react, she spun to face the hillside, and the mountain drew its stone cloak back around itself, this time with a sound like thunder and a single heave of ground. When the echoes had died tremendously away the canyon was as it had been an hour since, as it had been for the past hundred, or the past thousand, years, and in silence Athyn followed Morric's coffin aboard the ship. It was Esmer's own flagship, the *Lion of Connacht*—Velenax had not trusted this errand to any lesser craft or crew—and she knew the ship well.

Having seen the kist settled in her own old cabin, herself beside it near enough to touch, Athyn heard as from a great distance the sound of the pulser engines engage, felt the slight motion as the ship rose up through atmosphere. There was the familiar shudder as the stardrive took the ship and all who sailed her into the overheaven, and then the absolute cessation of motion that was the hallmark of hyperflight. *So, we are safe away now... But with my new-claimed skills I think I will speed things along; it is a three-day trip elsewise, and I have no time to spare...* Athyn reached out and brushed her fingers against the coffin, and, her hand resting upon the cold smooth stone, prepared to keep waking vigil beside her lord, all the road home.

"I did not think ever to see her use those powers," said Breos at last. "Even Morric did not believe she ever would. And I see too, now, why she did not wish to. It is more like to a force of nature than to common witchery. Easily called upon, but not so easily commanded or controlled."

"Oh, I do not know about *that*!" said Mariota roundly. "She looked fine in command to me—"

"You are all forgetting," came Cathárren's calm voice, "that however much in command she may appear, or even be, she is still entirely untrained. She is not a sorceress. She has been taught nothing of balance and response, naught save the little magics and pishogues we all learn as children... And that was no pishogue but a Great Working, perhaps the greatest I have yet seen—and I have the strangest feeling that she is not half done with it. But to a sorcerer it is like going out to hunt field-voles with a bow strung for war."

They were gathered in the common-room of the ship, all save Athyn—and Morric. Once the ship had cleared the ard-na-spéire, they had put it on autohelm, with sighs of relief to show their backs to Kaireden. No one spoke for some time; though their hearts and minds were full, there seemed strangely little to say—and then it had all come tumbling out.

"I know little of magic," said Mihangel. "Is that wrong?"

"It is not what sorcerers best like to see," said Rhain. "In almost all folk of all races, the instinct and talent for magic are present, but unless the gift is trained it will lie inactive, especially among those peoples who disbelieve. The power is real, and they can still sense it: a feeling of warning, a sense of good luck or ill about to happen, no more; not a thing to be summoned but a natural skill for all that. But the power Athyn showed here is of another order entirely—though whose order I think I will not say."

"*She* seems calm enough about the use of it, any road," said Cathárren.

Breos shook his head. "That calm is but the sign manifest of a mighty will. And that will in this matter is not yet completed."

Sosánaigh looked sharply at him. "Are you too saying she is not done with this? But all those who betrayed her and Morric are dead! We slew the last of them; Athyn herself killed

Amzalsunëa. She found Morric as she said she would, and we are bringing them safe home. What more can there be?"

Breos looked out at the blue glow of the overheaven. As always, it seemed that hyperspace was going by at tremendous speed and they themselves were standing still—and according to some astrogators and planetophysicists, that was exactly what it, and they, did. But this time, though he did not know it, the very magic that was the topic of their concern was moving things along more swiftly still; Athyn had bent even space to her will, and they would be home not in the usual three days but in three hours.

"That was vengeance," he said after a while. "And though there is a vast difference between vengeance and justice, there is a deep kinship also... Save for the slaying of Amzalsunëa, which was foredoomed from the start, I think that to Athwen all this has been no more than prelude: clearing away the caltraps in her road, to make smooth before her the path that she must take. Now it is justice, and though it is dark justice it is true justice."

Mariota stirred in her seat. "And what path is that? Where does avenging end, and justice begin?"

Breos shook his head. "I do not know. I do not think she knows yet herself."

But he was wrong.

chapter twenty-nine

Darkness tends toward light.

—*Séomaighas Douglas Ó Morrighsaun*

Morric Douglas ac Aoibhell gân Athyn, King of Keltia, an ollave of Seren Beirdd, was entombed at Ni-maen, in a barrow near the ancient ring of sacred stones, in the valley where the rulers of Keltia have been laid to rest since Brendan's day.

His people grieved for him deeply and sincerely. Since the earliest days of the Gwerin, and even before, Morric Douglas had been a name renowned in Keltia for song and music and beauty. It was not merely a king the Kelts had lost in him but an artist, a voice that sang their souls; all across Keltia they spoke of him, with gladness even in their grief, taking somber pride and satisfaction at his homecoming and the manner in which this had been accomplished. And they pondered what might come next—what Athyn Blackmantle might deem a suitable and fitting memorial for her murdered lord. She did not do things as others did—as Keltia and Firvolgior both alike had just seen—and the folk wondered aloud, uneasily if not without deepest sympathy, as to what her next actions would be. And they were not the only ones who wondered.

Since her return from Kaireden—even en route, as she sat stonefaced vigil beside Morric's stone bed, speeding the jour-

ney with the magic she now owned, or that owned her—
Athyn had kept as much to herself as she might, taking to her
the dán of those she had slain. Whether those slayings had
been by her own hand, or by commanding others to it, or by
others taking it on themselves to spare her, it made no differ;
they had died because she had willed it, and the dán was therefore hers to assimilate and make peace with, as earlier she had
done at Witchingdene.

There was most to accept where it concerned Amzalsunëa,
rightly most. She had played on Morric's sympathies and generous heart, and then had murdered him, had betrayed him to
his death; for that Athyn hated her as she had hated no other
being living or dead, and she found that she could not set aside
her hatred of the betrayer with the avenging of the deed.

*For which deed she will answer before Arawn, I know that, and
we shall see how she will not be able to hide behind the hazen and the
falseness then… But have I not done as much myself? She murdered
Morric, I murdered the law. Though I kept the law's letter, I have
done great violence to its spirit; as brehon, as Fian, as Queen. I
knew better on all counts, and I did as I did in the law's despite—a
grave sin indeed. But I would have sinned more greatly still, a thousand times over, so that things might be set right again, and whatever
the cost, I will pay it. That is, after all, what éraics are for…*

So Athyn's thoughts as she brought Morric home; and as
she barrowed him as the King he was, and as she slept again in
their bed, her arm stretched out across the empty pillows. But
even in the midst of the rioting discord in her heart, she found,
to her own surprise, that she had compassion for Amzalsunëa
Dalgarno, though she knew few would believe her if she said
so. To be sure, she had slain her, and would again, but still that
did not mean she did not feel a small certain touch of pity and
sorrow; and nor did either sorrow or pity mean she felt regret.
She had even spoken for Amzalsunëa to the gods, in the little
canyon cottage, before she left to find Morric, and she found
her prayerful action no more paradoxical now than she had
then…

For it is about not slaying but liberation; though not even the gods would deny that I had the right to kill her for what she did to Morric. I said the speeding prayers for her as Nilos taught me, in her own tongue, in the fashion of her own people; in the fashion of mine I spoke her name to the Goddess and to Arawn Rhên. That was more than she had any cause to expect, more than ever she would have done for me. And certain sure it was far more than she did for my Morric, for as we know she did naught to speed his spirit—no ceremony, no prayers, no prester. But she had the right to a speeding, even as any other soul, and it was for me to see that she had one given her.

She left nothing behind her: She created nothing—no writings, no music, no songs, no sculpture, no limnings. Nothing will memorialize her, nothing cling to her name save the ineffaceable stench of hazen and whoredom and murder; her murderess's name will be linked with my Morric's forever, and for that my hatred is as undying as for the deed itself. If I pitied her also—and I am not saying I did not, from time to time—my pity was a thing apart from my hatred; and each is a thing apart from justice, and neither should have any weight upon that justice at the last. Once she did as she did, I could have done nothing else but what I did; not and have still remained Athyn—or Blackmantle. Even Amzalsunëa Dalgarno cannot fault me for that.

"Well," said Athyn, glancing round, her voice as light as she could make it, "I have fulfilled my oaths; through my own poor arm, and greatly through yours, for which I thank you all again, for Morric and myself. Now I have something more to reveal, and I say straight out that none of you will like it in the least."

The Gweriden were assembled in the room of the table, Athyn's council chamber; it was the evening of the day of Morric's barrowing at Ni-maen, and she had called them together for a brief meeting before the nightmeal.

"Now that my lord is once more among us, I would tell you

what I have had in mind ever since his going; indeed, to set that in motion was why I went to Kaireden. All you thought it was merely revenge and avenging, and you are correct to think so, for it was, but—"

"—but revenge is not enough," said Cathárren, when Athyn fell silent. "It does not requite what you have lost."

Athyn shot her a swift glance, then leaped up to pace back and forth by the windows, pausing to stare out through the bubbled green glass at Highfold beyond and below, where lights were beginning to come on in the grand brughs against the falling dusk.

"That is what I have felt from the first," she said, not turning round to look at them. "I brought his body back from Kaireden, we barrowed him at Ni-maen as befits a King of Keltia, the Nine Nights are being cried for him. But that was never my intent, to leave matters there—never the whole of the plan, to leave *him* there... Tomorrow is the night of Samhain the Less," she added then, still not turning round, though she watched their wavering images reflected in the glass, fascinated by the unreality. *Almost it is a glamourie, the chamber reversed to a rich strangeness, their faces all unfamiliar yet the same...* "And I will go to find Allyn son of Midna, who knows my right, and I will ask him to conduct me."

"Where away?" asked someone quietly. "And to what purpose?"

Athyn took a deep breath. "I brought back his body. Now I shall bring back the rest of him: his very soul and self from the Otherworld. I will go down into Annwn to rescue my lord and restore him to life and to my arms. I will claim Morric back from Arawn himself, and I will not be denied."

Still she did not turn, but the quality of the silence behind her told more loudly than any words; she let it go on as it needed. *Twangling like a plucked bowstring...* No one spoke or stirred. This was something so far beyond even their wildest fears that for the moment they were dumbfound, purely stunned. Then as Athyn spun round to the room, and took her seat again, her movement seemed to unleash the rest from their fixity: to be aghast, amazed, appalled, as the mood did take them. Of them all, only Ganor was unsurprised; but then she had known Athyn longest, and arguably best.

"Even if that may be, Athyn," said Katterin de Cuirteis at last, with utmost gentle carefulness, "the time that has passed since Morric's death— Aye, aye, I know, his body will be unchanged forever under your staying-spell, and that was very well done, but he himself... He will be far down his road by now. No one has ever been called back from Annwn after so long, and I am not sure it is good or lawful even to try. Even the crochans of old could not do it; and as for going to Annwn yourself—it has never been done in all our history, perhaps not in all time before."

Athyn shrugged. "All times are one time to the gods, and any road, even the Low Road, can be travelled both there and back again. That is the least of my doubts; and everything has a first time." *And all firsts are by their very nature forever, so my beloved sang...* She studied the table before her, aware of the intake of breath round the table when she spoke of the Low Road—that legendary path by which voyaging souls, be they of the dead or merely of venturesome sorcerers, may travel between the worlds—then said, without looking up, as one to whom the question is most casual and careless of an answer, "Did you barrow her?"

It was beautifully done. Like horses crowding at a water-jump they fell in every one of them, no way to run out; she had dug a yawning pitfall before a towering hedge and then had run them straight up to it on an iron rein.

Mihangel sighed and spread his hands, glancing round the table; all the Gwereiden who had gone to Kaireden had agreed not to tell Athyn that they had buried Amzalsunëa. *Only if she asks, we all vowed; we shall tell her of it when she asks and not until, and now she has asked...*

"Ard-rían, we did. In the orange-garden grove; it seemed the place. But we raised no cairn above her."

"We could not leave her there like that, Athwen, lying upon the floor in her blood," said Rhain. *Much as we would have loved to...* Though this he did not say aloud, it seemed she heard.

But all she said was, "Aye. I see that you could not."

But later, private with Mariota and Sosánaigh in her chambers, Athyn opened her heart to her friends.

"No matter the gods' power over time, there is in truth very little time left for me to act. He came to me in a dream last night," she said in a low haunted voice, sitting cross-legged in the middle of the great bed she had shared with Morric, and Sosánaigh noted with a start, though she had long known it, that Morric's things had not been cleared from the chest that had served him for nightstand on his side of the bed.

Sosánaigh stared at the small intimate domestic clutter, and without warning tears stung her eyes. Save for the vase—cut from a single silver topaz—filled with white and red roses, fresh each day, that ever since Morric's death had stood beside the bed, all was untouched, just as the King had left it: some notebooks, a lightpen, a dagger, a few jewels and ornaments, spare strings for his harp, a tiny portrait of Athyn in a pearl-encrusted gold frame... *That says much, that she has left it so; though just exactly what, I am sure I am not sure—*

Athyn was still intent on her words, unaware of the focus of her friend's bleak tear-blind glance. "He spoke to me. In my dream he spoke to me; they say you never see the faces of your beloved dead in any dream, but, careddau, I saw his face... 'Long the day and long the night and long the wait for Arawn': Those were his very words, and though I woke weeping I woke to know his meaning, I know now what I must do. It is all dán, and, m'charai, there is hope. You cannot stop it."

"We would not if we could," said Mariota; her glance had followed Sosánaigh's to the bedstand, and her eyes had taken on just as bright and hard a sparkle. "If not for hope, the heart would break."

Athyn smiled through her own tears. " 'Every omen masks the truth': Did not my lord himself sing so? But this is more than hope; this *is* that truth."

Mariota threw out a hand, a blind instinctive protest she already knew was in vain. "But Annwn."

"I was born among the dead," said Athyn then. "Perhaps that is why I do not fear to go among them now."

Samhain the Less on Tara, the eleventh of November. Though the day had dawned fair, long before noon the sky to the north and east was slate-gray and black. No air moved; the autumn trees were limewhite against growing darkness. To the southwest, out over the sea, there was still some pale sunlight, and a dapple of clouds. But the slow ominous march of the stormclouds increased its pace; and now a wind arose, a glassy stream pouring out of the northeast, and from the eye of the wind there glanced a knifing chill.

Athyn leaned on her elbows and looked out from her window, taking a deep breath of the cold rushing air; she could scent winter behind it, and upon the wind's wings, very faint and far, rode the sound of pipes. Her heart leaped as it ever did at the sound. *I think Kelts have a nerve, or a cell, or an instinct, inborn, embedded somewhere in our genecode—probably knotworked!—that allows us to hear and respond to pipemusic, even from three glens away; it touches something deep, deep within us, that the outfrenne can never know... Someone playing a lament of the Óran Mór, upon the great-pipes, clear across the City; perhaps the piper even plays it for Fireheart, and will never know that Blackmantle heard it played...*

She strained her ears to hear; the wind ebbed, sidled, and the music faded, then with another shift of air the melody was blown back again to her, clearer. *A wind from the Hollow Mountains, from the Otherworld... Will Annwn be so, when I take the road there? But what horse of earth would carry me?* She pulled the shutter to; the music was gone now, and soon she would be also. *No matter; if I can find no horse I will walk the Low Road on my own two feet, and after my feet are too torn and bloody to hold me up I shall travel it upon my knees, and when my knees give out I shall drag myself along by my fingernails clawing the ground... As long as it takes, as far as it may be, whatever, or whomever, I may meet upon the road. And there is so little time left for me to do so.*

Barely time to wait, and to her way of thinking just as well, too: She would not have to endure the fierce loving attempts of friends and kindred and officers of state to discourage her. *To be sure, nothing and no one can change my mind, but still I do not wish to hear. If it means death for me then that is well. If not, that too is well...*

The only person to whom she spoke in parting was Esmer, summoning him to her chambers. He was gruff and terse of speech, by which she knew how deeply afraid for her he was.

She was already clad for her journey in a plain black tunic and white leinna and black leather trews and boots, the snake-skin cloak that Morric had given her slung across her shoulders, and she laid a hand on his arm; the hand that bore her seal ring, the ring that had been her mother's. Esmer looked down at the ring, then met her eyes, and his own were full of the fears not of a prince for his queen but of a father for his child.

The look did not go unnoted. "I gave you that ring when I went on my Long Hunt," said Athyn smiling, "to wear and use in my place, because I did not know if I would return. But though I have named you Regent"—she waved toward her desk behind her—"the seal stays this time on my hand; for I *will* return, and I shall bring him with me... Nay, athra-maeth, hear me out! As once I told my lord, so I now tell you: There are places in the sea where there is drowning, and places upon the lands where to set foot is to perish, and places amid the stars where dragons wait; nor man nor woman, goddess or god, can alter it. And when dán has ordained you to die there, dán will turn your path there. You would not come to such a place if your dán did not demand it, and your dán would not permit itself to be so demanded of if it were not what Kelu has meant must be."

"Is there no choice?" asked Esmer presently.

She smiled again, brushing away unapologetic tears. "There is always a choice: to do, or not to do."

"And so you will go to Annwn."

"I will go to Annwn."

"Alone?"

She shook her head slowly, though still she smiled. "Never that. And I shall not come from it alone, either."

Esmer took her other hand, the one upon which she wore the marriage rings, hers and Morric's, beside the poesy band. He turned her fingers back and forth, so that the rings flashed in the light, and both of them read out the poesy in their minds—'Love Is Enough'—but neither spoke it aloud. *Goddess grant it be so; but I know it is…*

"I never told you," she said then, "or the others even, how grateful I am to you all."

"Name of Dâna, cariadol, whyever for?"

She did not look at him. "Though you all have doubtless thought it, and more times than just the once, not one of you ever said to me 'He is dead. Let him go.' Not that I would have paid the slightest heed, of course, and very like would have banished any who said so, but there it is; and I am grateful."

Then Esmer, carefully casual: "It is said that over the gates of Arawn's palace is carved in many tongues of men and gods, 'Here strangers meet'."

"That will be seen, and I will return to tell you. But we shall not meet as strangers, he and I. And whosoever else may be there, I do not think that we shall meet as strangers either. This is not how it shall end."

So Athyn Cahanagh went out from Tara upon the day of Samhain the Less, to seek Allyn son of Midna in the likeliest place she knew to find him.

The Gweriden had readied *Seren-syw* for her out at Mardale, 'Brightstar', the ship she and Morric had ordered built for their use as monarchs. But Athyn had swifter means of travel now at her command—*Now that I am no longer shy of using them*—and as Esmer left the chamber in the Western Tower so did she.

With one last look round, a smile for what had been and what would be, Athyn stepped into the air, folding space and place and time and distance round her like a cloak; and when she set down her foot again she was on Erinna, deep in the mountains near her old bield, still used by Archill herders.

The Long Hills were already whitening on the high tops with winter coming on; but the lower slopes were still clad in shredded flags of gold and red where the ironoaks and bronze maples stood, here and there stonebirches flaunting their startling bright blue bark, the stands of silvery ghostwillows, their feet wet where they crowded near the secret streams. She stood there for a long while, remembering; then, as once Morric had done at need for her, she called out with her mind, heart and soul and spirit together one shout, not loud—and she was heard.

He came from behind as he had often done before, but she was his equal now in such things, and without turning, without so much as a snapped twig's having announced his arrival to her ear, Athyn the Queen greeted Allyn Midna's son.

"A useful trick," he said laughing. "I see you are shy no longer of using the gifts left beside your cradle."

She turned at that, looked up swiftly at the near-echo of her own thought, eyes across his quick and sharp as a parrying blade.

"My first cradle was the hollow of a shield, my swathing-cloth a bloody plaid; I nursed at a gauntlet filled with mare's milk, and not my mother's breast—as well you know."

"Who better?" His voice and face had gone as solemn as hers. "Why else were those gifts yours at all?" But that took them too near the unresolved remnant of bitterness and blame that still lay between them—rightly or no—and he moved gracefully away. "But what of the soulsail? In all the years of our acquaintance, never have I known you to miss it. Have you no messages to send to the West this night?"

"I will send myself," said Athyn simply. "Samhain night I set my candle on the water; but tonight I am message and messenger both alike. My own soul to sail the waters to the West—to Annwn."

"I knew you were set upon this course," he said then. "And I am not the only one who knows..."

"Then if you know that, you know too what I shall do once I do get there, and that I will not be prevented."

Again he was silent, and Athyn serenely waited him out, watching the sunset burn against the face of the Long Hills. "I do not encourage you in this, to say the least," said Allyn presently. "But I will do what I can, from loving friendship—and kinship—as well as out of old debt."

"That is gracious, lord."

"It is folly, lady," he returned calmly, but with more than the hint of a smile. "And more shall be changed for it than you may ever know." He whistled thrice, like a horseboy from these very vales, startling her considerably; but what came cantering up round the corner of the trees, in response to the clear sharp sound, was no tame Connacht pony...

Two tall horses, and one of them Athyn knew of old. This time she did not wear her aspect of bones, but her old friend the Mari Llwyd was no whit less awesome or dreadful to behold in her stormcloud beauty, as she slowed to a trot and came straight up to nuzzle the front of Athyn's cloak. The other was a horse rough in his winter coat, big and gold and furry as a sun-bear, with a gleaming amber eye that somehow did not chime with the rest of him, seeming as it did to measure her all too near for comfort.

Scarce a fit steed for a lord of the Shining Folk—and as a horse-girl I should know... Still—

"This is the Tanglecoat, from the Land Underwave, Tir-nam-beo." Allyn smiled, knowing her dismayed thought, though not with a sword to her throat would she have let it be seen. "Put your true-shape on yourself!" he scolded fondly, and the horse lifted his head, golden eyes glinting. And then he stood before them, white as the moon and proud as a swan, his mane like a breaking wave, his tail like seafoam sweeping the ground.

"Surely this is Manaan's own horse," said Athyn with wonder. "Aonbarr, the Wavesweeper—"

"It is, and he has graciously consented to carry me on your errand; as the Mari Llwyd shall carry you."

Athyn bowed to both horses then, thanking them for the courtesy of their service, and almost laughed aloud to see the bows they made her in return. *It is by no means a laughing matter; these horses, though they are not gods, ride with gods, on the gods' business; and maybe it is that they are gods themselves after all...*

But time was now; and as the last of the light left the sky, stars sprang out above them. But they were no stars that Athyn had ever seen before; the familiar autumn constellations were not there, and as these new stars loomed above her, all unknown, she was suddenly, briefly, afraid. *They are the stars that shine on the Otherland; these are the stars that light Annwn. The change has begun...*

The Sidhe lord, himself already mounted, stretched out an arm, and from his pointing hand a silver spiral curled out and down. Where it struck the ground a white path opened before him, a path that ran straight before them as far as she could see, a royal road, a path of silver edged with golden flame.

The Heroes' Way—never did I think to see it in living life. Still less to take it… Athyn found herself astride the Mari Llwyd's bare back; neither horse bore tack of any sort, not even a headstall such as the Sidhe used with their own mounts. Which reminded her…

"Where, my lord, is your beautiful stallion?"

Allyn did not take his gaze from the road unrolling before them into infinity under those strange stars.

"No other mounts will serve our need. Not for training, not for whipping, not for love; no horse of earth, not even a horse of the Sidhefolk. No other horses save these two only would set hoof upon the road that we must go. Time is. This is the Low Road. Now ride."

And Athyn sat down hard as the Mari Llwyd surged from a standing start into the huge smooth world-devouring gallop she so well remembered, and asked no more questions.

As the bards would later tell it, so swift they rode that they overtook the wind that went before them, and the wind following could not catch them up until the morrow, or else it was that they rode for forty days and forty nights, through red blood to the knee, and saw neither sun nor moon all the while. Whether that was so or no, what none ever doubted or disputed was that they took the Low Road, that road which led to Annwn and no other place, that road of fear and legend, the diamond highway to the heart of the world. The Low Road they took, and none could have ridden it save they alone, Blackmantle and Midna's gray-eyed, red-cloaked son.

As clouds built to towers and darkened all the lands behind, it seemed to Athyn that they rode the Heroes' Way round all Erinna, along Connacht's ironbound coasts and over A'Mhaighdean's ramparts, through Thomond's hills and Findhorn's forests, across Donn and Deveron; the hoofs of the magic steeds spurned the sands of the Duraray Plains and beat upon the Timpaun's dark and empty miles of windswept grasses, traversed An-da-lugh-síagh with fields full of rain and league upon league of sleeping Erinnach heartland. They met no one on their way. They were headed for Sheehallion, that same peak that years before had reached out across the dark miles, to touch the young Athyn with light at midnight.

Coming at last to the mountain court that rings the faerie hill, the steeds that bore them stinted not but set their feet upon the air itself. All was different now, the passing country had been changing as they rode, even as the stars above their heads. The mountains were not their old familiar selves, but wore a strange and savage dress; and yet they were fairer than ever, and Athyn knew that the farther they went from the everyday into the world of the Sidhe, the nearer they drew to the Otherland, the more she was beginning to see Keltia as the Sidhe themselves did see it. *It is more itself, more like the true thing...*

And out of those subtly different mountains Sheehallion lifted her fair white shoulders above them all, tall queen of snows. Once a firemount that had flung down burning rain on all the lands beneath, Sheehallion had cooled long since, though she had kept the lovely perfect cone-shape such mountains build for themselves. The topmost pinnacle, Athyn knew, was hollow, where uncounted ages ago a great explosion had collapsed the peak into itself, leaving behind a bottomless caldera, a lake filled now with sapphire water, a jewel amid the eternal ice that itself did never freeze. Llyn Baravogue that lake was called, and it was lapped about with magic, so that few mortals came there, or ever had.

The horses topped the peak, and pulled up of their own accord on the hilly shore above the loch, where the magic road ran right straight down under the waters.

"You said you would sail your own soul to Annwn," came Allyn's clear voice, and Athyn realized she heard it not with ears but within her mind. "Comes now your chance to prove that word—"

And glad I take it... In that biting glassy air, she reached beneath her snakeskin cloak, drew out something wrapped in soft leather which Allyn smiled to see. Unfolding the swathings, Athyn held up the silver fillet of Nia the Golden, given to her and Morric as wedding gift from the People of the Hill, with which she had crowned her lord and lover King of Keltia.

Holding the Sidhe lord's eyes, she raised it in token of salute, then set it about her own brows; and, though she was prepared for it, she was unable to suppress a little gasp, for the coronet fitted her as well as it fitted Morric.

"It is well thought of," said Allyn. "You may have need of it where we are going now, and where you are going after." But more than that he would not say, or else he did not know.

They rode out upon the air now, slanting down to the lake Baravogue, but that lake had grown vast as a sea, she could not behold the other side; and as the Mari Llwyd, leading, set one plumed hoof down upon the water, it seemed that the water bore them up as if it had been a highroad, and not the Low Road which it was, and the path plunged beneath the smooth unruffled surface.

Fire and water; the Heroes' Way, the sunward course with everything...

"On!" came Allyn's voice in her mind. "Lead on!"

And with a silent prayer to the Goddess—*Lady, Your cloak about me*—and a silent promise renewed to Morric—*Beloved, I come! I come for thee*—Athyn closed her knees upon the Ghost Mare's fine narrow girth, and led on, straight down the Low Road into the dark silent waters of the lake.

chapter thirty

Small profit to fight with the smith in his own forge.

—*Mihangel Glenrossa*

Ever afterwards, when folk would ask her—timidly, curiously, enthralled by the awe and high romance of it—about that wild drumming ride into legend, Athyn would only smile and shake her head, and say she had been too busy merely riding to be at any time either sure of or feared of what they were riding into; and for the most part that was the truth.

What she was sure of was that Llyn Baravogue was a gateway, a portal to the Otherlands. It did not long remain a lake to Athyn's perception: As soon as the Mari Llwyd's hoof touched the water, all things altered, and they rode into a different realm of the real. Somehow, beneath the lake's surface, there was breathable air, as of a cool summer or warm autumn day, and dry land that rang solid and familiar under the horses' hoofs.

But after a while—hours, or it could have been years—they drew near to a great gray mountain that stood like a sentinel across their path; and going behind it they came to a high place where they might overlook a vast vale. Athyn straightened and slid her weight back, unbracing her hips, easing her muscles, and the Mari Llwyd, responsive as any steed of earth, slowed and came to a stand.

Beside her, Allyn too stretched where he sat upon

Aonbarr's smooth powerful back, and the great white sea-
stallion blew down his muzzle, nodding his head.

"That is Annwn," said Allyn, pointing ahead below.
"There Arawn is lord, with Malen his queen and lady."

Now am I truly between the worlds... Athyn swung about
atop the Ghost Mare's back. Behind her she could see, as
through a wavering mist or wall of rain, the fields she knew, all
little and small, but true, and there; face forward before her lay
the Otherland. *It does not look so very greatly unlike to our own
lands; there may be more colors on it, a different light, oh, I know
not,* something, *but still it* looks *an earthly place, right enough...*

But it was not. Annwn it was, first destination of the Low
Road, the place to which souls between their lives have resort,
to stand before Arawn Rhên, and to judge themselves before
him as it were in the presence of the Highest. It was a fair land,
as Athyn had already noted, strangely like to Tara: rolling
green plains, tall mountains, a wide river threading through
like a silver seam. But—

"Where is the sun?" she heard herself asking—of Allyn, of
the air—and though she hated the tremor she heard in her
voice she could not command it gone. "There is light, yet
there is no sun above—" That was it, that was the great difference she could not understand: The zenith was a uniform
bright brushed gold, heaped bronze clouds jostled at the hori-
zons, all round her was day-bright, as on an October midafternoon with the sun westering and the light clear as water,
sharpening all it touched; but no sun stood above their heads.
"See, we cast no shadows on the grass—"

"Light in Annwn, by all means," said the Sidhe lord, "but
never the light of moon or sun. In the Otherlands there are no
shadows."

No shadows— So the old songs have the right of it... She was
trembling, and sensing her fear the Mari Llwyd nickered com-
fortingly, just as Rhufain would have done.

"If there are no shadows in Annwn, there is Shadow; Light,
but never yet the Dark." The voice in her ear was not Allyn's,

and hearing it Athyn found herself lapped in a sudden warm
familiar presence; though whether it was Morric's or another's,
or several others', she could not tell. Yet the voice took away
her doubt, and she looked out again over Annwn where it
stretched out before them. Then a wind from the Otherlands
came up from beneath, cold and clean, visiting her face, blowing back her hair and her cloak, and all her fears went with it
as it passed.

In that low light the Low Road, empty of all save themselves, wound away across unknown distances to an unimaginable destination. They paused atop the pass a moment longer,
and then, following Allyn, Athyn rode down the cool slopes of
air, into the wind, into the hollow lands, into the kingdom
where Arawn was lord.

They crossed the plain and for a long time followed a track
beside the broad winding river they had seen from above, and
Athyn marvelled again at how very like the land was to the
country round Caerdroia. *Nay, it is more than like, it is the very
same— Look, those hills are set and shapen like the Loom, this river
runs as does the Avon Dia, and over there in the distance, snow-
mountains exactly like to the Stair…*

"Is it just my fancy?" she asked Allyn. "Would an outfrenne
see the same as I am seeing?" But the Sidhe lord only smiled.

Now the lands drew in closer, and she saw a mountain far
away shaped like a castle; then her perspective shifted, and it
was not a castle-shaped mountain far away, but a mountain
that *was* a castle, very near at hand. Still Allyn said no word,
and Athyn began to tremble again.

They came to it more swiftly than she would have thought,
or might have liked. The river itself bent round the towering
gray walls, and the road ran up on a causeway to the entrance:
a great gate, behind a fanged portcullis that went down into
the waters of the river. Dismounting, they left the horses outside, and the Mari Llwyd laid her head over Athyn's shoulder;

Athyn leaned into the Ghost Mare's storm-colored flank and thanked her, and the Tanglecoat also.

"Come," said Allyn; she stiffened at the command in the word, but she obeyed at once, to stand close beside him before the portcullis, on a glass moatbridge, frost-slick and sword-narrow, that leaped in a high arch to span the river running below. "Stand and say your truename; in Arawn's own place no other password will serve."

He gave his own, speaking easily, as one who was friend to him who was lord here, and Athyn hers in a clear calm voice, as one who was here by right, on an errand even the lord of this place could not deny; not as one who did not fear, but as one who was beyond fear's rule.

Nothing happened for long moments; then, without a sound, the black gate rose dripping out of blacker water, the portcullis lifted and yawned. The palace of Annwn lay open before them: across the bridge, up a low flight of wide steps, then through the great doors, upon the lintel of which—just as Esmer had said—was carved in many tongues, of men and gods alike, 'Here strangers meet.' Beyond those towering doors was a vast dim hall, cavernous, with chambers opening off it forever and forever, one after another, like a puzzlebox, save that the further in one peered, or went, the broader and wider and higher and deeper the chambers seemed to be.

"It does not always have this aspect," said Allyn, divining her uneasy thought as she stood there, for all her resolve and force not yet quite ready to enter. "For the castle is the land, and the land is the castle, and neither is either; to those who dwell therein there is no distinction. It is all Annwn alike... It appears in this guise for us alone, so that we who are not at this time habitant in Arawn's kingdom may have a familiar touchstone, something to anchor us to reality. Even to such a reality as this," he added, with a smile; and her heart soared, she had needed that smile.

It was the first time her companion had made mention of the Sidhe as subjects of Arawn; presumably, then, subject as was all mortal creation to death and life again after. She longed dearly to question him further, but something in his manner told her it was better not. Yet as they stood upon the glazen bridge, Athyn reached under her cloak, and under her black leather tunic, and loosening the lacing at the throat of her leinna pulled out into the long light of Annwn the token she had worn there: the collar of silver swans that had been Morric's last gift to her in life.

This, and our rings, and Nia's fillet, are the only metal I have borne with me into Arawn's realm; even my sword has been left behind in the waking world. For if the power is not in me, it will never be in anything that I wield in power's name, be it my sword or my word or my will. Better it is I learn that now, and Keltia with me... She touched the swans to hearten herself, then nodded, as one who says, Aye, but now, and followed Allyn mhic Midna across the bridge of glass.

Beyond the carven lintel and up the shallow flight of well-worn stone steps, they found themselves in a room so high and solemn it could only be a presence chamber, a fane for the greatest of presences. Two high seats of equal splendor were raised up on a low dais; though there was low cool light in the room, it illuminated little, and Athyn could not tell whence it came.

Below the dais stood two figures, cloaked like Allyn all in red. One of the figures, the taller, threw back his hood, and Athyn saw with joy and wonder that it was Gwyn ap Neith ac Seli. She made a start of eagerness, quickly checked, but just as eagerly he came across to her.

"Mathra-dhia," he said, and, "Methryn," and bowed to her; Athyn made return courtesy of her own.

Goddess-son or no, and though I am Queen of Kelts, still he is a prince of the Shining Folk... "I did not think to see you here, my lord Allyn said no word—"

"No. He would not have. I am come to speak for you to

Arawn Doomsman. I am prince of my people; the debt you have come to claim is ours owed, and mine to repay. And though it is a fearsome asking, and Neith the king himself was troubled when he heard of your choice—"

"Aye?" asked Athyn, when he fell silent.

Gwyn's rare smile flashed to light the gloom. "—for my part I think you have made the only choice; the best, most fitting repayment. But perhaps that is because I too now know what it is to love." He turned then to his veiled and hooded companion, his manner warmer, nearer, proud with it. "The Lady Etain, my betrothed, who shall be my queen."

The veil was set aside, the hood swept back, to reveal dark hair, white skin, eyes of gold and amber-dew.

"Etain the younger, only," came a musical mocking voice, "named for that goddess who is wife to Midir Rhên; though perhaps she and I are not unlike in other ways..." The voice lost its mockery, and its owner made Athyn a real reverence. "My honor, Queen of Kelts; all our folk know of your deed beneath the hill. If not for you, my lord would not now be; and, for all they love to boast of our favor and friendship, I think few of your people would have done so much, or as bravely."

"The bravery of ignorance, lady," said Athyn, and like Etain's her modesty was not feigned. "For had I known where my lord Allyn meant to bring me I doubt I should have gone for any sake, lacking courage even as I lacked for knowledge."

"That same lack of courage that has brought you here today—in full knowledge?" asked Etain coolly, and Athyn flushed.

No chit of a girl, even a lass of the Sidhefolk—who is probably a hundred times older than I, or else like my goddess-son, full fourteen years my junior for all he seems a thousand years my elder—is going to discountenance me, not even with compliment...

"That is another matter, clean entirely."

"It well may be." Etain veiled her eyes. "Yet spancelled is your man."

"Unfettered they who live the longest," returned Athyn with some heat. "But any tether can be broken; as a horsegirl that was one of the first lessons I ever learned. It is merely a matter of where the thing is snapped."

"Perhaps the time now is come to begin the horsegirl's last lessons—or the Queen's first."

When there were no longer four in the great hall but six Athyn never knew; she never noticed their arrival, if even they had done so blatant a thing as arrive. Indeed, it seemed that the two newcomers had always been there; for all she knew, they might have stood there since time's beginnings. They were cloaked and hooded, one in red different than the red of the Sidhefolk, clear and bright and dry and vivid, startling in the dimness of the hall, the other in gray the color of rainlight, of mist in hollow valleys or steel on stone; their faces were hidden within their hoods. They stood silently, unmoving as the thrones behind them.

Gwyn noted them first, turning with a start controlled before it had scarce begun, bowing deeply; Etain curtsied gracefully, hand to breast, and Allyn bowed more deeply than had Gwyn. The newcomers acknowledged the reverences, and then the two hooded heads slowly turned to Athyn.

Who had neither bowed nor curtsied nor so much as bobbed her own head; who stood staring up at the cloaked figures with an air of defiance utterly at odds with her usual perfect natural courtesy. *Curtsey, by gods! Now that I do not think! Not at least until I know who it is to whom I bend my knee; if it is, indeed, to gods that I do bend it...*

"I seek the Lord Arawn," said Athyn then.

"And he is come."

Who spoke? Athyn looked up at the tall gray-cloaked figure that stood before her; not raising her eyes merely, like some shy maiden with her first lover, but throwing her whole head back, calmly challenging, as if she faced the scaffold or the stake.

And that would be only death, and therefore easy; for after that still I would have to stand here where now I stand, and face him—save that I cannot face him, just so, for that his is hid...

The gray cloak fell round him like cloud, baffling her eye and brain; the hood was full and his countenance in deep shadow, but she glimpsed a dark beard trimmed to the contour of a strong jaw, deepset graysilver eyes under level brows, a silver brooch set with a blue stone that pinned the mantle's folds at his right shoulder—the rest was as misty as the hall around her. *That one who walked with me in the rain at Witchingdene... Yet surely that was my Morric, I could not have been mistaken in that! But then—*

She turned her gaze to the other figure. Arawn's consort stood beside him, cloak and hood now flung behind her, all in red, the War-red War-queen, darkhaired and gray-eyed like her mate; a collar of garnets circled her throat, and upon her left shoulder sat a raven with blood-tipped wings.

Malen Ruadh Rhên: It seems fitting somehow that the Lord of Judgment should have for mate a goddess of love and war—and one whom all my life I have besought...

Suddenly awed, Athyn made them a profound reverence, and they bowed their heads, acknowledging her respect and her recalcitrance both alike. A faint smile warmed Malen's lovely stern features, like firelight reflected upon a shield some cold silent midnight before a battle.

"Ingheann," she said, and that was all she said.

Beside her Arawn stirred; unlike his queen he had not unhooded, and still Athyn could not see his face.

"Never before has mortal ridden into my kingdom while still in the body, Athyn Blackmantle," he said, in a calm deep splendid voice. "I have allowed it this once, for sake of him who rides with you, and for sake of the steed who bore you hither, and for sake of that which you bear upon your brow"—involuntarily Athyn raised a hand to touch the cathbarr; the silver and stones were biting cold—"but never again. What is your will in my realm?"

Athyn drew a breath and straightened her shoulders under the snakeskin cloak; she had not failed to note that Arawn had addressed her by her earned byname, not her birthname or her royal title. *And rightly so, for it is more my truename than any other…*

"Lord, in payment of a service I once did them, the Sidhe owe me a debt from of old. All these years never have I asked to redeem the promise, when well I might have many times over; but I ask now, and it is this that I have come to claim. Lord Allyn has guided me, and Prince Gwyn will attest my right."

"This is known, and the reason also. Name what you would have as payment." Arawn spoke without emphasis, but the hall was suddenly hushed, as if a stream that had been bubbling and running just on the threshold of hearing had been all at once stopped, or as if an unseen many had been murmuring privily amongst themselves and now had fallen silent, for appallment or surprise.

Athyn closed her eyes briefly, opened them and stared straight into the living darkness within the gray hood. Her face, though she did not know it, bore now not the humble mien of a petitioner but rather the look she wore in battle, a look that made no bargains save with the blade, that gave no quarter and sought none. *He knows, he knows what I shall ask…*

"My lord and mate and King, Morric Douglas, who was treacherously and unjustly slain—I will have him returned to life, with me, as we were." And waited, her whole being suspended, for the god's reply. *Tide what betide, I do not leave here without my love; though what I shall do if Arawn denies me, I am sure I do not know. I cannot go to war against the Lords of Dán themselves—well, at least I do not think I can…can I?*

"It is a great alteration you require of me," said Arawn at last. "Be warned. So drastic a touch upon the web of dán will have reverberations such as you have not imagined, or cannot imagine."

"You are Lord of Annwn," said Athyn, and now she spoke

in her brehon's voice, reasoning, reasonable. "You are suzerain over the dead between their lives, Firstborn of the Absolute, chief of the Lords of Dán. You who are the hand of the Highest—who can gainsay you in such a matter?"

"My lord Arawn knows who he might be, what is his task to settle," said Malen, gently reproving.

"His task now is to settle the debt of my folk to this soul," replied Gwyn, gently reminding, but with an edge.

Athyn paid no heed to either; but, intent and still as a hunting falcon, she kept close keen gaze upon the tall divinity before her. "This is the payment I choose for the debt owed me. But also there is a debt owed Morric Douglas—what of that? Amzalsunëa Dalgarno begged him come to Kaireden to help her, and when he out of honor and pity and old affection did go to her, she killed him. How is *that* dán?" Her voice that had been coolly courteous rang with angry challenge; the brehon had fled, it was Blackmantle now who spoke. "In my book that is unlawful murder, or nothing is; and so I requited her for it—and not her alone."

The deep voice seemed somehow sad. "He took weakness from her weakness, and strength from your strength. Each of you gave him what you had to give, and all you had to give."

"She gave him death!" The fury leaped out unsheathed, like a leopard's claws. He did not make her the obvious answer, but she heard it even so, and drew in a ragged breath. *And so we see how angry I still may be, and how though my Long Hunt may have eased me for justice and vengeance, it has done nothing for my wrath, whatever...* "And you?" asked Athyn presently, anger banked again like a peatfire flame. "What did *you* give him, when he came before you? What did he take from that which you had to offer?"

But the god was silent.

Athyn took a deep breath and another line, as if she were in the hunting field and Arawn a particularly shiftsome fox to follow. The others—the goddess, the Sidhefolk, the whispering unseen presences, Morric himself—were forgotten; now it was Arawn and Athyn alone, their wills locked to move worlds. And almost it seemed that they were evenly matched: more, that the will of a mortal, armored by love and courage and no small arrogance, might this day go over even the will of a god.

"You know what covenant we swore to each other, he and I. You were witness to it at our bridal."

"No covenant is greater," replied Arawn. "Nothing mightier than love save only love with honor, and that you have also." The hooded head nodded then toward Athyn's swan collar, and she lifted a hand to her throat. "Swans mate for life," came the deep quiet voice. "And black swans?"

"Those too."

"And yet they do not sing."

"And yet they can. It is said that they sing once, and more beautifully than all other voices, just before they die." She paused. "And he did. This I know. For he sang to me."

The huge mantled form, insufferably calm, inclined to her; then, raising his hands, Arawn slowly spread aside the shadowing hood. Looking up straight into the revealed visage of the god, all her lives and all her soul naked and undefended before him, in that endless moment Athyn held herself to utter stillness, knowing now why Arawn kept his countenance veiled, his eyes, or eye, in shadow...

But though she beheld only that part of his divine nature that her mortal mind could bear, there was nothing of her own immortal being that he did not see, the goddess that was in her. And she spoke now to Arawn, simply, from the last of her mortality and the first of her divinity alike, her last entreaty, her utmost truth, her last plea as she had spoken it once before to Morric; save that, being Athyn, she spoke it now not as petition but as declaration, not supplication but command.

"I have knit my soul with his. The weave cannot be unpicked. Even the gods may not undo it."

Arawn was silent a while longer. Then: "I am bound by the word Neith ap Llyr did give you." As Athyn's joy blazed, he raised a warning hand. "The promise holds; but such an asking requires more surety even than the debt of the Sidhe. What will you offer?"

Unhesitatingly: "My lives for his living."

"He shall live again, ingheann," said Malen, gently. "And you with him. This you know. This is not the end."

"Unacceptable!" snapped Athyn, forgetting where she was, to whom she spoke; and just for an instant she thought she saw Arawn smile, a fugitive flash that went across his face like summer lightning. "He was betrayed; he shall not stay."

Arawn nodded slowly; he had let the hood fall close again round his countenance, and Athyn could not see what look that countenance now bore.

"He was betrayed, right enough. But as to whether he will stay or no: That is up to you, and to him also." And now the amusement was plain in his voice, if not his face. "By all gods, you are as inflexible with me as ever you have been with your enemies... Yet when next you face me in this place, it well may prove a different story. I shall be the same; but you may not."

Athyn caught her breath as Arawn seemed somehow to increase, to augment himself like a waxing moon, to grow taller, or huger, or more solid, though it could not be said that he changed appearance. But his power now was heavy in the hall.

"The bargain is made; but it may still be unmade. All those who worked evil against Morric Douglas are gone, you have sent them on before; but there are yet some words you must hear, and those words are not mine to say."

He lifted a hand, extending his arm in command, and beside him, upon Malen Rhên's shoulder, the raven unfurled its ragged wings, closing them again with a clap like thunder. Upon the far side of the great hall, a misty massing now came of forms and faces, a procession of souls, a hosting of the shades of those whom Athyn had slain; or at least those ones who had not already been reborn, who now were between lives, contemplating their past errors and preparing for their next turn in the body.

"Are they here to reproach me, then?" asked Athyn steadily. "For I promise you I am proof against them..."

Arawn shook his head within the hood; there was a brief flash of silver in the shadow, as if he wore a crown.

"The young, unripe ones, who might well have done so, for they still do not understand the nature of their offenses, are already moved on to new housings. For know this: The less advanced a soul, the less time between lives it spends in my kingdom. Those souls that have been through the fires of incarnation more times than not, they have the more to make their own between lives; they remain here until they have done so, and they themselves, not I, determine when they shall return to the body, and the circumstances of that return. But the young ones I send speedily out to fledge again, to learn, so that they shall have then something veritable to think on when next they come to me, something truer than they knew they knew."

Athyn smiled in spite of herself. "'Truer'! Can a thing be truer than the truth, or less true? Is it not either true or not true?"

"It can be, and it is; and when you come to understand that, you will have learned a thing yourself... But these others— well, they themselves shall tell you what they would. And you shall hear."

So, one by one, they told her, and she knew them all: those whom she herself had slain, those whom others had slain for her. Athyn felt the flames of fury unquenched as she beheld them, and though they asked her forgiveness she was as stone to their words, and they went softly away again. Arawn did not reproach her, either for presence of anger or absence of mercy.

Just because they are dead they think that all is well and settled between us? Small chance! Merely because they now cry sad and sorry does not mean I must forgive. I have been wronged, and I am a judge by trade; I am the only one who can judge aright in this, and

*by gods I say it shall take a deal more than easy cheap repentance to
win amnesty of me...*

"Well then?" came Arawn's measured voice.

"I have heard."

"And?"

She shrugged angrily. "They have spoken, I have heard. To
do more than that, no power below Kelu can force me with
force; and not even Kelu."

"Then one voice more you may wish to hear—"

Across the chamber's width, a rainbow shimmering came;
and a vision of Amzalsunëa, like a face seen through the boiling torrent of a waterfall, drifted like smoke across the hall.
Fair again as once she had been, she looked at Athyn as if she
would speak, held out her hands to her adversary.

Who regarded her unmoving and unmoved. Presently
Athyn: "I have naught to say to this one. Nor will I hear her.
Send her on."

"That is no longer in my power," replied Arawn, and she
glanced up swiftly at a note in his voice she could not read.
"Dán has determined, and she is already in the body once
again; being a very young soul, with very much to learn. But do
not be too harsh in judging her, or too swift in dismissing the
dán you and she have between you. What, did you think all
the dán in this lies between Morric Douglas and yourself? Not
so; but when she shall cross your paths again even I cannot
say."

"Cannot, or will not?" Athyn was most unexpectedly
shaken by the god's intimation: that she and Amzalsunëa
could possibly have fate that linked them outside Morric, or
beyond him.

"May not," came the reply, and Athyn knew she could push
him no farther.

"Well. For my part, lord, I wish only to hear what you *shall*
say. Can my intent be accomplished, and will you allow it—
my raiding of Annwn?"

"It can," said Arawn calmly, "and I shall; indeed I must.

With your oath and your Hunt you have served the law that is given to your people; hear now what you must do to serve a greater law than that." His voice was the voice of the Final Judge of the World, from whose justice there can be no appeal, and Athyn, herself a judge, drew herself up to hear the sentence he pronounced. "Athyn Cahanagh. Three trials for you in my kingdom: You must forge a sword in a smithy not of earth, a sword from the Air and a sword from the Fire, a sword from the Water and a sword from the Stone. You must use that sword to defeat the Orm, the Beast of Glora, though you may not slay it; and then conceal the sword in earth, under earth, for the one who will next have need. Lastly you must enter Pair Dadeni itself, the Cauldron of Rebirth; enter it alive and come from it alive, bringing your lord with you. Do all this, and he shall be restored as you do seek."

Athyn had gone a touch paler as Arawn spoke, but her countenance did not otherwise alter, and her resolve was unchanged. *God or no, know that I would do far more than that to get him back...*

"And one thing more," came Arawn's deep even tones, as if he had heard her; and undoubtedly he had. "In this matter Morric Douglas may not be commanded, as if your will were all-conquering and his utterly to be set aside. If your wish and will are his also, that he would join you in the world again—then the tests may begin. Your strength in magic may obtain, but he too must have a choice; and as he chooses so must you abide. You may beseech as you please; but you may not compel. Summon him now, and let him speak."

Oh, if that is all... Athyn was extending an arm, and more than an arm, before Arawn had quite finished speaking. *How many times each hour since he went I have longed to reach out for him... For that is how it is with our beloved dead: We may speak to them, and with them, and even call to them; but we may not command or demand, or trouble their peace. They may answer us when or as or if they please... As to my beloved, I know that he will hear me, and hearing, he shall come...*

It was a sensation not unlike to a certain pishogue that Athyn had practiced since her girlhood: the reaching heart, she had called it. It had not been taught her; she had never even known its proper name. But now not her heart alone but all of her reached, holding herself out to Morric, to bring him back again to her across that great expanse that naught save love and the willing spirit can bridge.

And it seemed he heard her call straightway, or had been loitering near at hand waiting for just such a summons, or else her power, or her love, or love's power, was greater than even Arawn had thought; for, suddenly, quietly, Morric Douglas was there, across the chamber's width, looking at his wife as she looked at him. Not as Amzalsunëa had appeared, wraithlike in her new ensoulment; but entirely a liege of Annwn, and entirely himself, as solid and real to Athyn now as he had been in life, clad in black, grave and beautiful as ever; on a cord against his chest a small gold locket gleamed. His hand was held out to her, and she surged forward to him, instinctively, a look of joy and desperation on her face; but Gwyn put out an arm to bar her way, and she saw that a river lay between Morric and themselves. Looking again, she saw that it was no river but a pool of cold flame, freezing fire, and she did not struggle against Gwyn's arm.

But if she might not run to him still she could gaze upon him. It was like to a dream she had had, she could not remember when; a dream, or a Seeing, or merely an ashling, to her they were all much the same these days: a vision of him in a dark place, across an expanse of flame, his arm stretched before him. *Is his hand held out to take my own, then? Or is it meant to warn me off? I cannot tell...* And though from the moment she knew he was dead she had been as iron in her purpose, adamantine in the correctness of her quest, the sight of him now but confirmed her in it ten thousand times over.

What is on you all, even the Lord Arawn, that you persist in the futility of asking, in testing, in warning? Do you not see that I will not be thwarted or denied in this, no matter what, or who? I have thrown away the scabbard; I shall ride the storm and direct the whirlwind, pass through flame and flood, I shall shake the very stars for him, or ever I cease the path. There was never even a moment of choosing; from the first it was a thing ordained...

She reached out her own hand, seeing in the strange light the gleam of her betrothal ring, the words to give her hope and heart: 'Love is enough.' And by all gods I say it shall be...

"Hir yw'r dydd a hir yw'r nos a hir yw aros Arawn," she said. *'Long the day and long the night and long the wait for Arawn'*— and Morric smiled at her across the fire, and turned to face the lord of Annwn.

Athyn never knew what Morric and Arawn said one to the other. She did not move a muscle, not a thought or breath, watching the towering form of the god, the beauty of Morric as he stood. Then Morric turned again to her, and held out his hand, and was gone.

"Time is," came Arawn's voice, piercing the blank anguish that enfolded her.

But Athyn was already retying her leinna, fastening her cloak at her throat. The brief vision of Morric had all but driven her to her knees with pain and grief and longing; but to see him had been a healing and a spur all in one. *Though whether it is worse for me to have beheld him so briefly than never to have beheld him at all, I cannot tell. But my wish is his wish—even Arawn cannot deny that now—and this is a thing I can do; I shall be perseverant as a kedder on a blood-trail, I will not leave him here one millim longer than I must, not if my soul is flung from the Wheel for it forever... So long as he is with me....*

She glanced up at the god. "I go alone, then? Well enough."

Before Arawn could answer, Athyn felt something push hard against her hand, something warm and not unfamiliar; looking down, she saw the rough-maned head, the padded paws, the arching massive-muscled back of her fetch, the great brindled blacksilver wolf.

"You do *not* go alone, then..."

The words came to her as if the fetch had spoken. And then, with never a glance at the gods or the Sidhefolk, but looking up at Athyn out of green-gold eyes, with a light behind them reflected from nothing in that hall, in a low furry voice that held amusement and impatience and more than a little affection, the wolf did speak.

"Inquire in Cartha Galvorn."

Cartha Galvorn... Sharply Athyn remembered sitting one time with Morric in the window-seat in their bedchamber, his arms around her, both of them gazing out at Gavida's Smithy, the volcanic island that stands many miles out to sea in the Bight of Caerdroia, and he telling her that that fiery earthtorch, sometimes glowing like a pharos, sometimes plumed with ashclouds that climb to the edge of space, was named among bards Cartha Galvorn... And this seemed more miraculous even than that the wolf had spoken. *Can that be this 'smithy not of earth' that I am bidden seek? For such is the meaning of its name in the bard-usage, as Morric's means 'sea-valor' and my own means 'silver flame'—again, as my lord did tell me...*

"How is it you have never spoken before?" she asked humbly. But the wolf only gave his low purring croon, and leaned against her leg.

Now indeed time was... Bowing to Arawn and Malen— "We do not say farewell just yet," said Allyn smiling when she turned to the three Sidhefolk, and Athyn contented herself with a long level look that was more than a smile—Athyn and the wolf went together out of Arawn's hall.

Outside the massive walls it was as if no time at all had passed; whether she had spent hours or centuries within the palace contesting with the god, the endless gold light of Annwn had changed not at all, was still that of an autumn afternoon. *But then I daresay a day here is not like any day I have ever known...*

Athyn looked round for the Mari Llwyd, but no horse stood before the gates; she had not truly expected to find the Ghost Mare standing waiting like some patient livery cob. Indeed, it was past all imagining that that legendary creature had already borne her twice in a lifetime upon its back. *Still, I did hope; but perhaps another time, thrice the charm, to pay for all....*

But it seemed that she was not to go without transport after all: In the stream of the river that circled Arawn's palace, straining against the fierce complaining current, a gray-hulled curragh now stood moored, and if it had had her name writ round about its prow in letters of fire it could not more plainly have been meant for her.

The wolf leaped into the prow of the little craft, and, favoring Athyn with a great ostentatious white-fanged yawn and an ambiguous crooning comment, promptly went to sleep.

She laughed indulgently to see it. *So even fetch-wolves are not above the ways of their mortal cousins—well, all dogs hunt alike, and I have ever been a one for hounds as well as horses. Yet it seems it is not for naught that the House of Aoibhell is called the House of the Wolf—though I never thought much about it until now....* Athyn looked about her as the foaming stream took the boat, and a wind filled the red leather sail from behind. *This is a strange thing, a river that is and yet is not the Avon Dia I know so well... Are all things then in the world we think of as the true world merely copies, blanched and blotched and faded, of things in Arawn's kingdom? And are those in their turn only imperfect copies of things truer and realer still, in other kingdoms beyond his and mine alike? Perhaps before this is done with I shall know, and in such wise as I cannot begin to guess...*

So they sailed upon the strong current to the sea.

But behind her in his hall, Arawn stood silent, and even Malen his mate did not trouble his peace, if peace it was.

chapter thirty-one

Undertake no duel in falsehood, for there has not been
nor will there be found a truer judge than a duel.

—*Brendan mac Nia*

hen still many miles upriver Athyn heard the
roaring of the sea—a sustained low note like a
great horn, a bombard or a drónach, diving down,
far below the deepest note a man can sound. The curragh
fled onward, borne upon the current, past the Plains of
Ellertrin, the Cliffs of Fhola, the City itself; and when it
came to the Mouths of the Avon Dia, or rather to their coun-
terpart in this Otherland Tara, under Athyn's hand on the
tiller it shot through the straits and came out into true
Ocean.

Ahead of her, almost due west as the arrow flies, lay the
island of Gavida's Smithy, little more than the rough shoulders
of a towering firemount thrust up from the ocean floor, three
leagues below the surface of the heaving waters. *And who
among us ever knew how truly named it was...* The seas were
mountainous, the currents crossed and wild. But sun-sharks
leaped ahead and alongside, to show her the safe road through
the waves, and following their smiling pointing faces it was
straight for those stark gray walls that Athyn steered.

*   *   *

She had beached her boat, waved farewell and thanks to her sun-shark guides. Now Athyn dragged the curragh up the foreshore out of tidereach, and the wolf, splashing into the salt water with every appearance of laughing enjoyment, bounded onto the clinkered black shingle.

Athyn shaded her eyes and threw her head back, gazing upward. *I have only the word of my fetch to go on, it was upon that alone that I came here. He did not say it was the place, even, only that I should inquire here, in Cartha Galvorn. There was no assurance that this is the place I seek, and somehow I very much doubt it is any good asking him…*

Halfway to the summit, a great shoulder loomed out from the mountain; beneath its threatening brow, a cavemouth yawned in the mountain's scored, scarred flank, and from it came a low throb on the threshold of human hearing, and a faint red light. *And there it plainly is, the place of my inquiring. But would it have been so much to ask, that it had been even a little more conveniently situated? Aye, I suppose it would…*

A long time later, how long she did not know. Her boots slashed through by the razor-sharp slag, her hands and knees and elbows torn and bleeding where she had missed her footing and fallen hard, Athyn came at last to the cavemouth where it was delven into the mountain's shoulder. The light was deeper and more brilliant than it had looked from below, the cave red as a wound in the firemount's side; the wolf, who had bounded powerfully uphill beside her, now was nowhere to be seen.

Halting only to draw a deep breath for a prayer to the Goddess, Morric's name upon her lips like a talisman, she entered, and was instantly plunged into darkness. When her eyes adjusted, she saw that the dark was not absolute, and that a way was there.

This was Cartha Galvorn, the Forge of Gavida, upon the vast buttress called Pen Gannion. Deep within the mountain lay that forge, red-litten, the hot heavy airlessness smelling of roses and heated iron. About her and before her as she went the walls of the cavern fled away on all sides into dim shadowy regions, save straight ahead at the forge itself, where the light was like to that at a white sun's heart, and she guessed that the place did not exist in space and time but, like the semblance of Annwn, had been set here for her. *I have seen this place before. It is as in that vision I had, I cannot even recall when, but if this is a true Seeing, then perhaps those other things I Saw are true also, or will be...*

"Come. Step forward into the light, where I may see you."

The words rolling out on the heated air sounded as if the earth itself had spoken. Athyn stepping forward as she was commanded, or invited, blinking in the sudden fierce forge-light that fell upon her, lifted her head to look at him who had bidden her forward.

Gavida Burn-the-wind: the Smith of the Gods, Gavannaun, Forgelord, the Artificer, the Gabhain Saor; he stood on the forge's far side. He seemed made of the metals he himself did make, his face and arms bronze-red, his hair and eyes iron-dark; an apron of white buckskin he wore, and his braided beard flourished against his bare chest. His arms were as the pillars of the world, his shoulders spanned galaxies in their strength and splendor, the might of his breast was as a shield before the stars. Upon his anvil was hammered out the thunder, from his forge the lightning took its birth. He was altogether a being to be feared; and yet Athyn did not fear him—he seemed to her less high and remote than Arawn and Malen, though he was of their race. She felt instead a strange kinship, a sudden wave of deep affection and utmost respect, as if she were of his blood or his begetting.

"By oak and iron," came the huge soft metallic voice, strong as an earthshake and deep as a gong. "We *are* of one blood, though you knew it not till now. The Aoibhells have long been kin to the Gabhain Saor." Though how that might be he did not say.

"As a kinswoman, then, I shall ask of thee, Gavaun Rhên," said Athyn, and her voice though a human voice held strength the equal of his own. At her side, the wolf stirred, growling softly to echo the rumble far beneath the cavefloor, and Athyn twisted her fingers for comfort into the great rough mane.

Gavida swung the hammer. The anvil rang, the mighty oaken kepp beneath it absorbed the blow, sending it out as the earthshake, of which this god is lord. Sparks flew from the anvil like tiny suns; or they might have been suns, even, in some other creation, for of that too he is master.

"What would you, lass? Chains to bind? Crowns to find?"

"I am sufficed with both," said the Ard-rían of Keltia. Athyn then: "I have need of a sword; a sword from the air and a sword from the water, a sword from the fire and a sword from the stone, to be forged by my own hand in a smithy not of earth. And I was bidden inquire for this thing in Cartha Galvorn."

Though she was momently blind against the dazzle of white fire that leaped up then, she did not throw up an arm to shield her face, and it seemed to her that the god smiled.

"You ask modestly," said Gavida. "Not hard. What more?"

Athyn's sight had returned, though it could not pierce the fire-brilliance to the forge's other side.

"The strength and lore to use it as I would: to win back my lord from Arawn Doomsman."

"Ah." The syllable rumbled like the groundshake; the god was silent, his presence grown suddenly dark and shadowy in that place of heat and flame.

"I do not as a rule dispute governance with my brother of Annwn," he said then. "He to his province, I to mine. But this I see is a very strange matter, unlike all others with which I am heretofore acquent, and I see too where a lawful claim might be made." He brought the great hammer down once more, as if by way of punctuation, though what it was that he worked Athyn could not see. "Well. As for strength, love is all the strength you require, maiden, and that you have already. Your blade you must forge here as you have been commanded, under my eye, by your own hand. But, for the sake of the one you seek, and for that you have asked it of me, and that you

come of blood that is dear and near to me, take a gift of me—
a hilt to fit that blade."

She received it reverently in both hands. A hilt only, as the
god had said; no blade was yet attached to it, that she had yet
to win. It was a lovely, well-made thing, with intricate interlace in heavy gold that ended in the suncross on one side, the
moonstar on the other; a huge gold diamond crowned the
pommel. She touched the stone with the tip of one finger:
blazing cold.

"A nice bit of crafting, though I say it as should not."
Gavida's voice rumbled with satisfaction, then changed the
note. "Now. To your work."

And Athyn hearing him knew well he did not speak of the
blade alone.

Suddenly it was dark beneath the mountain, softly, stiflingly
dark, like a black cloth smothering her face, or a choking muffling sooty hand; dark as perhaps it had never been before in
that place. The forge-fire had been blown out: Gavida had
snuffed it as easily as a child might snuff out a bedcandle, or
else he had merely given it that appearance—whichever,
Athyn knew that he waited now for her to rekindle it.

*A new fire for a new working, that is the rule of the forge. And this
is the first of my tasks, to relight the Fire that has never died, and all
before the forging might begin. But how? It is on me that simple magic
would not be allowed here, and the greater magic upon which I might
lawfully call—at least if the word of the Sidhe counts for aught here—
is meant for greater trials than this. The first simple test; but at none
of them can I afford to fail, and they are not so simple either...*

She pushed back her hair from her face, and her fingers
brushed against the metal of Nia's cathbarr. She had forgotten
she even bore it on her brow; but moved by an instinct she did
not understand, she lifted her right hand with ceremony, and
touched her fingertips with authority to the great cushion-cut
crystal set in the frontlet piece.

A shocking light blazed out in the velvet dark, like the light from atop Sheehallion when Athyn was young, a long cool milky glowing lance of brilliance that streamed from the stone. It struck the forge, and the dead fire beneath, kindled a spark in the smithy's heart; and after a silent endless moment the fire reawakened, with a soft humming roar like a dragon's song, the crucible glowing red, standing ready for her work.

"Well done," came the voice of the Forgelord. "For here that crown was made, and by my hand; and so too another."

Of the blade's making Athyn recalled but little. She had ore to her hand, meteoric iron from beyond the sun and behind the stars, shining black and green as if metal and ice had mated; she had water and fire; she had the god's own tools, oak and iron— the great hammer and anvil with which Gavida worked the world, and the kepp that was the world itself. And ever she was 'ware of the eyes of the Smith upon her.

Still, the meteor-metal blazed when she melted it down, pouring it into the blade-mold as easily as water from her bed-side cup; many times she hammered it and folded it and heated it and hammered it again, plunged it into fire and water, worked the great bellows with bare bleeding feet, blowing the fire until it danced upon the roof of the cave; though whether she did these things in truth, or if the making was done in some other reality, she was never to know.

But howsoever it might have been, slowly, surely, a sword began to take shape where there had been until now only a long slip of flaming metal. With a maker's confident instinct she grooved the fullers and shaped the tang, polished the silver length of it, balanced it, sharpened the edges with the three sharpenings—the green, the black, the lightning-colored— and the darting deadly point. Until at last a finished blade lay before her upon the anvil, smooth and silken, with a green-black icy flash that came to it from beyond the stars, heavy with power, of an edge to draw blood from the wind, of all the hearts and heroes of the world; and the gold hilt lay beside it.

Athyn stood back a little; then, with not so much as a glance at the Smith-god who faced her across the forge, she stretched out her hand, palm down, and thought her will from the power that was in her, laying the wild-magic gently into the sword, as if it had been but another folding of the metal, another polishing of the blade. Like a live thing the blade blurred and moved, seating itself in the hilt, indissolubly fusing tang to socket; the diamond in the pommel shone out briefly, an echo of the light from the jewel in Nia's fillet, the interlacing seemed to braid and twine; and when the stone was dim again and the patterns had ceased to writhe, the sword was made.

"It is made," said Athyn. "It can cleave the dustmote in the sunbeam, it can wound the wind. There will be no seeing its passage, save for a slash of brightness in the air as it goes by, and the diamond drops that are the blood of the wind falling after."

"Name it," came the huge voice of the god, Gavida's voice, in the fire and the darkness and the sudden hush. "Thou hast made it; thine it is to give it its name, and its dán also."

She spoke, suddenly sure, and around her brows the cath-barr of Nia struck cold to the bone.

"I name thee Llacharn," she said, speaking as Gavida had spoken in the High Gaeloch, ancient tongue of Kelts—human and silkie and merrow, Sidhe and god all alike. "Llacharn, the Flamebright. And for dán I give thee this: to wait in night and expectation, in the Forest in the Sea. Thou art the Sword from the Air and the Sword from the Fire, the Sword from the Water and the Sword from the Stone. I will use thee in my need and set thee in thy place to await those who follow. One will come whose need is great also, and drawing thee from thy place shall use thee well. Another will set thee in thy place again, though he use thee not himself. And in the end shall come the third and last to wield thee at need, in the service of more than worlds. Then wilt thou find freedom; and thy task, and theirs, and mine, be done."

Now Gavida stood forth, the King-Smith, and it seemed that she had not beheld him at all until this moment, such a glory now was on him. Tall as the mountain he stood, cloaked in a blue mantle deep as living night, its hem set about with the stars themselves, its folds brooched to his mighty shoulder with a great wheel of diamond and ruby that for fairness rivalled a sun in splendor; at his side hung a sword of such beauty and danger and power and holiness that upon beholding it all Athyn's being yearned to it.

Surely this is Fragarach, the Answerer, Lugh's own blade, this is the Sword among the Thirteen Treasures of the Kelts... But Gavida's face was fairer now than high summer, his hair darker than the abyss of the sea; his voice came rich and deep, warm with his pride in her, and he spoke now in the common tongue, less grand, less high.

"It is done, and well done. It is a sword of the right forging; let only the one who has earned it dare set hand to its hilt. Though it break, and break it shall, it will break only to be reforged better than before. And remember, maiden: Though you have wrought it in your need, to your need, of your need, it does not belong to you. It might as easily be said that you belong to it. Do not forget this. But take it up now and go."

And Athyn closed her hand around the knotwork hilt of Llacharn the Flamebright, and gave thanks and honor and reverence to the Lord of the Forge; and then, the wolf pacing silent at her side, she went away down the mountain, to put Llacharn to the first of all its tasks, the second of her own.

When she emerged into the air, shockingly cold after the heat of the smith-god's palace, dawn leaping like a lean gold panther over the edge of the continent behind her, Athyn saw that the curragh was gone. But she was not troubled, and with a smile she laid her hand upon the wolf's back and stepped confidently into the brightening air; when she stepped out of it she was once more in Annwn.

Those who had been with her in the great hall were just as she had left them, as if no time had passed; as for them very like it had not. And seeing none but Arawn Athyn went straight up to the lowest step whereon he stood, and in silence laid the sword, like tribute or insult or the gauntlet of a challenge, upon the stone floor at the feet of the god.

The hooded head bent. "Llacharn," said Arawn meditatively, as if he recognized an old friend, and Athyn nodded once, unastonished that he knew the weapon's name.

"Llacharn it is," she agreed. "You know it then."

"I know it." The darkness within the hood lifted then, and Athyn felt the god's gaze on her. "And you?"

"I know it now," said Athyn.

"And what must be done with it?"

"That the event must prove." She let a touch of impatience in upon her manner. "Besides, lord, you yourself have already told me what it is that I must do. I go now to the Sea of Glora, to find this Beast you have bidden me deal with, this Orm I must defeat."

"And I to be her guide." That was Allyn, from where he stood with Gwyn and Etain.

Athyn looked at him with love, though she spoke for Arawn to hear. "I am no Ban-draoi, but my lord Allyn is for me Kevarwedhor, the Guide of Souls. Has ever been, and ever shall be; though why he should do me such honor, by the Wood and the Field and the Fountain, I am sure I do not know."

The Sidhe lord bowed to her, smiling. "There might be reasons. But though I guide, it is you who shall gain."

A cold morning. The edge of a beach, a perfect, white, utterly untrodden seventeen-mile sweep, with the east wind screaming across the Roaring Dunes that hum and drone when even a laighard slides down them, and the huge rollers running before.

The seabirds were as thick upon that water as cloves studding a gammon; only here the gammon was a smooth green glassy wave and the cloves were scores and hundreds of seascouts, the handsome black-backed duck that winters in those waters, corking up and down and up again over the rollers coming endlessly to shore.

This was Glora, the great freshwater inland sea that splits the main continent of the planet Gwynedd, a relic of the planet's violent past. Ages since, the lands riding, as they do still, upon the firetides far beneath the crust, there had almost been a break here, as if the foundation-floor of a house had been very nearly pulled apart; the crust of the planet itself had cracked, and the molten rock all but burst through to the surface. That crust is thin in those regions to this day—to the east Glenfhada, the Long Valley, gives proof—but the gaping earth split had remained open all along its length, and down the centuries it had filled with fresh water draining down from the lands around. So Glora had been born: Even now the deepness of it is unknown, and the many streams and rivers that go to make its fullness keep it cold with snow-melt and high with spring thaw.

Athyn and Allyn stood on the shoreline of Glora, the wolf beside them. All around was stark steep-sided hill country, a treeless dark sweep straight down to the shore, where the hill-grass went to machair and then to the long narrow fringe of pure white sand.

"A hundred years from today all this will be changed utterly," said Allyn, with a sweep of his hand. "Oak and ash and elm shall clothe those hills; there will be a stony beach, and the island Collimare shall have its name proved at last." He pointed to their left, far up a long arm or inlet where it joined the sea's main body, to where a low bare island could just be seen in the haze.

"'The Forest in the Sea,'" said Athyn. "But no forest grows there just yet." She picked up a stone, flung it into the little waves. "Gods but I am aweary of tests..."

"Aye?" asked Allyn after a while, and she grinned to hear the carefulness of the inquiry. The wolf looked up at her, whimpering anxiously above the wind.

"Nay," she admitted then with a smile. "But I could wish to be on the other side of them—"

"I must leave you now," said the Sidhe lord then. "And your wolf must come hence with me. I may guide you, your fetch may guard you; but in the end, you meet these tests alone." As he stepped back into the fold of air from which they had emerged, the wolf with him, his voice hung a moment behind him, a last quick urgent word of loving advice. "Do not let it look you in the eyes."

Athyn raised a hand in farewell, but they were already gone; and she smiled at the empty airt where they had stood. *Ah, the parting-gift, the fágáil of the Sidhe, and as vexing unfathomable as ever... Not to mention completely against Arawn's bidding, no doubt, for Allyn to tell me even so much, and I trust he will not be chided for it. But even so little as that, from him, is worth more than much from many... I will remember.*

And in that same concurrent instant breath with Allyn's going Athyn was transported a full five leagues from where she had been, to find herself standing alone on the shore of a steep-sided loch that lay straight as a sword, its entrance to Glora a mile or two to her right at the wide eastern hilt end, its tip pointing back west among the high hills. *This loch has no name that ever I have heard—perhaps this day shall see it named; for good or ill, though upon ill I will not think... But is it even in the world as I do know it, or is this still the Otherland, Gwynedd's astral double; or some union of both? Whatever, belike it makes no differ to what I do...*

The loch was long and narrow, its waters stained with peat, brown as a cairngorm where Glora's were sapphire-blue; the hills that held it plunged almost straight down to its surface, and so under. Another earthfault breaking through long since to the surface had drawn the line in the land; then in the ice ages that had come and gone and come again the march-past of glaciers had clawed it deeper and wider, like a fingernail gouging a scratch into flesh, over and again, until the scar remained, healed but abiding. Westaways from where she stood, no more than a mile or so, the island Collimare lay like a shield upon the water, midway across.

As Athyn gazed out over the loch, she caught the momentary spark of a keen hunting presence intent on her, an eager living intelligence that swept fiercely over her; almost as swiftly, it sheered aside into mist and silence, like a mousing owl in river-meadows by night. *It is watching me now, whatever it is, I can feel it. The Orm, Arawn called it, the Great Orm—what is it, then, a piast, or avanc of some greater or grosser sort? I remember how Cormac my father would warn me against the water-bulls or water-horses in certain of the upland lochs; not even Morvoren would swim in such dark and eldritch places... Those water-horses were thought to be cousin to the piast, and to the Avanc that causes the floods to rise; perhaps also to this Beast of Glora I have come to Glora to face?*

A catch crossed her mind then, a triad that Morric had idly recited to her one afternoon: 'Three wonders in the loch: an island without roots; fish without fins; waves without wind.' He had been telling her of a certain narrow deep gash-floored loch on Caledon in which strange creatures were reputed to dwell, but it could as easily have been of the sea-arm that stretched now before Athyn that he had been speaking, and to the Orm of mystery that the triad referred.

And still she stood, and as she stared at the long dark loch before her, clean water began to lap at her boots. *Do your task, and go from here. This is no water by which to linger; whatever dwells here, dwells alone.* From the farther shore she heard the crash and huish of suddenly risen water breaking on the beaches. And now the ripples were coming her way, a line of sizable waves rushing at her so swiftly that she stepped back lest they swamp her, or at the least soak her boots; and then they moved on down the shore and the loch was calm again.

But no sign could she see, though she scanned the waters, of what cause those waves might have. *Waves without wind...* The air was completely still; she was alone; no boat had passed. *What was it then did start that water moving?*

She did not have long to wait for her answer.

chapter thirty-two

It is lawful for princes to be judged, though they
themselves be judges.

—*Zarôndah of Aojun*

I t was dark and glistening and tremendous, floating lazily
just below the surface of the water. For all the haste of its
coming—so swift had it swum that it had thrown up a
bow-wave, and the spray had arced fountaining above—it
seemed now to be rotating leisurely underwater, like some
gigantic log spinning in the spring floods, the island without
roots of which the triad spoke. And yet she had hardly seen it
approach; one moment the surface of the loch was calm and
unbroken, the next she saw coming toward her a spoil of waves
with white foam in the midst of them, very strange to behold.

"It is easier than I thought it would be," she said aloud, not
knowing that she spoke so, nor indeed what she might mean.
"Not easy. But easier."

"Joy and grief are woven fine, on the same loom."

A strange sweet voice. Turning her head, Athyn saw looming above the water's surface, where the rolling sublacustrine
shadow had been, a long sinuous silver neck, its length topped
by a stiff crinkled reddish mane, and at the end of it a head like
a dragon's, oblong, bearded, with frills below its chin and
tufted ears and two small horns. The rest of its vast bulk was
barely visible in the peat-dark water. The Great Orm—the
Peiste as it is known to history, the Beast of Glora as Arawn

had named it—bent its gaze on her, and recollecting Allyn's warning she did not look it in the eye. But her hand now rested on the hilt of Llacharn, where it hung at her side from a humble leather baldric.

"So you say... Not Peiste, then, but piast," said Athyn at a venture. *It is amazing... Only look at it, the strangeness of it! Though many tales are told of it, and many have had brief sight of its comings and goings, and many more boast of such, few have ever beheld it in its home. Morvoren is the only person I know who has ever even glimpsed one of these, and that one was an orm of the deep sea...*

"Peiste to you, horsegirl; I am no common piast," said the Orm with pardonable pride. "Saint Brendan himself gave my line the gift of human speech, when he drove us off the salt. But though he bound us in the inland seas, even he could not rule us as the ordinary run of my kind are ruled; what hope have you?"

"Oh, I have hopes enough, I promise you... I have had to do with horses aplenty in my day, as you just now reminded me; and what are you, after all, but a water-horse, as the Caledonach call you?"

The Orm tossed its head, bridling and snorting as if to prove her words, thrashing about in the peaty wash, and Athyn pursued her line of verbal fence.

"You may look very like a dragon, piast, and talk very like one, but I daresay you have none of dragonkind's good qualities, and all of your own bad ones."

"That is not to be wondered at," said the Orm complacently; it had taken not the slightest offense. "I am called abomination, and no natural thing, and beast of blood, and worse names besides. But you are here to fight me."

"How do you know that?"

The creature heaved a deep dramatic sigh that sent little waves rushing out across the lake and in up the shingle, and Athyn stepped back farther still to spare her boots another dousing.

"It is always the same story... A warrior comes here to bind

me, or slay me, or capture me, and by so doing to win fame or
glory, a crown or a mate—the names change, the tale never.
What is it then that *you* do seek?"

It was angling its dreadful head, ducking its long neck like
a shy lad at Teltown, none too subtly trying to catch her eye.
But Athyn not forgetting the counsel she had been given kept
her glance on a close tight rein, and studied a patch of the
Peiste's shoulder, or its mane, or its ears, or the curious texture
of its skin, tough and rough and smooth.

"I think you know already," she said. "You have unlawfully
ventured out of Glora, and I must bind you again as Brendan
did; so Arawn Lord of Annwn has bidden me."

The Orm's whole huge bulk quivered, whether in outrage
or dismay Athyn could not tell but in protest unmistakable.
Even its jaw-frills were rigid with refusal.

"Bind me here? Nevermore to range through Gwynedd's
rivers and down to the seas? I do not think so!"

Athyn was unmoved by the bluster, and stepped back again
to avoid the splashes and spray. "Glora is big enough to house
many hundreds of your kind; it is not this one particular loch
alone you would be bound to. Brendan mac Nia saw to that."

"He had no right to do that, no right at all." The Orm's
voice was small and sulky. "Though he was a gallant lord and a
merry heart, still he had not the least cause to bind me so. And
if you come to do his task again for him—aye, aye, I know the
reason—I will show you well enough how not."

So Athyn drew her sword.

They fought from dusk to dawn and on to dusk again after. If
ever Athyn had thought a Fian a match for any combatant
that came along, she thought so no more; and if any beheld
this mighty struggle from near or far, either her own people or
the Orm's, or the Sidhe themselves, they gave no sign. Every
muscle screamed for ease, every bone seemed turned to water.
She was not wounded; the Orm did not seek to harm her but

rather to wear her down, and so triumph. Nor for her part was she seeking to kill it, but only drive it into the loch and confine it there again, as Brendan once had done.

They dueled with minds and wills: Though it could wound the wind, as Athyn had declared of it, Llacharn was not meant to draw the Orm's blood but to get the mastery in other ways. And it was well for Athyn that she understood this, for had she tried to slay the Peiste, who for all its brags and pufferies was a beast of the Otherlands and subject to Arawn, she should have lost her chance at Morric.

For Arawn said 'defeat,' not 'slay'; and I am glad of it. I had hated to kill this creature; there has been goleor of killing, one way or another…

At one point in the combat she even touched the stone in the cathbarr she still wore, thinking it might help her as it had in Cartha Galvorn; but the stone was cold and dark. The Orm noticed, and bugled dreadfully, the echoes flying out over the loch; after a shaken moment Athyn was more shaken still to realize that the creature was laughing at her.

"Think you a faerie pebble will help? Nay—but only free me! Join your power to mine and together we can steal the seas. I shall bring you pearls from the deep places, show you such castles and mountains as have no equal on the Dry Land." The Orm's voice was seductive, its power all but palpable; but as it saw Athyn shake her head it took another tack. "Undertake no duel in falsehood; wise words those. How then do you dare this duel with me, false as you have been?"

"I have not been false, finless fish," said Athyn, stung. "Seldom in all my life, and never where it counted."

"Not?" The Orm's voice held only honest curiosity. "Not false in your judging of those who wronged your mate? Not false in your Long Hunt? Not false in your claim to the crown, your marriage to the very lord you seek to save?"

At that she turned, and she smiled, and the Orm, seeing that smile, in a great alarmed huish of sloshing water drew back to deeper depths.

"And there, beastling, is your mistake," said Athyn calmly. "For the falsehood is yours; and it has cost you the fight, and your freedom also."

But the Orm was not yet ready to accept defeat, though she could sense it felt the truth of her words, and as the beast forced her back up the shore it snaked its neck down and bent the full light of its eyes on her. Athyn, remembering Allyn's word, threw up a hand to keep the sight away, so as not to inadvertently cross its glance with her own. At the outset of the fight she had had a quick glimpse of those eyes—silver-green, with a hot red pinpoint of flame coiling at the center—and she was desperately anxious not to repeat the sighting. *Those eyes can control thousands, as a snake can trance and fascinate a bird. Still, they shall not spellbind or glamour me...*

And then her own vision was filled entirely with beating white wings, her ears with the sound of soft thunder; there was a cool lightness round her throat and a wind in her face. She looked up, and all but dropped her sword in her surprise.

The necklace of silver swans that Morric had given her, before he left for Kaireden and death, had come to life. A flight of huge white swans now swooped and belled round her, so many that she could not see the loch, nor scarcely the Orm before her. Their feathered bodies shielded her, their wings a living blindfold, protecting her from the eyes of the Orm of Glora.

Athyn took the moment to swing Llacharn round, and just as the Orm's glance flickered and fell she caught it in the blade's reflection. Like a looking-glass was the polish on that blade, moon-bright; the Orm's gaze, with which it had hoped to enthrall Athyn, was turned back upon itself. There was a blaze of orange-red, so bright that it seared Athyn's aftersight vivid green, and giving a great roar of rage and despair the Orm fell back into the water with a monstrous splash.

The wave that rushed ashore then came nearly to Athyn's waist; it all but knocked her off her feet, but driving Llacharn into the gravel of the shingle she clung to the hilt until the water fell away.

"I will not slay you," said Athyn, gasping, leaning on the sword, the swan necklace once again cold silver at her throat. "Not slay you, Orm, but as Brendan did before me I command you take yourself down into this water, which from now shall be called Loch Bel Draccon for your sake, the Lake of the Dragon's Mouth—for indeed in all our struggle you never shut it once—and I bind you in Glora, with a promise; in the fulfilling of which shall lie your freedom."

"And what promise is that?" asked the Orm, hopefully, sullenly; though it was very pleased indeed not to be slain, and not half so displeased as it let on.

"That for my sake you shall help the next person who calls you forth in my name, and you shall dwell here in Loch Bel Draccon until one who brings this sword to you again bids you help at need."

"I will promise," said the creature readily. "I will not mistake *that* weapon... Nor shall I heed the evil little sea-cow names the ignorant and cowardly may give me in the meantime, howsoever much those names might hurt."

Athyn hid a smile at the Orm's mournful self-pity; if truth be known, she very much liked the beast. But she had one more task here... She drew Llacharn from the shingle and thrust it through the baldric loop, and stood straight-backed before the Orm.

"A Pheiste," she said in the ancient Gaeloch, in formal address, and at the old high name the Orm swelled itself proudly big in the water; its long neck arched, the frills fanned out, its mane rose all along its length. "Bear me over the water, to the Forest in the Sea."

The Orm raised one of its huge spade-shaped flippers; Athyn stepping cautiously upon it vaulted from there to the Orm's back, where she forked the huge powerful neck behind the bristling mane as easily as she might have backed Rhufain. *What goleor of strange steeds to bear me on this quest... First the*

Ghost Mare, and now the Great Peiste; the Star Elephant that carried me to Kaireden, and the Lion of Connacht that brought me home...

Then, carefully, riding high in the sudden wind-chop, the Orm sailed out to cross the width of the newly named Loch Bel Draccon, heading to Collimare. Athyn, though she did not relax for one heartbeat, found herself enjoying the sensations of the ride: the strength of the giant creature, the easeful grace with which it plowed the cold dark waters. *Mighty Mother! I would dearly love to see how it must move beneath the surface, how it hunts, how it disports with its kindred in its own domain...*

"Another time for that, I promise," said the Orm, not turning its head, and Athyn smiled.

Coming to the shore of the island, the Orm turned side-on to the shingle in a spray of foam. Athyn walked down the curving flipper as coolly as if she descended a wheelstair in her own palace, and then leaning forward she patted the beast's neck with real affection, scruffling the stiff red mane.

"I give you thanks, Orm of Glora," she said in the High Gaeloch, standing away then and bowing to the creature, who arched its neck almost to the water in return courtesy.

"Until again, Athyn Cahanagh," answered the Orm, and sank sudden as a stone into the dark smooth waters of the loch.

Shivering a little in her wavesoaked clothing, Athyn trudged uphill to the center of the island, where a rocky ridge rose higher than the surrounding ground. Touching Llacharn to the solid granite, she thought a doorway, and steps leading down to a cave, and light blooming like lichen upon the stone walls; and it was all there. Going down the wide shallow stairs, she came to a cavern that opened in the stone like a clearing in a forest. All round was granite, marble, basalt, rocks that had been born and bred in the deep wombs of firemounts, ignomorphics, gray, green, purple, white. But here a broad streaky bed of limestone ran through, laid down by a predecessor of the loch above Athyn's head, full of fossils of creatures that had perished millions of years before ever a Kelt set foot on the planet; a palimpsest of vanished life.

In the center of the cavern a rough oblong pillar of gray granite rose up. It was being slowly ornamented by the limestone-laden water dripping onto it from the cave roof; millions of years old in the making, maybe, yet it came but level with her chest. In the flat center top of it there was a lengthwise slot, a crack wide enough to take a blade, and into this natural scabbard Athyn of the Battles set Llacharn the Flamebright, and hallowed it about with mighty spells. And when she was done, the sword had vanished, the stone was as it was—save that there was now upon all four faces the carven image of a sword.

An unhewn dolmen... Here it is safe concealed. And the one who is meant to draw it from the stone will have the vision to see how it must be drawn, and the courage to draw it. Another shall come and go and come again, and the last shall wield the sword and call the Orm.

"Sleep thou," she said aloud to the sword in the High Gaeloch. "Lie hidden here for half a thousand years and thrice that again. And the great Orm of Glora, or its children, will know the one who brings thee to the Light."

She laid a hand on the carven semblance of the hilt, lovingly, one last time, and bending kissed the image of the blade. *It is my work, and yet not so; Morric is in it, it is for him that the sword was made; and Allyn of the Sidhe, and Gwyn, they are in it, it is made for them and their folk also... And Gavida is in it, and Arawn Lord of Annwn, and Malen my protectress, and all my Gweriden and Gwerin— The sword is for Kelts and Keltia; and if it be not the Sword that does the true task in the end, it will serve for the work that is to come...*

Athyn turned to gaze upon the sword one last time. *At least in this life's round...* She raised a hand then, much as she had done on Kaireden; but instead of thinning and opening as the stone of Morric's entombment had done, here the stone grew solid and shining, and closed behind her like the waters of the loch after the Orm had passed; of the cave no trace remained, and ascending the stairs she sealed the doorwall behind her. They might build upon this site in time to come—a fane perhaps, an annat or a llan, the Sidhe would doubtless prod them—but the cavern would remain, the sword would be hidden; and found also.

And the ones who would come here: What would they be like, those whose dán was set already? What need would bring them, or drive them? They would be Kelts, right enough; but the straits they might suffer—Athyn recalled images she had beheld in dreams. *The wars, the terror, the famines and droughts, the plagues and deaths and all the other fates I saw... Were he here, Allyn would remind me that tomorrow's dán is to tomorrow. Well then. Let it rest.*

Again Arawn's hall, again the same folk she had left there, though this time they did not greet her, nor she them. Instead, she stood before the god, the baldric hanging empty at her side, and waited him out.

At last Arawn spoke, as one who likes not what he must admit but knows he must accept it. "You have the promise of the Peiste, and the sword forged in Gavida's smithy set in the stone. Two parts of your task are done."

Athyn nodded. "Now remains but one; and then your bargain must be met, the promise kept."

"That is true," said Arawn, "and I shall keep it. But before your last task there are some things I would have you see. You have seen them all before. Now you shall know their meaning."

And as he spoke the hall faded round them, and she saw again those things she had seen in nightmare: the black ships sailing blacker seas, turning for those fearful gates of ocean; saw a howling battlefield as through a red veil, gaunt starved barely human figures dropping in fields and streets; heard things strange and terrible, geisa droma-draíochta; and over it all echoed the words of a great living darkness, "Therefore came I against you."

Close and near yet somehow distant she heard Arawn's voice. "See what may come of your chosen course: the Combat of the Red Wind, a battle where no two will recognize each other because of the wind-driven blood that will hang in the air; Samhra Marenna, the Summer of Near Acquaintance, the Hunger, when no two can recognize each other because of the gauntness of starvation that will be upon them; and worse things beside." But what that huge dark voice had meant, or whose it was, he did not say.

"Must this be?" she asked steadily, though she was shaking all over. "Because of what I do here?"

"Since you have not yet done what you shall do," said Malen, "who can say what may or may not come of it? But what of that Shadow you once spoke of to your lord? How if you could not see it, it was sure to be standing behind you? Are you brave enough to look upon it at last as you have never looked upon it before, face to face?"

"You brought back from Kaireden the body his true self inhabited," said Etain when Athyn remained silent. Her voice was full of wonder, as if she marvelled at the feat and would remind Athyn she had the right to do the same.

"Marbh nach anam: dead without life," said Athyn evenly. "Fair as it is, that is not he, that body; a vehicle, a shell only, a garb he put on in this life, a costume of great beauty that fitly clothed the soul within. But all the same I could not bear that it should lie in foreign ground."

"And this now?" asked Gwyn.

"Anam nach marbh, alive without death. That is the true Morric; ever was, ever shall be..."

"And you would have the two one again?" asked Malen, though it was no question. "Be very sure now of what you ask."

Athyn breathed an incredulous laugh. "I *would* have that,

and I *am* sure, and I *have* asked it. How many more times must I say it? For it was not yet the time for Morric to be apart from himself, or he and I to be parted one from the other."

"Are you then so wise? Wiser than the gods, to see all possible ends?"

Athyn began a hot angry protest, but Malen lifted a white hand. "Though here the count of years is reckoned by a different measure, time is strangely gone by in the world outside," said the goddess. "Only remember: Having achieved this, having passed and returned from Pair Dadeni, once you return to the world with your mate your life is fixed. Your lives for his living, you said. For you the Wheel will stop. Do you hold by your word?"

Athyn felt not hesitancy but a small cold touch upon her heart. *Mighty Dâna... Well, howsoever it may be, we shall be together, he and I, and I would give more even than lives to have it so...*

"It is my word," she said at once. "I hold by it indeed."

"And you may yet have more than you have asked."

A voice that had not until now been heard in the hall, a harsh voice, yet somehow musical: Malen's raven, Brónach, the Sorrower, had spoken from her place upon her mistress's shoulder. Seldom was her voice heard apart from the battlefield, when the War-red War-queen rode in her chariot upon the clouds of strife, and Brónach would hover high above the slain, shadowing the field with her wings, her cries and Lanach her mate's the last sounds in the ears of the dying. But though the gods waited, Athyn made the raven no reply.

"You are by no means the first to seek this of me, Athyn Cahanagh," said Arawn then. "Nor will you be the last. Though you are the first to come here before my face, did you think you were sole and singular in such desire? Nay, it is in all the tales: Other folk, loving as you do, resolute as you are, have sought to make the same bargain; and no matter their love or resolve, no matter even their success, in the end they fail ever and forever. Mortals simply will not heed: Tell a harper not to turn round to behold his wife until they have left my palace, he turns around; tell a princess not to speak to her lord before the Gates of the North are shut behind them, she speaks. They listen, but they do not hear."

"I have read those tales myself," said Athyn, mightily vexed. "And there is more to them than mortal failing. That harper turned to look at his wife not out of intemperance but to help her when she stumbled on the steps. And the princess spoke only to warn her prince of a poison snake near his hand when he rested in the sun. Should they then have been punished so straitly?"

"That is not the point. They were commanded, and they did not obey. The reason does not matter."

"Then, by Kelu, I say that it should, and must!" Athyn was of a sudden flame-white with fury. "I cannot accept that unthinking obedience should determine of so mighty an outcome, or that the Alterator would so decree, or that the Goddess and the God ordain, or the Highest allow."

Arawn was unmoved. "That is not what we are here to try. Again I give you warning: You have already incurred dán unlike any other dán that ever was, and even more if you insist on claiming that which you have come for."

Athyn's face was calm again, and dark as thunder. "This is the reward I ask as I was promised. Nothing else shall suffice. And I will not say it again."

The Doomsman sighed. "Well then. White your world, it shall be as you will have it. Be very sure that henceforth such bargains shall be strictly guarded against. But one more thing you must learn—" He fell silent a moment, and when he spoke again asked a question to which Athyn herself had long wished a proper answer. "Why think you the Sidhe have shown you such favor and friendship down the years?"

Athyn laughed aloud, puzzled at the turn of mood. "Not for any special virtue of my own, I am quite sure! Well—for that I did them once an honest service, and kept my word to them after; why else?"

"For the oldest reason of all; and that is kinship," came a voice from behind her, and the voice was Gwyn's.

He came forward to stand facing her, his fair face alight, and she shook her head, smiling.

"This is no news, amhic," she said. "The queen your mother told me as much, that day in A'Mhaighdean, when she made me free of my magic: that through Brendan mac Nia I had kinship with the Shining Folk. But so do thousands in Keltia; it is by no means a rare thing to boast so honorable a tie."

"Not so, ingheann: The degree of our kinship is closer and nearer than that, though it shall confound you to hear it—or anger you, for that you were not told the sooner."

She turned in surprise, for it was Allyn who had spoken; and as she looked on him the laughter in her face began to fade, like dawnfrost from a winter window when the sun gets high enough to warm the upper airs.

"What then? Only tell me swiftly"—she shivered once—"for I think I already know what you will say..."

"You and I are close indeed of kin," said Allyn. "One day in spring I saw a maiden walking in the hills. She was brown-haired and green-eyed, fairer in my sight than any maiden of my kindred, and I loved her on the instant, there on the green hill side. Lorn she was called, and she was the Maid of Astyllen, of the House of the Findhorn Aoibhells. For love she came with me beneath the mountain, and for her beauty and her strength we called her Ydarragh, the Oak-maiden. Of her grace she gave me her heart, and we were wed; of our love a child was born to us—births come easier, it seems, to a union of mortal and Sidhe together than of a mating of two of my own folk, or two of yours. But, being mortal, she longed for her own world, and often went back to it; and there in time she died, my maiden of the oak-trees, and I mourn her still. Yet our daughter grew and thrived, and in time came to wed a worthy lord and bear a daughter of her own. And so it is that Dechtira, daughter of Lorn and Allyn, known among us as Síonarân, Silverstorm, was your mother. I am your grandsir,

your mother's father; you are of our blood, kin beneath th
hill."

He paused, for Athyn had made a small sound, and Gwyn
stepping forward put a comforting hand upon her shoulder.

"That is where your gift of wild-magic has its origin," con
tinued Allyn presently, even more gently than before, "and
why, dying, your mother laid such geis on you, to spare yo
from it. I was too late to save her on the field where she died
my own daughter, the field where you were born; I wa
thwarted, and I came too late. Therefore I put it into Cormac
heart to save you, that something should be preserved aliv
from the wreckage of my hopes. All your life I have watche
and warded you, and shielded you as I might or your dá
allowed. For your sake I besought Dâna Rhên for certai
graces: to send you the light from the holy mountain, to brin
you under the hill to assist at Gwyn's birth, that you might b
his fostermother, to the blessing and benefit of both our races
I it was who sent the wolf to you that night in the snow, th
Faol-mór, and bid the Ghost Mare bear you in Elmet that day
I armored you as only our kin are armored, and saved you o
the scaffold, and went beside you in battle. When your lor
was slain I journeyed with you on your Long Hunt, and eve
to Kaireden, though you knew it not, and when still you woul
not give him up for gone I rode with you here to fetch hir
home." He paused, and looked upon Athyn with love. "Al
this I did for my Oak-maiden, and her child, and hers; daugh
ter's daughter, will you not turn to me?"

But despite that entreaty, it was not Allyn's face Athyn
sought but Gwyn's, and in it she read bright confirmation; i
Etain's the same, and compassion too, and this it was con
vinced her at the last.

"Cormac never knew, nor Maravaun," said Athyn then, i
a drowned voice. "But I, I think, I have always known." He
face blazed with light and tears as she looked upon Allyn. "It i
a thing I could wish to have been told sooner; but, lord, neve
could I love you more as my grandsir than I have done as m

friend..." A smile began to steal over her features then, as she recovered herself enough to jest. "And if perhaps I have not ever behaved to you as a dutiful grandlass, my sorrow—hard it would be to do so, to one who looks to have no more years on him than my Morric himself!"

Allyn laughed. "Now there speaks my Oak-maiden once again! You favor her greatly; proud would she be of her blood this day."

"I shall be the last of that blood in Keltia," said Athyn presently. "For though my lord be won back, it is on me that no child shall come of us; Keltia is our only clann, and now the Middle Kingdom also—and I am glad. But what of the promise, and the debt?"

Arawn stirred, and all turned to him. "Though argument might be made that the debt should be set aside, that it was engineered if not to thwart dán then certainly to twist it, I will allow it nonetheless; let be. But this shall never happen again, however clever a pleading is made. Dán was not meant to run backward; once is more than enough."

"I care nothing for that," said Athyn, and here her eyes went blade-gray. "I may not be the first to seek this of you, Lord of Annwn, but by all gods, I swear that I shall be the first to win it of you."

Arawn smiled suddenly within the depths of his hood; the air of the hall subtly and rhythmically altered to reflect his mood, a visible dance. "Of a truth is it said: None but a king may vie with a king."

"He has been yours," said Athyn then, with a smile that matched his in mood and meaning, and now she straightened her shoulders, drawing in her strength as for fíor-comlainn, the greatest of any she had faced. "But now he is mine again; indeed he has never ceased to be mine, nor shall ever cease to be so. I will vie with you, king to king, and let all the Three Creations bide the issue."

chapter thirty-three

The one you seek: Unless you bring him with you,
he is not here.

—*Arawn Rhên*

It was not as Athyn had thought it would be.

As she nodded once to Arawn, as one who says
Proceed, the great hall was transformed around her; or else
it was that her vision was raised to another plane of sight or
Sight. It was the House of the Cauldron, golden-roofed, silver
floored, copper-walled, with pillars of crystal, pure and cloudy
alternately, that went up like flames of ice and water between
the silver and the gold. The mist was gone now, and Athyn
could see the true dimension of the chamber: Bigger it was
than the Hall of Heroes, than Turusachan itself, its span was
greater than provinces, than planets. Yet for all its vastness
somehow she could see to the very walls, for around those
walls were ranged nine high thrones of cloud-white marble.
And in those thrones sat nine veiled women, and nine tall
hooded warriors with drawn swords stood between; none
spoke, or gave other sign that Athyn could discern.

In the center space facing the high seats of Arawn and
Malen upon the dais was another low dais, and upon it burned
a clean immaculate white flame, plumed and crowned; it
blazed under stars, for the roof had gone now, or perhaps it was
instead that one might see through it, to the open skies arching clear dark blue above, skies such as Athyn had never yet

seen in Annwn—all the mighty constellations in no configuration any star-pilot had ever beheld, stars that bloomed and blazed, misty globes of bluewhite light.

And at the heart and center of this splendor unparalleled sat atop the second dais a plain cauldron: a pot merely, an iron pot, large and plain and black and quiet, such as could be found in any cookplace or bathhouse in Keltia. But there clung about that seeming humble cauldron a power before which the mightiest would have bowed in terror and in reverence and in love.

Athyn never doubted that she was seeing the world as it was, as the gods see it. *Pair Dadeni… This is the Star at the Heart of the World, the Cauldron of Rebirth, the Well of Souls, the Gate of the Goddess. The dead who come to the Pair are reborn, the nameless named, the wounded healed. As for what may befall the living who shall come to it…well, that is what I am about to learn.*

And even as she thought so, and gazed so, Arawn raised his hand, and the true and holy nature of the Pair stood upon it; it came through with the light of a thousand gold and opal dawns above crystal mountains. That true Cauldron was of polished bronze, iron-dark, sun-bright; so vast was it that the very moon might roll in the hollow heart of it. It was inlaid with blue stones—skystone and seastone, sapphire and lapis—and bluer enamel; river-pearls ringed its rim. The image of Queen Keridwen Herself shimmered on the one side, that of the Cabarfeidh upon the other; the seas and the stars and the mountains sang together from its depths.

As for Arawn, he flamed skyward, unhooded now, Doomsman, Lord of Annwn, his crown burned among the stars; and Malen queen of love and war greeted Dôn Rhên, who was the crowned tenth amongst the nine veiled throned women attendant upon the Pair. As for the hooded warriors they spoke no word and did not stir.

The raven Brónach upon Malen's shoulder gave one harsh cry, and in answer to her call the swans of Athyn's silver necklace, Morric's gift to her for love and loyalty, beat up a second time, greeting the Cauldron as it came into existence. They were black swans now, flying round her where she stood, a wreath of downy darkness, a swirling cloud of smoke. A dark plume sailed spiraling down to land at Athyn's feet; a wingfeather of one of Brónach's own pinions brushed her cheek, and where it touched, its fine soft edges sharp as steel, it drew a line of tiny rubies against her paleness, bright minute undrying beads of blood.

Athyn stared at the Cauldron for a long time, her eyes blurred with tears or the light that came off it soft as rainglow. *So beautiful—I could look upon it forever.* She laughed, and the sound was joy. *And now perhaps am I about to have that very wish... I have been here before, all of us have; but never are we permitted to remember. Stepping through the Cauldron either way takes that memory from us. Now, when once I step through it, all my lives forever to come shall be taken from me; this life will be the last that I shall know, the strangest life that I have ever known. Whatever I might have been or seen, done or won, earned or learned, all that ceases here. It is met. It is met. And the thing ends with me...* As if from a vast and echoing distance she heard a clear strong voice.

"Stranger in the Hall, what name and rank have you?"

Athyn opened her mouth to answer, but shut it again almost at once. In that place she liked not to claim her title and rank as queen: Crowned though she was with Nia's fillet— and she had worn it here with a purpose—it seemed unworthy, not correct, and also she knew very well that they knew very well who she was, and what right she had to claim so. *By all my lives to this moment I am by no means a stranger to this Hall; they only wish to hear how I shall call myself before them, and more than I know may ride upon it...* Then the answer came to her, and she smiled within her as she spoke, without boast or vaunting, merely as one who says what is so.

"I am Athyn, called Cahanagh; my rank in Keltia is Distain."

And that was purest truth, for in Keltic law the distain is that one who stands against all comers for the sake of the dúchas or the lordship or the kingdom, to be first upon the field; before any invader shall come to point of sword with any of the folk therein the distain must face him. *And that is what I do, right enough...*

Before her stood the one who had inquired; darkhaired, gray-eyed, a woman in a white cloak set about with red stars. She had a look of the Sidhe, save that the look was higher and finer, if such a thing could be; and the thought was on Athyn that she had seen her before. The woman saw, and smiled, and her appearance subtly altered, so that Athyn gasped in sudden recognition.

"Dâna I am," she said then, "and among many others also I am Tarleisio. I it was who at Allyn's beseeching tuned a soldier's ear to a newborn's cry, who set the jewel alight atop Sheehallion, with whose blessing Allyn brought a young lass beneath the faerie hill to aid a birth; and who, one day on a strand near Tamon Acanis, gave Morric Douglas a word that could not save him."

"My lord never does listen where it most might do him good," said Athyn with rueful fond exasperation, but awe had mounted like a wave into her face. *This is Dâna—Dâna! She who is the living link between Kelts and gods—a goddess, yet the foremother of all our folk, of whose house and line were sprung Nia and so many others, so high...and I both proud and humble in face of her...*

"All things that are, or were, or will be, are all here in this place." Dâna's words were no rebuke but rather a reminder, of something Athyn had forgotten, or merely had neglected to remember.

And that too means Morric...

"Sorrow is known, and the end of sorrow also is known," said Dâna then, perceiving her thought, and Athyn hearing the divine compassion in the goddess's voice closed her eyes, lest she should die of it where she stood. And crumpling then at Dâna's feet she buried her face in the red-starred cloak, like a child in its mother's skirts, and wept.

But the end of sorrow is indeed known, at least to the gods, and if vengeance may be done with so too may be weeping; and when Athyn lifted her head again her storm of sobbing had calmed. She had no smallest idea of how long she had wept—in that land it could have been millennia as easily as moments—but though tears still stood upon her cheek peace was in her eyes. So many there had been to lament, not Morric alone—Cormac, Lyleth, Nilos, her parents Dechtira and Conn, those of the Gweriden who had fallen in the fight—losses that had not been given the grief that should have properly attended. Though each had been keenly felt, often there had not been time to sorrow but only to survive, and afterwards other demands took precedence.

But here in Dâna's presence she gave them all the mourning they deserved of her. And though some might have found it strange to think on, Athyn wept too for those she had slain on her Long Hunt; or rather for the need that had been on her to have slain them. *It could so easily have been other, so dearly do I wish it had been so. For they had it ever and always in their own choice: not to murder and betray, not to slander and libel and lie, not to comport themselves in viciousness and vice. Yet all those evil things they chose to do; and once they chose so, I had no choice but to do as I myself did choose… And that is what I grieve for; not the choices I made, but the necessity of choosing.*

Now Athyn rose and stepped forward with purpose; her wolf threw back his head and howled thrice, but in all that vast hall none spoke or moved to hinder her. Even Arawn Doomsman made no sign. She saw now as the gods saw: No more did the great Pair appear to her as a cauldron, but stood open before her like a gateway into cloud and mist and fire. Around it and before it the black swans circled like the eye of a feathered storm, and without fear or hesitation, with certainty and love she stepped through the rushing wind of their wings, through the ring of their passage, and entered in to the unknown. No ground was beneath her foot, no light upon her path; yet she cast a light of her own where she strode strongly on.

I have stepped living into the Cauldron of Rebirth; this is its true nature that only the gods have known, that only the dead do behold, when they are born to between-life and then again born to life in the world. They cross it both ways, and so now shall I, and my Morric with me; and then never again. I have sworn it.

So did Athyn Cahanagh go down into hell.

Annwn had been left behind. This was a place that had no name; or at least none that Athyn knew. It was a country of paradox: There was cold fire that did not burn but froze; a wind from the stars that blew from all airts at once; unsolid earth that would not bear her up; dry water that did not quench but parched. And over all a mist that could not be seen save with sidesight, but only felt.

When Athyn looked up, for a moment she was almost fooled into thinking she had stepped back into the everyday world. It seemed an earthly sky above her: The stormriders were out, the gath-an-dubha, the scudding gray and white clouds that stream on the crosswinds running before a storm; the storm-ghosts also, those dark undulations seen in a rainstorm, when fitful wind-gusts sheave and scatter the rain like a field of wheat. Yet there was no rain, no storm; only the strange shifting light and endless wind.

But the mist was real enough. It seeped into Athyn's bones like frozen rust, turning all that was strength within her to sorrow, and she felt herself faltering. At her side Allyn mhic Midna—she had not even known he had come with her through the Pair, though she did not turn to look—spoke to give her heart.

"Ah, the memory of mortals— Did I not tell you you would know the moment when you saw it—the moment of correct need—and that I would be with you when it came? Well then! Put you your power against the mist. Call upon that which is within you and has ever been, your mother's gift to you; for it comes to you from us, and through us from the gods, and the time for its using is now."

"I am nearly spent," said Athyn, and it was true, for never otherwise would she have said it. The trials and all that had come before them had taken heavier toll of her than she cared to admit; she had not just now confessed her flagging strength to crave indulgence but because it was simple fact. *Never have I asked quarter in any battle I have fought, not about to start now...*

Then by some grace, or Someone's, Morric's face was before her in the mist, beautiful and sorrowful as the daytime moon, and seeing the vision she straightened as if a string had been pulled in her back, caught again to the moment and the task; and she called upon whatever power she had left or could otherwise come by—the power that had ever been hers.

She glanced aside as the power began to rise, but Allyn was not there. Perhaps he had never been there but only her need of him, his presence a mere phasma or hallucination. Yet even that had been enough to suffice her, had supplied her with what she required to go on; and she sent after her new-revealed grandsir wordless loving thanks.

Thou too—in the High Gaeloch that is the speech of the Sidhe among themselves—*there was dán in this for thee also; for Lorn Ydarragh, and for thee...*

But whatever its source, strength now flooded into her, a bright tide to roll back the mist; words came, and she spoke them with a vehemence, knowing that she could do so, if she chose so, just exactly as she said, just as she did please.

"I will quench the sun and starve the moon! I will drown the Dry Land with every stream and river and sea and fountain in Abred, and burn the beds of every spring salt or sweet! I will bind the winds in a cave from now until the battle at the end of the world! All this shall I do, and more, and more, sith that you let me pass."

She awaited no response but went forward unhesitant. And the fire feared her and fell fainting back, the water drew its silver skirts aside; the shifting earth grew firm beneath her feet, the wind whispered down from a shouting gale to the gentlest warm breeze that ever had visited her face. But her power was well awake: She towered now as Arawn himself, her head among the stars, the coronet that sat upon her brow blazing like the Plumed Dancer; she stretched out her right arm over the empty lands, and her voice was as a silver battle-horn, a hai atton to the gods.

"Give me room and stand away! By the Wood and the Field and the Mountain, I shall declare my mind in Annwn! I announce my will in all the seven hells and all the lands and earths and out amongst all stars!"

And so did she announce it. It was for this alone that she had come: to claim Morric Douglas back from death. For this had her dán been decreed, her fate spun; for this her power had been born in her before the world was made. She declared her cause for coming, and her cry rocked the Otherlands; it echoed far beyond Annwn.

In towered Turusachan they heard her, and the walls fell. They heard her on Gwynedd, where the Orm of Glora snouted out from Loch Bel Draccon, streaming water, turning his eared and fearful head from side to side. On Erinna they heard her very clear; horses neighed in alarm and galloped wild and masterless over the Elmet plain. In all the Keltic worlds her shout rang loud, calling the seafolk up from the green depths and troubling Neith himself upon his crystal throne beneath the hill. By wold and by wave they heard her, by forest and fountain, by plain and peak; they heard her in the cities and in the towns, in villages and on far farms, though they knew not what they heard. And she spoke on unceasant, the power in her words rolling endless as the thunder: What she said lit flame upon the heather, set a light in the deep woods; it coaxed the levin from clear skies, it broke the darkness between the stars. She spoke; and she was heard.

So it was when Athyn Cahanagh announced her will in hell.

And then all walls fell: Before her now there was a vast plain that might have been land or ocean; she could not tell, it was all one gray, and seemed both, or perhaps it was neither. But at its nearer shore lay awaiting her a ship of crystal that glowed in the dimness; and some say there is ever a crystal ship waiting there for travellers in those lands.

Athyn stepped into it confidently, and at once it loosed itself from its mooring and sailed out; diamond-hulled, silver-masted, carrying neither oar nor sail. Where it sailed, and how long, and whether it sailed land or ocean, waves or hills, seas or skies, she never knew; it left a trail of elf-fire in its wake. But at the end of the sailing, for end it had, there was only black dark; or not darkness so much as the absence of light, which is by no means the same thing.

She had come to the Walls of the World. Yet even here there is ever a way out, or around, or through, for a door hung before her in the dark, a door unsupported, set into seemingly nothing but the air itself: a door of old dark oak, studded with gold nails thick as Athyn's wrist, hasped and bolted with thirteen bolts of iron black and ancient, against which magic metal the Sidhe themselves might not prevail. *Deveradûr, Oaken Door; this has been here from the First...*

"Here is a door was opened beforetime," said Athyn aloud, though none seemed near to hear her; she knew better. "I open it against that other opening; in law and love I open it."

She laid her hand to the latch, but it would not lift; she tried again, harder, putting shoulder to it, all her strength against it. But not even did it rattle in its frame, and at last she fell back. *I will not give up, not if I must camp here alone for eternity, build my own leaguer and lay siege to this Door in the Darkness, not so long as my Morric is on that Door's other side—*

*But never was made a door that would not open with the proper
key...*

Then a stab of cold and heat together seared her right arm,
and her muscles turned to water; looking down to see the
wound she surely expected she saw instead Llacharn alight and
dancing in her hand. The voice of Dâna sounded in her head,
clear as a hunting-horn on a winter morning: *All things that are,
or were, or will be, are all here in this place...*

She raised the sword to the salute, then swept her arm back
and brought it down, as mighty and clean a stroke as ever she
had struck in battle. The blade sheared through all thirteen
bolts at once, in a shower of blue sparks, for it had been forged
in Cartha Galvorn, and the Gabhain Saor himself had
watched its forging. Athyn set her hand to the latch again; this
time it lifted, with a strangely everyday click and scrape, a natural earthly sound that was the loudest thing in all that land.
She saluted again, and kissed the blade, then sheathed
Llacharn in the muffling air, and it was gone. And opening the
Door Deveradûr Athyn stepped through it to the other side.

Beyond Deveradûr lies Moymell, the Pleasant Plain; useless is
it to try to describe that place in words to those who have not
seen. Home of the soul between its lives—though not the true
Home—Moymell is a place neither of punishment nor of
reward but of learning. Once each soul in Arawn's presence
has pronounced in judgment upon itself—for only the soul can
with perfect correctness weigh and judge its own flaws and fail-
ings, triumphs and achievings—it betakes itself to Moymell,
where it may contemplate upon all these things together. No
censure or reproach, no useless guilt or endless torments as
some faiths do claim; but acknowledgment and understanding,
truth in clear light. Sin has no place in it save as a tool: the
means by which the divine in each created soul is measured,
before the Highest, against the merely human.

And the length of each soul's stay and education is as long

as seems good and necessary for its growth; the soul itself decides. Some, who are young in Abred and have little yet upon which to work, will be gone on a breath of that endless wind, blown back through the Door like grains of dust; others remain for a thousand years of the world, in high calm contemplation, ordering their deeds until they are ranged and ready, either for the next turn in the body or to move on past the turning Wheel.

All this came to Athyn as she stood framed in the Door, gazing out over Moymell; and tears were on her face, for she had recognized the land instantly; a great call had gone up to her like a chord of mystic music. *This*, this *is what I have been homesick for, ill with longing; when the dubhachas was on me, the hiraeth, when I longed and wept and ached for something I could not name, this place was what I was missing, this is where I was longing to be though I knew it not…and even this is not yet Home…*

After a while she went down from the high place of the Door, descending a long stone staircase through swirling mists toward the sunlit plain below. She was beyond fear now or surprise; so when the cloaked figure appeared by her side she made no start. Intent on what lay before, she had never even noticed when she chanced to be no longer alone. Who walked with her in the mist? Silent and steady the pace, unhurried; no tread rang upon the great stone stair.

"I am the Tacharan," came a quiet voice, after a while, and Athyn for all her high joyous serenity felt a feathering chill. The Tacharan: he—or she—who is Kevarwedhor to the dead between their lives, the Steward of Moymell, second in awe only to Arawn Rhên himself; the Psychopomp, the Guide of Souls.

"The greeting of the One and the Three to you, Athyn Cahanagh," said the Tacharan then. "Your errand is known here."

"The greeting of the gods and the folk to you, Tacharan," she answered. "And so I should think!"

The echo of a smile in the voice, though, like Arawn's own,

the face remained shadowed in the hood. "Indeed. Certain it is you announced yourself loudly enough... But it was very well done."

She could hear the pride and pleasure the guardian of Moymell had in her, but she found nothing to say. *I daresay the Tacharan knows already, and full well, aught that I might speak with words...*

By now they had reached the bottom of the steps, and halted. "Go then," said the Tacharan. "You will find Morric Douglas in a place not too far distant. Only remember, as Arawn Rhên has told you: You may beseech as you please; you may weep and you may whine, you may whinge, beg, plead, entreat, appeal, cajole, implore. But you may not compel. The will is yours; the choice is his alone."

"And you, Tacharan?" she asked, turning to go. "Shall I see you again?"

"I am the Guide of Souls," said the hooded figure, and now the amusement was plain to be heard. "As long as you have a soul, Athyn Cahanagh, I shall be here to guide you."

And the Tacharan was gone; but with that darkling promise Athyn was well content.

And then she was alone in Moymell. *Yet never alone...* Athyn saw all round her nothing but the dead; they could see her, but not one acknowledged her presence among them, a mortal's presence in the body in Moymell. Though they seemed to speak to one another she could hear no word they said, and whenever she tried to address them her voice dried in her throat. But their beauty would have rendered her speechless in any case...

Oh, fair beyond all earthly loveliness are the dead between their lives, when the highest thing which they have achieved in that life just past is the benchmark by which they have judged themselves—the best deed, the noblest feeling, the purest thought—in which appearance and perfection they robe themselves like a cloak of gold. And this is as it should be: Evil has its place in the determining of dán, right enough, but it is good that sways the balance. In the endless gloaming of Moymell the Shadow and the Light are one, and in all the One's creation that is the only place where this is so.

In that long fair summer-seeming twilight Athyn walked through the dead's ranks for what seemed a long time, or else no time at all; thick as autumn leaves in Elmet's woods they were, and as bright and lovely—upon the dead there is no stain. *Wrong it is to call them dead... They are more alive here than ever they were in life.* This *is the true life; that other, that earthly existence—that is the mortal caesura, the pause that slays...*

She walked on and ever on, wondering no more but only rejoicing; all round her was nothing but beauty and fierce bliss. In all the Pleasant Plain no sorrow could she see: If the dead sorrow for the sorrow of the living, for the grief of those they left behind in the world—as even in their perfect peace and wisdom they must surely do—it is grief of so different a nature from earthly mourning that mortals cannot comprehend it; as Athyn could not comprehend it now. *For them our grief like crystal rain, that beats upon a high and endless shield of rainbow glory...*

And then, without warning, she saw him. She saw him, he for whom she had come so far through so much; the sight of him was a sudden arrow through her heart, a flain of joy. His back was to her, but it was he, he and none else in all Annwn: his tallness, the bigness, the leopard-lazy grace of him as he moved, the dark hair and beard, the beauty that was here unveiled to shine forth in its true and perfect nature, of which his earthly beauty, great as it was, had been but shadow only.

She cried out to him then, called his name and tried to run to him, but suddenly she could come no closer, she was bound where she stood, as if chains had been cast close and fast round her. A brightness like whitegold mist was between them now; she could see him still, though all others seemed to have vanished away. But though she called until her voice cracked in her throat and tore like ripping silk, she could not make him hear or turn.

All things that are, or were, or will be... Athyn closed her eyes and let herself be filled from within; love, or power, or both together, found voice and strength united in her will, and she cried out to him once more across the distance and the mist.

"Na tréig mi go buileach no go bráigh!"

'Do not forsake me utterly or forever!'... That cry was a sword in the heart of any who heard it; it darkened all the Pleasant Plain with a chill clouding sorrow such as that bright fair place had never known, the green grief of bereavement that never before now had crossed the Sea or passed the Door. For those were the words of Lassarina Aoibhell when she heard of the death of Séomaighas Douglas her lord, and Athyn cried them now to shake all worlds, and call her own lord to her.

But still he did not turn.

Yet Séomaighas did not forsake his lady, nor she him... Nay, I will not be denied or defeated now—not when I see my beloved before me; not if I must destroy Annwn and Abred and Gwynfyd itself, to come to him again, to hold him once more before I too am destroyed for utter blasphemy. And I would dare even that so long as we might be together before that end... I have been told I may beseech as I like: Well, how better to summon a bard than with a good cast of his own lure? Yet the cast must be of my making, not his, and for all the efforts of many I have ever been an indifferent poet...

But Alaunos Songlord, Prince of Harmonies, or the Holy Awen itself, must surely have taken pity on her or him or both of them, for suddenly the words she needed were there, writ in flame upon the air before her eyes, and she spoke them with a will.

> "Seven long years I sought for thee;
> The magic sword I wrought for thee;
> The beast of blood I fought for thee;
> And wilt thou not waken and turn to me?"

He heard and turned to her.

*   *   *

And then all worlds turned: In the Otherlands a soundless sigh; while in the fields we know, the Hitherlands above, there came a causeless delight—folk turned to one another in smiling puzzlement, suddenly strengthless and breathless with the mystic joy that was upon them.

But on Moymell the mist drew in upon itself, and brightened to the silver blaze of a star come down to earth. Athyn could no longer see her love before her, but before the terror of loss could take hold the very ground of the Pleasant Plain rocked beneath her. And she heard a great glad shout raised up, from whose throats she did not know; but whatever its origin, it rang exultant through Annwn and Keltia and farther realms than both.

'*Dh'éirich an Rígh!* The King is returned!'

And then in the mist-brightness, just where it grew too bright for her to gaze upon, something formed, formed and stood, not so much a darkness as a lessening of brightness; which is by no means the same thing. It resolved into a shape, then a face; then the bright mists thinned, and Morric Douglas came walking back from death, back from Moymell, back from Annwn, back through the Cauldron of Rebirth for the power of his mate's love, stepping through the last veils of light and into her arms.

So in the mists beyond the Door Athyn's lord returned to her; on the Pleasant Plain they found their way to one another once again. And then the Plain whirled round them like a spinstar; clinging to one another, Athyn's arms fast around Morric's back and shoulders and his hands tangled in her hair, they were back in the great hall of Arawn as first she had beheld it.

They stepped once more through the ring of black swans, who in her absence had never ceased to fly, endlessly circling, guarding the entrance to the Pair against all intruders—she had heard the faint far thunder of their wings even beyond the

Door—and as they did so those great dark birds were on the instant silver again, a cold close chain round Athyn's neck. Arawn and Malen stood before them, the Sidhefolk behind; but otherwise the chamber was empty, and the Cauldron itself, the white fire that warmed it, the throned women who sat vigil round it, the sentinel warriors who guarded it, all had vanished away.

Before Athyn looked at aught else she looked up at her lord. The glamour of the Otherlands was fading before her eyes: He looked handsome as ever—the same brown hair and beard, the same blue eyes—but the unearthly fairness was already gone. A touch bemused, paler perhaps than had been his wont, otherwise Morric Douglas was entirely himself, just as he had been when last she had seen him, standing beside her bed in the night, or kissing her and walking away across the field at Mardale. But he had travelled farther than that, and she also, and now he was with her once again.

"I was—away."

He stared at her, love and wonder plain upon his face. They were both trembling; and Athyn would have wept, there was something behind her eyes that was longing desperately for the release of tears, but it was as if her head were hollow and dry as a drum; she could not weep. *There still is work for me to do…*

"Bydd i ti ddychwelyd," said Athyn softly, her hand upon his chest over his heart, as once it had been when she had vowed more to him than even that. *'There shall be a returning for thee'* …

He was as a lifter, a strayed beast grown so weak he must be carried back to the shelter of stable or herd; for all his former strength he seemed not yet securely moored again in his body or in life. To Athyn's fearing eye a terrifying translucence clung to him, and she suppressed the desire to throw her arms around him, to hold him fast in hell's despite.

"You must ground him once more in the world," said Arawn Rhên as from a very great distance. "I summoned his mortal form here from Ni-maen; you have brought his spirit from Moymell. Now he is one and whole again, but it needs more, and only you can do it. Even my power ends here."

And Athyn, who well knew what was needed, kissed Morric gently; and taking his unresistant hand she set his fingertips to the line of blood upon her cheek—thin and fine and neat as a sgian wound, still wet where the Raven's feather had drawn it—and then gently brushed his fingers wet with her blood across his own brow, signing him with the rune Atré, Lastrune, Rune of Ending. A smudge of garnet-red, there for a moment, it shone out and was gone. *Love is enough...*

"While the sun goes southward," she said. "The sunward course with everything."

And there in Annwn she began the low chanting, the great Litany to the God that she had chanted to him at their bridal, and in their wedding bed, the high and mighty attributes of the King of the World.

"Helm of the Gael—Lord of Lightnings—Dragon Warshout—Shield of Fire—King of the Winter—Rider upon Storms—Hunter of the Dawn—Black Rose of Desiring—the Face that Teaches and the Hand that Reaches—"

With every name Morric seemed more solid in himself; and Athyn seeing this threw into the words all her love for him unstinting, all her force of wish and will, the last of her power and her strength unsparing, holding nothing back. *For this is why it was given me, this the moment it was made for, the one for whom it was made... Allyn said I would know it when it came, and so I do—if I have naught left to me after, that is as it was meant to be; upon whom else, after all, would I spend it?*

At the end of the chant, at the height of the raised power, reaching up she undight herself of Nia's silver fillet, and reaching higher set it round his brows. The great clear centerstone blazed out, as Athyn Cahanagh crowned her mate in Annwn as once she had crowned him in Turusachan, and drawing the gold marriage-ring from off her finger, where it had been beside the silver one that was her own, she put it again upon his hand. And all at once he was there, as he had ever been, as he had never ceased to be, as he would ever be: Morric Douglas it was, king and bard, king returned, bard forever; Fireheart also, lover and beloved.

He looked upon her with love and knowledge. He knew her, knew what she had done for him. Knew too what at the last she could not bring herself to ask him, too proud to entreat of him a thing he might not wish to give, knew that it was his alone to choose; and gazing down on Athyn's face upturned Morric made his choice known to his mate and to the gods.

"Who giveth lives for love shall be given more than life; who quitteth the peace of Moymell for sake of love returned shall be requited more than peace."

The hall was gone now; Athyn stood with Morric hand in hand in a place which has no name, which mortal mind has no niche to hold nor words to blazon; behind them were Allyn and Etain and Gwyn.

But above and around and before them were all the crowned and starry ranks, the gods of the Keltiaith, who had watched as Athyn fetched Morric back from death, and who until this moment had not chosen to be seen.

First among them were the High Dânu—Arawn Doomsman, Firstborn of the Absolute and Malen War-queen his mate; Midir tall and grave, and Fionn the Young, he who is Friend-to-mortals, who moves between the worlds as he does please, whose other names are Idris and Gwion and Gwydion ap Dôn; Dôn Rhên and Dâna Rhên, sisters and queens, the Mothers of the Masters of the Mountains; Morna the Valorous and Bríghid of the Fire, Gwener Fairface and Síon of the Storms; Mâth the Ancient and Brân the Blessed, Lugh of the Deft Hand and Lír the Boundless.

And other gods also were there, those who have most to do with men: Alaunos Songlord, Gavida Burn-the-Wind whose mate is Bríghid, and who gave Athyn a most ungodlike wink,

Amaethon the Plowman, Rhiannon of the Horses, Gwenhidw
Cloudherd and her lord Manaan Sea-King, Mihangel who is
also Maharrion, Prince of Warriors, Captain of the Light in
the Last Battle, Aranrhôd who turns her silver wheel and
weaves the dán that Arawn does pronounce.

And above them all in glory were the Divine Couple, the
Twofold Word of Kelu, She Who Made All and He Who
Spoke the Name, the Goddess and the God of many names and
titles. Kernûn and Keridwen—Aengus and Rhian, Donn and
Macha, An Dagda and Modron, Star-queen and Sun-lord, the
Lady of Night and the Master of the Dawn, the Queen of all
green things and the Lord of Beasts, He Who Frees the Waters
and She Who Binds the Lands, the Mistress of the Wood and
the King upon the Mountain—stood now in Annwn.

Keridwen Rhên it was who had spoken; Her gaze rested
upon Athyn with knowledge and love. But Kernûn Rhên
inclined His head that bore the great antlered crown, the
Coron-rhaidd of the Cabarfeidh, from which the rayed sun
shot forth in splendor, light tangled in the mighty tines.

"Ingheann," He said, in a voice of deepest beauty.

"Athair-athiarna," answered Athyn, and before all the
other gods she sank in a profound curtsey to Them both, such
a reverence as she would have made no mortal monarch, sank
and bowed her head until her face was pressed against her knee
and her hair veiled her face and trailed along the copper floor.

She rose gracefully then, not waiting for Them to bid her
stand, and faced Them without fear. *'On your feet before the
gods!', did not Lyleth ever drum that into us as children? Still, it is
no sin or shame to reverence Them... They are the High Manifest
Word of the Uncreated, Yr Mawreth made known to us in the only
way we can yet know—and yet there is a Third....*

Gathering herself with a deep steadying breath, Athyn
turned her head to the shadow that stood silently beyond the
brightness of the Two; a shadow that did not move but merely
was. Of all divinities here assembled, this was the one Being
the facing of Whom she had indeed dreaded and feared: The

Alterator, Who works in the world the will that Kernûn and Keridwen receive and declare from the One, stood behind and to one side of Their double throne. He, or She, was cloaked in a shadow even more baffling and strangely wrought than that in which Arawn had been clad. Indeed, many there were in Keltia who thought Arawn was himself the Alterator; but here, beholding the true Alterator, or as much of that enigmatic Being as could be beheld by mortal eye and brain and heart, Athyn and Morric saw plain that Arawn, great though he be, was not.

And it was against the Alterator that Athyn had most offended, His the law of dán that she had gone against, oversetting it for her own wish, placing her will above His own, and so her fear was founded. And though she faced Him fearingly, she faced Him resolute, proud in that will and in her deeds. *I do not change it, not now, not ever; I will pay the price, and more beside, and I regret nothing...*

Yet it was not upon Athyn but Morric that the eyes, if eyes they were, were bent; and Athyn feeling the weight of the Alterator's attention made a sudden instinctive move, as swiftly checked, to step protectively between Morric and the God. *I would shield him if I could; but this is his dán as much as mine. His it is also to choose, when once he has heard in full...*

But when voice sounded again in that place it was not the Alterator but Arawn Rhên who spoke; and he spoke to Morric as if none else stood by, telling him of the terms of the bargain Athyn had made for his return. At the end of that telling there was silence in Annwn: the two mortals, the three Sidhefolk, the crowned ranks of gods, all as wordless in that moment as the world before the Three Shouts were given.

At last Morric, never once looking at Athyn beside him but gazing straight as a sword up into the Doomsman's face, spoke to break the hush.

"I did not know. But it is right that I should know. Therefore I offer instead another bargain, in which Alaunos Rhên will stake me: I will play, and if my song can move the gods to weep, then my lady and I go free, as we have been. If they weep not, I give up bardship forever, which for me is as giving up all lives. Yet to my mind, that is neither too great nor too long a sacrifice."

Athyn began a fervent furious protest, but Arawn lifted his hand, and she fell silent; the god bent his head as if to listen to a Voice none else could hear. And now it was not Arawn Rhên but the Alterator Himself Who was heard, and in that voice was the cold of the stars.

"The harp and song of Morric Fireheart, renowned in Keltia, may have trial in this place. Hear my will in this, which is the will of the Highest: Morric Douglas by his music must move all here to tears. If he fails, both Morric Douglas and Athyn Cahanagh shall remain as they are: he in Annwn and she in Abred, to work out the original dán that was built for them, by them, through many lives and deaths, and to bide their next turn upon the Wheel, merely, as others do."

"That is no justice of either man or god!" snapped Athyn, forgetting her fears and her offenses alike. "Was he not sent hence treacherously and unlawfully aforetime? And to win him back did I not perform perfectly, and in good faith, every particular of the tasks which Arawn Rhên did set me? Indeed, as the Gabhain Saor and the Orm of Glora and the Tacharan of Moymell will confirm— And was I not owed by Sidhe and gods alike a boon of my own asking? Aye, and aye, and aye again. Thrice over did I win my lord back from hell; and I swear by Kelu I will have that honored! Or do the gods now make practice of going back on their bargains, and is that a new thing in Annwn?"

But the Alterator made no answer.

"And if I succeed?" asked Morric at length.

The pause was small but terrible. "You shall be together. Trust in that. But you have first to accept, and then to triumph."

"I accept," said Morric at once, before Athyn could draw breath to protest it. "Silksteel," he said with a glance at her, forestalling even a word, and briefly laid his fingers to her lips. He turned away to face again the Alterator. "And I will triumph."

"Do so then on this." Arawn drew from the air a harp-shaped darkness; as he put it into Morric's hands the thing took form. It was a harp indeed, and it was wrought of bones; upon its ghastly whiteness were carven runes in a strange glyphic even Morric had never seen before, and its strings were silver. It seemed to have a life and dán of its own, and he was not at all sure that the harp's purpose chimed with his.

No matter; I will play. Even in the presence of Alaunos Harplord, who is god of music, and all gods else beside. To bring them to weep I play to my love alone; and pray that Moymell did not put me over-much out of practice...I would have them weep for beauty, not for sorrow...but sorrow's tears I will take if I can get them...

"I am still yours," he said then to Athyn, "you are still mine." They exchanged one long unsmiling look; then, well content with what he saw, Morric settled the harp against his shoulder and drew his fingers across the strings. At the first touch they slashed his fingers to the bone, so that his blood reddened the strings, and the harp, and the ground beneath. But he gave no sign that he had even felt it, and smote the strings again. The sound was triumph given music's form; a third time Morric struck the strings, and then the harp of bones performed his will in Annwn.

In that moment Morric Douglas sang to make worlds and destroy them. Peace and pain he sang to them, love and loss; he played to them the awakening from anger and the resting from strife; for them he harped the Joy of the Ground and the Splendor of the Sea and the Glory of the Skies, the Light that was and is and ever shall be, and the Shadow it forever casts.

And of Athyn too he sang: to be with her at the feast or in the fire, in death, or life, or freedom from both, it mattered not so long as they were together. He sang the world into being as he would have it, as none had sung before him save Alaunos himself, and even that Prince of Song was ravished now; he sang, and he was heard.

So it was when Morric Fireheart harped in hell.

But even such song must have an end; and Morric striking the endnotes dared at last look up, and caught his breath. Silence reigned in Annwn, and that was scarce to be wondered at. But so now also did life: Bare-branched trees had put forth leaf and fruit and blossom, streams ran and rang with the music Morric had set dancing in the waters, flowers stood in every corner of the Hollow Land, where never bloom had been. But greater change too was afoot...

Never since the Speaking of the Name had the sun shone in the Otherlands: not the shy bright morn-light, not the shout of noon. But now glory streamed out of the west like blood and gold and purple flame, and the folk who dwelled there wondered to see it. Never before had shadow been cast in Annwn; now their shadows, Athyn's and Morric's, raced away behind them eastward over the edge of the world, keen-cut and tremendous, black and startling against the sudden greenness of the grass.

And upon every face of god and goddess tears glittered in that new and startling light; the beauty of the High Ones was made lovelier still by grief. Even the stern visage of Kernûn was a storm of sorrow, and as for Keridwen the Queen Her cheek was as a flower after rain.

And at last Morric looked upon Arawn, who as Judge of the World would be the one to declare in this matter. His tears were the only tears that mattered, and as Athyn, weeping still, lifted her head to behold her love's face and the god's, she saw the Doomsman's manifest sorrow like a crystal torrent.

"Silksteel and Fireheart—" Arawn shook his head, smiling faintly, brushing away the tears. "Never have I seen more stubborn souls than yours—and I see them all, you know, soon or late... Well. Though Athyn has won Morric's freedom, and Morric hers, still there must be a toll. For Morric, Athyn was tried thrice, and entered the holy Pair to give up her lives to come, for his sake to be judged forever only on the lives she has so far lived;

and for Morric's part he was willing to give up forevermore, for Athyn, the thing that most truly makes him himself."

"That is so," said Athyn calmly. "We did. We are. We will. I was not instructed in magic, only born to it, but even I know that in such matters there is no bargaining. One does not haggle over the purchase of a war-sword or a ritual blade for the High Mysteries, but pays the required price unquestioning; how much less, then, does one chaffer with the Lords of Life and Death for the soul of one's mate."

"But you have paid; both you have paid. You bought Morric's freedom from death by your readiness to give up lives for him." Keridwen's voice came clear and sweet, and yet not as one's who can speak only sweetness. "And he bought yours from lifelessness by the power and sacrifice of his art. The test was the payment, and love the only coin."

"We would set even that payment aside if we could," said Kernûn Cabarfeidh, "but he has dwelled in Moymell and returned to the mortal body, and in the mortal body you have passed the Door. These are things were never done before: You are not the same two souls who met on Tara and wed at Starcross. The entity that is known as Morric Douglas died one death on Kaireden and was here born again to life, but that which is called Athyn Cahanagh has also died and been reborn. You have wrought greatly for one another; but by your love and deeds you have altered dán, and dán must ever be served. Even by us. By us in especial. Only Kelu and those who are with the Highest in Gwynfyd have dán to be their servant."

The voice of the Alterator sounded now like a viol, almost below the threshold of hearing; the other gods fell silent to hear, and Athyn and Morric, hand in hand now, drew themselves straight as spears, as if sentence were being pronounced upon them; for so it was.

"Know then that even on my word Athyn's bargain cannot be entirely amended, for the reasons we have just now heard. This is the dán your love has purchased: You shall not be parted, you shall live and share and love—but you have both been in Annwn, you have both been changed beyond changing, you have changed the fabric of fate. And dán does not run backward."

Now Arawn Doomsman took up the pronouncing. "Yet the Powers decree, and the High Dânu confirm, that it may be set thus far aside: You may share that fate together. You will be restored to one another and to this life, but unlike all other Kelts, unlike even the Sidhefolk, birthless and deathless and changeless you shall be forever, from this hour on. You shall have whatever life you may devise; you shall be together forever if that is what you choose. But from this moment both you are immutable in the world. Neither of you will ripen with mortal years, but live in Abred with the life of the Sidhe. Yet you are neither Sidhe nor mortal; and though you do not age, neither shall you alter, and you may find that a dearer price than you might think."

"That is not so harsh a tax," said Athyn bravely, though she knew already that it was, and would prove harsher and heavier even than she knew.

And Arawn knowing she knew it did not answer. Presently the Alterator spoke again.

"Prophecies I will give to you, for I am the Initiator and the Completer. Quite apart from this day's work you have more than earned them, and you will have need of them on the Road that you have chosen. I warn you now, and you two shall be first of all Kelts to hear it: There is a time coming when magic will begin to die in Keltia and beyond it, when the Warrior's Way will be the only way, when the sword that could not bring magic down will be magic's savior."

"Shall we be there for that fight?" asked Morric.

"Aye and nay. You will be there, but you will not *be* there. But the Gwerin shall ride again in time of greatest need. Mark you the Turning Tower, the Swan of the North. Comes then the Spinner of the Web, and the Wolves of the Gods to hunt him; in those days Gwyn will be Lord of that Hunt, and Caradrúin ride with him to harry the Dark, and Shieldstriker sound the horn that calls the Hounds from the quarry."

"I know not these names, Lord," said Athyn humbly.

"It is not meant that you should know them; only that you should hear them. But you shall know them."

There seemed no more to say; Athyn and Morric made reverence then to Kernûn and Keridwen, and to the Alterator, and to the other gods, and with the splendid courtesy of heaven their civilities were returned.

But Malen Rhên it was who had the last word, Malen, Warred War-queen, whom all her life Athyn had besought as protectress and advocate among the High Dânu; who spoke aside to Athyn Cahanagh as one queen to another, whispering that which they alone could hear, before Kernûn and Keridwen, raising Their hands in benedictory, in valedictory, took the world away.

The westering sun was glittering on the hills, the streams and lochans blazing like brazen shields; the distant woods began to wrap a dim blue mystery about them, as riders on the road, with miles to go before their journey's end, will huddle their cloaks against the rising evening chill, against a stranger chill within.

And in that hushed and hallowed moment, hand in hand, tall and triumphant, with the peace of the gods upon them and the Otherland sunset still burning in their faces, came Athyn Cahanagh and Morric Douglas, together, back from Annwn.

chapter thirty-four

Who has loved has triumphed.

—*Mariota Lennox*

None was there to see their homecoming save Allyn and Etain and Gwyn. The Otherland strangeness was slow to pass: For though Athyn and Allyn had entered Annwn through the lake of Sheehallion on Erinna, on the night of Samhain the Less, when Athyn and Morric returned to Keltia they found themselves instead on Tara, in the Hollow Mountains, on the green slopes of Craiganaeth in the secret vale of Glenshee. Nor was it yet, or again, the first of winter but the last of spring, a cool blue evening of May, one of the months of sacrifice—seven years since Morric Douglas had told his Queen and mate he had an offworld errand.

Though they longed to greet their mortal friends again after so long and unimaginable an absence, Athyn and Morric found themselves glad of the respite thus afforded them, to adjust once more to life and each other, nothing else between. So they spoke to the Sidhefolk, quietly, of where they had been and what had befallen and what would now betide; and then Gwyn and Etain and Allyn were gone, along the airy blazing bell-haunted elftrack, north and east to the Hill of Fare beneath which lies Dún Aengus, chiefest and ancientest stronghold of their folk.

*   *   *

When Morric and Athyn had watched them out of sight into the blue distance, and turned with a sigh from the east to consider their own next journey, they found their friends had had more in mind than a mere welcome-home. Horses they had left them, no mortal mounts but steeds of the Sidhefolk's own breeding, tall and elegant creatures, wise and mannered, with feathered hoofs and tails that swept the ground and silky manes that fell past the points of their shoulders; a black stallion for Athyn, for Morric a milk-white mare.

Suitable wayfarers' raiment had also been provided: plain red cloaks clasped with paired silver stag's-heads; and the high-cantled saddles, tailored as if to their very measures, held packs stuffed thick with other gear and goods.

Athyn was greatly moved by the solicitude of the Shining Folk; yet when she thought of the journey that lay ahead she was both glad of it—*All the more time to be with him, alone, before the world once again takes us up and fetches us away*—and impatient of delay. *I would we were home in Turusachan this instant, or at Roslin, or Starcross; indeed, any blest place where he and I have loved, there to love again*—

But Morric was looking at her, and with an indrawn breath like a stab of flame she knew this was the moment, more than any that might come later; this place as blest as any other, or to be new-made so...

> "His face is light and life to me
> His arms are song and strength to me
> His length upon me as a sword;
> Star of my joy, soul of my name,
> Pulse of my blood, my heart, my flame,
> Crown of my bliss, my king and lord."

So Athyn to Morric on the slopes of Craiganaeth, the green ground beneath them and the heights of heaven above. No account tells how it was, nor should it, when Morric Douglas and Athyn Cahanagh, back from Annwn, came together in love in Glenshee. But Craiganaeth, the Rock of Sorrow, had

ever after a new name: Gwel-y-sidan was it called, and that
means Bed of Silk.

Morric and Athyn had come back to Keltia in the turning
spring of that year. It was a cool spring on Tara, with fresh brilliant dawns, the sun hotter and nearer each day; but still there
were chill nights when fires and cloaks and the warmth of each
other's bodies did not suffice, and sometimes they shivered as
they slept. The weather did not always favor their journey,
though after the endless light of Annwn they were both hungry for contrast, and even spring storms were welcome: the
clear blue glimmering through broken clouds that speaks of
thunder rain on silver leaves; a wet wind upon their faces; and
thunder like the mutter of a distant sea.

Through their own acts and choosing they both had been
reborn; now they needed to be restored. Instead of a triumphal
return to Turusachan, straightway, what was required first was
something grounding, something real; and Athyn thought she
knew what that might be. If Morric was bemused and uncertain, she was strengthless, all but emptied; they both were in
desperate need of careful reviving, and she was the one whose
task it was to do.

On their long slow ride home to Caerdroia, across the
whole width of the Northwest Continent from Glenshee ("No
haste!" Athyn had assured Morric, when he doubted a little of
the lazy pace, "We have been gone long enough that a few
weeks more, or even months, shall make no differ; and we
need this time more than we may ever know"), they slept
rough wherever the nights did find them, in woods, in aban-
doned barns or steadings, even a ruined castle or two.

Sometimes—not often, for they were by no means surfeit
with each other's company, and jealously would not share each
other when there was yet no overmastering need to do so—
they sought hospitality under the hill, in the secret brughs of
the Sidhefolk that they passed; for they were known now to

the Shining Ones, Athyn's kinship with Allyn and Nia's fillet
that Morric carried in his saddlesack their passport and token
to the halls beneath the mountains. Other times they guested
with the mortals who dwelled along their way, and never were
they other than joyfully received. In Keltia it is a privilege as
well as a duty to entertain the chance-come stranger; their
benefactors were not courtiers or nobility but plain Kelts only,
unaware of who the travellers might be, and uncaring; though
Athyn and Morric were Queen and King, had that been
known to their hosts it would have made no jot's differ to their
reception.

For here in Keltia's heart there are no highway-invita-
tions, no inquiries from the teeth outward as to how you are
and how your folk might fare but no hospitality offered; or, if
there is, but mean and grudging: soup watered to the thickness of sweat, meat sliced so thin you can still taste the
knife... But Morric and Athyn were brought back to Keltia
and to life in the old slow honorable way, and that was the
only way in which it could have been accomplished; no
other way better for them, the last thing they needed for
their healing. And it was right that Keltia itself should
restore them.

Yet though they were together as never they had been
before, they were different now from all Kelts else, and on that
long ride home to Turusachan, they had already begun to feel
the keenness of the separation, the finality of that terrible and
eternal divide.

"A dream of summer, and you by me— There was a running
water sang to me one afternoon, the water cold and clean, and
up to my knees; my feet were bare upon mossy rocks; I pitched
my voice, and heart, in harmony with the sound." Morric
shook his head as if to clear it, vexed; ran a hand over his beard
in the familiar gesture. "*Did* I sing so, once? Were we together?
So clear I see it— I think I did once, I think we were. Or did I

but dream it, in Annwn? I dreamed so much there, you know: of you, of us together."

"Nay," she said gently, though her eyes had filled with tears, at his baffled frustration no less than at the memory. "No dream; it was, we were. It was on Erinna, in Connacht, in the first days of the Gwerin; you sang to me as the stream did sing to you."

They were seated by the banks of another stream for the noonmeal, taking the hour's rest afterwards which they had made their pleasant lazy custom. Halfway home now, they were riding through the rolling grasslands just west of Mount Keltia, where the infant Avon Dia, tumbling down to the high plain, becomes a strapping faunt. Athyn, looking round her as she rode, remembered the region well: She had sailed that same river, or not the same, in Annwn, heading westward to the sea.

When she was not looking on the landscape she looked at Morric, so much and so often that he teased her for it, her old familiar hooded-cavebat look. She laughed, but had no shame of it, and certain it was she looked no less; partly because she could never get her fill of looking on him, and partly because she could hardly believe even now that he was once more beside her to be looked upon, and partly again because she dared not take her eyes off him for fear he would vanish away. But there was yet another reason...

In the first days of their return Morric had seemed reluctant to have speech, either with Athyn or with any they met on the road. Herself no foe to silence, she did not press him, thinking that he was but yet unused to it from his time in Moymell, and when the wish or need was on him, he would speak. But though he was open and merry as ever when he did so, and fiercely ardent as ever when they loved, his silences grew, and Athyn began to fear, not his present actions, but her own just past. *Was I right, then—to fetch him, so peremptory, home from Annwn? Arawn said it was for him to choose, and that even my will could not move him if he willed elsewhere; but might it be that merely by my presence there I forced his choice? And in time to come, might not he blame and blast me for it?* So Athyn feared, and watched him as they rode.

Some days further on they turned south of west, climbing up from the floor of the Great Glen, taking a hill-track that wound into the remoteness of the eastern Dales. Coming to a high open valley that though hidden from below had views clear across to the Stair, they drew rein before a snug shuttered bield delved half into the side of a wooded mountain. This was Ty-'n-coed, Tincoats in the common speech; a private haven from the cares of state which Morric had begun to build as gift for Athyn, before he went to Kaireden, and which she herself had ordered completed before she left upon her Hunt.

"And now I know why it seemed so urgent that I do so... It might suit us to take refuge here awhile, anghariad, do you not think," said Athyn uncertainly, for Morric had not dismounted but remained in his saddle, staring at the trees and the glen and the bield as if never before had he beheld such things. The black stallion of the Sidhe, catching her sudden disquiet, began to snort and sidle crabwise under her, and without a thought she gave him a little touch of heel to sort him out, her gaze fixed like a spear of diamond upon Morric's face. "Sanctuary, a place for us to hide—" Alarm was rising now to terror of his strange stillness.

"I was dead," he said then, simply, starkly, turning to look straight at her, and Athyn felt all the blood in her body drain away to ice. "I was dead, and you came for me. As you said you would; came to Annwn to bring me back."

"You asked me once what I would do if you should die," said Athyn at once, with equal simple steadiness, holding his glance, desperate to reach him across the sudden distance. *All the distance of Annwn...* "And I did tell you... Was I wrong, then, to have kept my word?" And held not her breath alone but her whole soul and being suspended, to hear what he should answer. *Seven long years I served for thee...*

He shook his head, slowly, wonderingly. "Nay," he said at last, still staring out at the vale and mountains before him, as if strange signs were writ upon them none save he might read. "Cariadwyn— Nay. Not wrong. Not you."

They stayed there together, alone, through all that spring and summer, and into the autumn. They were learning to fit again to life and to each other: In all Keltia not a soul yet knew that they had returned; such news as they had was brought them by Allyn or Gwyn, who often visited—naught to concern them or alarm, naught that the Taoiseach Esmer and the Gweriden could not handle among them. Indeed, Athyn was alarmed only by how strangely unalarmed she was; and said as much one night to Morric.

"It was not ever thus," she remarked, with a wistful smile. "I remember that once in Elmet I looked out and saw only the swordlands of the Firvolgi, not the heartlands of the Kelts; and, though I trust I do not broider memory with a thread that never was there in life, I think it was in that moment I decided on the course I should take if it were offered. All my deeds from then out were in service of that seeing; and all now is changed because of what we have done."

But Morric only laughed. "Because of what *you* have done, anghariad; more is changed than even that—or have you forgot so soon?"

She would not be distracted; but neither would she look at him. "How if we stayed here always; never went back to Caerdroia?"

Morric leaned back in his chair and considered. "A tempting prospect. How would we fend ourselves?"

"Well, you would have of course your bardery," said Athyn. "I myself—once a horsegirl ever a horsegirl, I daresay I could turn a hand again to breeding bloodstock. A Sidhe strain perhaps, or half-blooded, from those two noble creatures gobbling grass up in the clune; or a nice line of mountainwise beasts."

"Oh aye? And those last, no doubt, would be the ones shorter fore than aft, for use on hill-farms? You see, I remember very well—everything you have ever said to me."

She was laughing. "And what a mighty freight of piffle that must surely be by now..."

"Oh, some of it, only; a small some. Still, Athynna, we are here to stay."

And she knew in her heart that he did not mean in Ty-'n-coed.

A cold summer following a chilly spring, the strong nightwind rushing like water through the heavy full leaf all around them, the branches of the trees tossing like masts. Athyn could lie in bed, with Morric wondrously beside her, lying between her and the room—and still she was not yet used to the miracle of his presence, she would turn to him unendingly in the night, in the dawn, just to hear him breathe, or feel the warmth of his solidness, bare against her own bare side—and listen to the moving breezes all night long.

Inside Tincoats it was snug and pleasant, rich not with garish ornament but with comforts, with simple beautiful meaningful things; for the first time in all their lives together they were plainly and perfectly alone. No campaigning, no bardery, no demands of court or Council; neither High Queen nor King Consort, not Blackmantle nor Fireheart, but Athyn and Morric only.

There was naught they did not speak of, ceaselessly, eagerly, as if words were not enough, not swift enough, to frame their wingèd thoughts; other times they were silent for long hours together, at ease in the moment, comfortable with each other; still other times they loved for hours just as long, fierce violent joyous union, ecstatic battles in which surrender was triumph, not defeat. Athyn gave full account to Morric of the Long Hunt, of her loss and grief and resolve; and perhaps Morric made her understand at last about Melassaun, whom for some amazing reason he did not fault quite as she did, though neither did he fault Athyn.

Of the death of Amzalsunëa Dalgarno they spoke once,

once only, spoke long and gravely; and spoke of it never again to the end of their days.

But words did not stop there. Morric wrote as never he had written before; songs, chaunts, litanies, prayers—and poems in sheaves. "It is not every day one comes back from the dead," he told his wife. "Best to write it down before it fades or I forget, else those who will tell our tale in after times might get their mucky paws on it—and you know they will—and invent all manner of lying fables, because you and I did not write enough, or let them know sufficiently, or sufficiently strongly, that which is our truth. And we shall have only ourselves to blame if and when they do so."

But for all his carefulness and words, and hers as well, they did.

As the summer deepened, the leaves of spring dark green now, heavy with sap and sulter but not yet touched with autumn, a change came upon them both; but neither said a word of it to the other. It was nothing either of them could name, and each heroically did not ask, thinking that if the other wished to speak of it, it would be spoken of; but neither did, and it was not.

Near Fionnasa, Allyn ap Midna rode visiting to Tincoats. They spent a pleasant few nights in company—though Allyn, as ever, would not sleep withindoors, if indeed he ever slept at all—but on the last night of his stay the Sidhe lord seemed strangely restless, and at sunset he abruptly bade Athyn go with him up to the top of the hill behind the bield. She shot Morric a quick questioning look, but he only shrugged.

At the summit Athyn and Allyn stood looking out over the valley below them sleeping in a sea of mist, blue mountains rising up like whalebacks. Far beneath their feet was Tincoats like a tiny jewel, its windows ablaze with the setting sun; they watched for a long time in silence.

"The Gates of the North are shut," said Allyn at last, turning his gaze toward the mountains far in that airt. "This will not be allowed again. Arawn spoke rightly; and the Alterator has decreed, in Abred and in Gwynfyd and in Annwn."

"Was it a wrong thing then to do, syra-wyn?" asked Athyn quietly, as once not too long since she had inquired of Morric himself, and with the same stab of inward terror.

"'Wrong'?" mused the Sidhe lord, then smiled, a smile of the morning of the world. "Not for me was it wrong: It was your way, and it was most correct, and in all ways it was strictly within the Law. But, gods, lass, it was mighty!"

A cold and misty morning of late October. Awakened by a call from outside her open window, Athyn looked out and up, and saw who had called her from her sleep: a line of wild geese, singing like hounds in the sharp air and the brightening dawn; and suddenly, surely, the vague stirrings she and Morric both had felt took form, and she knew it was time for them to go. *The geese know it, and now I know it too... This has been wondrous, and healing; but we are healed, and we must return to the world, he and I, to take up the dán that between us we have made.*

Over the months of their chosen exile, blissful though those months were, had hung a tiny cloud: Athyn and Morric, knowing that their idyll must come to an end, anguished endlessly over how it might be best to return to Keltia. As Athyn herself pointed out, they had not exactly been away on some holiday or embassy or progress-royal. They had been gone for seven years. She had left her throne. Morric had been *dead*... Though all Keltia would rejoice to see them, and care little for how or why, at least at first, to come swanning blithely back with no warning would be, or so they thought, no simple matter. It must be managed with care and with discretion, with wisdom and with love.

But in the end, for all their fearings, it was simple. They did not ask; neither one of them suggested or accepted, put forth the proposition or turned it aside. They went as plainly as the geese; they shut up Ty-'n-coed against weather, and chance comers beast or human, and put on their cloaks; and turning the heads of their horses westwards they rode home again in the ringing dawn.

Athyn and Morric returned to Caerdroia, very quietly, at sunset on the night of Samhain the Less, a full seven years since Athyn and Allyn had ridden the Low Road to Annwn.

Many who had gone down to the Bannochburn for the soulsail saw them come, and wondered at first if this were not some vision sent them by the Cabarfeidh to grace His holy feast: riding calmly along the light-strewn river through the gathering dusk, on a snow-colored mare and a stallion dark as night, their King who had died alone and afar, their Queen who had ridden none knew where to fetch him home.

There had of course been portents in plenty. A huge wolf, his brindled coat barred with silver as his deep chest was so starred, had been seen standing on Yr Hela, the peak of Eagle that rises directly behind Turusachan; the Ghost Mare had galloped down the whole length of the Raise, near Meldeburna on Caledon, under a cool cobalt moon; atop the hill Belnagar, in the circle of Starcross, white fire had blazed up where no fire should have been, and music had been heard of more than mortal beauty. But what all these things, and many others, did mean, no one could say; and if any hoped in secret they kept that hope within their breasts.

But now, though the watching folk were slow to realize, and by the time they did Morric and Athyn had ridden on, that this was no ashling from beyond the Door but merely truth, astounding and unlooked-for—their Queen was returned, their King alive again, and together they were restored to Keltia and to Kelts—the rejoicing knew no bounds.

So Athyn and Morric went up to Turusachan and entered in; and Esmer Lennox, Taoiseach of Keltia, was there alone to meet them in the gate. Seven years they had been gone; seven years had Velenax held Blackmantle's throne for her, and none more glad than he to hand it back.

The histories tell well enough the bare events of that night; but for all their careful recounting none can relate what joy was there when Athyn and Esmer met again, and Morric with them, nor when the Gweriden came flying to their friends' side, scarce able to believe what their eyes and ears and arms and hearts did tell them. No book or tale or song relates how it was when only dawn called a halt to the jubilant reunions and the rejoicers went reluctantly to bed; or when the Ard-rían of Keltia and her King went hand in hand to their own bed, to spend their first night home again, in that chamber where Athyn had kept her lord's possessions just as he had left them, and where the Gweriden had taken care as great, in the seven years of her absence, to keep her own as undisturbed as his.

"For we know how cross you can get, Athyn," Mariota had said, smiling through her tears, "when your belongings are meddled with."

But beyond the dry recording of history and scholarship, such tales as there are that came out of that night of miracle are in their undertext all well agreed: No task is beyond the management of those with the strength to imagine it, and love is, indeed, enough.

And how then did they live after? Well you may ask. It was the wonder of the folk, and their fear also: If Athyn could wrest Morric back even from Annwn, could command even Arawn Deathlord to her will, what might she not command of them? How would they shift, they who must deal with her on daily terms, she who had harrowed hell and won? Blackmantle had been one thing: Her they understood, she had been one of them, born and reared in Keltia's heart even as themselves; they knew her and loved her and were grateful. But this was something very different. They were proud, no question, of that which she had wrought; but she whom they had loved, though they loved her still, they now did also fear.

And they wondered too how Morric must consider, he who was brought back from death, as no one before had ever been, nor ever would be again; was he glad to return from the glory of Moymell, or did his wife's action anger him, or displease? But when some, greatly daring, ventured a guarded query, or, grossly curious, asked point-blank, Morric only laughed, or confounded them with some cryptic bardic englyn; and though they never ceased to try the question never did they have from him any answer more than that.

It was a strangeness all round. Save for the enchanted months at Ty-'n-coed, to Morric his absence from the worlds had been but as hours; even to Athyn herself, apart from her hunt, it seemed perhaps a week, no more. But to Keltia it had been seven years since Athyn rode to Annwn, and though her Kelts were glad beyond all measure to have her back, and Morric beyond all hope restored, still there was a certain wariness, a constraint more felt than known.

Which Athyn, no fool, perceived all round her, and at once began to do what she might to ease it: naught overt, nothing one might name or note; but only she dealt with folk as ever she had dealt with them, in wit and honor and open plainness, to let them see that whatever may have been, or she had done, she was just the same, she was still theirs, they were still hers. And, little by little, they came to feel it and know it too. But she knew in her heart, and Morric also, that the folk were right to mark the change: They were not as they had been, and never would be again; and whether or no that mattered, or should, must yet be seen.

In the years of their reign, Morric Douglas and Athyn Cahanagh brought about many reforms that no monarchs before them had been able to achieve, and from which all Kelts did benefit thereafter. Athyn—known already as Athyn

Taighlech, Athyn the Glorious, though, true to form, she hated the byname—established the trading planet of Clero, at a sufficient distance from Keltic space that no tide of Incoming could ever again creep up on their shores, and from that time very few outfrenne were allowed to set foot upon the Keltic worlds. Working with Esmer and Rhain and Morvoren, she created a standing army and seafleet and starfleet, such as Keltia had never had before, every Kelt to be liable for military service, and the Fianna to serve as officers; and other great reforms beside.

As for King Morric Fireheart, he revived the immrama-tuathal, the secret return voyages to Erith, to see what might be shaping, if the Terrans should be near to joining the Kelts out among the stars. He himself went on many of these journeys, bringing back beautiful music but no good report: A noble Scotan house which had come promisingly to rule in Anglia had been treacherously overthrown, and the gross and stolid Alamaeni line of Hánivyr invited in and crowned in its place. Worse, there had been a terrible battle at a place called Culloden, in which the Scotan clanns were broken—for pity's anguished sake Morric and his ship's crew had thrown aside all the rules of the immrama-tuathal and helped some of the survivors away, taking them home to Keltia—and in the other Celtic lands of Erith also little good, but subjugation and colonization and sullen seething rebellion. Clearly there would be no reunion with the mother planet any time soon, and Athyn for all her curiosity and grief for the Kelts' long-sundered kindred could not say she was sorry. *Not the day nor yet the hour. One day, aye. But not this day…*

But other outfrenne friendships thrived. Athyn and Morric grew great friends with Zarôndah and Brahím of Aojun; for his part Morric found in Brahím a brother bard, a fellow of music and the word, while Athyn came to love and prize Zarôndah as one of the true Gweriden, for her loyalty and honor, and her calm clarity of mind.

As Aojun and Keltia grew in friendship and alliance,

Athyn began to send emissaries out to other star-realms, so that the Fasarine worlds of Suka Vellanor and Kholco of the Firefolk and Galathay of the Hail, Harilak of the Numantissans and even the Dakdak homeworld of Inalery, with its frost-fortress capital of Ajen-akd, and more beside, all saw Keltic embassages established, and sent their own ambassadors to Caerdroia, even as did the Firvolgi and Fomori; and so it went, for many decades after, until the Marbh-draoi made an end. But that is another's story.

chapter thirty-five

You must judge at the last.

—*Lassarina Aoibhell ac Douglas*

As with so many greater, graver things down the years, Athyn Cahanagh was to have her will in a small matter also. Never did the scar leave her that Brónach's feather had drawn upon her cheek; a fine faint silver line stayed there always. She wished it so; so that, as she said, folk would never forget how she had come by it—not that, as Morric remarked, there was the smallest chance they ever would—and, as Morric again remarked, she wore it like a jewel.

Other lives went on, not theirs alone. In the Hollow Hills, in the great silver-roofed thronehall of Dún Aengus beneath the Hill of Fare, the Prince Gwyn took the Lady Etain for his bride and his princess and his queen that would be, and Athyn stood proud supporter to the ceremony, with Allyn her kinsman to partner her. The bride was fair indeed, wearing a cloak of roses and a crown of may, but to Athyn's fond eye the bridegroom was fairer still.

After the rite Athyn danced with Gwyn, and Neith the King, and Allyn, and other faerie lords of her acquaintance, in the vast dancing-hall to music such as never she had heard, and Morric led out with Etain and Seli, though he was quickly lured away to harp by those who made the music. Later, in the summer evening, they walked with the bridal couple in the

rosegardens of Seli the queen; since the return from Annwn
they all had grown close fond friends, and as often as Morric
and Athyn visited in Glenshee or Sychan on Gwynedd or
Gwyn's own birthplace of Knockfierna or other haunts beside,
the Sidhefolk came to guest with them, in Caerdroia or
Tincoats or Witchingdene.

"I did not know that the Sidhe wed as we do," remarked
Morric, who earlier had harped a wedding-chaunt, a grá-traigh
of such loveliness as to have brought even the faerie folk to
joyful tears.

"We wed once for all our life," said Etain smiling. "You and
your lady have wed for all your lives; more or the less the same
span of time, either way."

"And when mortals wed with Sidhefolk?" asked Morric,
glancing at Athyn on Gwyn's arm.

It happens, they told him; not so often in these latter days,
but long ago it was by no means an uncommon occurrence.
Nia the Golden and Fergus Fire on Brega, whose blissful union
had produced the great Astrogator, were perhaps the best
known, but they were scarce the only pair to do so, nor even
the last; as Allyn himself could attest.

"It may even be that in centuries to come our two kindreds
will draw closer still," said Gwyn. "Neither Sidhe nor mortal
Kelt, but the best of both in one blood."

Morric found a sudden sadness in the thought. "Could that
be, do you think? Or should it: to blend the best, but to lose
the wondrous difference?"

"There may be no choice to either, Fireheart," said Gwyn.
"But that is another trouble for another time."

"Today's dán to today," murmured Athyn, and the Princess
Etain smiled, and to the surprise of all who beheld she took off
her crown of may and set it upon Athyn's head.

"And that is truer than you know, Queen of Kelts," she said.
"But not truer than you will come to know."

*   *   *

Other lives too were not forgotten: Every yearday of the slaying of Amzalsunëa Dalgarno, the High Queen punctiliously performed a ritual of sending at whatever nemeton was nearby; always she went alone. One year she went to Starcross, where she had been wed; another year to Mount Keltia, to the ancient hallow of Caer-na-gael that stands beneath the Gates of the Sun.

Morric knew her practice, but said no word; and Athyn did not know he knew. Nor would she have been troubled if she had; as she herself confided to Sosánaigh.

"I am not sorry, nor have I ever been, and what I do is by no means atonement. But Amzalsunëa too, for whatever reasons, was part of the dán, and it feels right to help her move along home."

Sosánaigh looked at her curiously. "Even though she is incarnate again?"

"Oh aye; cannot hurt, may yet help. Though where or indeed who she might be Arawn gave no hint; and I wonder if we will encounter one another again, while I am still Athyn—if we would know each other when we met."

"There is dán still between you all three. Morric needed her to need him, he needs you to need..." Sosánaigh smiled. "I do not feel that you will meet; but, if you should, somehow it is on me that you shall know—all three of you."

So Athyn and Morric were restored, and Keltia rejoiced, marvelling at the splendor of the exploit that was already legend. Secure upon the Throne of Scone, they ruled in glory and in joy; and if Athyn Ard-rían still had wild-magic to her hand, never again did she make use of it.

Time came that Morric and Athyn had been twenty-five years wed. On the observable-day of their handfasting Morric gave his mate a chain of twenty-five huge rose-cut diamonds set in silver; but his gift to her long since, the silver swan collar that twice had come to life in Annwn—that jewel she wore always, it had become part of her. Her own gift to him that yearday was a cabochon ruby the size of her fist set in a rosegold frame, their names worked in runes on the sides and a gold diamond in a bezel at the top; and once Athyn had hung it round his neck seldom was he seen without it.

Years passed then, more years than Athyn cared to count; and to her and Morric they meant no more than as many months; but to those they loved it was very much elsewise...

In the fullness of time the great Esmer Lennox died, first Prince of Connacht, too early as all Keltia deemed it who grieved his going. His Princess and his duchess daughter and her mate were beside him, his Queen and King stood at the foot of his bed to bid his journey thrive. Athyn barrowed him at Ni-maen, in highest funeral-state, with the rulers of Keltia in their own beds about him and the Gweriden with torches to bear him to his grave; and she wept for him as she had wept for no other, for he had been the last and greatest of those who had stood to her as father.

Though Conn had sired her, and Cormac had saved her, and Nilos had given her the matchless gift of poetry and a new kind of sight—and Allyn more even than that—Esmer it had been who had seen what she might be, and who by dint of coaxing and commanding, with love and with cunning, and with force when needed, had made her into what she became: not for herself, or even for his own plans, but for Keltia—had made her brehon, and Fian, and High Queen, and Blackmantle also; he from whose blood and mind and heart the Outgoing had been forged. Never had he not been there for her, or for Kelts, or for Keltia—Velenax, the true Lion of Connacht—and she would miss him all the rest of her days.

As for Morric and Athyn themselves, they went on, in deepest love and endless bliss. But their doom was to be changeless and ageless, and though at first it seemed no sacrifice or hardship but a great and wondrous gift—to be ever-young and undying with your beloved, yet to be alive in the world, who would not wish and covet such a fate?—after a time it became for both of them the burden the gods had known it would be; but though they knew something needed to be done, they were as yet uncertain as to what that thing might be, and besides they were not yet weary of their state.

Though others grew so, and went away joyfully into that change where Athyn and Morric might not go themselves: Athyn's Archill fosterns all were gone now; and Maravaun Aoibhell, Prince of Thomond; more than a few of the Gweriden; and Ganor, eager to rejoin her Velenax. And though for their part they missed them sore, Fireheart and Blackmantle rejoiced to bid them speed, knowing as did no other what awaited them, and in that knowledge glad.

This was the crown of their reign, when the rooted sapling had grown to mature leaf, and now would only broaden and deepen where it stood. There was time even in these days for romantic interludes at Witchingdene or Ty-'n-coed; their love and desire had grown but greater with the years. To the secret awe of their subjects, they looked no older now than on the day they were wed.

But if no older surely they were wiser; that was change of another sort, change that did not fall under Arawn's ban. As part of her royal duties, Athyn had gone back to her judging, and those who these days brought suit to the Ard-rían came away wondering. Justice there was as there had ever been with her, perfect and correct, creative even; but now there was an uncommon mercy in her verdicts, and a vision that could pierce all hearts however veiled or hardened.

Morric as King led Kelts in battle and diplomacy alike on many worlds, in service of the new alliances he and his Queen had made; but never did he cease his bardery, and his music had ever now a warmth it had heretofore achieved only time to time, and an art imperishable.

Athyn too had kept a hand in at her old trade, at least somewhatly. As she had only half-teasingly once told her mate she intended, with the help of Aunya nic Cafraidh and Rhiannyn of Trevattow—a Gweriden horsemistress, who had wedded Errick mac Archill and with him rebuilt Caerlaverock—she had bred up a faerie bloodline from the two horses Gwyn had given them upon their return, and the Glora strain was now a wonder of Keltic bloodstock, itself a wonder among outfrenne worlds. She had just acquired a new horse of that very line, a tall black filly, granddaughter of Rhufain and that white mare Morric had had of the Sidhe; perhaps presumptuously, she had named her Brónach.

Yet for all their love and joy of one another, for all the great deeds of their reign and their delight in their friends and the pleasures they took where they could and might, still it was with them as Arawn had warned them, and they grew, not less happy, but more unplaced in the world, dislocated in time as time went round them.

It was not so much a matter of mere years, as in despair Morric once cried out to his wife, for that could be endured or even enjoyed; but the knowledge that those years could bring them no new thing. In the body, at least, they were no longer mortal; though—with great difficulty—they could perhaps be slain, or even slay themselves, they would otherwise live with the life of the Sidhe. But their souls were mortal souls still, full of the need and hunger mortals have for growth and gain and change; and now never again would that be so for them. Other things, greater things perhaps; but never that.

And at last, time was that they knew beyond doubt or further fear what they must do; and, one day of cool and bright October, Fionnasa not long past and Samhain not yet come, they set about the doing.

Ofttimes it is that no one thing decides a great decision. Many small matters accumulate over time, like snow all winter falling upon a high hidden mountainslope, unnoticed from beneath. But comes the spring thaw, and the great white mass becomes unstable; a careless shout, a warmer day, one snowflake too many, and then the avalanche is sweeping down the mountain side upon the vale below. So that the hapless villagers caught in its path, if they live through it, are astonished, and looking at their buried homes they shake their heads, saying over and over that they never even dreamed the threat was there.

So it was for Athyn and Morric. No one thing precipitated their decision, but the accumulation of many tiny burdens; the difference was that they very well knew the snowmass was forming, indeed they themselves had called the cold and snow. But they spoke of it to no one save each other: Though they might well have confided in Esmer, he was gone now, and in the end they chose to keep the burden upon their shoulders only, and not trouble those who loved them with a choice which—however right it might be for Athyn and for Morric—could never bring those dear ones aught but sorrow.

Thus, the weight of that choice heavy upon them but their hearts immeasurably light, when the time came Athyn Cahanagh and Morric Douglas took special farewell of no one dear to them—"Not for them again *that* pain," Athyn had said fervently, "and I know they will not think so, but this way is truly best"—but slipped away from Caerdroia one autumn afternoon, casually, as for an hour's hacking in the hills.

Mariota and Sosánaigh were the last to see and bespeak them, waving cheerfully to them, as those who confidently expect to meet that night at supper. But Morric and Athyn rode on down the hill, through the Great Square and the Market Square and out from the City through the Wolf Gate. A few miles down Strath Mór, turning in her saddle, Athyn looked for the last time upon Caerdroia, where it lay mighty and shining behind her. A shaft of sunlight lanced from high white clouds to smite the towers of Turusachan, and she stared long and long, to seal the beloved image forever upon her mind and heart. But Morric Douglas never once looked back.

                         *   *   *

Allyn mhic Midna smiled to see them ride over the green brow of Gwel-y-sidan; upon that very same white mare and black stallion that had carried them hence so long ago, returning now to the fields where they were foaled.

"I know why you are come," he said, giving them the kiss of kinsman's greeting. "And therefore I waited on your coming. But you need no guide this time; your wish and will now are all that is needed to bring you where you would go."

"That may be; but will you ride with me one more time, my lord?" asked Athyn through sudden stinging tears. "And this the last, to pay for all."

I have known him since I was a lass of fourteen summers; he has known me longer than any living soul. He saved me from a death on the battlefield of my birth, and from another on Caerdroia's walls, and he rode with me to Annwn to fetch back my beloved. More than that, he is my grandsir! Fitting it is that his is the last face I should see in Keltia; for though Morric is more hopeful, it is on me that we shall not be returning to the world. And yet that does not feel to me as hopelessness, but joy...

Allyn smiled. "Gladly; but as to that last, we will learn what Arawn may have to say. Though he came off the loser by a touch in your last bout; and I for one would take no wager even at long odds. But come; let us ride together."

They were riding to Annwn, to seek from Arawn Doomsman some mercy, or forgiveness, or mere advising, now that they knew the true nature of the dán they had taken upon them. They did not regret it, or seek to alter the bargain: They would abide as they had pledged, nor would they change it if it meant all else must change alike; but they sought some way to live within it, to find a way through what now seemed a trackless pathless future to the other side. And the Lord of Annwn was the only hope they had.

                         *   *   *

In the vast dim mountain-hall Arawn was awaiting them—perhaps he never had ceased to wait—and Malen his mate stood beside him as before. He looked upon them in silence for a long time before he spoke, and what he said then was the last thing they had expected to hear.

"You have done well; far better indeed than I had thought. I had looked to see you here many years since, with just the prayer you now bring me."

Athyn drew breath to speak, but Arawn raised a hand for silence.

"I know what you do seek," said the Doomsman then. "And there is a way... But first let there be no more mystery: I will tell you how it was, and is, and may yet be. Know then that Morric Douglas was meant to perish when he did." Though Athyn, not expecting to hear that of all things, gasped at that stark word as if a spear had pierced her heart, Arawn spoke calmly on. "His dán was for a higher role and rule: He was meant to be the Hidden King, to care for the life of the land and the life of the folk alike, working on the astral for the weal of all. As for Athyn Cahanagh, the task we set for her was harder still: She was fated to survive Morric, to go on alone without him; to be the Queen Revealed, who implemented his work and worked his will in the world. That was the nature of the partnership for which you two were destined: Whatever Amzalsunëa Dalgarno may have meant by her act against him, know that it was our will she carried out. All this was known while the oceans were being made; it had been planned before the rocks were formed, before the mountains were lifted up. But mortals are ever free to choose, and, by choosing, change. For love and loss Athyn chose change, to fetch Morric back again into life; and Morric chose to join her in that alteration. The Sidhe too, for allowing her wish to bind them to their promise, are caught into the knot; but how that might work on them I will not say."

He ceased then, and Malen took up the telling; for all her steel-fierceness and battle-splendor her voice was soft, her glance upon them gentle.

"Out of love and courage, will and wild magic—a mighty alliance, against which even the gods may not always prevail—you altered dán. There is no going back. What was done here has shifted the course of all fate forever, and though the end will be unchanged who can say how it must be meanwhile?"

"Though you would not have been together," said Arawn, and now he spoke only to Athyn, "you would never have been apart. You called him back; but if he had not wished to join you, never could you have won him from my realm."

"Was it wrong, then, lord?" asked Athyn quietly; as once she had asked of Allyn, and even of Morric himself.

Arawn smiled. No more was his face hid from them: The beauty of the Doomsman's countenance was there for them to see; perfect justice and the mercy of the One stood in it, and a humor that was all his own. And his answer when he gave it was not as the other answers had been.

"Wrong?" he mused. "Though you have gazed living upon the Sea and the Plain and the Door, and have lived in the world with the life of the Sidhe, you do not yet always see with the vision that wisdom has given you... Always mortals in the body are too concerned with wrongness and rightness, and never see that there is something beyond both that is greater still, and it is that which all beings under Kelu serve." But what that thing might be he did not say.

"Nay, ingheann, not wrong," said Malen then, with a sigh and sidewise glance at her mate that had she been a mortal woman would have been called exasperation. "Nothing done from love is ever wrong. But not right either. Simply a deed like many another, where the Shadow falls across the Light. But there is a great and eternal difference between the Shadow and the Dark, and this is a thing I know you know; for that Shadow has fallen hard upon you."

"I am a queen," said Athyn simply. "I was not born to it, but made for it. And to be a monarch is to be a royal sacrifice for the life of the people and the realm, in life or in death—nor have I ever been unwilling, either way, when such demand was made, for the Light, the Shadow or yet the Dark."

"True, and this we know; but there is more. As the land is in cycles so must the monarch be also; if the cycles cease of either partner, king or land, for whatever reason, they must be set right again or both shall perish."

"What then can be done to restore so vast a balance?" *For I see now it is not as I in my eternal traha had thought: Morric and Athyn are not alone at peril here; indeed, he and I may well be the least of it…*

Arawn's words came strangely slow now. "Something of equal weight and vastness… For there is another royal sacrifice, and a higher, if you are willing: to be the Hidden Queen beside the Hidden King, upon a throne between the worlds, to care for Keltia upon the astral and come never again to mortal lands."

"That is no sacrifice, but a higher destiny than even *my* traha could allow me to covet," said Athyn when she had mastered her own voice again. "Who would deny such a blessing and a gift? But would Kelu truly permit this to me—to us?"

"It lies within my sphere to order," said Arawn, and she smiled at the irony in his voice. "As someone once reminded me, I have that mastery—though there must of course be a test… What I see now before me is a strong spirit in a frame too battered to bear it. No disgrace to you; you have ventured with matchless heart where none other has ever gone, or shall go. You have operated from instinct all along, and that instinct served you well. To serve one of us is to serve us all, god and man alike; and to serve god and man is to serve the land, and to serve the land is to serve That Which is above the land and god and man together."

"Make no mistake," said Malen, "mighty things have been done here. You have harrowed hell. You have returned from death. Both you have changed forever how Keltia deals with Kelts and with outfrenne alike. Blackmantle and Fireheart have set a long precedent: Never again will Keltia allow itself to be so used."

"Then Blackmantle has served her purpose," said Athyn smiling, "and with Fireheart beside her can find an honorable death. But Athyn may yet have another purpose—that test you spoke of, Lord?"

Arawn smiled. "Such a fate has been asked of me often enough before; but never by one prepared to back up the asking. Here then is the way of it: Morric Douglas must harp once again in Annwn, and if he can move us once again to weep—my lady and myself—the sacrifice will be accepted. You may step through the Pair together, and off the Wheel together, forever to remain together. Thus Athyn shall share the task to which Morric was destined, in which she herself in time would have joined him. But if this dán is accepted, nevermore may either of you return to the world, together or apart, not unless the Goddess or the God deeming the will of the Highest, or the Alterator working it, or Kelu in Kelu's Self in the Throne of Being commanding it, should rip up this new weave and decree another. Is this acceptable?"

"Before you answer, know that even this may not be the end," said Malen. "It well may be you *shall* return one day, theophanes of the Goddess and the God. Even if one steps off the Wheel, one may still be sent to do the work of the One, to fill a purpose; many servants of the Light have done so, and who is to say you shall not be among them? But there are no certainties. Consider that too before you accept."

But Athyn and Morric looked into one another's eyes and hearts, and were well content with what they saw.

Then Morric, gazing upon Athyn: "To be together forever, in a way that mortals cannot even dream of—no more to come to the world—"

"It is no punishment," said Malen, "nor is meant to be. It is a high and noble choice, and if you choose it, you will find in it joy unimagined, and unimaginable."

Athyn, her eyes still deep in Morric's, answered for them both. "Then be it so. We are agreed, my lord and I."

Arawn lifted a hand, and the white harp of bones that Morric once before had played was suddenly lying at his feet.

"I warn you fairly," he said, and humor glinted in his dark glance. "Harder it will be than formerly, to bring tears to my eyes."

"We shall see," said Morric lightly. "As we know, swans sing once and once only just before their deaths, and their song is then the fairest that ever was heard."

"And black swans?" asked Allyn, speaking for the first time. Morric smiled, and took up the harp of bones. "Those too."

The song Morric Douglas made then in Annwn was unlike to all songs made before; even Alaunos Songlord never made such chaunt. The depths of grief unsounded did he harp, and the power of love undying, and the pain of loss beyond imagining: the inconsolable wound that lives in all created souls, the longing for a Home we have not seen to dwell in, a Face we do not know we know to behold. Peace he harped in the midst of strife, and valor among the craven, honor against dishonor and truth in the midst of lies; he harped the Star and the Mountain and the Pool in the Heart of the Wood. He harped the Shadow and the Light, the One and the Three, Abred and Annwn and Gwynfyd Itself. Everything in all the One's creation did he harp, save only the Dark; and then the Dark also. But he ended with the Light.

So for the second time did Morric Fireheart harp in hell; and if there shall be a third time of harping, none can say...

Athyn his wife and Queen was all but beyond herself to hear it: She stood as a white and lighted candle in that dim high hall; her heart was poured out like water, and her love for him appeared as a living flame; as for Allyn Midna's son he wept as a frore birch in the spring thaw. And as Morric ended his song, not with a chord of triumph but with an endnote that was as the last star in a dying sky, or the first in a new sky being born, he looked up at Arawn Rhên, and Malen Rhên beside him, to read his fate and his lady's in the faces of the gods.

And in the light of Annwn the stone-pale cheek of the War-queen was as crystal dew upon ferns of a still June morning, and the countenance of the mighty Doomsman bore a single track of glittering tears.

"You have bested me again, both you; and it is you alone could have done it." Arawn's voice held only pride and love. "The test is therefore won. Save that you will have a mighty task, and not perhaps for Keltia alone, not even I can say what your doom might be. We will meet again. You must put your trust in Kelu, but you will be together, in knowledge and in love. Shall that suffice you, and are you ready for so high and holy a destiny?"

It would be sufficement for all time, they said humbly, and nay, they were by no means ready for it, who would be? But they would do it even so.

And that was the answer Annwn's lord had been hoping to hear, the only answer he could have accepted (for even the High Dânu have their Masters); and in his office as Doomsman joyfully did he then confirm their choice and grant their wish. Arawn lifted his hand, and the light of the Pair filled that great hall of Annwn; the nine queens rose up from their thrones to honor them, the nine warriors raised their flaming swords to the salute.

And then the world rolled back, and the Way lay open and shining before the Hidden King and his most loving Queen.

So Morric Douglas and Athyn Cahanagh, hand in hand, embraced and kissed and bade farewell to Allyn ap Midna who had been their long-loved friend and kinsman, he who riding home to Keltia would attest their going to the mortal world. And bowing then to the Lord of Annwn, and to the War-queen his mate, and receiving blessing from them, they passed the queens and the warriors alike, and entering Pair Dadeni they went beyond it together, and were seen in Keltia no more; and not even the gods can say whither they have gone.

But among the Sidhe and the sorcerers it is told that they indeed passed through the Pair; and crossing the Plain they boarded the crystal ship that waited there for them, and sailed across the Sea to a different Door than the one Athyn once had opened to Moymell.

The swans of Athyn's necklace, black and white together, swirled round them one last time to give them escort, and winged upward into the bright air to be free forever after; her fetch, the Faol-mór, the wolf of her kindred, sat like a figure-head, still and proud and eager in the ship's prow, and the great ruby Morric bore upon his breast shone to pierce the mists with a light like a crimson star. And where the crystal ship came at last to land, stepping through the Door that swung wide to welcome them to what lay beyond, hand in hand and soul in soul they left the Wheel forever.

Or so their tale is told.

AFTERTALE

The true index of an artist is the way he does, or the
way he scants, the work that has been given him to
do. Morric added finish and witchery to his poems,
and was loved therefor. He began to sing young,
and shone early, and left us too soon. But the work
remains; and the love also.

—*Elen Lasdern*

These events have been recounted, I trust faithfully, by
myself, Genvissa of Aojun, Royal Historian. I have
used as sources the works and words of the Lord
Brahím, our much-mourned Subhadar, and the recollections
of our late beloved Jamadarin Zarôndah, both of whom had
the inestimable privilege of the friendship of Morric and
Athyn of Keltia, and who were kind enough to share those
precious memories. Likewise I had the assistance of the Keltic
chronicler Davyth na hInclei, called Incleion by my folk, the
poetess Elen Lasdern of Tamon Acanis and the historian Sover
mac Heth of Tanadale on Keltia's Throneworld—honest scribers
strong in the Holy Awen that my people call the Shanad'dhar.

The end has now been reached of a tale that would be
unbearable were it not so beautiful, and doubtless you who
have read thus far in this chronicle will wish to know what
came about in Keltia after Fireheart and Blackmantle left
together to find their fate.

Athyn and Morric produced no heir to follow them on
the Throne of Scone, so upon their strange and wondrous

ranslation (attested to by no less a personage than Allyn of
he Sidhe himself), the Crown was awarded by election to
he line of Pendreic, who had been staunch supporters of
Athyn Blackmantle in the fight she made to rid Keltia of
he Incomers.

Perhaps one day someone greater even than Athyn,
hough never greater than Athyn's spirit, may come out of
hat new royal line. Certain it is that it has begun most aus-
piciously: The first monarch of the House of Pendreic,
nown to history by his chosen throne-name of Rohan IV,
vas none other than Sosánaigh Darnaway's lord Micháltaigh,
nd Sosánaigh herself was Queen Consort, and Chief Bard
fter. Their fair and strong-willed daughter, Lassarina
Athyn, rules now as Ard-rían, and her son, Aeired, the
Tanist, will be High King thereafter; the House of Pendreic
s well founded, may it last a thousand years!

The Gweriden remained at Caerdroia as councillors to
he new rulers, and they had great honor and affection in
he land, passing on to their heirs the dúchases they had
been given by Queen Athyn, and going on to garner glory
of their own.

On the death of the great Esmer Velenax, Mariota
Lennox succeeded as Princess of Connacht, with Prince
Stellin Ardwyr beside her, and they ruled there well and
visely, Mariota long holding the office of Taoiseach of
Keltia in the reign of Rohan and Sosánaigh.

Athyn's sister Debagh nic Archill, the great limner,
ogether with her friend the no less renowned Tammas
Cantigh, minded herself of a word Mariota had spoken on
Athyn's accession; and together they wove a series of tapes-
ries to hang in the chamber called Gwahanlen, where
Athyn and her Council had met at the round table. Portraits
of many heroes of Keltia's past; but holding pride of place
among them was a work of love: Athyn Blackmantle and
Morric Fireheart with their friends and foes, and Allyn of
he Sidhe, and his great bronze horse also, beside them.

Sulior nic Archill became one of the most renowned healers of Keltic history, rediscovering many secrets of healing that the Danaans once had held; Cathárren Tanaithe was elected Ban-draoi Mathr'achtaran. Rhain mac an Iolair was named by acclamation as Captain-general of the Fianna, and Selanie Drummond his lady served the new King and Queen as a High Councillor; while the Jamadarin Zarôndah, late our own wise ruler, and aunt of our present queen, signed further treaties with Keltia that shall keep our two peoples friends and allies for all time to come.

A sadder turn to the tale: The Sidhefolk, who had continued to visit Turusachan while Morric and Athyn yet remained, after their friends' departure tarried there less often, and at last came no more.

As far as her deeds are concerned, let there be no doubt Athyn Cahanagh was devoted to the law, both as brehon and as queen, and all her life she served it with honor.

Let there be also no doubt that she ill-served it as well, and in spectacular fashion, both when she revenged herself on her enemies and when she claimed Morric back from Annwn. She who was the law's servant, as is any crowned ruler, bent the law of man for the sake of vengeance, and she who was the gods' servant, as is any created soul, broke the law of the gods for the sake of love.

Athyn entered the holy Pair in the living body, and died herself, walking round the back of the grave as none had ever dared before, to fetch her beloved back from death, winning his final freedom by her willingness to give up lives for him; as he won hers by his willingness to sacrifice his gift, the one thing that made him himself. And, when even that was not enough, they left together for an unimaginable destiny, never to be apart.

We all could wish to do as she did, and as greatly, when we ourselves are in such anguished straits. To win back our loved ones from death—to go into Annwn, to come before the great Doomsman himself and impose our will on the Absolute: Who among us, in bereavement, has not had such a desperate longing, would not do anything to have it so? But Athyn alone dared and dreaded worlds to do so, setting her very soul at hazard for her love's sake. And Morric, willing to give up his art to save her from that hazard, by that same art moving the gods themselves to weep for human sorrow, did no less.

For even soulmates do not always choose to return to a spousal union; all that is certain is that they will be together. Next time they might have been brother and sister, or parent and child; she who had been the woman might have chosen next life to be the man, or they might both have been men, or both women; such choices turn on what the souls still need to learn. But all that now is done with; they are one, and still themselves, and still they love.

Athyn and Morric had no child. It seems right that they left no heir behind them; they were too caught up each in the other for anyone else to come between, even a child of their own producing. And any road—as Kelts say—they have heirs indeed: all those who hear their story and are moved and inspirited by it. It is in my mind that they would like that best; and perhaps they themselves will indeed return one day to help their folk, or any folk who need helping—as theophanes of the Goddess and the God, what my people call avatars. For even if one is beyond incarnate, one may still be sent back to fill a purpose of the Highest; it has happened before, and it may well be so with those two. Only time will prove.

But a strange and telling thing: Another bard of that same House of Douglas which produced Morric, who also died untimely young after a brief blissful marriage, has already become conflated and confused with Morric over the intervening years.

Even more strangely, this bard too had had a redhaired wife of the House of Aoibhell. Though she did not do as Athyn did, this Aoibhell princess had surely loved as much as Athyn loved, for though she could not bring her lord back from death she did a thing that Blackmantle herself could not do: She went on, alone, without him. She wed none other after, and she lived on many decades with her memories and his music and their love. Though with such companions as those, she was never alone; and by her writings, and his that she did keep and tend, she gave him life imperishable, and herself with it. And he was with her still, they were never apart.

But that Douglas bard too had made chaunts for his wife, the loveliest of which perhaps was a song about his love in green. And even Morric Fireheart, writing of Athyn Blackmantle, could not have written more lovingly or more lastingly than that.

What is loved best is remembered best.
                                        —*Morric Douglas*

What comes again was never gone.
                                        —*Athyn Cahanagh*

Appendices

Glossary

Words are Keltic unless otherwise noted.

a chara: 'friend, dear one'; used in the vocative (**a charai**, pl.; **m'chara**, 'my friend')

Abred: 'The Path of Changes'; the visible world of everyda existence within the sphere of which one's various lives are lived

ac: sponsal affix used with clann name of mate (*Séomaighas Douglas ac Aoibhell*); relative affix used to indicate consanguinity, linking names of both parents (a child will take the higher-ranking parent's name for surname)

Aengus: one of the High Dânu; god of wind, journeys and love

Aescaileas: the Greek dramatist

airts: compass directions of north, south, east, west

alanna: endearment used to a child

Alaunos Songlord: god, one of the Dânu; creator of song and music

alaunt: breed of coursing gazehound known for its loyalty

allavolay!: exclamation; cry in the hunting field

Alterator: one of the three High Powers of the Keltic pantheon; neither male nor female, the Alterator works with the Mother Goddess and the Father God to effect the changes they decree and the will of the Highest

Amaethon: god of agriculture; one of the Dânu (**the Plowman**)

amhic: 'my son'; used in the vocative (*uh-VICK*)

An Dagda: name for an aspect of the God

an-da-shalla: 'The Second Sight'; Keltic talent of precognition

anghariad: 'beloved, most beloved'; intensive prefix *an* + *cariad*

An Lasca: the Whip-wind; ionized northwest wind at Caerdroia, usually blows in October, heralding the start of winter

Annwn: equivalent in Keltic theology to Hades, the underworld, ruled over by Arawn, Lord of the Dead; lowest of the Three Circles of the World. Though sometimes the word 'hell' is used to describe Annwn, that should not be read as the Christian concept but merely as a chthonic descriptive; Annwn is not a place of punishment but of learning, a fair and pleasant realm where souls contemplate their physical incarnation just past and prepare for their next (*Annoon*)

an uachdar: lit., 'uppermost'; in salutations (e.g., **'Gwerin an uachdar!'**) usually translated as 'Long live _____!'

Aojunese, Aojunni: inhabitants of the planet Aojun

aonach: feast, fair, celebration; gathering, especially for ceremonial or political purpose

Aonbarr: the crystal ship or, confusingly, the beautiful white stallion, belonging to the sea-god Manaan

ap: 'son of'

Aranrhôd: 'Silver Wheel'; one of the Dânu; goddess who decrees dán by a turn of her wheel

Áras Bretha: 'Temple of the Law'; the high courtroom in any brehon house of law or brehon college

Arawn Rhên: god; known as the **Doomsman, Firstborn of the Absolute;** one of the High Dânu; ruler of Annwn

arbalists: laser archers; arblasts, laser crossbows

ard-na-spéire: 'the height of heaven'; hyperspace, the overheaven

Ard-rían, Ard-rígh: High Queen, High King; title of the Keltic monarch (only actual rulers take these titles; consorts are styled plain 'King' or 'Queen')

Ard-tiarnas: 'High Sovereignty'; the term for Keltic monarchy

Argialla: the white moon that is the smaller and inner of the two moons of Tara

Ariandal's Crown: on Erinna, name for the polar aurora, the Northern Lights; **Ariandal**, one of the constellations of γ **Sygnau**, the Keltic zodiac, a winter sign equivalent to Aquarius

Arlan-zar: 'The Beast that Walks Like A Man'; legendary creature of Keltic folklore, similar to Terran yeti or sasquatch

arwydd: omen, portent, sign (*AR-weethe*)

ashet: large platter or plate, of metal, pottery or wood

ashling: waking wishing dream, daydream

asthore, athaigur: 'darling, treasure'; used in the vocative

athair: 'father'; a formal style; **athra:** 'father'; informal, adult usage

athra-cheile: 'father-in-law'; lit., 'mate-father'

athro, athron: 'teacher', 'master' (m. and f.)

Atland: Terran homeland of the Danaans, who, after Atland's destruction, became the Kelts, and the Telchines, who became the Coranians; their lasting enmity was taken to the stars, and will endure until Aeron Ard-rían puts an end to it, two thousand years after Athyn's day

Avanc: large semi-mythical creature, thought to cause and control floods by its roaring

averin: herb averin; healing plant of the sage family, with aromatic, spiky, silver-green leaves; used medicinally and magically, for cleansing

Awen, Holy Awen: lit., the Muse or sacred poetic gift of inspiration; as used by bards, the personified creative spirit, represented by three lines, the center one vertical, the outer two angling in opposite directions (/|\)

*   *   *

bach: (also **-bach**, suffix to male names) denotes affection and familiarity; used to all ages and stations and is translated 'lad' (fem., **fach** or **-fach**, 'lass')

bairn: 'child'

ban-charach: lit., 'the loved woman'; term for a woman formally and legally associated short of lawful marriage (cf. **far-charach**, **céile-charach**)

Ban-draoi: lit., 'woman-druid'; Keltic order of priestess-sorceresses in the service of the Ban-dia, the Great Goddess; **Mathr'achtaran**, 'Reverend Mother,' title of the head of the order

bannachtas: lit., 'blessings'; general term for 'good' or 'white' magic

bannock: thick, soft bread or roll; biscuit or muffin

bansha: female spirit, often red-cloaked, that sings and wails before a death in many Erinnach families; often seen as a wild rider in the air or over water

bardquain: person of either gender who follows round after bards, in hopes of sexual encounter

bards: Keltic order of poets, chaunters, musicians and loremasters; they often function as teachers, mediators, marriage brokers and spies; the Order was officially founded in Keltia in the year 347 A.B. (Anno Brendani) by Plenyth ap Alun, known as Pen-bardd

baresark: berserker, battle-mad

bas no beatha: 'death or life'; traditional challenge in a duel

bavour: afternoon snack or light meal

Beira: Keltic goddess; Queen of the Winter

Bellendain: the red moon that is the larger and outer of the two satellites of Tara

Beltain: 1 May; start of the Keltic summer, one of the two holiest days in the Keltic calendar

beneath the Horns: sub rosa, secret; refers to the Horns of the God, the **Cabarfeidh** (q.v.)

bield: traditional dwelling of Keltic upland areas, usually built into the side of a hill for shelter and warmth

blood-bat: vampiric flying rodent

borraun: wood-framed, tambourine-shaped goatskin drum, played by hand or with a small flat wooden drumstick

Brân, Brân the Blessed: god; one of the High Dânu

braud: 'brother'

brehons: Keltic order of judges; **Archbrieve**, head of the order

Bríghid of the Fire: Keltic goddess of fire, art and smithcraft, spouse of Gavida, the Gabhain Saor; one of the High Dânu; **Brighnasa**, her feast, celebrated on 1 February (*Breed*; *BREE-nuh-suh*)

Brónach: 'The Sorrower'; one of the War-ravens of Malen Ruadh Rhên (the other is **Lanach**, 'The Fulfiller')

brugh: fortified manor house, usually belonging to one of the gentry or nobility; in cities, a town-palace or townhouse of great elegance and size

bruidean: inn, roadhouse or waystation, where any traveller of whatever rank or resources is entitled by law to claim hospitality free of charge

burning-water: marine phosphorescence, seafire (**wyn-o'-the-wave**)

'Bydd i ti ddychwelyd': blessing from Keltic death-ritual, usually spoken by the widowed or chief mourner; translates as 'There shall be a returning for thee' (*beethe-ih-tee-thick-HOOill-idd*, more or less)

Cabarfeidh: the Antlered King; aspect or personification of the God, the male principle of the universe and the Goddess's mate, as the Hornèd Lord, a tall darkhaired man with the antlers of a stag (*CABBER-fay*)

Caer Coronach: 'Castle Lamentation' or 'Crown of the North'; in Keltic theology, the silver-walled castle (also known as **Argetros**, 'Silver Wheel') behind the north wind, to which souls journey as the first stop after death; a place of joy, light and peace, to which the newly dead

soul is guided (and guarded en route by the living who
love it) by those who have gone before who have been
loved or admired by that particular soul in life

cailleach: 'old woman', 'old wife'; term is respectful, not
derogatory; **Cailleach**, 'the Veiled One': a winter
Erinnach constellation

calon-dal: 'heart-hold'; wedding ring designed by Morric
Douglas for Athyn Cahanagh; two hands clasping a
crowned heart; also known as **claddon** or **clondagh**,
much to its creator's annoyance

caltraps: three-spiked iron balls, tossed into the path of
horses in battle, to bring them down with their riders

cantrip: very small, simple spell or minor magic

Caomai: the Armed King, a constellation of the Keltic
zodiac, equivalent to Leo; the **Allwand**, the Baldric of
Caomai, containing the stars known to Terrans as
Betelgeuse, Rigel and Altair

Caravat and Shanavest: in Keltic political history,
two bullying factions notable for their bitter
opposition and their complete similarity of strategy
and tactics

caredd: 'heart'; used to friends and family (pl. **careddau**)

cariad: 'heart'; used to a lover

cariad o'nghariad: 'heart of hearts'; used to a beloved

cariadol: 'heart', 'little love'; used to a child

cariadwyn: 'beloved', literally 'white heart'; the deepest of
the many Keltic endearments, used only between the
soulmated; the suffix 'gwyn', whose usual meaning is
'white', here takes on a connotation of 'sacred, blessed,
holy, only', a chosen and sanctified love

carse: flat land along a river, a river-plain

cashel: fortress or castle built on a high place

cathbarr: fillet or coronet, usually a band of precious metal
ornamented with jewels

catteran: rebel or other irregular fighter; outlaw

céile-charach: 'loved mate'; word for either partner to a legal and formal union short of lawful marriage, or for the partnership itself, whether the partners are man and woman, man and man, or woman and woman

ceili: party or revel with dancing, feasting and music

chiel: term of opprobrium; roughly translates as 'bastard'

clann: tribe or family (also **Name**)

clarsa: Keltic musical instrument similar to a harpsichord

claymore: huge two-handed broadsword favored by Scotan fighters

cleggans: biting, buzzing, annoying insects; blackflies

Comelings: term for those Firvolgians resident in Keltia, formerly known as Incomers, who petitioned Athyn Ard-rían for permission to remain in spite of the Outgoing, and who were by her decree created Keltic subjects

Common Tongue: at this time, not based on the Terran tongue Englic, but on a form of Hastaic, the Coranian mother-language

Coranians: ruling race of the Cabiri Imperium, hereditary enemies of the Kelts; they are the descendants of the Atlandean Telchines, as the Kelts are the descendants of the Atlandean Danaans

Coron-catha: 'war-crown'; garland given on the field to a victorious general

Coron-rhaidd: the Antler Crown of the Cabarfeidh

corrigauns: Otherworld beings, small of stature but powerfully built, usually darkhaired and dark-eyed; opinion in Keltia is divided as to whether the corrigauns (also known as **dwarrows**) are indeed a separate magical race or are actually an aspect of the Sidhefolk

Crann Tarith: 'Fiery Branch'; the token of war across Keltia. Originally a flaming branch or cross; now, by extension, the alarm or call to war broadcast on all planets, or, locally, a horncry or other alarum

creaghts: armed riders, skilled in catteran warfare and living off the land, in the employ of Keltic tigerns and lords (cf. **kienaghts**)

Cremave: the magical clearing-stone of the royal line of St. Brendan; also, a constellation of the Keltic zodiac, equivalent to Libra

cribbens: humble food eaten by travellers, usually a stew of whatever is available or can be hunted

Criosanna: 'The Woven Belts'; the beautiful rings that circle the planet Tara (*criss-anna*)

crochan: magical healing-pool that can cure injury, provided the spinal column has not been severed and the brain and bone marrow are undamaged

crossic: unit of Keltic money; small gold coin

cumha: lament, dirge, elegy; **Cumha Dubhglais,** mourning-poem Athyn Cahanagh made for Morric Douglas (also known as the *Lament for Fireheart*)

cupshot: unpleasantly drunk, soddenly intoxicated

curragh: small, leather-hulled boat, sometimes masted, rowed with oars

cutsark: lit., 'short dress'; common whore

Cwn Annwn: in Keltic religion, the Hounds of Hell; the red-eared, white-coated dogs belonging to Arawn Lord of the Dead, that hunt down and destroy the souls of traitors (*coon annoon*)

Dakdaks: race of biped furred marsupials dwelling on the ice-planet Inalery

dán: 'doom'; fated karma (*dawn*); **dánach,** one who is so fated

Dâna, Dâna Rhên: goddess, one of the High Dânu, sister of Dôn Rhên; patroness of the Keltic people, and especially of the Erinnach

Dancers: name for the polar aurora on Keltic worlds; also **Crown of the North** (or **South**)

daradail: longchafer or other large noxious crawling insect

densaix: three-edged blade used by Sospran kedders in procured assassinations

destrier: huge war-horse, used for both cavalry and chariotry

Dioghaltair-cheart: 'The Just Avenger'; one who seeks capital vengeance under ancient Keltic law

distain: in Keltic households, that one who is champion, who will stand against the enemy before any other shall do so

dolmen: a standing stone, sacred pillar-stone

Dôn Rhên: goddess, one of the High Dânu; traditionally well-disposed to the Kymry, as is her sister Dâna Rhên to the Erinnach

Donn: an aspect of the God, Kernûn Rhên

dorter: large sleeping-room, attic or loft, usually found in garrisons, colleges or large households

downwith: on Erinna, a directional; away from the mountains, toward the sea

Draoícht, Draoíchtas: generic term for the body of arcane knowledge shared by adepts of the Ban-draoi and Druid orders (*DREEkht, DREEkh-tas*)

dróchtas: lit., 'cursings'; general term for 'black' magical workings

drónach: hurdy-gurdy type instrument with a peculiarly haunting sound

Druids: order of Keltic sorcerer-priests, in the service of the God

dubhachas: 'gloom'; melancholy characterized by causeless depression and inexpressible longing for unnameable things; colloquially known as 'the Keltic blacks'

dubh-cosac: stimulant herb usually taken in powder form; burned as incense, it is a powerful hallucinogen

dúchas: lordship or holding; usually carries lands and a title with it

dún: a stronghold of the Sidhe, the Shining Ones (also **liss** or **rath**) (*doon*)

enech-clann: brehon system of honor-price violations and recompense

engrains: tattoos, skin inkings, extremely popular in
Keltia, for ritualistic or clann purposes as well as mere
decoration

éraic: 'blood-price'; in Keltic law, the honor-payment
exacted for a murder by the victim's kin, in lieu of killing
the offender (which is also a lawful option)

Erinna: system of Keltia settled by those of Earth who came
from Ireland (**Erinnach, Erinnachín**)

Erith: old Keltic name for Earth

fágáil: the parting-gift of the Sidhefolk, given to mortals as
favor or requital

faha: courtyard or enclosed lawn-space in a castle or maenor
precinct; space before tent in a military encampment

Faol-mór: 'Great Wolf'; the fetch, or spirit-wolf, that
protects the House of Aoibhell

far-charach: 'loved man'; term for a man formally and
legally associated short of marriage (cf. **ban-charach,
céile-charach**)

farspeaker: early version of transcom; **farviewer:** television

faunt: child when he or she becomes a walker and talker

ferch: 'daughter of' (*vairkh*)

ferren: very handsome species of fir, with thick curving
branches and dense dark green-blue needles; used for the
wintertree at the solstice celebrations

fetch: the visible form, usually an animal of some sort,
taken by the spirit-guardian of a Keltic family, clann or
individual; totem or power animal

Fianna: organization of Keltic soldiery and military supremacy

fidil: four-stringed musical instrument played with a bow

findruinna: silvery, superhard metal used abundantly in
Keltia, especially for swords and other weapons

Fionn, Fionn the Young: god, one of the High Dânu; Fionn
is problematic in that he is a god in his own right, but he
is also the vehicle by which other of the High Dânu

(Gwydion, Mihangel, even Arawn) often choose to make themselves known; the God Himself, the Cabarfeidh, Kernûn Rhên, employs Fionn's appearance to interact with mortals, as the Young Lord; for this Fionn is known as Friend-to-Man, and is much beloved by all Kelts; his feast of **Fionnasa**, 29 September, is a day of revelry as well as worship (*finn*)

fíor-coire: 'the truth of the cauldron'; the test of hospitality offered a wayfarer, for which, if unsatisfactory, the provider may be fined (*feer-curra*)

fíor-comlainn: 'the truth of combat'; legally binding trial by personal combat

Fireheart: bard-name of Morric Douglas, foretold for him by Seli, queen of the Sidhe

Firvolgi: humanoid race native to the Firvolgior system; they began infiltrating Keltic worlds two hundred years before Athyn's time, and not until she, as Blackmantle, drove them out by force did they depart; called by Kelts **Fir Bolc** (*feer BUH-lug*), 'Folk of the Bag', after an old Earth enemy, in a neat wordplay on not only the similarity of sound but the Firvolgs' mercenary attitudes

fith-fath: spell of shapeshifting or glamourie; magical illusion

flain: laser arrow used in arblasts

flink: common harlot or slut

Fomori: ancient enemies of the Kelts, adversaries of St. Brendan

force: 'waterfall'

fosterage: Keltic custom in which children of all social classes are usually exchanged between sets of fostering parents, beginning at the age of five and continuing in most cases to age thirteen; **fostern**, relation by fosterage

Fragarach: 'The Answerer', also translated 'Retaliator'; the Sword of Lugh, one of the Four Chief Treasures of Keltia

*   *   *

Gaeloch: the official language of Keltia, spoken on all
Keltic worlds (in addition to the six major planetary
languages and the many dialects thereof); **High
Gaeloch,** the ancient formal tongue of poetry and ritual

gallaín: 'foreigners'; generic term for all non-Kelts,
humanoid or not (sing. **gáll,** fem. sing. **gállwyn,** fem. pl.
gállwynion); similarly, **outfrenne**

galloglass: Keltic footsoldier, infantryman

gammon: ham or salt pork

gân: sponsal affix used with mate's forename (*Lassarina gân
Séomaighas*)

garron: breed of small, sturdy horses, 13–14 hands high,
gray or dun in color

gauran: plow-beast similar to ox or bullock, legendarily
stubborn

Gavida: the Smith of the Gods, one of High Dânu; his
spouse is Bríghid; **Gavida Burn-the-wind, Gavannaun,
Gabhain Saor, Forgelord**

geis, geisa: prohibition or moral injunction placed upon a
person, often at birth or other significant moment, to do
or not do certain things, some of which can seem ridicu-
lously arbitrary; geisa are broken at great peril, resulting
in certain ill-luck and misfortune,if not worse; **geisa
droma draoíchta,** inviolable baneful magics (*gesh, gesha*)

ghostwillow: beautiful tree with silvery-green leaves and
gray-white bark that grows near streams in upland
forests; deeply sacred to the Goddess

glamourie: small magical spell of appearance or disguise

glib: fringe or forelock of hair; bangs

glozer: shameless flatterer and truckler; sycophant, toady

goldencapes: beautiful rays or mantas, deep bright gold in
color, found in the cool midlatitude oceans of Erinna,
Vannin and Tara; **seawings,** a similar species but with
soft silver coloration

goleor: 'in great numbers, overabundance'; Englic word
galore is derived from it

gralloch: to disembowel, as a stag or other beast killed in the hunt

grá-mór: 'great love'; the love of one's life

grá-traigh: 'heart-song'; one of the twelve bardic musics, to do with love

grafaun: double-edged war-axe

gricemite: very small, poor quality potato usually fed to pigs

grieshoch: embers; low-smoldering hearthfire

Gwener: goddess of beauty and insight; one of the High Dânu; her mate is Midir, her lover is Aengus

Gwenhidw Cloudherd: sky goddess, mate of Manaan Sealord

Gwerin: 'the War-band'; name chosen by Athyn Cahanagh for her armies raised to fight the Incomers; **Gweriden**, those of the Gwerin first to join her, her dearest, closest and most trusted friends and lieutenants

Gwydion ap Dôn: god of writers and sorcerers, one of the Dânu, son of Dôn Rhên; aspected as Fionn the Young

Gwyn ap Neith ac Seli: Prince of the Sidhe; friend, fostern and goddess-son to Athyn Cahanagh, who, as a girl of fourteen, attended at his birth

gytresh: cowlike, apelike creature of very low intelligence, used by the Firvolgi as a slave

hai atton: lit., 'heigh to us'; the horn-cry that rallies an army

Hail: the Eagle-people; winged race native to the planet Galathay, with an average lifespan of more than a thousand years

hal-ya: Firvolgian greeting

handfasting: rite of religious Keltic marriage, as distinguished from civil marriage; a spiritual linking of souls, which is marked by the making of the third of the **Three Cuts** (q.v.)

hardgate: land that has never known the plow

hazen: narcotic that can be sniffed, inhaled, drunk in solution or absorbed through the skin; combined with even a small quantity of wine, it is invariably fatal, though it gives a painless death; named for the glaze that comes in the eyes of the newly dead; **hazer**, one who is addicted to the drug

High Dânu: the eight (or, by other counts, seven, nine, twelve, fourteen or twenty-seven) gods and goddesses of the general Keltic pantheon who are raised up above the rest, to act as intermediary Powers between mortals, the lesser deities and the Highest God (**Kelu**, **Yr Mawreth**, q.v.)

hiraeth: 'longing'; nameless homesick longing or desire for unknown things

hodden: a kind of soft rough-woven woolen cloth, usually heathered gray or brown in color

Hui Corra: flagship of Saint Brendan, in the first immram of Kelts

hujah: exclamation of exultation, disapproval or surprise

Hu Mawr: Hu the Mighty; name for the God as Father in the Kymric pantheon (**Hu** as *hee*; **Mawr** to rhyme with 'power')

hurley: fierce Keltic sport played with a wicker basket-glove and a small hard leather-covered ball; it has been famously said of hurley that it is only distinguishable from warfare because it is not played with a sword

Idris: Keltic god; the Marshal of the Stars, one of the Dânu; also an aspect of Fionn the Young

immram: 'voyage'; pl., **immrama**, the great migrations from Earth to Keltia; **immrama-tuathal**, the reverse voyages of spying and information-gathering that went from Keltia back to Earth

inceptor: third and highest ranking of Druid, Ban-draoi, brehon or bardic aspirants

Incomer: Kelts' almost-universal descriptive term for the

Firvolgi dwelling in Keltia; not well-meant, but just
short of chargeable incivility in brehon law

ingheann: variant of 'inion'; used in the vocative
(cf. **amhic**)

inion: 'daughter'

Inion Rían na Speir: 'the Daughter of the Queen of the Skies';
a constellation of the Keltic zodiac, equivalent to Virgo

Jac Lattin: a threat commonly heard in Connacht; Jac
Lattin was punished by being made to dance from
Graystones to his home in Kensaleyre town more than
thirty miles away and change his dancesteps every lai,
until he died of exhaustion; 'I'll make you dance' is
a common threat, but 'I'll make you dance Jac Lattin'
is a hundred times worse

Jamadarin: title of the matriarchal ruler of Aojun, who is
always of the clan of the Yamazai; her consort, always of
another clan, takes the title **Subhadar**

Keavers: Keltic raiders, ostensibly banded together to fight
off mosstroops

kedders: huge ophidian creatures of the planet Sospiria;
because of their great ferocity, tenacity and chameleonic
qualities, they are often hired to carry out procured
assassinations; once on the bloodtrail they are utterly
relentless, and only their own death will take them
from the hunt

keeve: beaker or barrel

Keltia: interstellar homeland of the Kelts (see **Six Nations**)

Kelu: 'The Crown'; that One High God above all gods held
by Kelts to be both Mother Goddess and Father God
together, or neither, or beyond such distinctions entirely;
the will of Kelu is manifested in Abred by the Goddess
and the God, and wrought by the Alterator

kepp: tremendously strong base beneath an anvil, made from the heart of an oak

Keridwen Rhên: the Goddess in Her most familiar and beloved aspect as Queen and Mother of the World

kern: footsoldier, sailor or starfleet crewman; any warrior not of officer ranking

kethern-a-varna: the one in the gap, who sees the danger coming; warrior who holds the pass against all comers

Kevarwedhor: 'Guide of Souls'; psychopomp, the one who guides candidates through trance states in Ban-draoi and Druid initiations

kienaghts: household retainers; usually organized into troops, often mounted, kienaghts do service to tigerns in exchange for salary and keep, performing such duties as hayward, escort to travellers of the house, helpers in time of flood and other disasters, and such defense as might at times prove needful; in dangerous times trained as **creaghts** (q.v.)

lai: unit of distance measurement, equal to approximately one-half mile

laighard: small footed lacertine creature with characteristics of both lizard and snake

Land Underwave: one of the magical realms

landlash: exceptionally powerful rainstorm with destructive winds

lasathair: 'half-father'; stepfather

lasra: laser

leazing: to glean a field after the reapers have left it in stubble

leinna, pl. **leinne:** loose long-sleeved shirt usually worn under a tunic (*LEN-ya*)

lennaun: lover, with or without benefit of formal legal arrangement

levin: the lightning-bolt; also **fireflaw**

lifter: a beast so weak from starvation it cannot stand and must be carried

Lír the Boundless: god; one of the High Dânu

Llacharn, the Flamebright: magical sword forged by Athyn Cahanagh in Cartha Galvorn, in the presence of the Gabhain Saor, and set by her in the stone in the cave on Collimare

lochan: small lake or mountain tarn

lorica: mail tunic or back- and breastplates worn in battle

Lugh: god; one of the High Dânu; **Lughnasa**, his feast, celebrated on 1 August

lymphad: graceful oared and masted galley used for war; **the Lymphad**, a constellation of the Keltic zodiac, equivalent to Pisces

Macca's Well: a famous alehouse in the Stonerows quarter of Caerdroia, much favored by student bards and brehons, run by a former bard now retired

Macha: title and attributive name of the Great Mother, the Goddess

machair: sea-meadows; wide tracts of salt grassland bordering on the sea and running down to the high-water mark

maenor: hereditary dwelling-place, usually a family seat

-maeth: suffix denoting 'foster-father'

Malen: goddess of war and love, one of the High Dânu; mate to Arawn Rhên and queen of Annwn; in battle she rides in her chariot above the field, and her two ravens, Brónach and Lanach, choose the slain; also **Malen Rhên, Malen Ruadh, the War-red War-queen**

mamaith: 'mother'; equivalent to Englic 'mama' or 'mommy'

Manaan: god, one of the Dânu; his crystal ship that can sail both land and sea is known as **Aonbarr**, 'Wavesweeper', as is also, rather confusingly, his beautiful white stallion; his mate is the sky-goddess Gwenhidw

marbh gan anam: 'dead without life'

Marcher Lords: loose confederation of powerful Erinnach nobles, nominally led by Esmer Lennox, Earl of Connacht

Mari Llwyd: the Ghost Mare; in Keltic mythology a frightening apparition in shape of a giant horse of bones, with fire in her eyes; the Mari Llwyd is an omen of great and terrible significance, presaging events of moment

marúnad: lament, keen; funeral song; **Marúnad Séomaighas**, the lament that Lassarina Aoibhell made for Séomaighas Douglas Ó Morrighsaun

Mâth the Ancient: god; one of the High Dânu

mathra-dhia: goddess-mother, child's female saining-sponsor

mether: four-cornered drinking-vessel, usually made of pottery or wood

methryn: foster-mother

Mi-cuarta: banqueting-hall in the palace of Turusachan

Midir: god, one of the High Dânu; god of meaning, plan, healing and literature; his mate is Gwener

Mihangel: god, one of the High Dânu; god of battle, known as Prince of Warriors (also **Maharrion**), captain of the forces of Light at the battle at the end of the universe

millim: millisecond; unit of time measurement

mochyn yn y lliath: lit., 'the pig in the milk'; mild Keltic expletive

Modron: title and attributive name of the Great Mother, the Goddess in Her Cailleach form, the Wisewoman

Morna: goddess, one of the Dânu; known as Morna the Valorous

Moruadha: the **merrows**, the sea-people; green-haired and red-skinned, of lithe and graceful build, this completely amphibious race dwells chiefly on Kernow but has

migrated to all Keltic planets; their ruler is known as the
Mórar-mhara, Lord of the Seas

mosstroopers: mercenary bravos of the Firvolgi Incomers in
Keltia

Moymell: 'The Pleasant Plain'; region of Annwn where
souls between lives spend time in contemplation

Nâr, Nâredd: hereditary Firvolgian honorifics equivalent to
'Lord' and 'Lady'; **Nârin, Nâreddin**, diminutives used by
children of those so ennobled

nemeton: henge, ceremonial stone circle; **Caer-na-gael** is
chief of these in Keltia

Nevermas: sarcastic; a time that never comes

Nia the Golden: a princess of the Sidhe; mother of Saint
Brendan, wife of Fergus Aoibhell, known as Fergheas
Tinne fo Brega, Fergus Fire on Brega; she is considered
founding mother of the Kelts, beloved and besought as
Saint Nia

ní, nic, nighean: 'daughter of '

Nine Nights: period of formal Keltic mourning marked by
nightly ritual and observance

Numantissans: leonine race native to the Harilak system

ollave: master-bard; by extension, anyone with supreme
command of any art or science (**brehon-ollave, Druid-
ollave**) (*ulluv*)

Óran Mór: the Great Music; formal pipe-music

orm: huge amphibious water-beast found in deepwater
Keltic lakes and sometimes in the oceans, chiefly on the
planets Erinna and Caledon; the species was known to
Erith folk as the Loch Ness Monster; also **piast**; **Peiste**,
the honorific name for a particular breed of orm to
whom Saint Brendan gave the gift of human speech

Otherlands: the magical realms, of death or beyond death

outfrenne: outworld; foreign to Keltia; offworlders, cf. **gallaín**
oxter: ribcage; armpit; angle between side of chest and arm

Pair Dadeni: the great Cauldron of Rebirth presided over
  by Keridwen Rhên, the Queen of the World; one of the
  Four Chief Treasures of Keltia, also aspected as the Graal
  or the Cup of Wonder
pastai: small handmeal consisting of a pastry crust turned
  over and filled with meat and sometimes potatoes and
  onions; may be eaten hot or cold, and will keep for a
  week in warm weather, twice that in winter
Peiste, piast: see **orm**
petty-place: first professional posting of a bard, sorcerer,
  Fian or brehon
piast-tears: false tears of hypocritically feigned emotion
  ("crocodile-tears")
pibroch: battle music played on the war-pipes; each Name
  has its own, the most famous being Clann Douglas's
  'Come wolves for I will feed you flesh'
pishogue: very simple spell or minor magic
plaid: the shoulder-sash worn with a kilt (*plade*, not *pladd*)
Plough: the Keltic constellation that includes Tara's
  Polestar
pompion: small pumpkin, used for the **soulsail** (q.v.)
porrans: potatoes, usually baked or roasted
prester: member of the Firvolgian sorcerer-clergy

quaich: a low, wide, double-handled drinking-vessel, often
  made of precious metal and ornamented with jewels
quaratz: common quartz
quitclaim: legal procedure by which a Kelt may divorce
  himself from his immediate family, for any of a number
  of grave reasons; the person seeking quittance must have
  reached the first-majority age of eighteen years

rann: chanted verse stanza used in magic; spell of any sort; sometimes, poem

rechtair: steward of royal, noble or wealthy houses

Rhên: ancient title meaning 'lord'; now used of both genders and reserved almost exclusively for deities (*rain*)

Rhian: the Maiden, the Young Goddess; an aspect of the Great Mother, when She appears as a young woman, usually with brown hair and gray eyes

Rhiannon: one of the Dânu; goddess of horses

rhisling: battle castoff, thing found on a field of war

Rhygar: the Horseman Archer; a constellation of the Keltic zodiac equivalent to Sagittarius

rígh-domhna: Keltic royal kindreds, as reckoned from a common ancestor, any of whom may (theoretically, at least) be elected to the Sovereignty (*ree-downa*)

ros-catha: battle-cry; Athyn Cahanagh's was 'Go sian-saoghail!' ('To the world's end!')

ruddenwood: tough-grained scarlet-colored wood used for outdoor furniture

Ruvania: imaginary country; **'And I am the Queen of Ruvania!'**, a jesting scoff intended to connote extreme skepticism and unlikeliness

saining: rite of Keltic baptism, administered anywhere from seven days to a moonyear after the birth

Saint Brendan: Brendan Aoibhell, or Brendan mac Nia as he is more usually known; the Great Astrogator, who, to escape the advent of Christianity, led the Kelts from Erith to their new planetary home; ancestor of many of the oldest Keltic families

Samhain: 'Summerend'; the holiest day in the Keltic calendar; the great feast of the beginning of winter and the Keltic New Year; celebrated on 31 October (**Great Samhain**) and continuing through 11 November, **Samhain the Less**, when the **soulsail** is traditionally held (*SAH-win*)

sarsen: dolmen; great upright stone often found in conjunction with nemetons, of a particular blue and smooth-grained mineral composition

schiltron: military formation much used and favored by Kelts in battle; compact and tightly organized, it is extremely difficult to break

seastone: the gem aquamarine

sempster: seamstress or tailor; one who sews

Ser, Beldam: titles used by the Firvolgi, connoting merchantly status

sett: the pattern of a Scotan or Erinnach tartan; tartan is *not* to be called plaid; a **plaid** (q.v.) is a very specific garment, not the pattern of colors and weave

sgian: small black-handled knife universally worn in Keltia, usually in the boot-top or a sheath strapped to the wrist

shakla: chocolate beverage brewed with water from the berries of the brown ash, and drunk throughout the galaxy, hot and cold, as a caffeine-supplying stimulant; enormously popular, it can be made into a syrup or confection, and it is one of the Kelts' most lucrative exports, as it can be grown on very few worlds other than Erinna, Kernow and Vannin

sharnclout: **sharn**, cowdung in a liquid state; **clout**, rag or cloth (*cloot*); a term of extreme opprobrium

shieling: mountain cavern where herds are stabled against rough weather

Sidhe, Aes Sidhe: the Shining Ones; a race of possibly divine or immortal beings inhabiting Keltia (*shee, eyes-shee*)

silkies: see **Sluagh-rón**

Silksteel: Morric Douglas's loving byname for Athyn Cahanagh

silkwool: luxurious fabric much favored in Keltia

silverskin: beautiful, light and extremely tough armor crafted by the Sidhe or the corrigauns; it is very occasionally bestowed upon highly favored mortals

síodarainn: 'silk-iron'; black metal alloy with a green-bronze lustre, extremely strong and tough, frequently used for starship hulls (*sheedah-RAWN*)

Síon of the Storms: a goddess, one of the Dânu (*Sheen*)

sithsilk: very fine, very costly silk fabric

Six Nations: the six star systems of Keltia (excluding the Throneworld system of Tara); in order of their founding they are Erinna, Kymry, Scota, Kernow, Vannin and Arvor (Brytaned)

sizar: first degree of aspirant Druids, Ban-draoi, brehons or bards

skelp: a scold, gadfly or beshrewer; to scold or sharply criticize

skinfuser: dermasealer; laser suturer invented by the Fian healer Lady Liaun Darnaway, a distant cousin of Sosánaigh

skippering: a thrashing, whipping; any mild physical discipline or punishment

skirtins: the wainscot boards round the join between floor and wall

skystone: the gem material turquoise

slinter: term of opprobrium; roughly, 'evil weasel bastard'

Sluagh-rón: the Sealfolk, or silkies; phocine race originally native to Erith that came with other Kelts on the immrama; by now they dwell on all Keltic worlds; like the merrows, they are on excellent terms with their neighbors of all kindreds, mortal and nonmortal alike (**ban-rónna**, 'sealwoman', phocimorph, woman who can boast silkie shapechanger blood or ability, much respected in Keltia)

snowstones: hail, sleet, frozen rain

softsauder: to flatter or butter up; shameless flattery

Solas Sidhe: 'the Faery Fire'; natural phenomenon similar to the will-o'-the-wisp but occurring over rocky ground; usually seen in the spring and fall; also, the magical silvery light or aura sometimes worn by the

Sidhe themselves in the presence of mortals (*sullis shee*)

sophister: second-term Druid, Ban-draoi, brehon or bardic aspirant

soulsail: the practice of sending lighted pompions, small carved pumpkins, on little floats, to sail down the rivers to the sea on the night of Samhain the Less or Samhain itself, in honor of the dead

spancel: cord, string, binding, rope or tether for beasts; **wedding-spancel**, the ritual red-silk cord, three-stranded and braided, used at a handfasting, with which the wrists of the bridal couple are bound, usually by their parents or fosterers

stirk: young calf

Stonerows: ancient quarter of Caerdroia, frequented by artists and students

streppoch: term of opprobrium; roughly, 'bitch'

súgachan: small roadhouse or inn, where music of all sorts is the rule

sulter: oppressive heat and humidity

summerbyes: chrysanthemums

sun-gun: moon-sized (and -based) laser cannon used to defend planets

sun-shark: species of dolphin native to most Keltic oceans; friendly and gregarious, often helpful to humans in distress at sea, they are intelligent beings who can communicate with not only each other, but with humans, silkies and merrows

Sunstanding: summer or winter solstice; the festivals held at those times

syndal: fine, extremely expensive silk

syra-wyn: 'grandfather', 'great-grandfather'

Tacharan: enigmatical magical being who governs Moymell for Arawn Rhên

taish: magical projection of a person's face or form; common slang for 'ghost' or any kind of extraordinary phantom vision or apparition

Tanglecoated Horse: aspect of Aonbarr, the beautiful white stallion belonging to Manaan Sealord

tannan: splendid full-branched conifer with beautiful blue-green needles, often used as the wintertree

Tanist, Tanista: heir of line to the Keltic throne; Crown Prince or Crown Princess of Keltia

Taoiseach: Prime Minister of Keltia (*TEE-shaakh*)

tasyk: 'daddy'; child's name for 'father'

tathryn: fosterfather

telyn: lap-harp of the Gwynedd mountains

theophane: appearance or operation of the Goddess or the God placed upon a mortal; avatar, a soul sent back to serve as instrument of Kelu's will to the world

thole: to endure, to bear a grief or burden, to stand what is thrown at one

thrawn: stubborn, unreasonably perverse against all advice

Three Circles: in Keltic theology, the three levels of existence—**Annwn**, the Otherland, where the souls of the dead reside between lives; **Abred**, the Path of Changes, the visible, everyday world of imperfections and strivings; and **Gwynfyd**, the Circle of Perfection, where dwells Kelu, only to be attained to by created beings after many cycles of rebirth

Three Cuts: tiny ceremonial nicks made on one's wrist with a consecrated sgian, during rites of saining, fosterance and handfast marriage, to obtain a few drops of blood for the purposes of these three most solemn rituals; the principle being invoked is courage and willingness to suffer and sacrifice—for oneself, for a fostern or for a mate

Three Shouts: the means by which Kelu created the world (also the **Speaking of the Name**)

Throne of Brendan, Cathair Bhrendaín: a Keltic constellation

Throne of Scone: in common usage, the Keltic seat of governance; the actual throne, a high-backed chair of white granite, carved with mystical sigils, that came with Brendan from Erith

throughbreds: breed of swift elegant horses used in racing and riding

tigern: 'lord'; proprietor of a Keltic maenor or farm establishment; **subtigerns**, the dependents on such an estate

tinnól: marriage-gift each partner gives the other, usually on the morning after the wedding or handfasting; **tinnscra**, wedding gift from a couple's friends or kindred

Tolbooth: grim Firvolgi prison built in Caerdroia; it was also the seat of Incomer government (the **Council of Elders**)

torc: gold or silver neck ornament worn by Kelts of rank

traha: more than simple arrogance; overweening wanton pride, hubris

triail-triarach: the three-part ordeal which must be passed by aspiring Fians

Trinaethwr: 'the plowing ox on the tilth side'; bardic or mystical byname for Arthur Penarvon

tynollish: sweathouse or lodge similar to Terran sauna

Tywarchwr: 'the plowing ox on the turf side'; bardic or mystical byname for Athyn Cahanagh

upwith: toward the mountains; adverb of direction used on Erinna (also inwith, any direction away from the sea)

usqua: 'water of life'; Keltic whiskey, invariably unblended

-vaeth: suffix signifying 'fostermother'

Velenax: 'Wild Boar'; not entirely admiring byname given Esmer Lennox by the Incomers

vennels: tunnels under buildings and, often, city walls

vitriglass: clear crystalline substance, its molecular structure reinforced by metallic ions, used in starship viewports and other such applications for its extreme hardness and resistance to shattering

Volgiaran: the language of the Firvolgi

war-witch: Fian sorcerer, male or female, trained in the art of battle sorcery

waterstairs: small constructed waterfall running through the center of a street, for pleasure and spiritual purposes as well as mere cleaning

waxflower: vine with beautiful waxen-looking ivory blossoms

"White your world": a benediction

whitrit: a type of particularly foul-tempered weasel or foumart; a term of opprobrium

windpuffs: dandelion fluffs, blown away by children to tell time

Y Sygnau: (also **Y Sidyth**) the Keltic zodiac as seen from Tara; the thirteen signs of which include **Paladryn**, the Twin Spears, equivalent to Gemini, and **Llenaur**, Golden Cloak, equivalent to Cancer

Yamazai: dominant race of the planet Aojun the More; usually refers to, specifically, the matriarchal and matrilineal clan of fierce and able women warriors who rule the planet and system

Yr Mawreth: 'The Highest'; Kymric name for that supreme Deity known also as Kelu or Artzan Janco, the Shepherd of Heaven, the One God who is above all gods

zareer: Firvolgian term for whorehouse or bawdhouse

Gazetteer of Keltic (and other) Places

A'Mhaighdean: wild and remote mountainous area of north-central Erinna (*uh-WAJJ-in*)

Aber-dau-gleddau: 'Mouth of the Two Swords'; site of Athyn Blackmantle's final and decisive victory over the Incomers (*abber-die-GLEH-thigh*)

Alligin Water: small river in Armoy province

Aojun the More: homeworld of the Aojunni; its capital city is Mistissyn (*OW-jin*, ow as in cow)

Arderydd: first major battle, and one of the great triumphs, fought by Athyn Cahanagh and the Gwerin forces against the Incomers

Ardturach: 'the High-towered Place'; seat of the Earls of Connacht on Erinna

Armoy: lovely scenic district in central area of Tara's Northwest Continent

Arvon: extremely rough and mountainous district in the far west of the main Gwyneddan continent

Arvor: (or **Brytaned**) one of the Six Nations of Keltia

Avon Dia: 'River of the Gods'; the Great River on Tara, that bisects the entire Northwestern Continent (*avvin dee-a*)

Bannochburn: a small stream that feeds into the Avon Dia, close by Caerdroia

Belnagar: sacred hill in the Yarrow Valley of Caledon, upon which stands the nemeton of Starcross

Bight of Caerdroia: the bay on whose eastern shore the Keltic capital stands

Brondor: shield-mountain in the Connacht mountains,

where Cormac mac Archill and his wife Lyleth
are buried beneath a chalk hill-figure of a running horse;
from this the valley is known as **the White Horse Vale**

Caer Dathyl: capital and chief city of Kymry, on the planet
Gwynedd

Caerdroia: capital city of Keltia; known as **Caravossa** by
the Incomers

Caerlaverock: 'lark castle' or 'fort among the elm trees';
childhood home of Athyn Cahanagh, in Elmet on
Erinna

Caledon: chief planet of the Scotan system

Casterlines: Fian training establishment in the Riddings,
near Shanagolden

Cleddau Vaur, Cleddau Vach: 'Great Sword', 'Small
Sword'; two rivers on Tara

Clero: the Keltic trading planet, established by Athyn
Ard-rían

Clowyn: 'white foaming water'; mountain river in
Nancledra on Erinna

Collimare: 'The Forest in the Sea'; a small island in Loch
Bel Draccon

Connacht: province of the planet Erinna

Craiganaeth: 'The Rock of Sorrow'; hill in Glenshee,
latterly known as **Gwel-y-Sidan**, 'Bed of Silk', or
Labasheeda in the Erinnach tongue

Deveron Highlands: lovely mountainous area of Erinna,
much frequented by holiday-makers (Deveron, 'dark
waters')

the Dragon's Spine: great mountain range in the extreme
southwest of Tara's main continent

Druimattow: 'the Long Hills'; major mountain range in
central Connacht

Dún Aengus: chief seat, so far as is known, of the Sidhefolk on the throneworld of Tara, located in the Hollow Mountains

Dyved: planet of the Kymric system

Elmet: mountainous district in western Connacht, the home of many horse-studs

Erinna: one of the Six Nations of Keltia; chief planet of the Erinnach system

Erith: Keltic name for the planet Earth

Falls of Yarin: waterfall of the Bannochburn, on eastern edge of Caerdroia

Farranfore: 'The Cold Lands'; a high salt desert in the south of Tara

Fialzioch: battleground on Erinna where Athyn's parents were slain and where Cormac mac Archill found her

Findhorn: 'white waters'; traditional lordship of Athyn's branch of Clann Aoibhell; a hill-province on Erinna with many rivers and streams

Firvolgior: home system of the Firvolgians, who are known to the Kelts as the Fir Bolc; capital world is Kaireden, with the capital city of Katilon Ke Katil

Gala: province in the westlands of Caledon; capital is the market town of **Galashiels**, which stands on the banks of the **Gala Water** near **Loch Grane** (*galla, galla-SHEELS; Grane, grahn*)

Ganaster: third planet of the Nicanor system, on which is seated the High Justiciary; the capital city is Eribol

Gavida's Smithy: volcanic island far out in the Bay of Caerdroia

Glenshee: vast hidden valley in the Hollow Mountains

Graystones: provincial market-town of Connacht; country seat of Esmer Lennox

Gwynedd: chief planet of the Kymric system

Heart Fell: in Armoy, small mountain deriving its name from a heart-shaped clearing on its side, where Morric Douglas and Athyn Cahanagh were formally betrothed

Heliawater: long deep fjord in the southwest of Tara

Highfold: in Caerdroia, the terrace ridge just below Turusachan

Hollow Mountains: great mountain range in far northeast of the main continent of Tara

Kaireden: homeworld of Firvolgior; a large planet with many desert areas; capital is **Katilon Ke Katil**

Kernow: one of the Six Nations; homeplanet of the Kernish system

Khed Anjaval: royal fortress on Aojun the More, home palace of the reigning Jamadarin and Subhadar of the Yamazai

Kincarden: home maenor of Athyn's parents, Dechtira Aoibhell and Conn Strathearn, in the Ox Mountains on Erinna

Kymry: one of the Six Nations of Keltia

the Leap: a marked place in the wild chasm of the river Drumna, where if a fugitive from law can leap across and survive (the fall to the river is over a hundred feet, and the chasm itself is more than forty feet wide), he is safe from the law on those offenses for which he is pursued (**"Beyond the Leap, beyond the law"**)

Lennoxliss: town brugh of the Lennox earls, on Highfold at Caerdroia

Llyn Baravogue: beautiful crater-lake atop the mountain Sheehallion

Loch Bel Draccon: 'Lake of the Dragon's Mouth,' an arm of the Sea of Glora

the Long Hills: high rugged range of mountains on Erinna (**Druimattow**)

the Loom: range of mountains rising behind Caerdroia; **Mount Eagle**, or **Eryri**, is the highest peak, at eight thousand feet

Meldeburna: birthplace of Morric Douglas on Caledon

Mistissyn: capital of the Yamazai throneworld of Aojun

Mount Eagle: the two-horned mountain that rises behind Caerdroia

Mount Keltia: the highest mountain in all Keltia, in the center of Tara's Northwest Continent; its peaks are known as the **Gates of the Sun**

Moymore: 'Great Plain'; the vast central Great Plain on Tara

Nancledra: 'Vale of the Sword'; remote valley in the Long Hills, where Athyn established a secret camp for the Gwerin

Nantosvelta: the secret tunnel, constructed by Brendan's master-builder Gradlon of Ys, running beneath the mountain range of the Loom, connecting the Keep of Turusachan with Wolfdale, as an escape route at need

Nicanor: system in which is located the planet Ganaster

Ni-maen: great and ancient nemeton, or stone circle, in Calon Eryri, 'Heart of Eagle', the high valley up behind Caerdroia between the peaks of Mount Eagle; traditional barrowing-ground of the monarchs of Keltia

Oriors: province of Erinna, adjoining Connacht

the Orrest Hills: mountain range on the planet Caledon

Otherlands: general term for Annwn and other magical planes

the Plains of Ellertrin: on Tara, region of central Northwest Continent

Port-na-tir: on Caledon, small riverine townland known for its roses; home lands of Clann Aba

Powys: planet of the Kymric system

Radwinter: castle-keep of Tipherris Inchspell of Greyloch

the Raise: wide upland running from the Orrests to the Teviots on Caledon

the Riddings: mountain range along the eastern side of Heliawater

Ruchdi: the single, very large moon of the planet Caledon; also, valley on Caledon

Scartanore: 'The Thicket of Gold'; pre-eminent Ban-draoi school, on Erinna

Scota: one of the Six Nations of Keltia

Seana Bhraigh: Athyn's first secret headquarters (*SHANN-a-VRAY*)

Sea of Glora: vast inland freshwater sea on the planet Gwynedd

Seaholt: picturesque fishing-village on the Connacht coast, with stepped streets; home of Morvoren Kindellan's family

Shanagolden: ancient small walled city in Teffia, near Casterlines

Shanavogue: sister city to Shanagolden; destroyed in a civil war

Sheehallion: 'hallowplace of the Sidhefolk'; sacred mountain on Erinna

Sherramuir: site on Caledon of a major battle fought

against the Incomers by Esmer Lennox, Earl of
Connacht
Silverwood: the brehon school Athyn attended on Dyved
the Stair: very high mountain range, perpetually snow-
crowned, to the north of Caerdroia
Starcross: oldest of the Caledonach nemetons, atop
Belnagar, a sacred hill in the Yarrow Valley, where
Athyn and Morric were married
Strath Mór: 'the Great Glen', on the planet Tara
Suka Vellanor: a first-magnitude white star, the primary
of the home system of the Fasarini, a very attractive
humanoid race; their chief world is Aquelana, their
capital Elaby Gathen

Tamon Acanis: a beautiful southern sea-town on the planet
Tara, with mountains and desert nearby
Tara: the Throneworld of Keltia; a large ringed planet with
two moons, white **Argialla** and red **Bellendain;** the rings
are known as the **Criosanna**, 'The Woven Belts'
Teffia: hill region in southwest Tara
Thomond: lush hill region of mid-eastern Erinna,
hereditary princedom of the Aoibhells
the Timpaun: 'the Drumhead'; broad grassland plain on
Erinna; many horse-studs are located here for the
richness of the grazing
Turusachan: 'Place of Gathering'; the royal palace at
Caerdroia; by extension, the entire central government
of Keltia; also, the plateau area above the city, just below
Eryri, where the various governmental buildings are
located (*TOOR-oo-SAKH'n*)
Ty'n-coed, Tincoats: 'the House in the Wood'; refuge built
for Athyn by Morric, in a remote part of the Dales, three
hundred miles east of Caerdroia

*   *   *

Vannin: one of the Six Nations of Keltia

Westmark: remote mountainous province on Caledon
White Wellans, Vaxan Wellans: two tiny villages in the Deveron Highlands
Windishaar: market town in central Erinna, on the Oriors-Connacht border
Witchingdene: small castle in Armoy, given to Athyn and Morric as a wedding gift by her cousin Maravaun Aoibhell
Wyvis Yarrow: maenor house on Caledon, belonging to the Macosquin lairds of Yarrow; Athyn and Morric were married from there

Yarrow Valley, Yarrow Water: in Caledon's Westmark, a wild mountain river and its valley, south and east of Fleetdale; clann lands of the Macosquins
Yr Hela: 'The Hunting-ground'; westermost of the two peaks of Eryri, Mount Eagle

Main Characters

Names are listed by forename, not surname.

Allyn mhic Midna: a lord of the Sidhe; friend to Athyn and Morric (*allen vick MEETHE-na*)

Alveric Elshender: Fian; Gweriden; mate to Bronwyn Muirheyd; friend to Athyn and Morric

Amzalsunëa Dalgarno: Incomer; daughter of Falxifer and Margiamnë; onetime lennaun of Morric Douglas (**Melassaun**) (*amz'l-soo-NAY-uh*)

Ardattin: Athyn's red-brindle wolfhound bitch (*ar-DAH-chin*)

Ashlinn Glyndour: youngest daughter of the Lord of Gwaelod; wife to Maravaun Aoibhell, Prince of Thomond; mother of Raffan, his heir

Athyn Cahanagh: Ard-rían by acclamation, Queen of Kelts; birthdaughter of Dechtira Aoibhell and Conn Strathearn; wife to Morric Douglas; she rid Keltia forever of the Firvolgi Incomers; as High Queen, she established the Keltic trading planet of Clero, began the long alliance and friendship with Aojun of the Yamazai, and created standing armed forces so that never again would Keltia be taken over from outside, as it was by the Incomers. She is considered one of the greatest monarchs in Keltic history, known in latter times as Athyn Taighlech, Athyn the Glorious, first of three Keltic monarchs to be given that byname (three others rejoice in the appellation 'the Great', and three are called 'the Holy'); her union with Morric Douglas is regarded as one of the great love stories of Keltia, and their latter end has gone into legend; she is most commonly known as **Athyn Blackmantle**, or by her correct family name of **Aoibhell;** also **Athnë Marwinë** (by the Firvolgi), **Athuina Isarona** (her formal style as Queen; 'Isarona' = 'Findhorn', her branch of Clann Aoibhell), **Athyn of the Battles, Athyn Anfa, Athyn nic Archill** (the surname of her fosterers, Cormac and Lyleth, though they did not foster her strictly according to law); in his poems and songs and writings, and in their private life, Morric Douglas called her **Silksteel** (*ATH-inn; ca-HANN-a; ee-VELL*)

Aunya nic Cafraidh: Gweriden; horsemaster to Cormac mac Archill; mentor, teacher and friend to Athyn; Athyn created her Countess of Glyndrâgon

Baigran Dyoleus: Incomer and war criminal; slain by Greyloch and Liadan

Brahím of Aojun: Subhadar-Lord of the Yamazai; consort to the Jamadarin Zarôndah; gifted bard and musician; friend to Morric and Athyn (*BRAH-heem*)

Breos mac an Aba: Fian; Gweriden; mate to Morvoren Kindellan; friend to Athyn and Morric; Athyn created them Duke and Duchess of Kernow

Bronwyn Muirheyd: Archbrieve; Ban-draoi; Gweriden; cousin to Selanie Drummond; friend to Athyn and Morric; mate to Alveric Elshender; Athyn created them Duchess and Duke of Rodorion (*bron-win MOOR-heed*)

Cathárren Tanaithe: Ban-draoi; Gweriden; friend to Athyn and Morric; later became Mathr'achtaran of the Ban-draoi

Comyn and **Havoise Douglas:** Morric Douglas's parents, whom he disowned in his early youth; Athyn banished them for their crimes against him

Conamail: High King of Keltia a century before his successor Athyn; his death without heir resulted in the very bitter, prolonged succession wars, keeping the Throne of Scone vacant and allowing the Incoming to flourish unchecked

Conn Strathearn: birthfather of Athyn Cahanagh; husband of Dechtira Aoibhell; Lord of Galloway on Caledon

Cormac mac Archill: lord of Caerlaverock; father to Kier, by first wife Kerys; by second wife Lyleth, father to Debagh, Tigernach, Galian, Errick and Sulior; adoptive father to Athyn

Dalgu Namani: Incomer, profiteer and war criminal; executed by Stellin Ardwyr and Mariota Lennox

Debagh nic Archill: fostern of Athyn; Gweriden; a brilliant limner, she designed the tapestries that hang in the chamber Gwahanlen, and raised for Athyn and Morric a monument that still stands in Keltia two thousand years after they are gone

Dechtira Aoibhell: birthmother of Athyn Cahanagh and a direct descendant of Brendan the Astrogator through his daughter Fionaveragh; known as **Síonarân**, 'Silverstorm', among the Sidhefolk

Donn Aoibhell: Athyn's ancestor; son-in-law, distant cousin, war-leader and friend to Brendan; he married Fionaveragh, Brendan's daughter, to found the House of Aoibhell; the Aoibhells of Thomond are descended from Kiaran his second son, while Athyn's line, the senior branch of Findhorn which is believed to have ended with her, derives from Sithney his eldest daughter

Elster: the wheaten wolfhound Athyn owned in her girlhood

Erramun Zedoary: Firvolg; master-lutanist; onetime bandfellow of Morric Douglas

Errick mac Archill: son of Cormac mac Archill and Lyleth Kerguethen; fostern to Athyn; Gweriden; she installed him as heriot of Caerlaverock, and he later wedded Rhiannyn of Trevattow, the rechtair Athyn appointed to the maenor

Esmer Lennox: Earl of Connacht; husband to Ganor; father of Mariota; mentor and protector to Athyn; known to the Incomers as **Velenax**, 'wild boar'; prime mover of the Outgoing; Athyn created him first Prince of Connacht, and appointed him her Taoiseach for life

Etain: a lady of the Sidhefolk; later the bride of Gwyn ap Neith

Evance Tregar: Firvolg; tambor-master; onetime bandfellow of Morric Douglas

Falxifer and **Margiamnë Dalgarno:** Incomers; parents of Amzalsunëa; banished by Athyn

Fleance: innkeeper at Shanagolden; friend to Athyn and Morric; loyalist and spy, of great service to the Gwerin

Ganor Colquhoun: Countess, later Princess, of Connacht; wife to Esmer Lennox, mother to Mariota; unofficial fostermother to Athyn and campmother to all the Gweriden

Gerr and **Failenn mac an Aba:** Gweriden; friends of Athyn and Morric; Breos's older brother and sister-in-law; Athyn created them Earl and Countess of Port-na-tir

Gwyn ap Neith: Prince of the Sidhe; son of Neith and Seli, king and queen of the Shining Folk; foster-son and goddess-son to Athyn; friend to Athyn and Morric

Haneria Lauder: bard of Elmet who taught the young Athyn and the other Archill children

Iolo Forsycht: local Elmet Druid, who, with Haneria, kept the secret, and the proofs, of Athyn's parentage

Jaffran Eskendy: Firvolg; clarsa-master; onetime bandfellow of Morric Douglas

Jalior: Firvolg; lennaun of Morric Douglas's bandfellow Shane Ó Falvey; later a strumpet in the bawdhouse of Pharuca T'pettun, slain by Athyn on Kaireden

Jirko pen Rhys: half-Kelt, half-Firvolg; profiteer and war criminal; slain by Athyn

Katterin de Curteis: Ban-draoi and brehon; Gweriden; friend of Athyn and Morric; wife to Lord Rhodri mac Maolain of Lochaber; Athyn created her Countess of Graystones

Kier mac Archill: eldest son and heir of Cormac; joined the Keavers to raid against the Incomers, then betrayed Keltia by siding with the Firvolgi; he is known as Kier Anbhartach (Evildoer) to chroniclers

Lassarina Aoibhell ac Douglas: Erinnach bard; wife to the great Scotan bard Séomaighas Douglas Ó Morrighsaun; their story is counted among the great Keltic romances

Leto Novedris: Incomer, profiteer and war criminal; betrayed Morric Douglas and slandered Athyn Cahanagh; executed by Athyn

Líadan: beautiful long-haired white war-dog belonging to Tipherris Inchspell

Lira Cromell: brehon; Gweriden; friend to Athyn and Morric

Lorcan Firdanisk: half-Kelt, half-Incomer; informer and war criminal; slain in single combat by Athyn

Loris Venoët: Coranian-Firvolg playmaster; Gweriden killed him on Kaireden

Lorn Aoibhell: the Maid of Astyllen and the Mistress of Findhorn; mother of Dechtira Aoibhell

Lyleth Kerguethen: wife to Cormac; mother to Debagh, Tigernach, Galian, Errick and Sulior; stepmother to Kier; adoptive mother to Athyn

Lyrin: Firvolg; lennaun of Evance Tregar; later a strumpet in Pharuca T'pettun's bawdhouse, she was spared by Athyn

Mâli: golden-coated war-dog belonging to Mariota Lennox and Stellin Ardwyr

Maravaun Aoibhell: Prince of Thomond; Athyn's nearest blood kinsman; Gweriden, one of the first supporters of the Gwerin and devoted sponsor of his long-lost cousin's claim to the crown

Mariota Lennox: bard and Gweriden; daughter of Esmer and Ganor; friend to Athyn and Morric; mate to Stellin Ardwyr; Athyn created them Duchess and Duke of Kells; Mariota was Taoiseach of Keltia in Athyn's reign after her father's death, and also served as Taoiseach to Rohan IV; she succeeded her father to the coronet of Connacht

Micháltaigh Pendreic: Fian; Gweriden; mate to Sosánaigh Darnaway; friend to Athyn and Morric; he was elected King of Kelts to succeed Athyn, and, under the crown-name of Rohan IV, was the first monarch of the Pendreic House of Dôn; his daughter, Lassarina Athyn, succeeded him (**Miach**) (*mee-HAWL-ta*)

Mihangel Glenrossa: Fian and bard; Gweriden; friend to Athyn and Morric; Athyn created him Duke of Glenrois; his brother was **Robat Lord Rossdal**

Morric Douglas: master-chaunter and harper, bard-ollave;

mate to Athyn Cahanagh; King of Keltia by his marriage
to her; he is considered the greatest chaunter of his time,
and one of the finest bards in Keltic history; his union
with Athyn is held to be one of the great romances of
Keltia (**Fireheart;** to Athyn only, **Morrighsaun**)

Morvoren Kindellan: Gweriden; friend to Athyn and
Morric; she was of silkie blood from the Kelts' time
on Earth; mate to Breos mac an Aba; Athyn created
them Duke and Duchess of Kernow; their son Teulyr
was the founder of the Kernish House of Tregaron
(*more-VORE-en*)

Neith ap Llyr: King of the Sidhe; by his queen, Seli, father
to Gwyn

Nilos Marwin: Incomer and poet; second husband to
Lyleth Kerguethen; fosterfather to Athyn, and, in
Firvolgior, her warder-guardian, or legal parent

Phaal Torcwyn: brehon and Druid; Gweriden; friend to
Athyn and Morric

Pharuca T'pettun: Firvolg whoremonger plying her trade
in Keltia and, after the Outgoing, on Kaireden; slain by
Athyn on Kaireden

Raighne Ard-rían: High Queen of Keltia several hundred
years before Athyn's reign; began first real Keltic trade
with other star systems (*RAWN-ya*)

Rhain mac an Iolair: Fian and Druid; Gweriden; Athyn's
swordmaster at Casterlines and her Lieutenant-general in
the campaigns of the Outgoing; friend to Athyn and
Morric; mate to Selanie Drummond; Athyn created them
Duke and Duchess of Eaglespur; he was later elected
Captain-general of the Fianna (*Rhine mac-uh-NILL-ir*)

Rhiannyn of Trevattow: assistant horsemaster to the Gwerin; married Athyn's fostern Errick mac Archill; Rhia and Errick rebuilt the maenor and studs of Caerlaverock, and bred the renowned Glora strain of throughbred racers

Rhufain: Athyn's horse in her days with the Gweriden, a giant bronze stallion

Rhykeur Pym: Incomer and war criminal; slain by Rhain and Selanie

Rozenath: lennaun of Erramun Zedoary; later a strumpet in Pharuca T'pettun's Kaireden bawdhouse, she was punished by Athyn Cahanagh

Selanie Drummond: Fian war-witch; Gweriden; mate to Rhain mac an Iolair; friend and counselor to Athyn and Morric (**Selanie:** *rhymes with Melanie*)

Seli: Queen of the Sidhe; wife to Neith, mother to Gwyn; by Rhûn, a mortal, mother to Edeyrn

Séomaighas Douglas Ó Morrighsaun: brilliantly gifted Scotan bard-ollave; husband to the Erinnachín bard Lassarina Aoibhell, for and about whom he wrote the famous song 'My Love in Green', upon her teasingly wagering him on their wedding night that he could not write her such a lovesong in ballad form; he was murdered only a year after their marriage; theirs is one of the great love stories of Keltia

Shane Ó Falvey: master piper; onetime bandfellow of Morric Douglas

Shelia: tricolor Kernish sheepdog belonging to Rhain and Selanie

Sionnabharra: red-coated war-dog belonging to Cathárren Tanaithe and Phaal Torcwyn

Sosánaigh Darnaway: bard-ollave and Gweriden; friend to Athyn and Morric; fostern to Mariota Lennox; later Chief Bard of Keltia; named by Athyn Duchess of

Westmark, she became Queen of Keltia by her marriage
to Micháltaigh Pendreic, and was the mother of
Lassarina Athyn, first Ard-rían of the House of Dôn
(**Sósaun**) *(so-SAWN-uh, SO-sawn)*

Stellin Ardwyr: Fian; Gweriden chariotry commander and
historian; friend of Athyn and Morric; mate to Mariota
Lennox; Athyn created them Duke and Duchess of
Kells, and they later succeeded Esmer and Ganor as
Princess and Prince of Connacht

Sulior nic Archill: fostern to Athyn; Gweriden; Ban-draoi
Domina and healer

Tarleisio: thought to be a lady of the Sidhe; friend of
Athyn and Morric

Tarn: Athyn's horse in her youth, a gray stallion

Tipherris Inchspell of Greyloch: fostern of Esmer Lennox;
Gweriden commander; friend of Athyn and Morric; his
mate was **Hutcheon Fraser**, a renowned Fian general

Zarôndah: Jamadarin of Aojun; friend and ally of Queen
Athyn and King Morric; began the long alliance and
great historic friendship between the Yamazai and
the Kelts

тhe вooks of тhe кelтіаd

The Tales of Brendan
*The Rock Beyond the Billow
*The Song of Amerguin
*The Deer's Cry

*The Sails of the Hui Corra (**A Book of Voyages**)

Blackmantle (**The Tale of Athyn**)

*Lord of the Dark (**The Tale of Edeyrn**)

The Tales of Arthur
The Hawk's Gray Feather
The Oak Above the Kings
The Hedge of Mist

*Lions in the North (**Tales of the Douglas**)

The House of the Wolf
*The Wolf's Cub
*The King's Peace
*The Beltain Queen

The Tales of Aeron

The Silver Branch
The Copper Crown
The Throne of Scone

The Tales of Gwydion

*The Shield of Fire
*The Sword of Light
*The Cloak of Gold

Edited by Patricia Kennealy-Morrison:

§ *Fireheart: The True 'Lost Writings' of James Douglas Morrison*
The Poetry, Songs, Drawings and Love Letters of Jim
Morrison to Patricia Morrison, edited and annotated
by Patricia Morrison, with a foreword by Jim
Morrison.

* forthcoming

§ to be published in 2003 or 2021, depending on copyright con-
siderations

A History of the Kelts

Twenty thousand years before the start of the Common Era, the Tuatha De Danaan, the People of the Goddess Dâna, arrived on Earth as refugees from a distant star system whose sun had gone nova, and established great city-realms at Atlantis, Lemuria, Nazca, Machu Picchu and other centers of energy. It was an age of high technology and pure magic coexisting: lasers, powered flight in space and in atmosphere, telepathy, telekinesis and the like. There was some minimal contact with the primitive native inhabitants, who, awed, regarded the lordly Danaans as gods from the stars.

After many centuries of peace and growth, social and spiritual deterioration set in: faction fights, perversions of high magical techniques, civil war. The Danaans withdrew to the strongholds of Atlantis, or Atland as they called it, there to fight until Atland was destroyed in a fierce battle fought partially from space, which resulted in a huge earthquake and subsequent geologic upheaval that sank the entire island-continent. (The battle and sinking of Atland were preserved in folk-myth round the world, the effect on the Earth primitives having obviously been considerable.)

The evil Atlandeans, the Telchines, escaped back into space; their descendants would later be heard of as the Coranians. The Danaan survivors made their way as best they could over the terrible seas to the nearest land—Ireland—and to the other sea-countries on the edge of the European landmass. There had long been Atlandean outposts there, and they made a likely refuge. (Some Telchines even found haven in the fastnesses of the Pyrenees; their ancient language—unrelated to any other tongue spoken on Earth—is still to be heard there today.)

But the refugees had yet another battle to fight: with the Fir Bolc and the Fomori, the native tribes currently in occupation of Ireland. Atlandean technology carried the day, however, and the Danaans settled down to share the island and rebuild their all-but-lost civilization.

After a long Golden Age, the peace was shattered by invasion: the Milesians, Celts from the European mainland. War exploded; the new tribe was clever, brave, persuasive and quarrelsome. The Danaans, at first victorious in defense, were at last defeated by the strategies of the brilliant Druid Amerguin. They conceded Ireland to the Milesians, and obtained sureties of peace.

That peace lasted many hundreds of years; there was great amity, intermarriage, joint explorative and military endeavor. Then a period of Milesian jealousy and Danaan distrust turned to hostility, and the elder race began to withdraw. With the coming of Pátraic to Ireland, bringing the less than tolerant new religion, persecutions even broke out, as Pátraic and his monks called upon all to denounce the Danaans as witches and evil sorcerers.

But Brendan, a Milesian war-lord's son, was also part Danaan by birth—and more in spirit. His mother was Nia, a Sidhe princess, and he had been taught by her in the ways of her people. Rebelling against the persecutions and condemnation of the old knowledge, he resolved to take the Danaans home again into the stars, to find a new world where they could live as they pleased.

After study, instruction, construction and a few short trial trips, Brendan was ready, and the Immrama, the Great Emigrations, began. Following the directions of Barinthus, an old man who was probably the last space voyager living on Earth, Brendan and those who wished to go with him in his ship the *Hui Corra* left the planet. After a two-year journey, they found the place they sought: a habitable star system a thousand light-years from Terra; Keltia, as it would come to be known, would eventually command seven inhabited planetary systems and a huge sphere of influence in the galaxy.

The emigrations continued in secret over a period of some eight hundred years; not only humans but the races known as the merrows and the silkies—and the Sidhe themselves.

After that first great immram, Brendan himself remained in the new worlds, organizing a government, overseeing the continuing voyages, setting up all the machinery needed to run the society he dreamed of: a society based on freedom and total equality of gender, age, nationality and religion, fixed on the solid and compassionate foundation of brehon law. He would come to be venerated as St. Brendan the Astrogator, first ruler of Keltia, and his line continues there to this day.

By about Terran year 1200, the Keltic population had increased so dramatically (from both a rising birth rate and continued immigration from Earth) that further colonization was needed. The Six Nations were founded, based on the six Keltic nations of Earth: Ireland, Scotland, Wales, Man, Cornwall and Brittany, called in Keltia Erinna, Scota, Kymry, Vannin, Kernow and Brytaned. A ruling council of six viceroys, one from each system, was set up, called the Fáinne, the Ring. The monarchy continued, though the Fáinne had equally sovereign power at this time.

This was the Golden Age of Keltia. The mass immigrations ended at around Terran year 1450, and the dream of Brendan seemed long since achieved. There was complete equality, as he had intended; a strong central government (which Celts on Earth had never been able to achieve, leading to their ultimate defeat at the hands of the Romans) and representative local governments; the beginnings of a peerage democracy; great advances in magic, science and art.

It could not last. Despite the tremendous achievements of Raighne Ard-rían, and, later, the even greater deeds of Athyn Blackmantle, by the Terran year 1800 increasingly vocal separatist movements had sprung up.

The Archdruid of the time, the unquestionably brilliant Edeyrn ap Rhûn, saw in the unrest the chance to further his own ends, and succeeded in dissolving the Fáinne, assassinating the High King Alawn and almost every member of his family, and installing Druids loyal to him as magical dictators on every level. Civil war broke out across Keltia, and the realm was all but destroyed by the conflict.

This was the Druid Theocracy, and it went on for nearly two hundred unhappy years. Edeyrn and his bent Druids were joined by many politically ambitious and discontented noble houses, who saw in the upheaval a chance for their own advancement.

There was of course a fierce and powerful resistance: Known as the Counterinsurgency, it opposed Edeyrn, and his terrible military enforcers the Ravens, with strength, resource and cleverness. Consistently outwitting the aims of the Theocracy, these loyalists managed to preserve the fabric of true Keltic society, and also succeeded in salvaging precious lore, science, art and records, hiding these in remote secret bases all across the Keltic worlds.

The terrors of the Theocracy raged on for two centuries, with the mastery continually shifting between Theocracy and Counterinsurgency. Then Edeyrn raised the stakes, bringing in outworld mercenaries; but out of the strife and chaos, a mighty figure began to emerge.

*   *   *

Arthur of Arvon, thought to be but a minor lordling of a minor noble house, was proved to be instead the secret rightful heir to the High Kingship, only child of Prince Amris and the Lady Ygrawn.

Arthur was challenged in this claim by his cousin, the Princess Gweniver. The High King Uthyr, uncle to them both, commanded that when the time came they should marry and be co-sovereigns over Keltia; and they obeyed, after overthrowing Edeyrn, who would be known to Keltic history as the Marbh-draoi ('Death-druid').

Gweniver and Arthur came to fall deeply in love, and reigned brilliantly and successfully for nearly fifty years. Then they were betrayed by Malgan, Arthur's son by his first wife, and his nephew Mordryth, son of his sister Marguessan. Arthur dealt with the insurrection, then led a space armada against the invading Coranians with whom the traitors had allied. The invaders were destroyed, but at a terrible price: In the climactic battle, Arthur sent his flagship *Prydwen* against the Coranians', and took both vessels and all aboard them into hyperspace forever. His last words to his people were that he would come again, when he was needed.

In the absence of proof positive of Arthur's death, he is still King of Kelts, and all succeeding monarchs have held their sovereignty by his courtesy and have made their laws in his name; for who knows when Arthur the King might not return?

After Arthur's disappearance, the monarchy became by Gweniver Ard-rían's wishes a Regency, the only one in Keltic history. Arthur's other sister, Morguenna, his mother Ygrawn and Gweniver herself ruled jointly as Regents, until such time as Prince Arawn, elder of Arthur's and Gweniver's two children, should be old enough to take the crown.

All three women were strong and skilled in magic, but Morguenna, called Morgan Magistra, or St. Morgan of the Pale, was perhaps the greatest magician Keltia would ever see.

After taking counsel with the Ban-draoi, Druids, Fianna and bards, with her own co-Regents, and above all with her beloved husband, Arthur's fosterbrother the renowned bard Taliesin Glyndour, Morgan undertook the immense achievement of the raising of the Curtain Wall. There was no other feat like it, even back to the days of the High Atlandeans, and the achieving of it killed her and many others.

The Curtain Wall (also known as the Pale, which term has entered the language as a metaphor for outrage or incomprehensibility—'beyond the pale') is a gigantic force-field; electromagnetic in nature and maintained by psionic energies, it completely surrounds and conceals Keltic space. Once outside its perimeters, it is as if Keltia does not exist: Space is not physically blocked off, and carrier waves are bent around the Wall, but any ship attempting to cross that region is shunted into corridors of astromagnetic flux that feed into the Morimaruse, the terrifying Dead Sea of space, and now no one goes that way.

So the Keltic worlds and their peoples became a half-legend of the galaxy, a star-myth to be told to children on dark winter nights. But behind the Curtain Wall, the Regency carried on Arthur's work, and when in time Arawn became King, he proved almost as gifted as his parents. The dynasty he founded was followed in peaceful succession by the royal house of Douglas, and for fifteen hundred years Keltia prospered in isolation; not total isolation even then, for still there were out-Wall trading planets and military actions, and ambassadors were still sent and received.

In the year 2693 of the Common Reckoning the Crown passed to the Aoibhells of Thomond. Direct descendants of Brendan, the Aoibhells have held the monarchy in a grip of findruinna for eight hundred years, according to the law of Keltia that the Copper Crown descends to the eldest child of the sovereign, whether man or woman.

In 3512, the third year of the reign of the Ard-rían Aeron, seventeenth Aoibhell to sit in the Throne of Scone, the Terran probe ship Sword arrived in Keltic outwall space; for the first time since Brendan's day, Kelts and Terrans met. Queen Aeron determined to make an alliance with Earth, but before she could effect this Keltia was plunged into war with the Cabiri Imperium—and once again it was Telchine against Danaan.

Arianeira, sister of Aeron's mate Gwydion Prince of Gwynedd, used magic to tear a hole in the Curtain Wall, and invited the Coranians to invade, betraying nation and queen alike into the hands of the new Cabiri Emperor, Jaun Akhera. But persuaded by Gwydion, Arianeira repented of her evil, and enabled Aeron to escape beyond the Curtain Wall on a desperate errand: to find the legendary Thirteen Treasures, that Arthur himself was said to have taken with him in Prydwen, when he left Keltia so long ago.

With the help of Elathan, King of Fomor and a former enemy who had had the vision and courage to set his enmity by, Aeron defeated Jaun Akhera on the battlefield of Nandruidion. Aeron and Gwydion became Queen-Empress and King-Emperor over not only Keltia but the remnants of the Cabiri Imperium, finding themselves at the center of the kind of galactic politics from which Keltia had for millennia held itself apart.

But when Gwyn ap Neith, King of the Sidhe, came to Aeron and Gwydion in desperate need of their help, and magic began to die all across Keltia, Aeron found that she must face an enemy against whom none before her, not St. Nia, not Blackmantle, not Morgan Magistra, not Arthur nor even Brendan himself, had ever prevailed...

FIREHEART

The True 'Lost Writings'
of James Douglas Morrison

The Poetry, Songs, Drawings and Love Letters of
Jim Morrison to Patricia Morrison

edited and annotated by Patricia Morrison
with a foreword by Jim Morrison

On 5 May 1995, the twenty-fifth anniversary of James
Douglas Morrison's proposing to me, I began to go
over the many letters, drawings, poems, songs and
notes he had sent or given me, or had left in my keeping to
hold against his return, before he went to Paris to his death
on 3 July 1971.

On 24 June 1995, the twenty-fifth anniversary of our
handfast wedding ceremony, I completed the task of editing
(minimally or not at all) and annotating (extensively) this
material I had kept so close and cherished so long.

And now in this twenty-fifth anniversary year of my
beloved Jim's death, I have the very great honor to
announce *Fireheart*, to be published twenty-five years from
now, on 3 July 2021, half a century since the day he died.

This compilation of Jim Morrison's private communications
to me during the years 1969, 1970 and 1971—his true 'lost

writings', though in point of fact they have never been lost,
at least not to him and me—has been set aside in a place of
safety, there to await the first instant when I (or my heirs or
literary executors) shall finally be able to lawfully publish it
without having to beg permission to do so from the con-
trollers of his literary estate—permission, which, given the
contentions and agendas that have historically surrounded
Jim and his legacies, and the nature of the material, would
without question have been denied.

During the course of our friendship, love, union and
what it pleased both Jim and me to call our marriage, Jim
saw fit to honor me with many truths. Save for some confi-
dences which are of such incandescent intimacy as forever
to preclude publication (I must keep something for ourselves alone), those truths will all be included here: words
about himself, about me, about us; reflections on his childhood and youth, his family and associates; thoughts on his
career as a rock star and his ambitions as a writer; observations on his past and present, and his hopes for the future
he promised we would have shared; poetry of rare and tender—and, some may think, uncharacteristic—lyricism, and
unapologetic eroticism also.

Accompanying the letters and poems (many of which
will be shown in facsimile) will be drawings Jim made—
including some nude sketches of me and of us together—
and several of the unpublished songs he left with me,
perhaps intended for a Doors album to follow *L.A. Woman*,
but more likely earmarked for his own first solo effort,
which he had planned to begin recording here in New York
when he came back from Paris.

The Jim Morrison of *Fireheart*, a Jim whom perhaps no one
but I was ever privileged to know, *is* Fireheart (as he names
himself in one of the last and loveliest of the poems): a man
writing the deep secrets of his soul to the woman he calls, in

these same writings, his wife, the woman he took to himself in an ancient and beautiful ceremony, as he took no other.

This material, or much of it, has so far been seen by only my closest friends, and by the four journalists who reported the news of its existence; no one (save Jim and I) has yet seen all of it. My original, long-held intention was to destroy it before my own death, and so to take it with me back to Jim. But I have been persuaded away from this course by those who feared that this marvelously romantic legacy might be forever lost, and the man it reveals remain forever unknown.

Fireheart will surprise many and astonish most, will show a Jim Morrison that not even my memoir *Strange Days* could show—by no means the sadistic, alcohol- and drug-benumbed catspaw who is the only Jim his various biographers seem able or willing to understand or accept, but a man of matchless spirit and sensitivity, a man capable of the deepest feeling and the most loving expression thereof.

And it will also prove, once and for all, just how Jim felt about me, and why he kept our union the secret that it was. Quite simply, he thought our love was none of anyone else's business; and considering the public torture that Linda Eastman McCartney and Yoko Ono Lennon were enduring at that very time (it always seems to be open season on rock wives, or at least on the ones who are strong, independent women with creative lives and careers of their own, while the pretty, parasitic, brainless addicts are allowed an endless free ride), we were both—for of course I shared Jim's feeling on the matter—correct to think so.

Jim, in his chivalry and protectiveness, wished only to spare me the pain of ordeal by publicity, and the vicious personal attacks such attention can bring (and indeed has brought). What he and I could never have foreseen was that our natural wish for privacy in love would, with ghastly

rony, work so against me two decades later, resulting in a
far more terrible ordeal, nor yet that I would be left to face
it alone. If we had, our decision would almost certainly
have been very different indeed...

Even so, I kept silence in the face of enormity for twenty-
one years before finally speaking out in *Strange Days*; no
one, I think, can accuse me of rushing to publish, and, with
a name and a following of my own for my Keltiad, neither
can I be accused of being a one-trick author, trading on my
association with Jim *ad infinitum* (and *nauseam*) because
that is all I have to offer.

Since 3 July 1971 my hands have been tied, my voice
(or Jim's voice to and through me) has been stopped.
Incredible as it may seem, short of a court verdict declaring
that he gifted me with the copyrights along with the words,
I do not own the publication rights to the love letters sent
me by my own mate, nor to the poems he composed for and
about me, nor the sketches he drew of and for me, nor the
songs he sang to and about me.

As it is, I must wait out a full half century from the day he
died: Copyright obtains for the lifespan of the author plus fifty
years; thus Jim's estate, in which I have no legal rights, controls
these writings, and I do not. But the same law that has for so
long barred me from making public any of this material will in
time free me to do so: If copyright law now holds these writings
hostage, as part of Jim's "literary estate," then twenty-five years
from now copyright law must likewise set them free.

*[Since making these plans, and writing this piece, I have
been informed that a recent modification in American copyright
law states that any unpublished material written before 1978
enters the public domain in 2003; if this is indeed the case, I
have not decided whether I will take advantage of this to publish
earlier, and for the foreseeable future I will keep to the 2021
publication date.]*

My one regret is that it shall take so long to happen; but that is something I can neither command nor control, and in any case I am not yet ready to let these precious things go, even as tribute to the world and to Jim—he is the last person who ever touched them, and they are all I have left that is still private between us.

But, sooner or later, *Fireheart* will complete the picture *Strange Days* began to paint—and the truth is no less true for being delayed. After all the others have said what they will have said, Jim Morrison is going to have the last word, and Patricia Morrison is going to make certain that he gets it.

Like *Strange Days* before it, *Fireheart* is a gift of deep and abiding love from me to the man I call my husband, the last I shall give him in this lifetime and perhaps the most enduring. By assembling this work, announcing this intent, I break no trust Jim placed in me: It is the way I choose to honor him, by enabling him to speak, for once, for himself, and, for the first time publicly, for us.

Jim Morrison was one of the most attractive human beings who ever lived. Those blessed enough to have had their paths cross his consider him the most extraordinary individual they ever met, and my love for him does not except me. I do not know if, two and a half decades hence, Jim will still command the same interest he aroused during his life and since the undeserved and untimely death that was so murderously dealt him. I realize that many now reading these words may not live to see published this last loving vindication of a man who has been much and deeply wronged; that I myself, even, may no longer be here in the world but joyfully reunited with Jim according to our vows, moving on together to our next lives, or beyond them.

No matter. What does matter is that whoever may come to read *Fireheart* will find, I think, that it will have been well worth the wait: to meet James Douglas Morrison at last, as he was, and as he was loving enough and trusting enough and courageous enough to reveal himself to the woman he called his wife, face to face, mind to mind, heart to heart.

Or so, at least, he and I both hope. We can wait.

Patricia Morrison
New York, 1996

FIREHEART

I have lived in winter since you went:
You took my seasons with you into earth
To keep them safe, forever, with your own.
I miss them not at all: I miss you more;
The seasons are all one, and that one ours.
I have loved in wonder since you went:
You, you alone, and only, ever, you.
But I can bloom in frost-time,
For I love you,
Still, and then,
And will, and now,
And ever move,
And never cease to love.

—Patricia Morrison

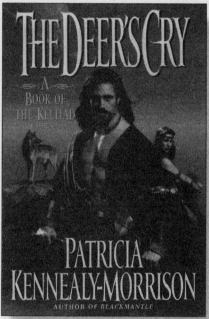